Laura Dean

keeps breaking up

with me

MARIKO TAMAKI

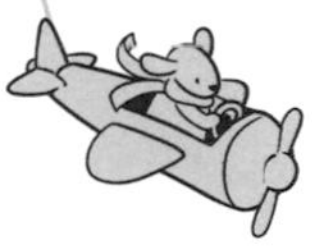

Laura Dean Keeps Breaking Up with Me

ROSEMARY VALERO-O'CONNELL

First Second
New York

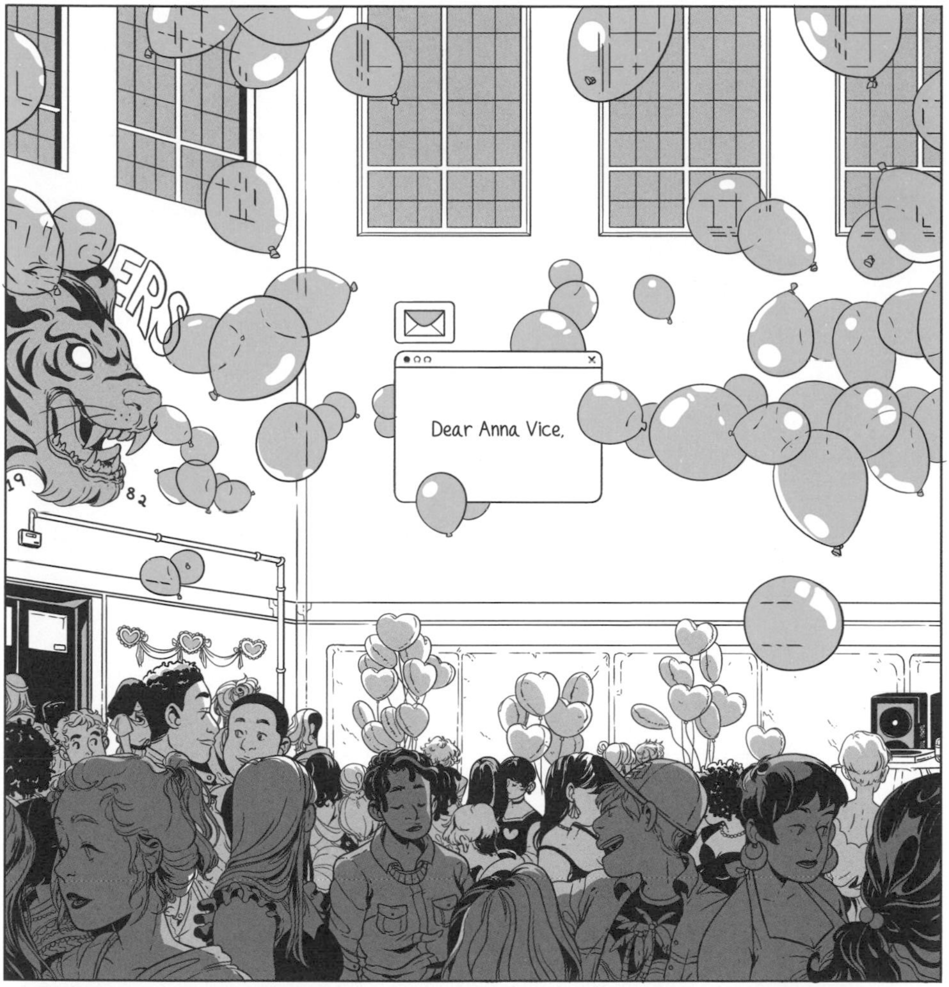
Dear Anna Vice,

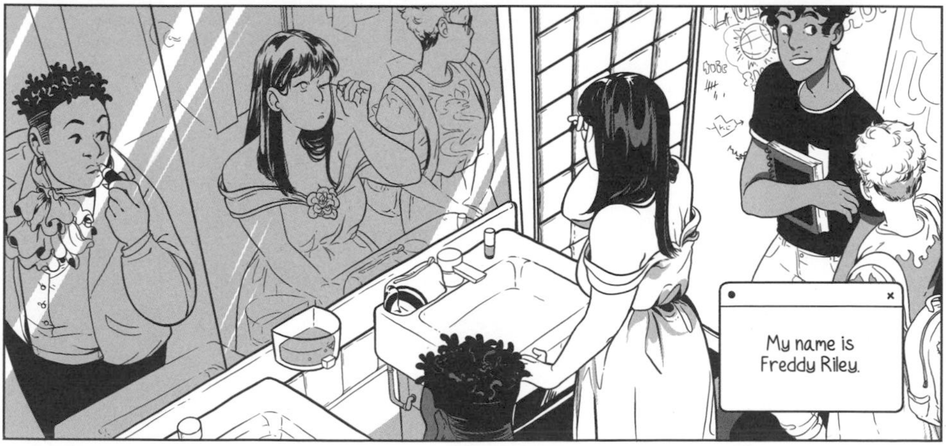
My name is
Freddy Riley.

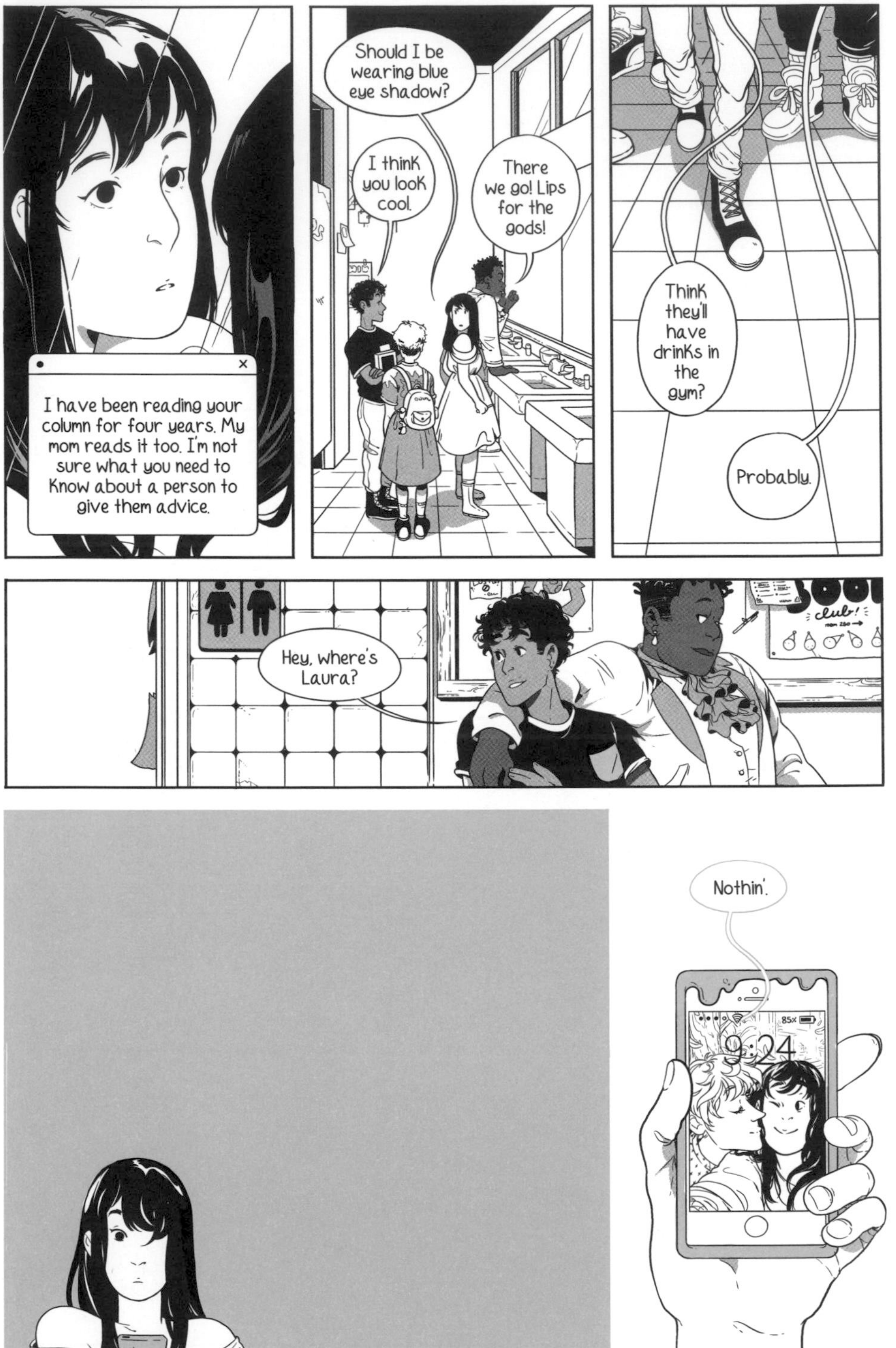
I have been reading your column for four years. My mom reads it too. I'm not sure what you need to know about a person to give them advice.
Should I be wearing blue eye shadow?
I think you look cool.
There we go! Lips for the gods!
Think they'll have drinks in the gym?
Probably.
Hey, where's Laura?
Nothin'.

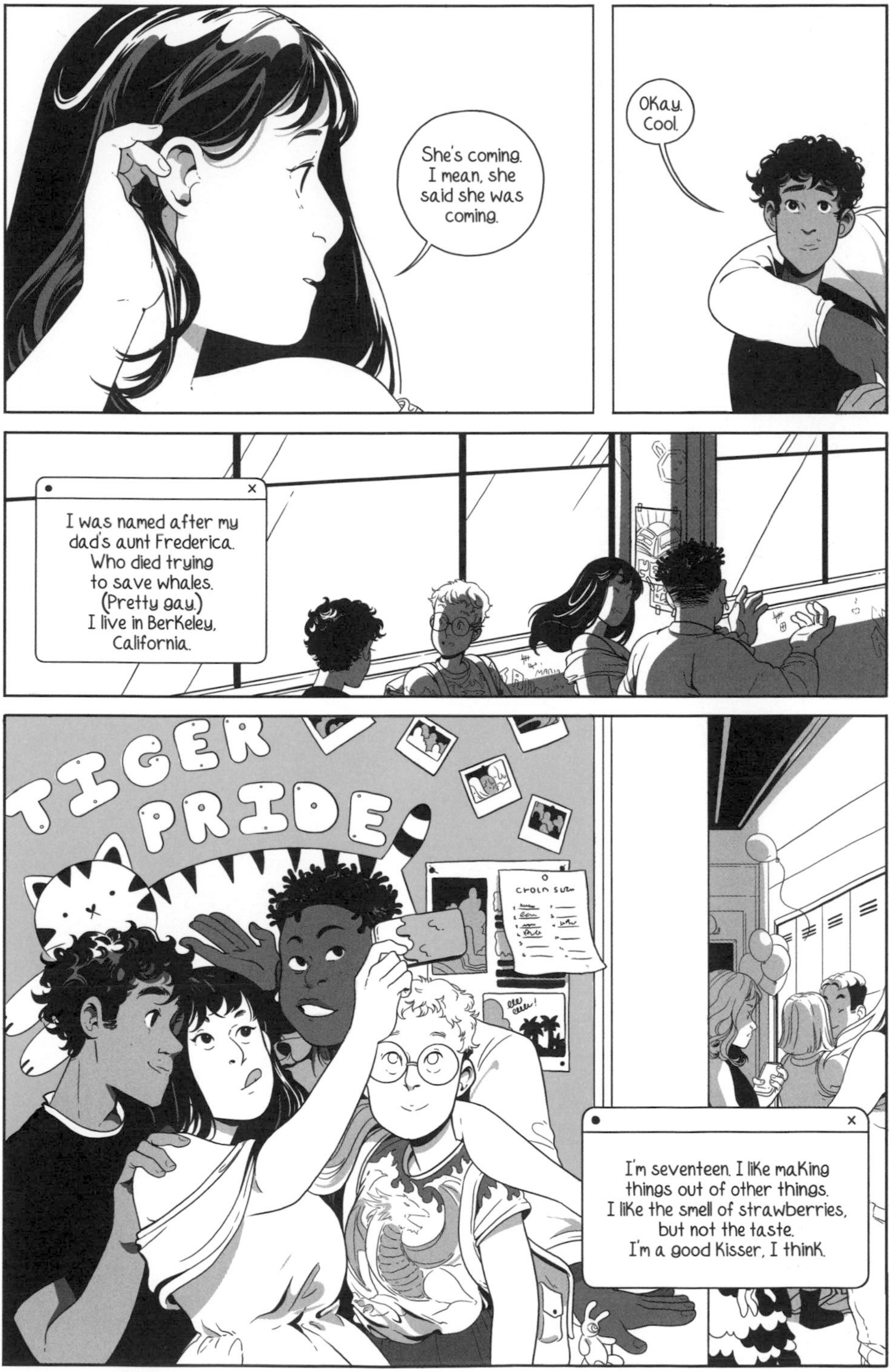
She's coming. I mean, she said she was coming.
Okay. Cool.
I was named after my dad's aunt Frederica. Who died trying to save whales. (Pretty gay.) I live in Berkeley, California.
TIGER PRIDE
I'm seventeen. I like making things out of other things. I like the smell of strawberries, but not the taste. I'm a good kisser, I think.

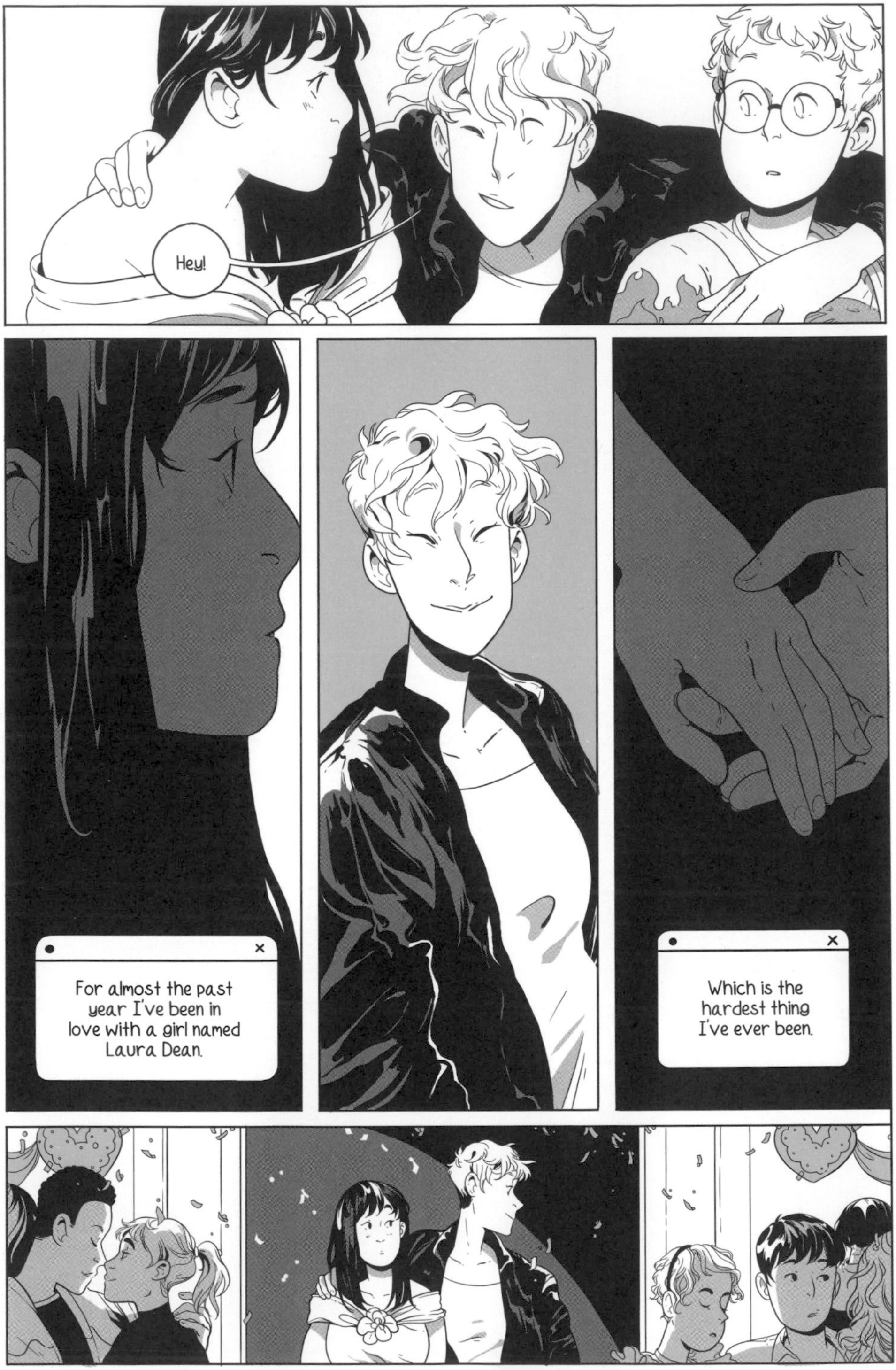
Hey!
For almost the past year I've been in love with a girl named Laura Dean.
Which is the hardest thing I've ever been.

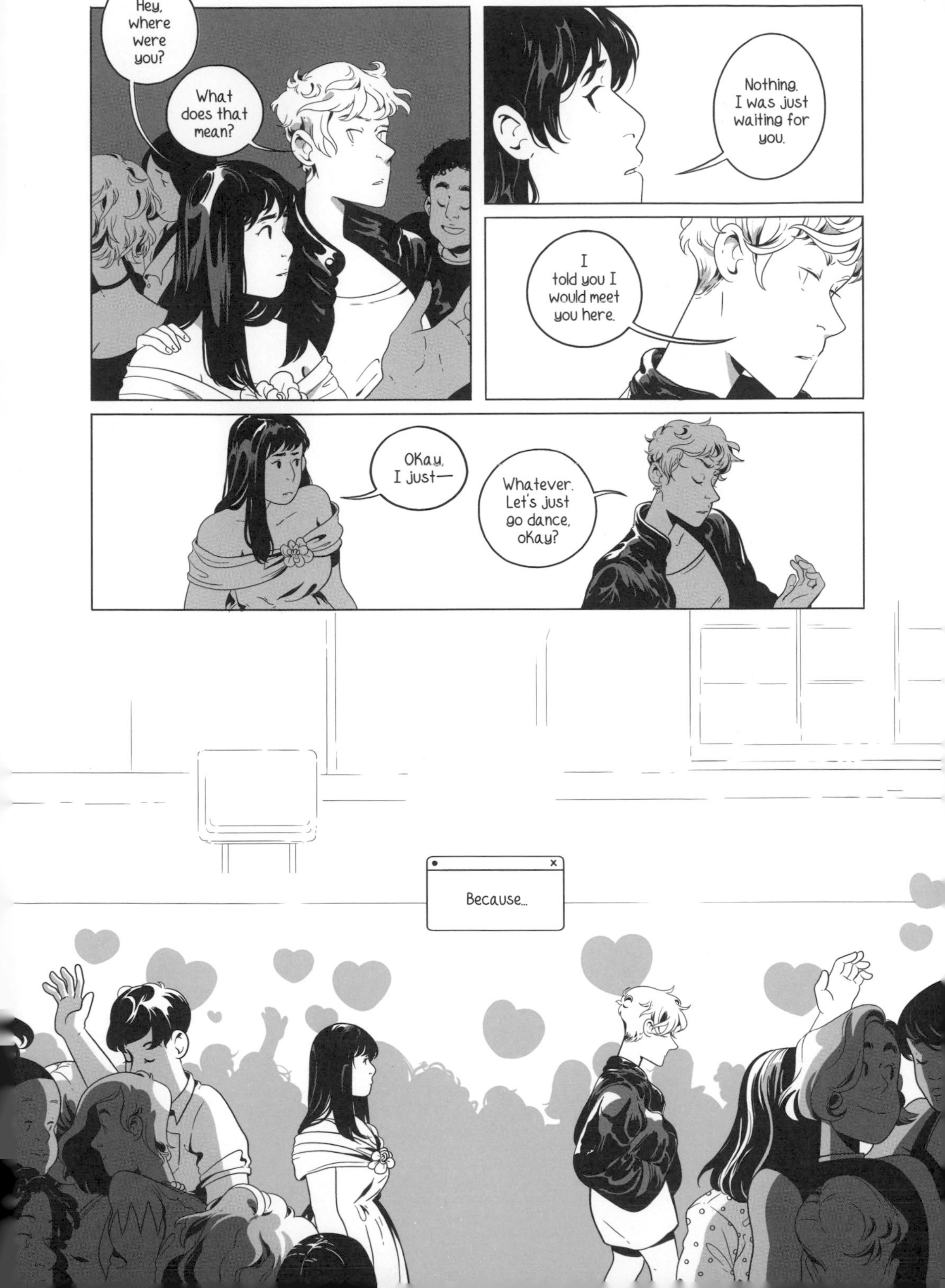
Hey, where were you?
What does that mean?
Nothing. I was just waiting for you.
I told you I would meet you here.
Okay, I just—
Whatever. Let's just go dance, okay?
Because...

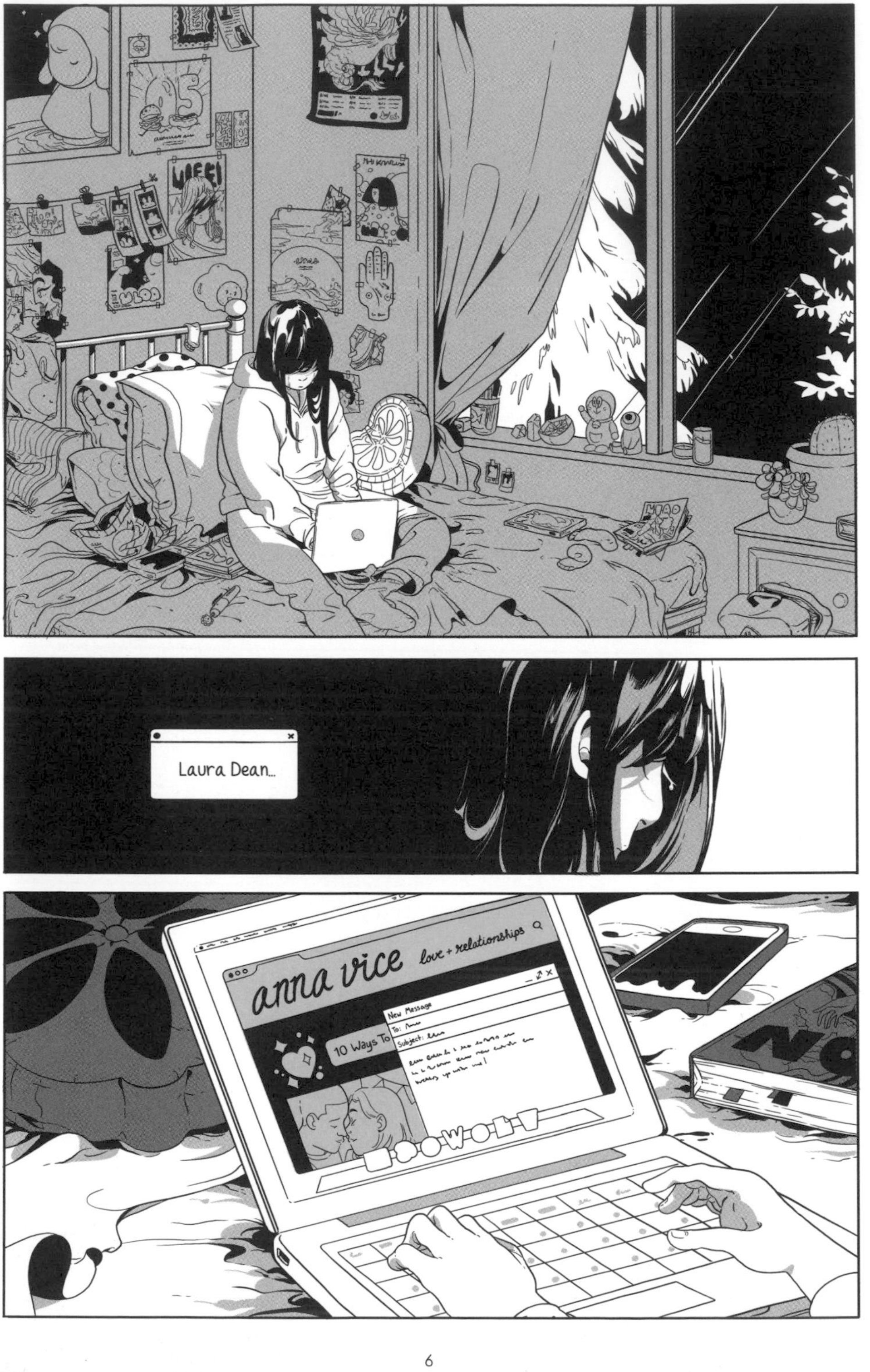
Laura Dean...
anna vice
love + relationships
10 Ways To
New Message
To:
Subject:

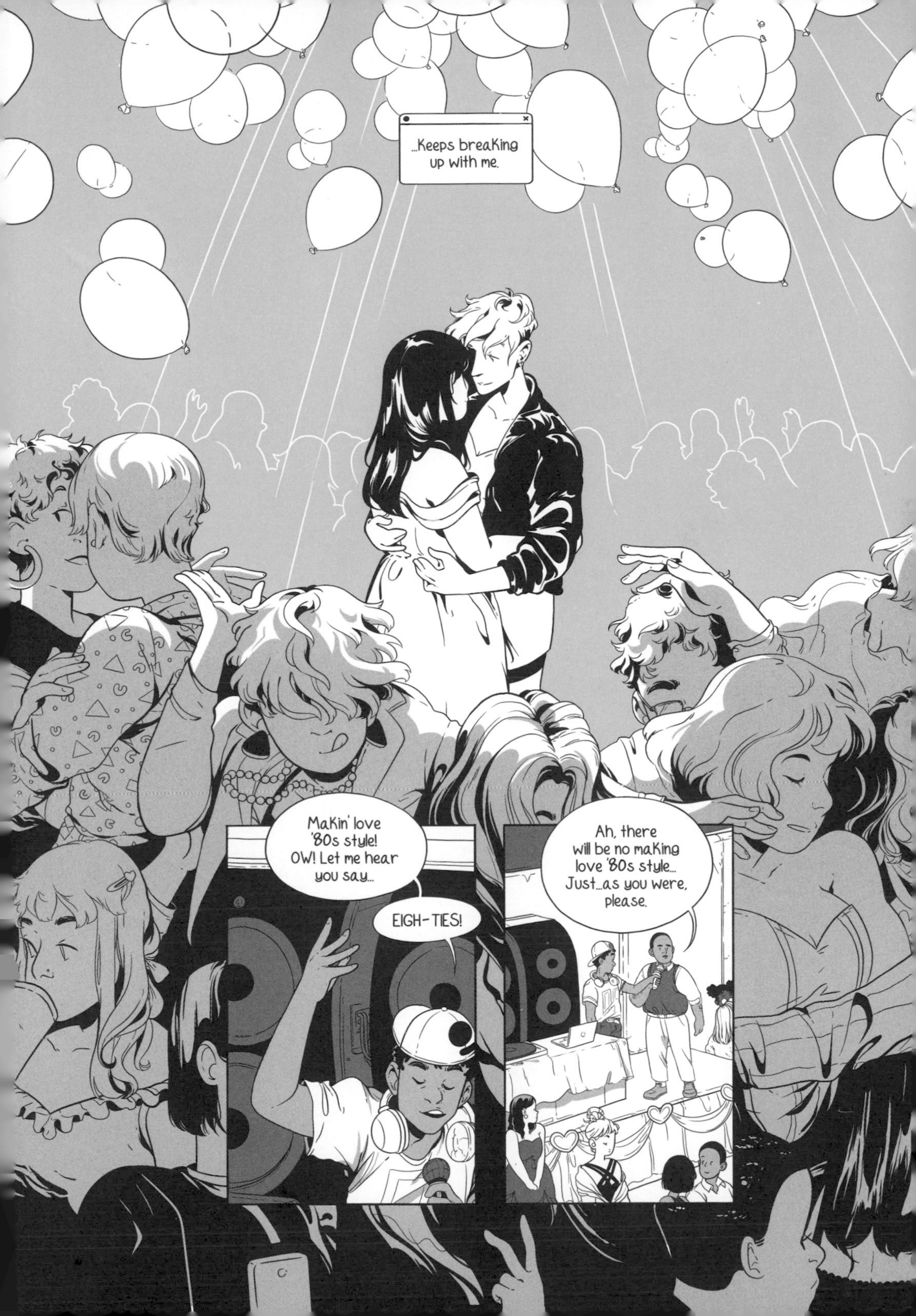

...Keeps breaKing up with me.
MaKin' love '80s style! OW! Let me hear you say...
EIGH-TIES!
Ah, there will be no maKing love '80s style... Just...as you were, please.

Yo, Dean!

Be right back.

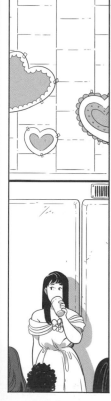

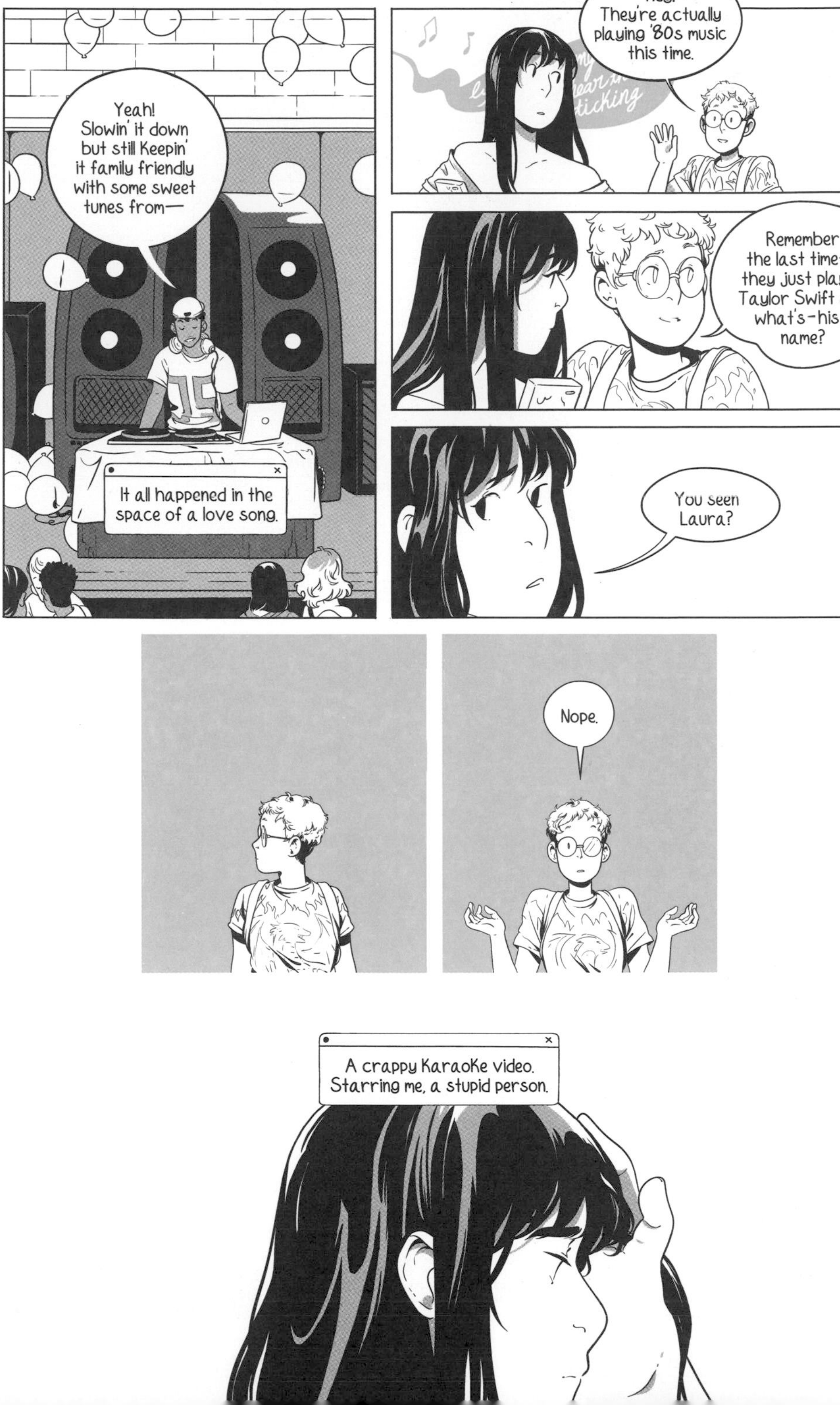
Yeah!
Slowin' it down but still Keepin' it family friendly with some sweet tunes from—
It all happened in the space of a love song.
Hey! They're actually playing '80s music this time.
Remember the last time—they just played Taylor Swift and what's-his-name?
You seen Laura?
Nope.
A crappy Karaoke video. Starring me, a stupid person.

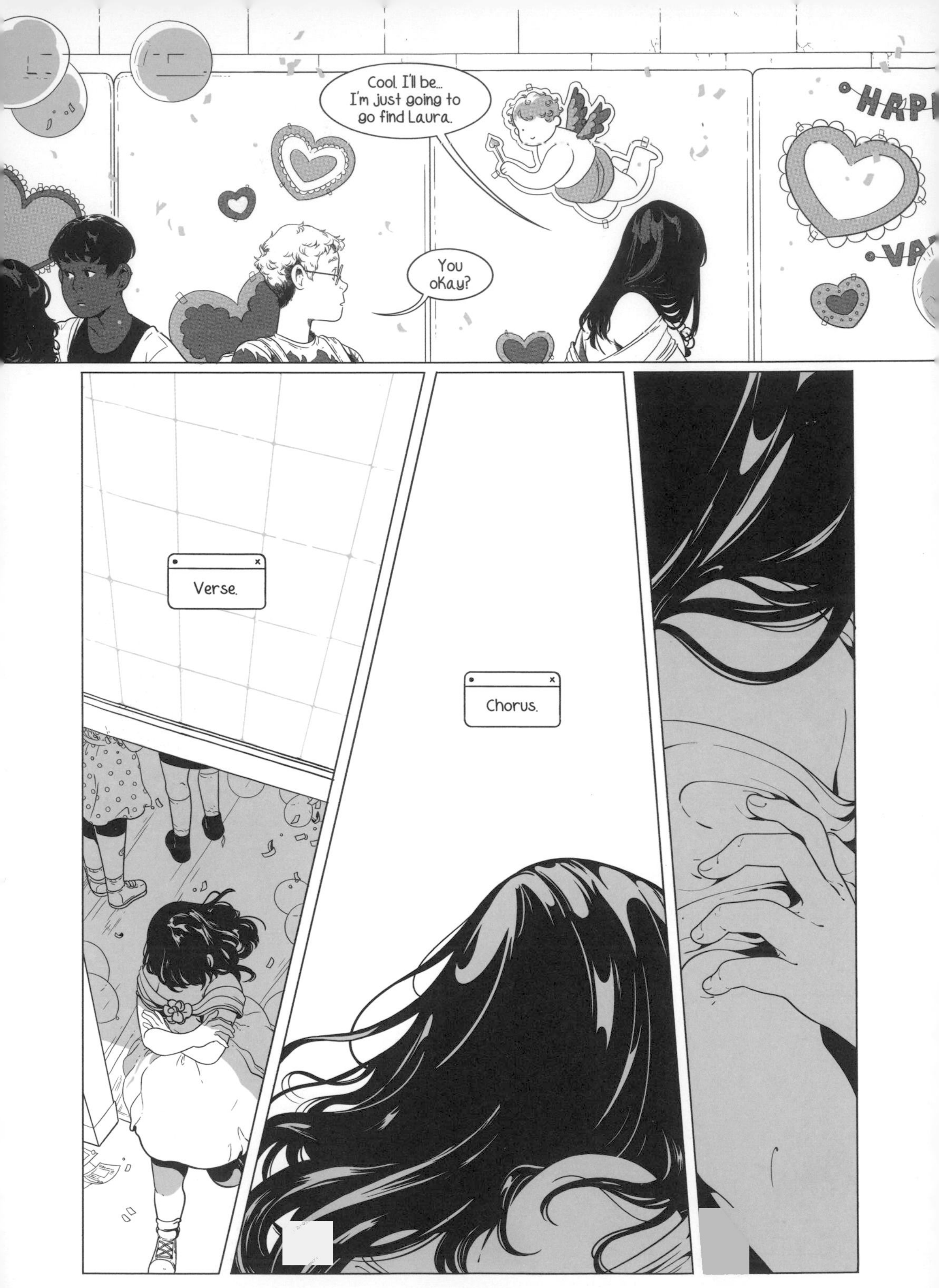
Cool. I'll be...
I'm just going to
go find Laura.
You
okay?
Verse.
Chorus.

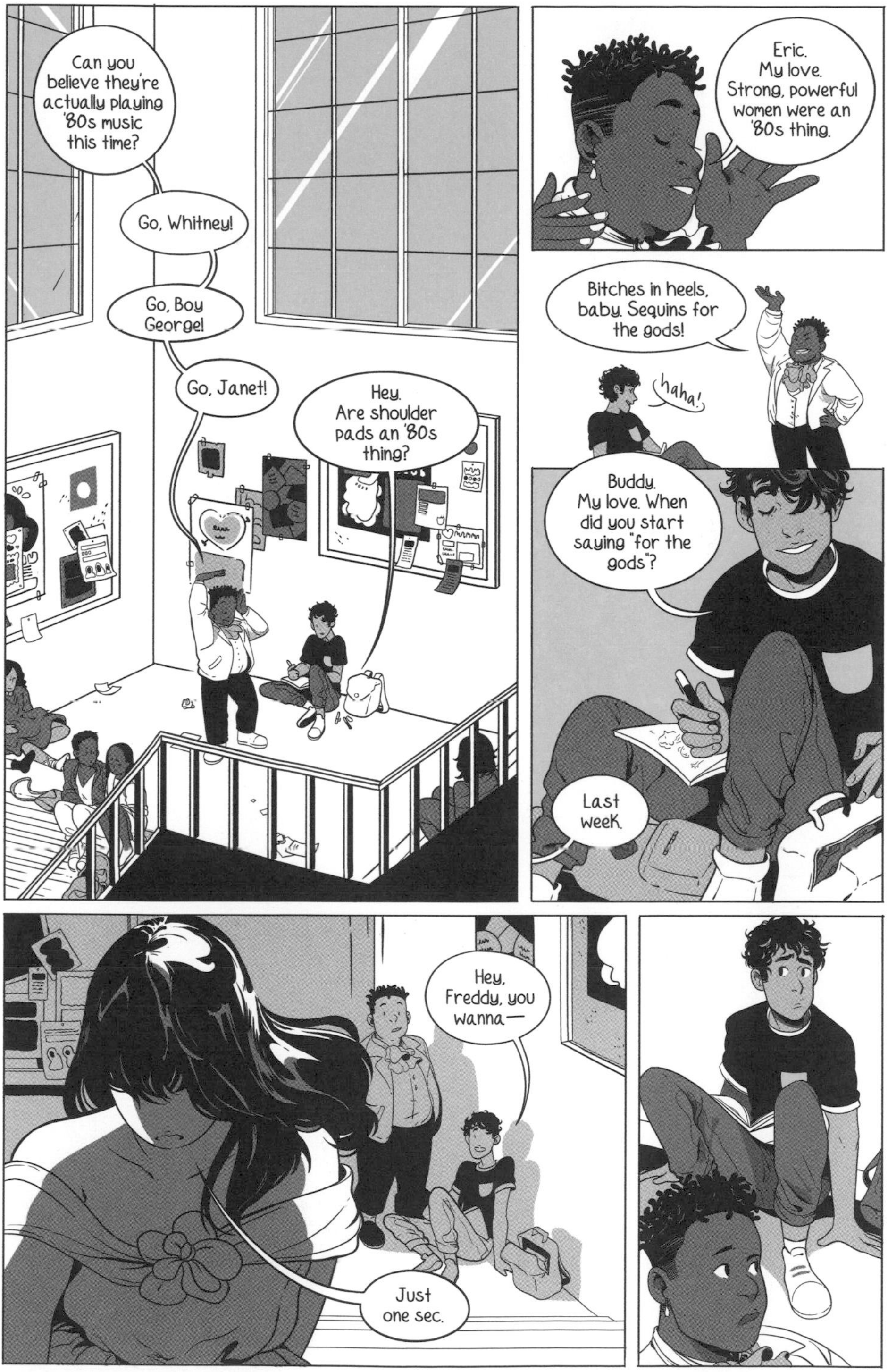
Can you believe they're actually playing '80s music this time?
Go, Whitney!
Go, Boy George!
Go, Janet!
Hey. Are shoulder pads an '80s thing?
Eric. My love. Strong, powerful women were an '80s thing.
Bitches in heels, baby. Sequins for the gods!
haha!
Buddy. My love. When did you start saying "for the gods"?
Last week.
Hey, Freddy, you wanna—
Just one sec.

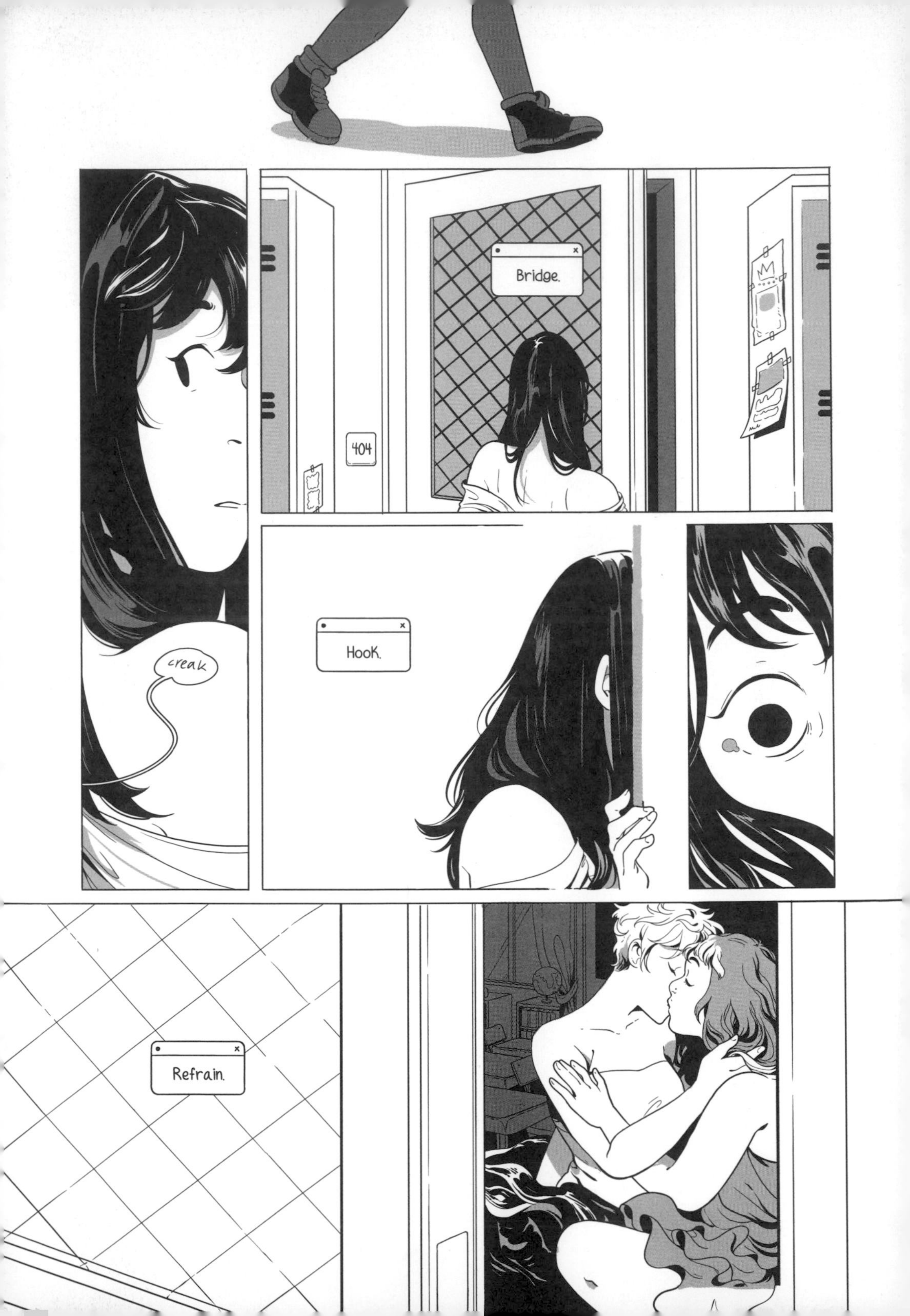
Bridge.
404
creak
Hook.
Refrain.

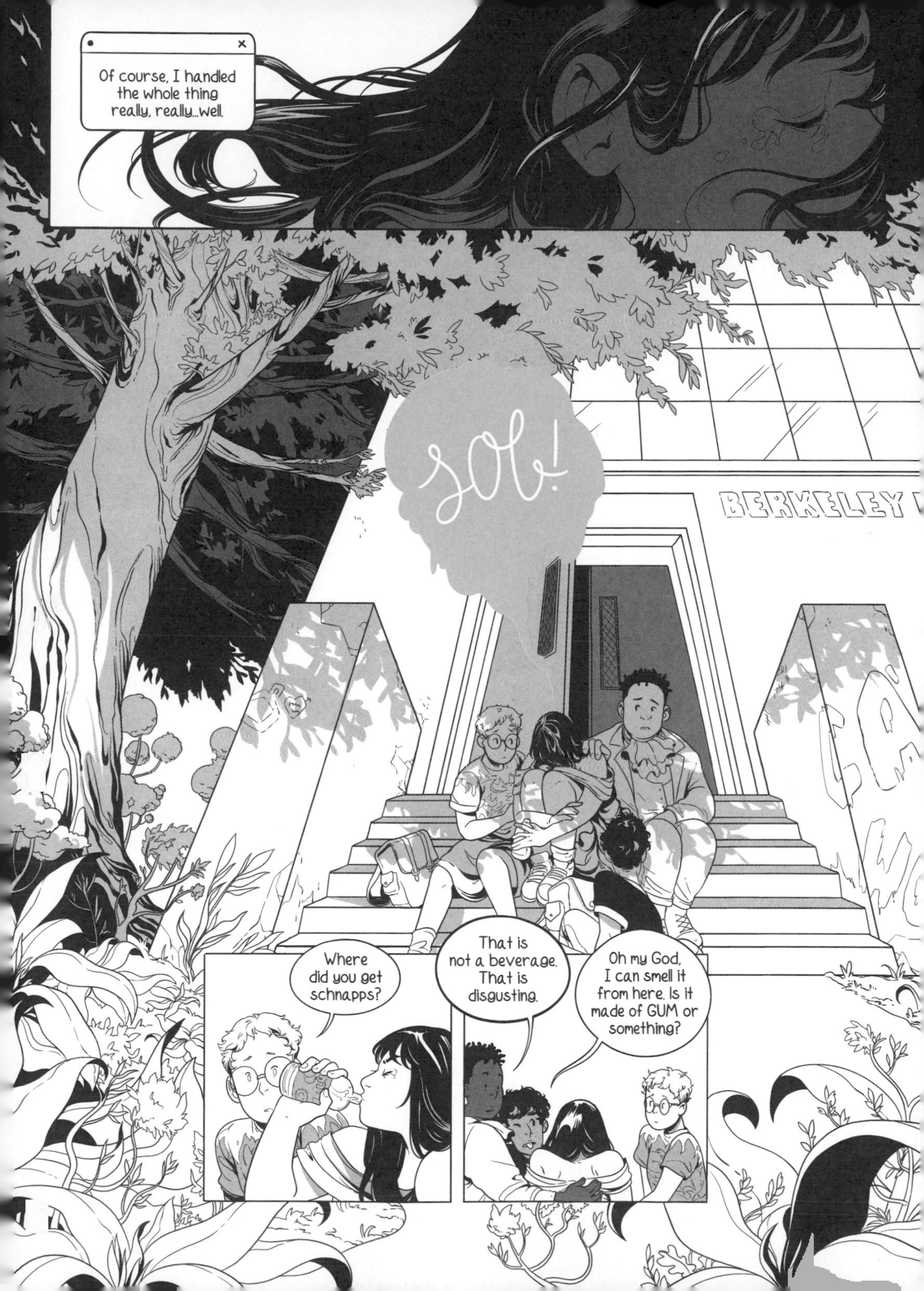
Of course, I handled the whole thing really, really...well.
sob!
BERKELEY
Where did you get schnapps?
That is not a beverage. That is disgusting.
Oh my God, I can smell it from here. Is it made of GUM or something?

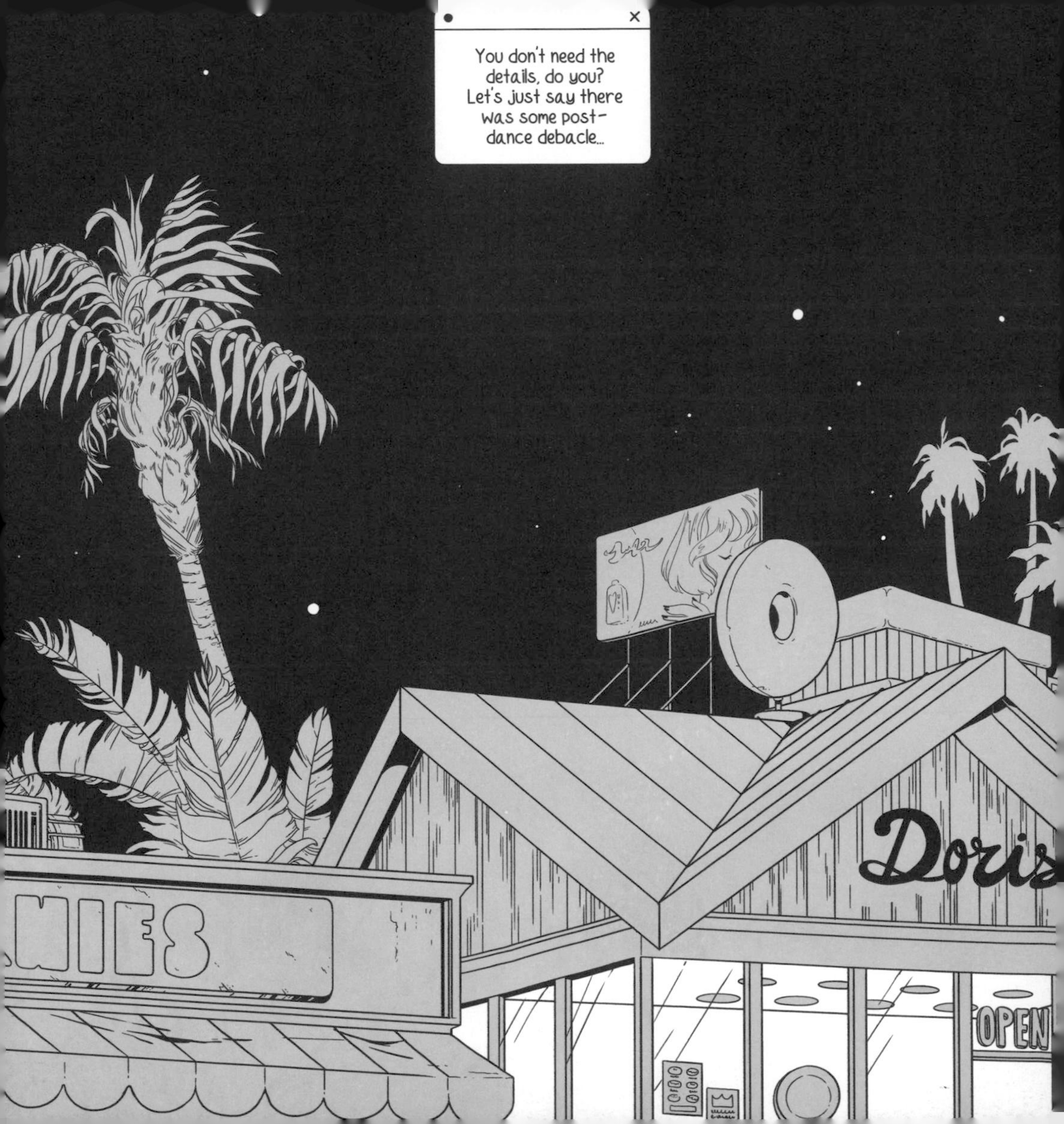
You don't need the details, do you? Let's just say there was some post-dance debacle...
MIES
Doris
OPEN

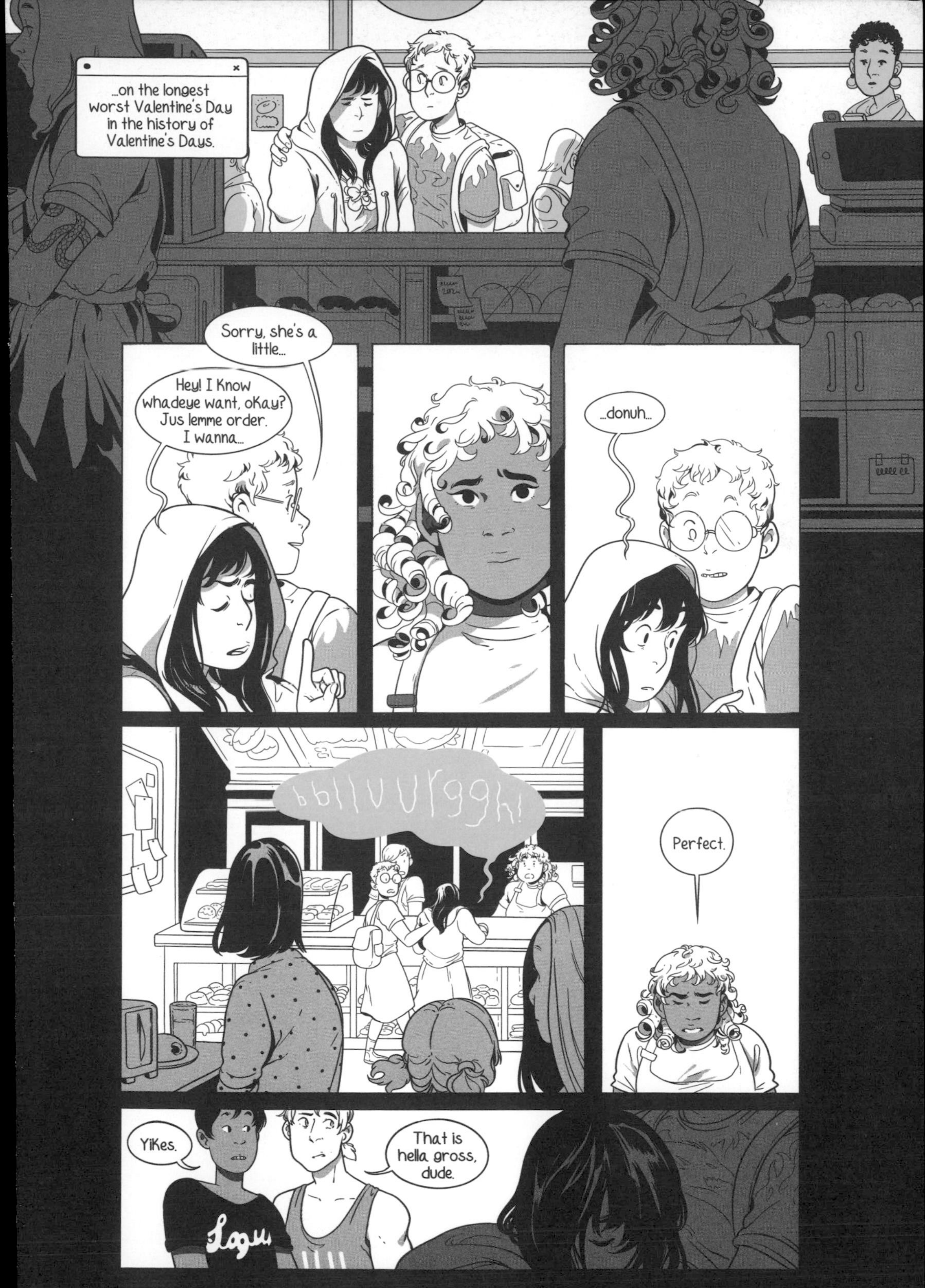
...on the longest worst Valentine's Day in the history of Valentine's Days.
Sorry, she's a little...
Hey! I Know whadeye want, oKay? Jus lemme order. I wanna...
...donuh...
bbllvvrggh!
Perfect.
YiKes.
That is hella gross, dude.

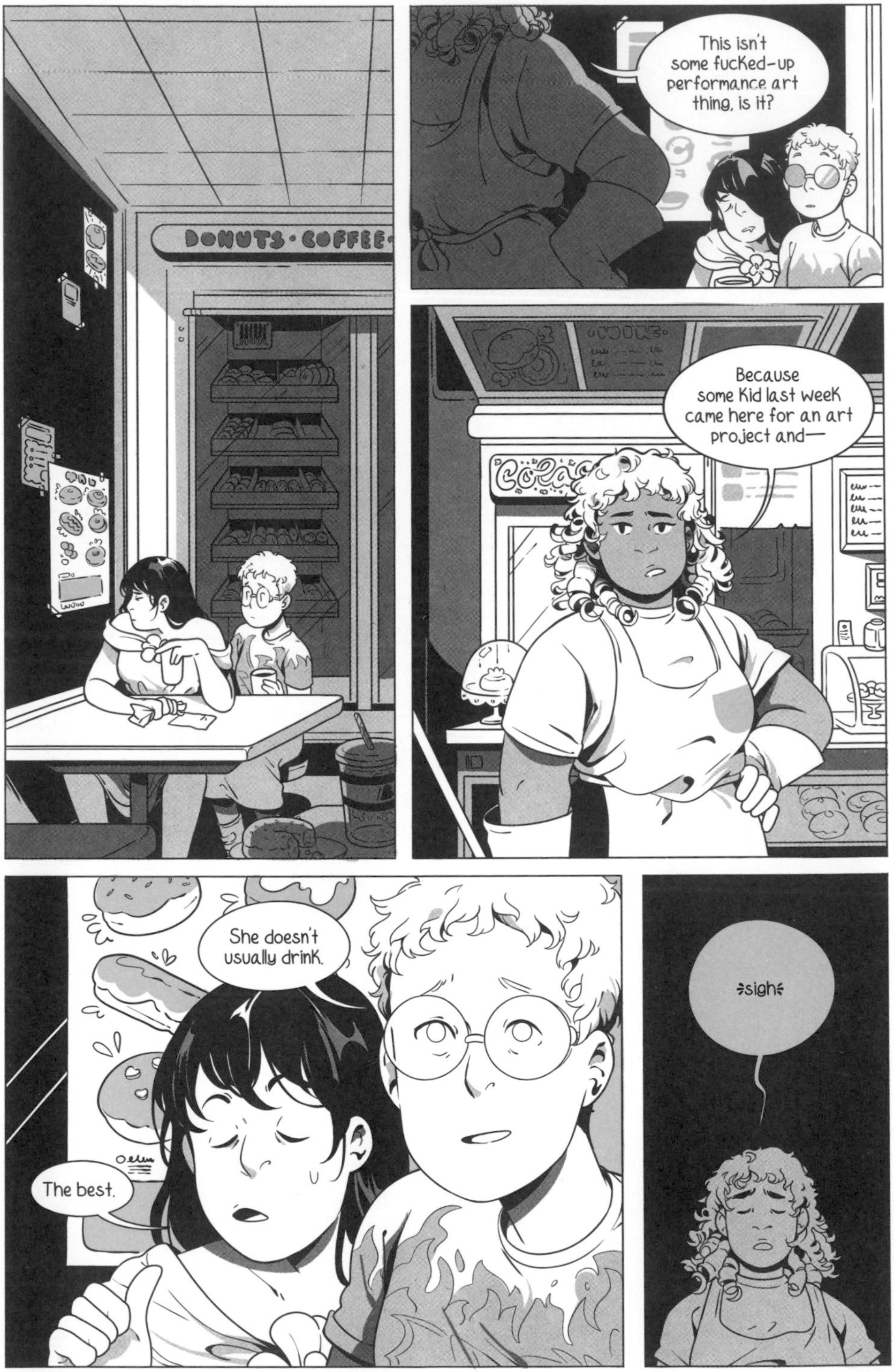
DONUTS · COFFEE
This isn't some fucKed-up performance art thing, is it?
Because some Kid last weeK came here for an art project and—
She doesn't usually drinK.
The best.
sigh

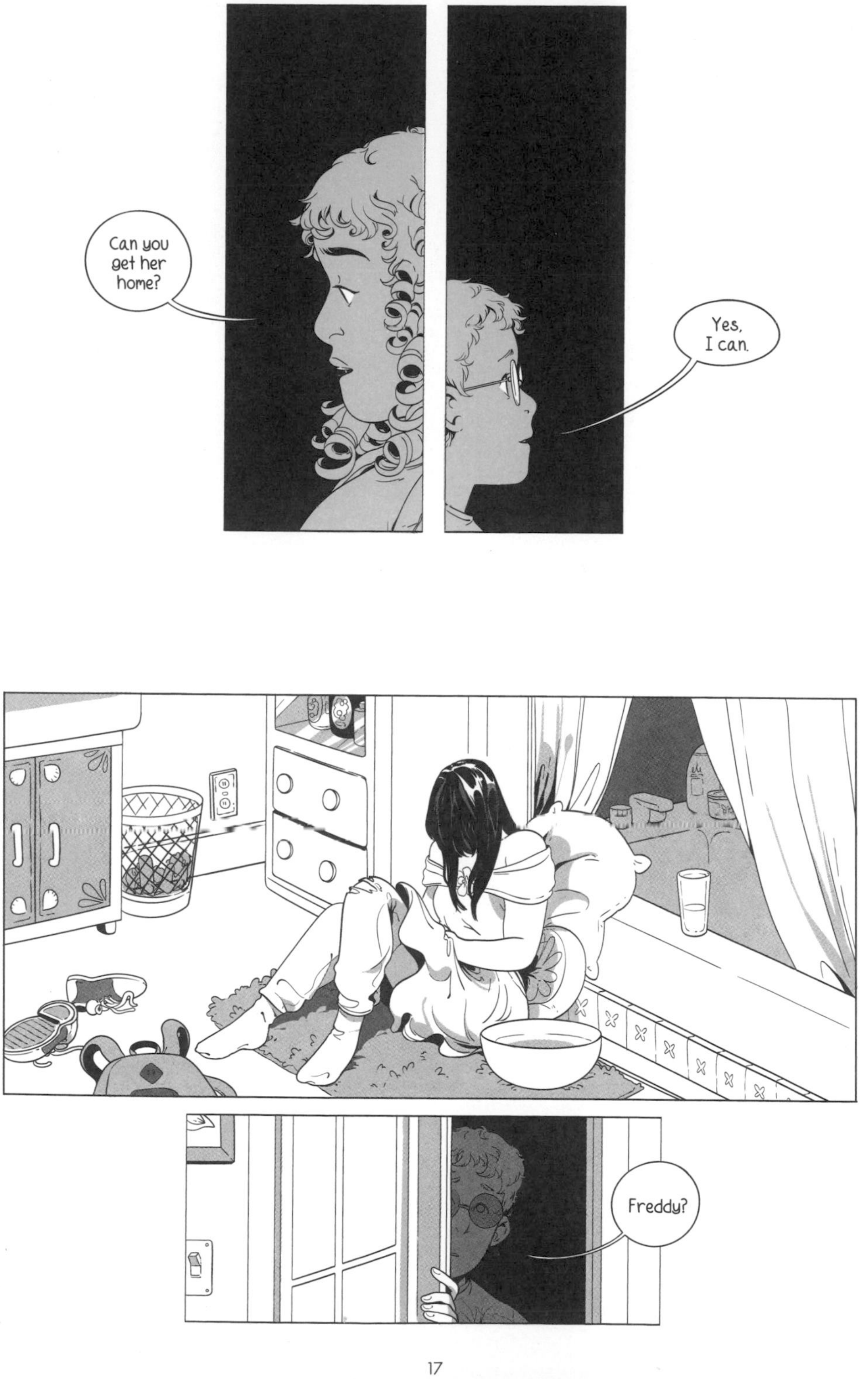
Can you get her home?
Yes, I can.
Freddy?

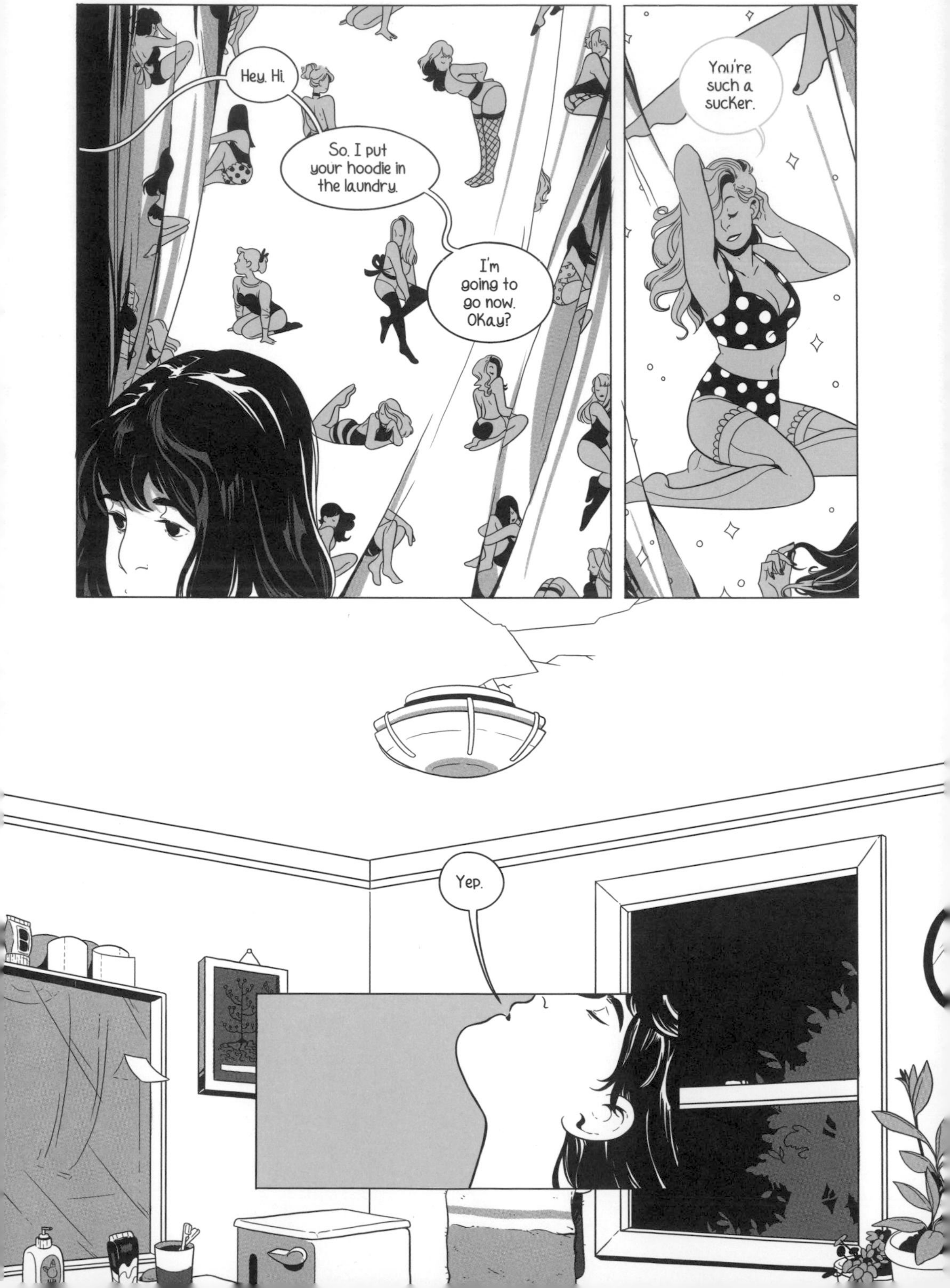
Hey. Hi.
So. I put your hoodie in the laundry.
I'm going to go now. OKay?
You're such a sucker.
Yep.

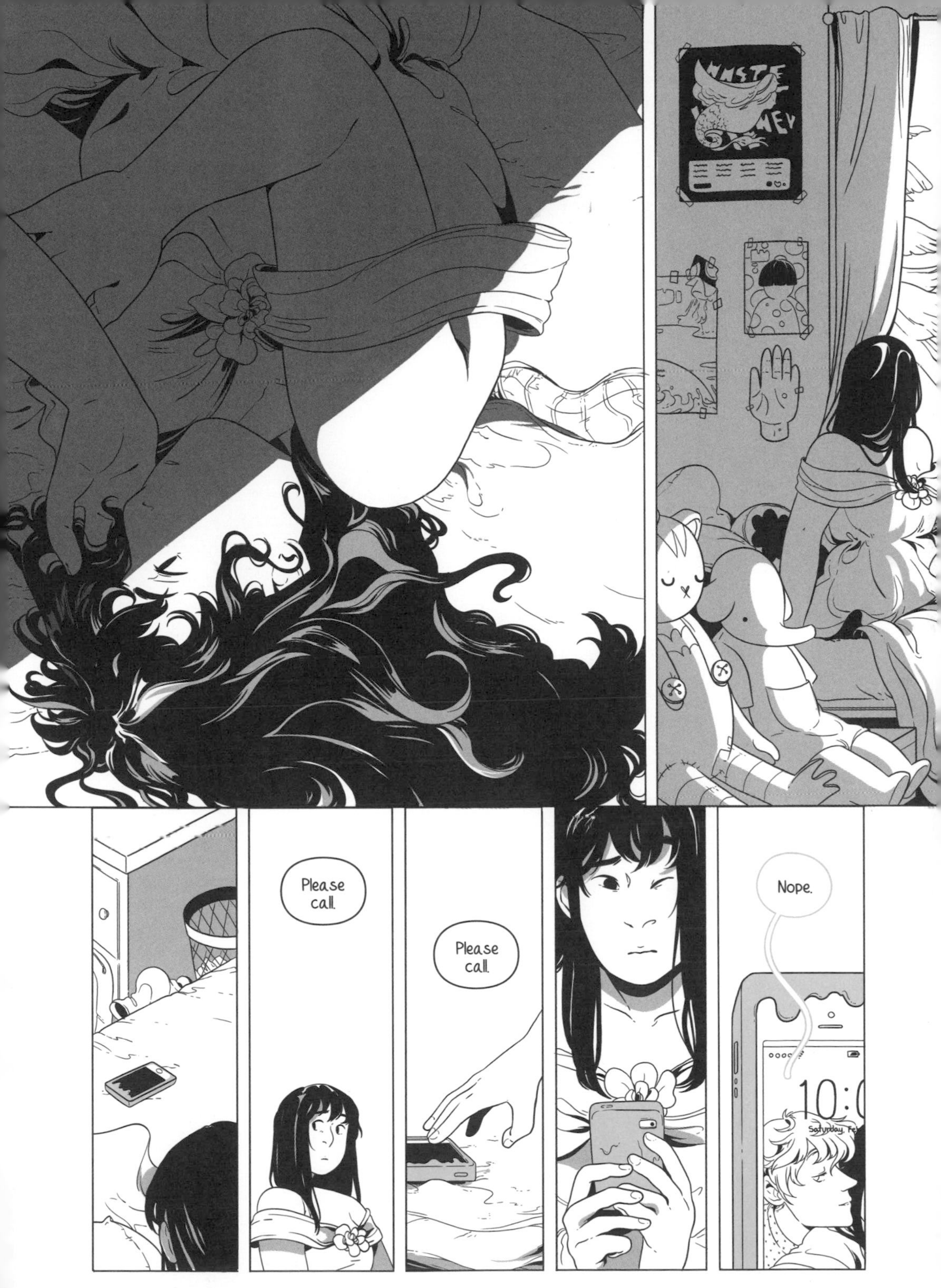
Please call.
Please call.
Nope.

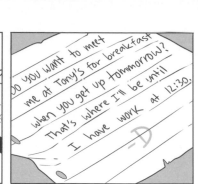

Do you want to meet me at Tony's for breakfast when you get up tommorrow? That's where I'll be until I have work at 12:30. -D

bzz

0000 LTE   11:32 AM

‹ (1) Laura 🐾🐾...

Hey! We're heading to the gym, so I guess you can just meet us there?

Hhow cou ld u!!! I/// tho ught aa x!..t!!

Lra!!-

Today, 11:31

don't be mad. xoxo

20

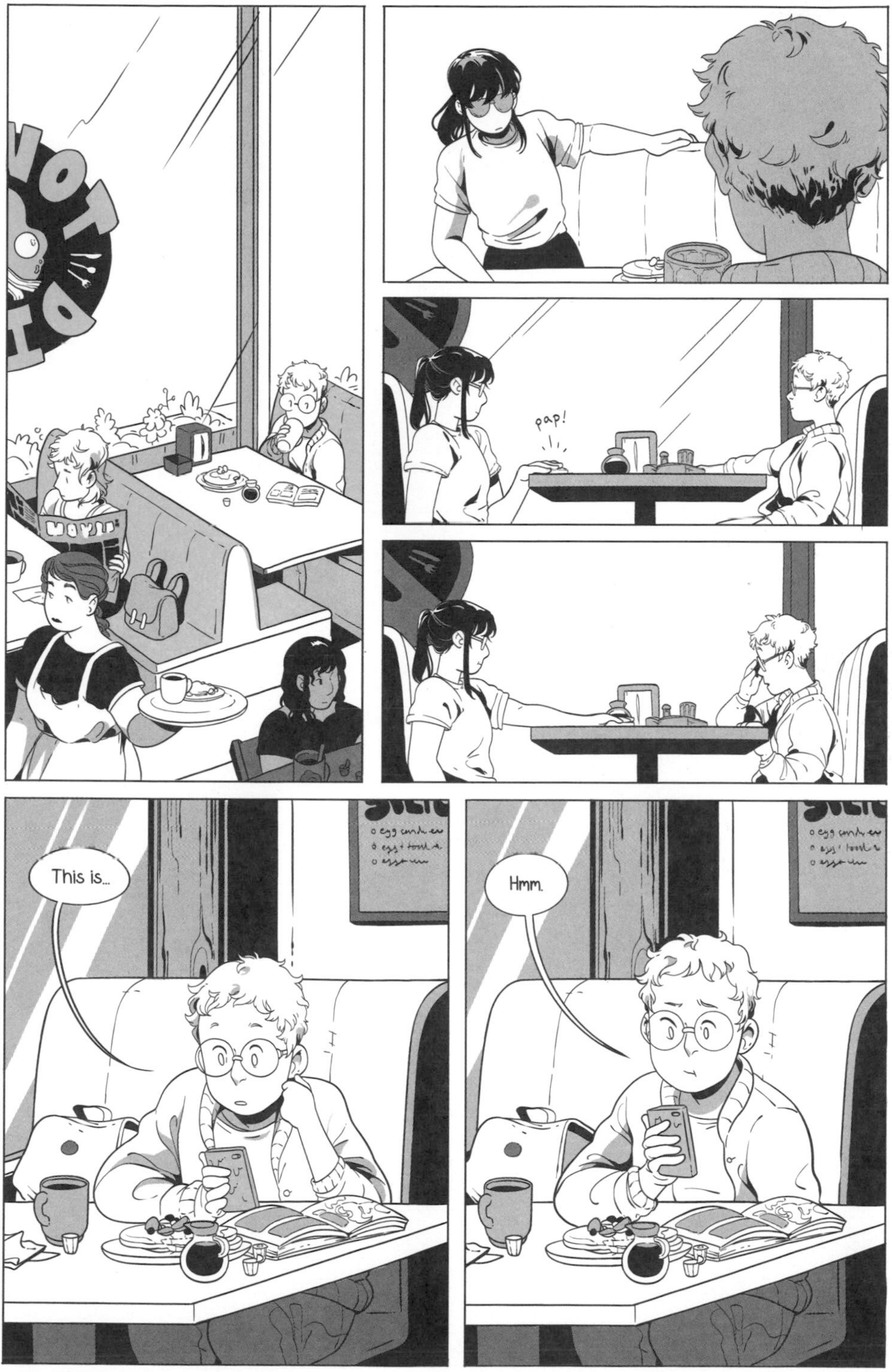
pap!
This is...
Hmm.

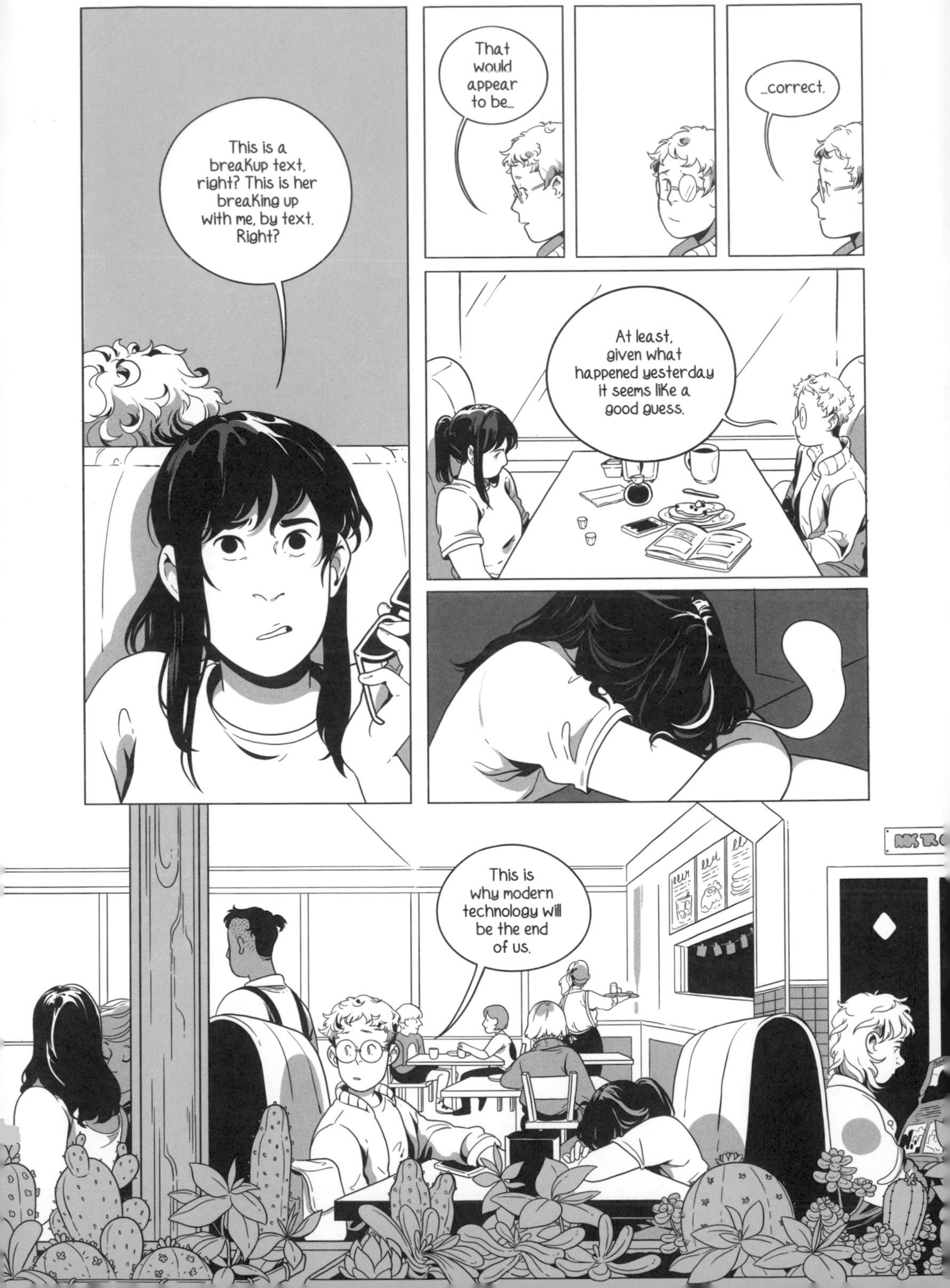
This is a breaKup text, right? This is her breaKing up with me, by text. Right?
That would appear to be...
...correct.
At least, given what happened yesterday it seems liKe a good guess.
This is why modern technology will be the end of us.

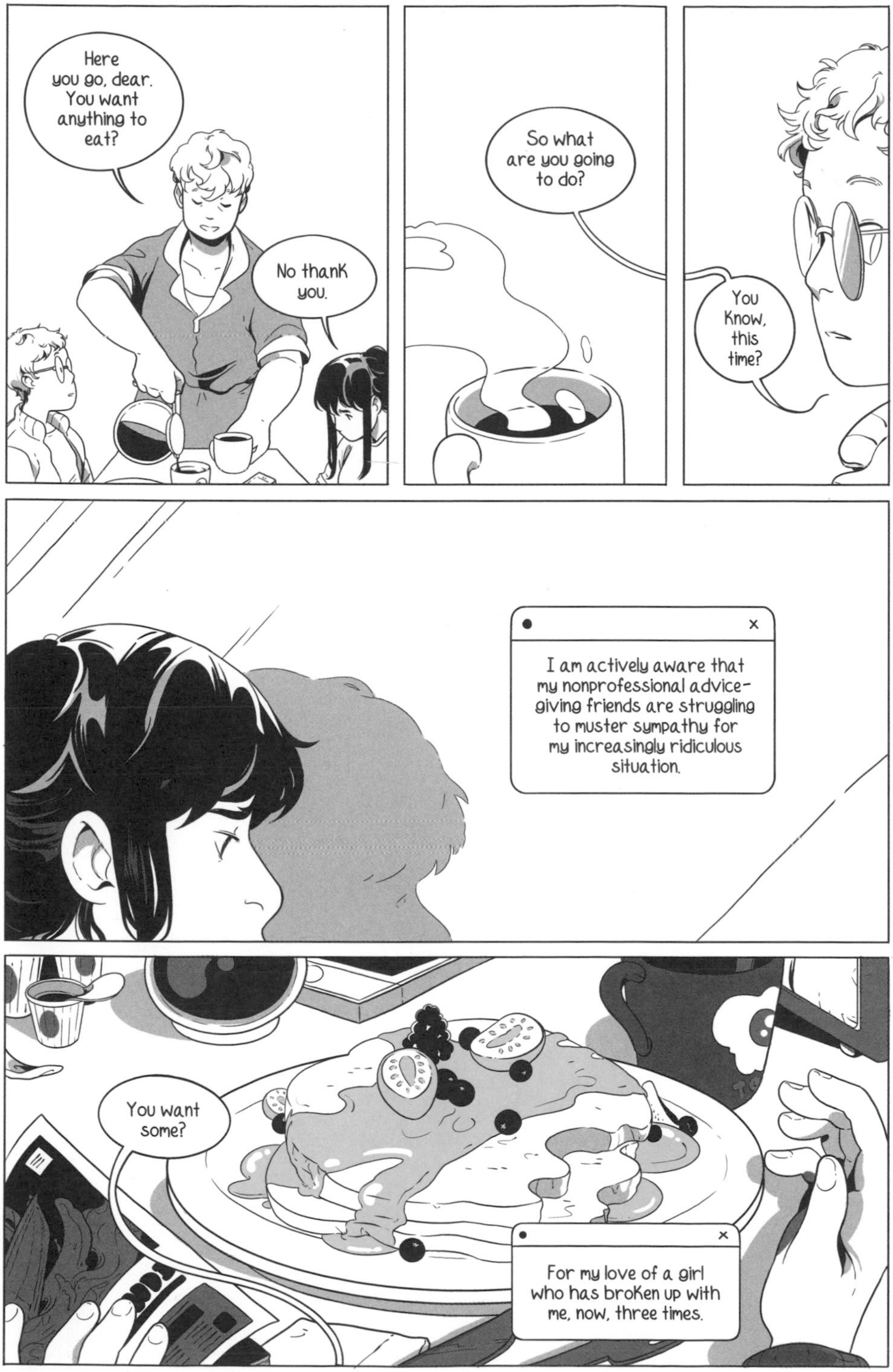
Here you go, dear. You want anything to eat?
No thank you.
So what are you going to do?
You know, this time?
I am actively aware that my nonprofessional advice-giving friends are struggling to muster sympathy for my increasingly ridiculous situation.
You want some?
For my love of a girl who has broken up with me, now, three times.

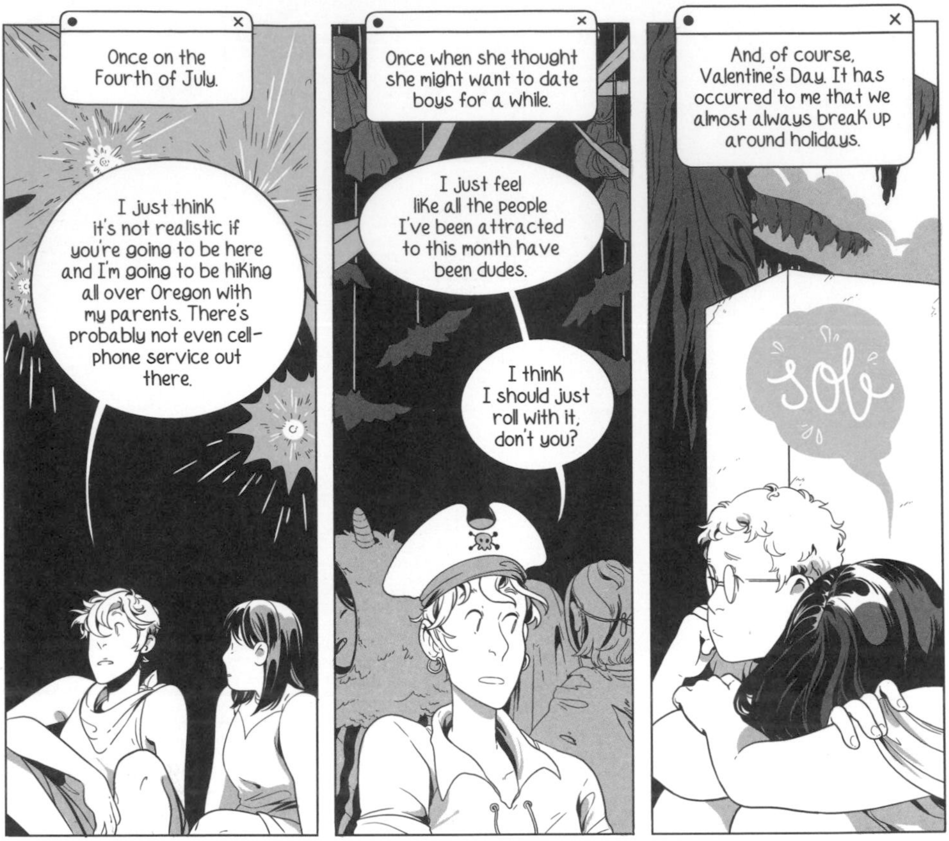

Once on the Fourth of July.
I just think it's not realistic if you're going to be here and I'm going to be hiking all over Oregon with my parents. There's probably not even cell-phone service out there.
Once when she thought she might want to date boys for a while.
I just feel like all the people I've been attracted to this month have been dudes.
I think I should just roll with it, don't you?
And, of course, Valentine's Day. It has occurred to me that we almost always break up around holidays.
sob

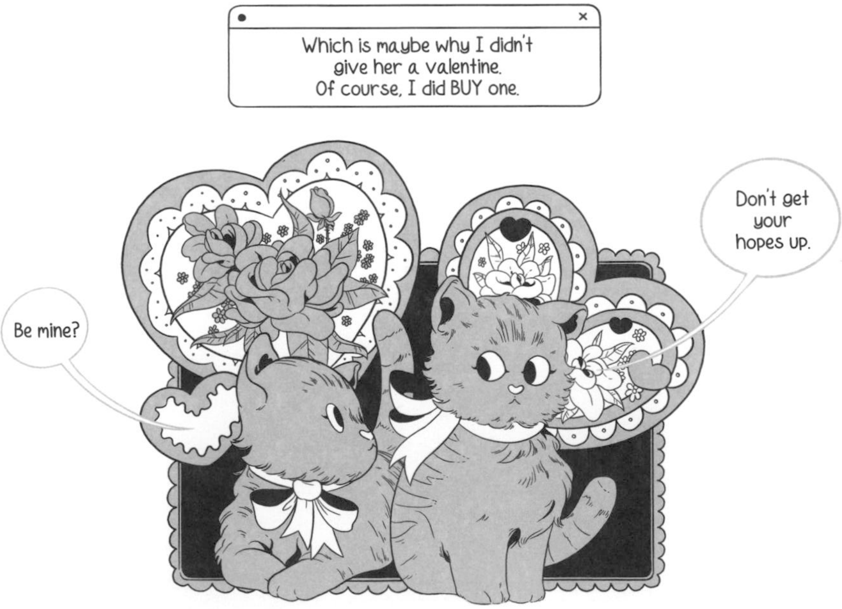

Which is maybe why I didn't give her a valentine. Of course, I did BUY one.
Be mine?
Don't get your hopes up.

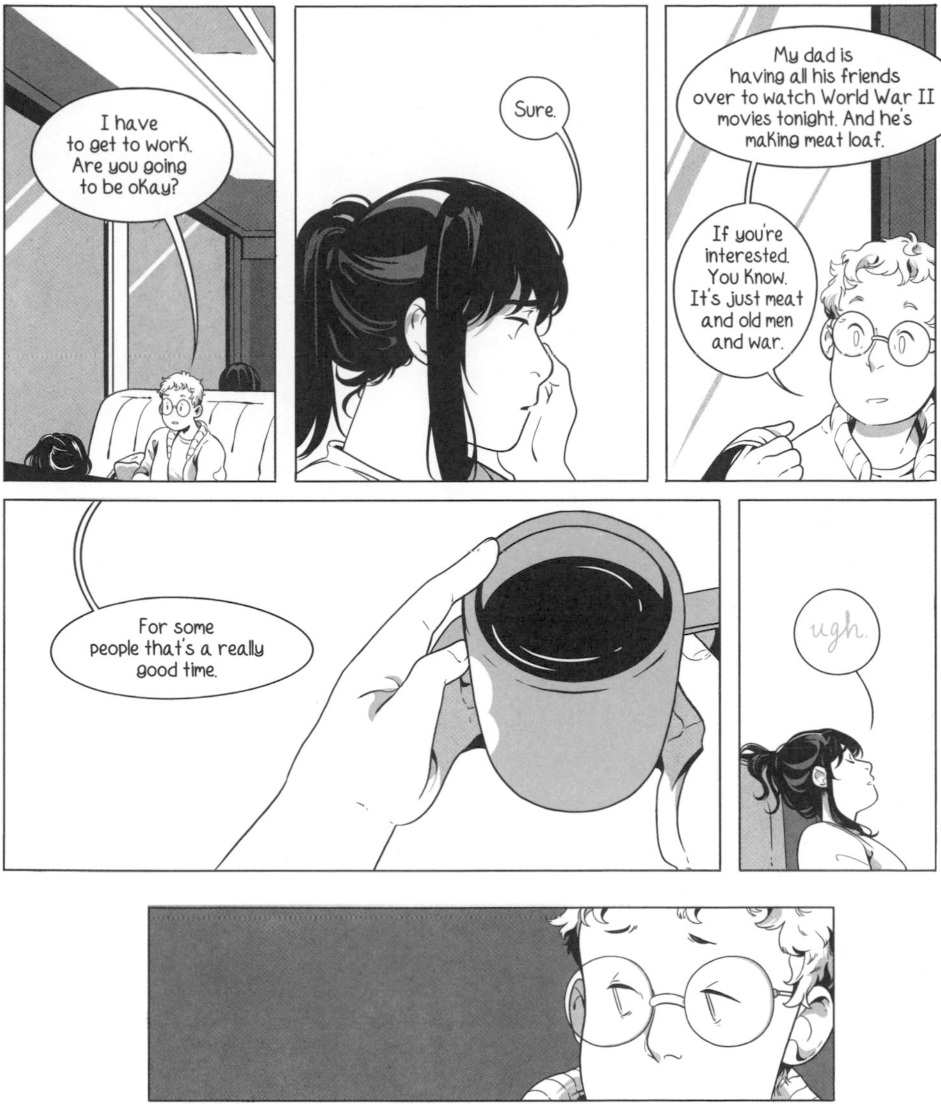
I have to get to work. Are you going to be okay?
Sure.
My dad is having all his friends over to watch World War II movies tonight. And he's making meat loaf.
If you're interested. You know. It's just meat and old men and war.
For some people that's a really good time.
ugh.

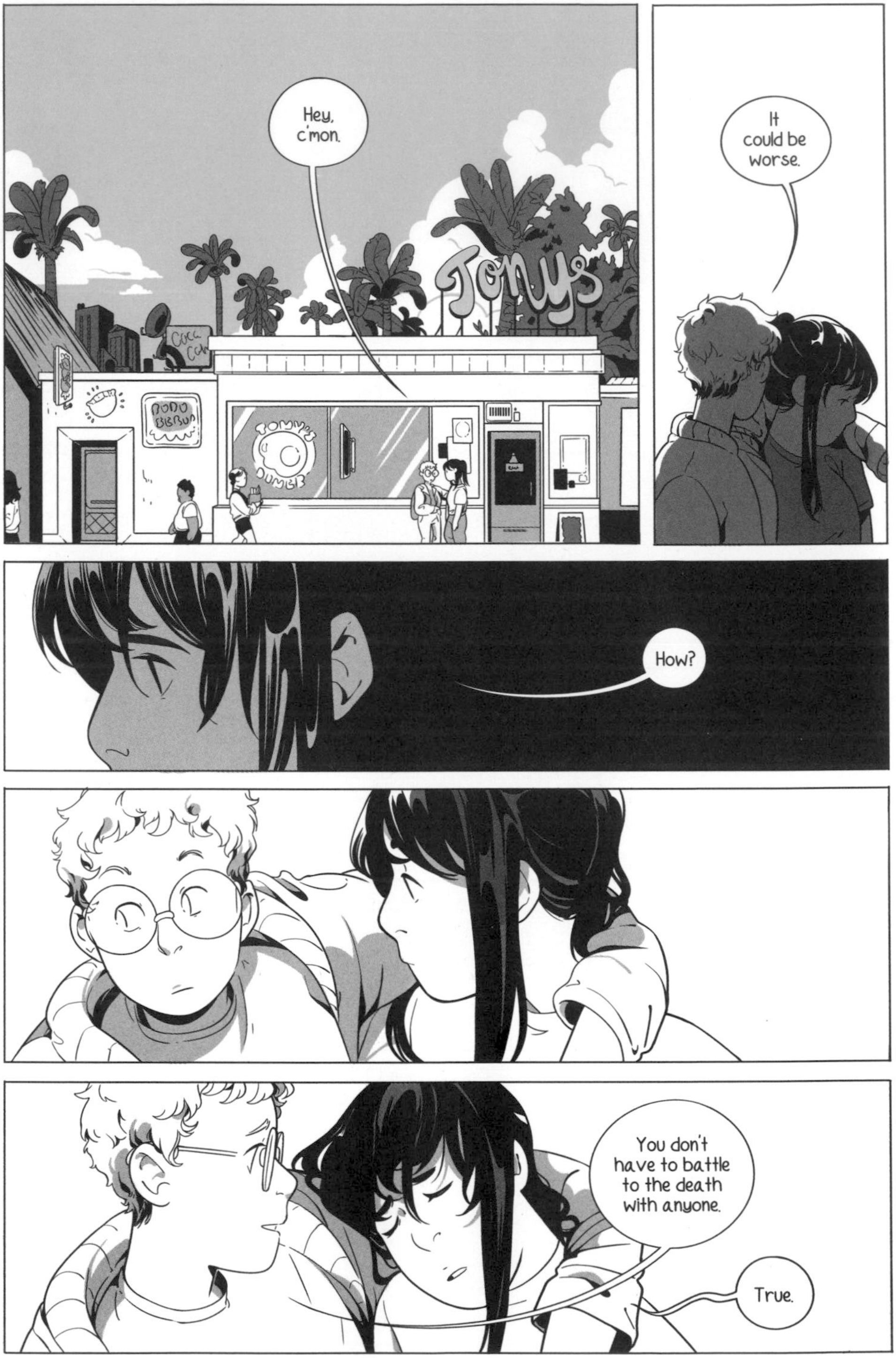
Hey, c'mon.
It could be worse.
How?
You don't have to battle to the death with anyone.
True.

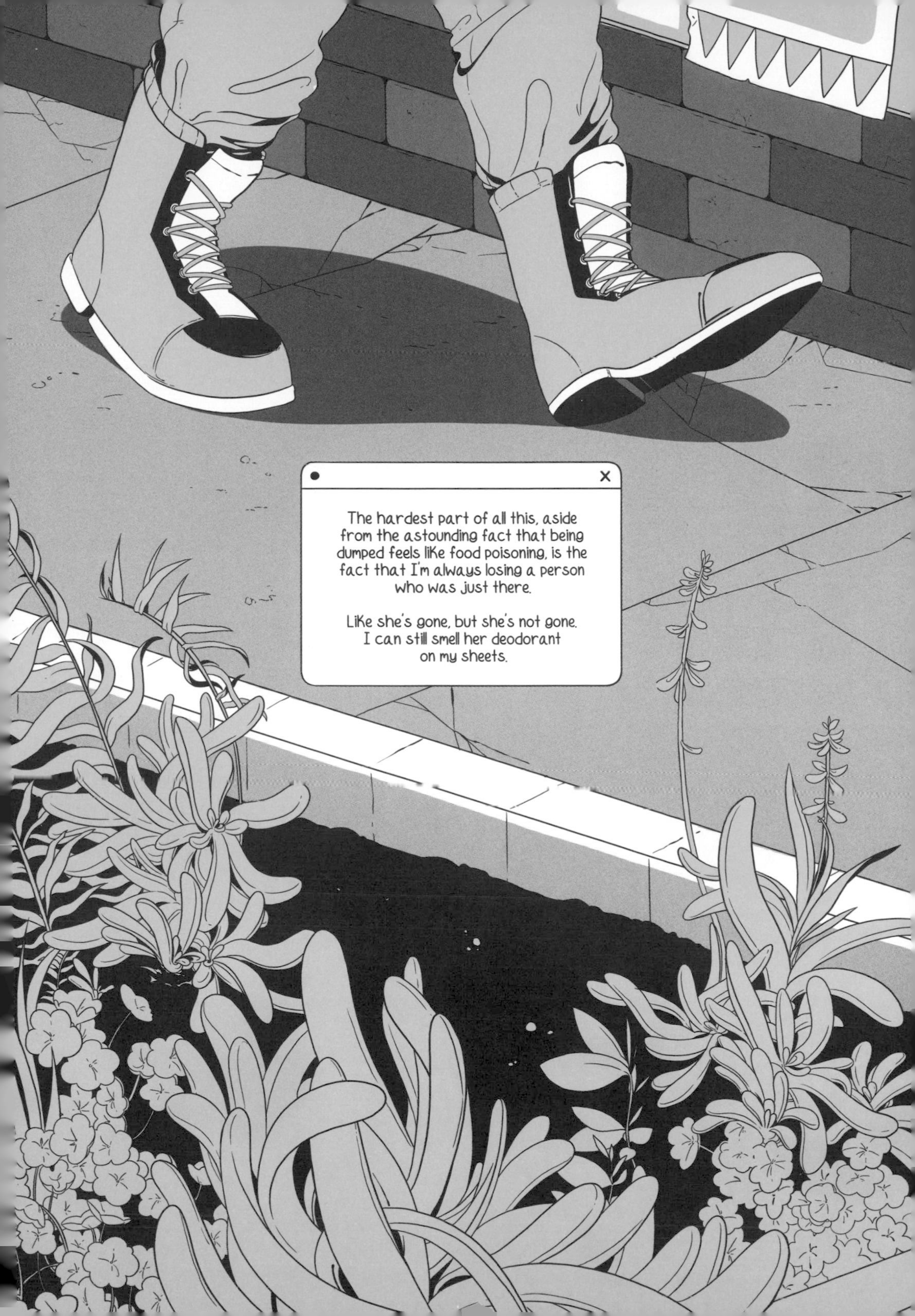
The hardest part of all this, aside from the astounding fact that being dumped feels like food poisoning, is the fact that I'm always losing a person who was just there.
Like she's gone, but she's not gone. I can still smell her deodorant on my sheets.

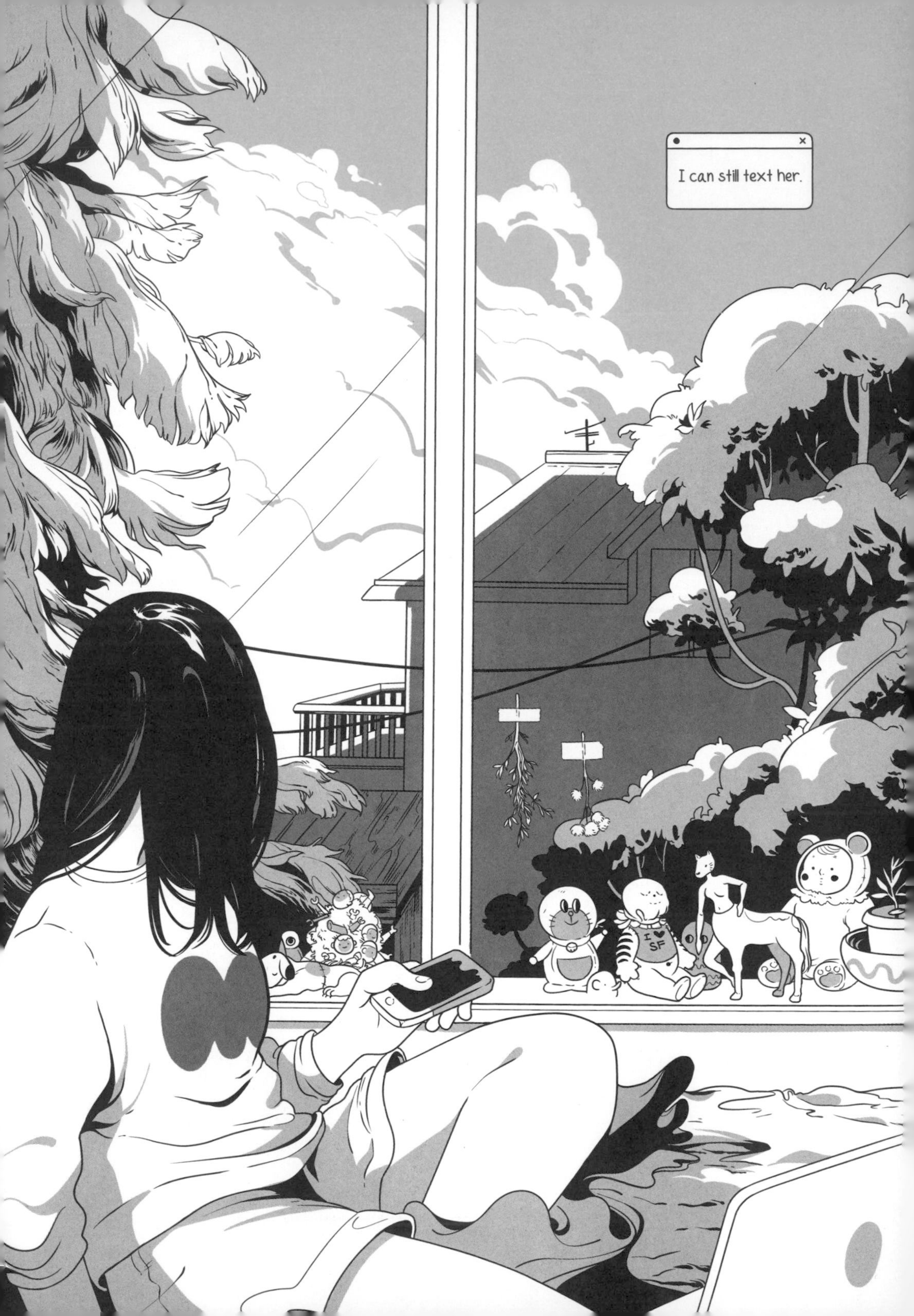
I can still text her.
I ♥ SF

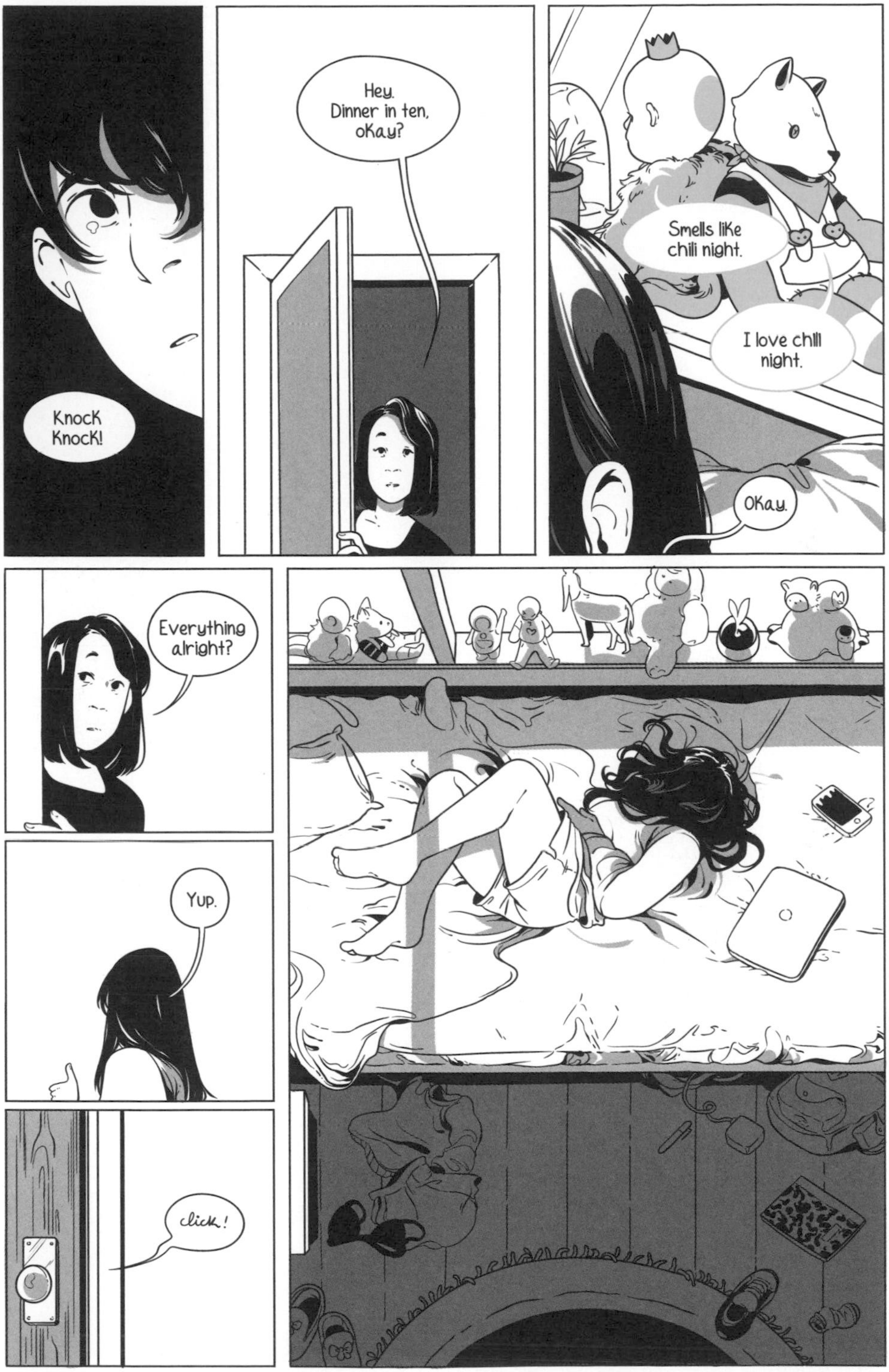
Knock Knock!
Hey. Dinner in ten, okay?
Smells like chili night.
I love chili night.
Okay.
Everything alright?
Yup.
click!

Of course, I know there are LGBTQIA activists out there who fought for centuries for me to have the right to fuck up like this.

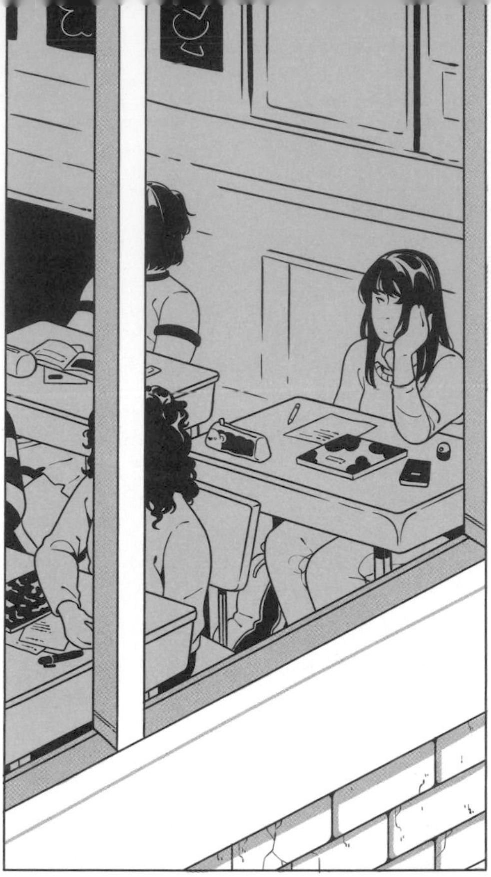

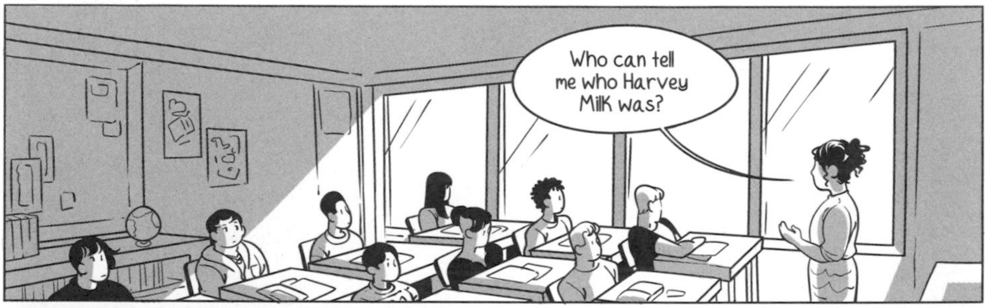
Who can tell me who Harvey Milk was?

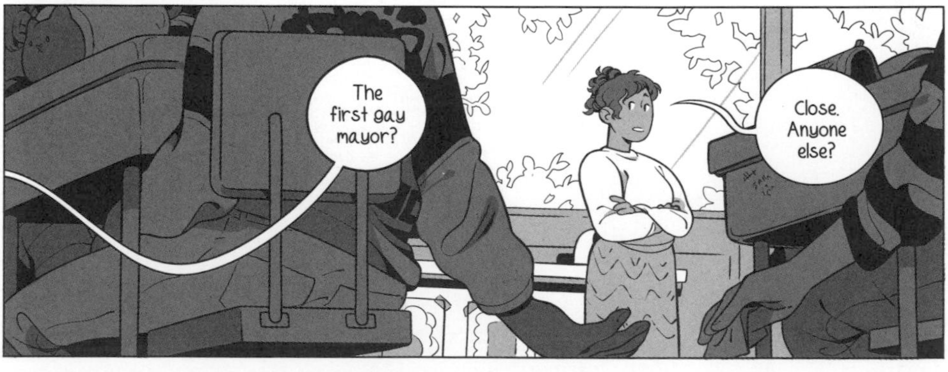
The first gay mayor?
Close. Anyone else?

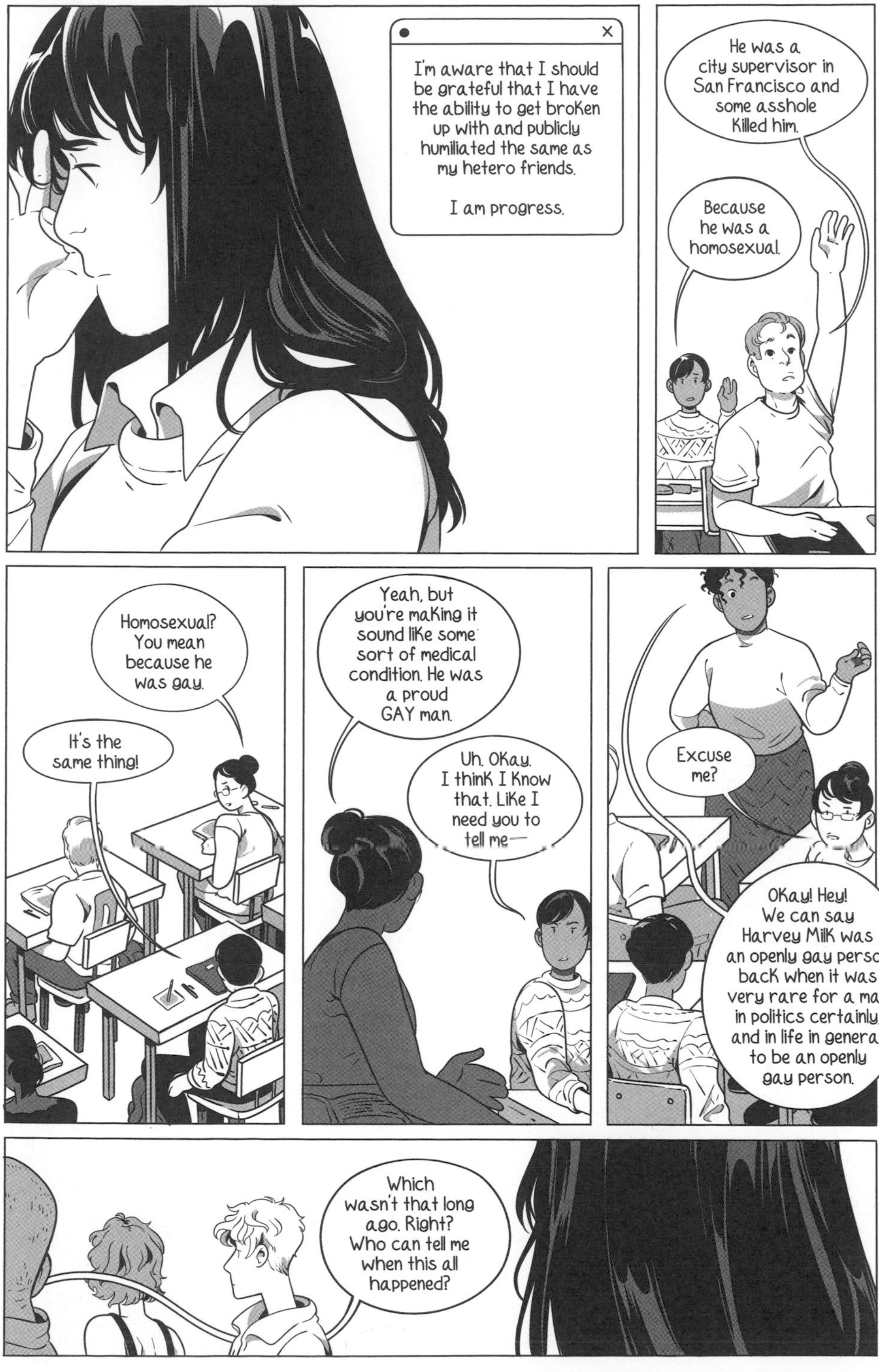
I'm aware that I should be grateful that I have the ability to get broken up with and publicly humiliated the same as my hetero friends.
I am progress.
He was a city supervisor in San Francisco and some asshole killed him.
Because he was a homosexual.
Homosexual? You mean because he was gay.
It's the same thing!
Yeah, but you're making it sound like some sort of medical condition. He was a proud GAY man.
Uh. Okay. I think I know that. Like I need you to tell me—
Excuse me?
Okay! Hey! We can say Harvey Milk was an openly gay person back when it was very rare for a man in politics certainly, and in life in general, to be an openly gay person.
Which wasn't that long ago. Right? Who can tell me when this all happened?

Embarrassing. Progress.

Second hardest part of this?

There are no secrets in high school.

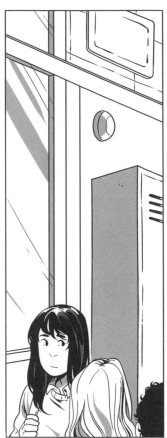

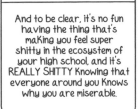
And to be clear, it's no fun having the thing that's making you feel super shitty in the ecosystem of your high school, and it's REALLY SHITTY knowing that everyone around you knows why you are miserable.

WHAT?

Uh, nothing?

Jesus. Chill.

In case that wasn't, you know, clear.

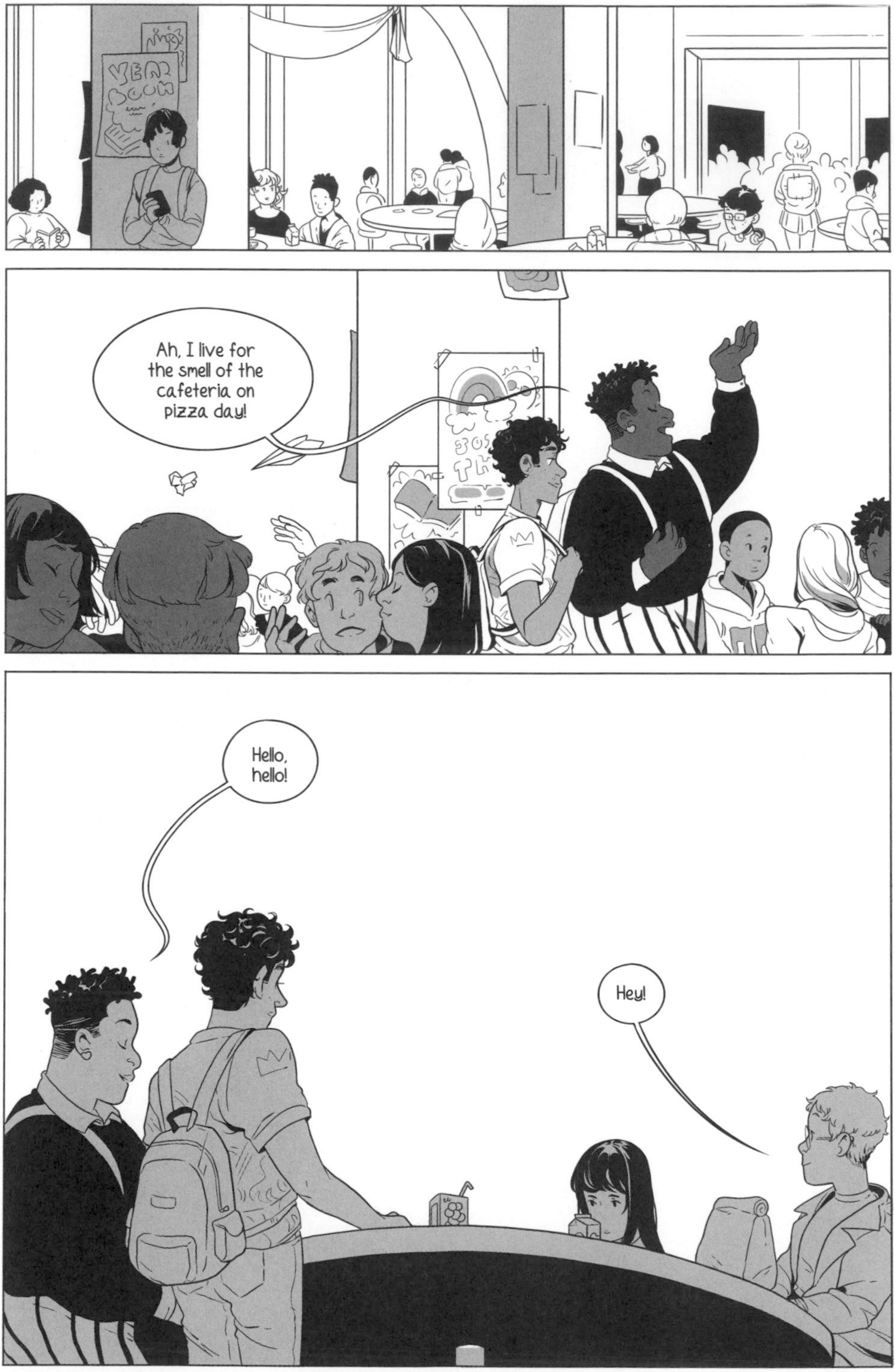
Ah, I live for the smell of the cafeteria on pizza day!
Hello, hello!
Hey!

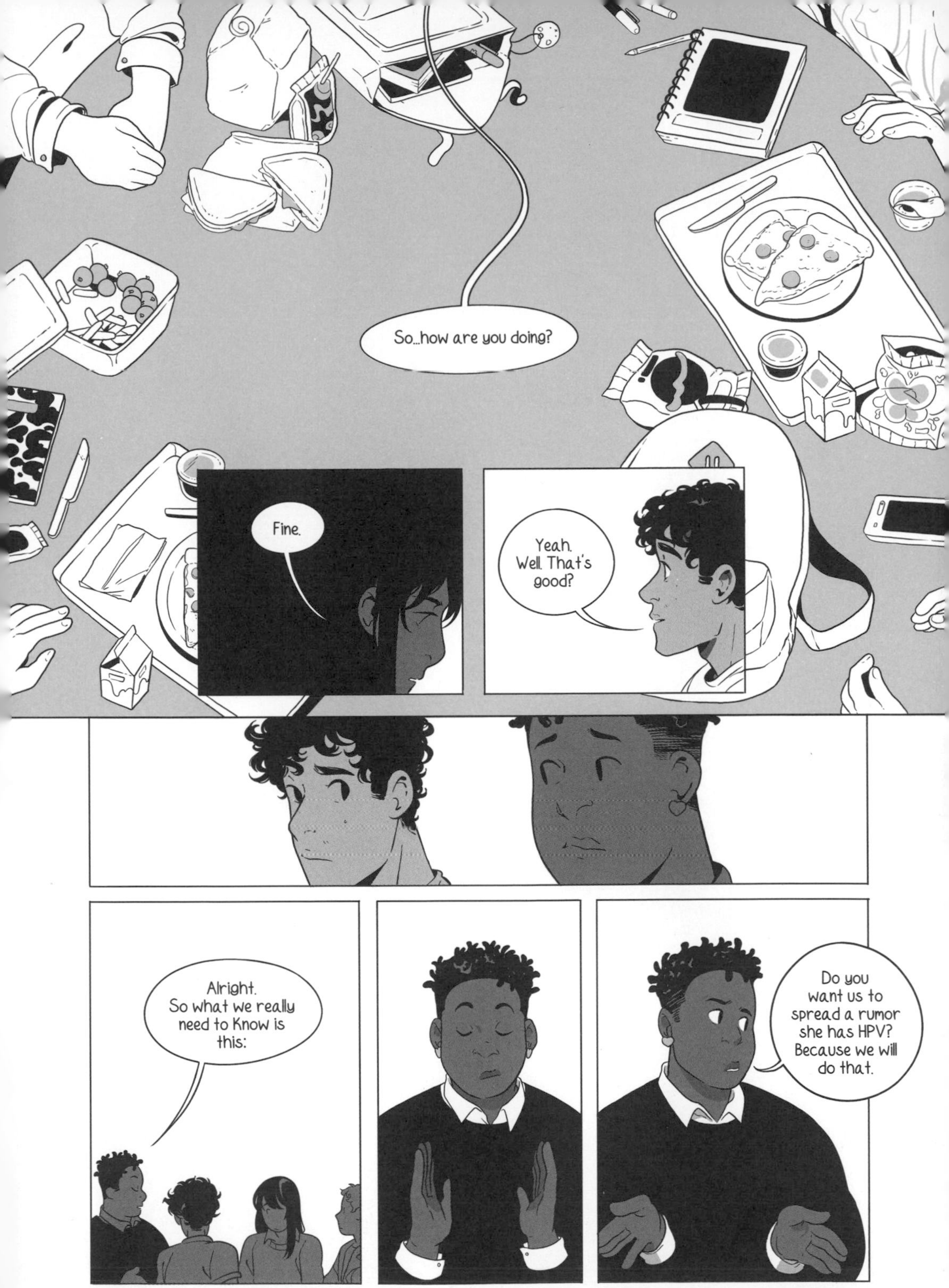
So...how are you doing?
Fine.
Yeah. Well. That's good?
Alright. So what we really need to Know is this:
Do you want us to spread a rumor she has HPV? Because we will do that.

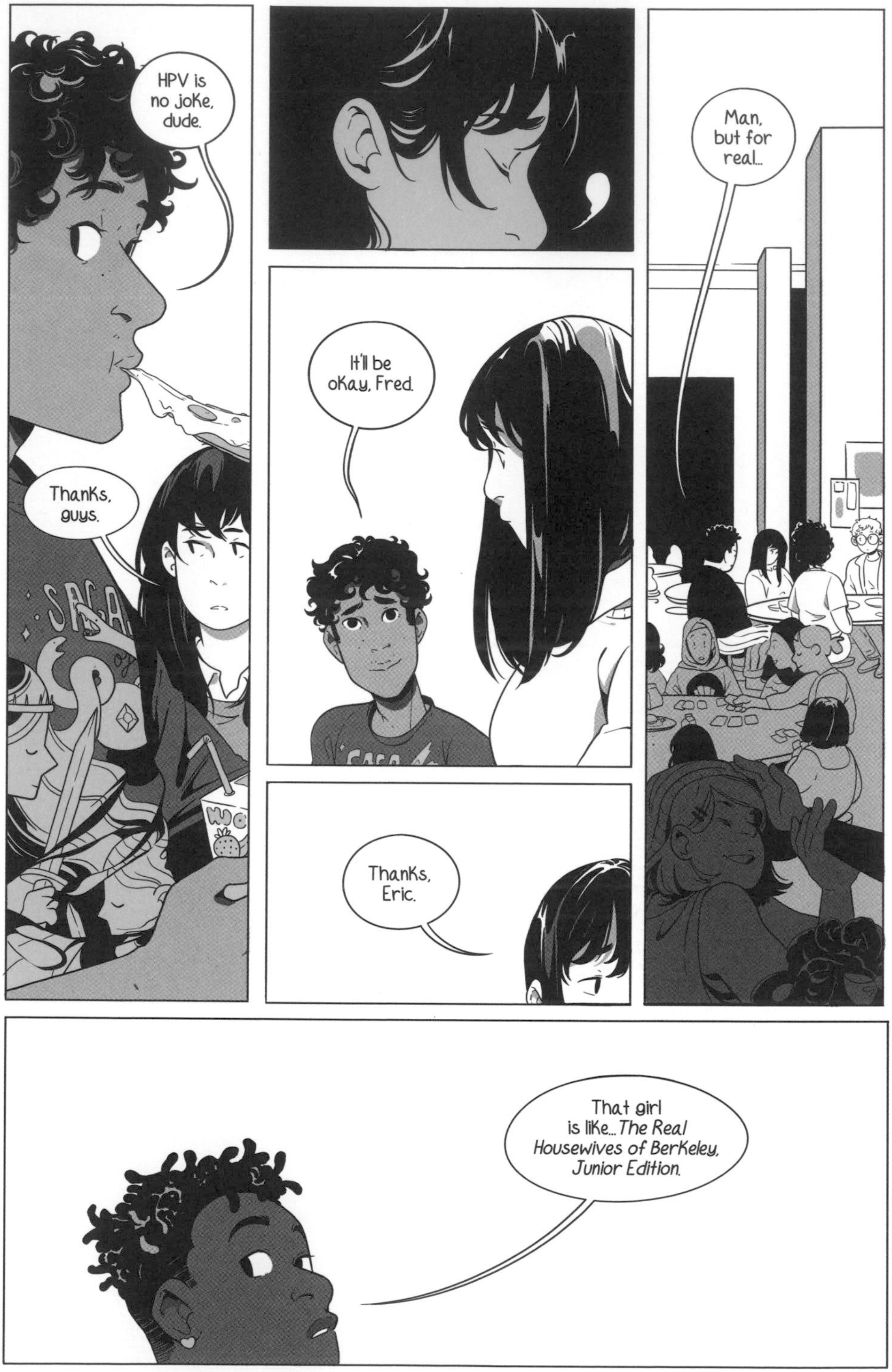
HPV is no joKe, dude.
ThanKs, guys.
It'll be oKay, Fred.
ThanKs, Eric.
Man, but for real...
That girl is liKe... *The Real Housewives of BerKeley, Junior Edition.*

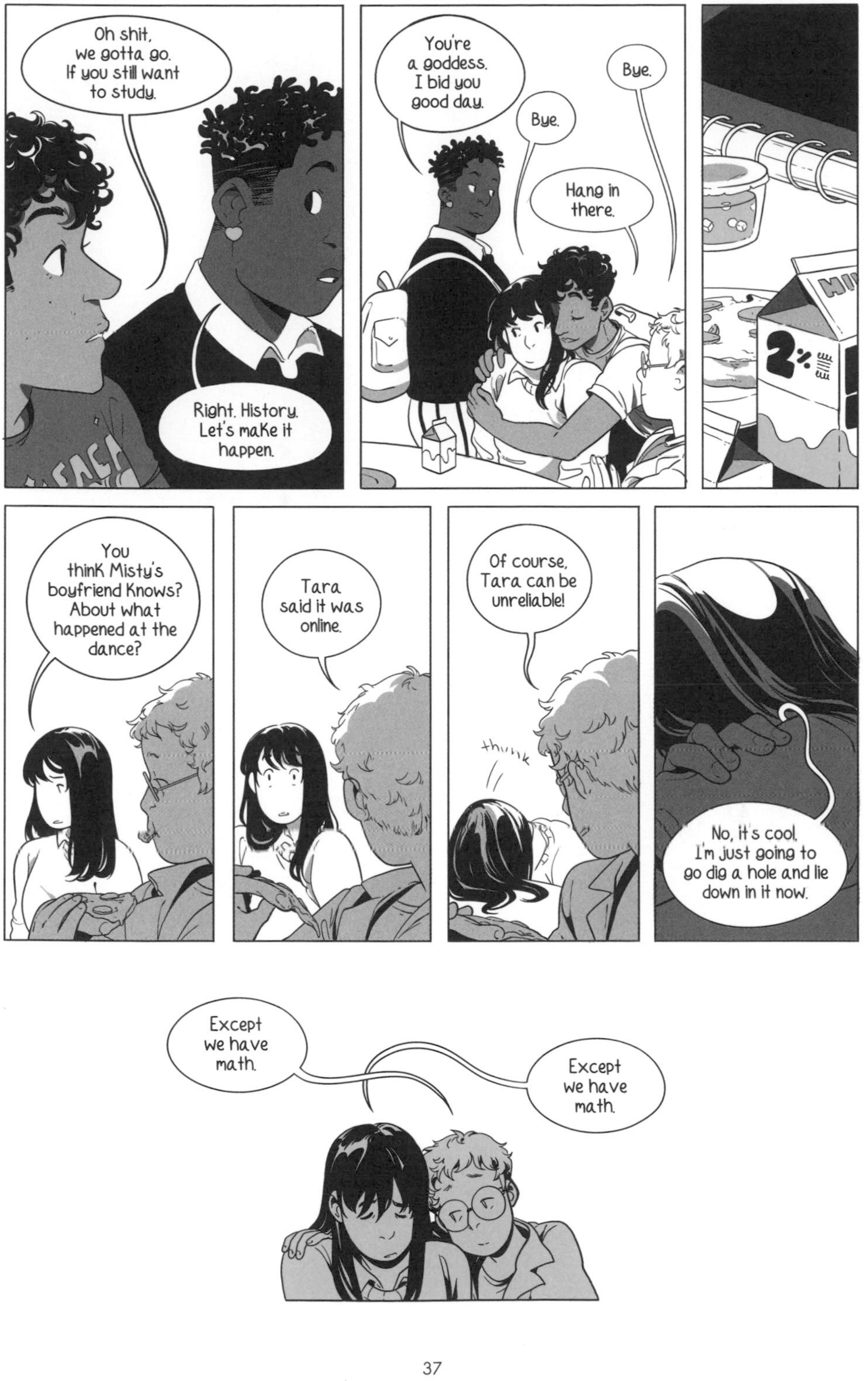
Oh shit, we gotta go. If you still want to study.
Right. History. Let's make it happen.
You're a goddess. I bid you good day.
Bye.
Bye.
Hang in there.
2%
You think Misty's boyfriend Knows? About what happened at the dance?
Tara said it was online.
Of course, Tara can be unreliable!
thunk
No, it's cool. I'm just going to go dig a hole and lie down in it now.
Except we have math.
Except we have math.

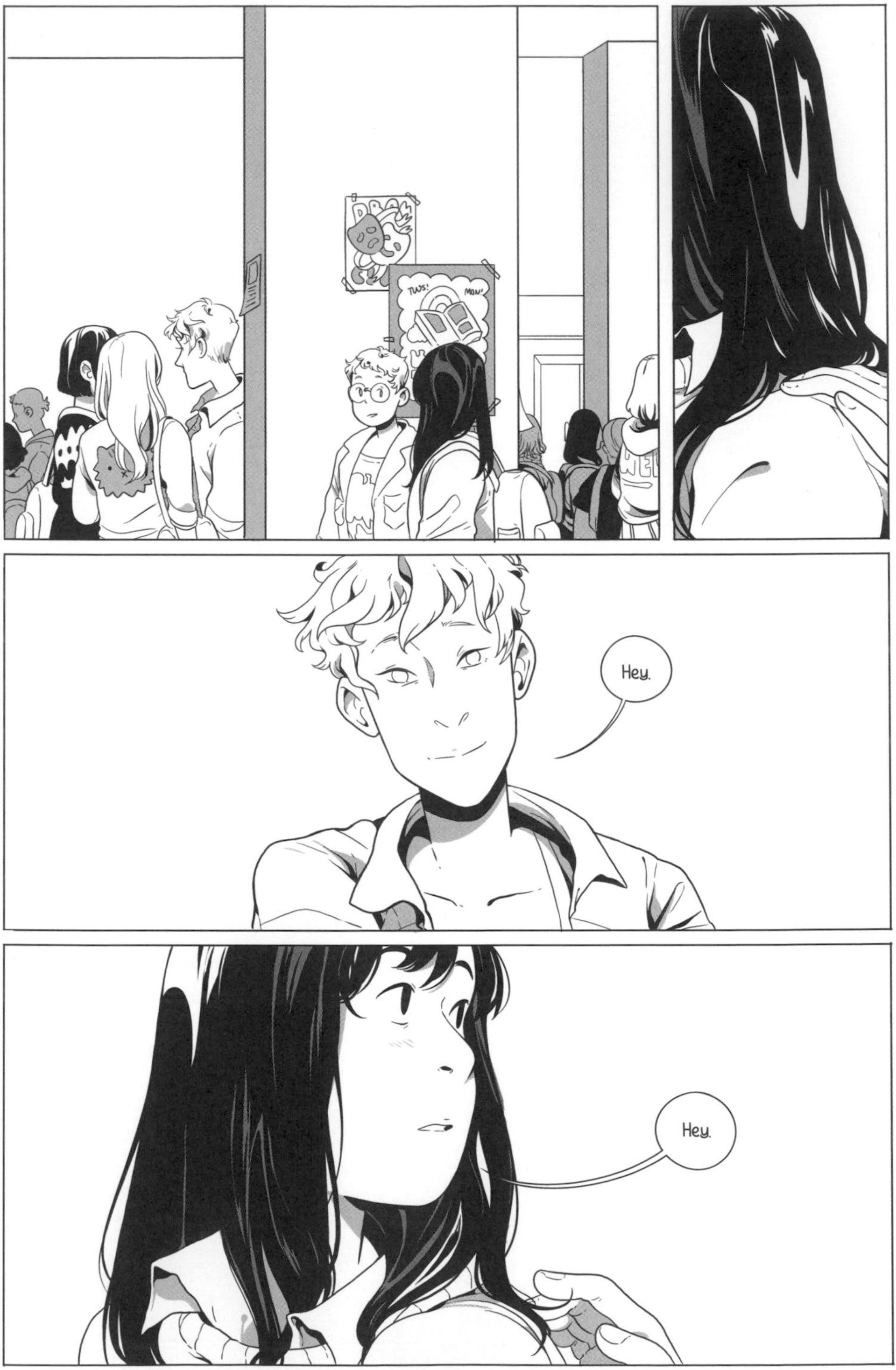
Hey.
Hey.

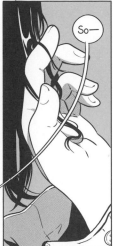So—

Freddu.

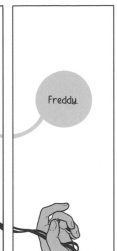

Math?

Please bus t

Yeah.
I mean...
I gotta go
to class.

OKay.
Cool.

Talk
to you
later.

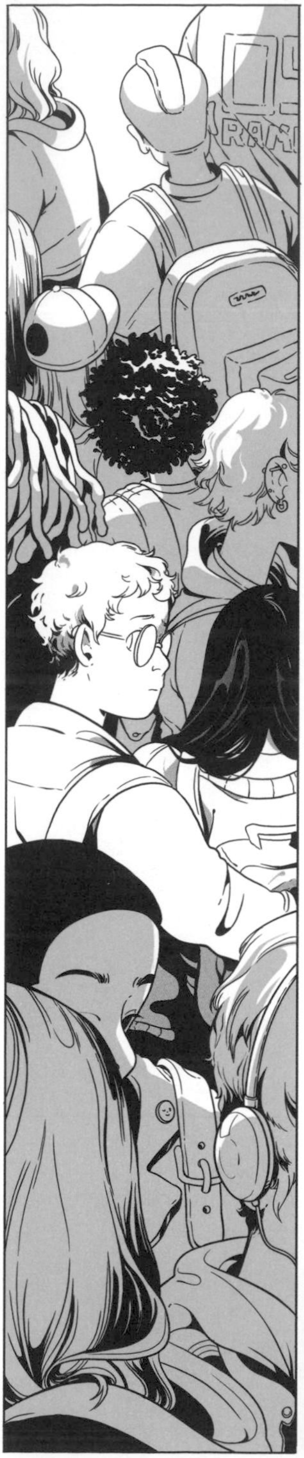

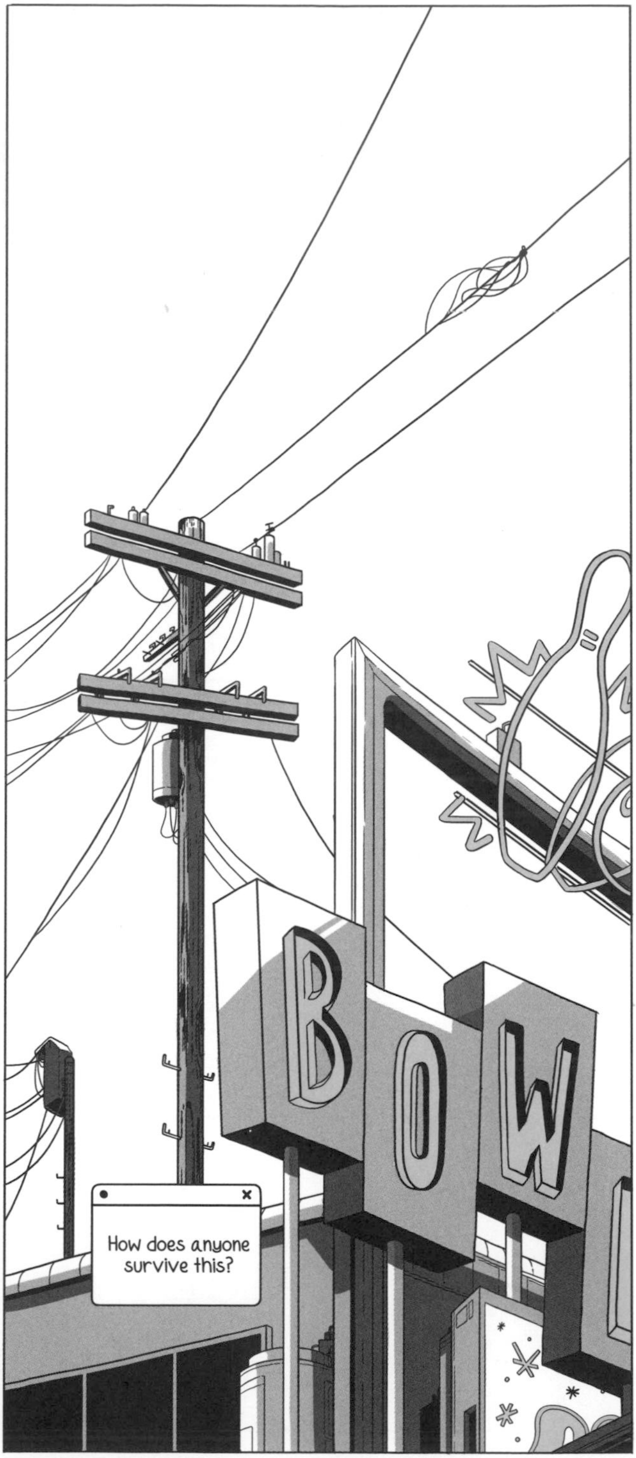
BOW
How does anyone survive this?

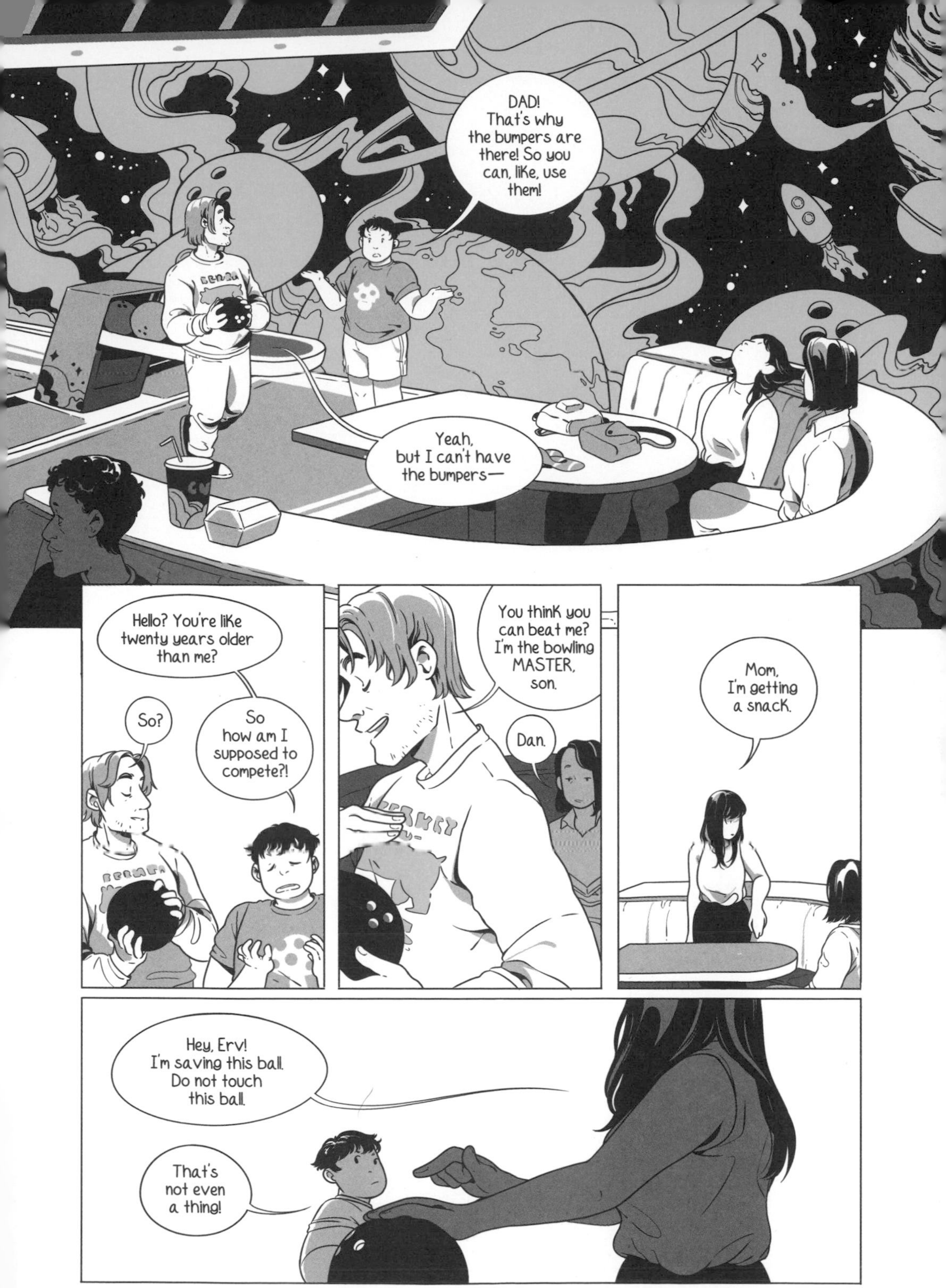
DAD! That's why the bumpers are there! So you can, like, use them!
Yeah, but I can't have the bumpers—
Hello? You're like twenty years older than me?
So?
So how am I supposed to compete?!
You think you can beat me? I'm the bowling MASTER, son.
Dan.
Mom, I'm getting a snack.
Hey, Erv! I'm saving this ball. Do not touch this ball.
That's not even a thing!

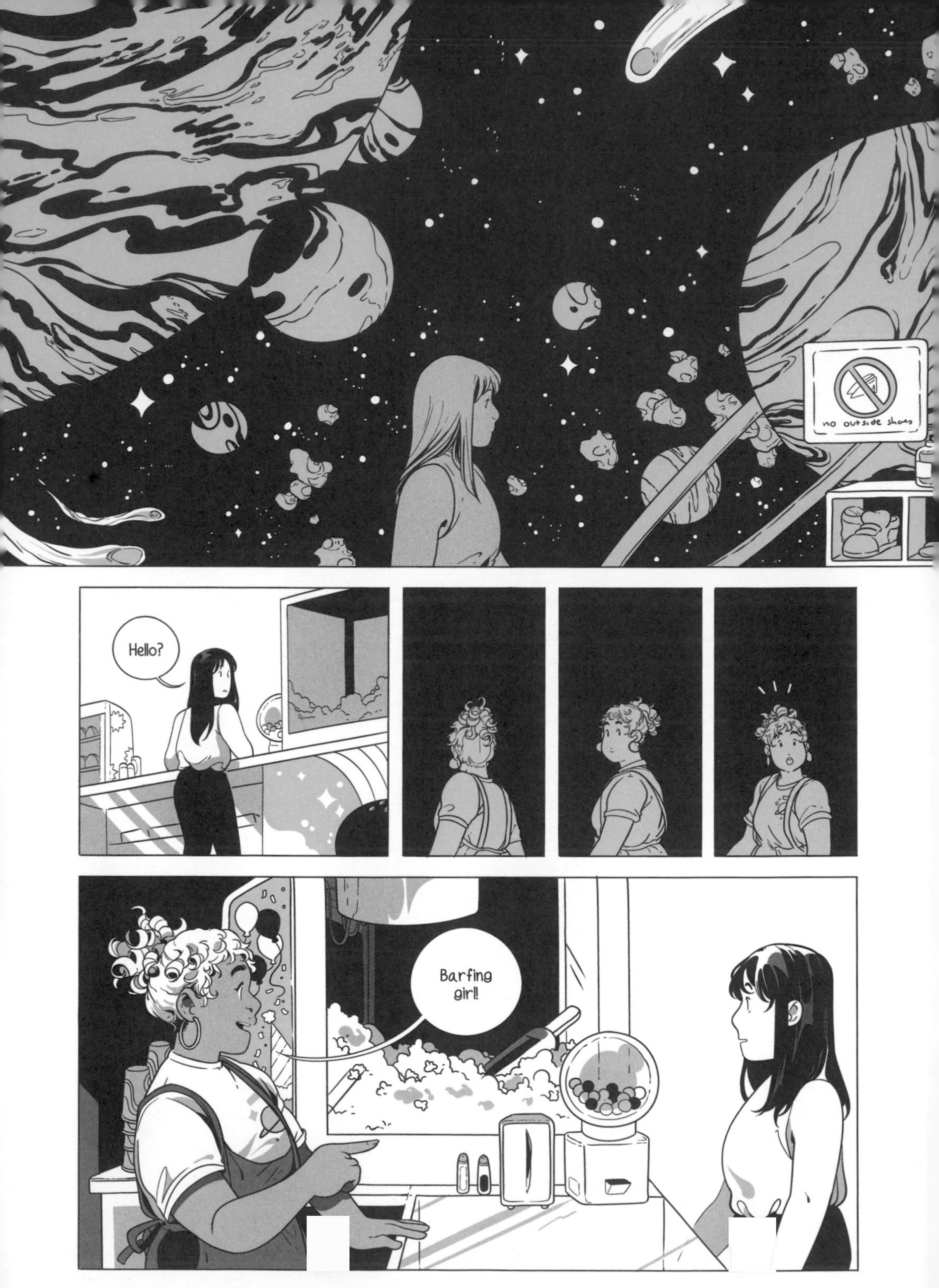
no outside shoes
Hello?
Barfing girl!

Uh. Hey. Doris's Donuts, right?

Ding ding ding! What can I get you?

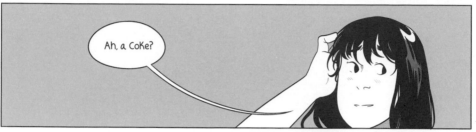

Ah, a Coke?

So how's it going?

Oh! Better. Um, sorry about last Friday. I didn't have the best night.

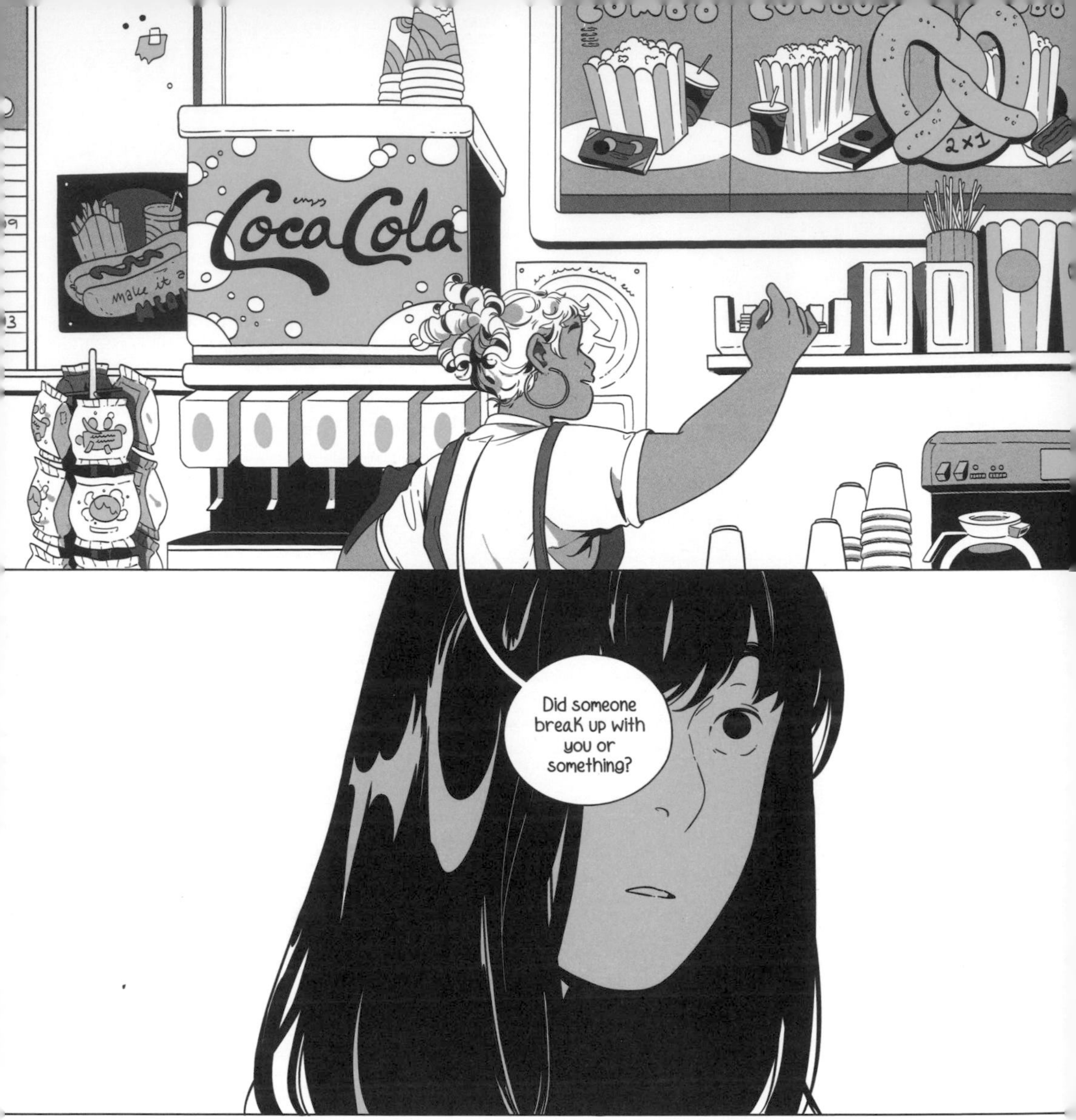
Coca Cola
make it a
2x1
Did someone break up with you or something?

Sorry. I forget sometimes that you're supposed to talk to people you don't know differently than the people you know. You know?

I'm rude.

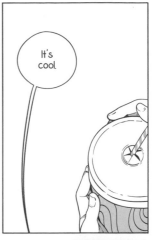

It's cool.

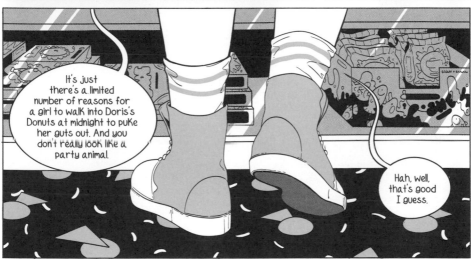

It's just there's a limited number of reasons for a girl to walk into Doris's Donuts at midnight to puke her guts out. And you don't really look like a party animal.

Hah, well, that's good I guess.

Freddyyy. Mom said to get her a bag of pretzels.

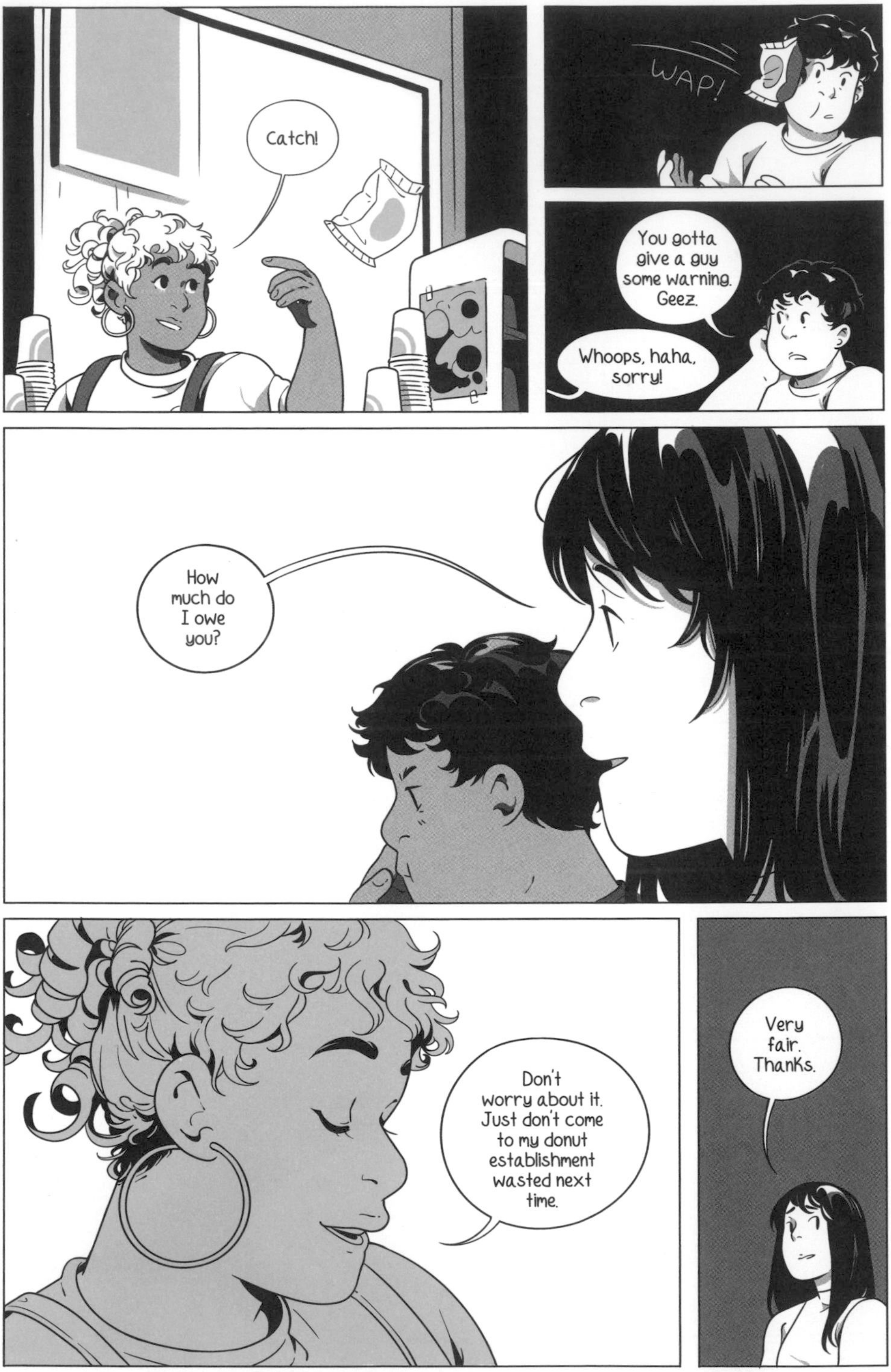
Catch!
WAP!
You gotta give a guy some warning. Geez.
Whoops, haha, sorry!
How much do I owe you?
Don't worry about it. Just don't come to my donut establishment wasted next time.
Very fair. Thanks.

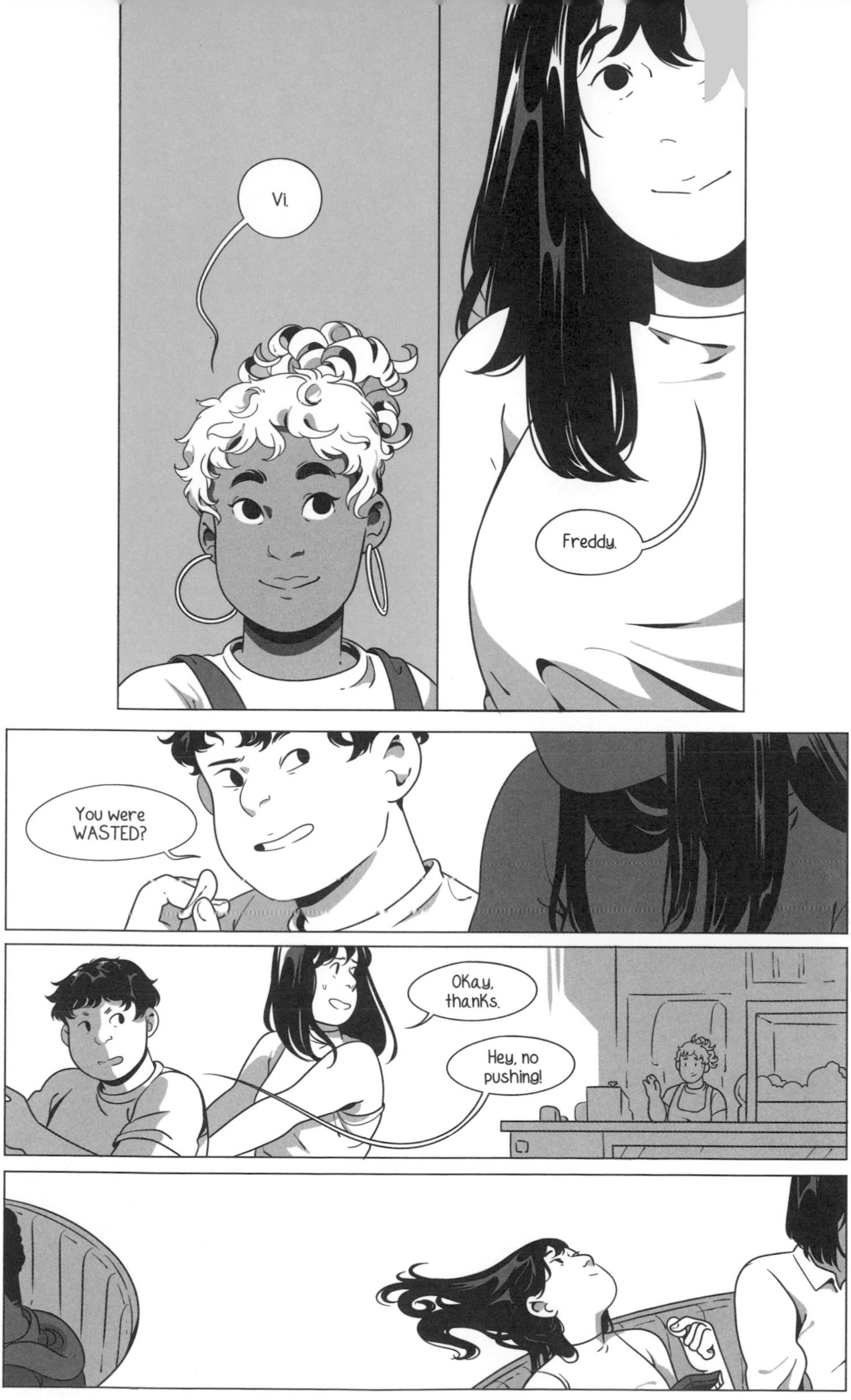
Vi.
Freddy.
You were WASTED?
Okay, thanks.
Hey, no pushing!

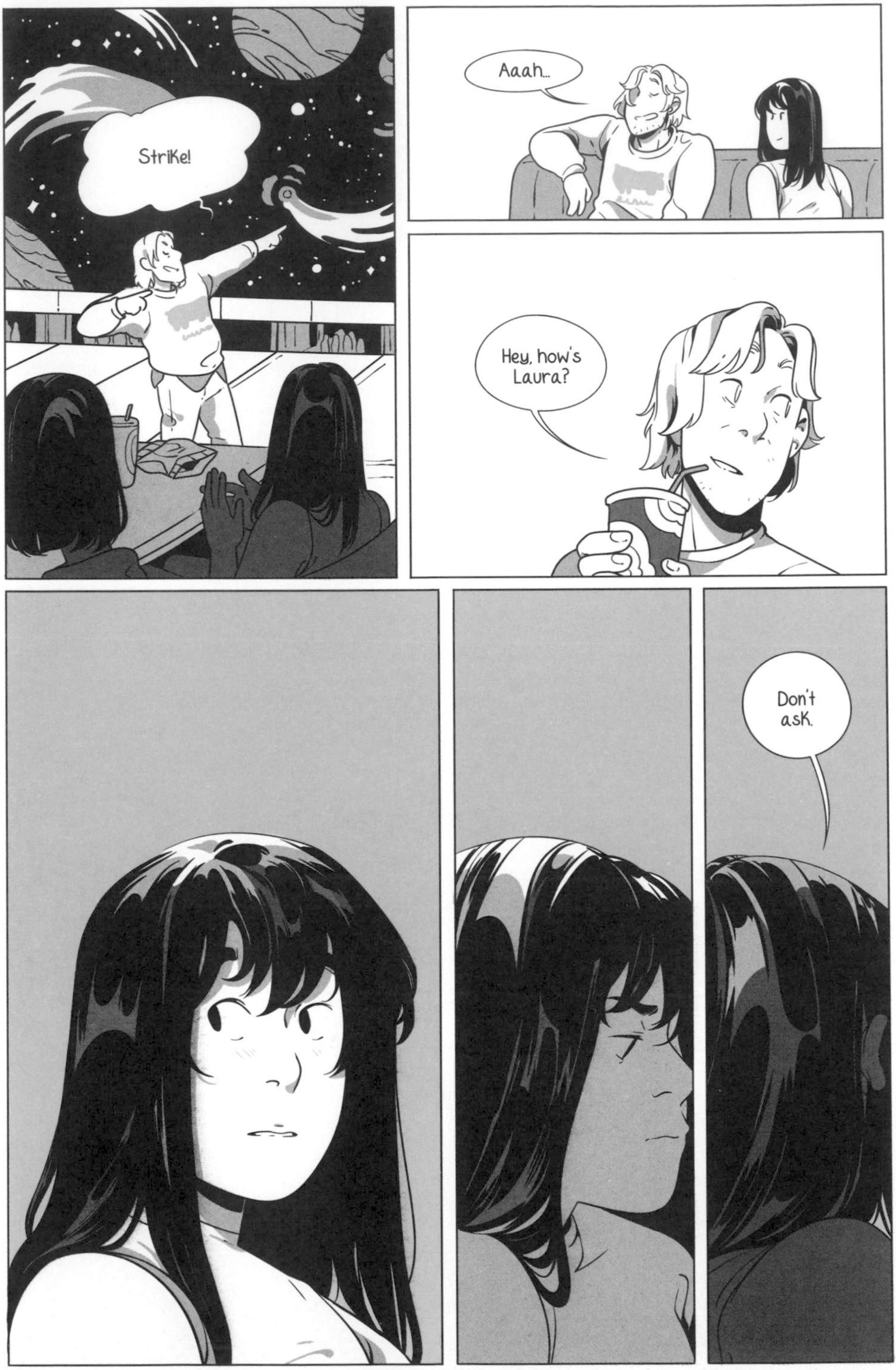
Strike!
Aaah...
Hey, how's Laura?
Don't ask.

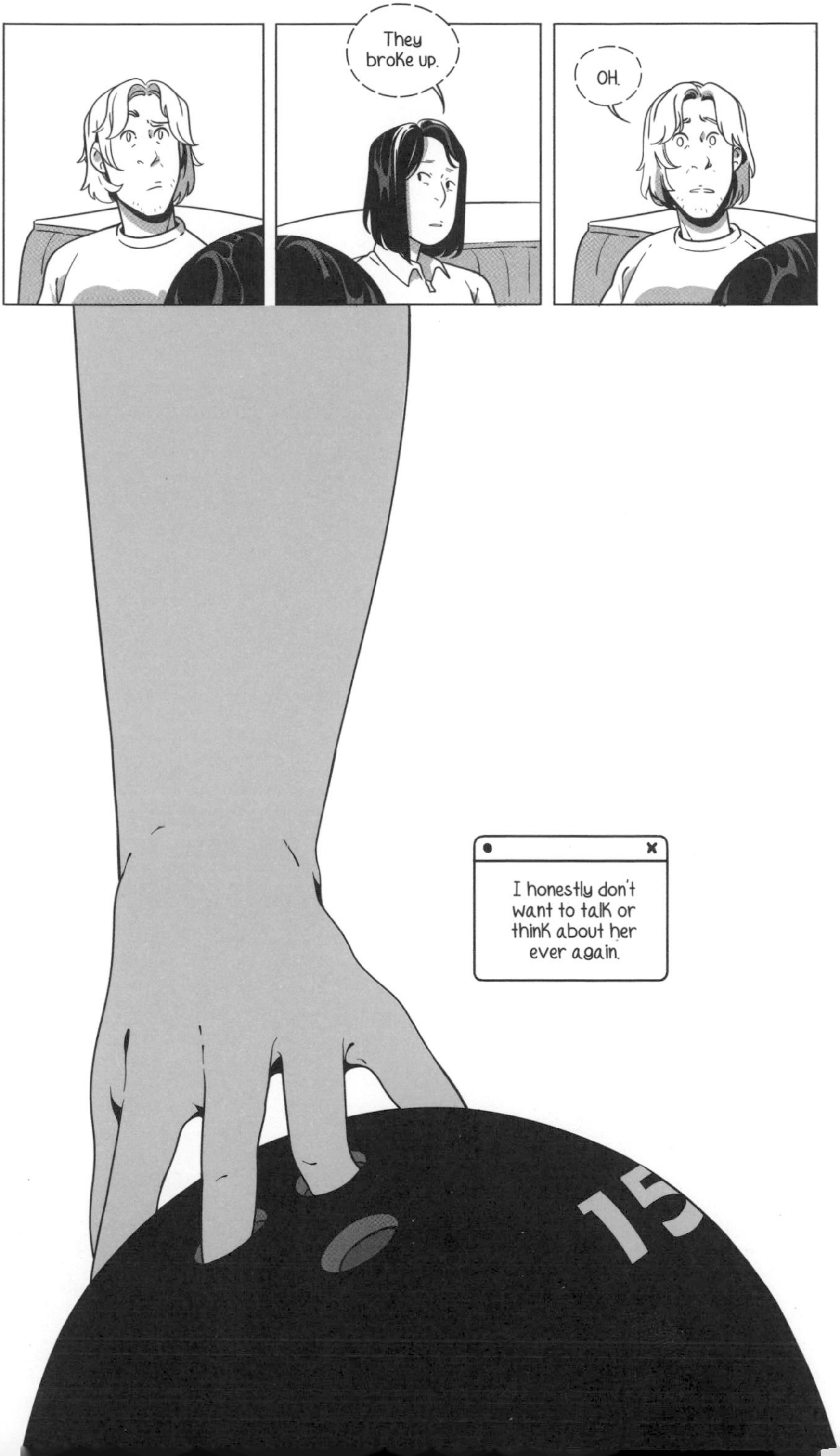
They broke up.
OH.
I honestly don't want to talk or think about her ever again.
15

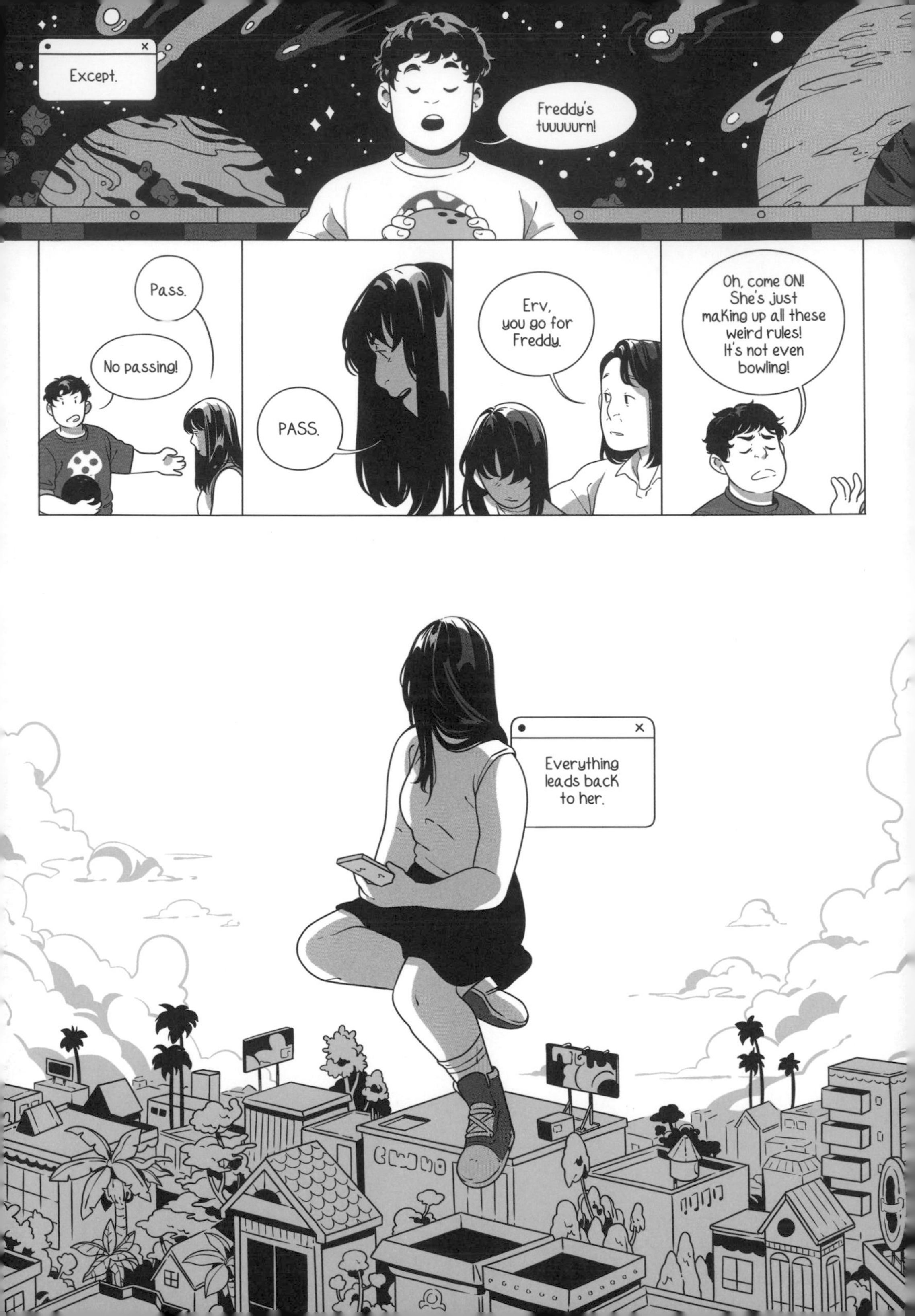

Except.
Freddy's tuuuuurn!
Pass.
No passing!
PASS.
Erv, you go for Freddy.
Oh, come ON! She's just making up all these weird rules! It's not even bowling!
Everything leads back to her.

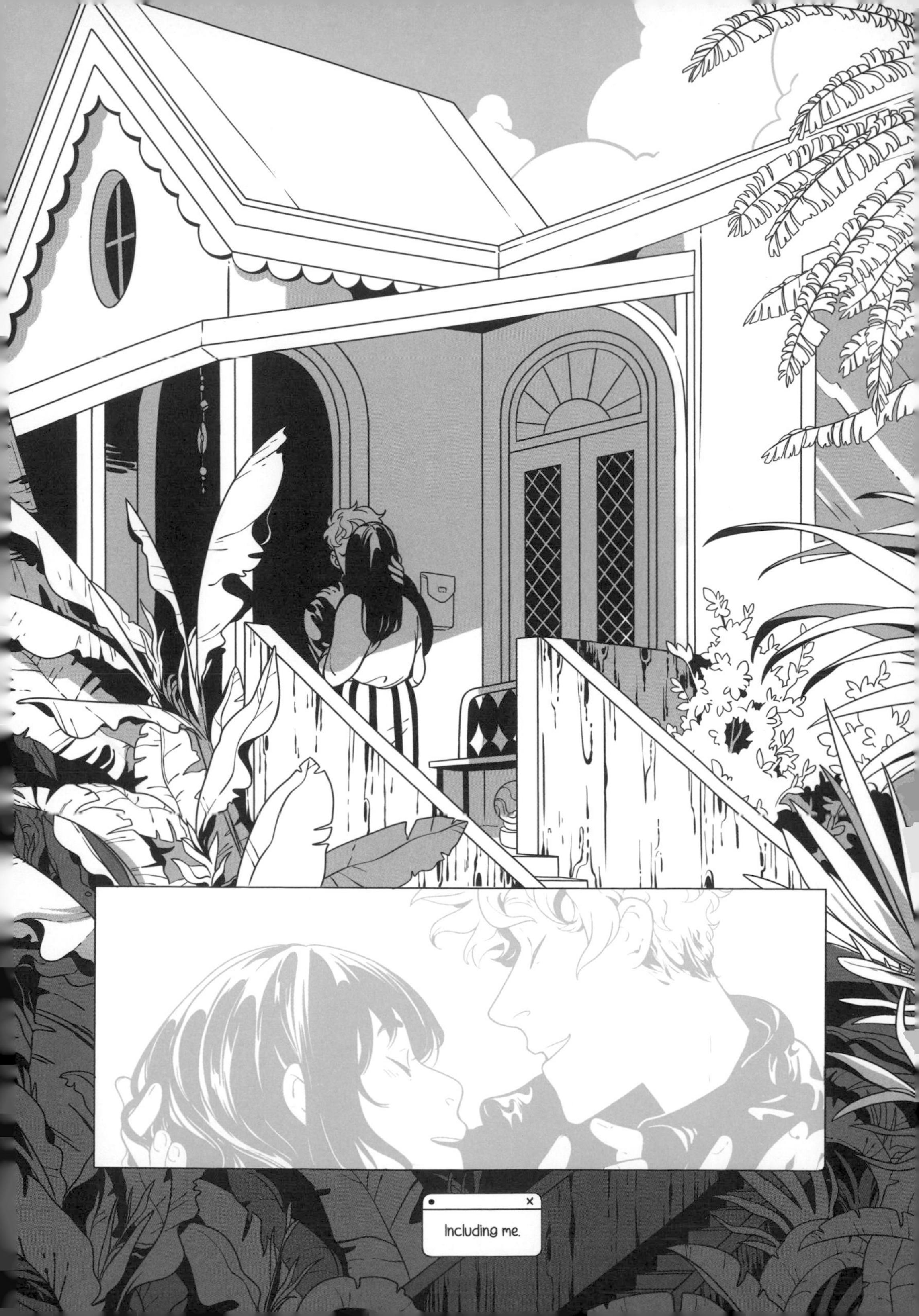
Including me.

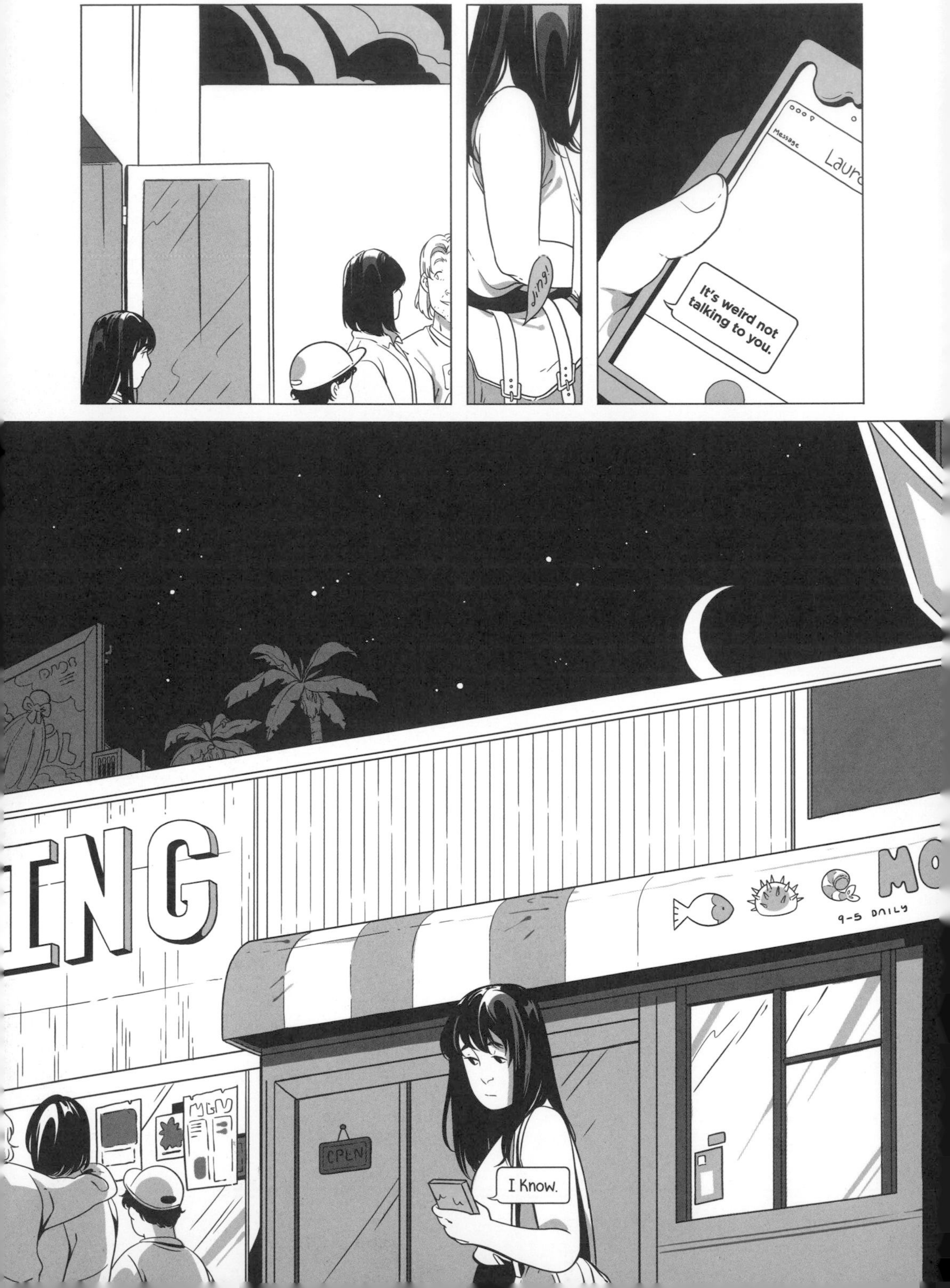
Jing!
Message
It's weird not talking to you.
9-5 DAILY
I Know.

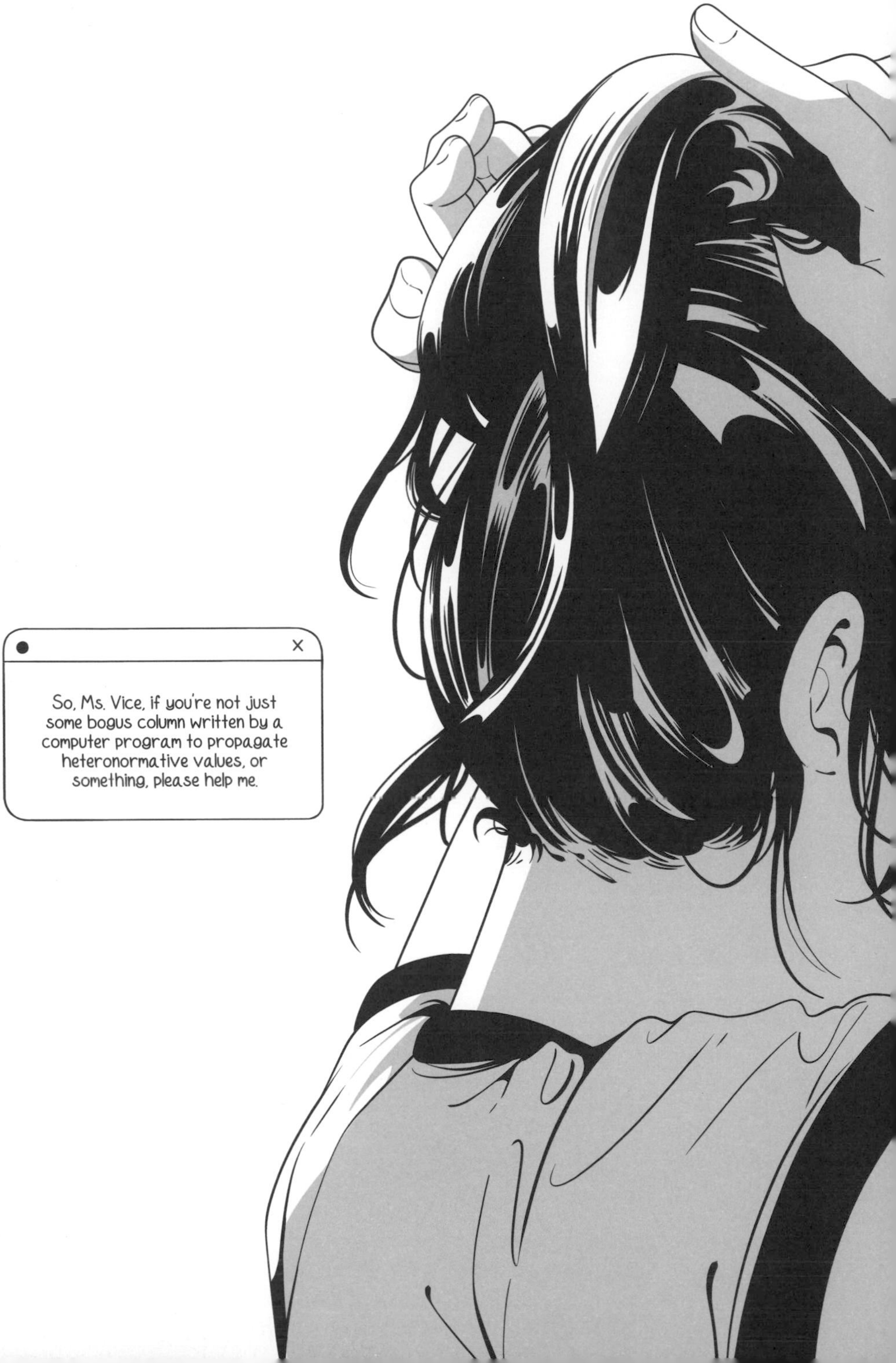
So, Ms. Vice, if you're not just some bogus column written by a computer program to propagate heteronormative values, or something, please help me.

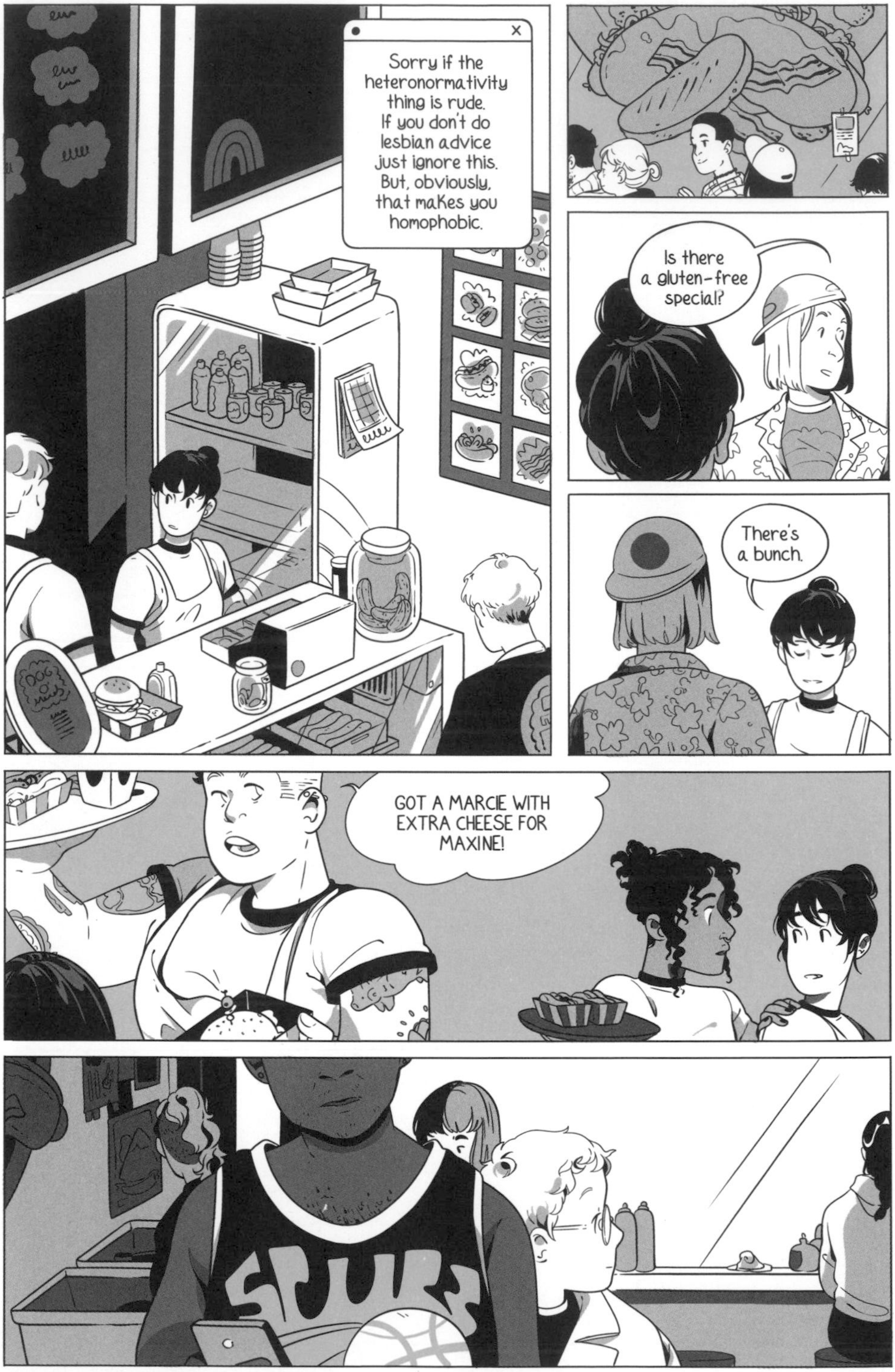

Sorry if the heteronormativity thing is rude. If you don't do lesbian advice just ignore this. But, obviously, that makes you homophobic.
Is there a gluten-free special?
There's a bunch.
GOT A MARCIE WITH EXTRA CHEESE FOR MAXINE!

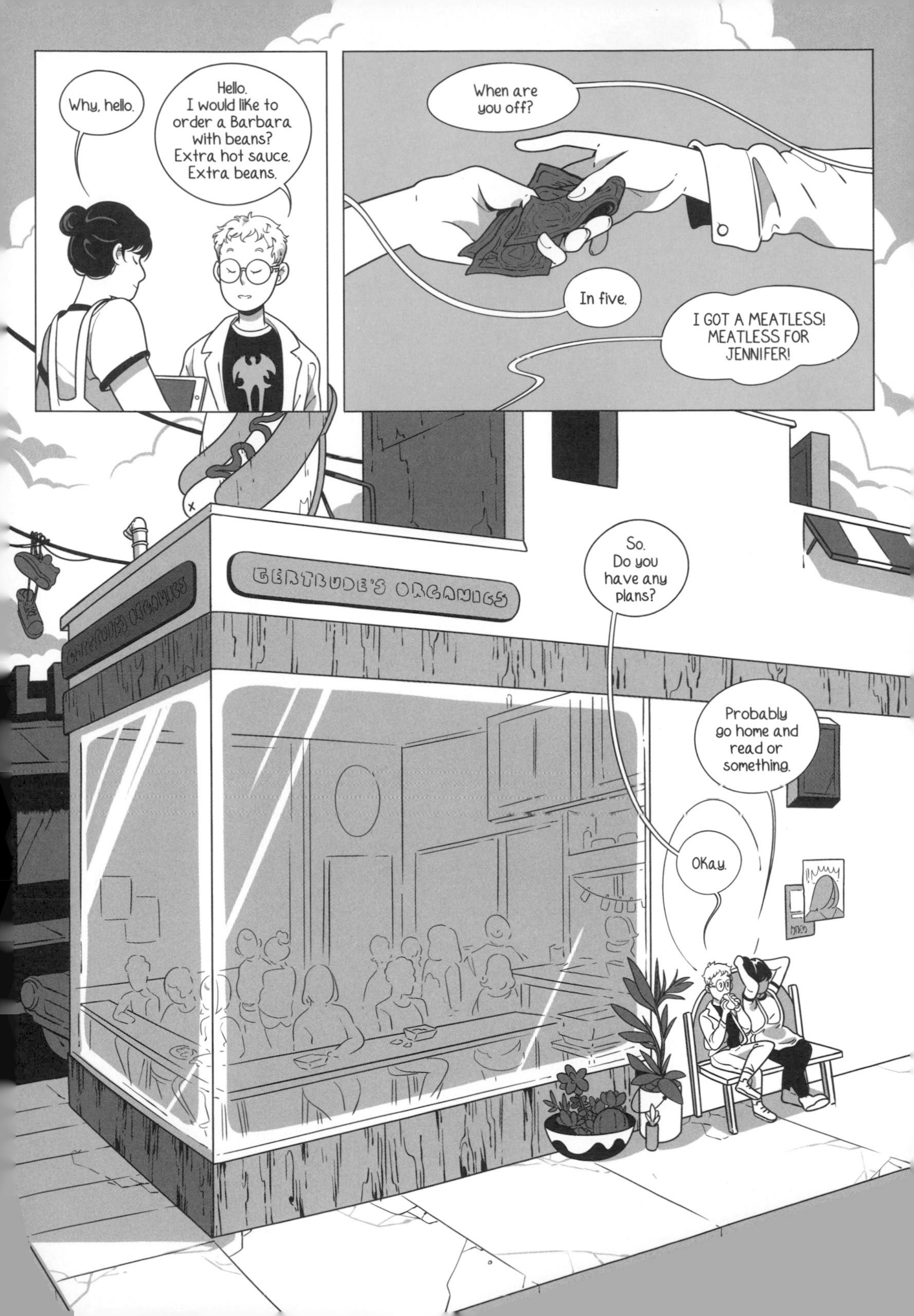
Why, hello.
Hello. I would like to order a Barbara with beans? Extra hot sauce. Extra beans.
When are you off?
In five.
I GOT A MEATLESS! MEATLESS FOR JENNIFER!
GERTRUDE'S ORGANICS
So. Do you have any plans?
Probably go home and read or something.
Okay.

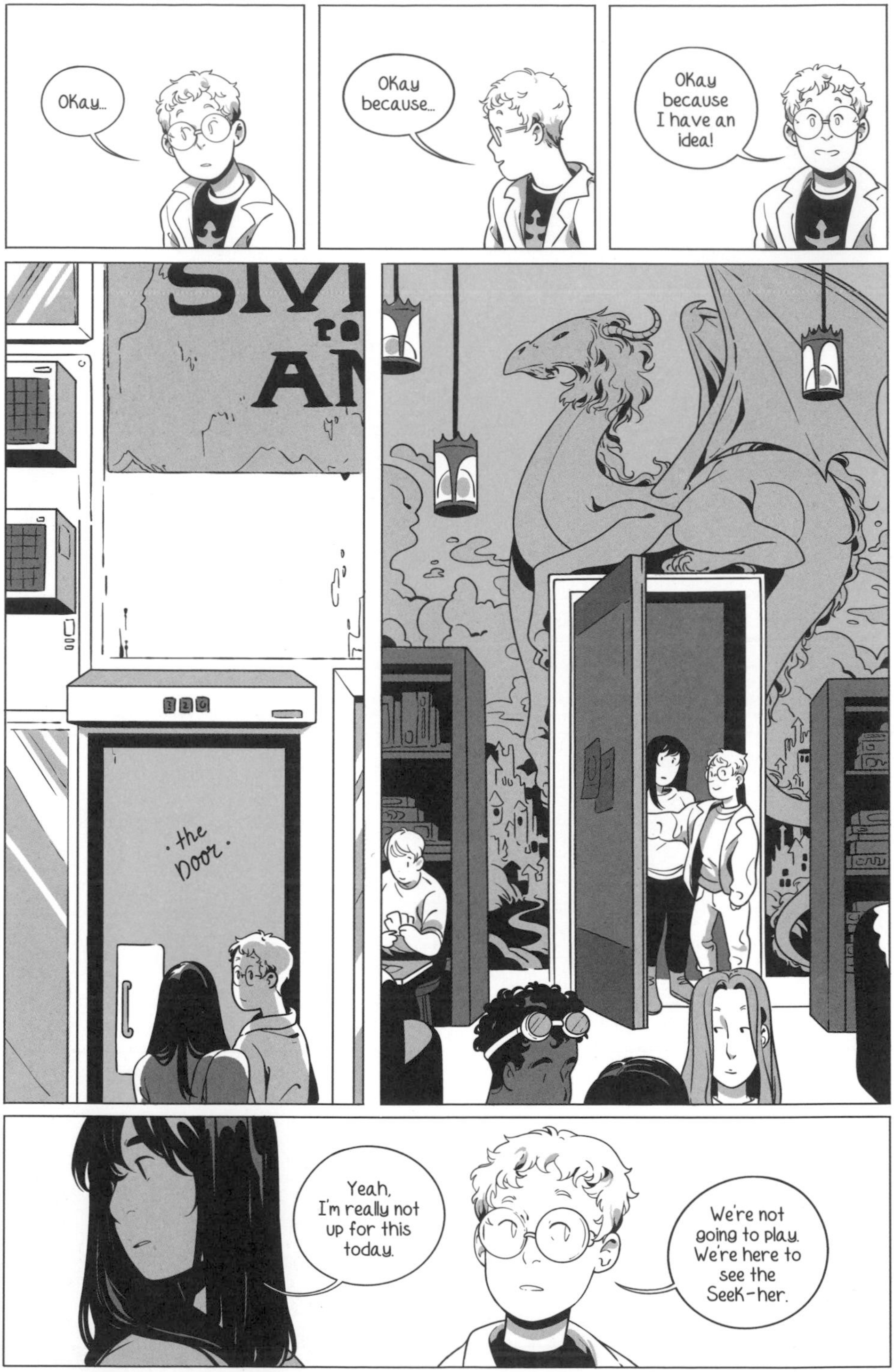
OKay...
OKay because...
OKay because I have an idea!
the Door
Yeah, I'm really not up for this today.
We're not going to play. We're here to see the SeeK-her.

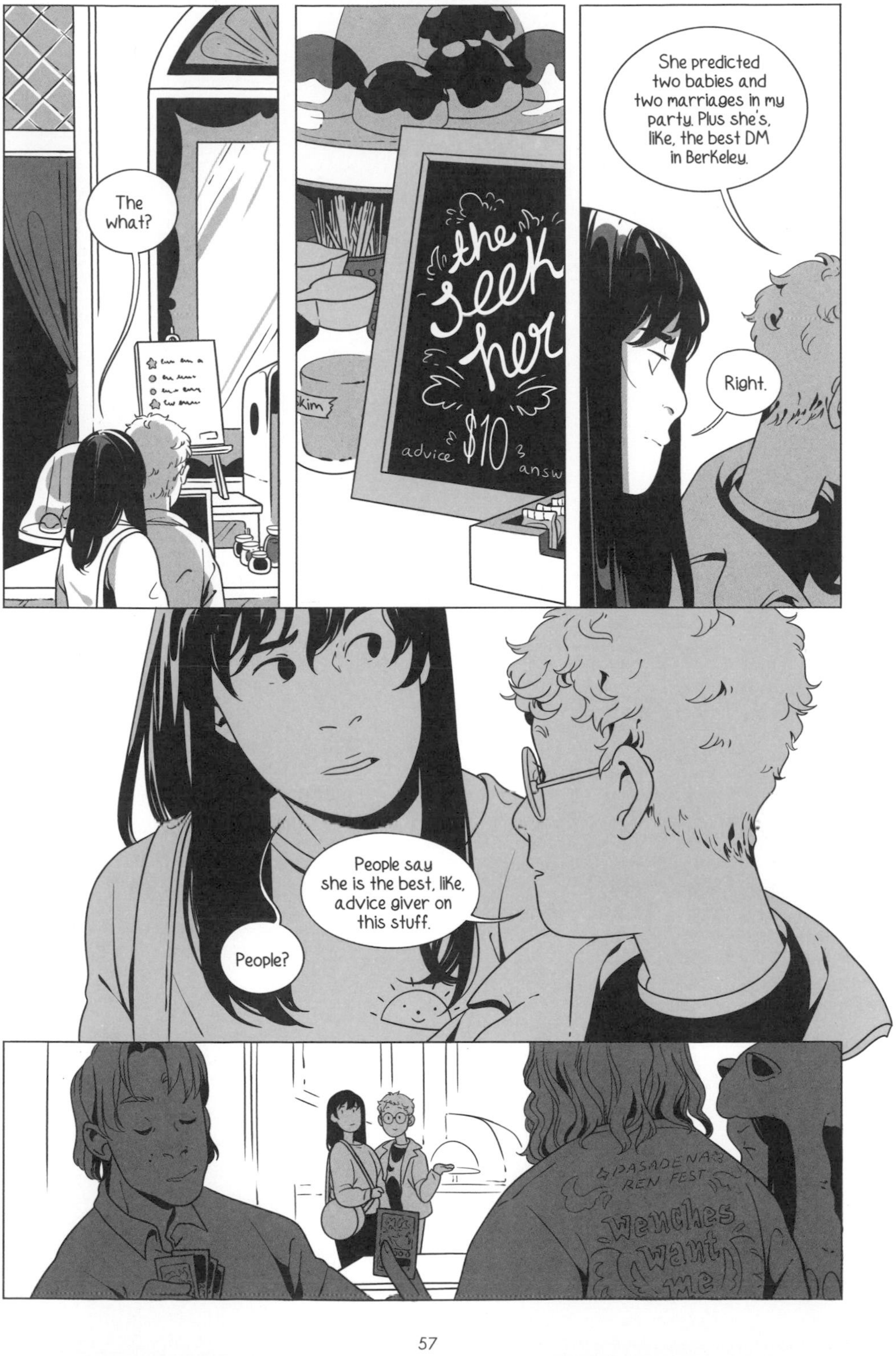
The what?
the seek her
$10
advice
She predicted two babies and two marriages in my party. Plus she's, like, the best DM in Berkeley.
Right.
People say she is the best, like, advice giver on this stuff.
People?
PASADENA REN FEST
wenches want me

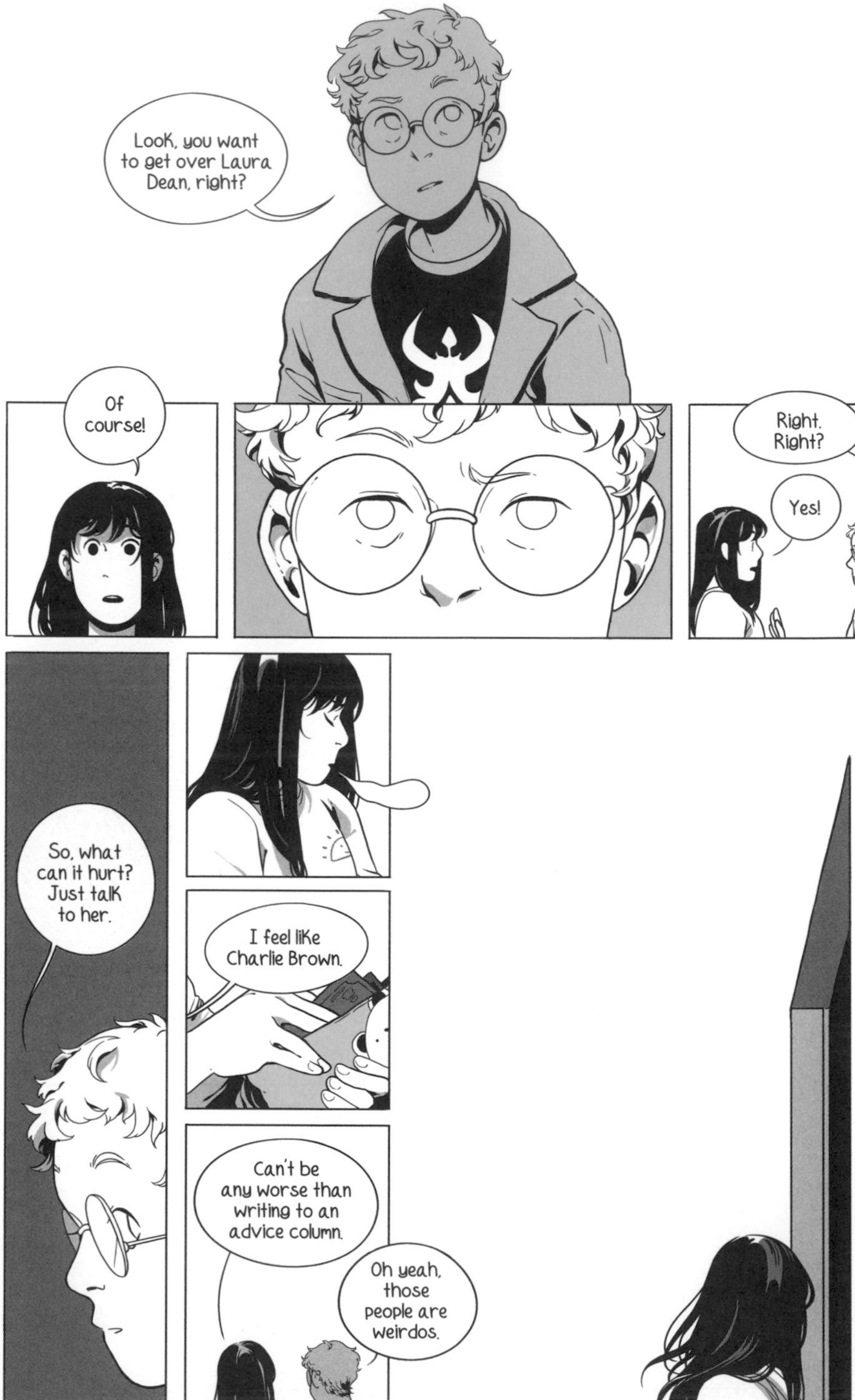

LooK, you want to get over Laura Dean, right?
Of course!
Right. Right?
Yes!
So, what can it hurt? Just talK to her.
I feel liKe Charlie Brown.
Can't be any worse than writing to an advice column.
Oh yeah, those people are weirdos.

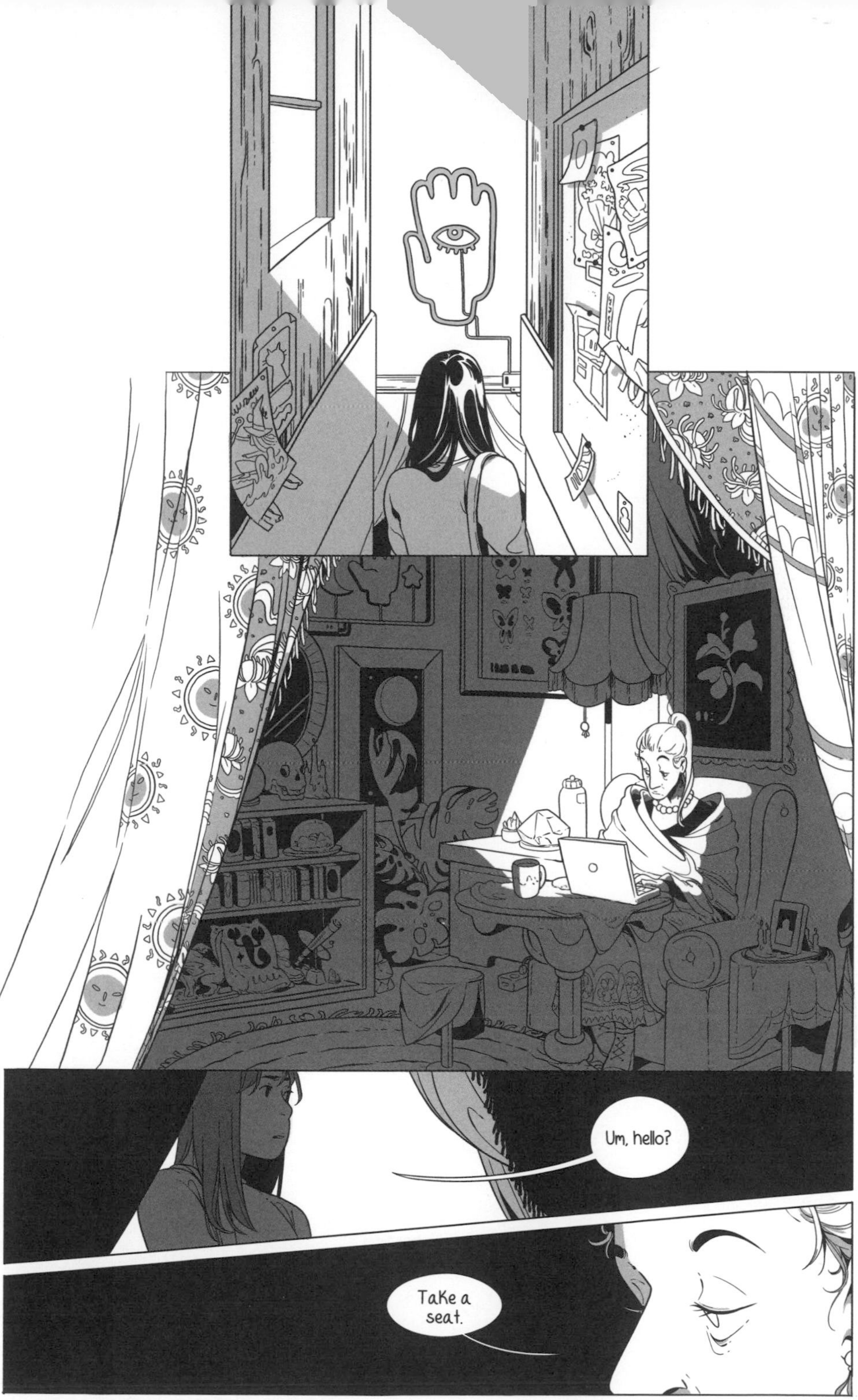
Um, hello?
Take a seat.

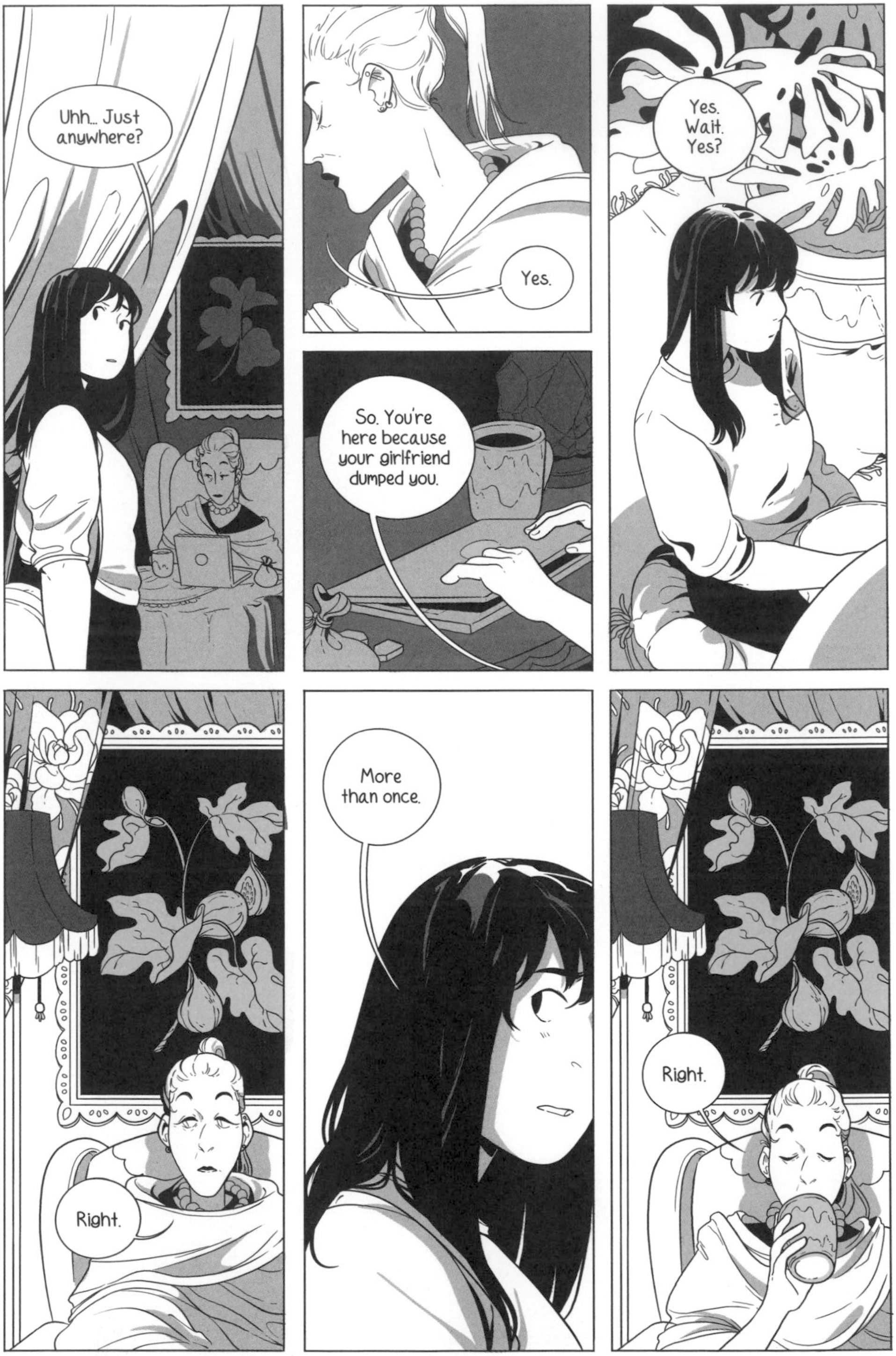
Uhh... Just anywhere?
Yes.
So. You're here because your girlfriend dumped you.
Yes. Wait. Yes?
Right.
More than once.
Right.

So, uh...

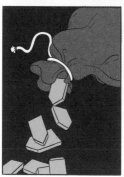

Okay... okay, yes.

I'm getting a weird pattern here.

Hmm...

Interesting.

Tell me how you fell in love.

O-oh! Do you mean where we met?

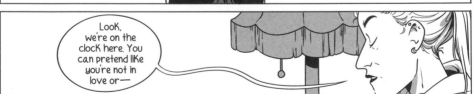

Look, we're on the clock here. You can pretend like you're not in love or—

Square dancing.

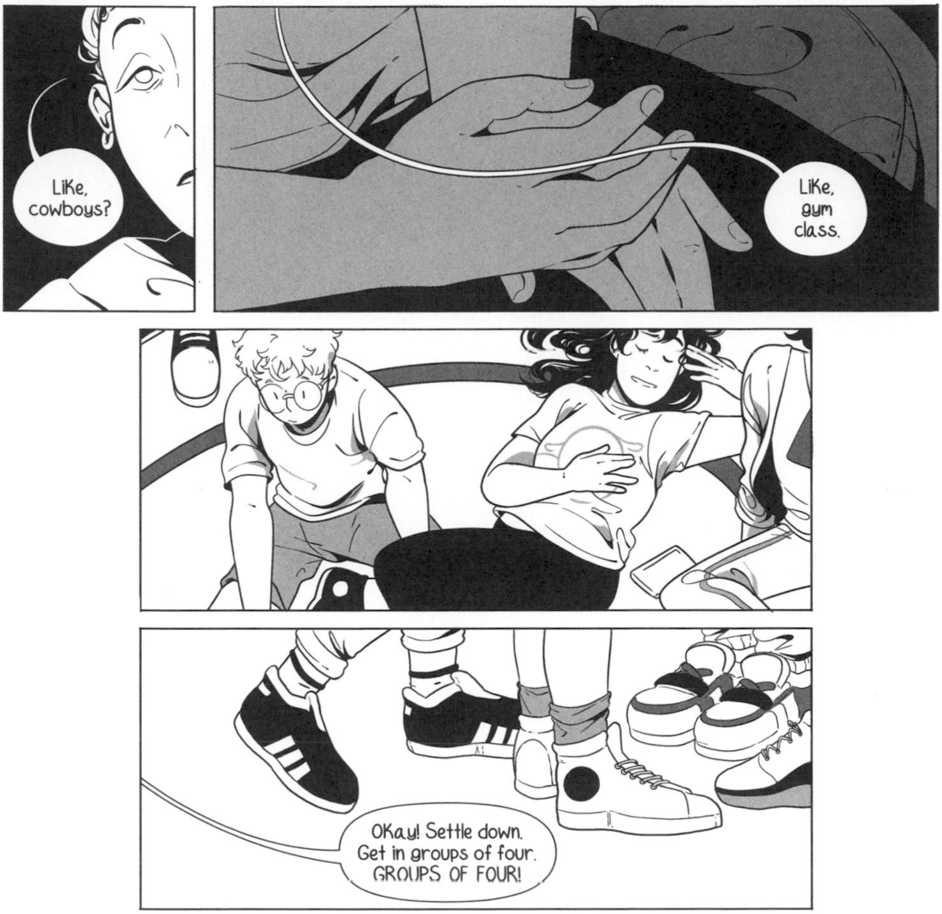
Like, cowboys?
Like, gym class.
Okay! Settle down. Get in groups of four. GROUPS OF FOUR!

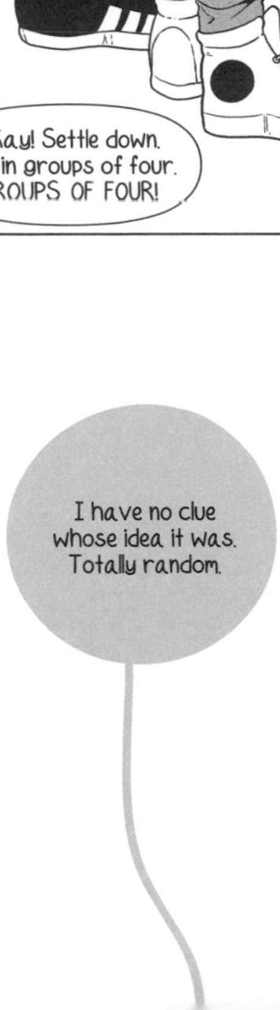
I have no clue whose idea it was. Totally random.

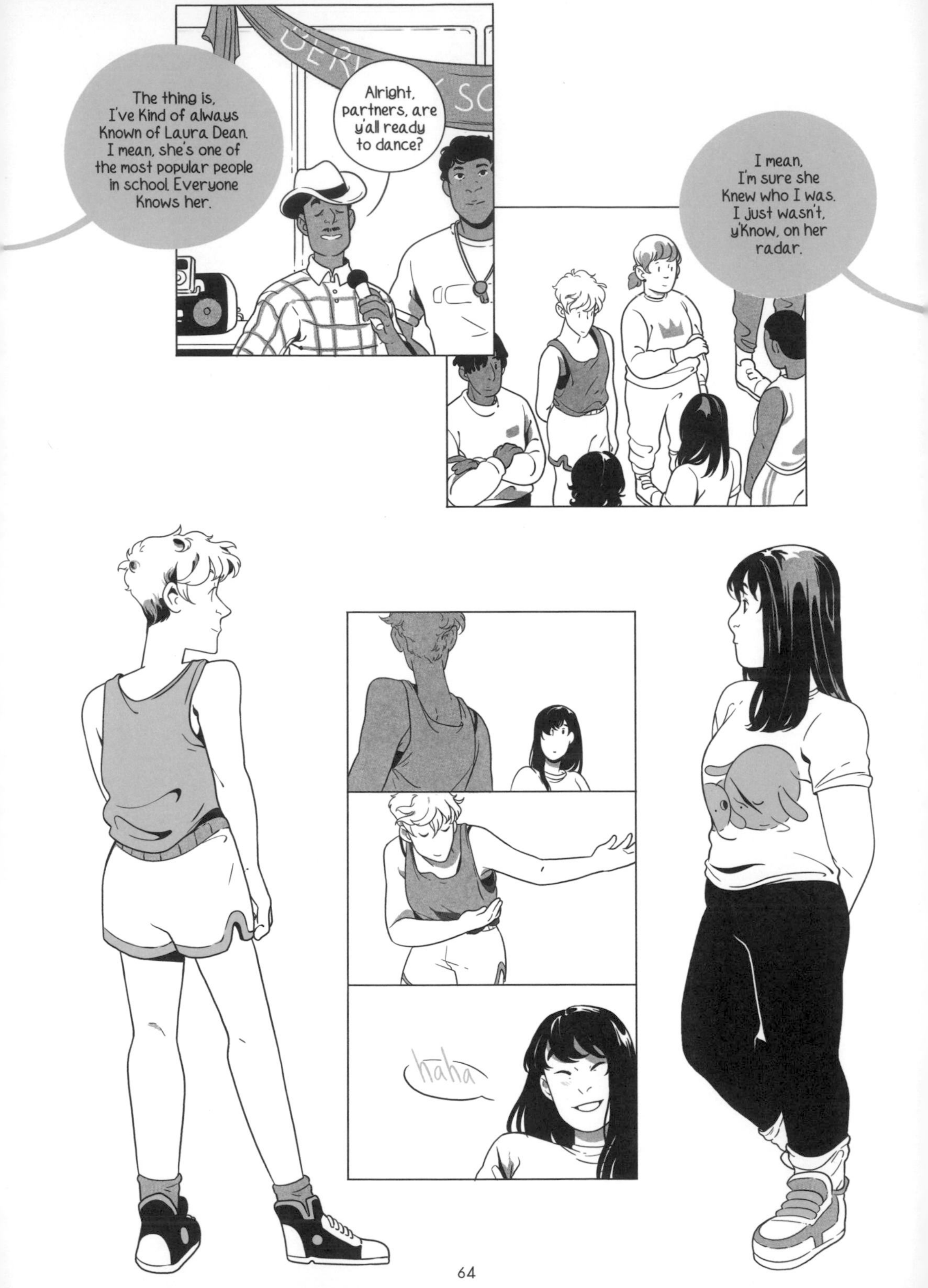
The thing is, I've Kind of always Known of Laura Dean. I mean, she's one of the most popular people in school. Everyone Knows her.
Alright, partners, are y'all ready to dance?
I mean, I'm sure she Knew who I was. I just wasn't, y'Know, on her radar.
haha

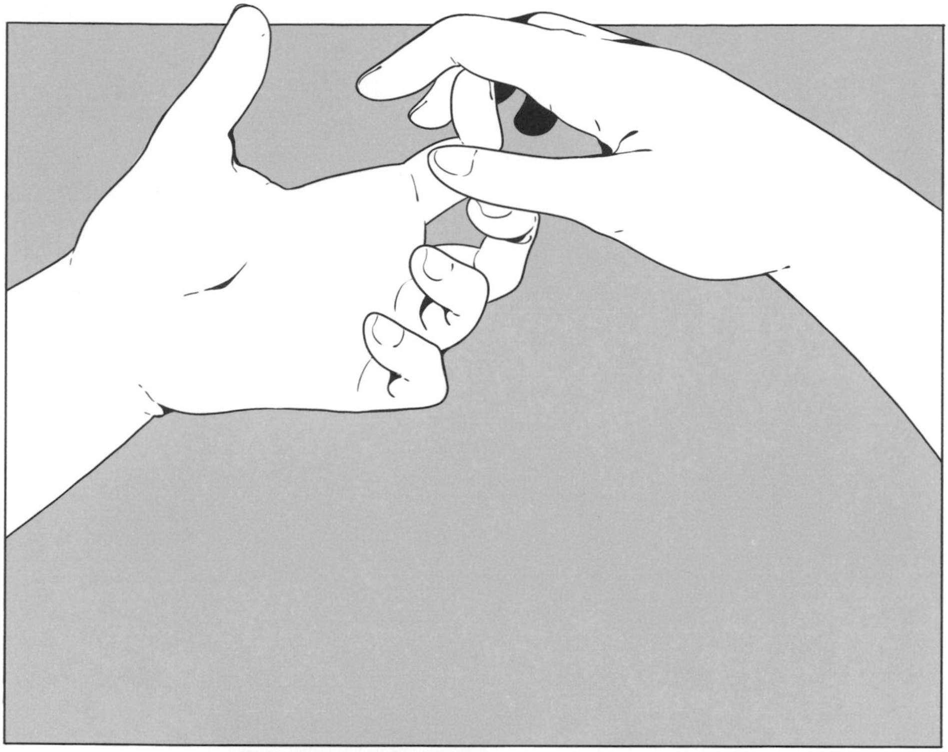

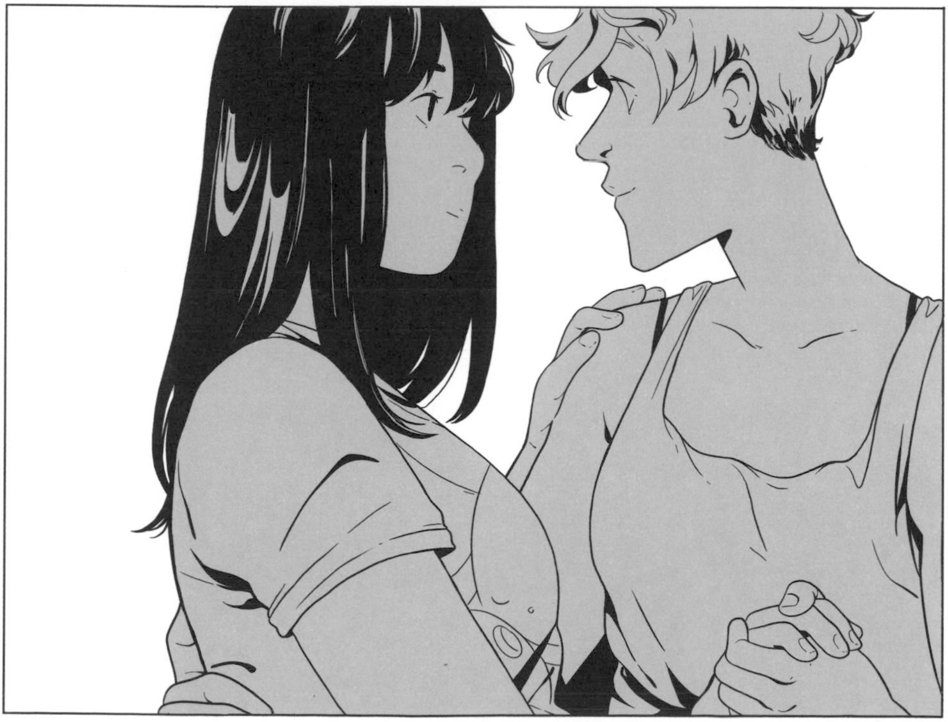

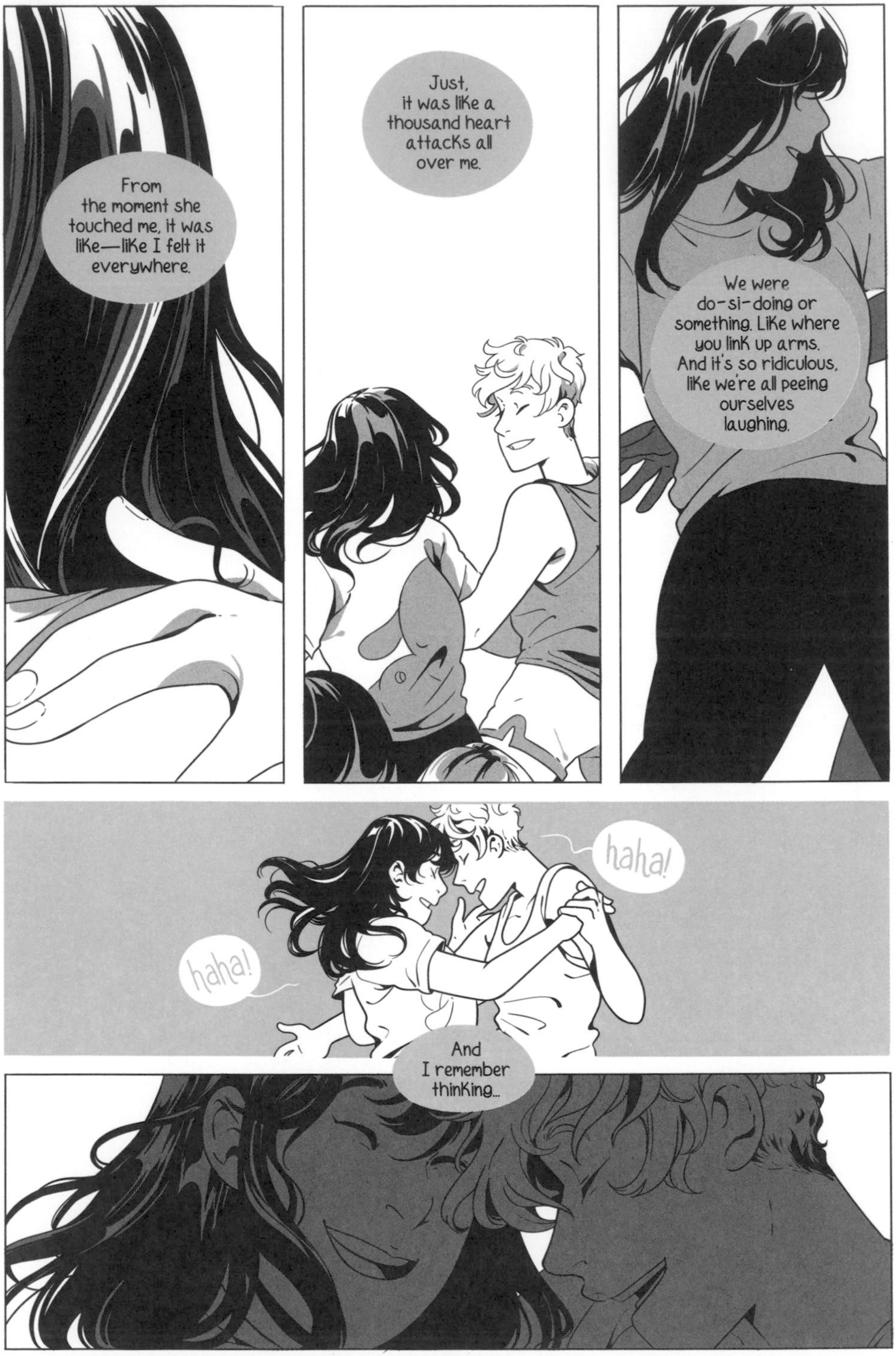
From the moment she touched me, it was like—like I felt it everywhere.
Just, it was like a thousand heart attacks all over me.
We were do-si-doing or something. Like where you link up arms. And it's so ridiculous, like we're all peeing ourselves laughing.
haha!
haha!
And I remember thinking...

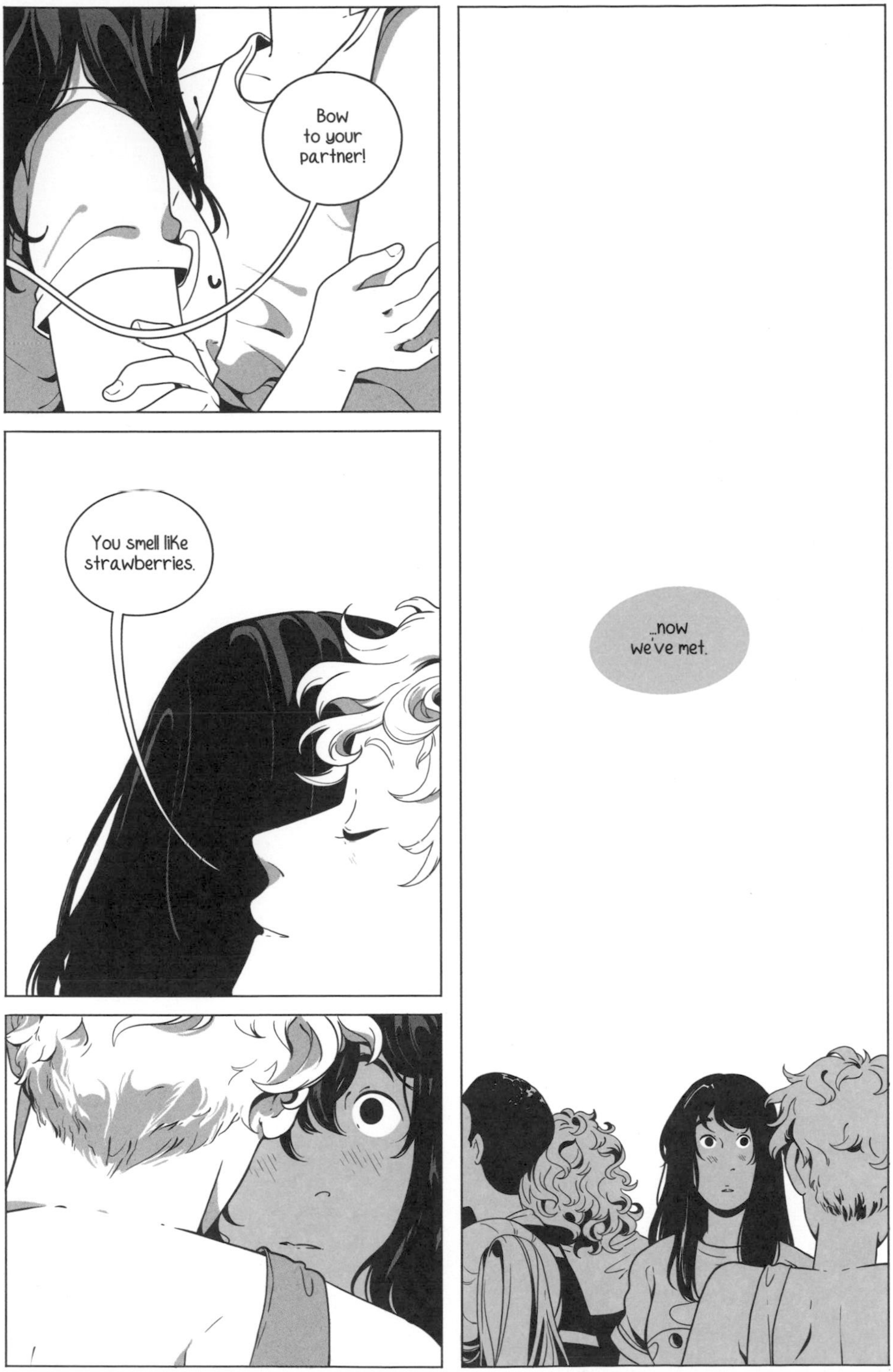

Bow to your partner!
You smell like strawberries.
...now we've met.

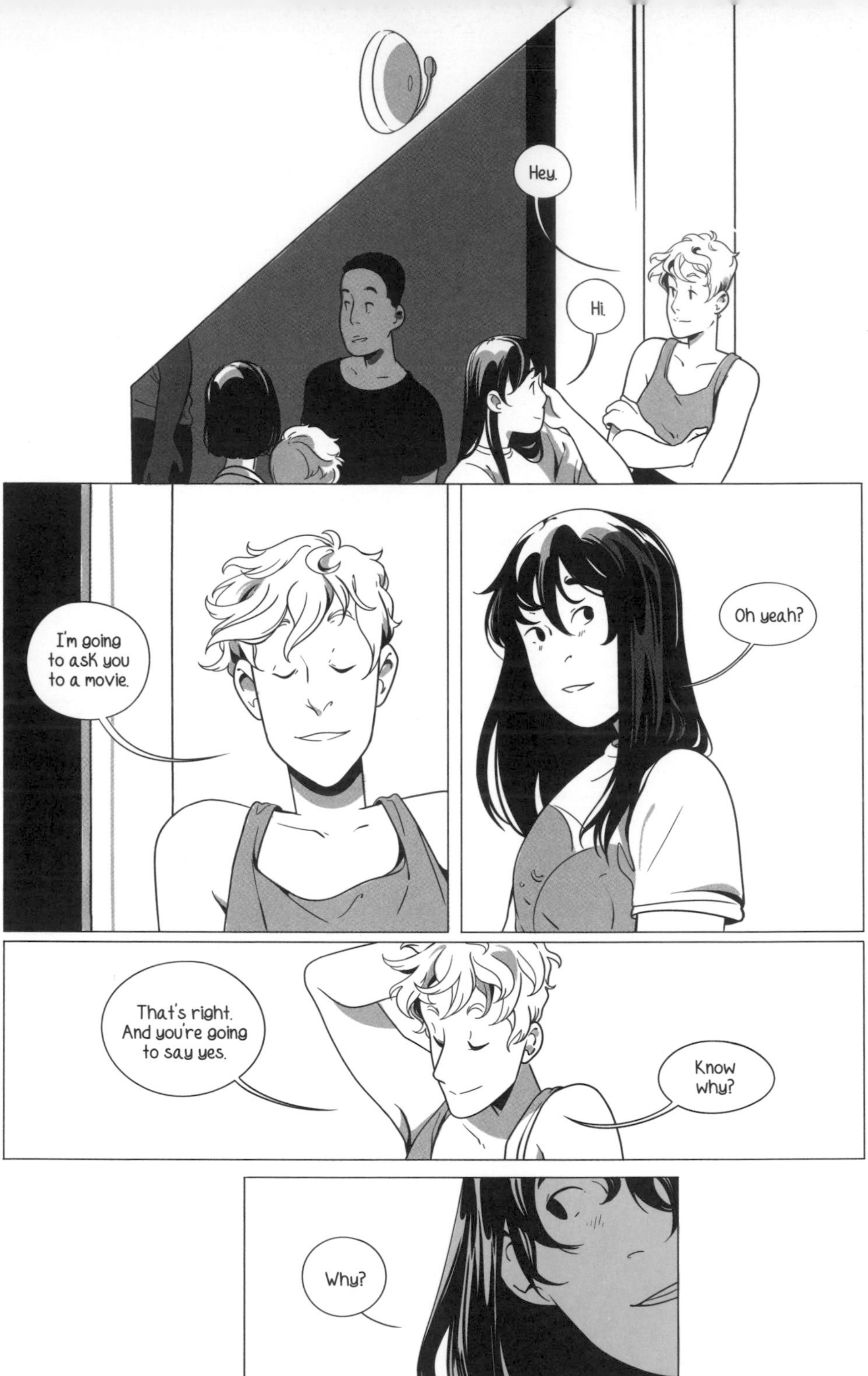
Hey.
Hi.
I'm going to ask you to a movie.
Oh yeah?
That's right. And you're going to say yes.
Know why?
Why?

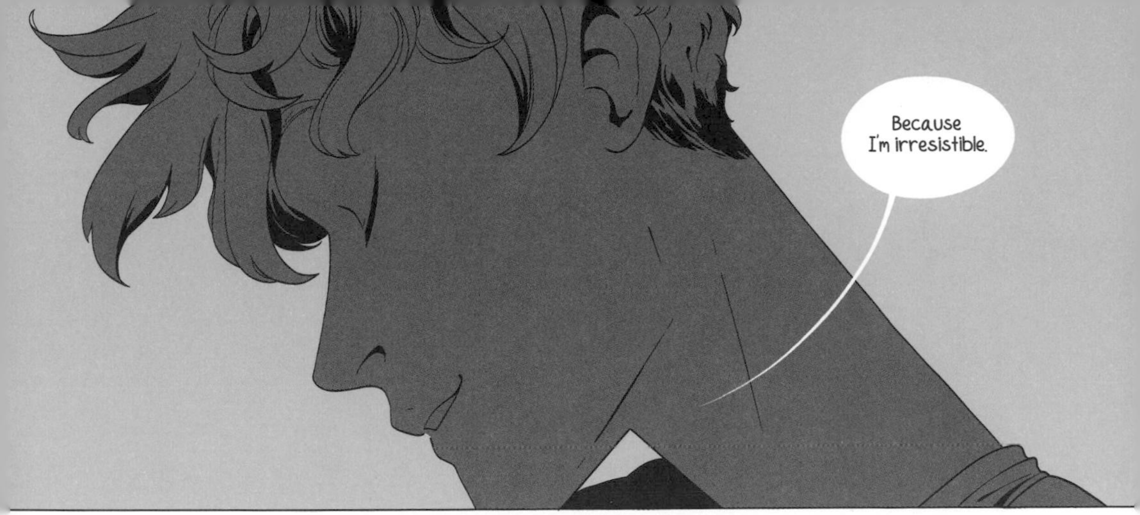
Because I'm irresistible.

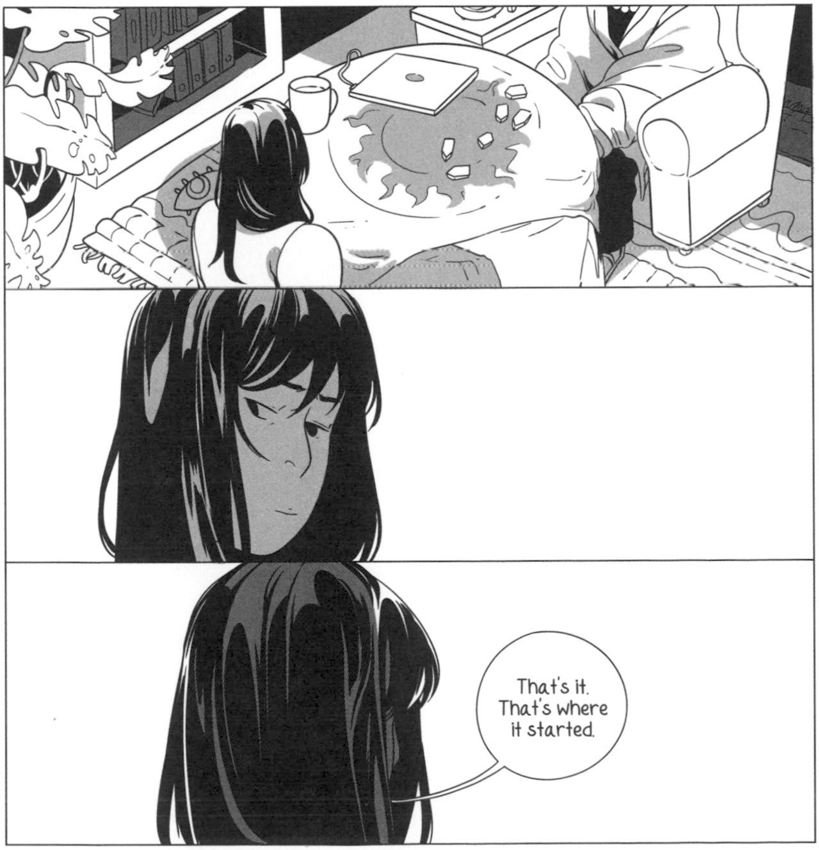
That's it. That's where it started.

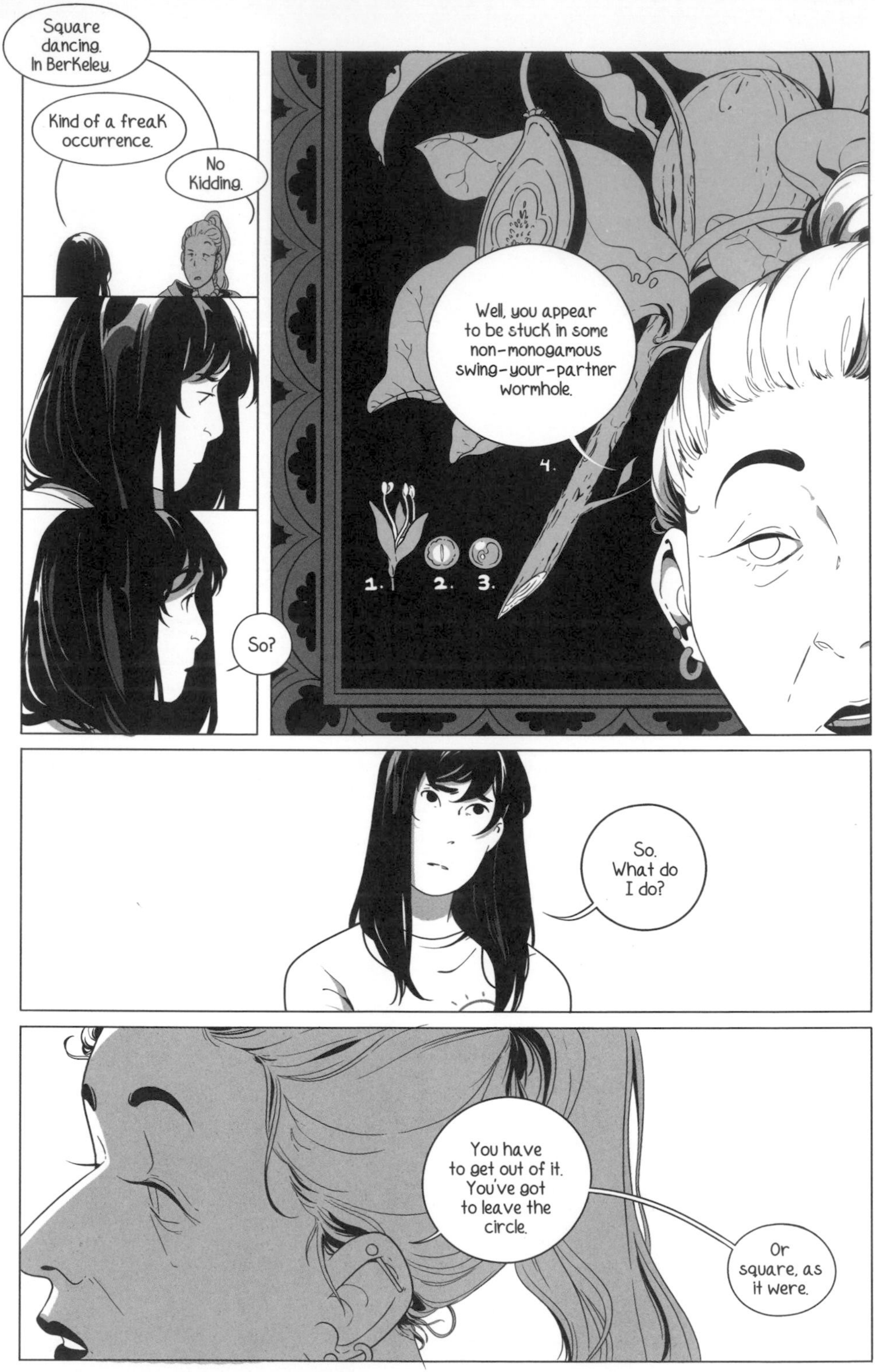

Square dancing. In Berkeley.
Kind of a freak occurrence.
No Kidding.
So?
Well, you appear to be stuck in some non-monogamous swing-your-partner wormhole.
4.
1.
2.
3.
So. What do I do?
You have to get out of it. You've got to leave the circle.
Or square, as it were.

OKay, but HOW?

You have to break up with her.

Good luck.

Wait, I don't understand.

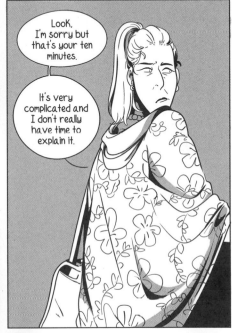

Look, I'm sorry but that's your ten minutes.

It's very complicated and I don't really have time to explain it.

How do I break up with someone who's broken up with me?

Well, that's what you've got to think about, isn't it?

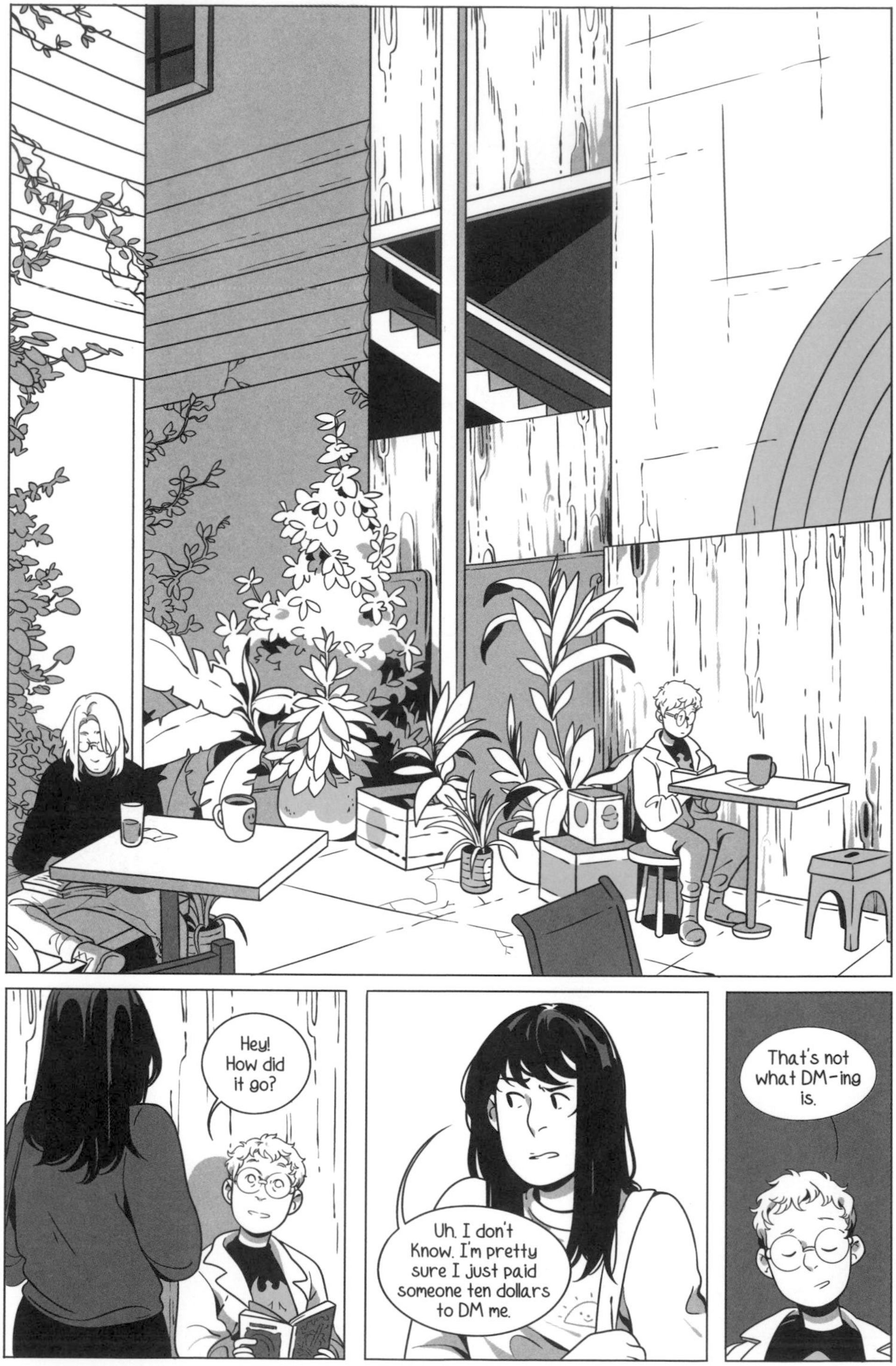
Hey! How did it go?
Uh. I don't Know. I'm pretty sure I just paid someone ten dollars to DM me.
That's not what DM-ing is.

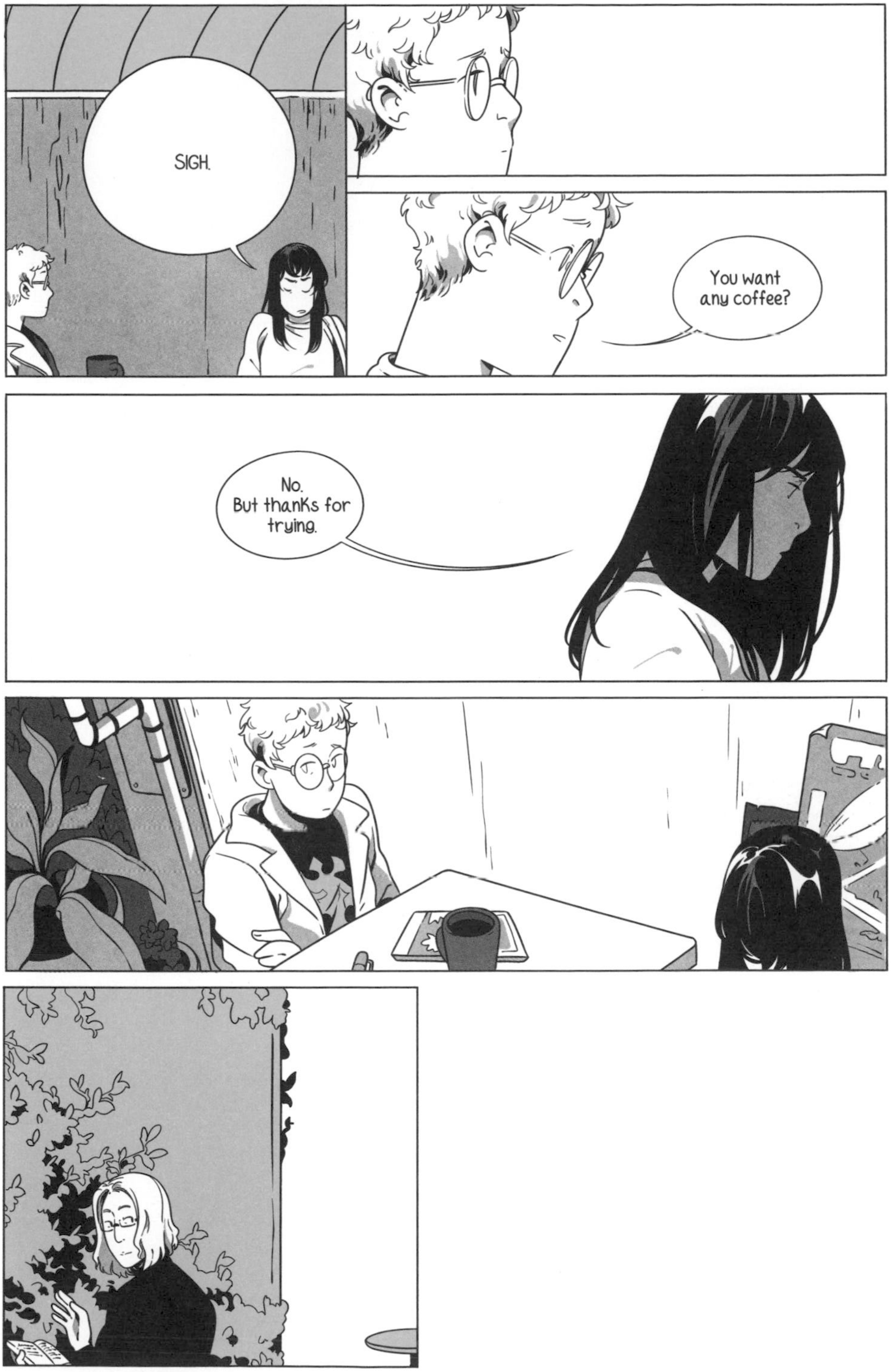
SIGH.
You want any coffee?
No. But thanks for trying.

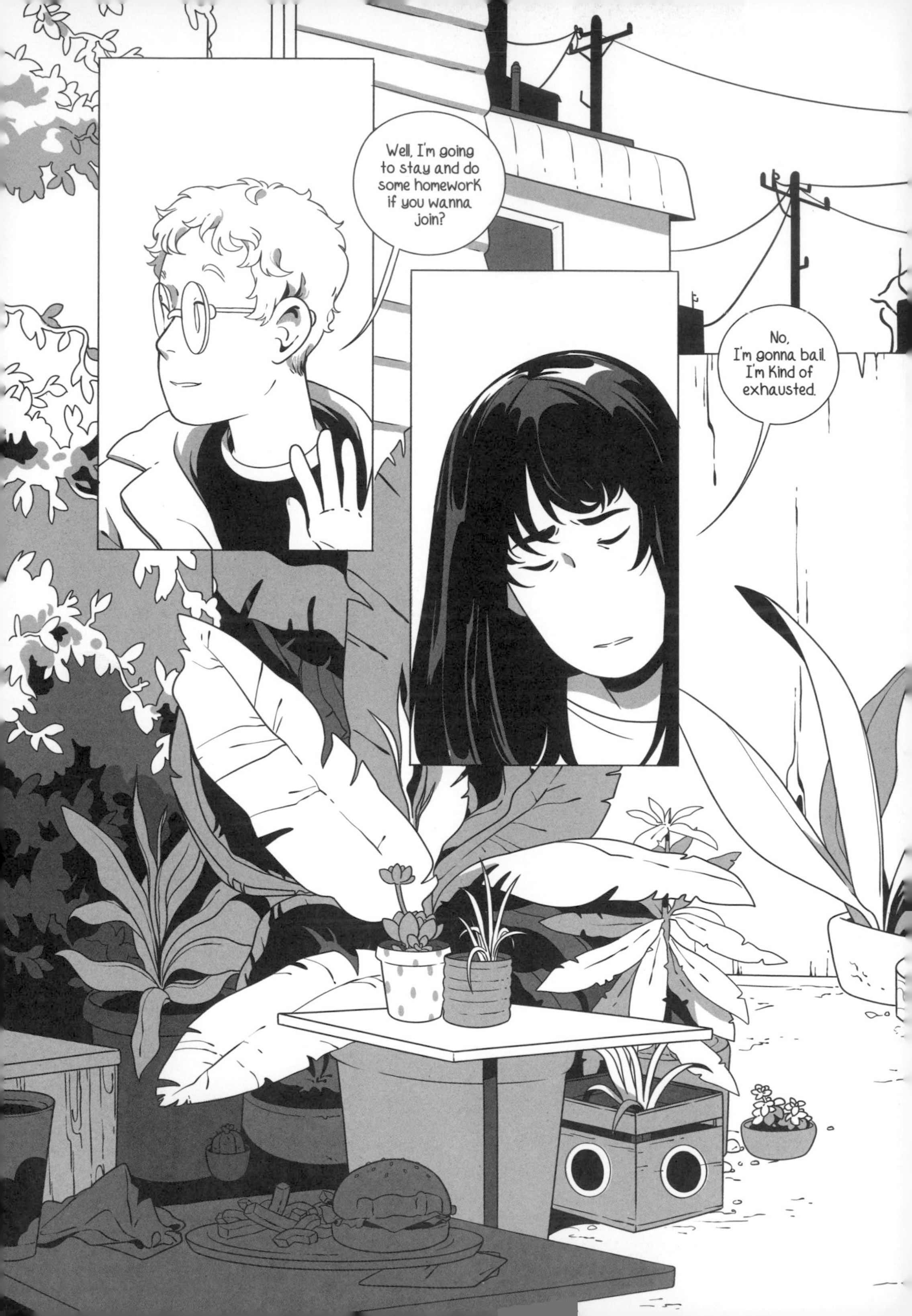
Well, I'm going to stay and do some homework if you wanna join?
No, I'm gonna bail. I'm kind of exhausted.

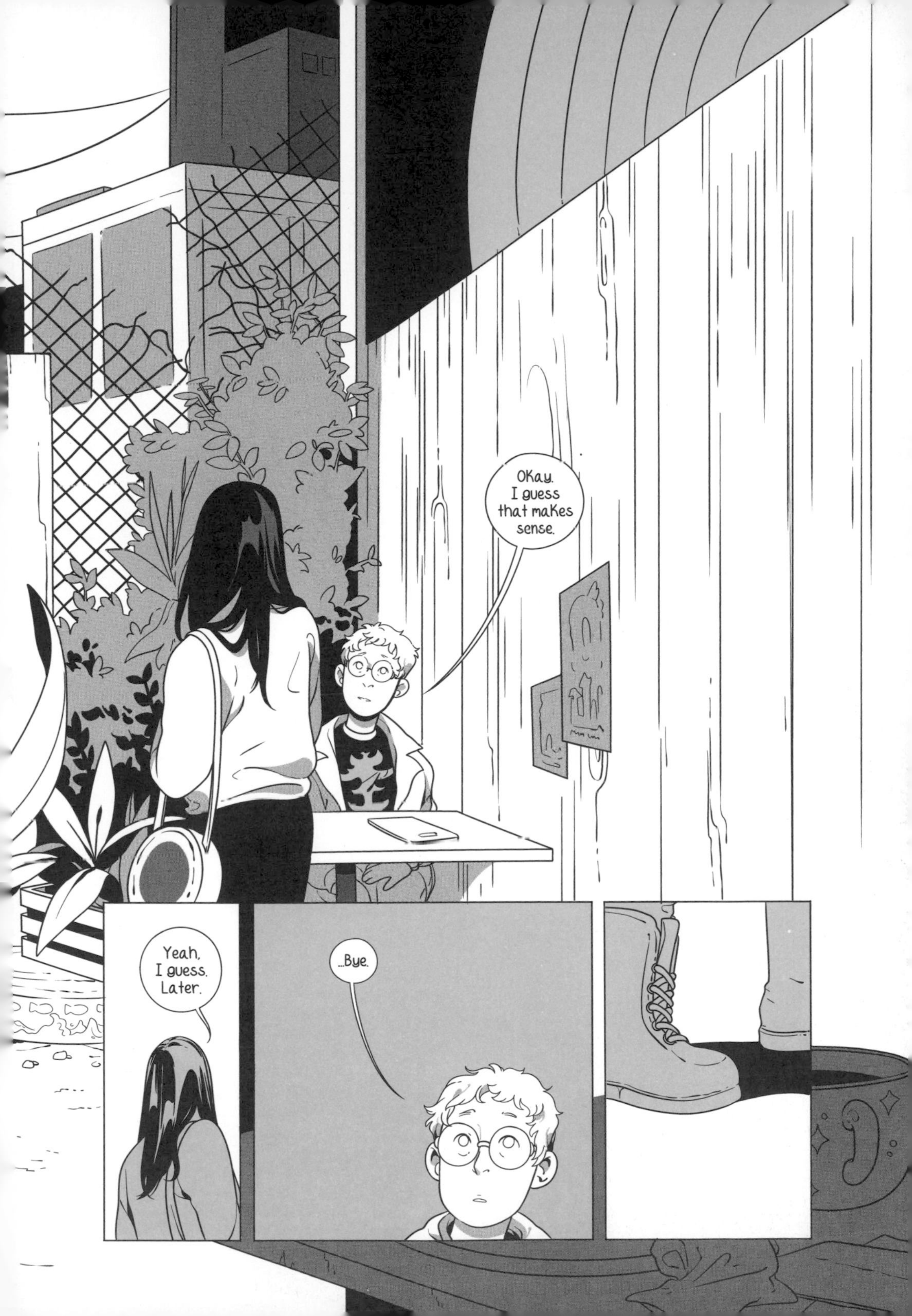
OKay. I guess that makes sense.
Yeah, I guess. Later.
...Bye.

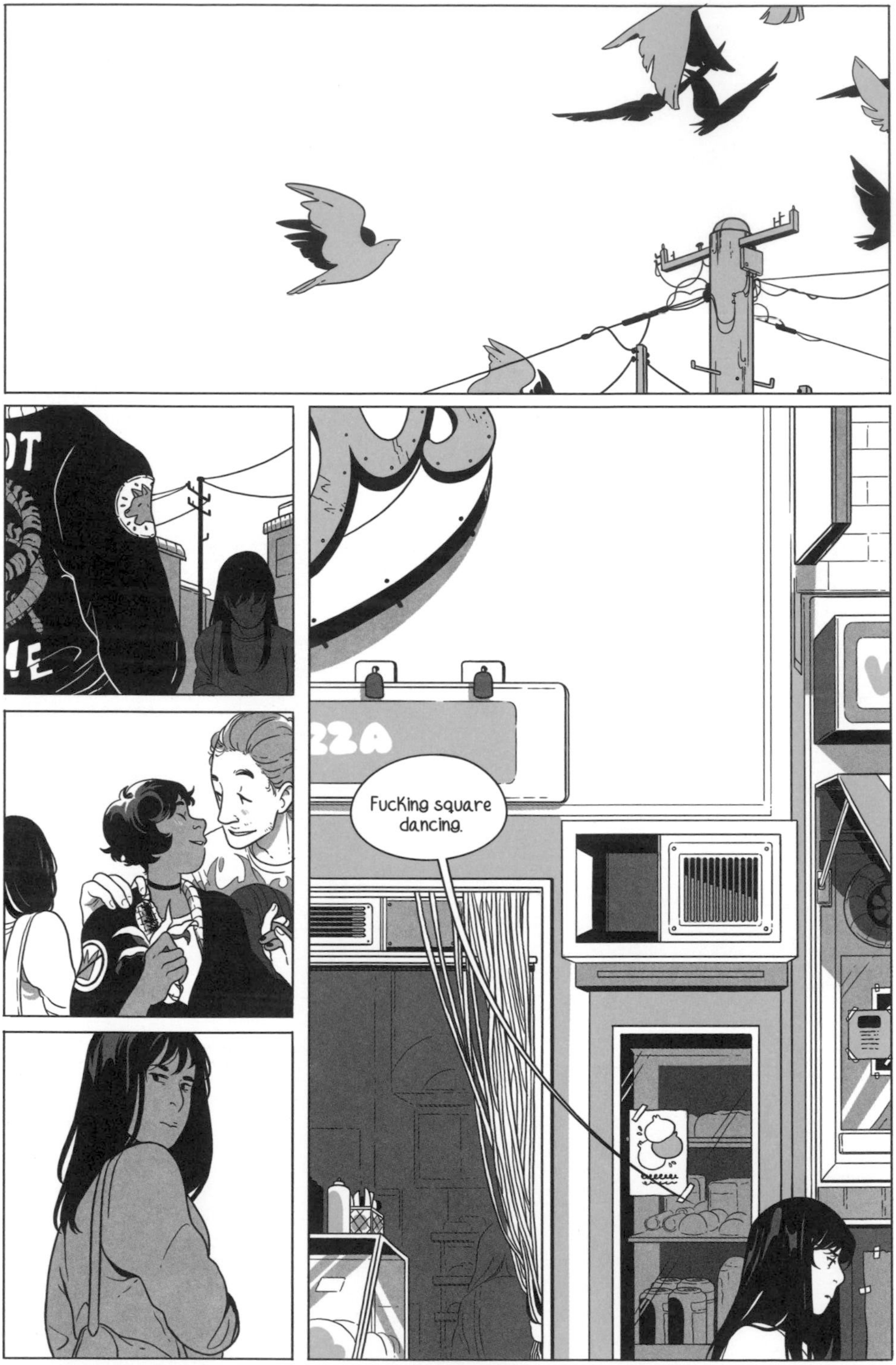
Fucking square dancing.

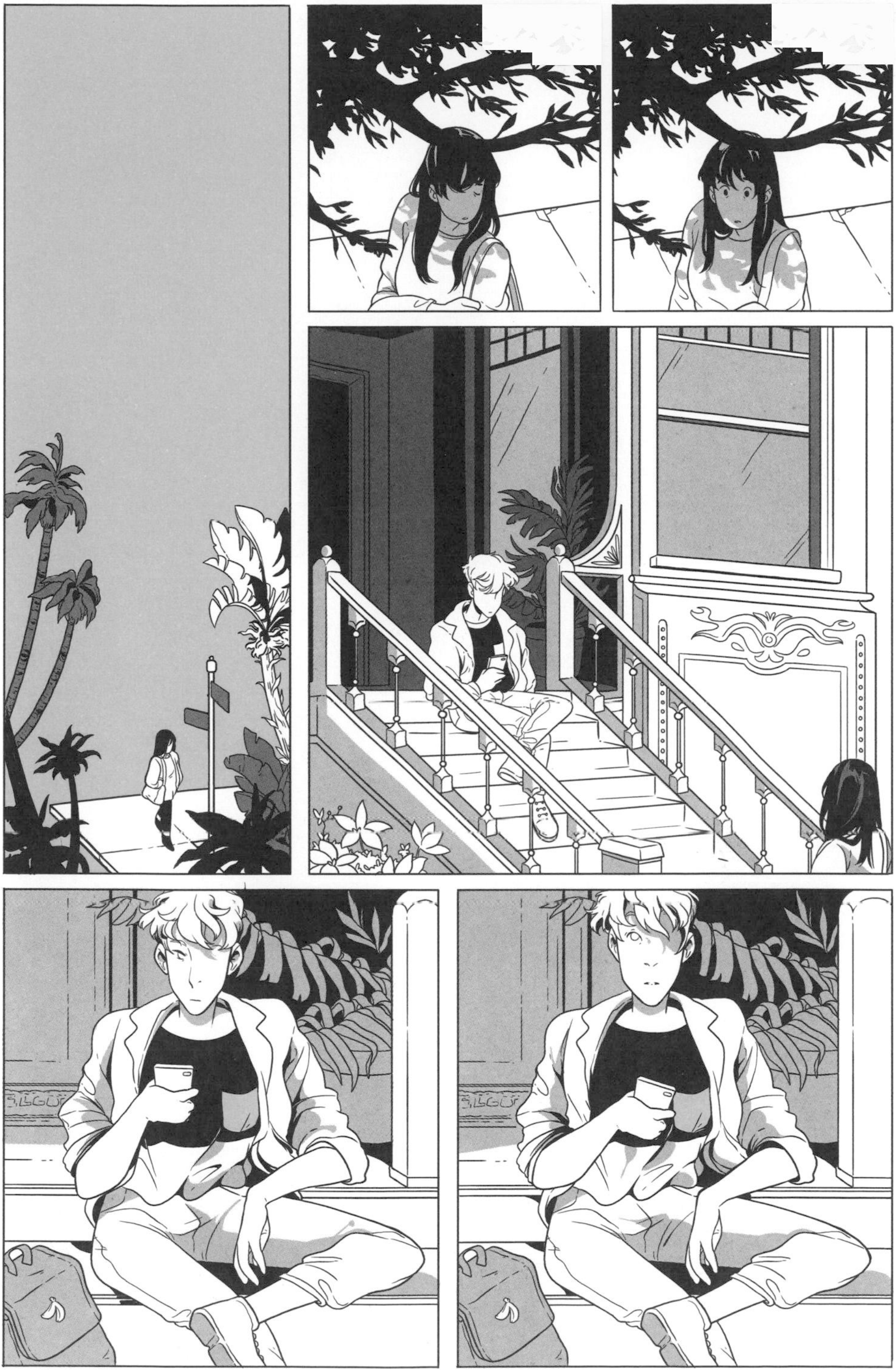
[redacted]
[redacted]

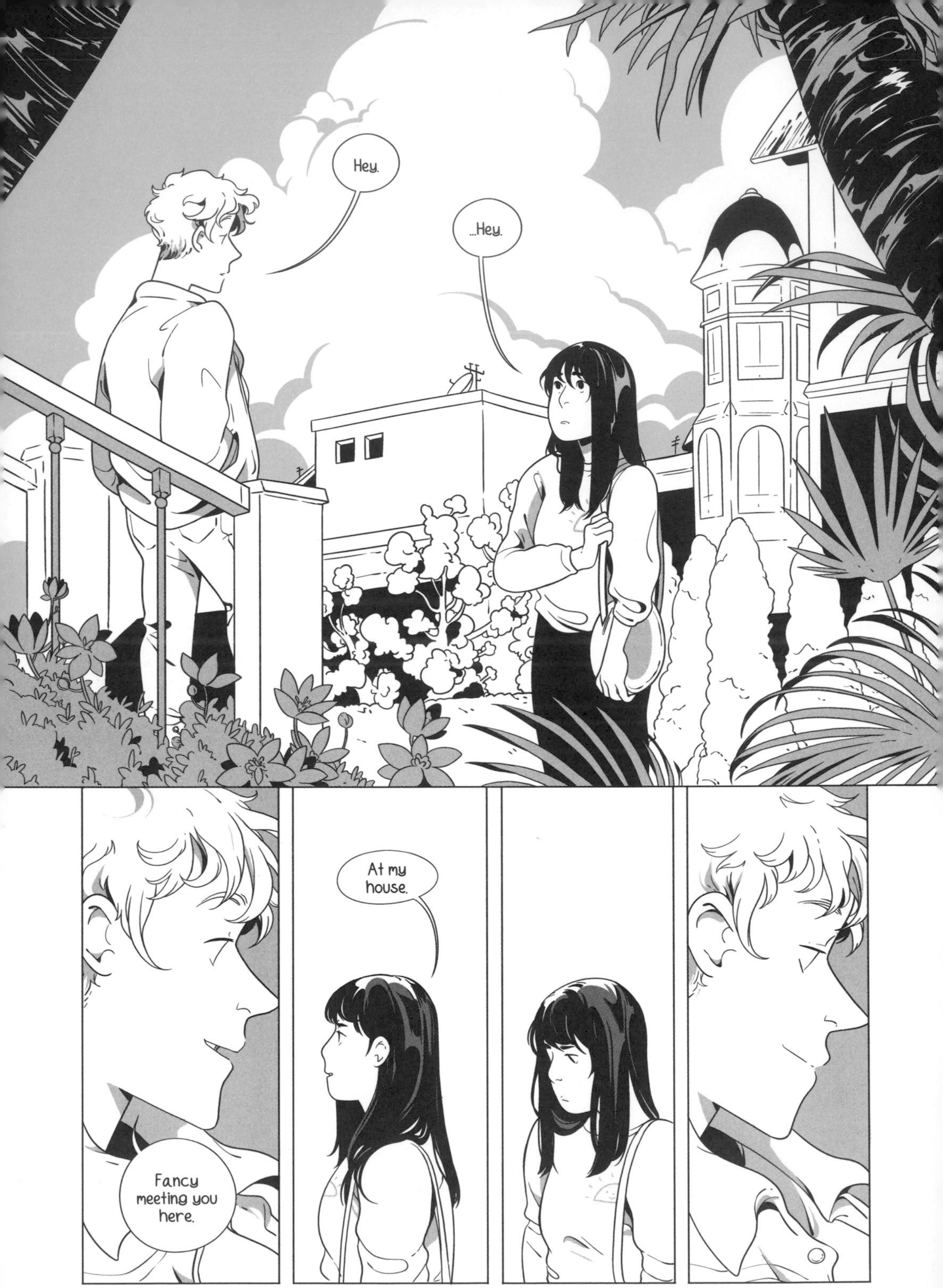
Hey.
...Hey.
Fancy meeting you here.
At my house.

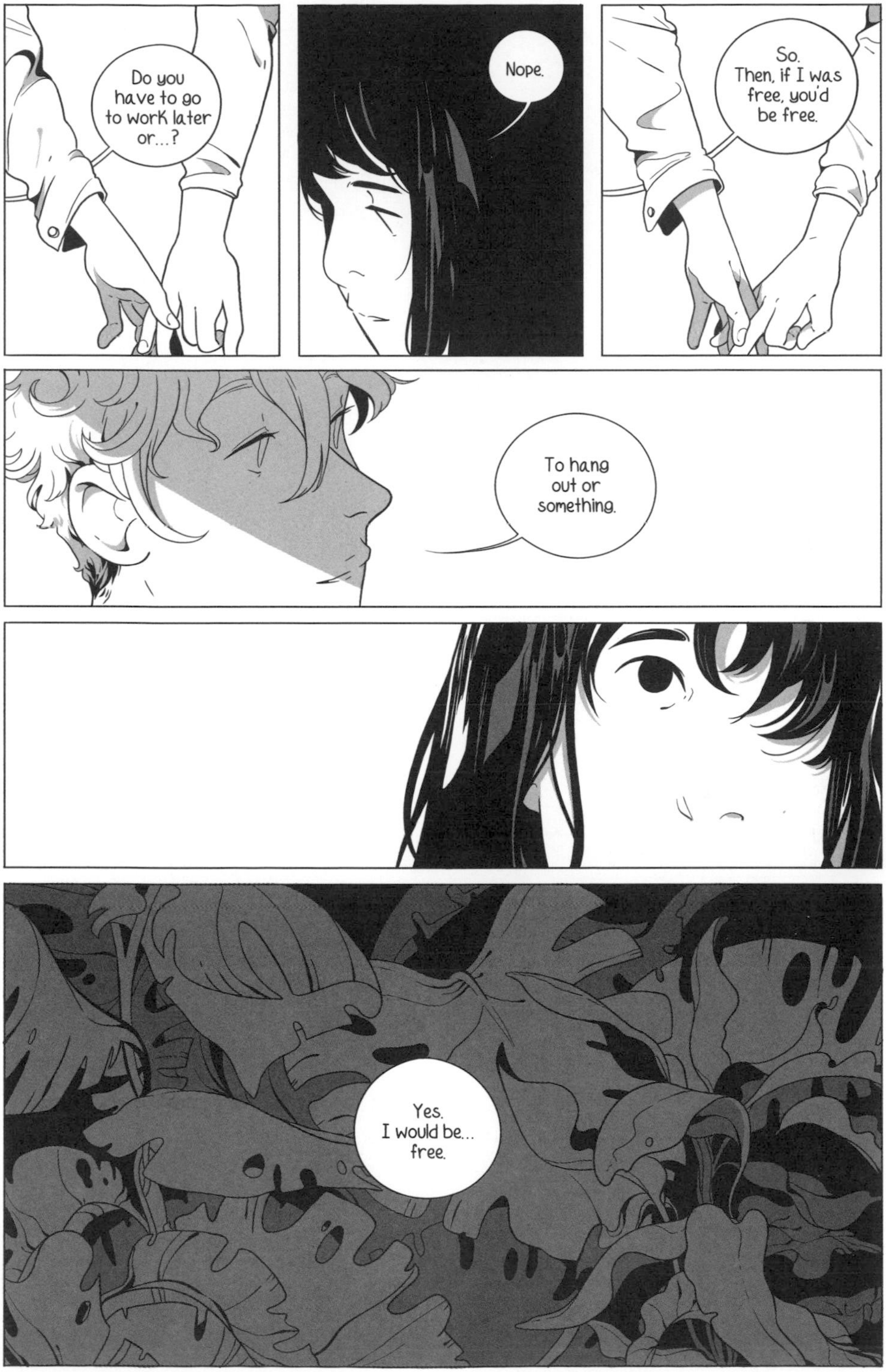
Do you have to go to work later or...?
Nope.
So.
Then, if I was free, you'd be free.
To hang out or something.
Yes.
I would be...
free.

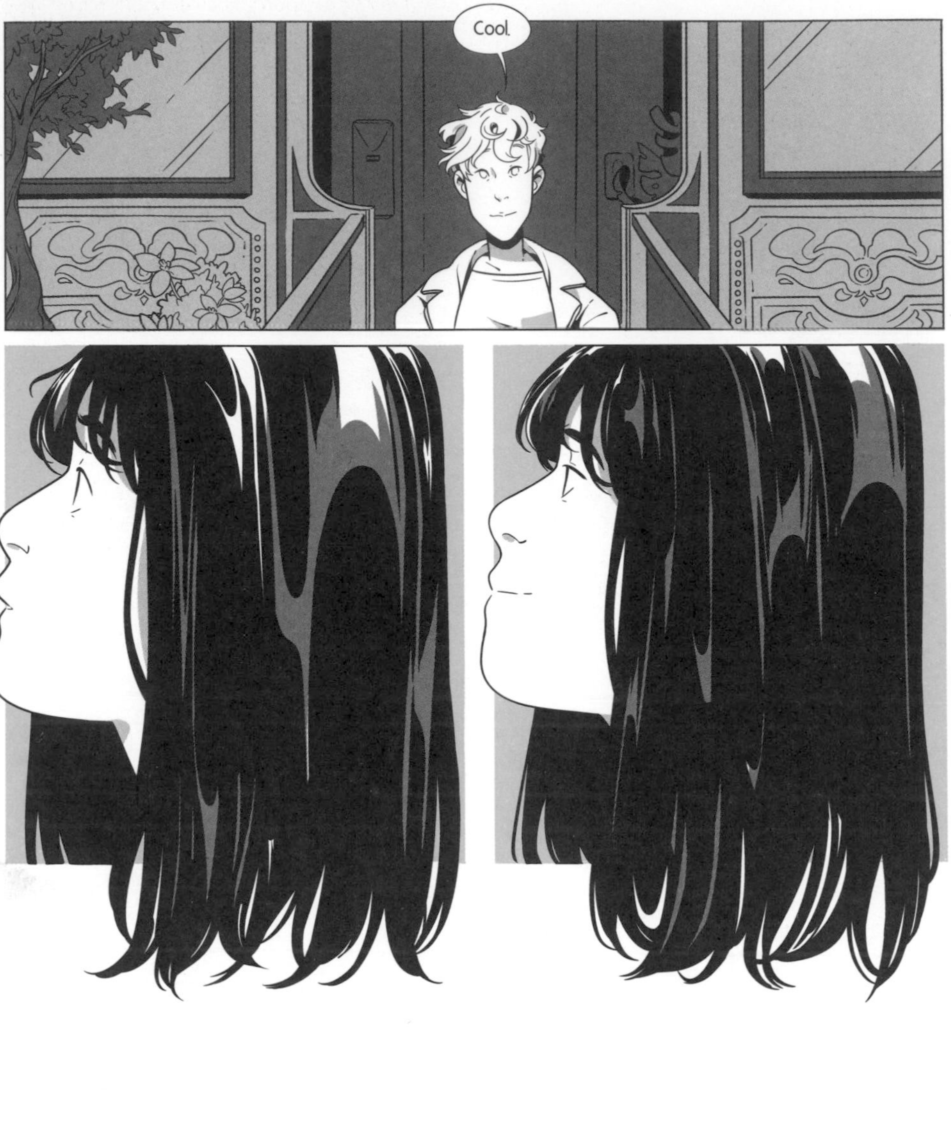
Cool.

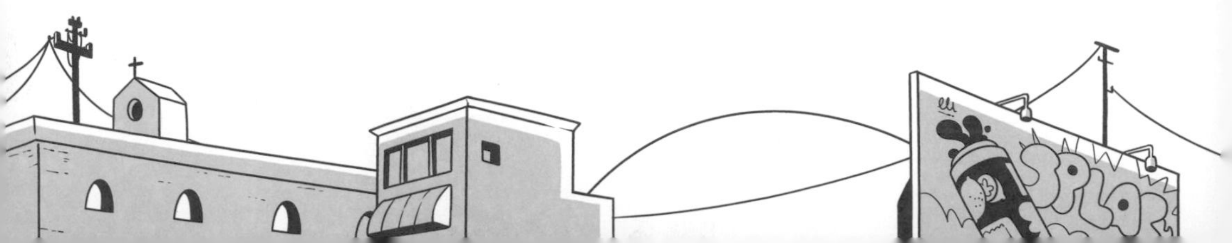

Dear Anna Vice,
Me again.
So. Update.

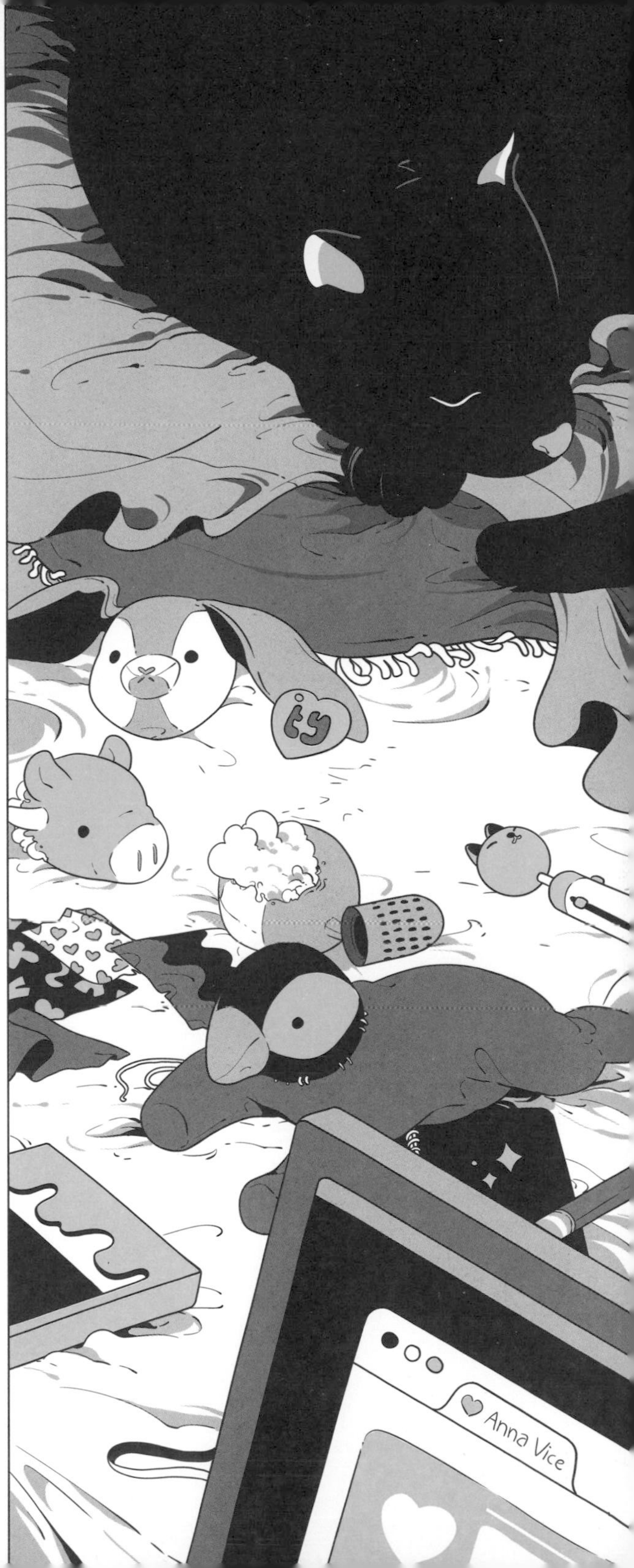
ty
Anna Vice

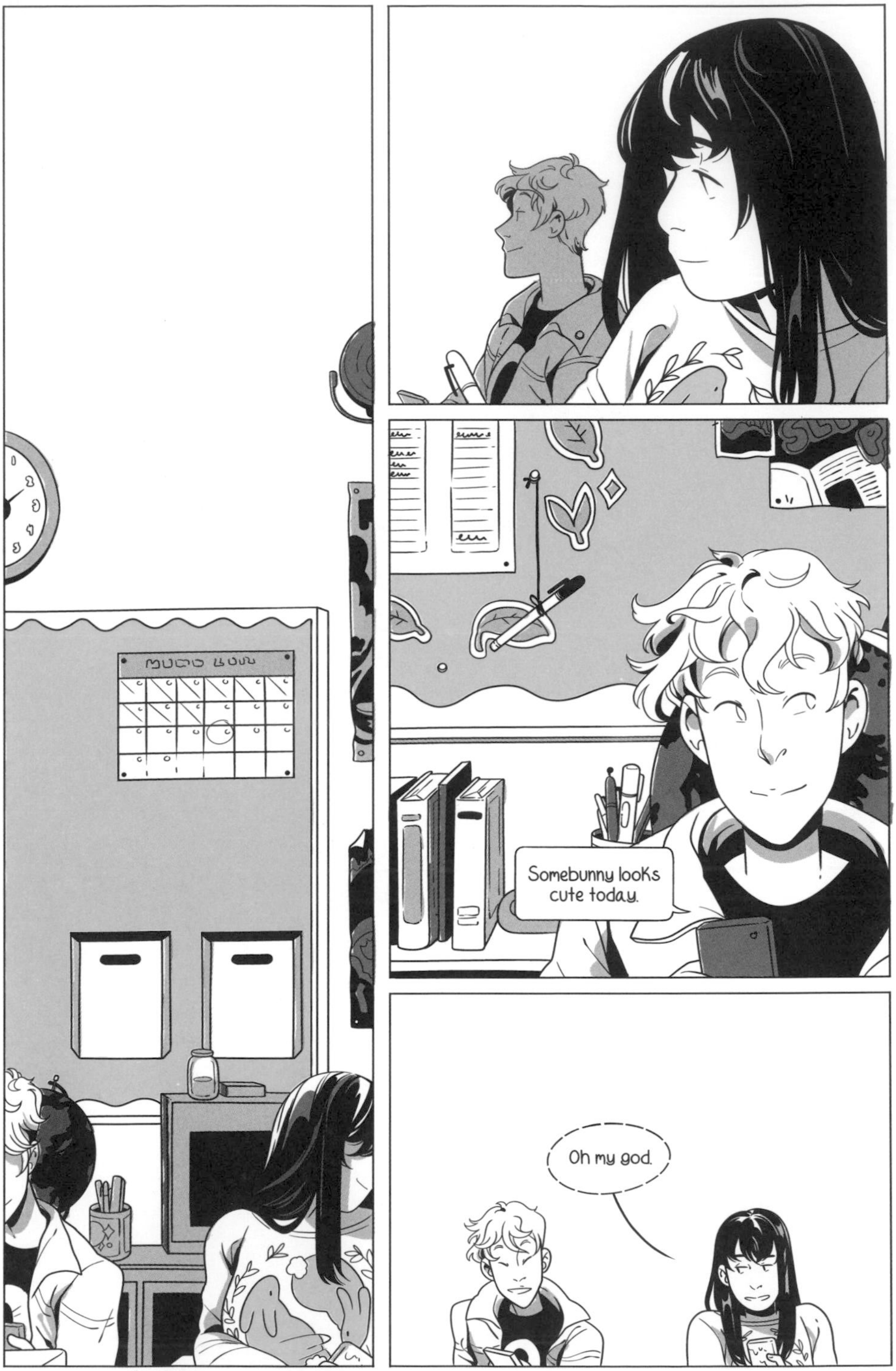
Somebunny looks cute today.
Oh my god.

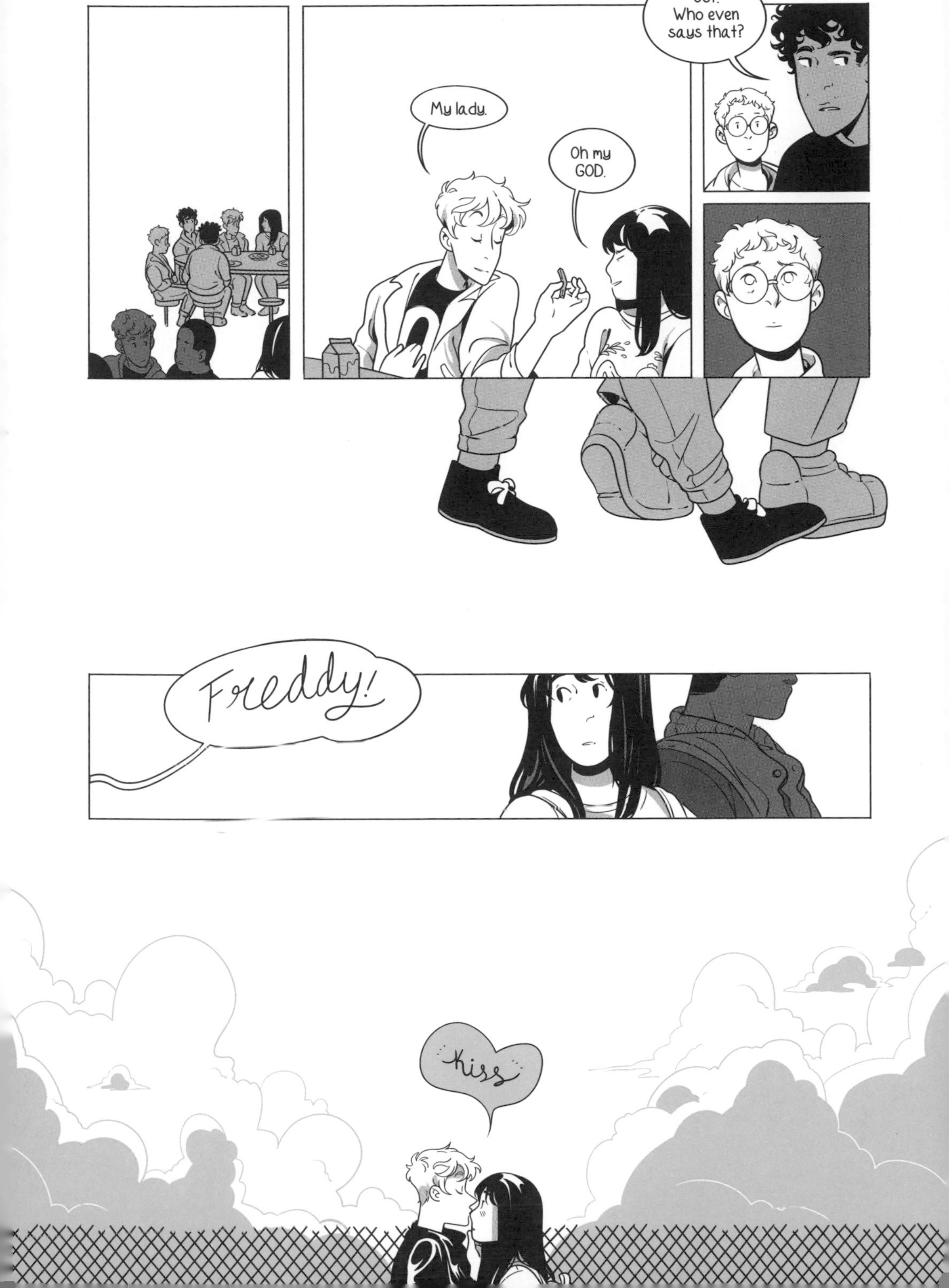

My lady.
Oh my GOD.
Oof. Who even says that?
Freddy!
Kiss

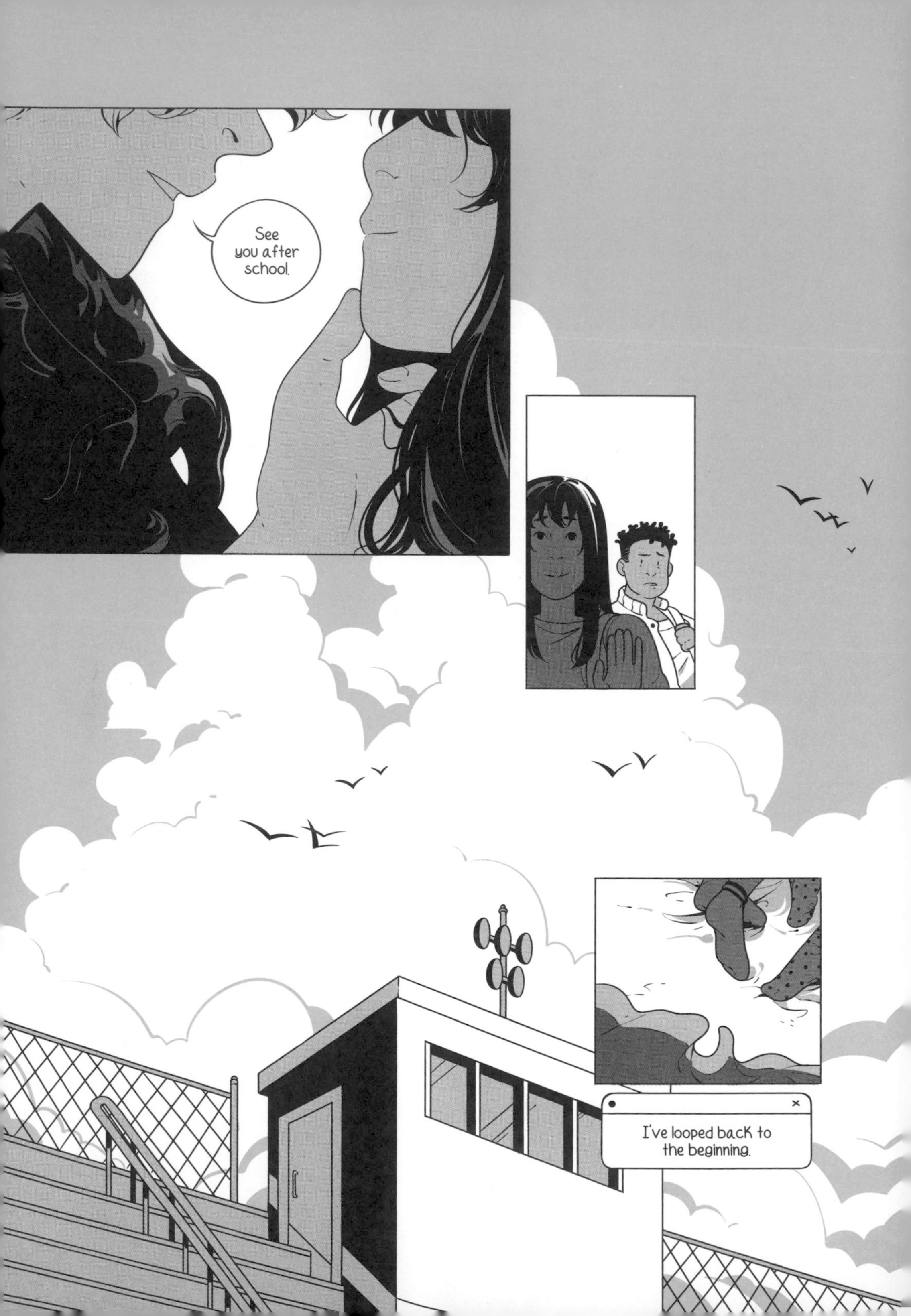
See you after school.
I've looped back to the beginning.

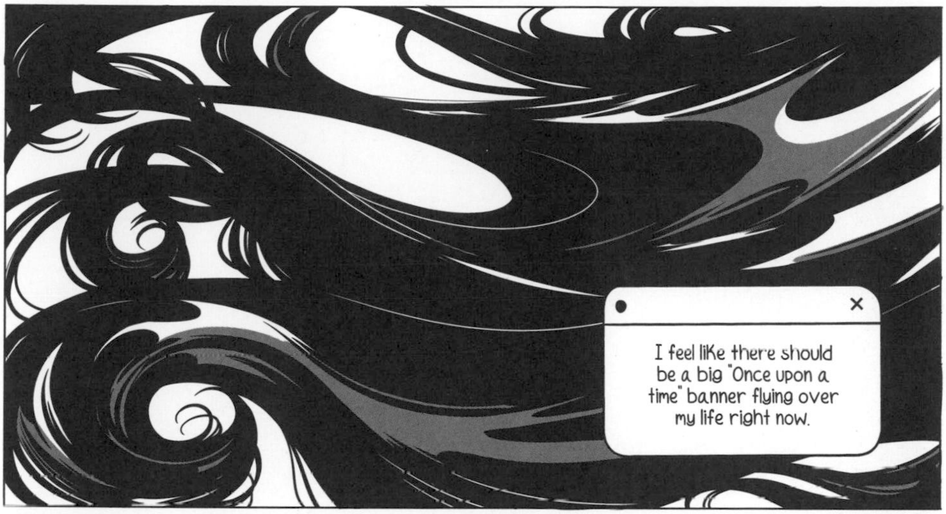
I feel like there should be a big "Once upon a time" banner flying over my life right now.

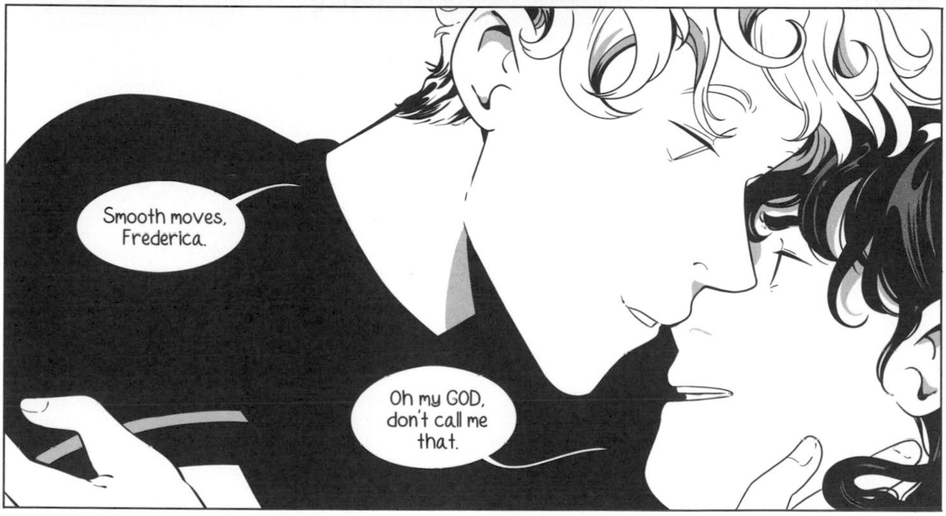
Smooth moves, Frederica.
Oh my GOD, don't call me that.

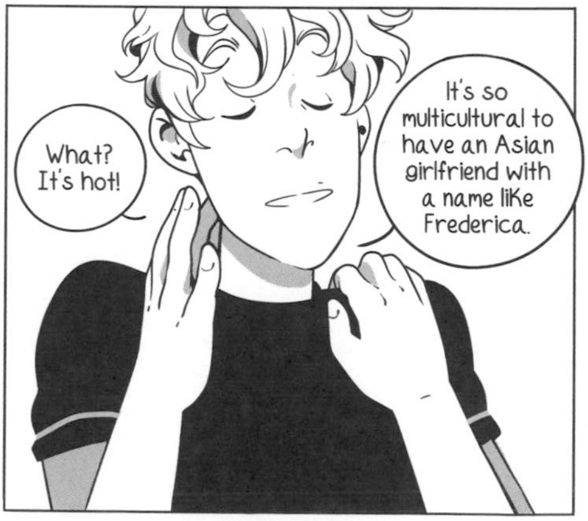
What? It's hot!
It's so multicultural to have an Asian girlfriend with a name like Frederica.

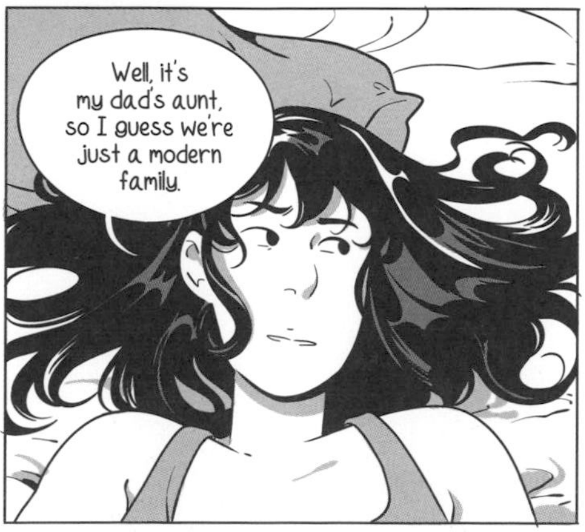
Well, it's my dad's aunt, so I guess we're just a modern family.

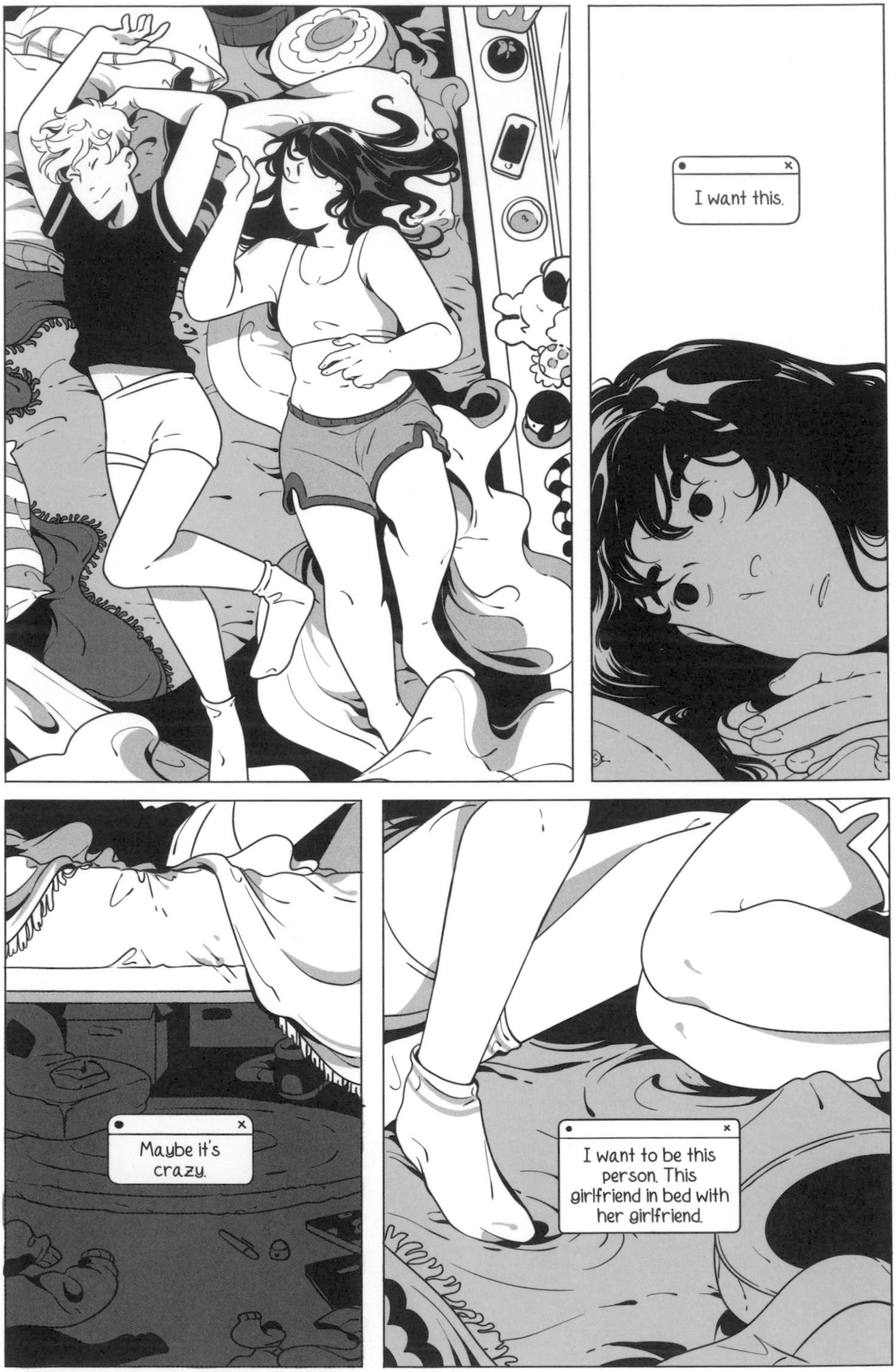
I want this.
Maybe it's crazy.
I want to be this person. This girlfriend in bed with her girlfriend.

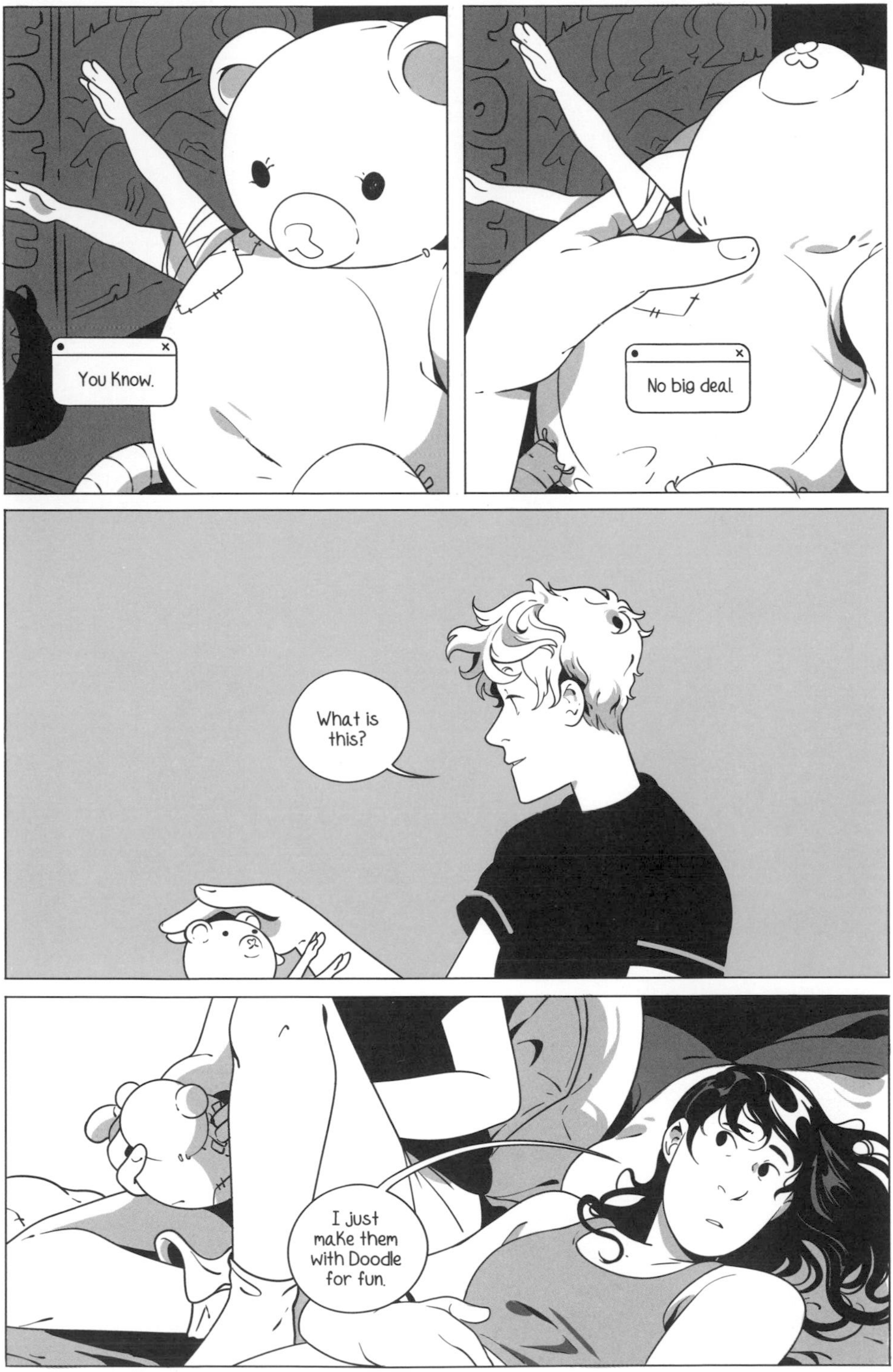
You Know.
No big deal.
What is this?
I just make them with Doodle for fun.

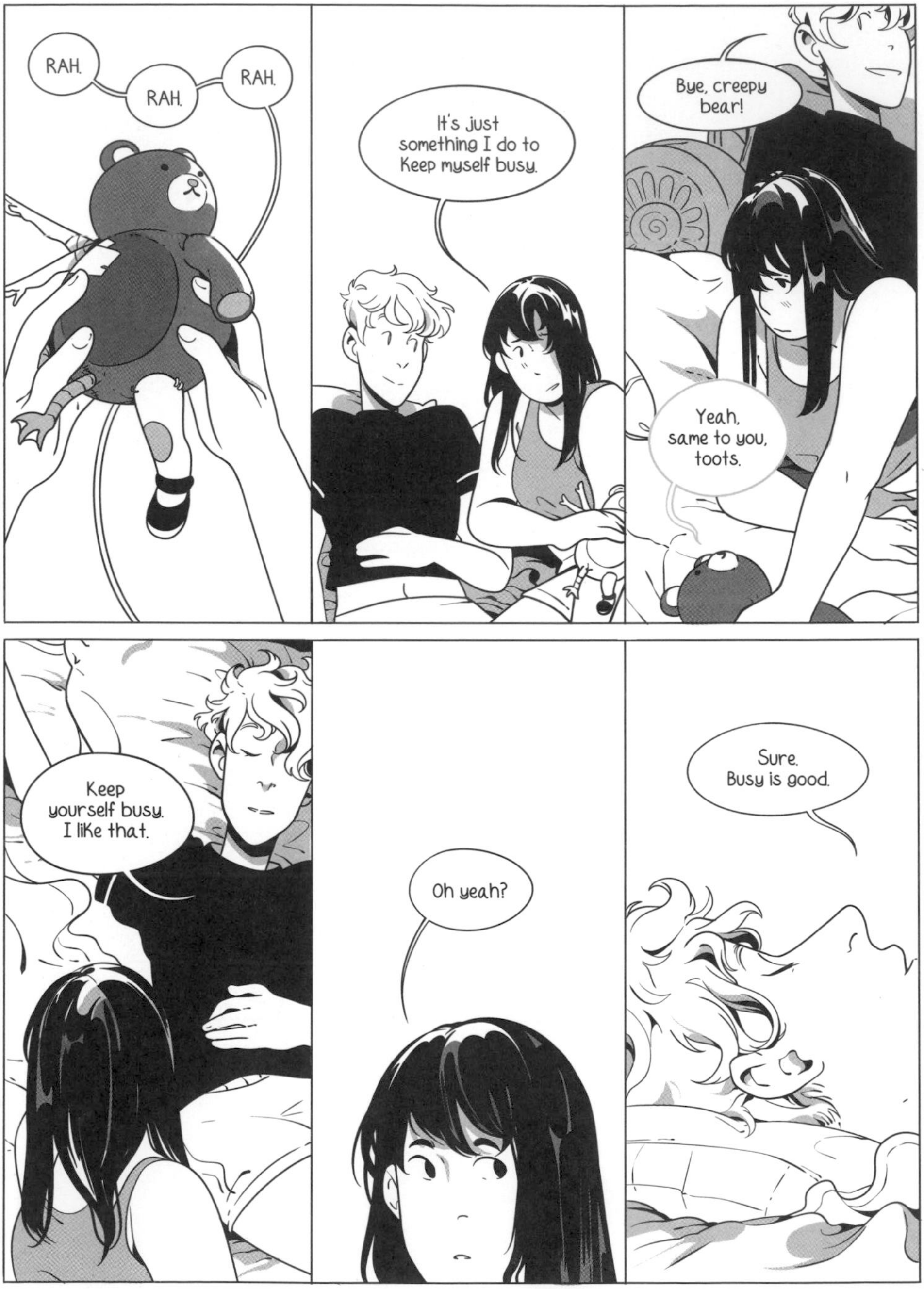
RAH.
RAH.
RAH.
It's just something I do to Keep myself busy.
Bye, creepy bear!
Yeah, same to you, toots.
Keep yourself busy. I like that.
Oh yeah?
Sure. Busy is good.

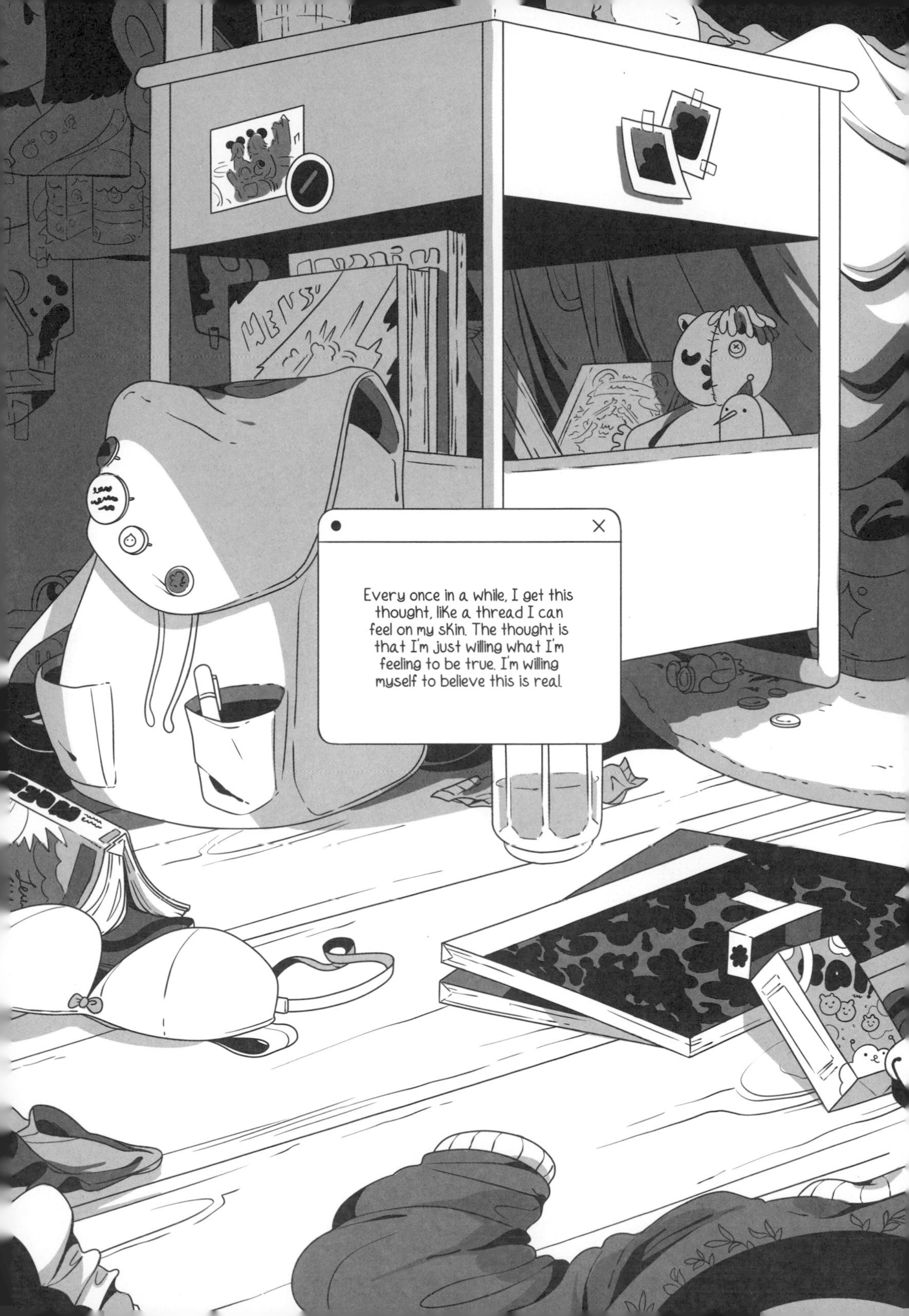
Every once in a while, I get this thought, like a thread I can feel on my skin. The thought is that I'm just willing what I'm feeling to be true. I'm willing myself to believe this is real.

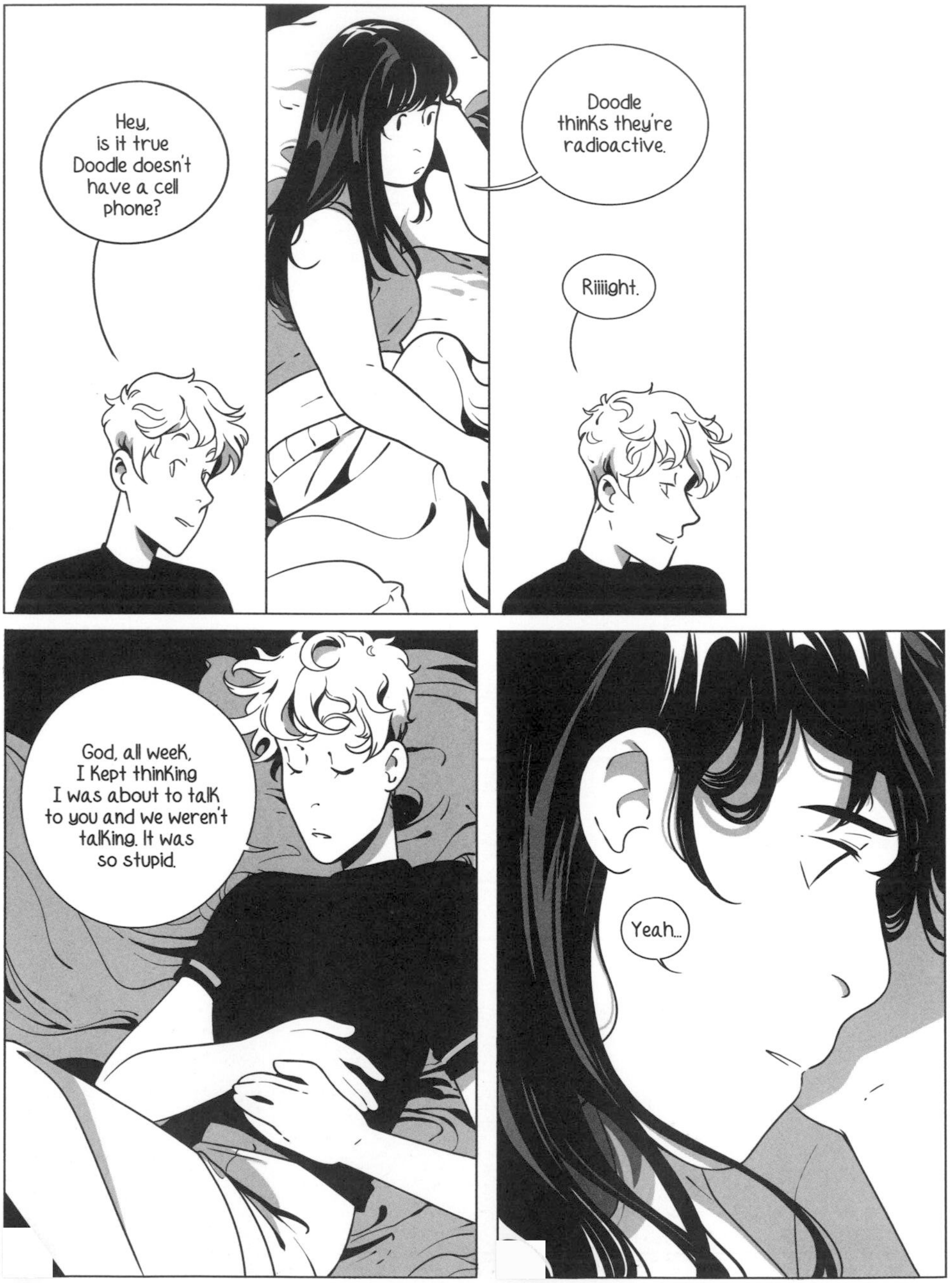
Hey, is it true Doodle doesn't have a cell phone?
Doodle thinks they're radioactive.
Riiiight.
God, all week, I kept thinking I was about to talk to you and we weren't talking. It was so stupid.
Yeah...

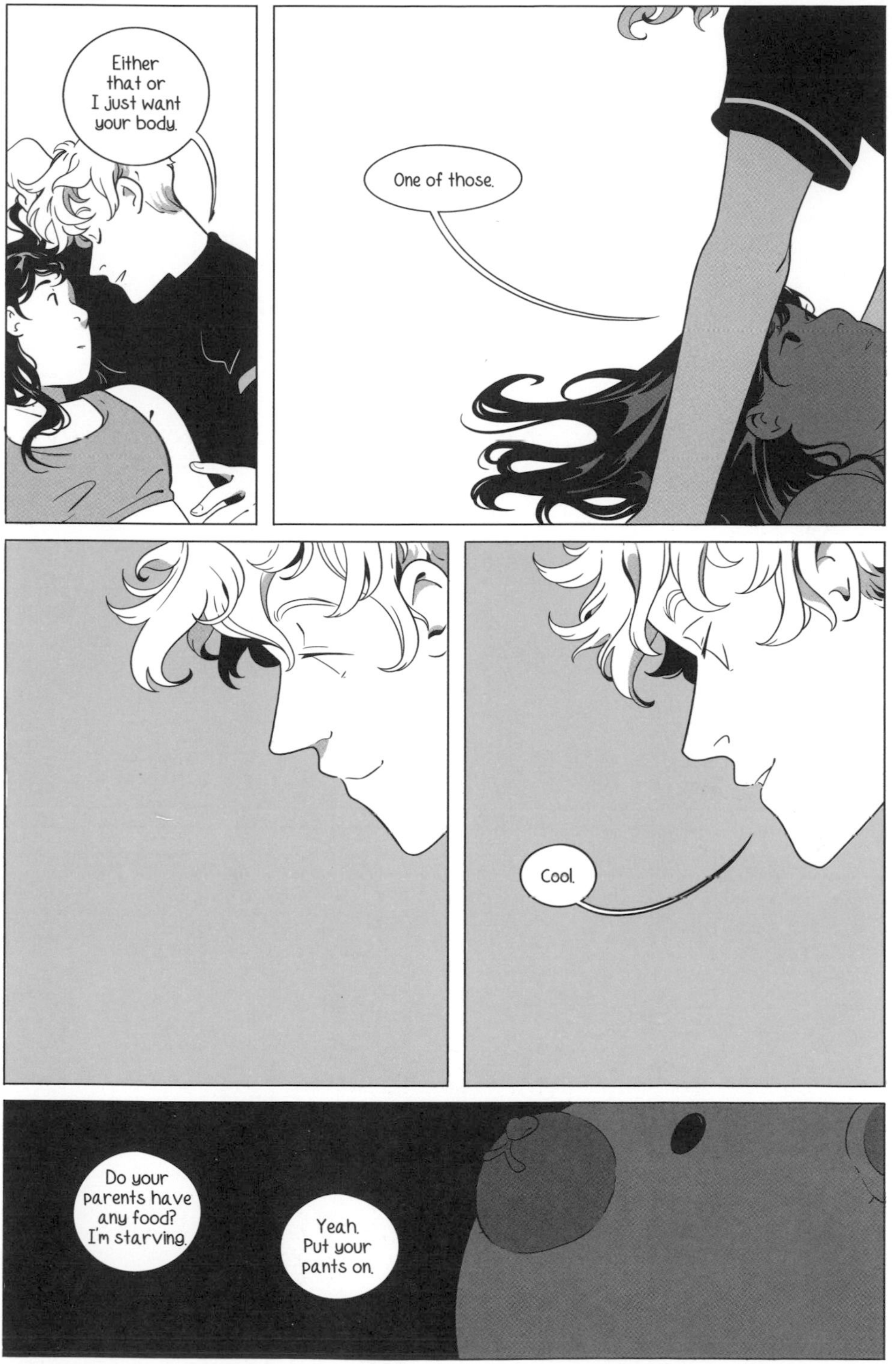
Either that or I just want your body.
One of those.
Cool.
Do your parents have any food? I'm starving.
Yeah. Put your pants on.

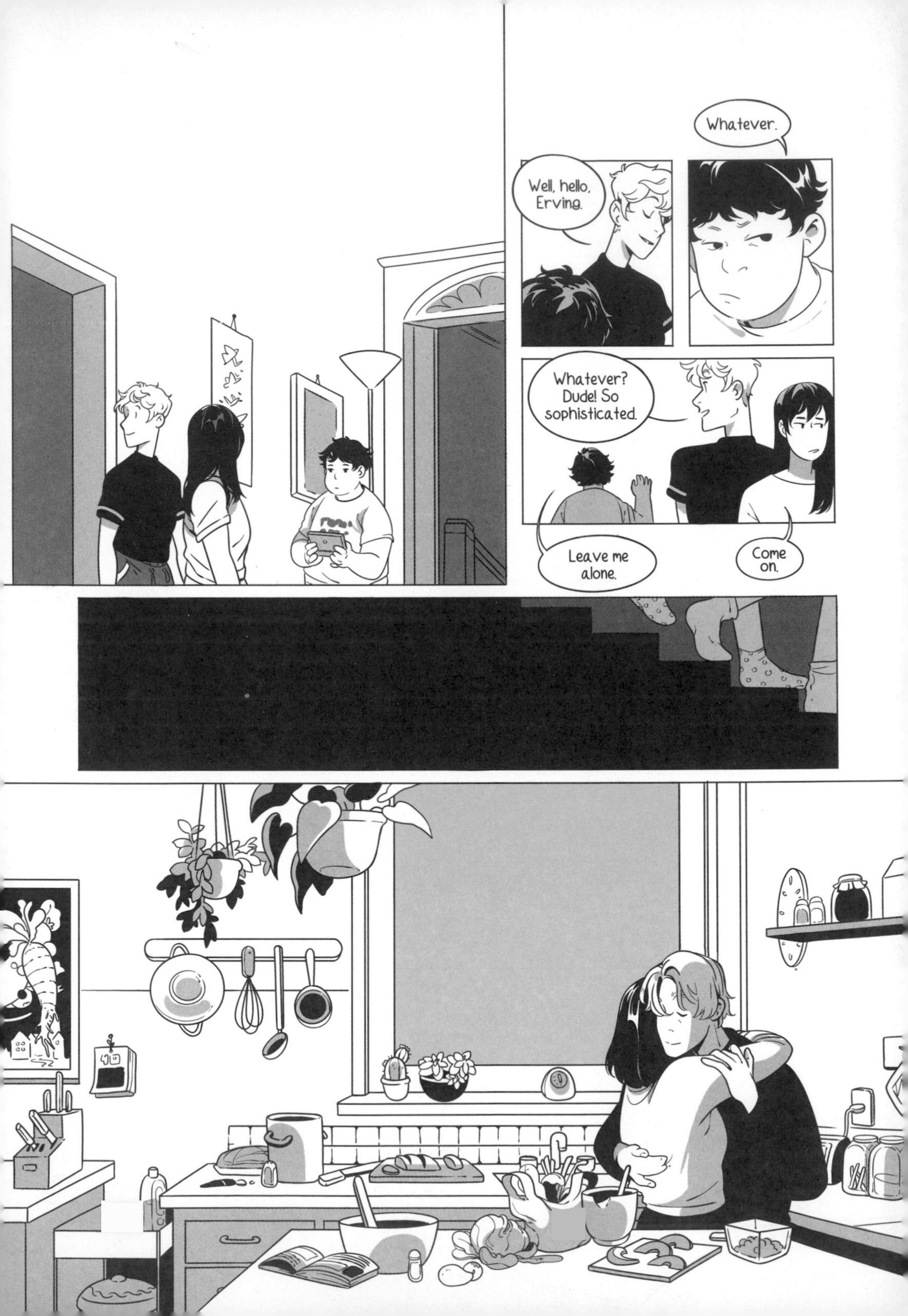
Well, hello, Erving.
Whatever.
Whatever? Dude! So sophisticated.
Leave me alone.
Come on.

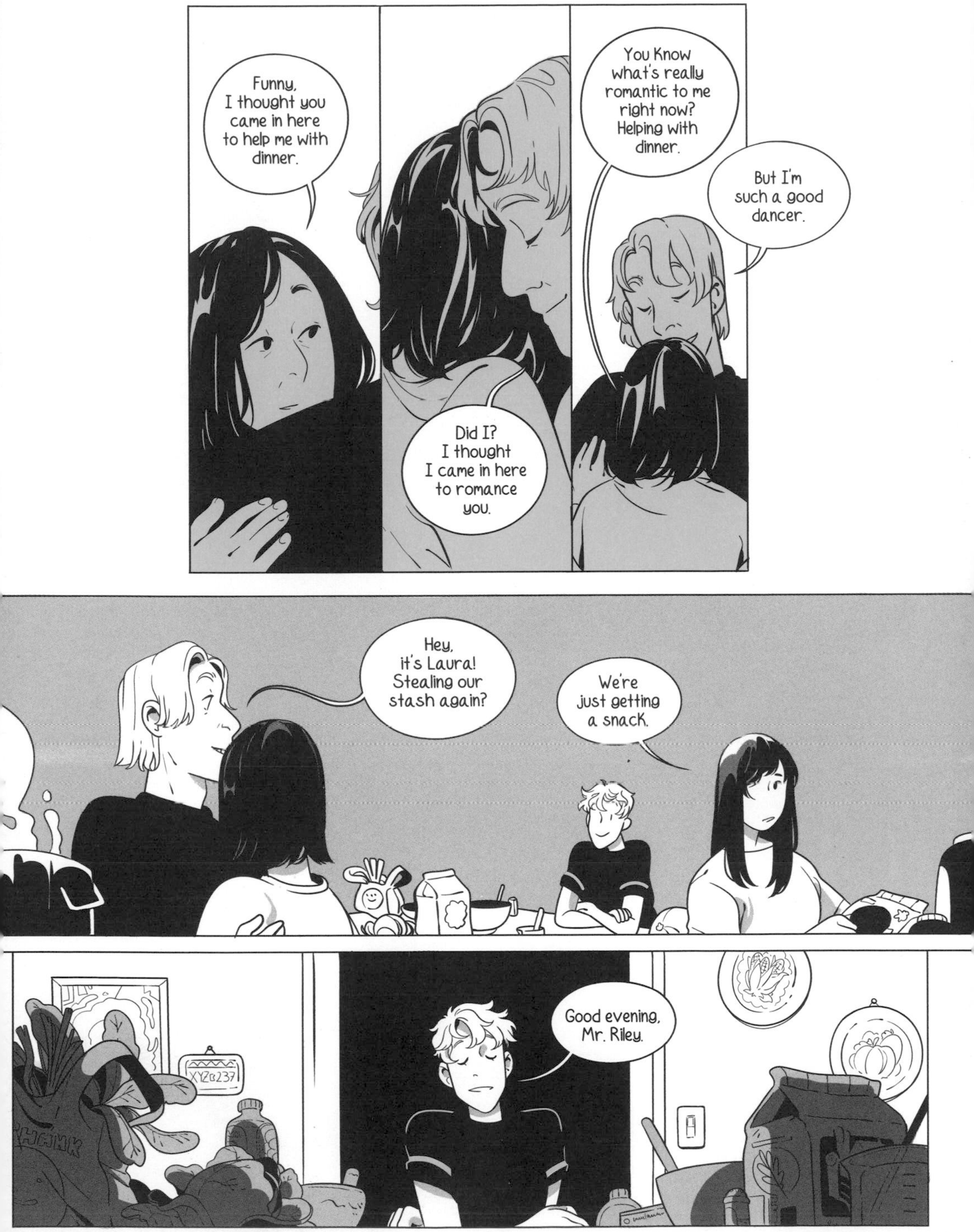
Funny, I thought you came in here to help me with dinner.
Did I? I thought I came in here to romance you.
You Know what's really romantic to me right now? Helping with dinner.
But I'm such a good dancer.
Hey, it's Laura! Stealing our stash again?
We're just getting a snack.
Good evening, Mr. Riley.

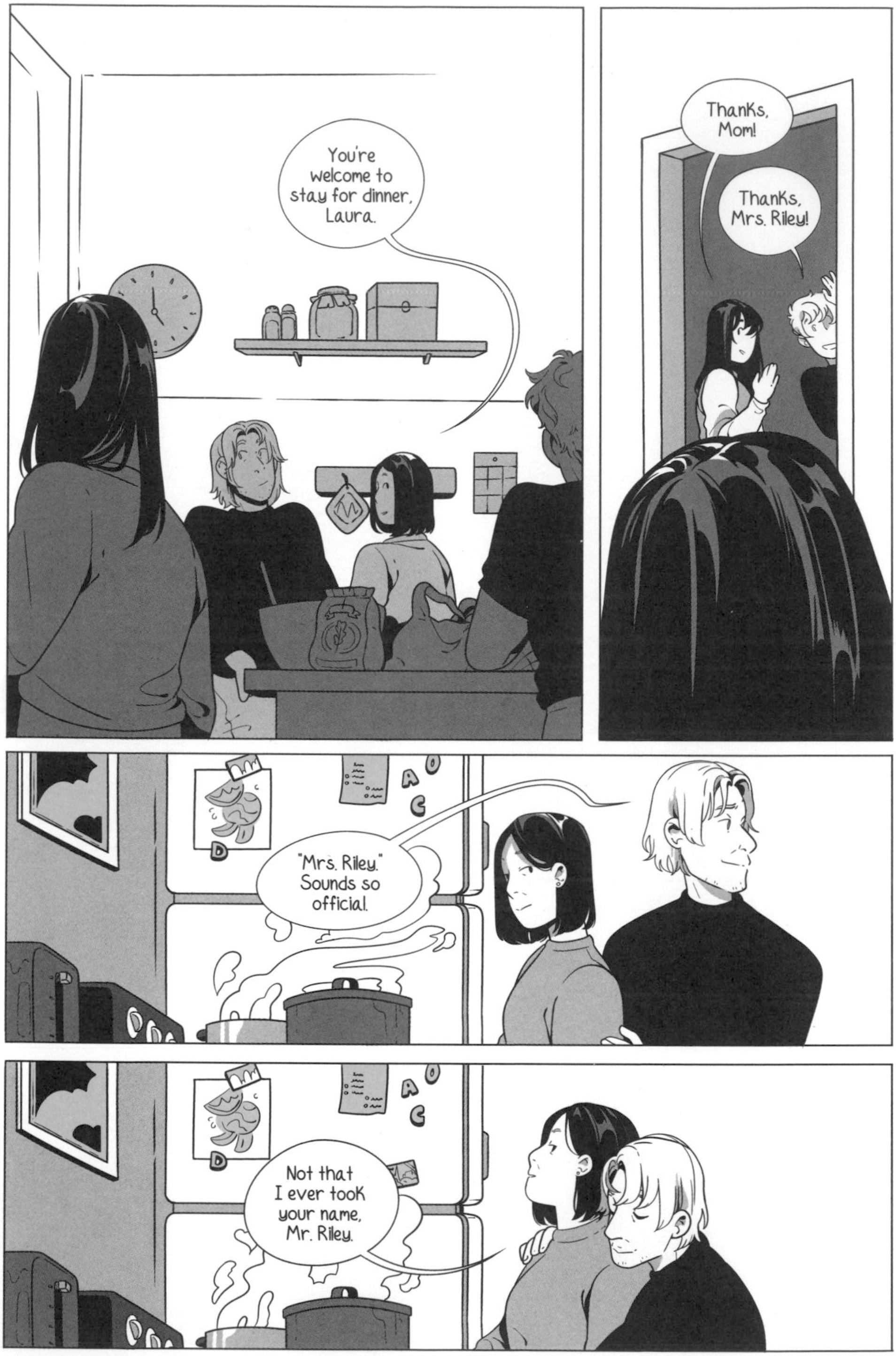
You're welcome to stay for dinner, Laura.
Thanks, Mom!
Thanks, Mrs. Riley!
"Mrs. Riley." Sounds so official.
Not that I ever took your name, Mr. Riley.

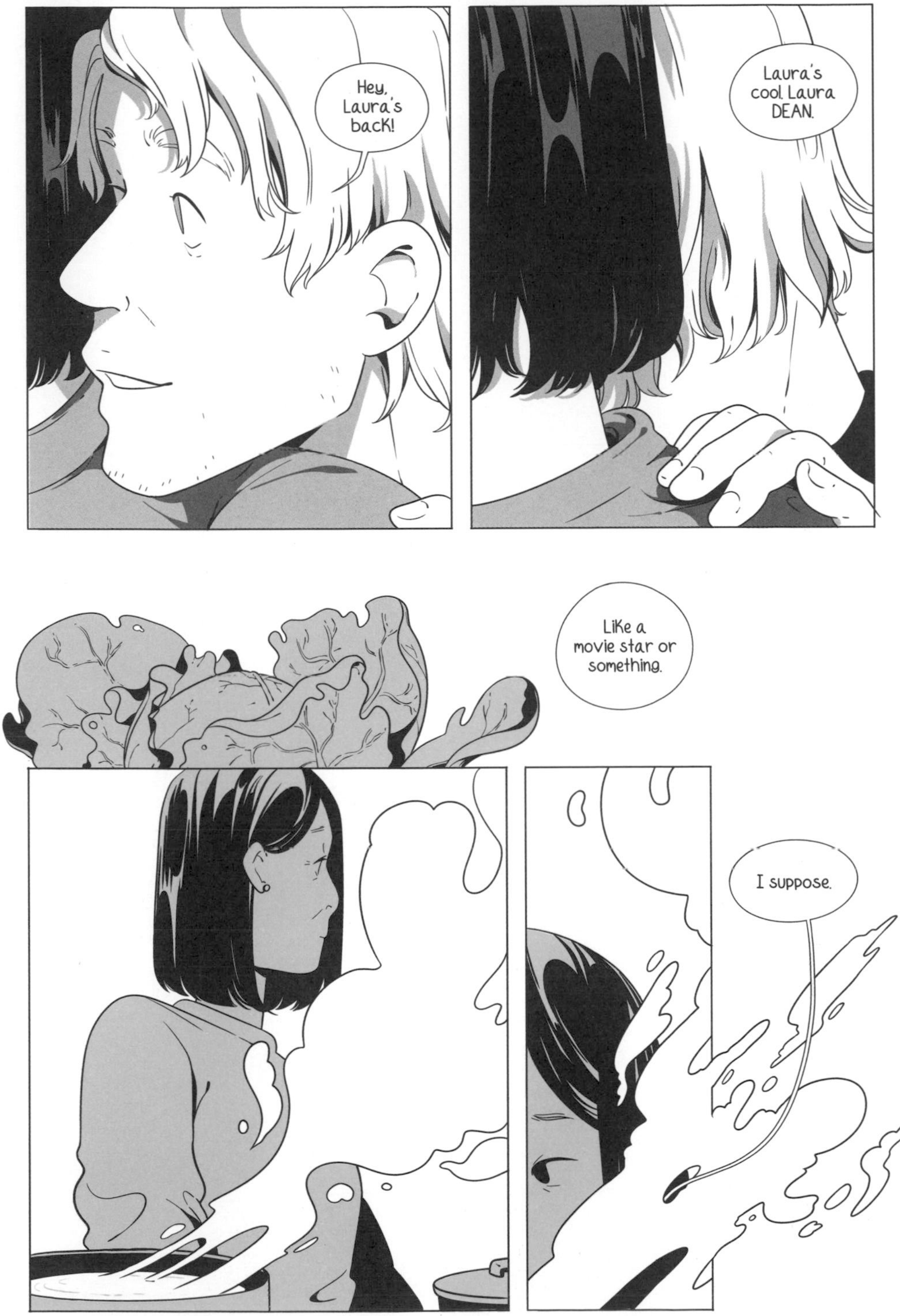
Hey, Laura's back!
Laura's cool. Laura DEAN.
Like a movie star or something.
I suppose.

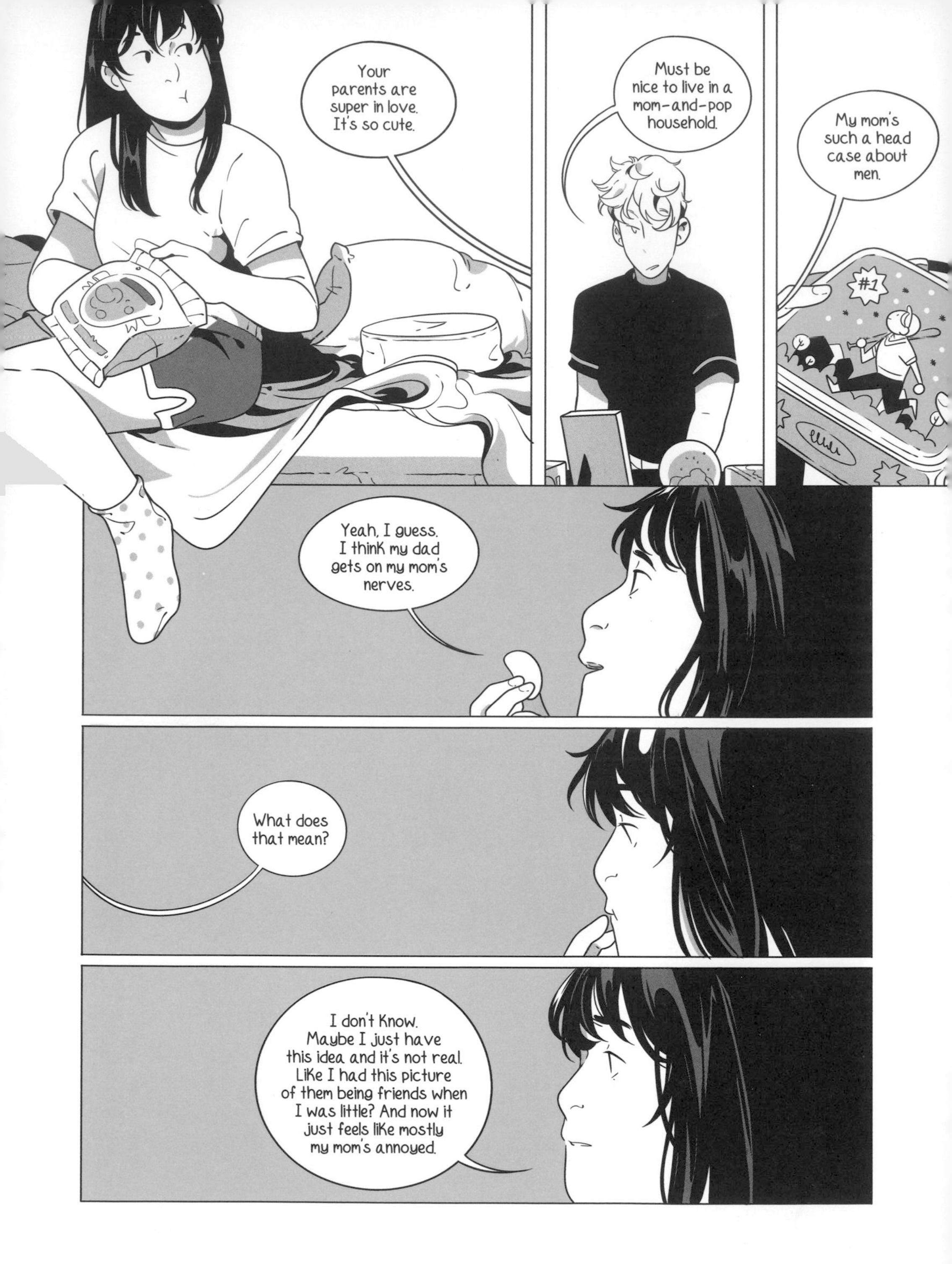
Your parents are super in love. It's so cute.
Must be nice to live in a mom-and-pop household.
My mom's such a head case about men.
#1
Yeah, I guess. I think my dad gets on my mom's nerves.
What does that mean?
I don't know. Maybe I just have this idea and it's not real. Like I had this picture of them being friends when I was little? And now it just feels like mostly my mom's annoyed.

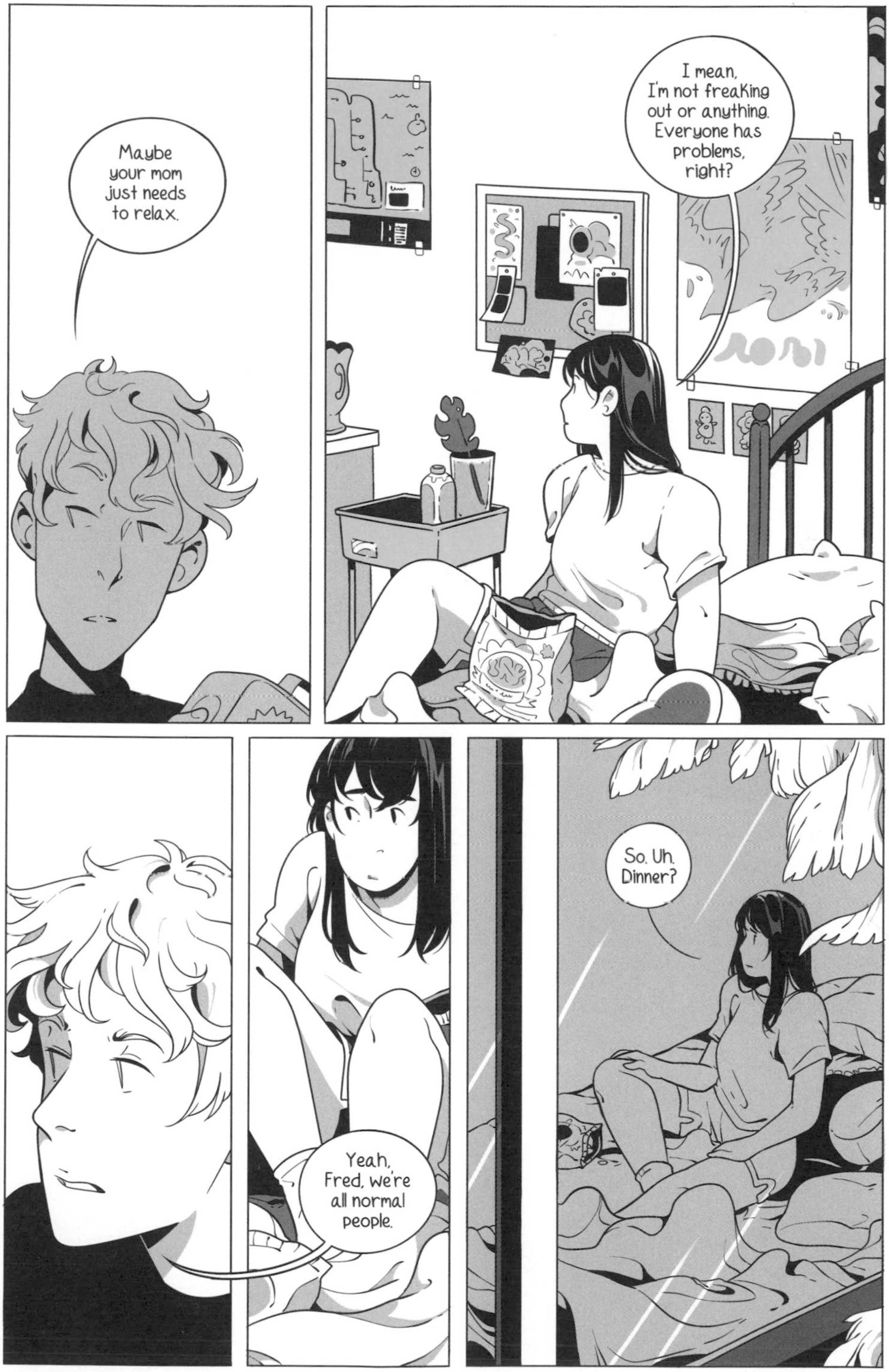
Maybe your mom just needs to relax.
I mean, I'm not freaking out or anything. Everyone has problems, right?
Yeah, Fred, we're all normal people.
So. Uh. Dinner?

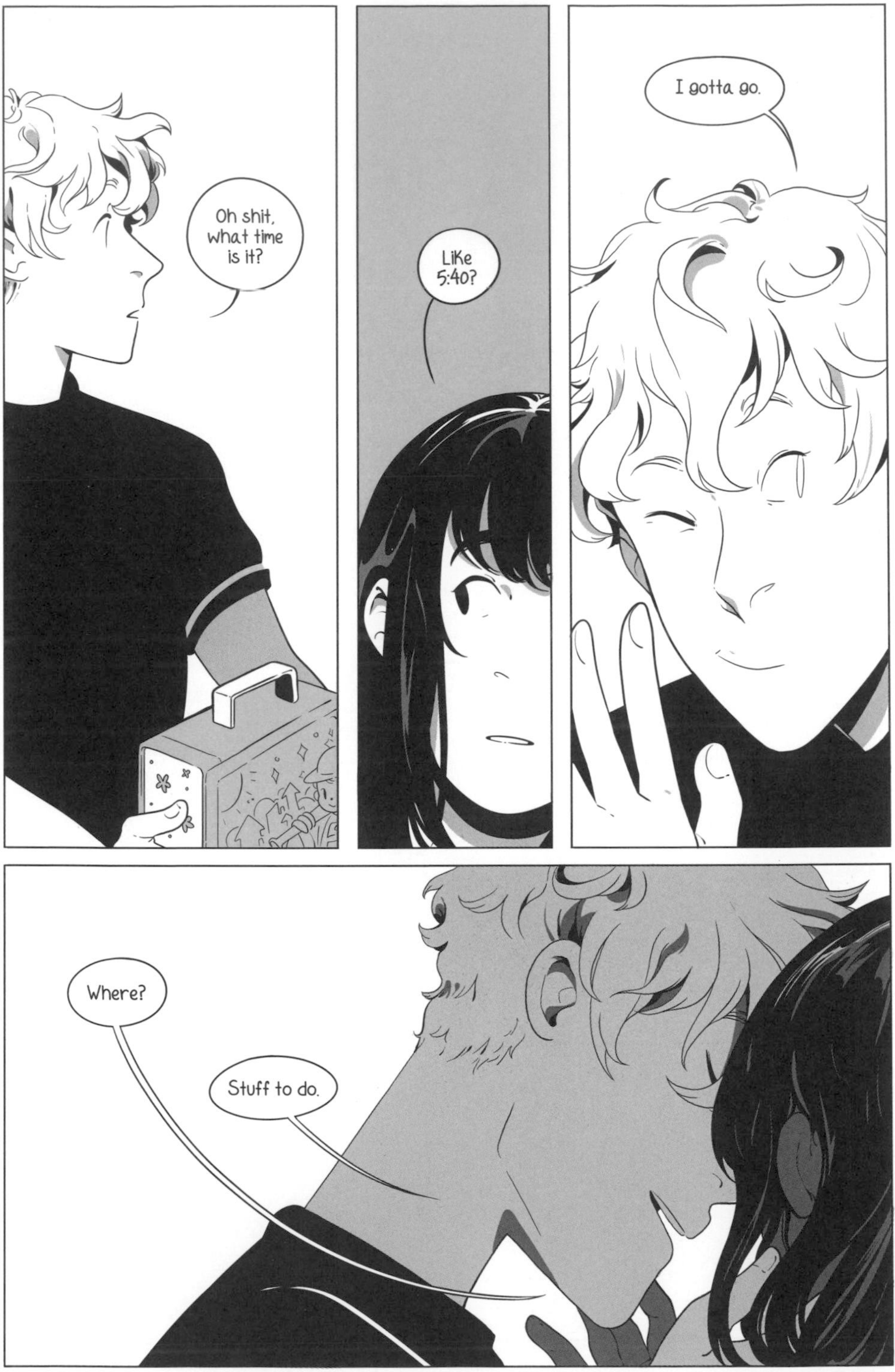
Oh shit, what time is it?
Like 5:40?
I gotta go.
Where?
Stuff to do.

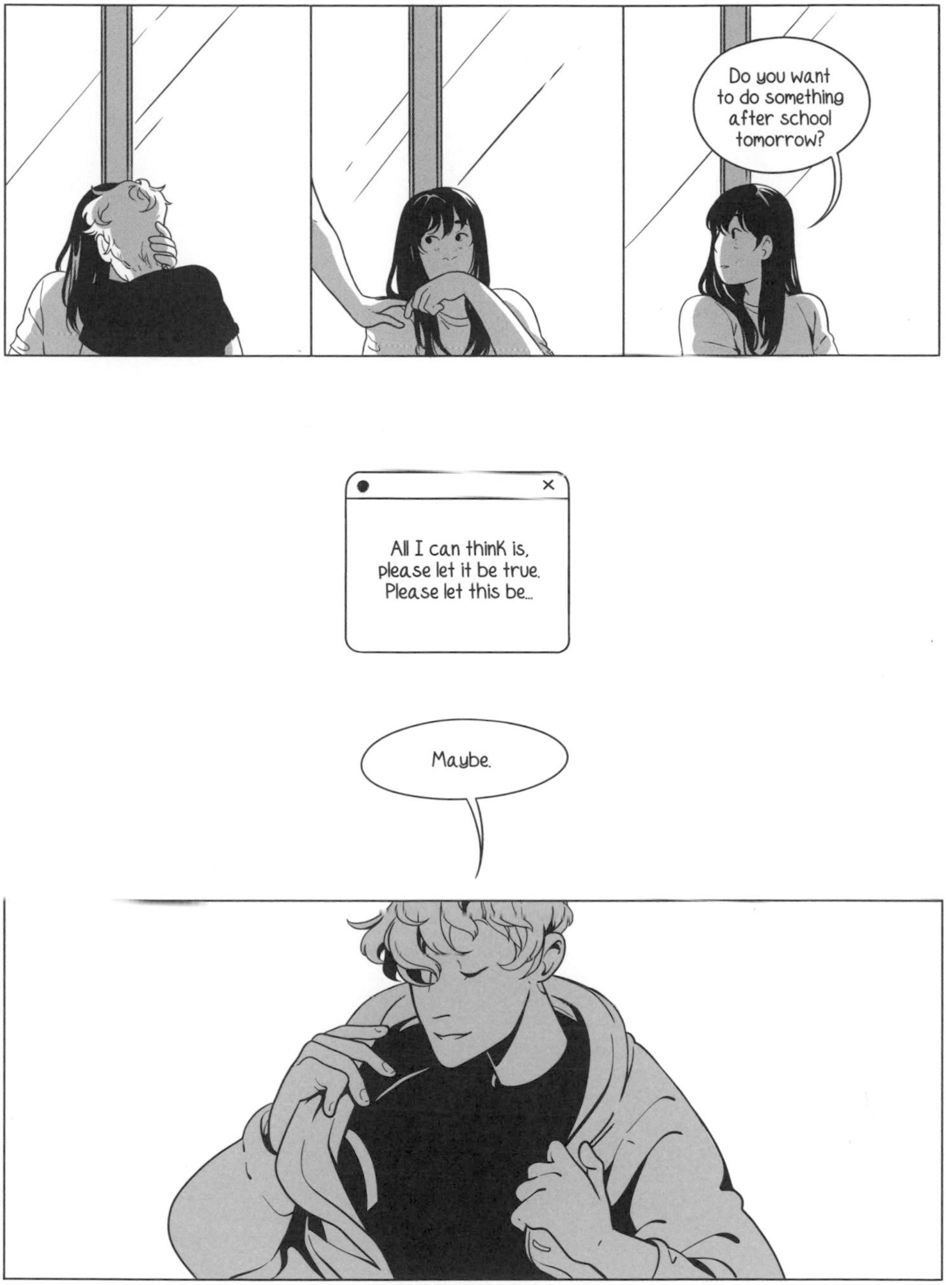
Do you want to do something after school tomorrow?
All I can think is, please let it be true. Please let this be...
Maybe.

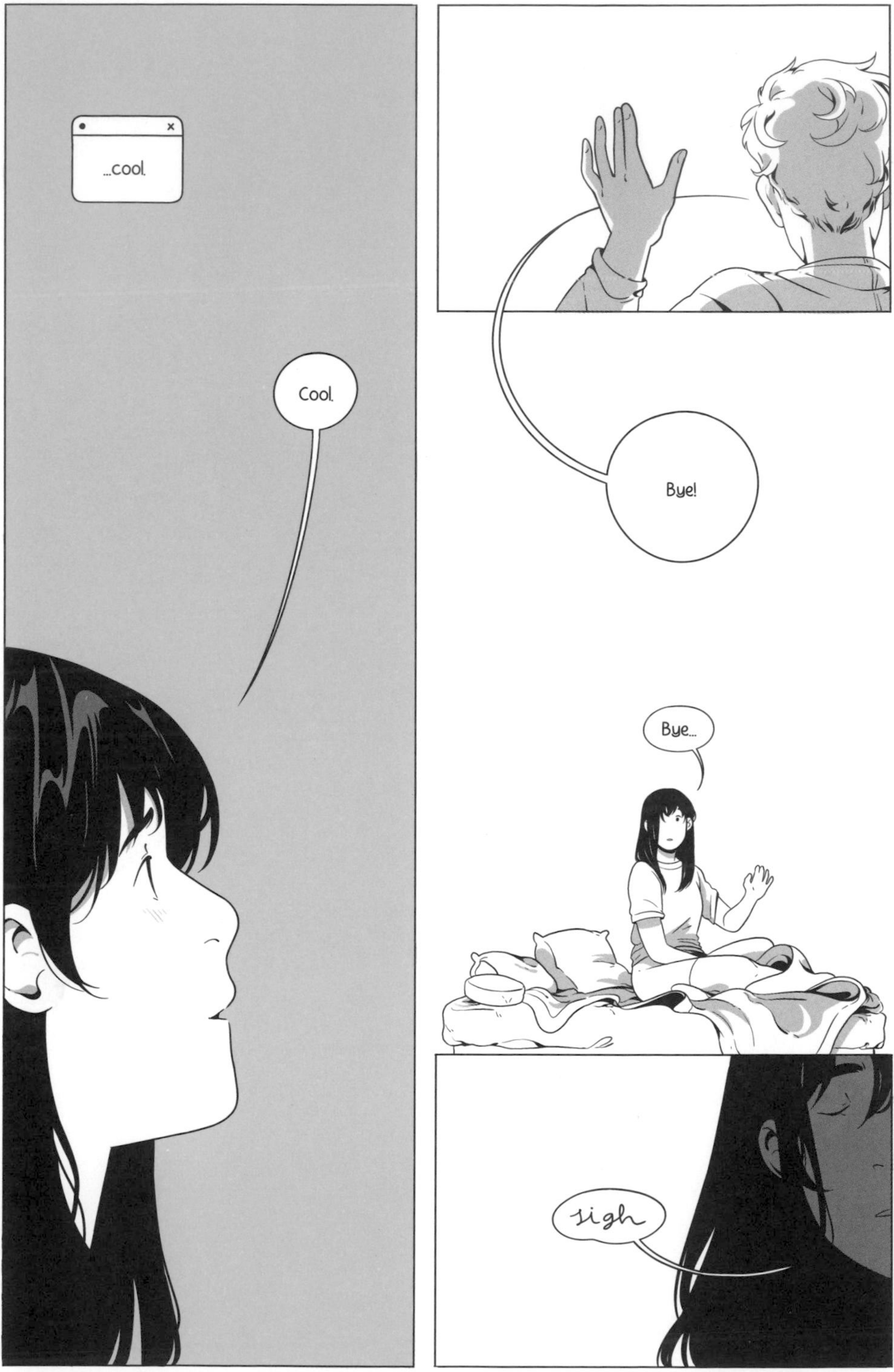
...cool.
Cool.
Bye!
Bye...
sigh

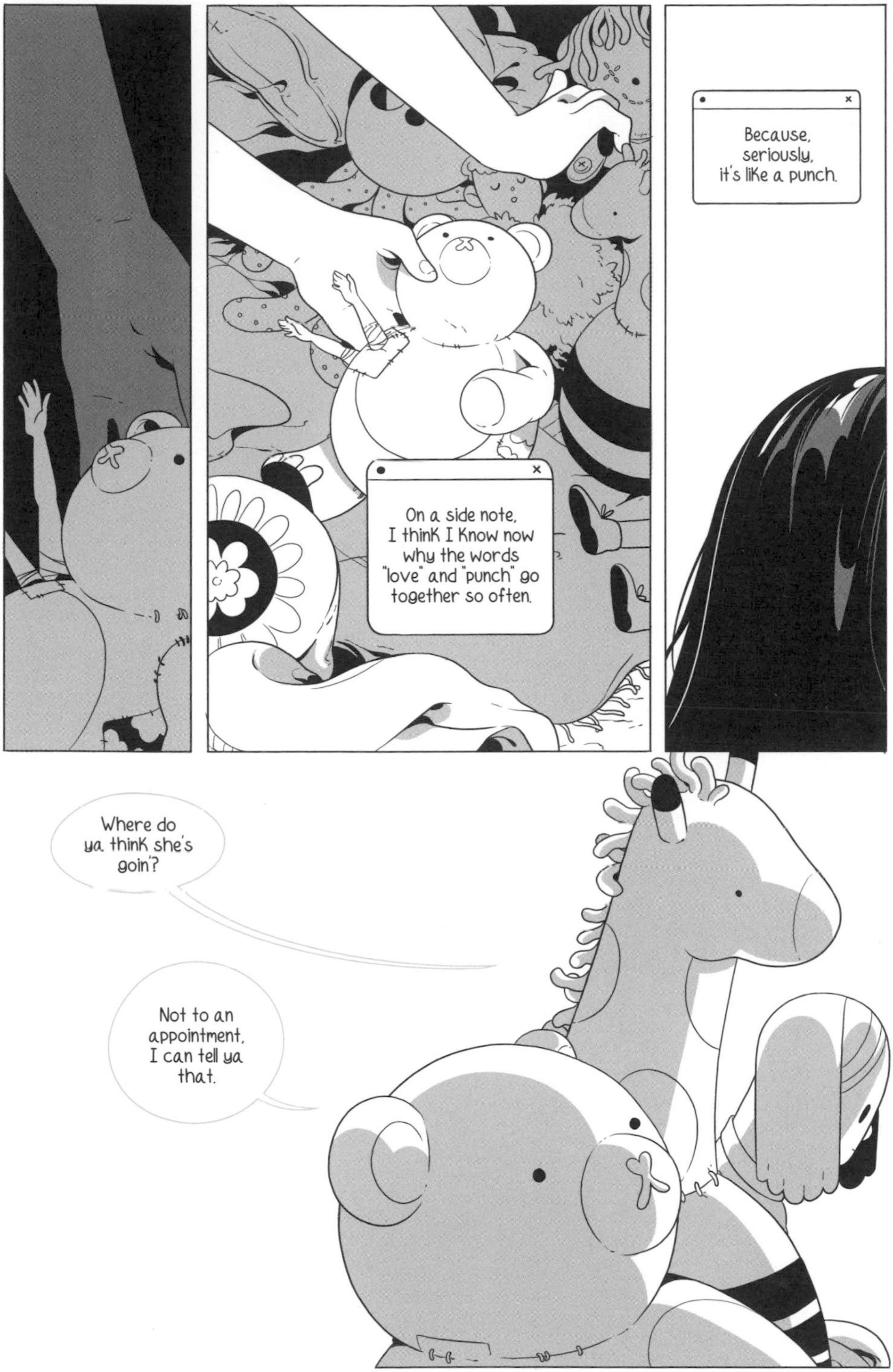
Because, seriously, it's like a punch.
On a side note, I think I Know now why the words "love" and "punch" go together so often.
Where do ya think she's goin'?
Not to an appointment, I can tell ya that.

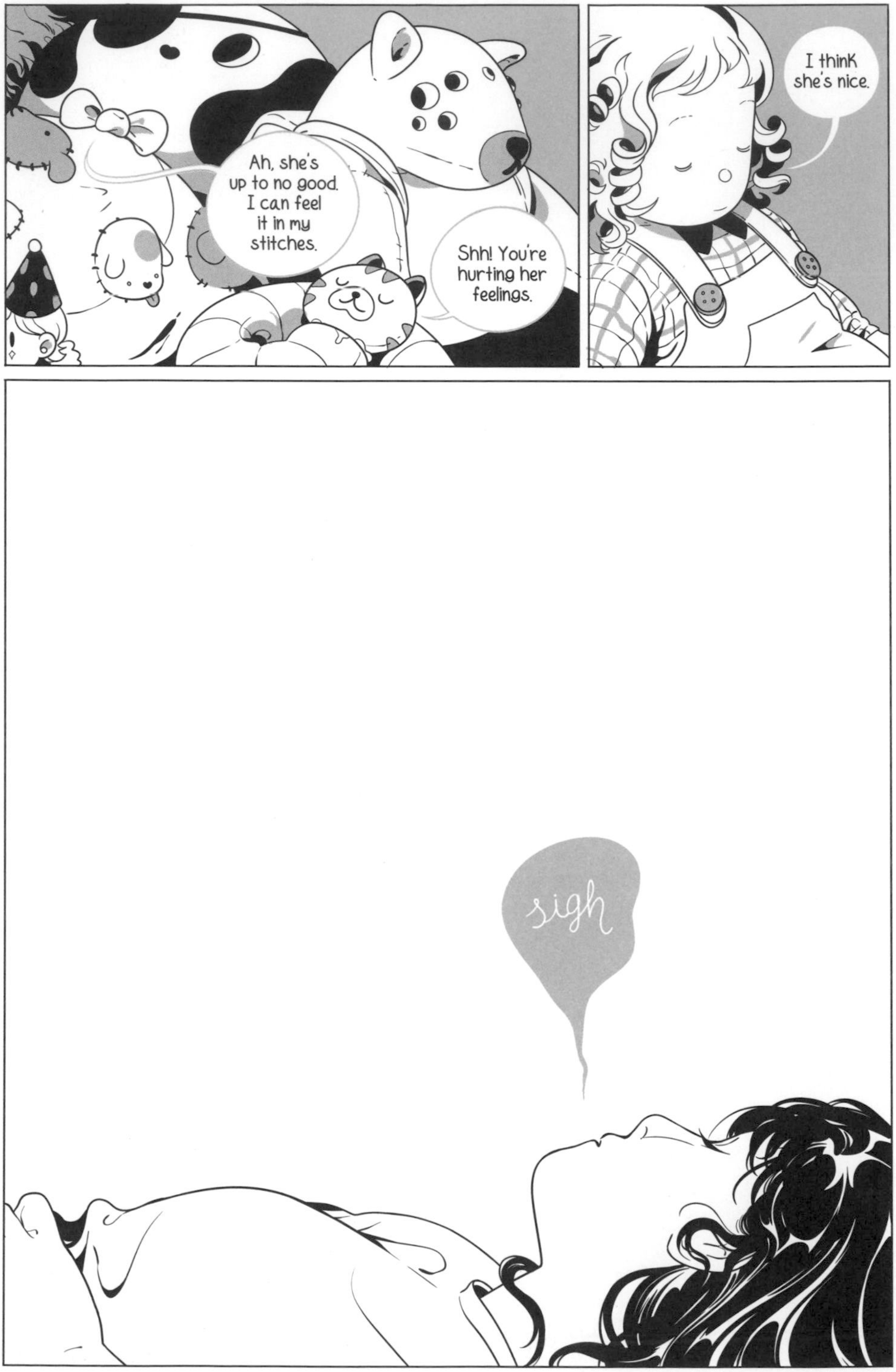
Ah, she's up to no good. I can feel it in my stitches.
Shh! You're hurting her feelings.
I think she's nice.
sigh

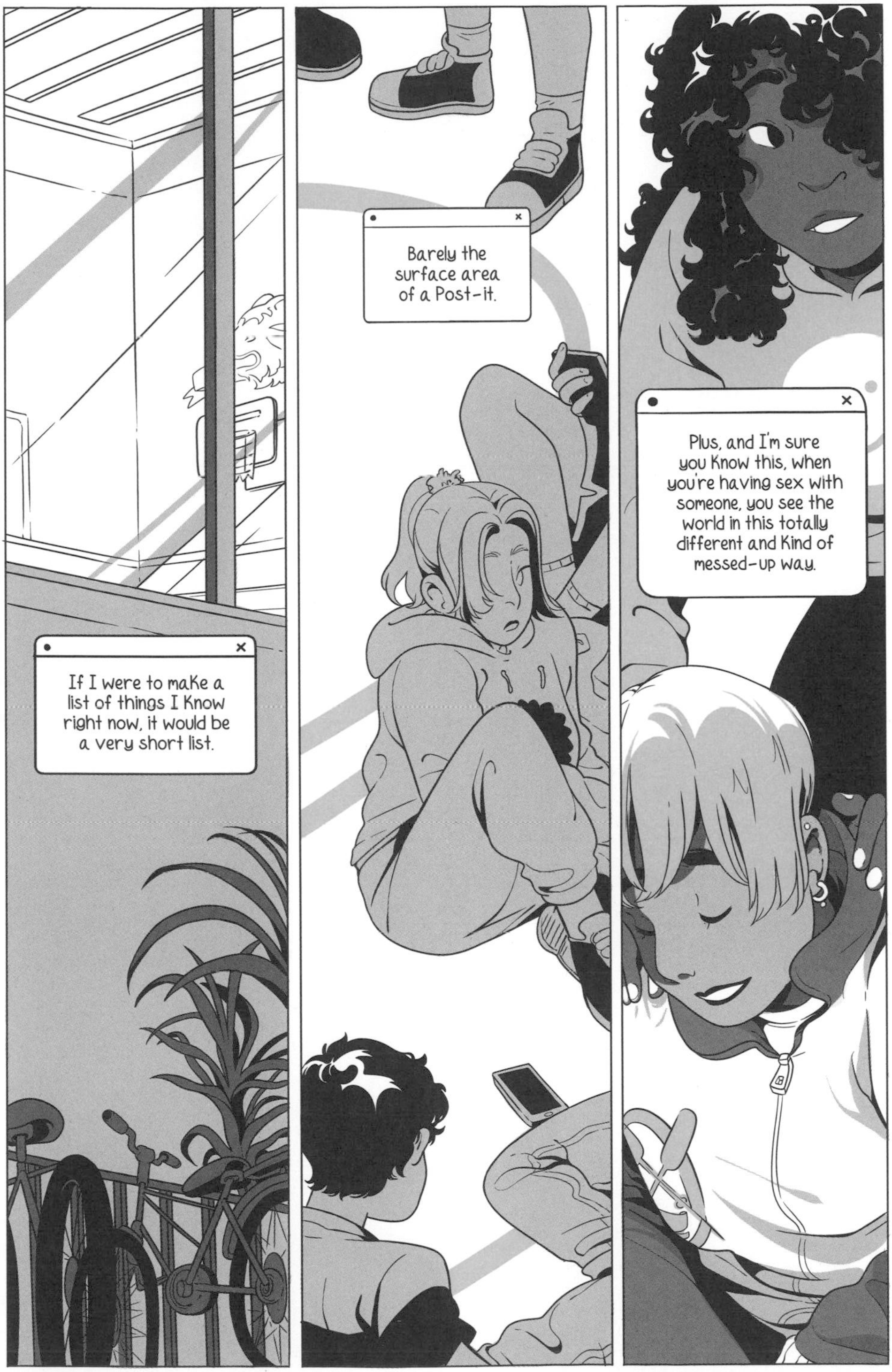
If I were to make a list of things I know right now, it would be a very short list.
Barely the surface area of a Post-it.
Plus, and I'm sure you know this, when you're having sex with someone, you see the world in this totally different and kind of messed-up way.

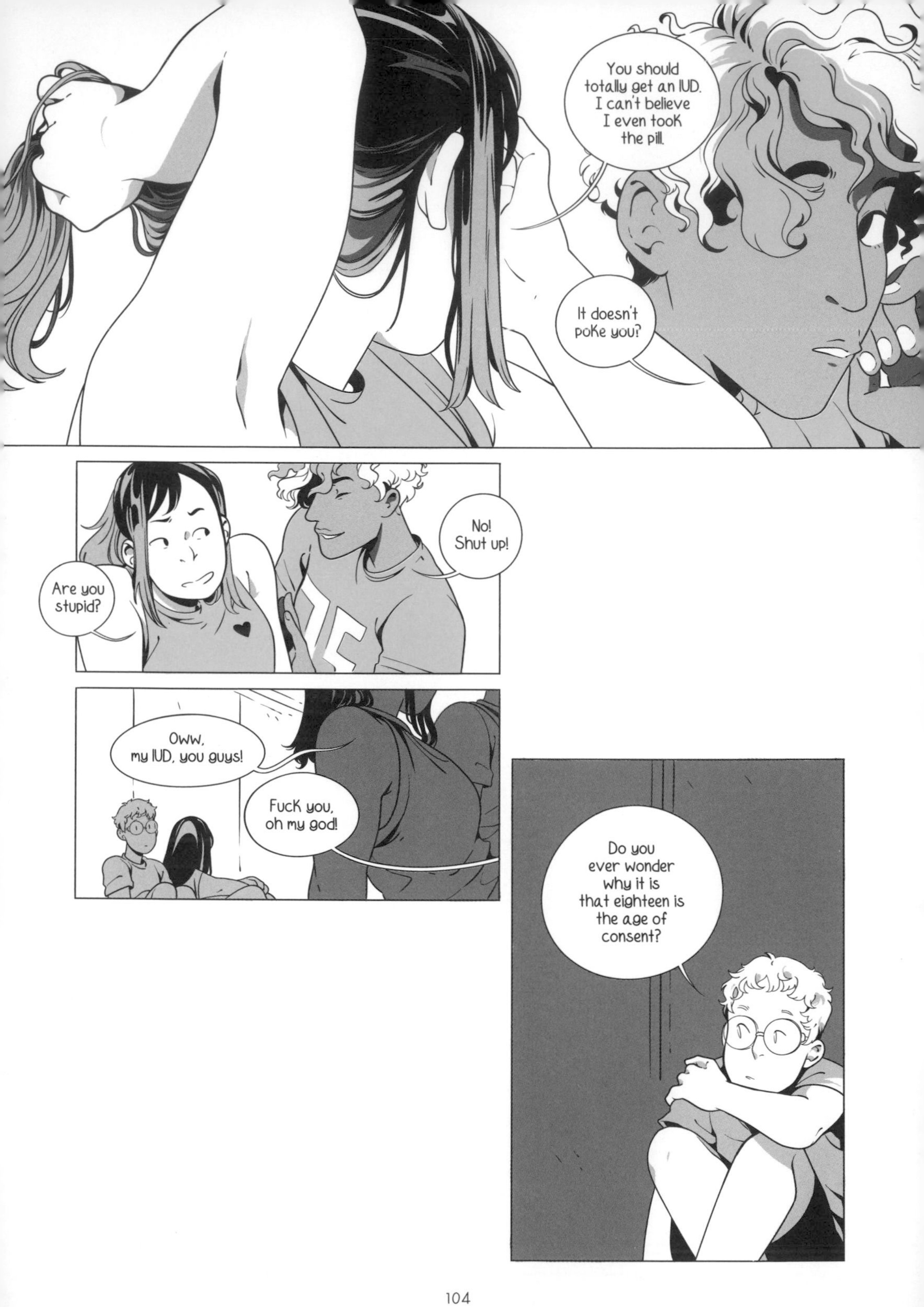
You should totally get an IUD. I can't believe I even took the pill.
It doesn't poke you?
Are you stupid?
No! Shut up!
Oww, my IUD, you guys!
Fuck you, oh my god!
Do you ever wonder why it is that eighteen is the age of consent?

Not really. Do you?

Yeah, I mean, age is subjective. You can be a really mature sixteen-year-old or a really immature twenty-year-old... Like, what IS eighteen?

What are you talking about?

I'm saying "the teenager" is essentially a societal construct...

Yeah, but AGE isn't. And the whole consent thing is so adults can't take advantage of younger people.

But in some states it's sixteen. So then what does that mean?

I dunno.

Hey, didn't you read something that said that in Japan people, like, aren't having sex?

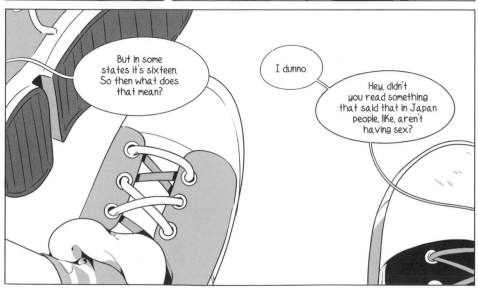

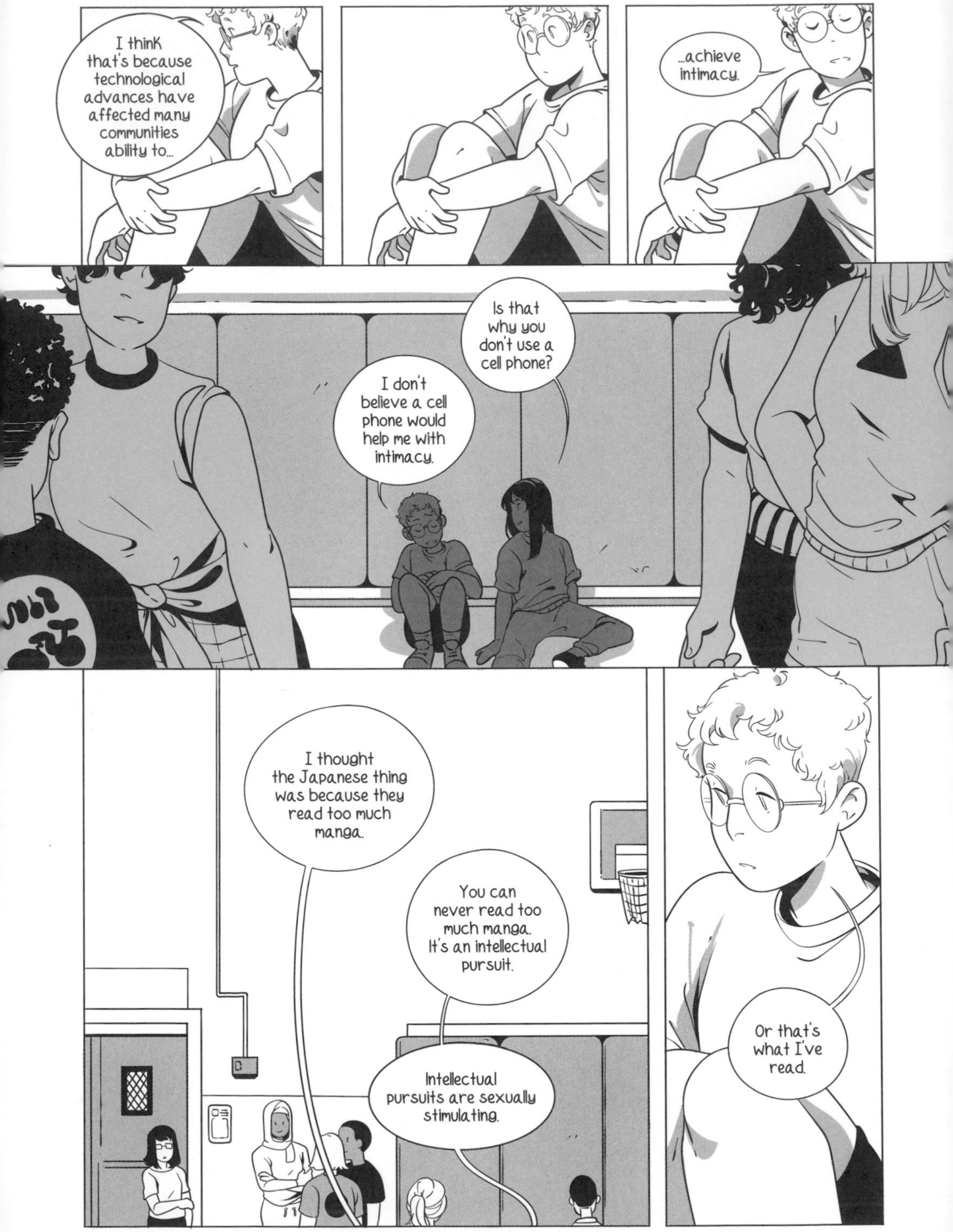
I think that's because technological advances have affected many communities ability to...
...achieve intimacy.
Is that why you don't use a cell phone?
I don't believe a cell phone would help me with intimacy.
I thought the Japanese thing was because they read too much manga.
You can never read too much manga. It's an intellectual pursuit.
Intellectual pursuits are sexually stimulating.
Or that's what I've read.

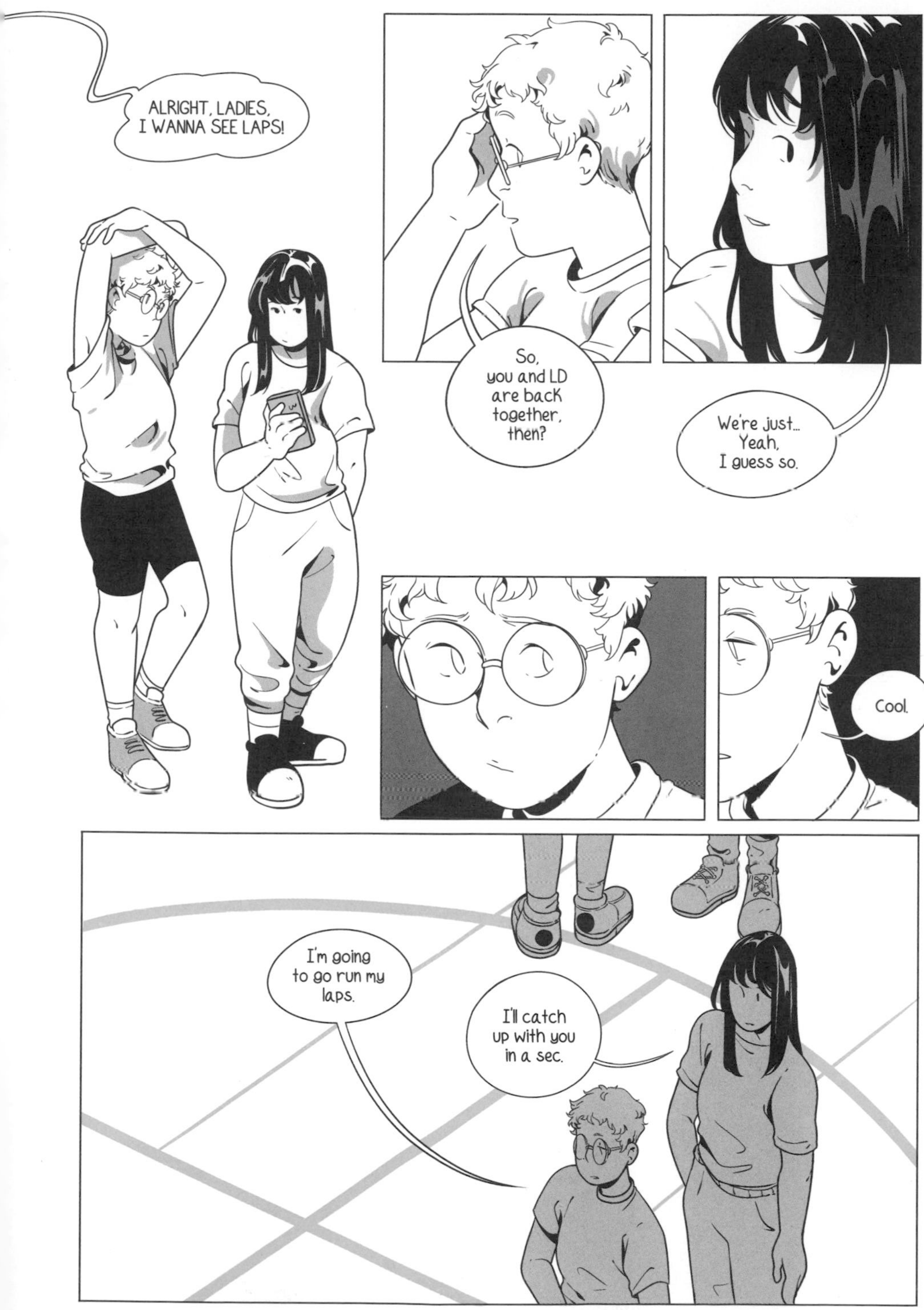
ALRIGHT, LADIES, I WANNA SEE LAPS!
So, you and LD are back together, then?
We're just... Yeah, I guess so.
Cool.
I'm going to go run my laps.
I'll catch up with you in a sec.

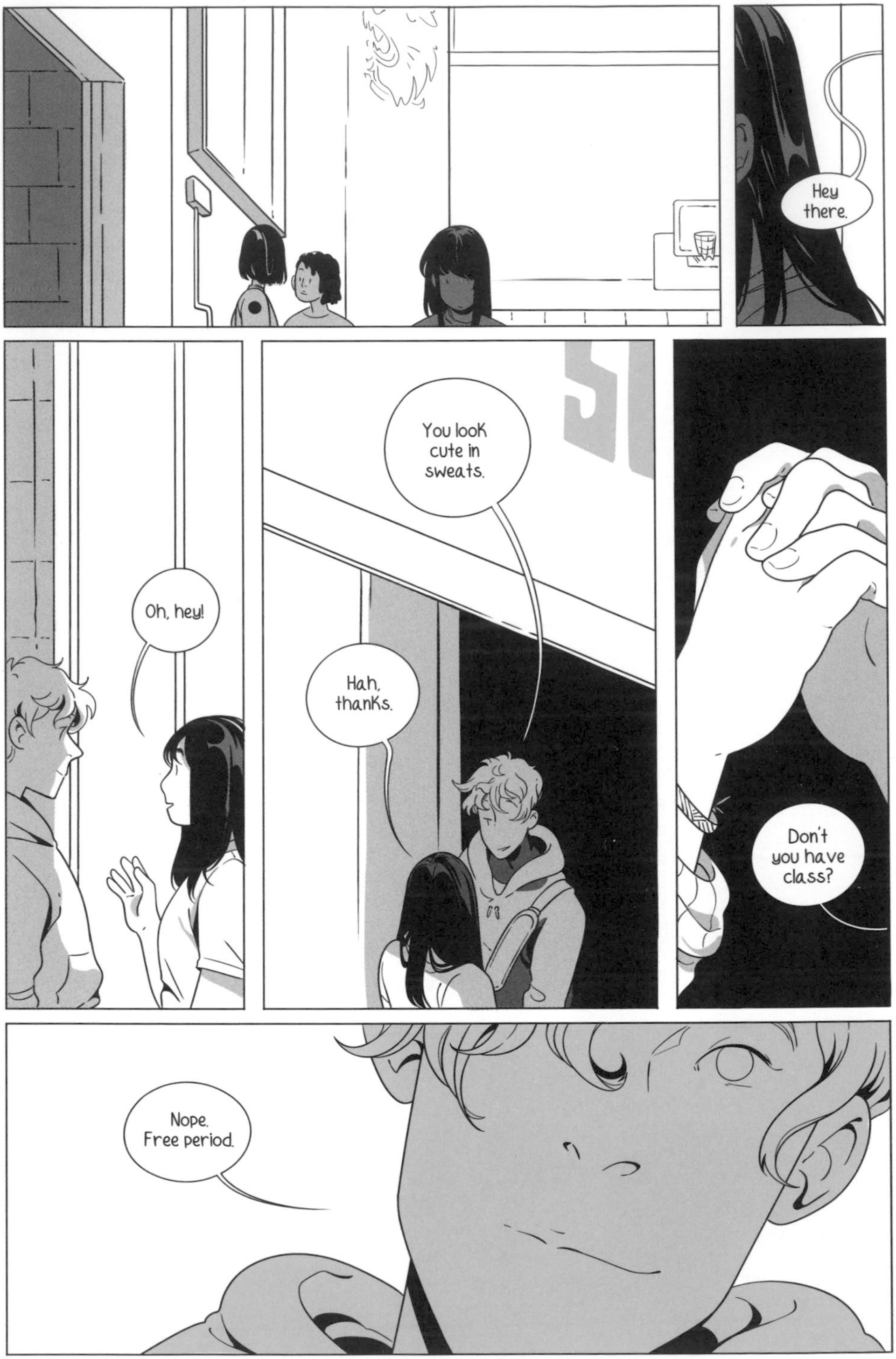
Hey there.
Oh, hey!
You look cute in sweats.
Hah, thanks.
Don't you have class?
Nope. Free period.

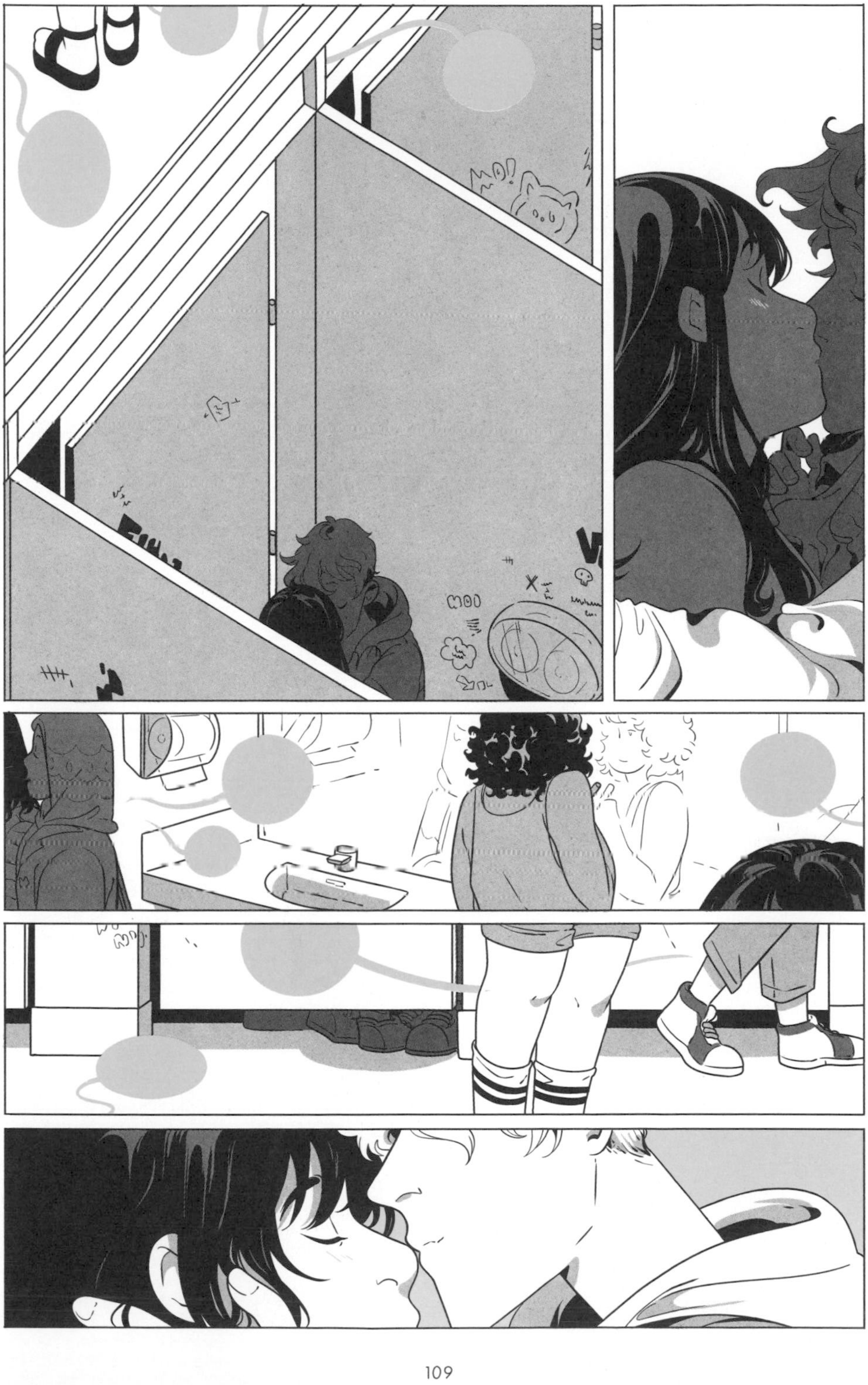

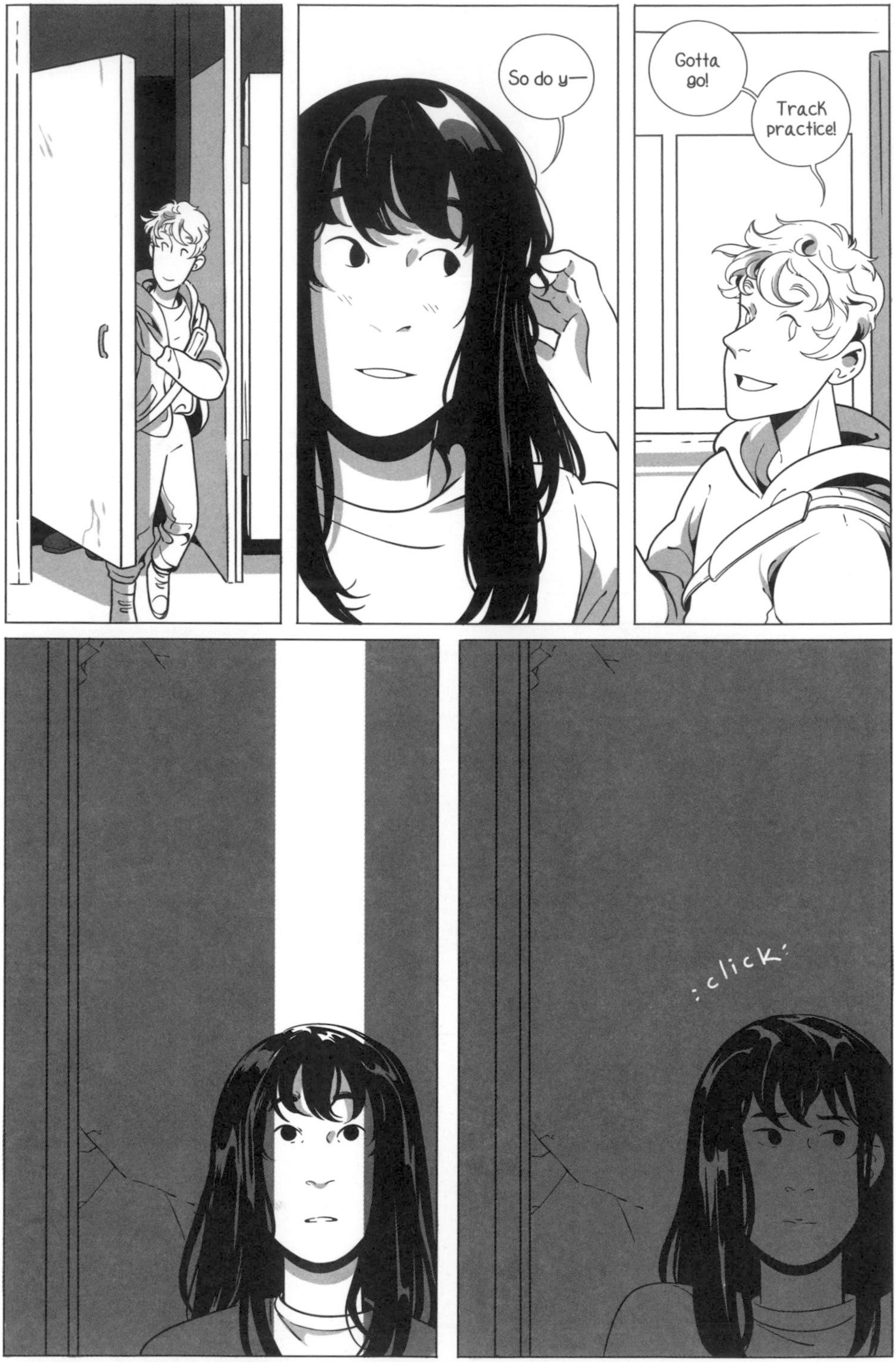
So do y—
Gotta go!
Track practice!
: click :

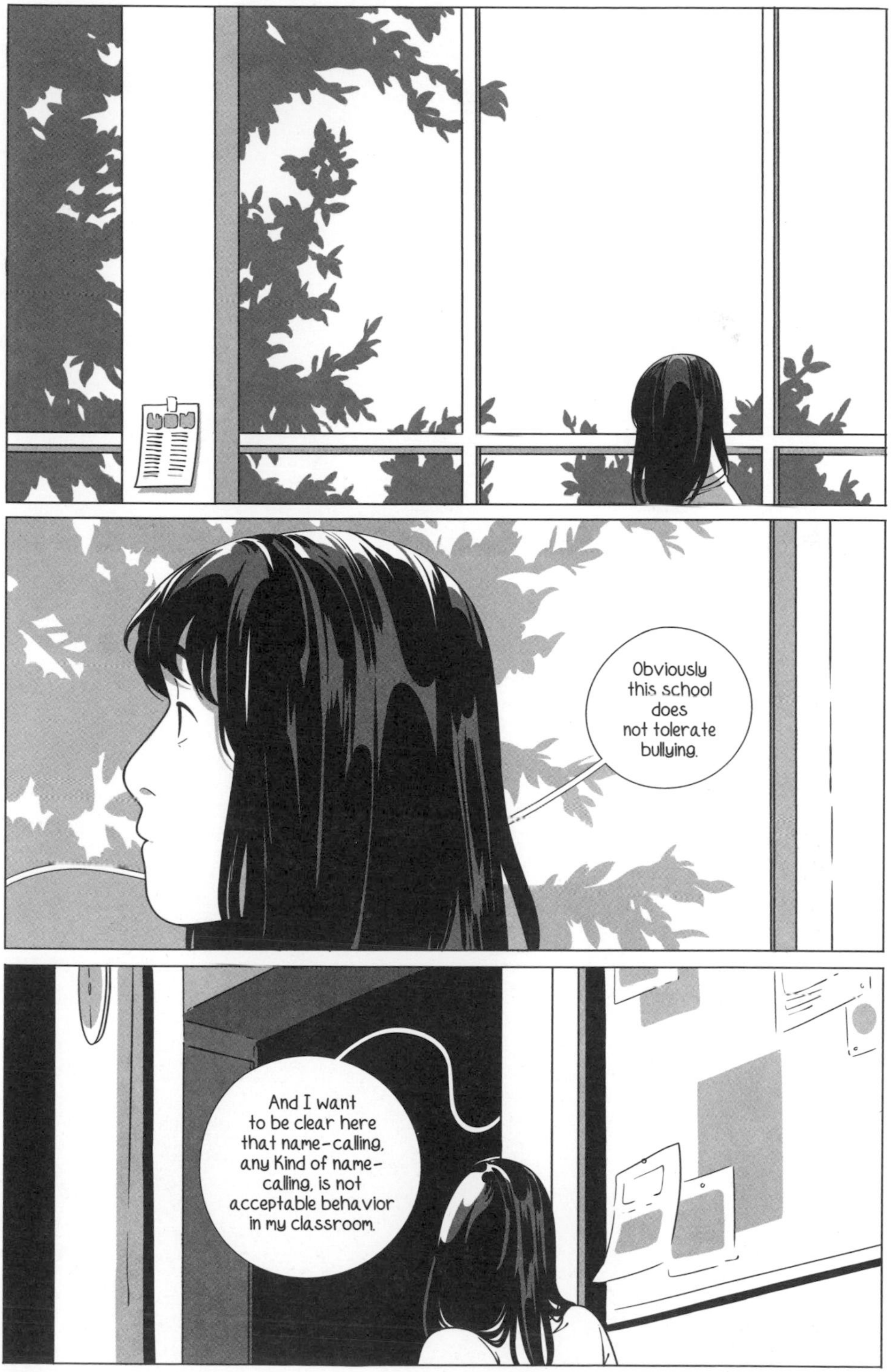
Obviously this school does not tolerate bullying.
And I want to be clear here that name-calling, any kind of name-calling, is not acceptable behavior in my classroom.

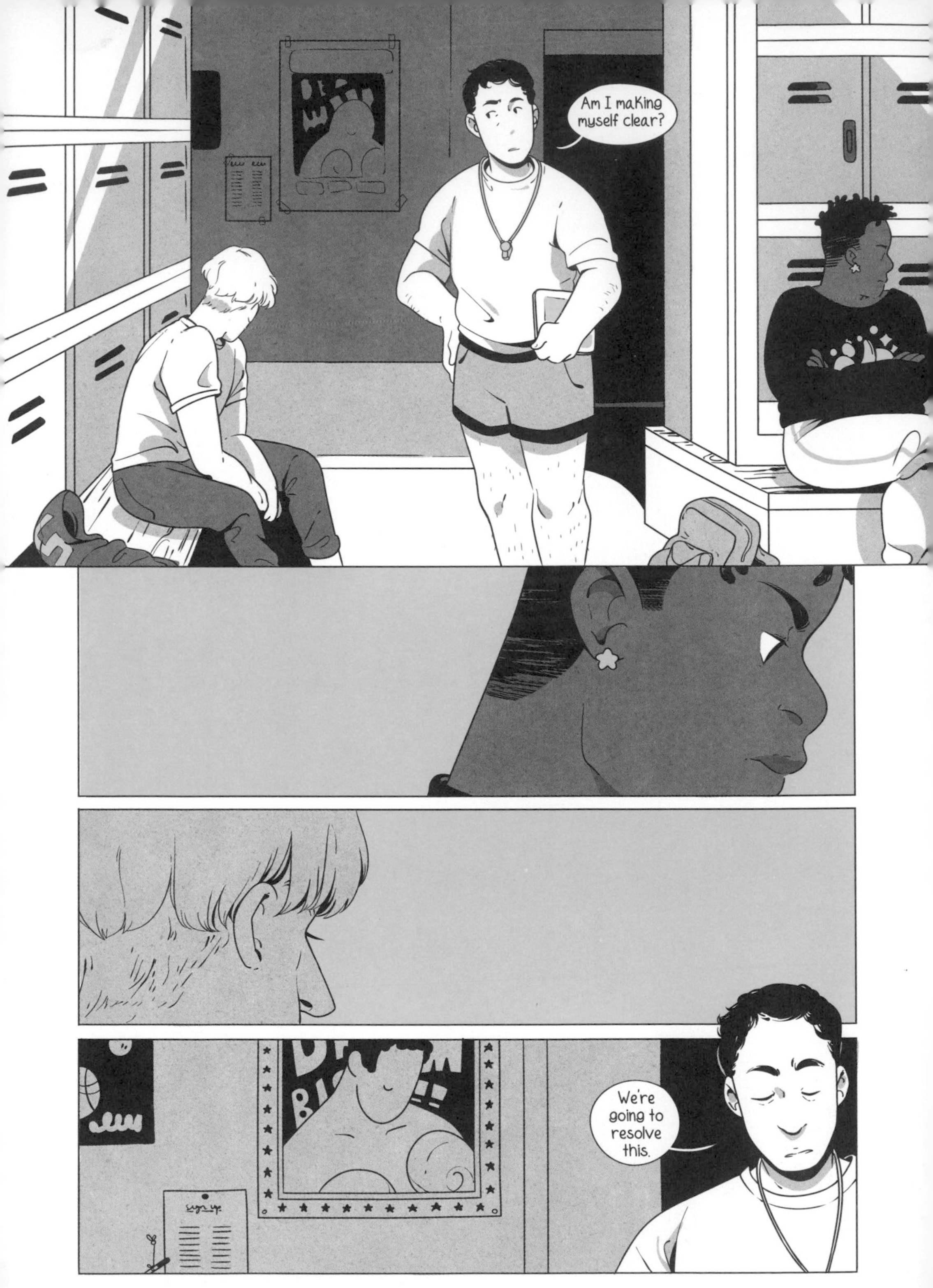
Am I making myself clear?
We're going to resolve this.

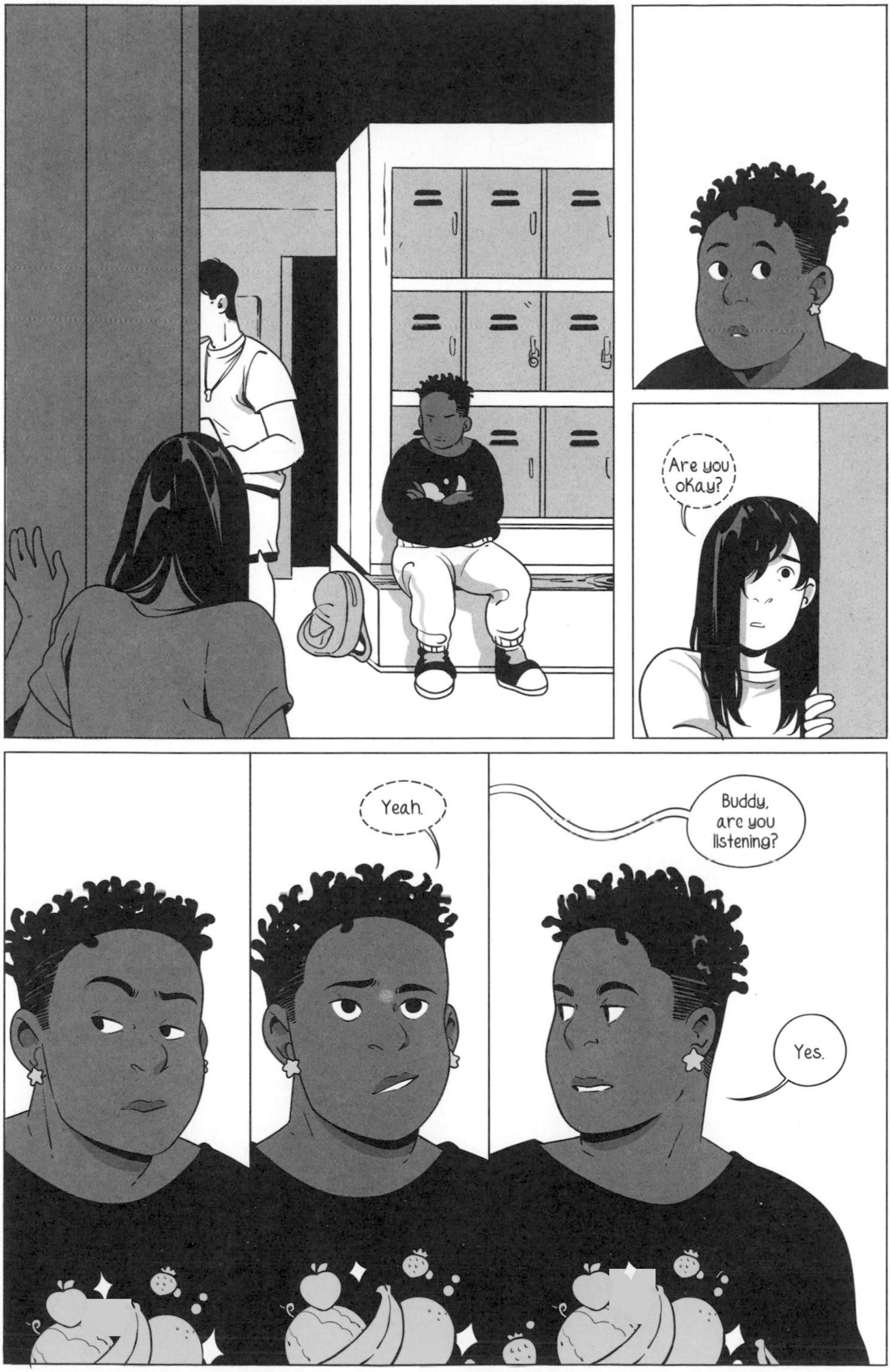
Are you okay?
Yeah.
Buddy, are you listening?
Yes.

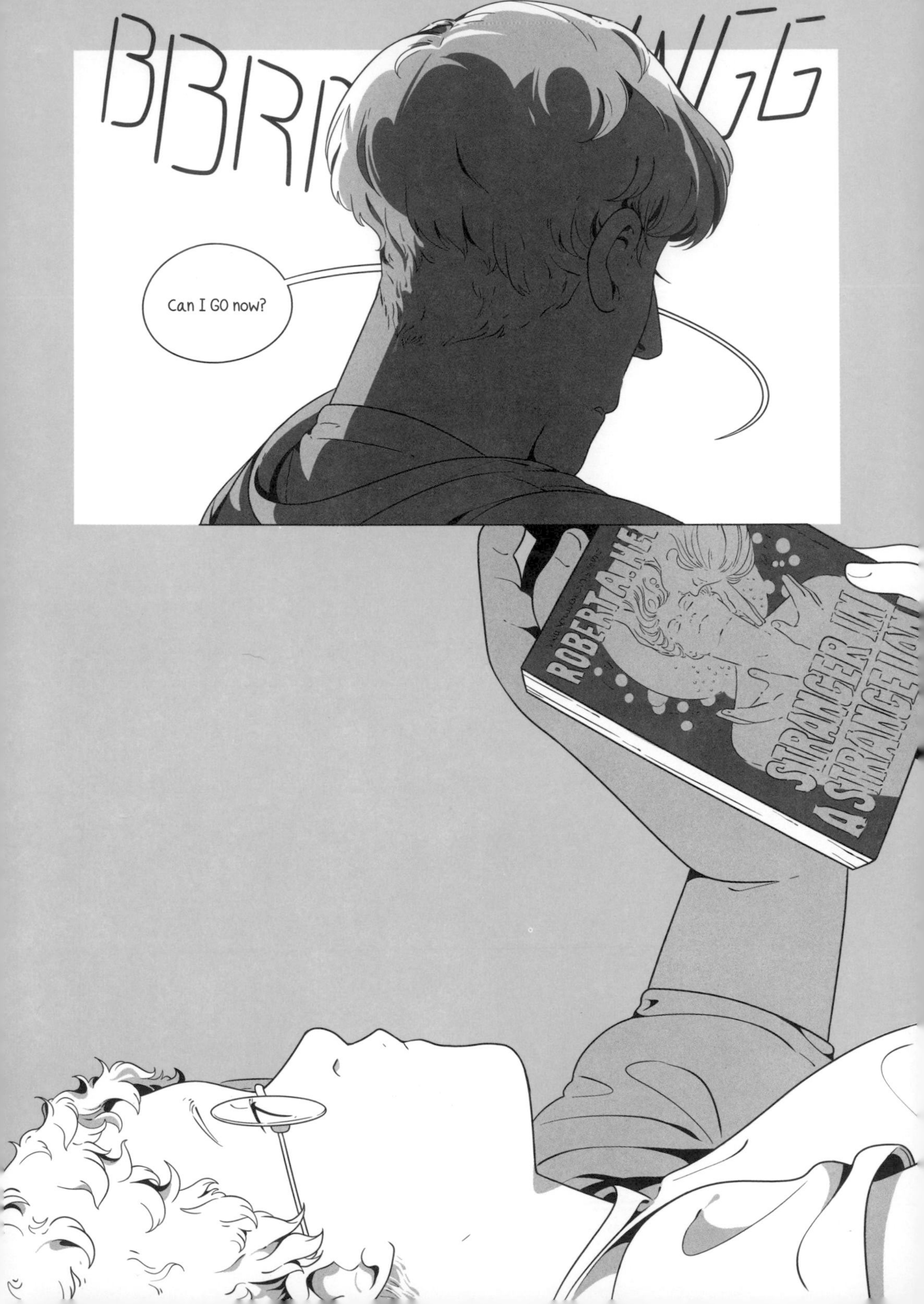
Can I GO now?
STRANGER IN

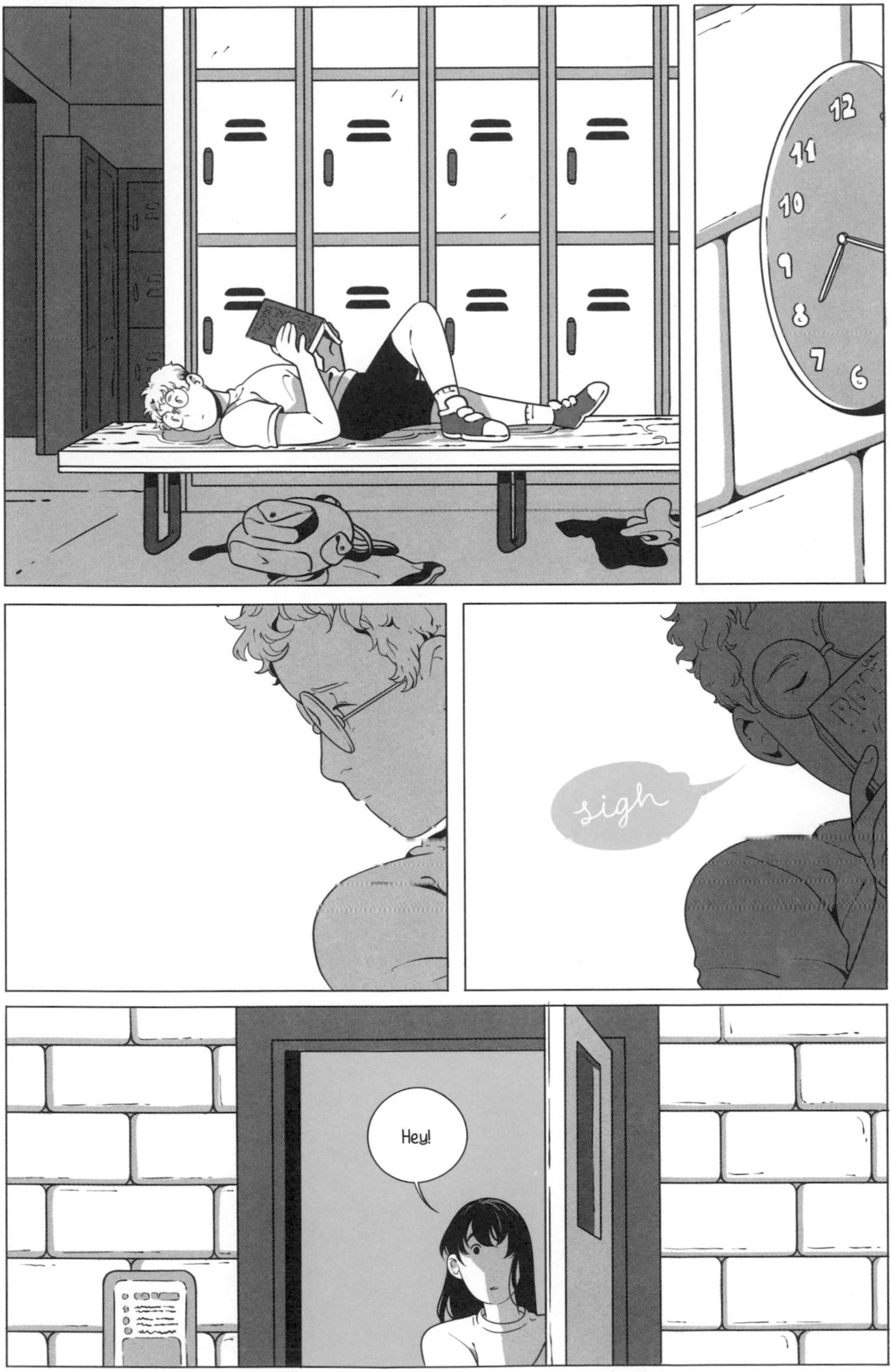
sigh
Hey!

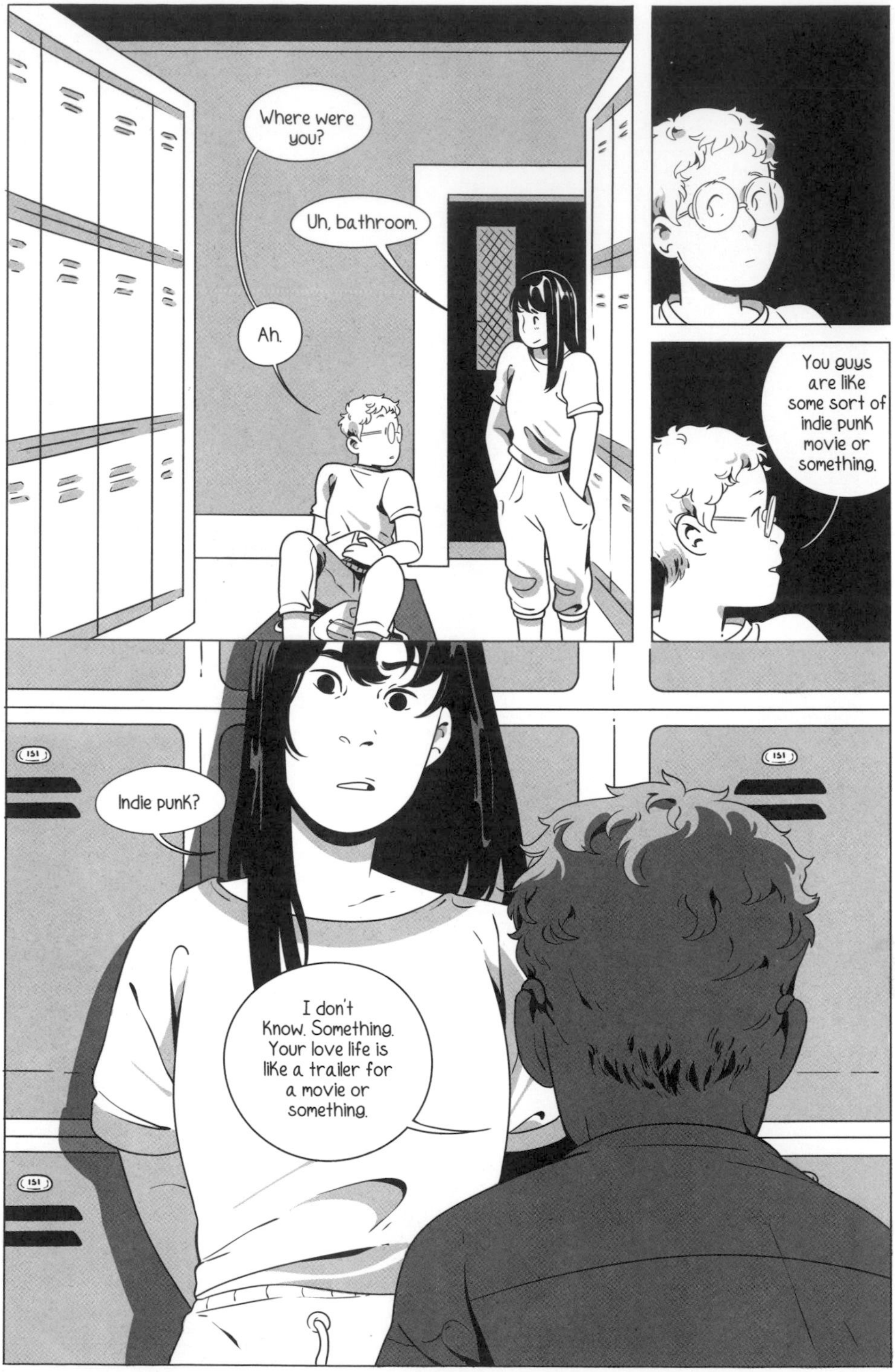
Where were you?
Uh, bathroom.
Ah.
You guys are like some sort of indie punk movie or something.
Indie punk?
I don't know. Something. Your love life is like a trailer for a movie or something.

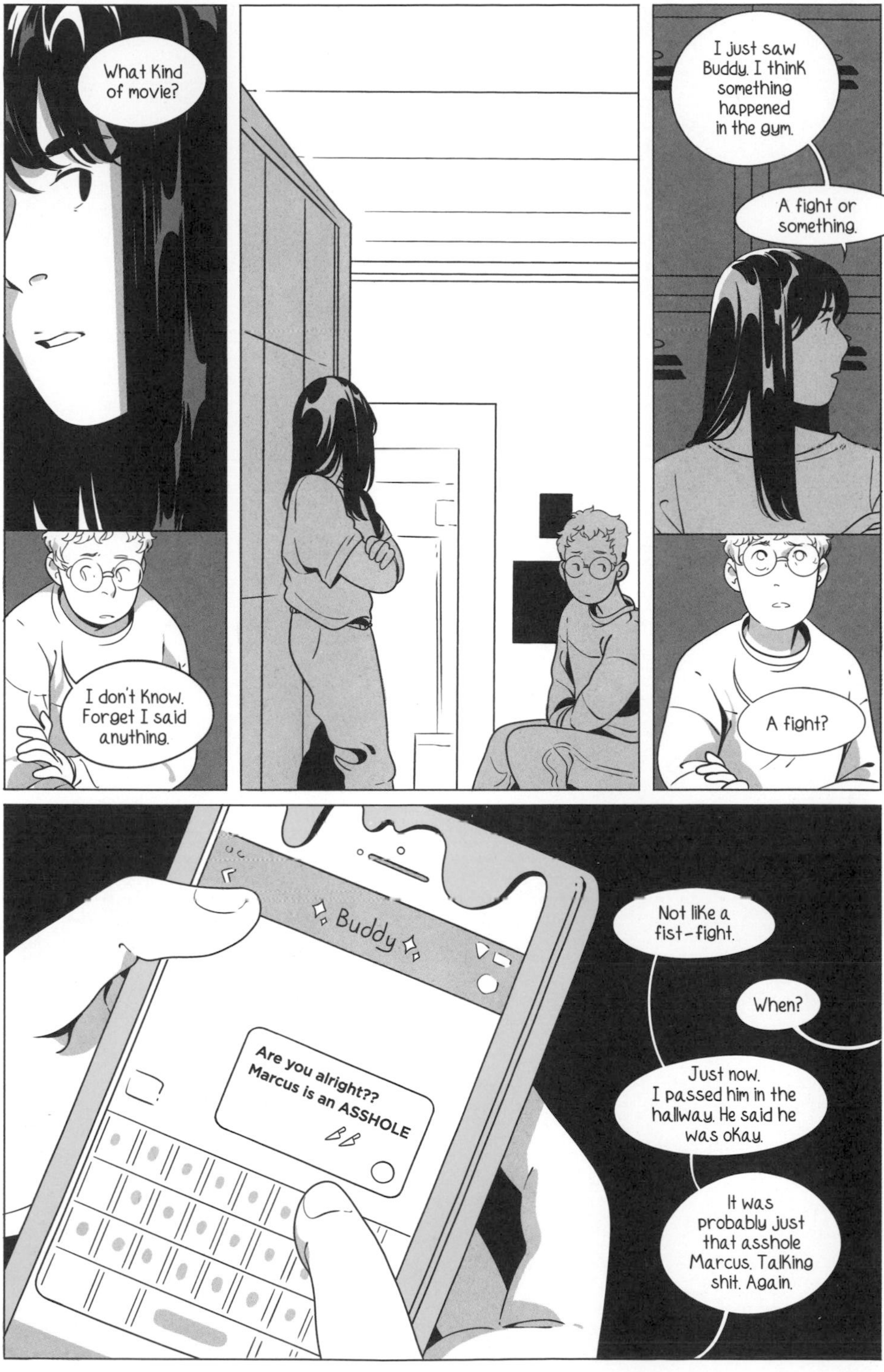
What Kind of movie?
I don't Know. Forget I said anything.
I just saw Buddy. I think something happened in the gym.
A fight or something.
A fight?
Buddy
Are you alright?? Marcus is an ASSHOLE
Not like a fist-fight.
When?
Just now. I passed him in the hallway. He said he was oKay.
It was probably just that asshole Marcus. TalKing shit. Again.

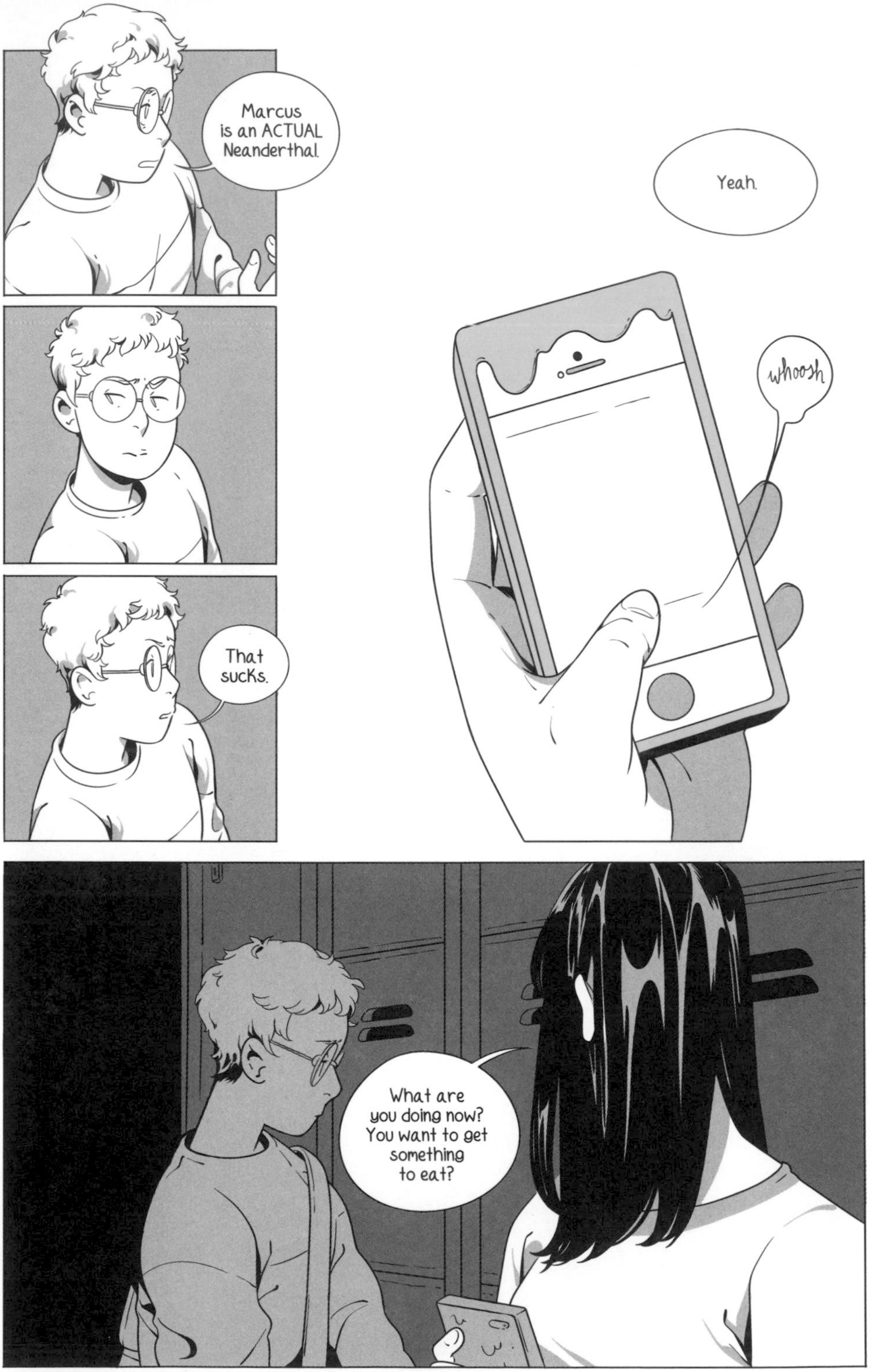
Marcus is an ACTUAL Neanderthal.
Yeah.
whoosh
That sucks.
What are you doing now? You want to get something to eat?

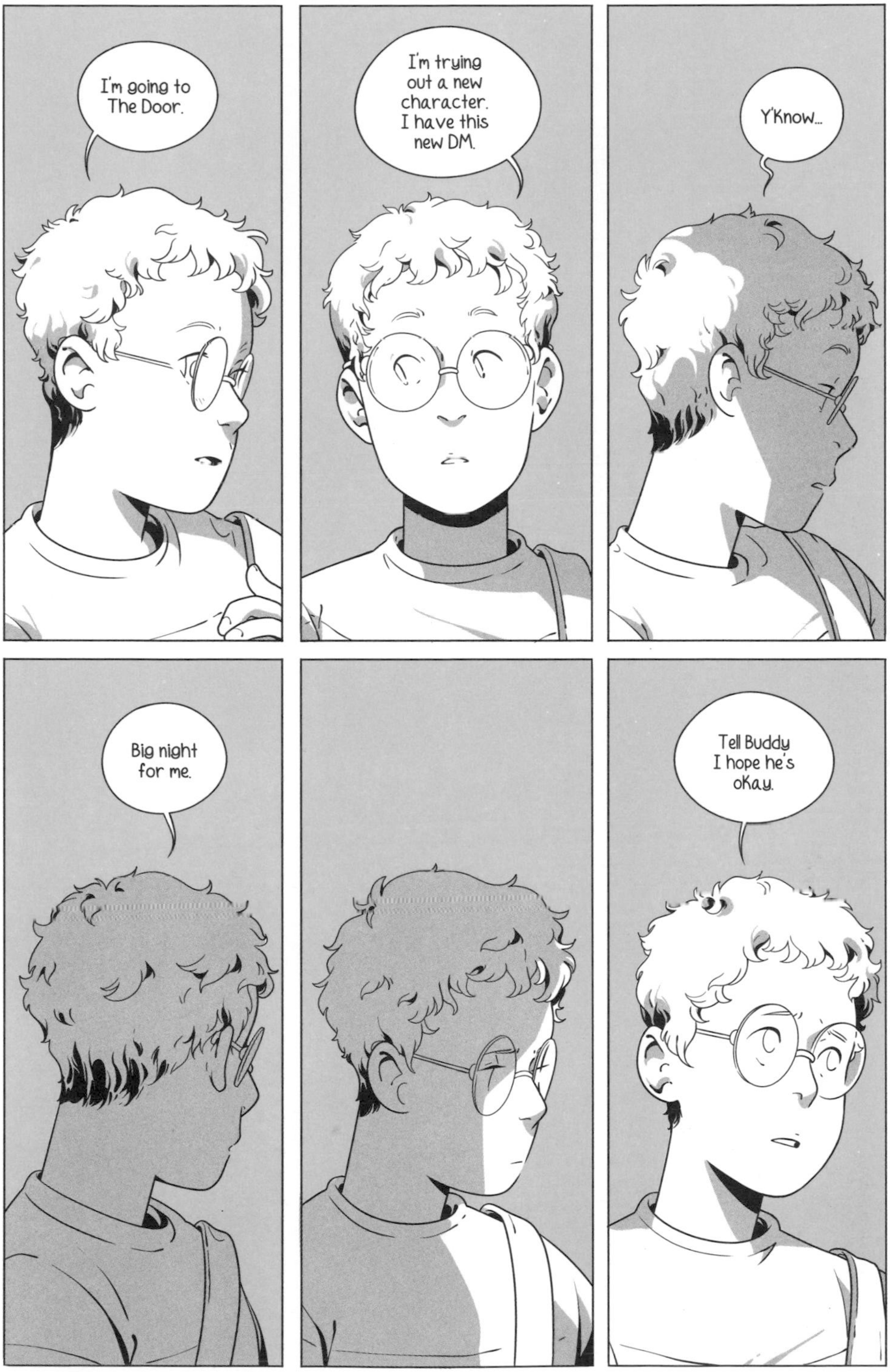
I'm going to The Door.
I'm trying out a new character. I have this new DM.
Y'Know...
Big night for me.
Tell Buddy I hope he's oKay.

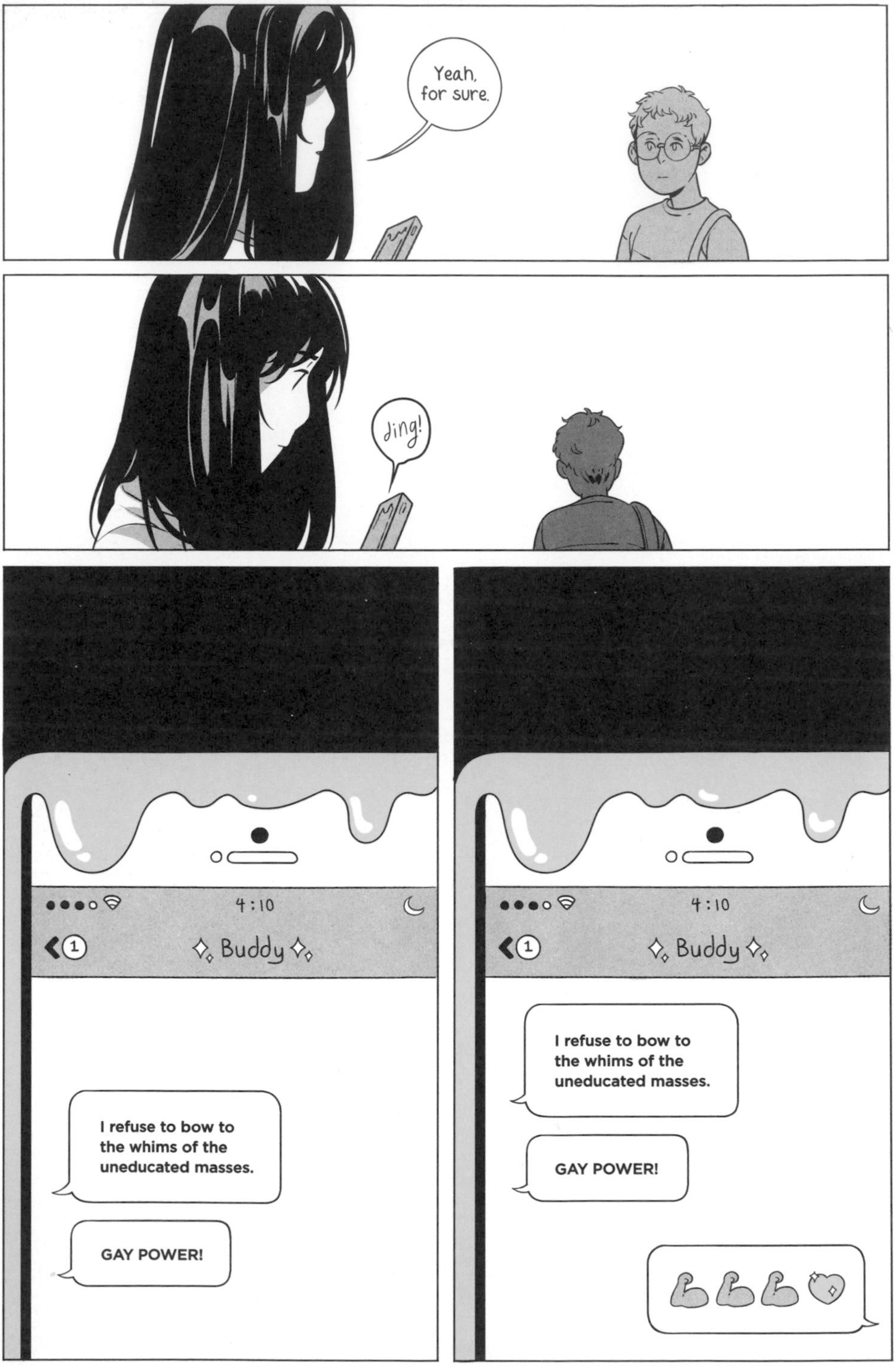
Yeah, for sure.
ding!
4:10
Buddy
I refuse to bow to the whims of the uneducated masses.
GAY POWER!
4:10
Buddy
I refuse to bow to the whims of the uneducated masses.
GAY POWER!

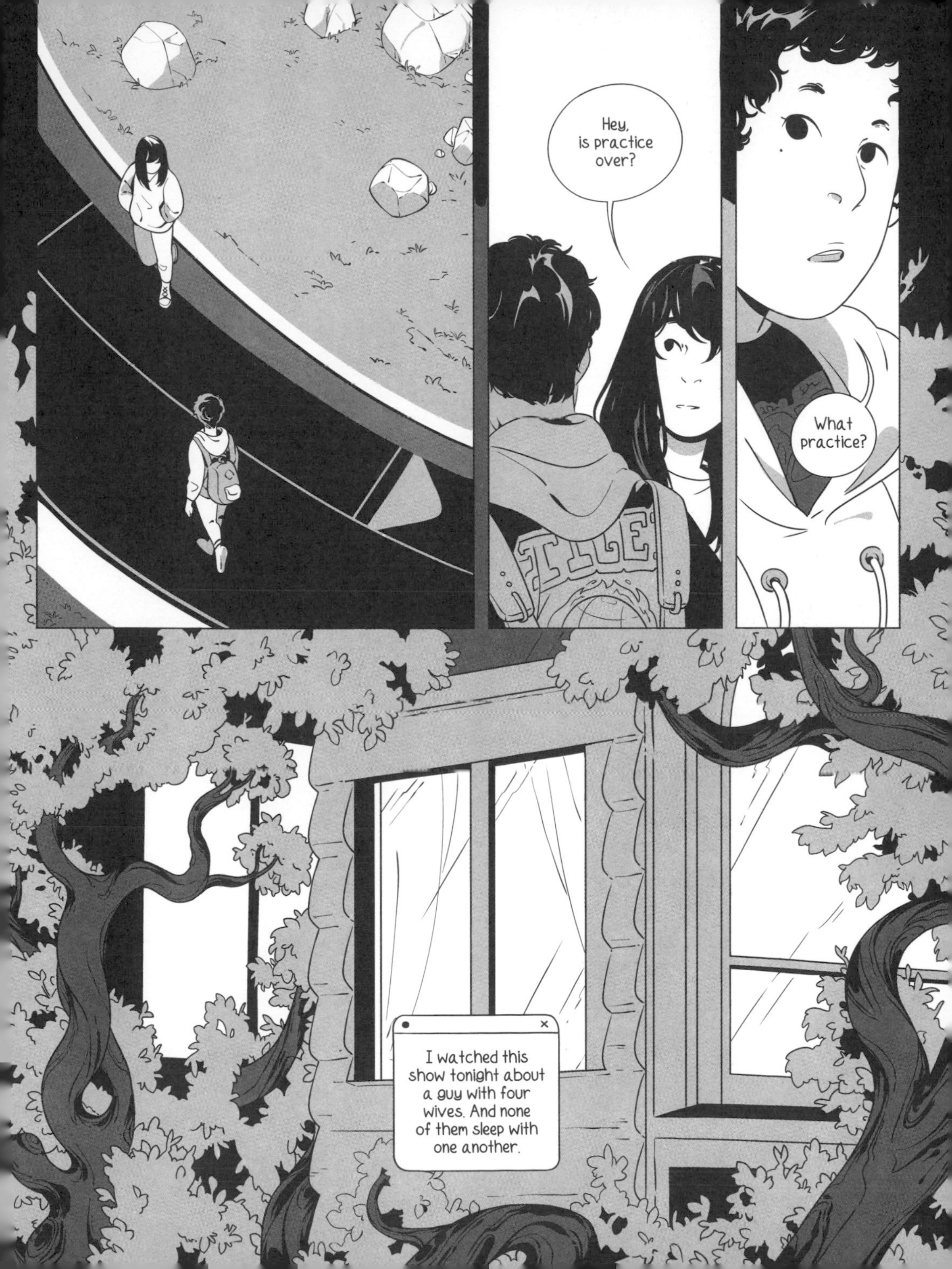
Hey, is practice over?
What practice?
I watched this show tonight about a guy with four wives. And none of them sleep with one another.

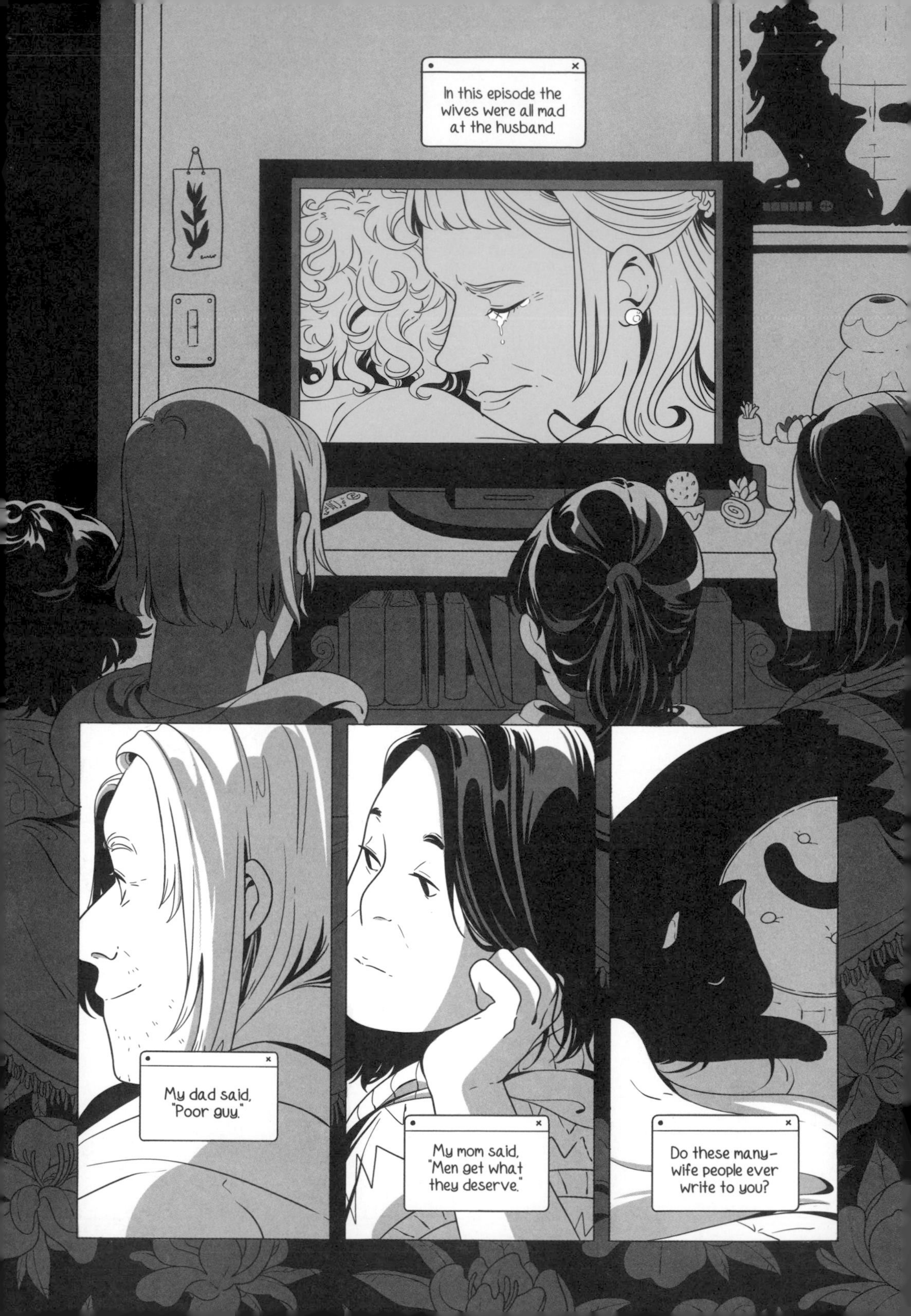
In this episode the wives were all mad at the husband.
My dad said, "Poor guy."
My mom said, "Men get what they deserve."
Do these many-wife people ever write to you?

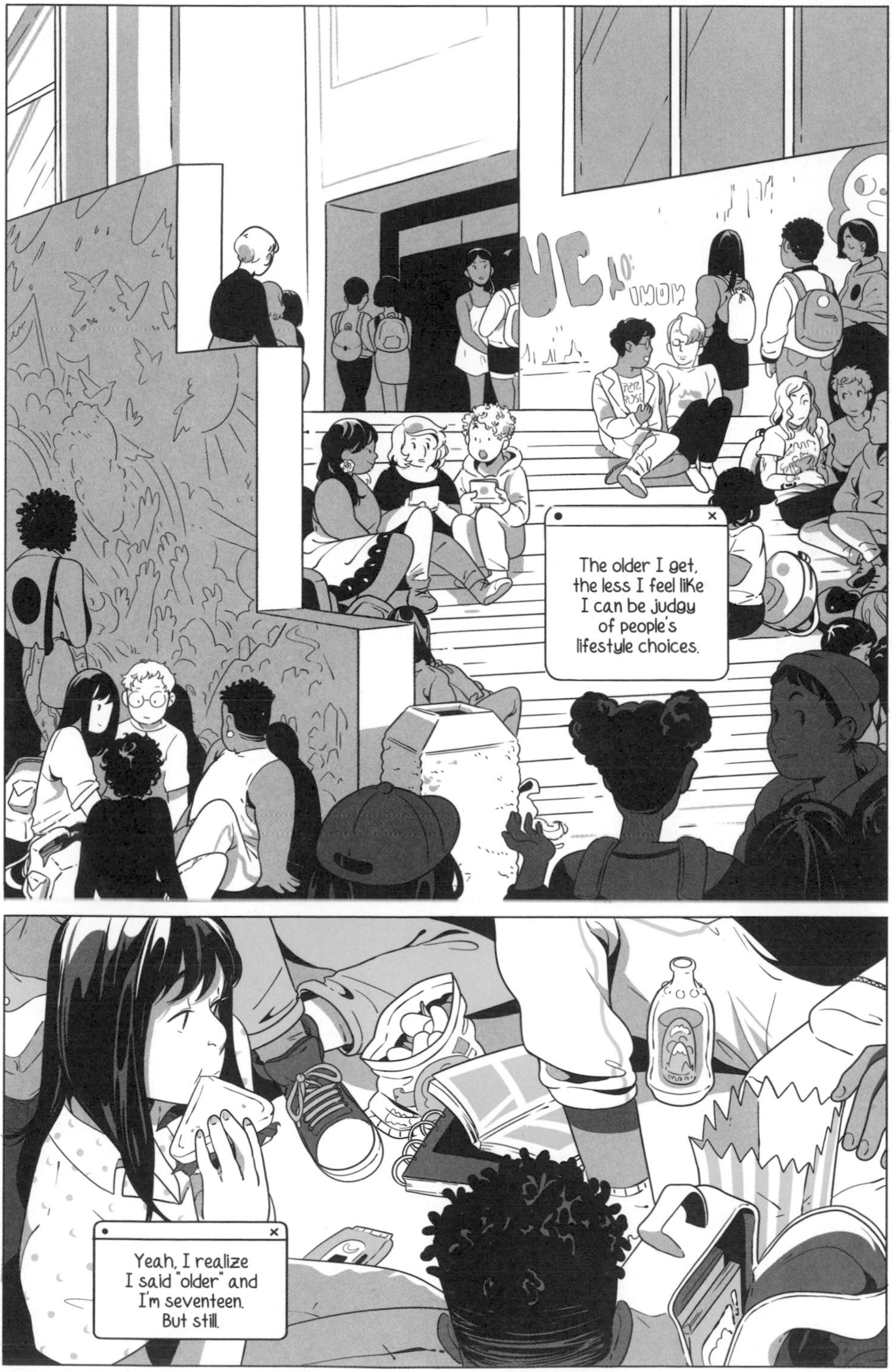
The older I get, the less I feel like I can be judgy of people's lifestyle choices.
Yeah, I realize I said "older" and I'm seventeen. But still.

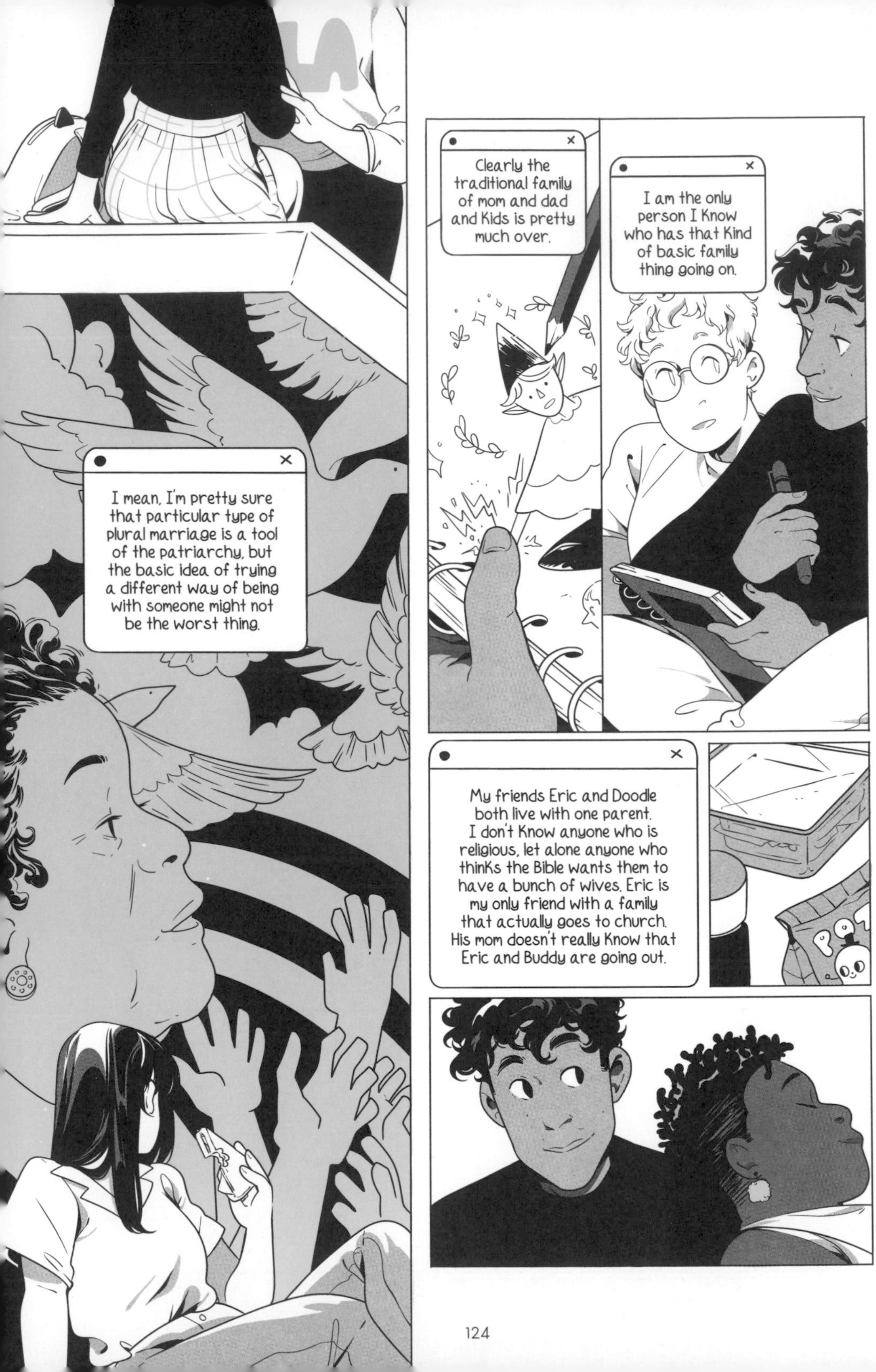
I mean, I'm pretty sure that particular type of plural marriage is a tool of the patriarchy, but the basic idea of trying a different way of being with someone might not be the worst thing.
Clearly the traditional family of mom and dad and kids is pretty much over.
I am the only person I know who has that kind of basic family thing going on.
My friends Eric and Doodle both live with one parent. I don't know anyone who is religious, let alone anyone who thinks the Bible wants them to have a bunch of wives. Eric is my only friend with a family that actually goes to church. His mom doesn't really know that Eric and Buddy are going out.

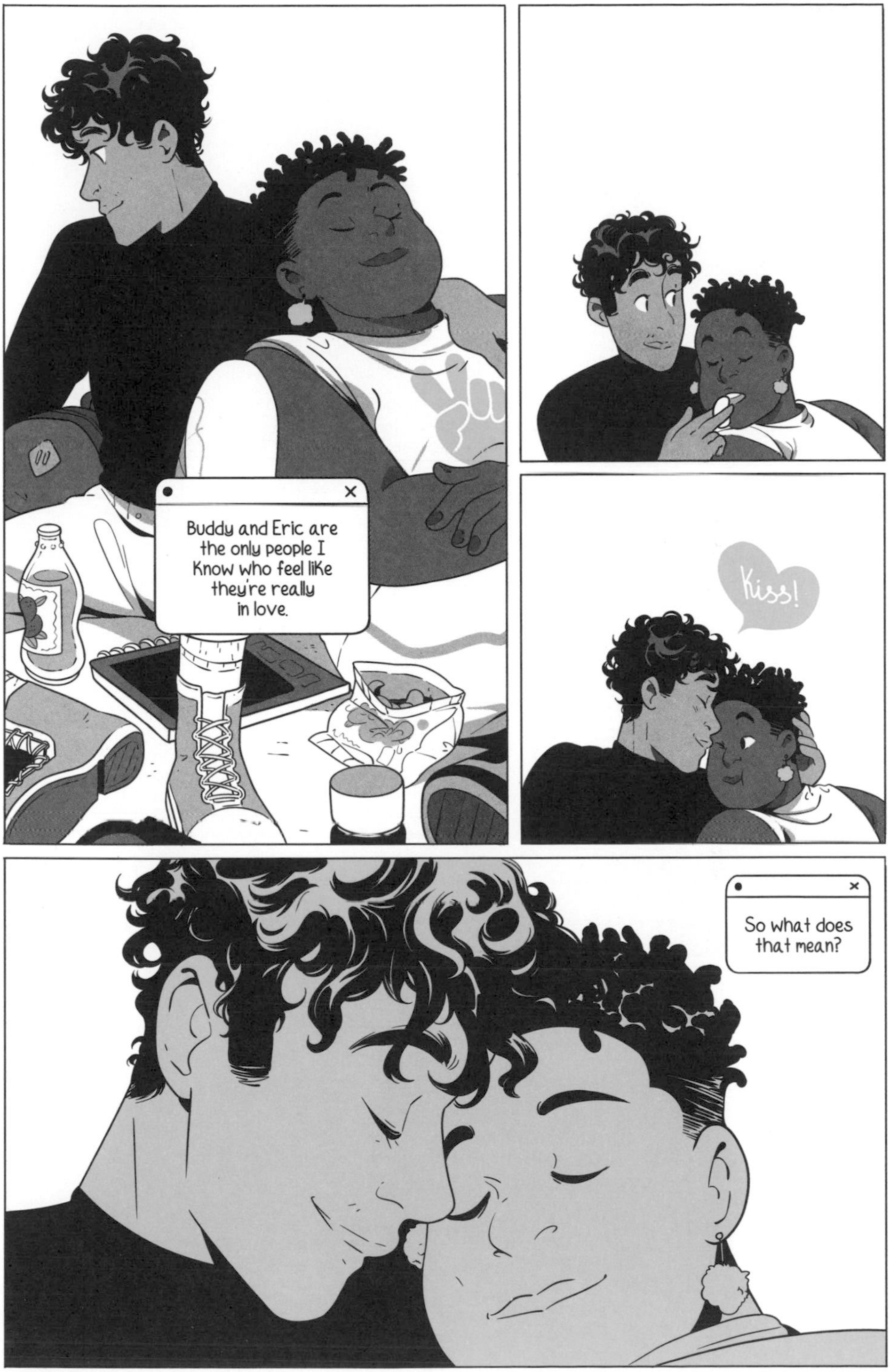
Buddy and Eric are the only people I know who feel like they're really in love.
Kiss!
So what does that mean?

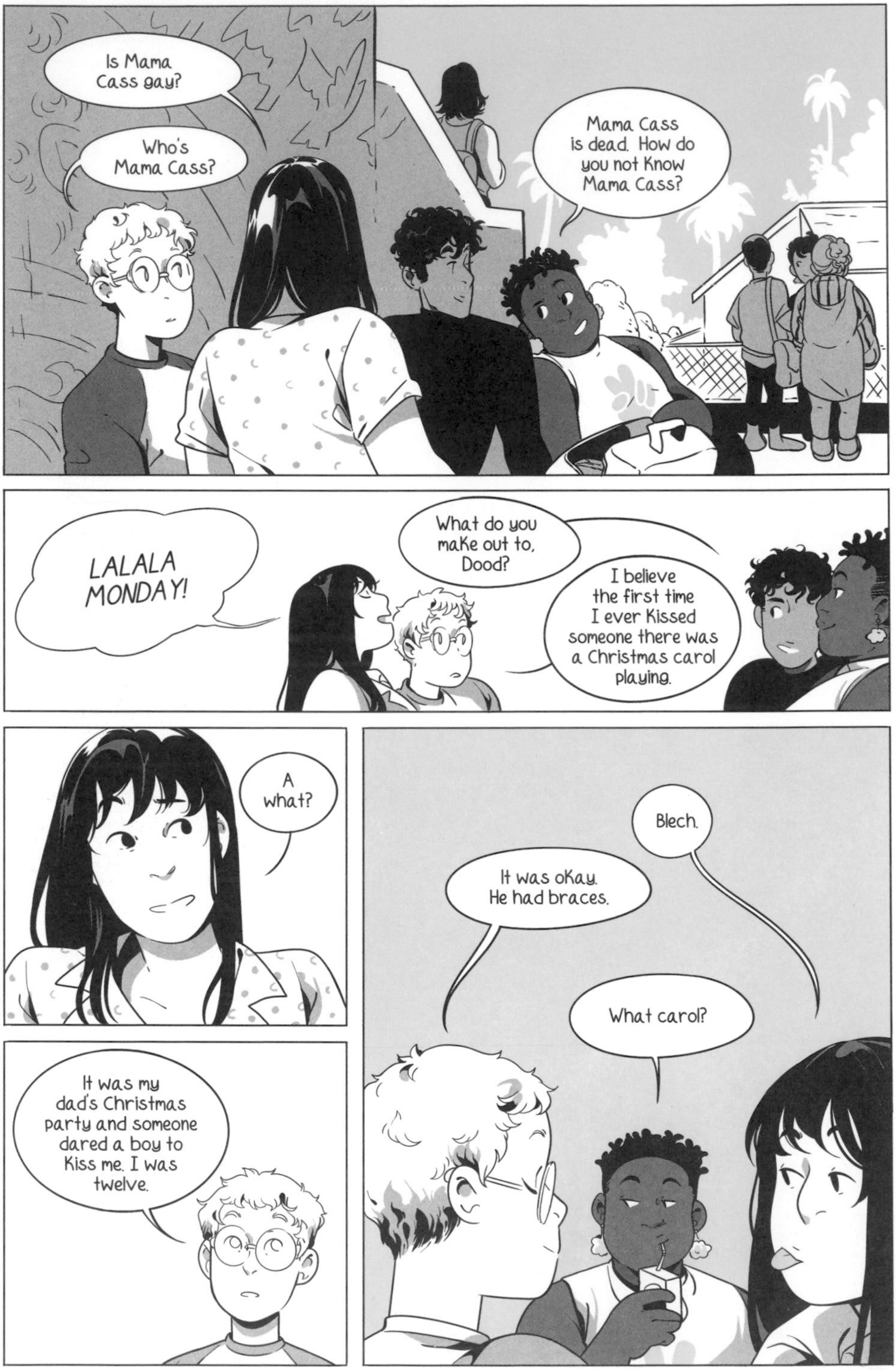
Is Mama Cass gay?
Who's Mama Cass?
Mama Cass is dead. How do you not know Mama Cass?
LALALA MONDAY!
What do you make out to, Dood?
I believe the first time I ever kissed someone there was a Christmas carol playing.
A what?
It was my dad's Christmas party and someone dared a boy to kiss me. I was twelve.
It was okay. He had braces.
Blech.
What carol?

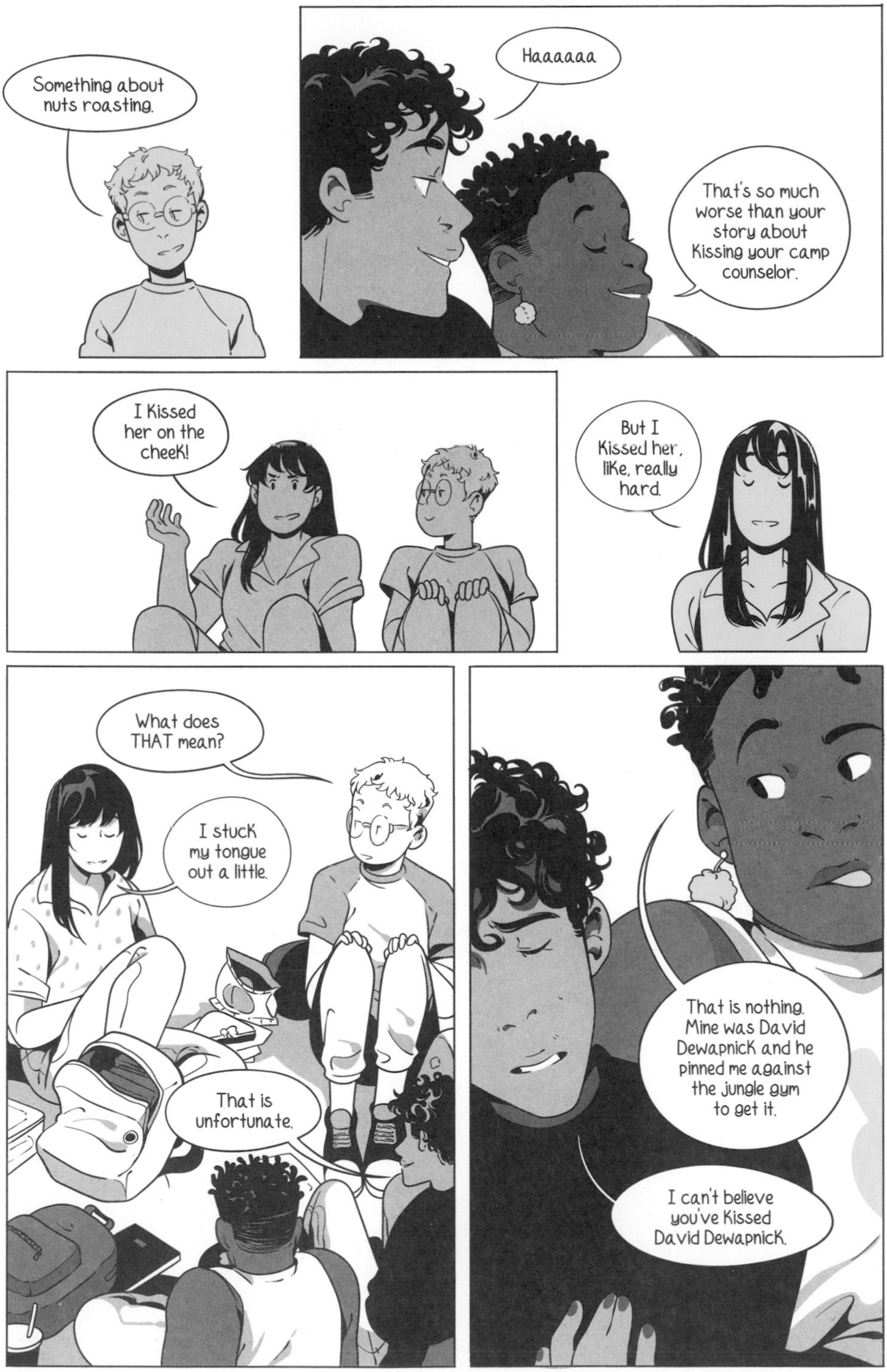
Something about nuts roasting.
Haaaaaa
That's so much worse than your story about Kissing your camp counselor.
I Kissed her on the cheeK!
But I Kissed her, like, really hard.
What does THAT mean?
I stucK my tongue out a little.
That is unfortunate.
That is nothing. Mine was David DewapnicK and he pinned me against the jungle gym to get it.
I can't believe you've Kissed David DewapnicK.

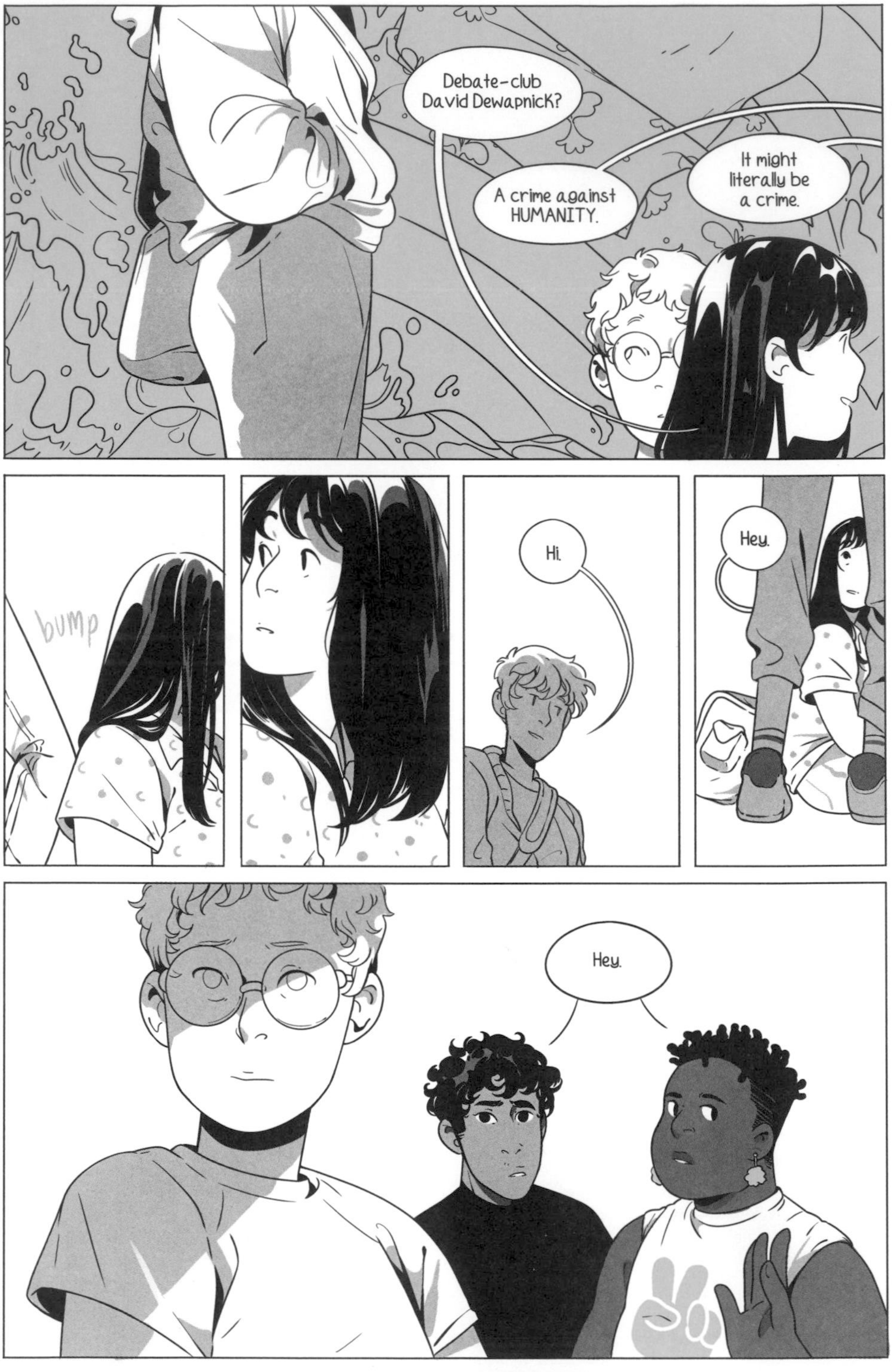
Debate-club David Dewapnick?
A crime against HUMANITY.
It might literally be a crime.
bump
Hi.
Hey.
Hey.

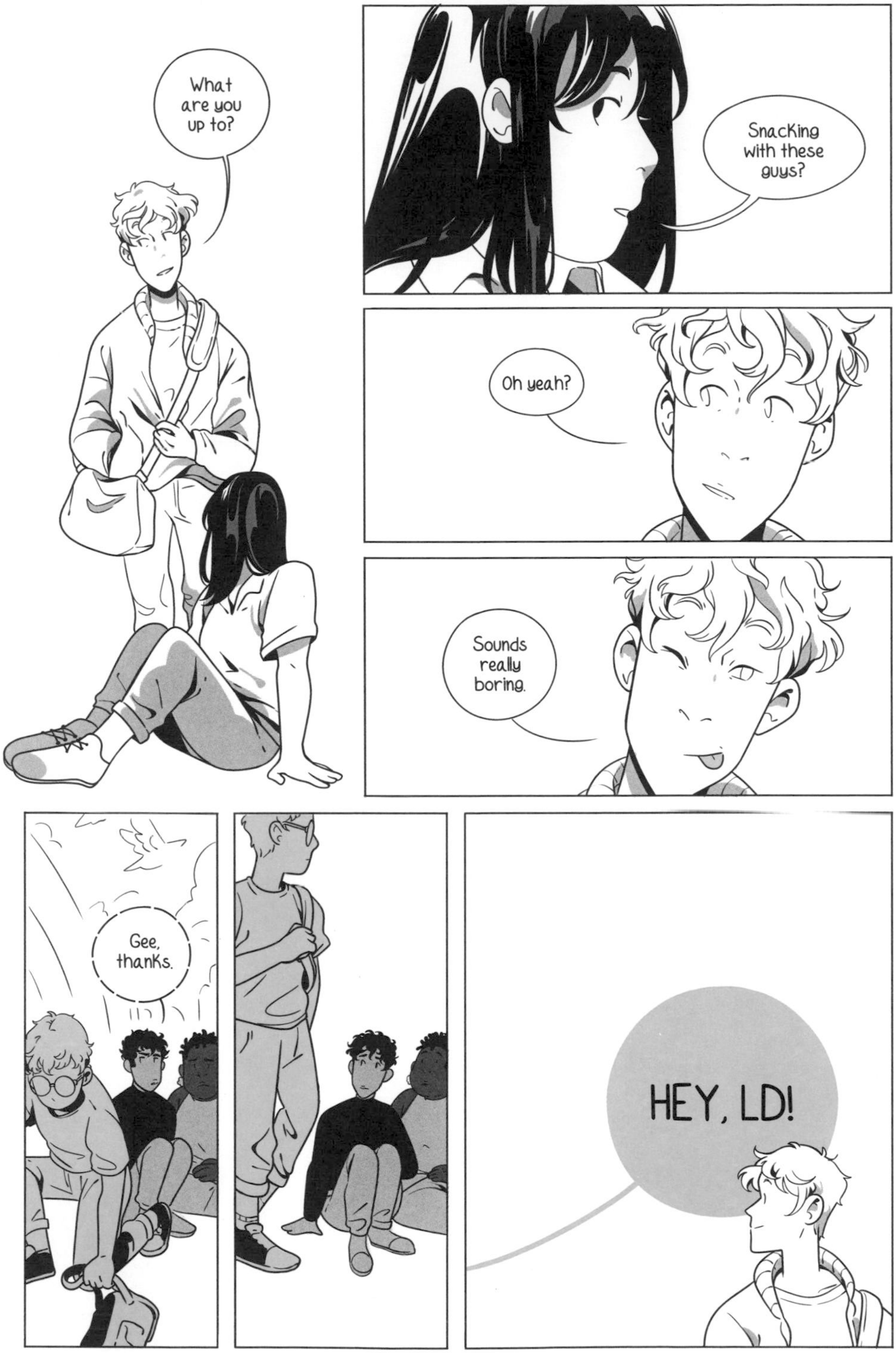
What are you up to?
Snacking with these guys?
Oh yeah?
Sounds really boring.
Gee, thanks.
HEY, LD!

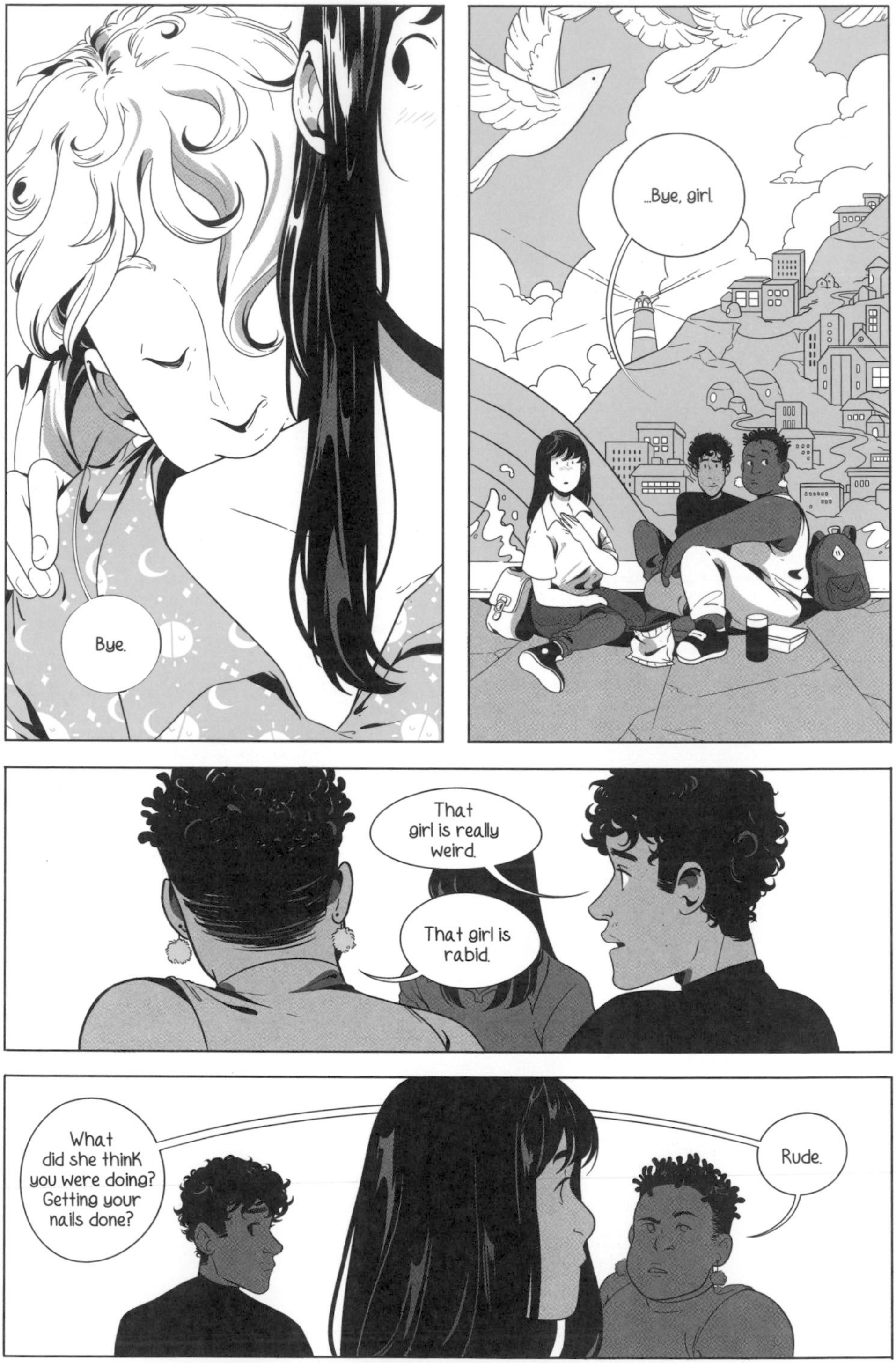
Bye.
...Bye, girl.
That girl is really weird.
That girl is rabid.
What did she think you were doing? Getting your nails done?
Rude.

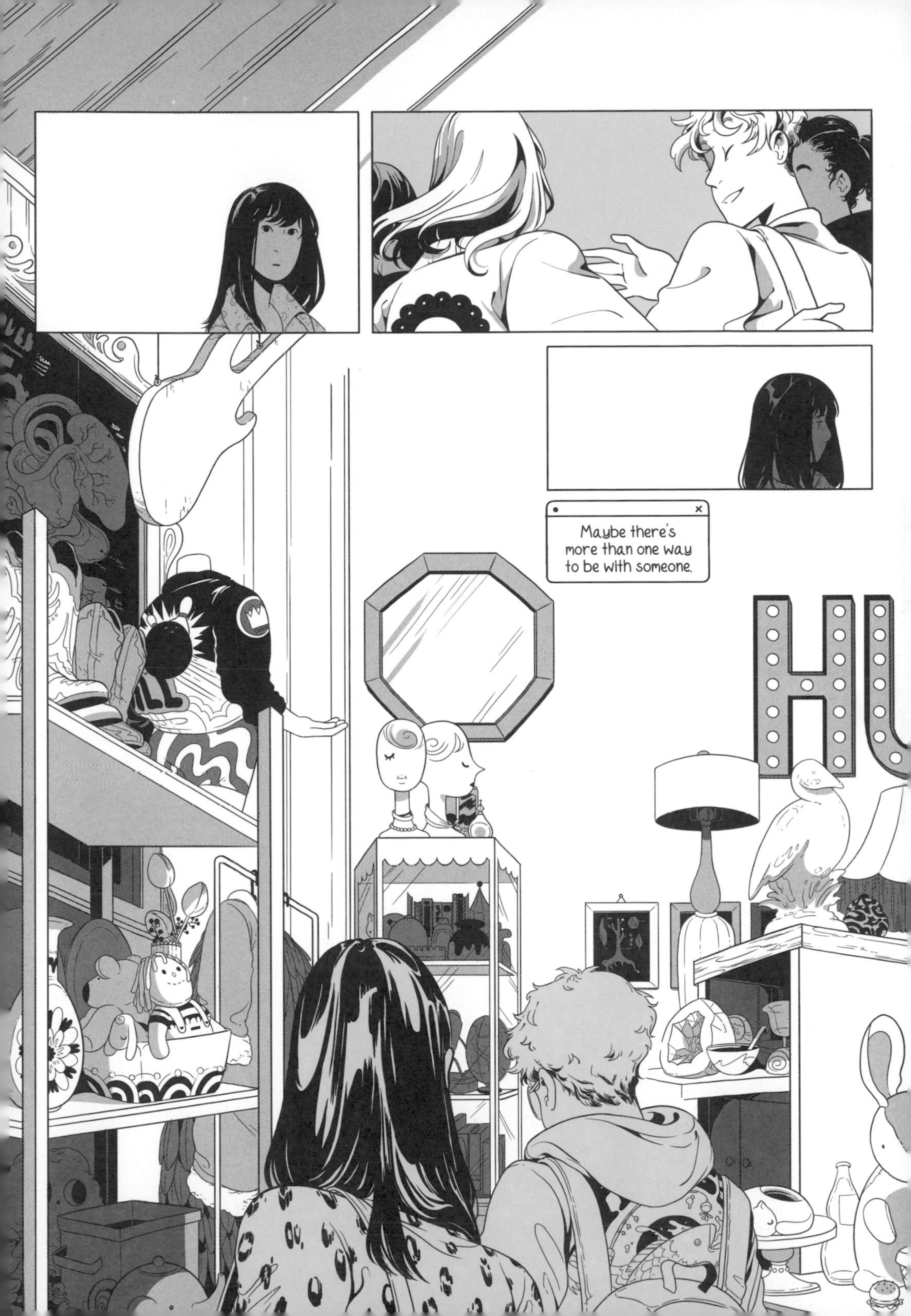
Maybe there's more than one way to be with someone.

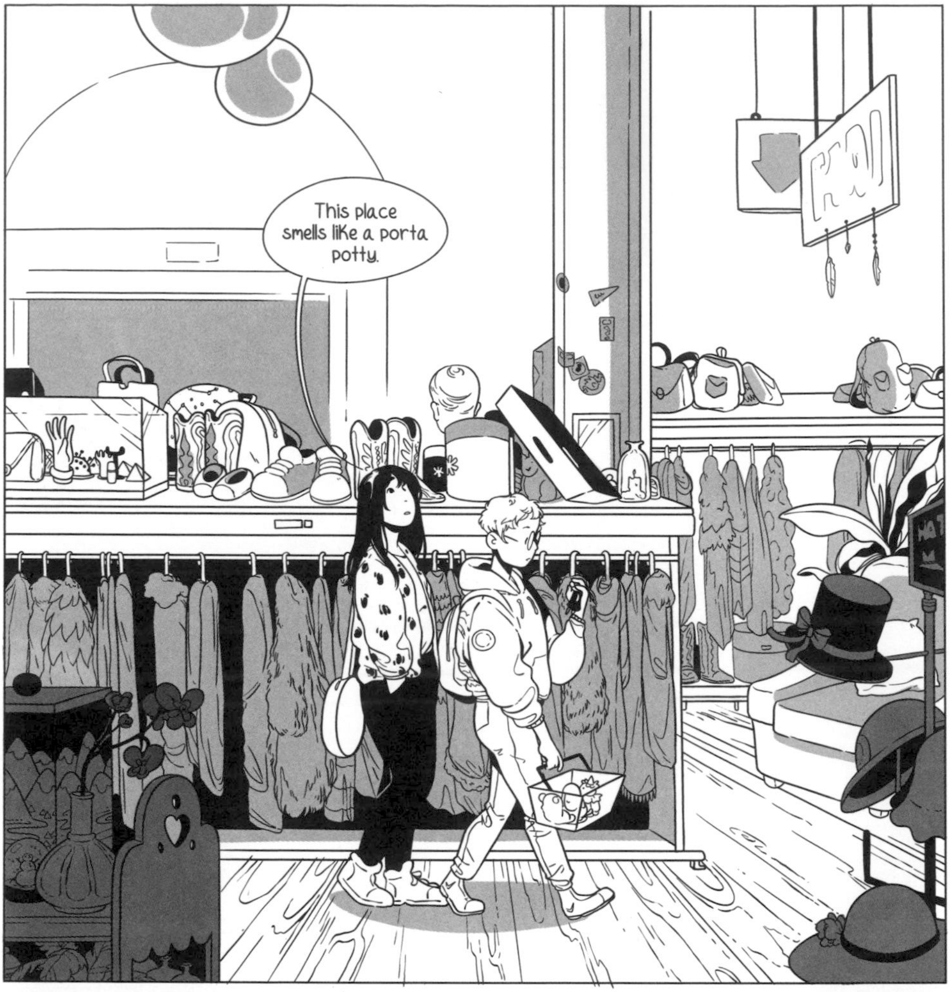
This place smells like a porta potty.

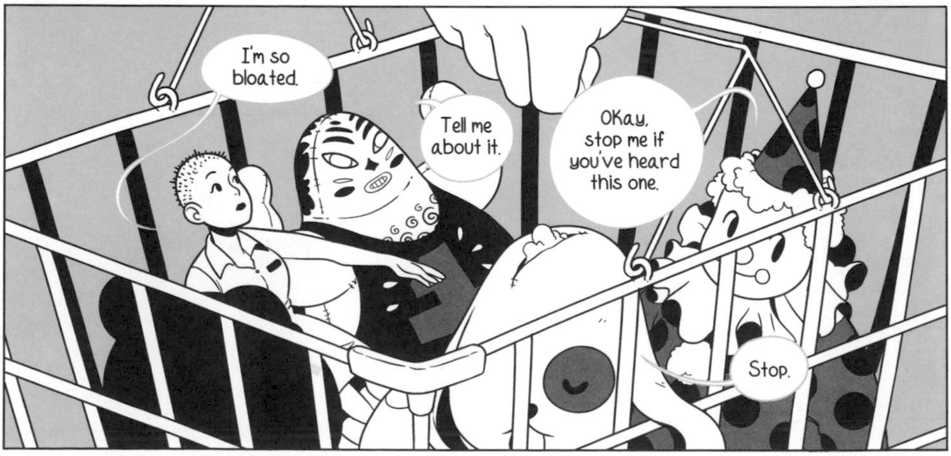
I'm so bloated.
Tell me about it.
Okay, stop me if you've heard this one.
Stop.

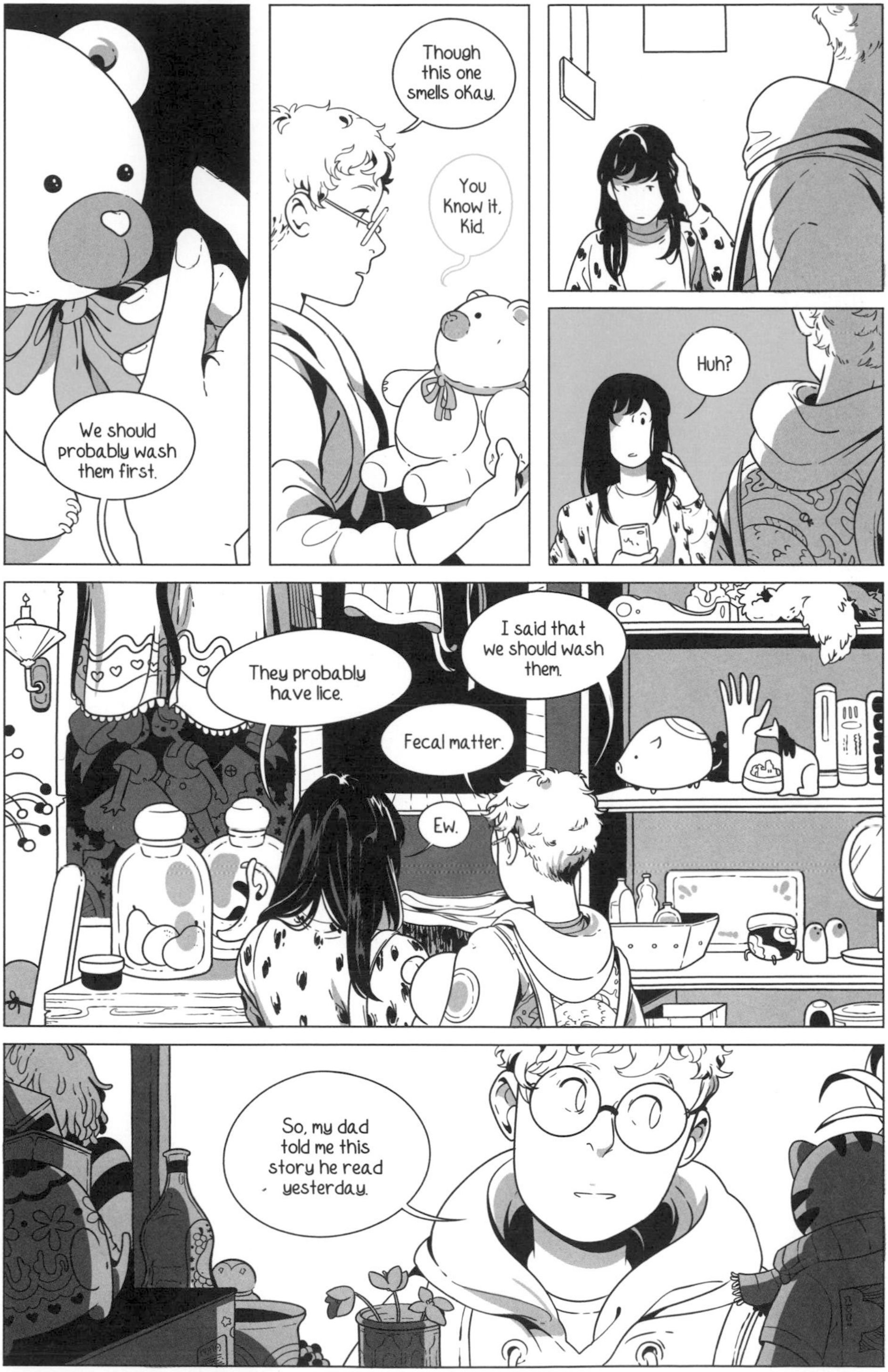
We should probably wash them first.
Though this one smells oKay.
You Know it, Kid.
Huh?
They probably have lice.
I said that we should wash them.
Fecal matter.
Ew.
So, my dad told me this story he read yesterday.

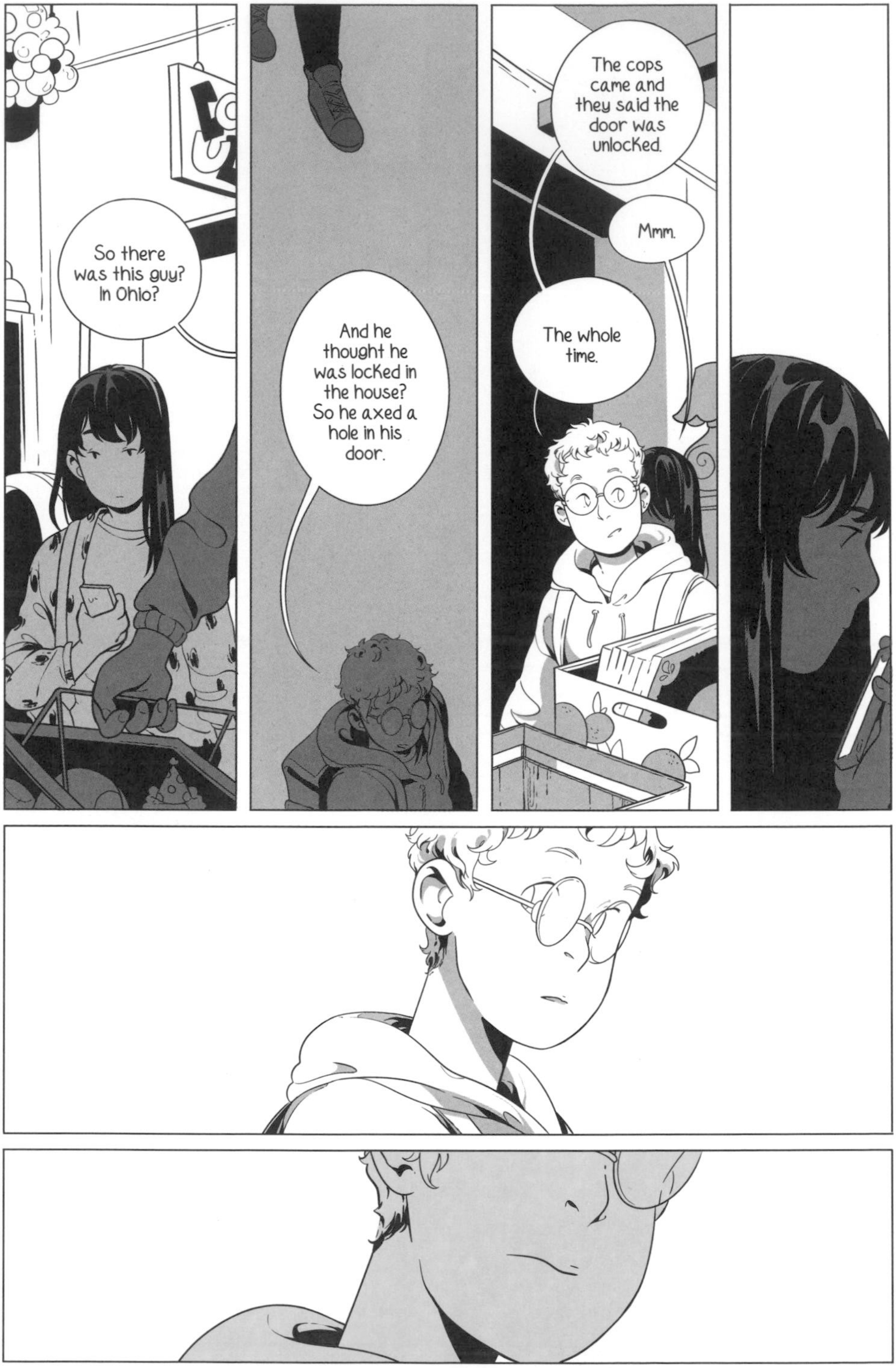
So there was this guy? In Ohio?
And he thought he was locked in the house? So he axed a hole in his door.
The cops came and they said the door was unlocked.
Mmm.
The whole time.

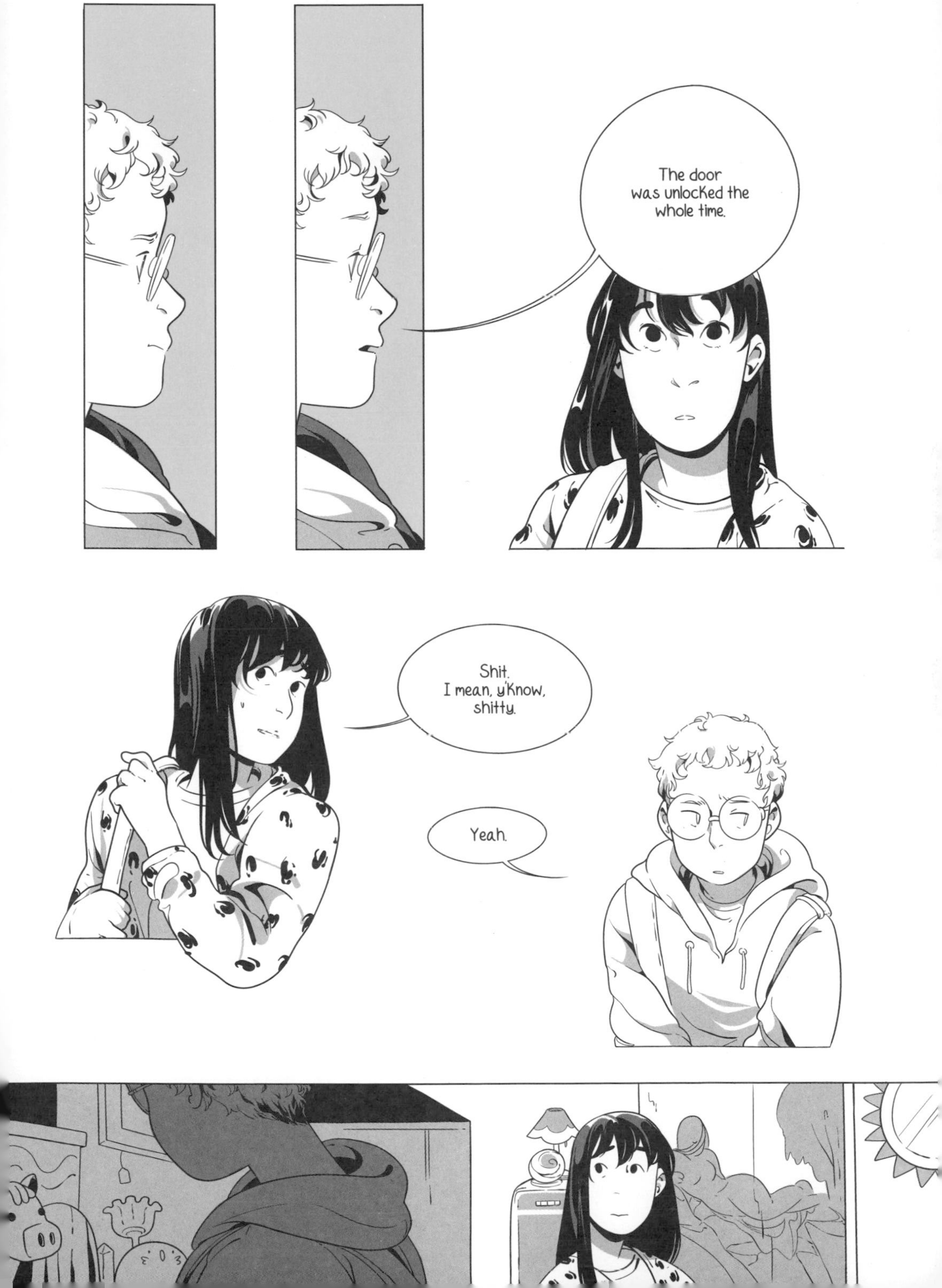
The door
was unlocked the
whole time.
Shit.
I mean, y'know,
shitty.
Yeah.

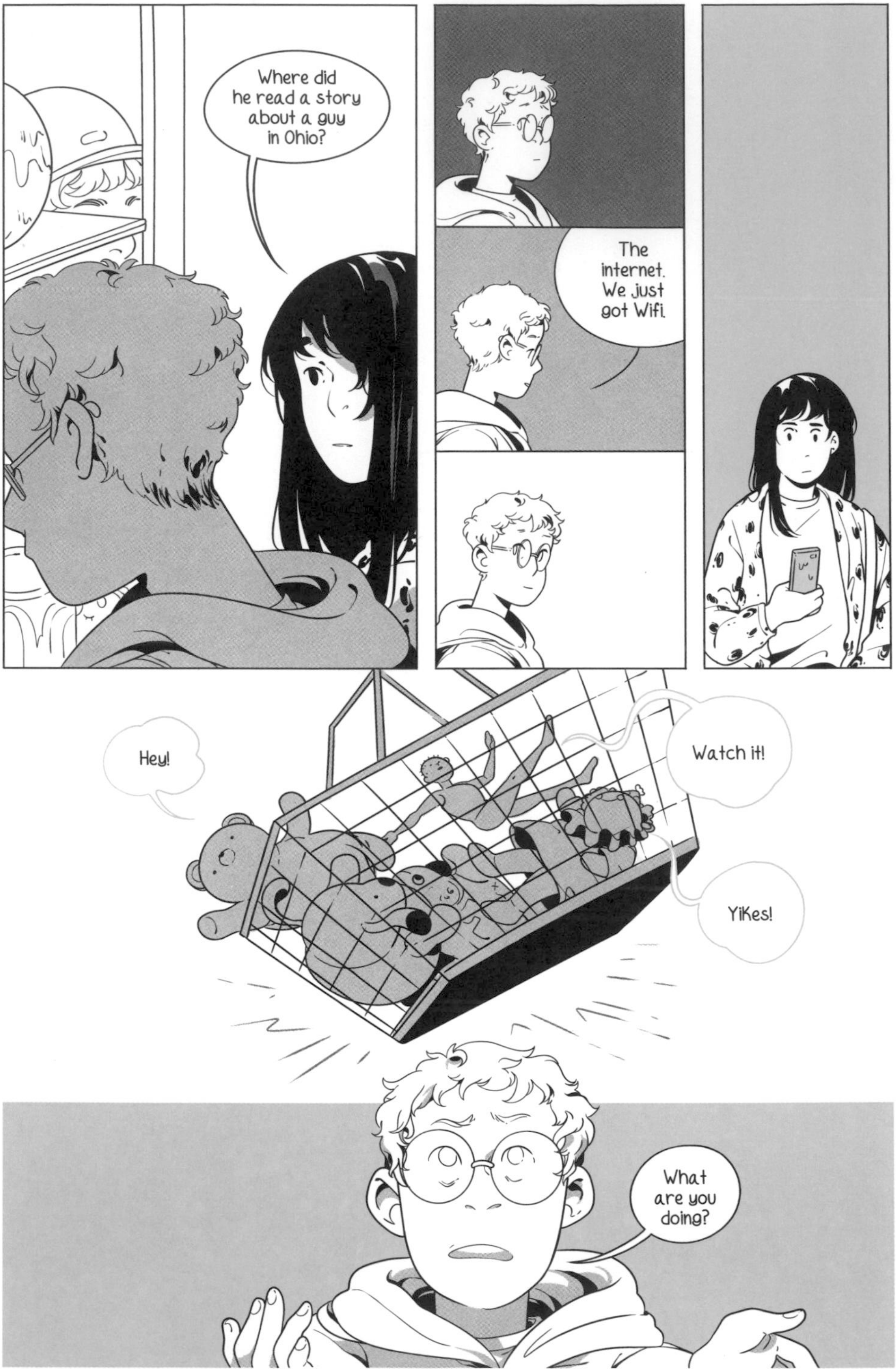
Where did he read a story about a guy in Ohio?
The internet. We just got Wifi.
Hey!
Watch it!
YiKes!
What are you doing?

Are you waiting for a call?

No, I just asked someone something earlier. It's nothing.

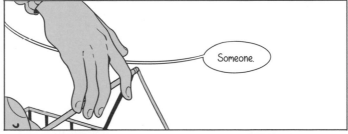

Someone.

I—I keep thinking I feel it vibrating.

Yeah.

Alright.

Yeah, I mean, I think that's fine.

But. Aren't we going to your house tonight?

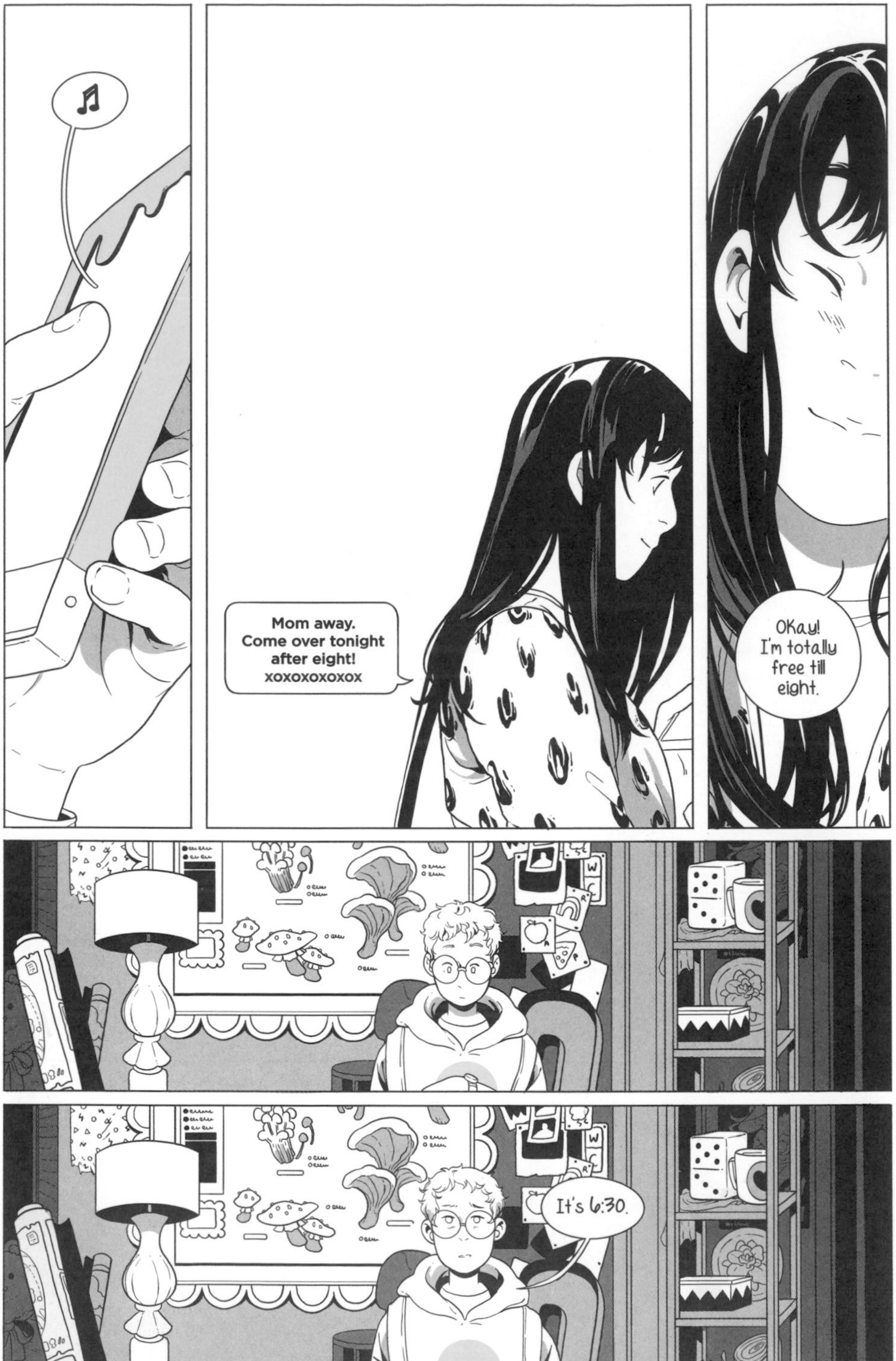
Mom away.
Come over tonight
after eight!
xoxoxoxoxox
OKay!
I'm totally
free till
eight.
It's 6:30.

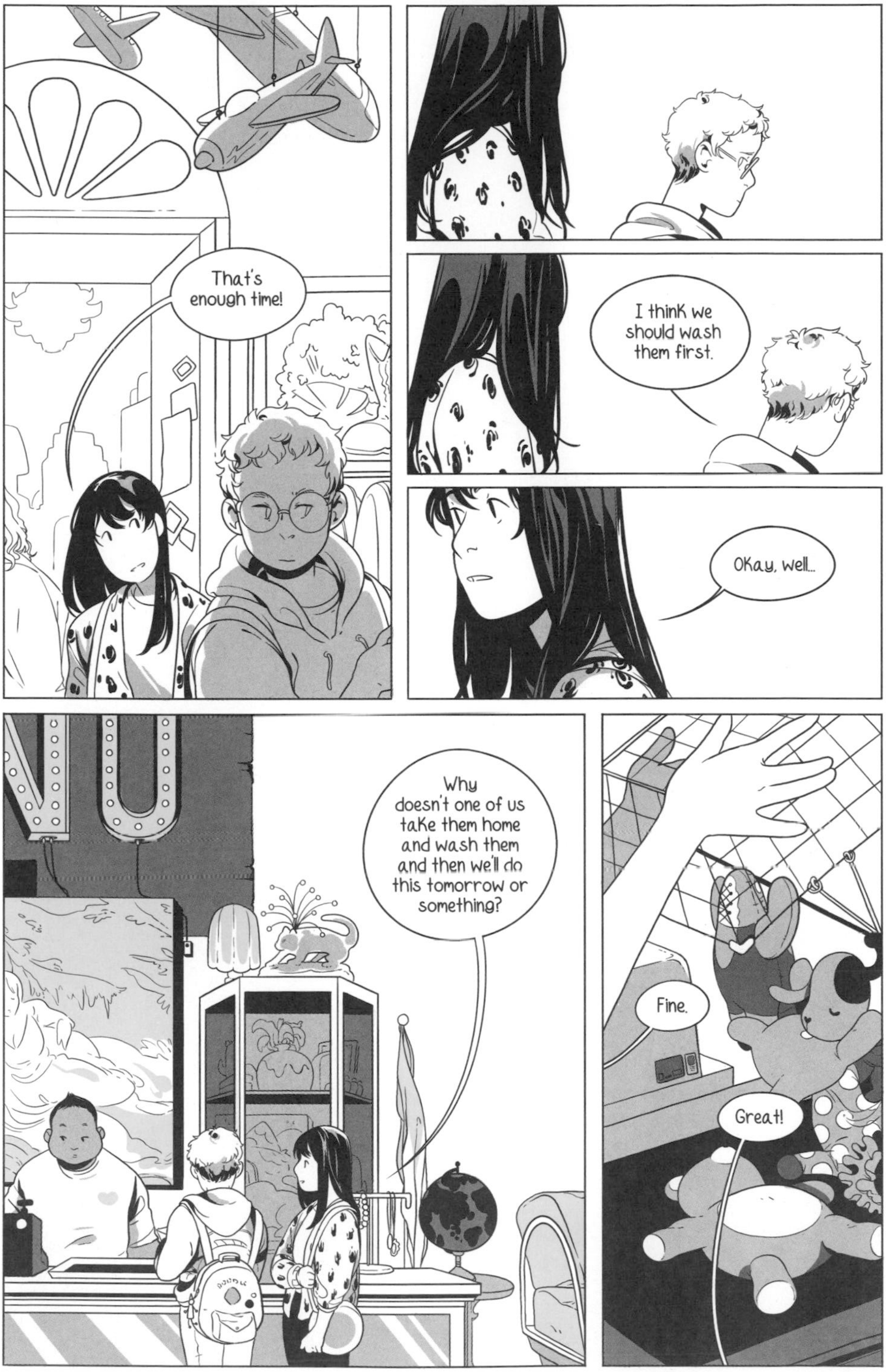
That's enough time!
I think we should wash them first.
OKay, well...
Why doesn't one of us take them home and wash them and then we'll do this tomorrow or something?
Fine.
Great!

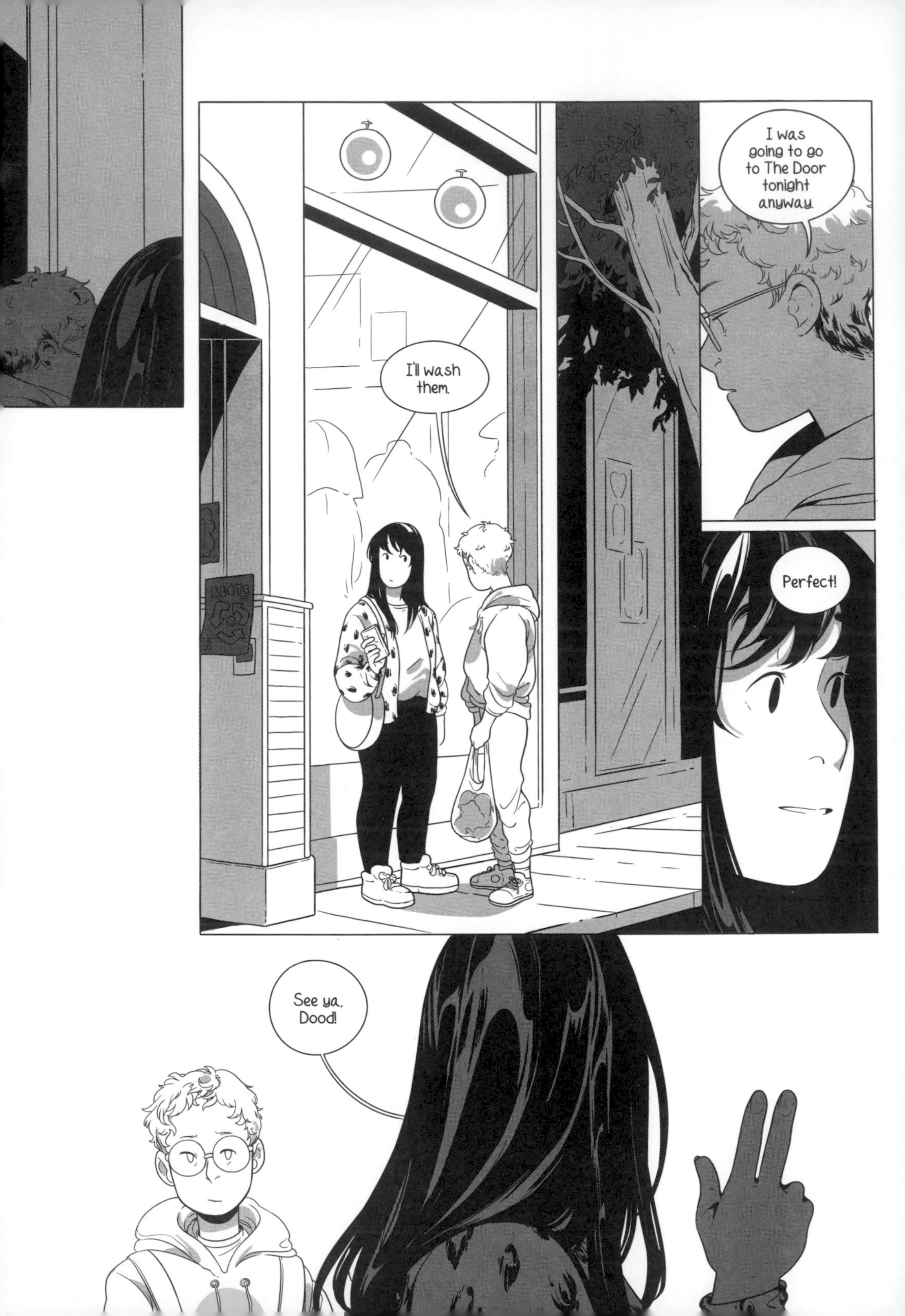
I'll wash them.
I was going to go to The Door tonight anyway.
Perfect!
See ya, Dood!

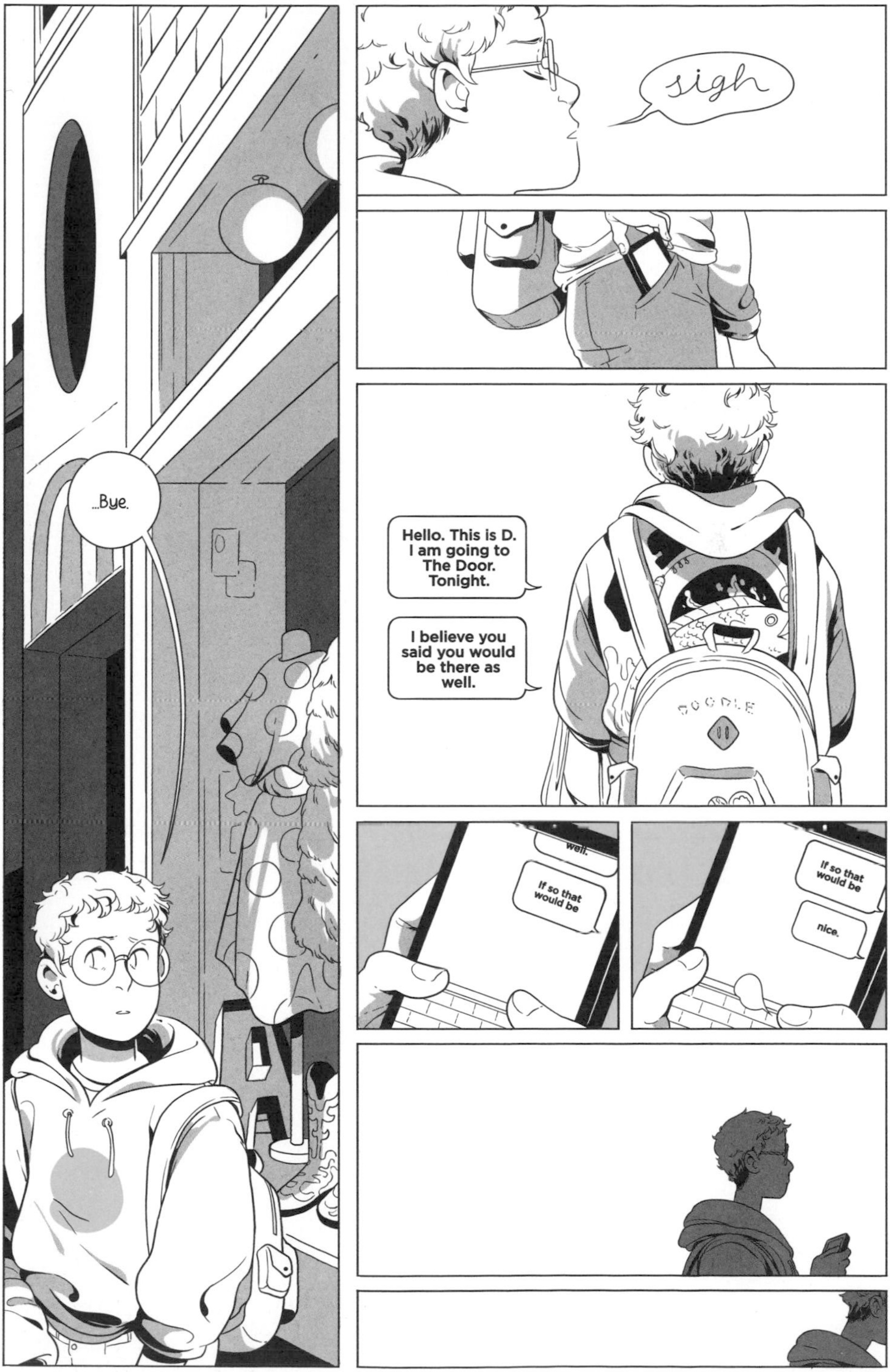
...Bye.
sigh
Hello. This is D. I am going to The Door. Tonight.
I believe you said you would be there as well.
well.
If so that would be
If so that would be
nice.

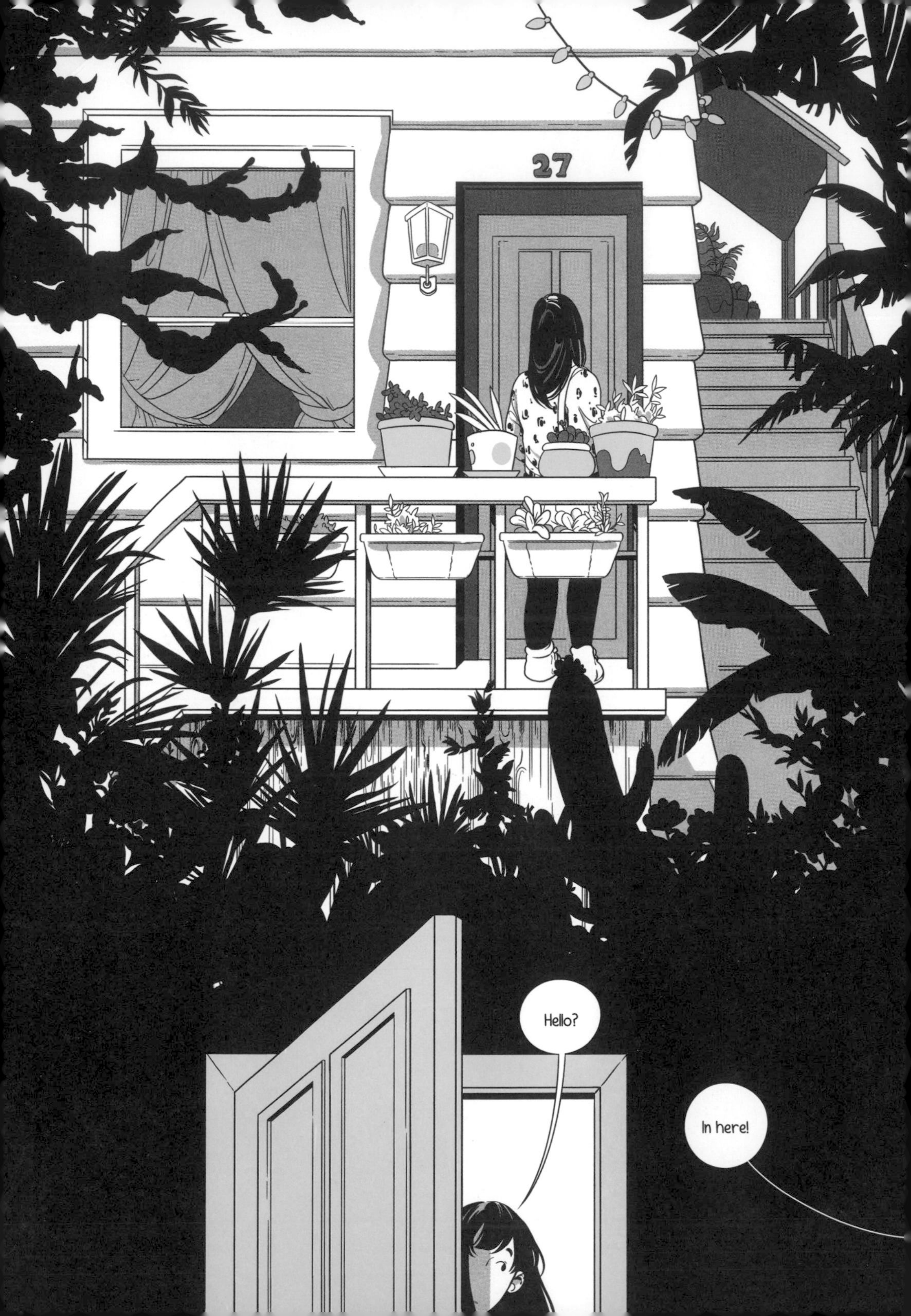
27
Hello?
In here!

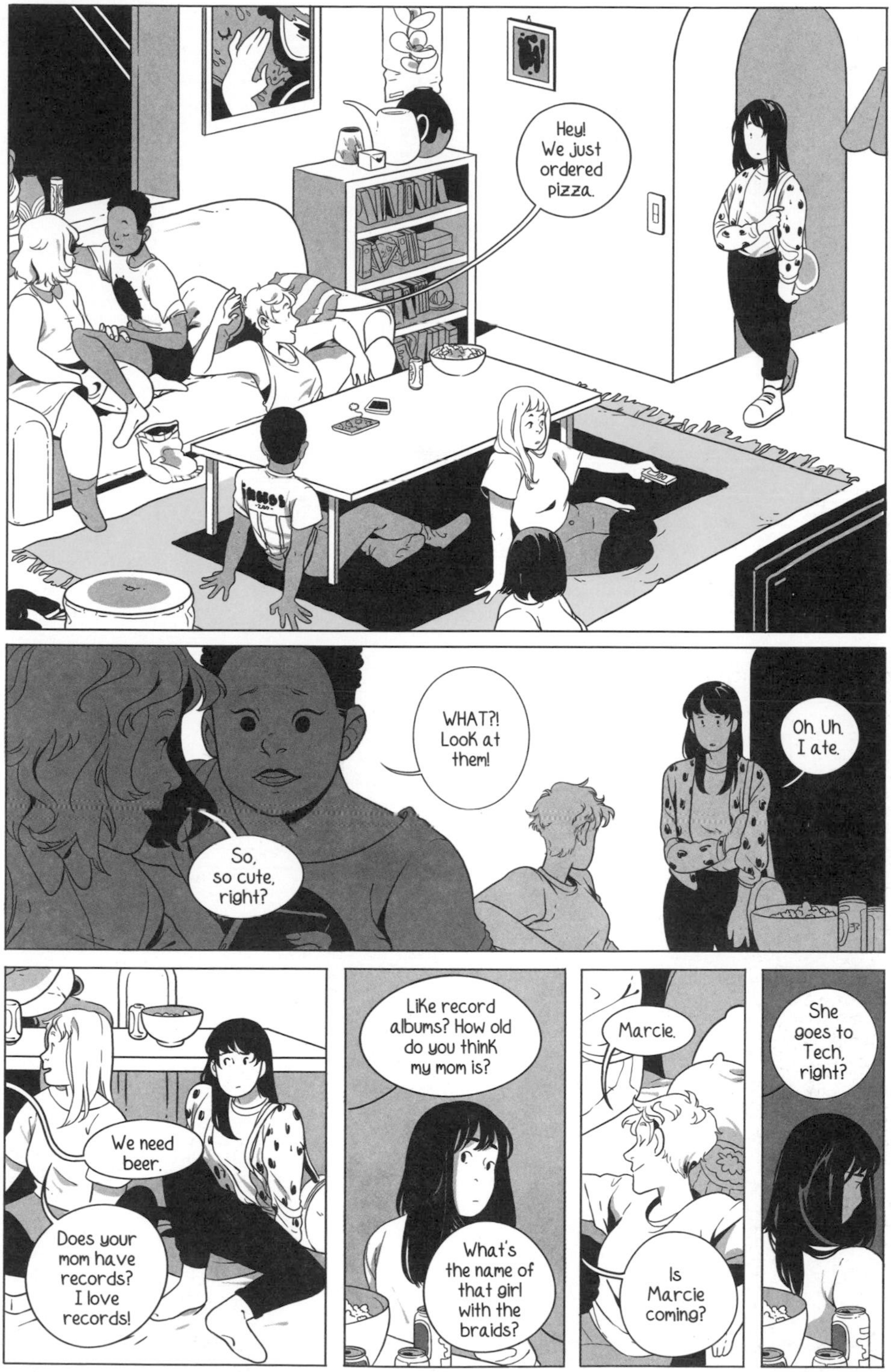
Hey! We just ordered pizza.
WHAT?! Look at them!
So, so cute, right?
Oh. Uh. I ate.
We need beer.
Does your mom have records? I love records!
Like record albums? How old do you think my mom is?
What's the name of that girl with the braids?
Marcie.
Is Marcie coming?
She goes to Tech, right?

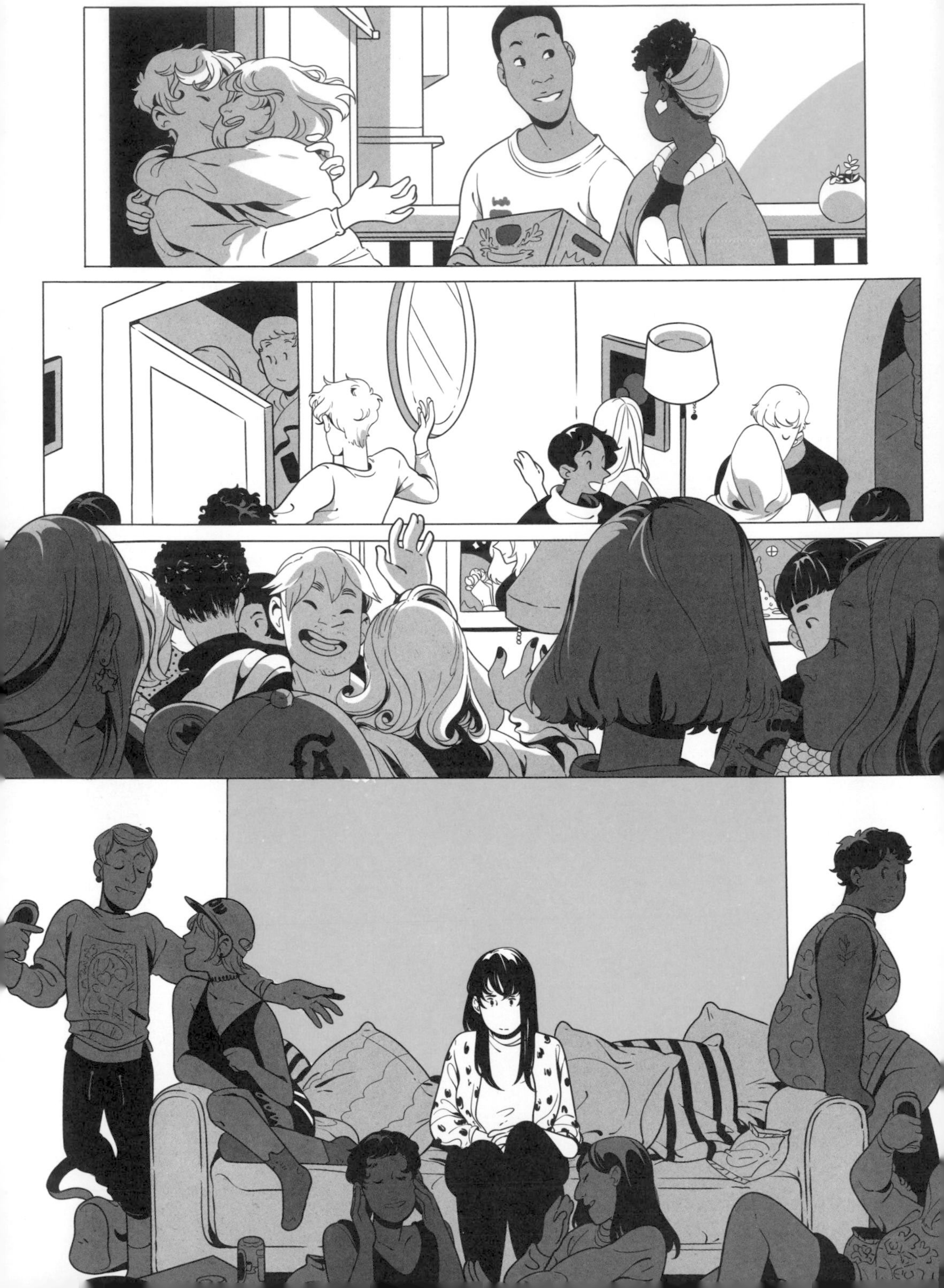

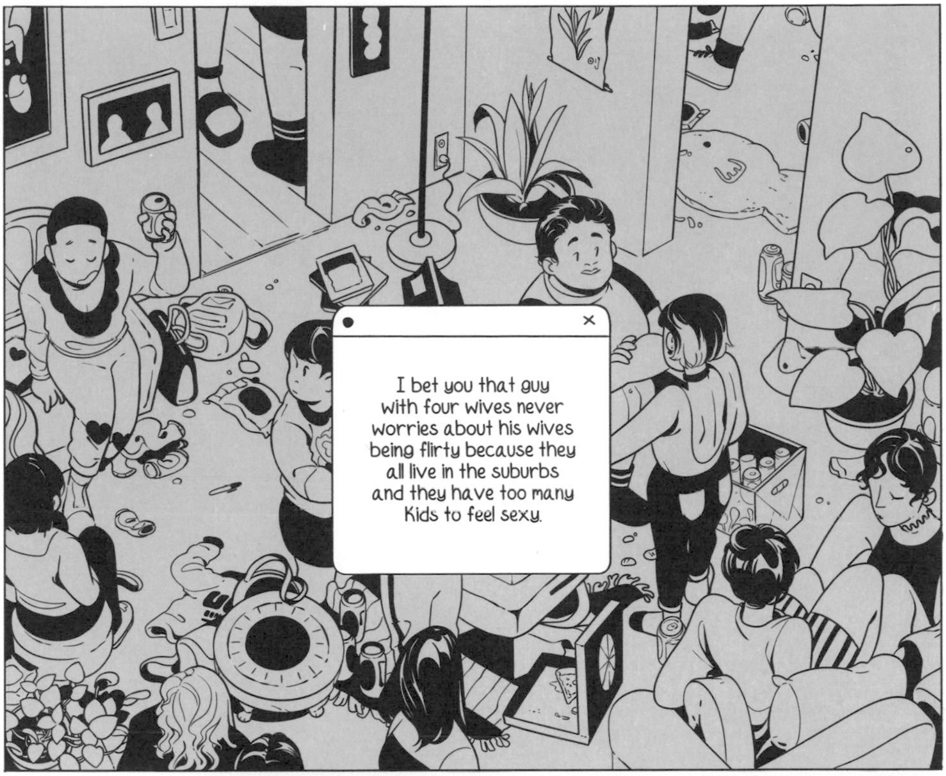
I bet you that guy
with four wives never
worries about his wives
being flirty because they
all live in the suburbs
and they have too many
Kids to feel sexy.

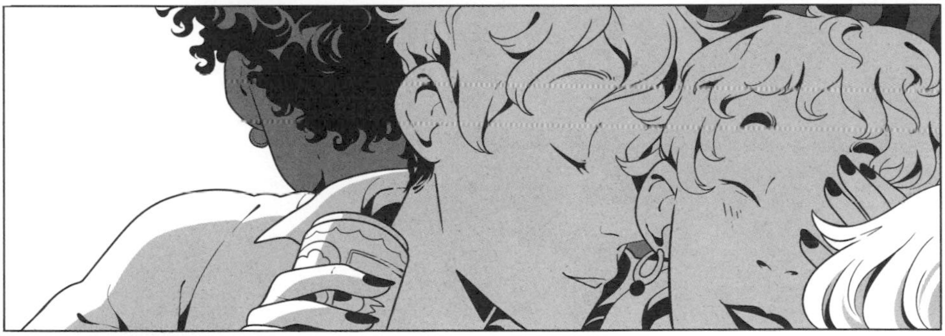

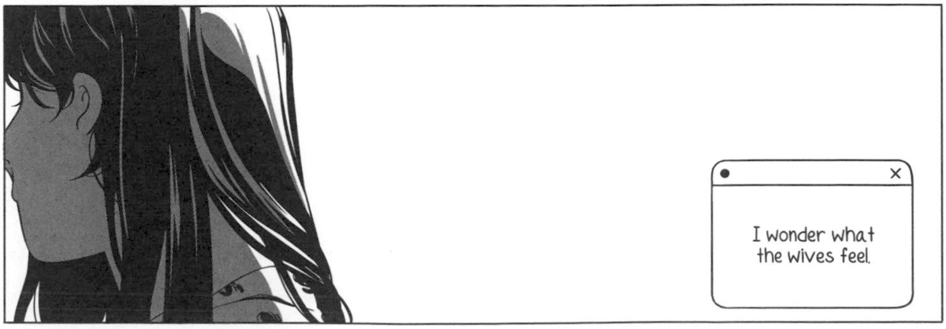
I wonder what
the wives feel.

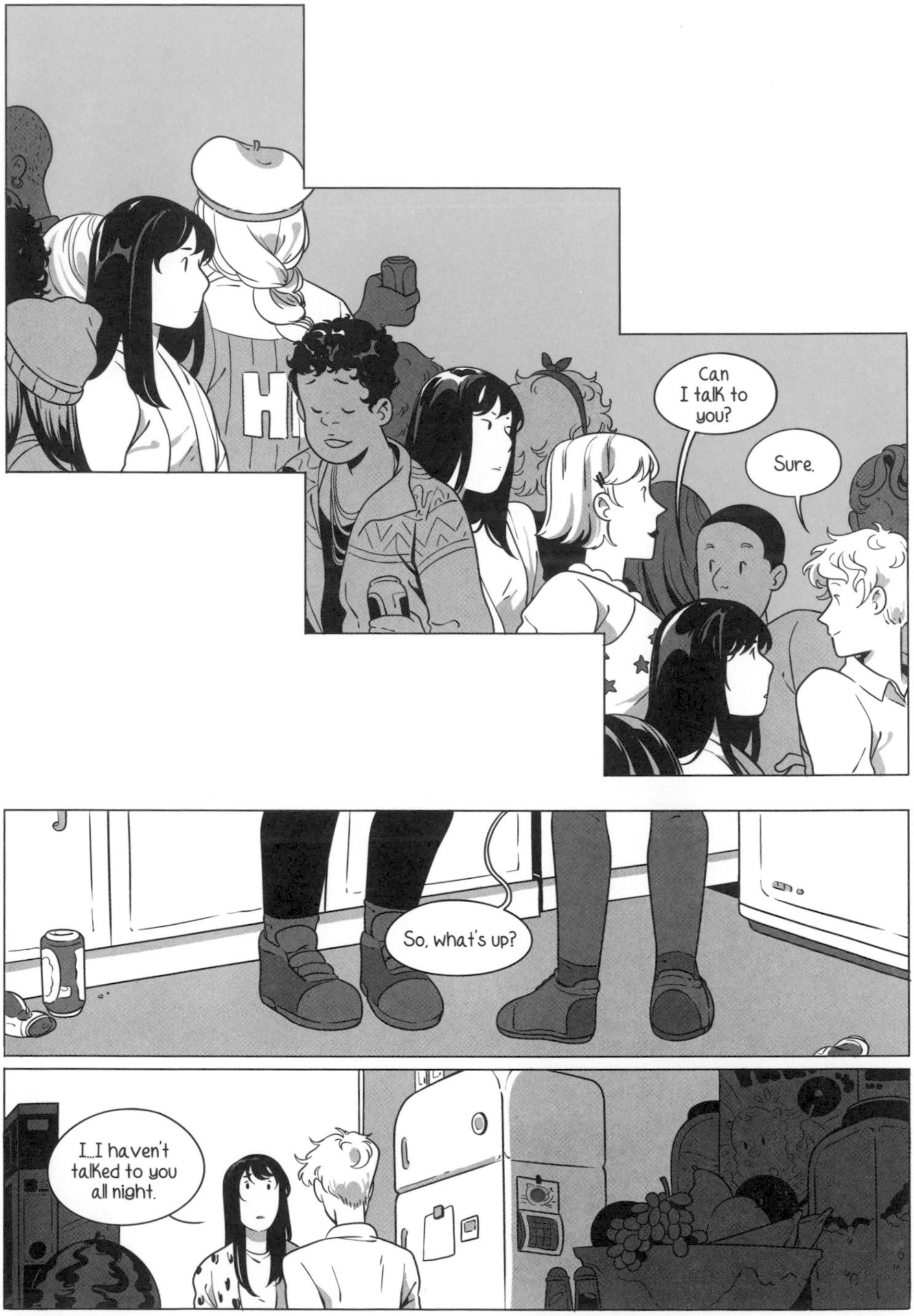
Can I talk to you?
Sure.
So, what's up?
I...I haven't talked to you all night.

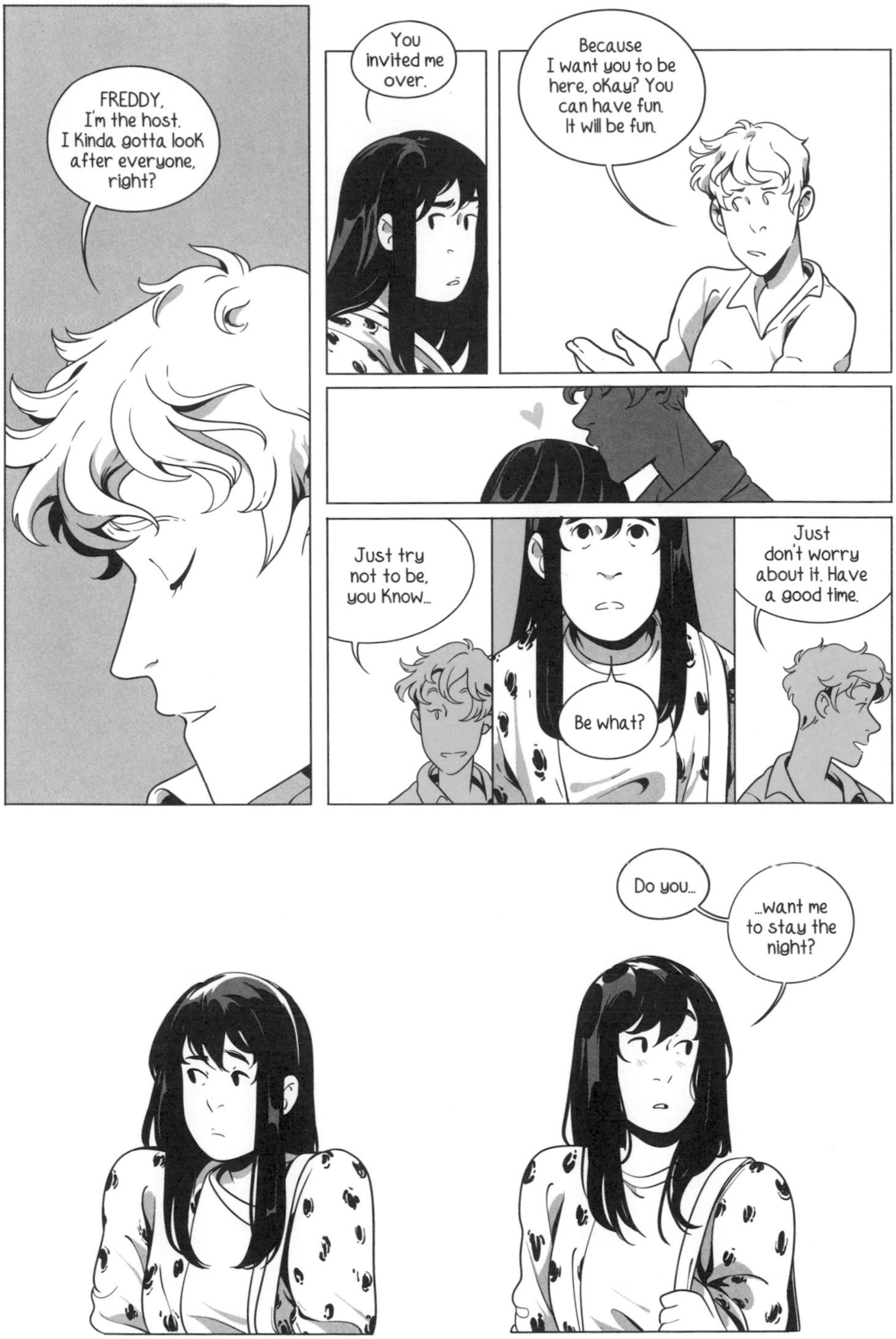
FREDDY, I'm the host. I Kinda gotta looK after everyone, right?
You invited me over.
Because I want you to be here, oKay? You can have fun. It will be fun.
Just try not to be, you Know...
Be what?
Just don't worry about it. Have a good time.
Do you...
...want me to stay the night?

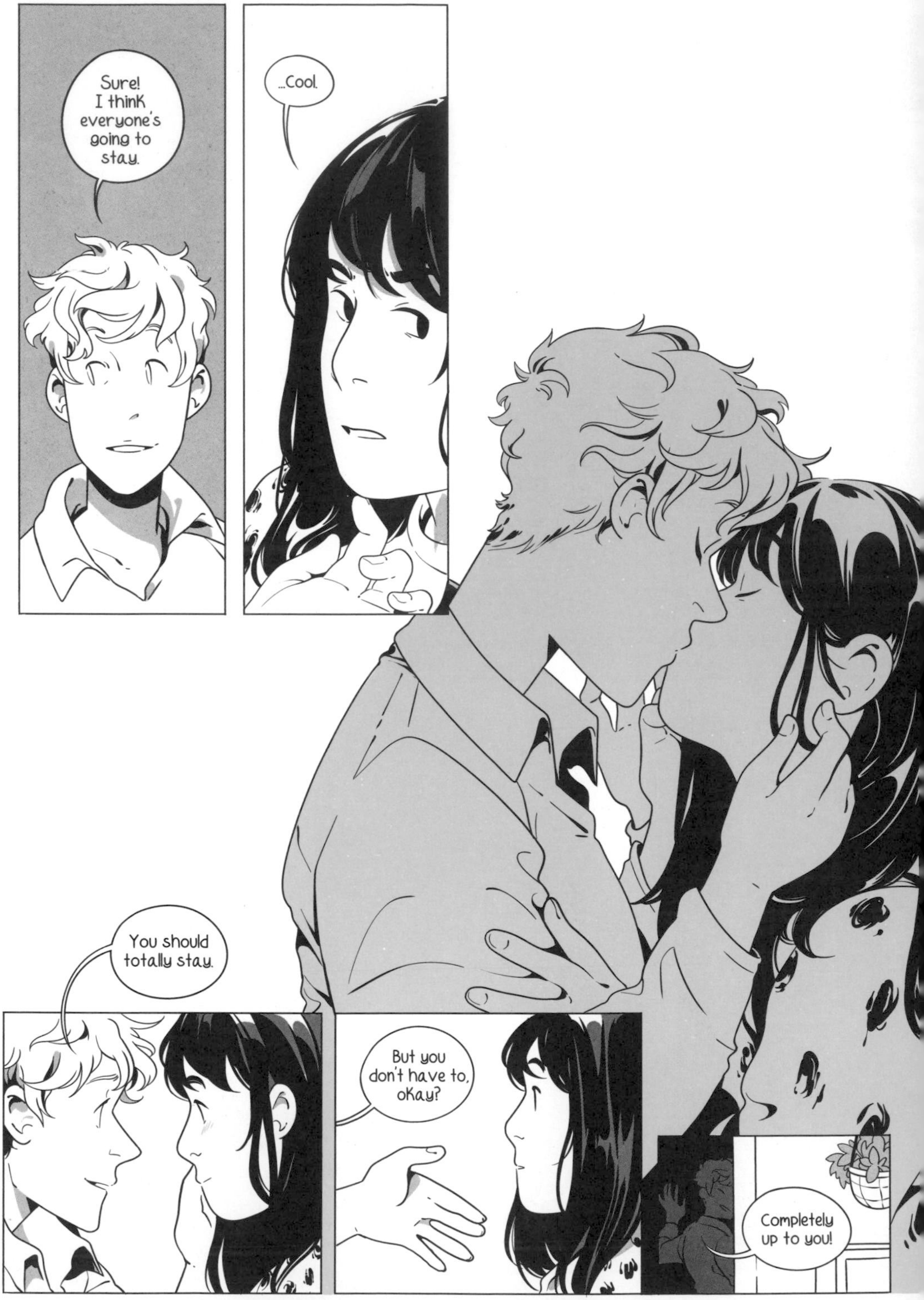
Sure! I think everyone's going to stay.
...Cool.
You should totally stay.
But you don't have to, okay?
Completely up to you!

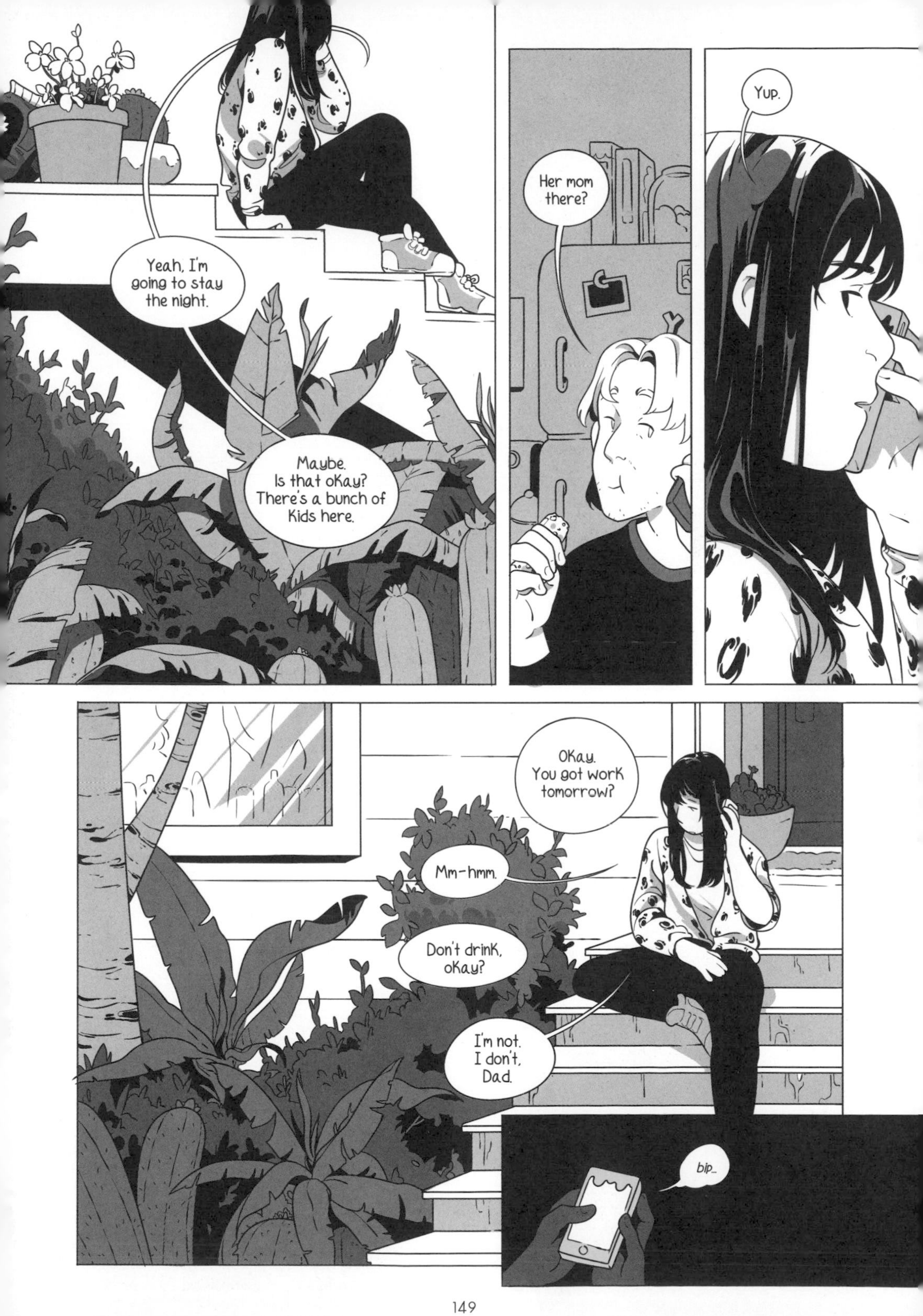
Yeah, I'm going to stay the night.
Maybe. Is that oKay? There's a bunch of Kids here.
Her mom there?
Yup.
OKay. You got work tomorrow?
Mm-hmm.
Don't drink, oKay?
I'm not. I don't, Dad.
bip...

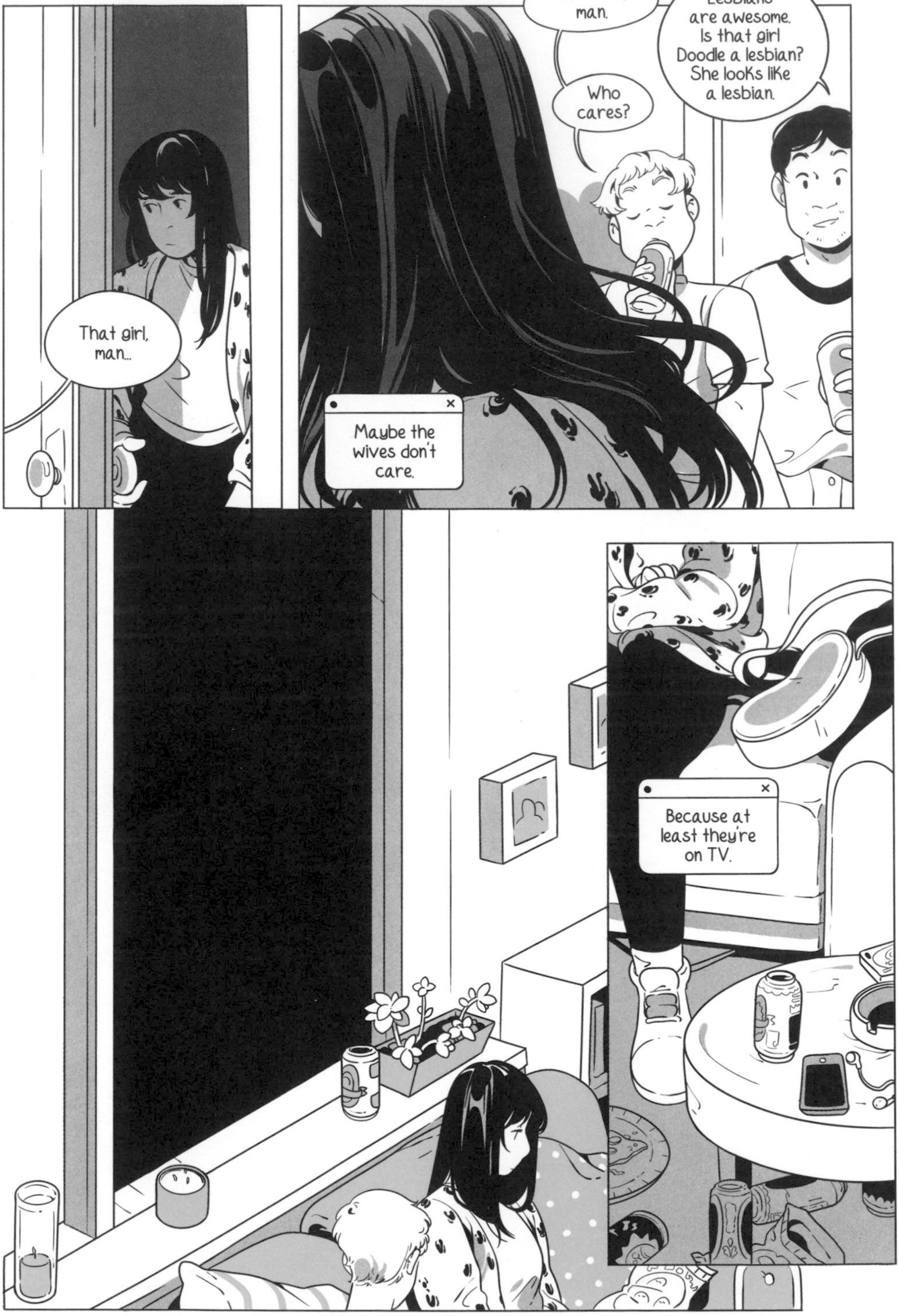

That girl, man...
Lesbians, man.
Who cares?
Lesbians are awesome. Is that girl Doodle a lesbian? She looks like a lesbian.
Maybe the wives don't care.
Because at least they're on TV.

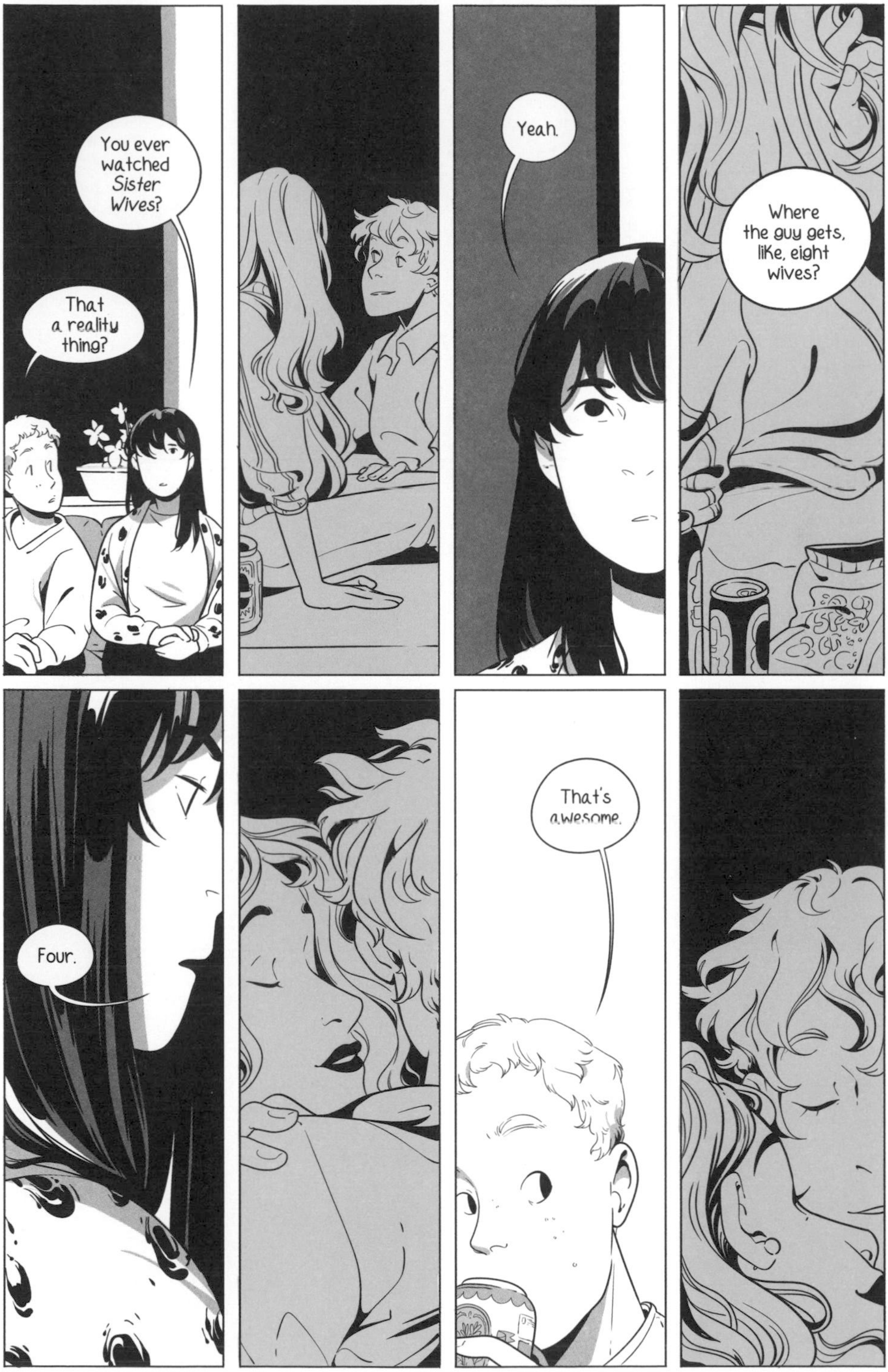

You ever watched Sister Wives?
That a reality thing?
Yeah.
Where the guy gets, like, eight wives?
Four.
That's awesome.

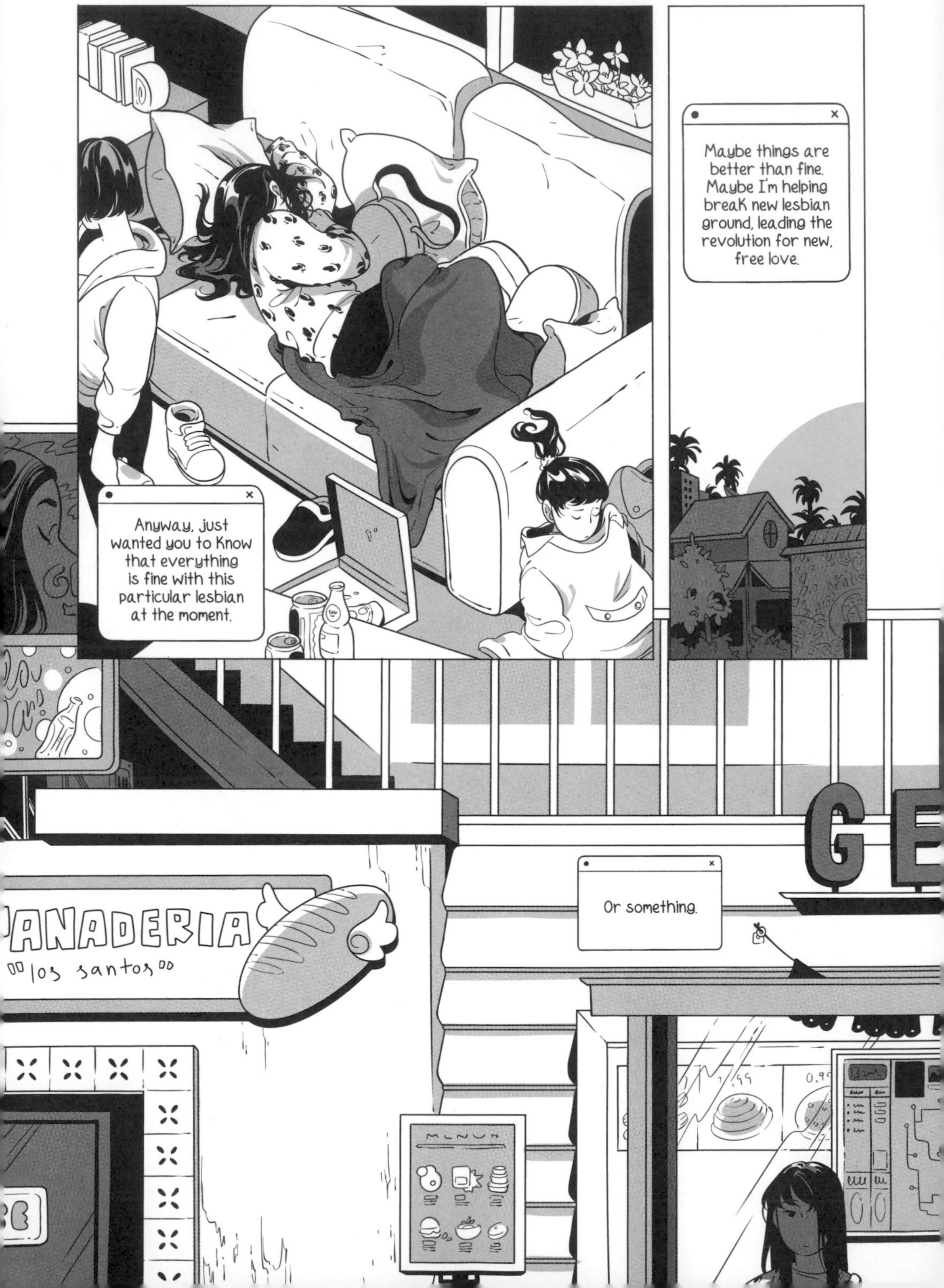

Anyway, just wanted you to Know that everything is fine with this particular lesbian at the moment.
Maybe things are better than fine. Maybe I'm helping break new lesbian ground, leading the revolution for new, free love.
Or something.
PANADERIA
"los santos"
GE

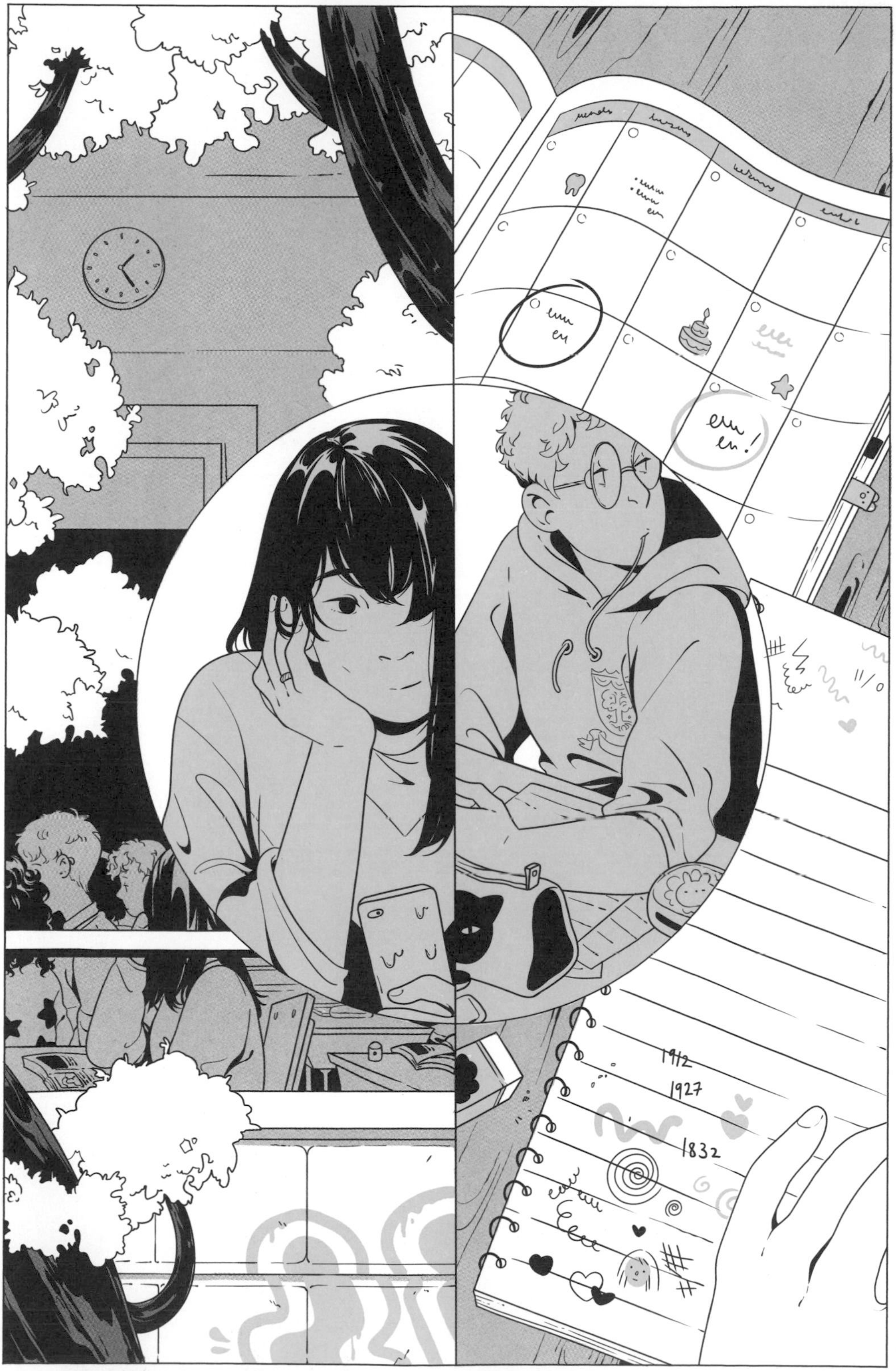
1912
1927
1832

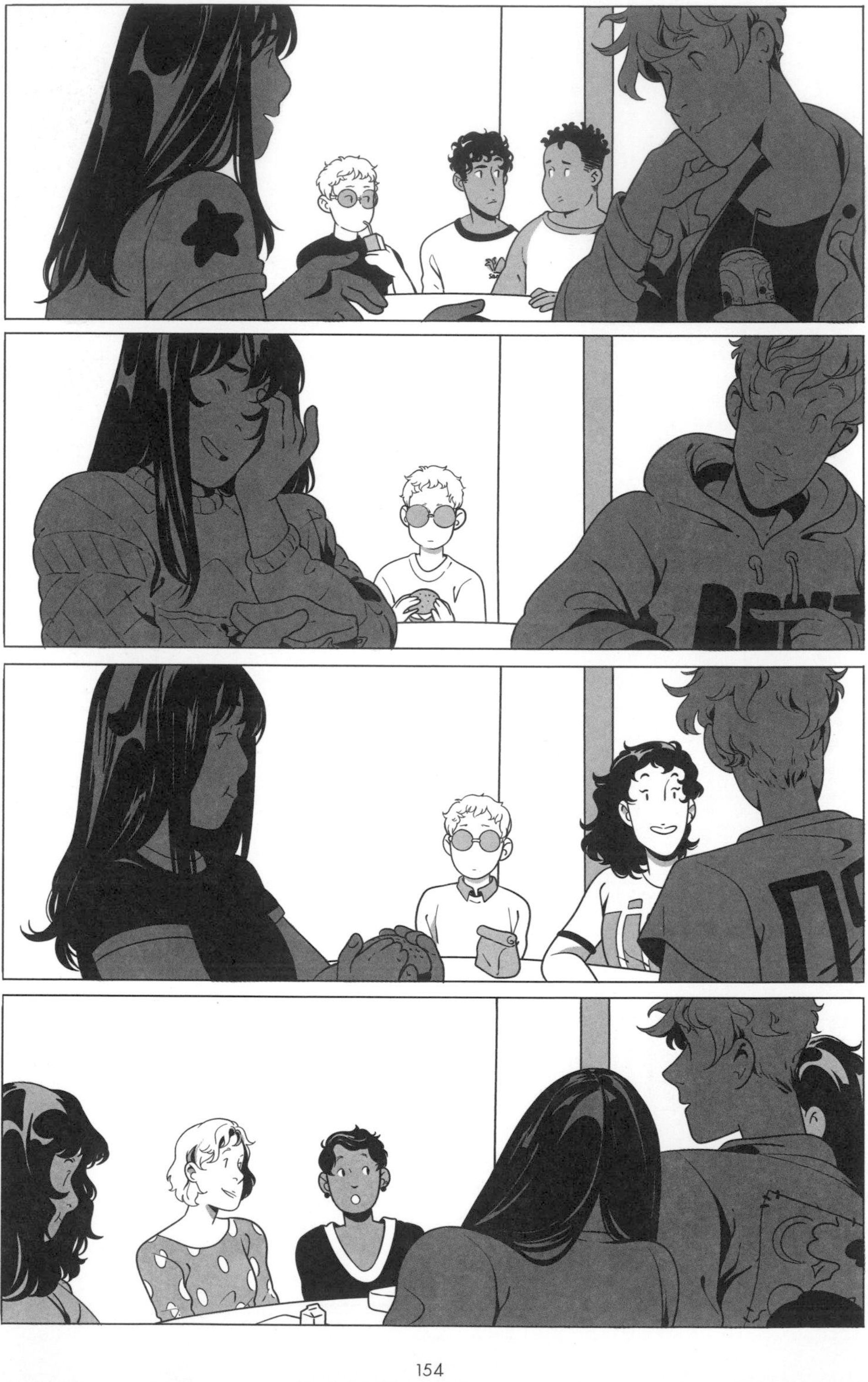

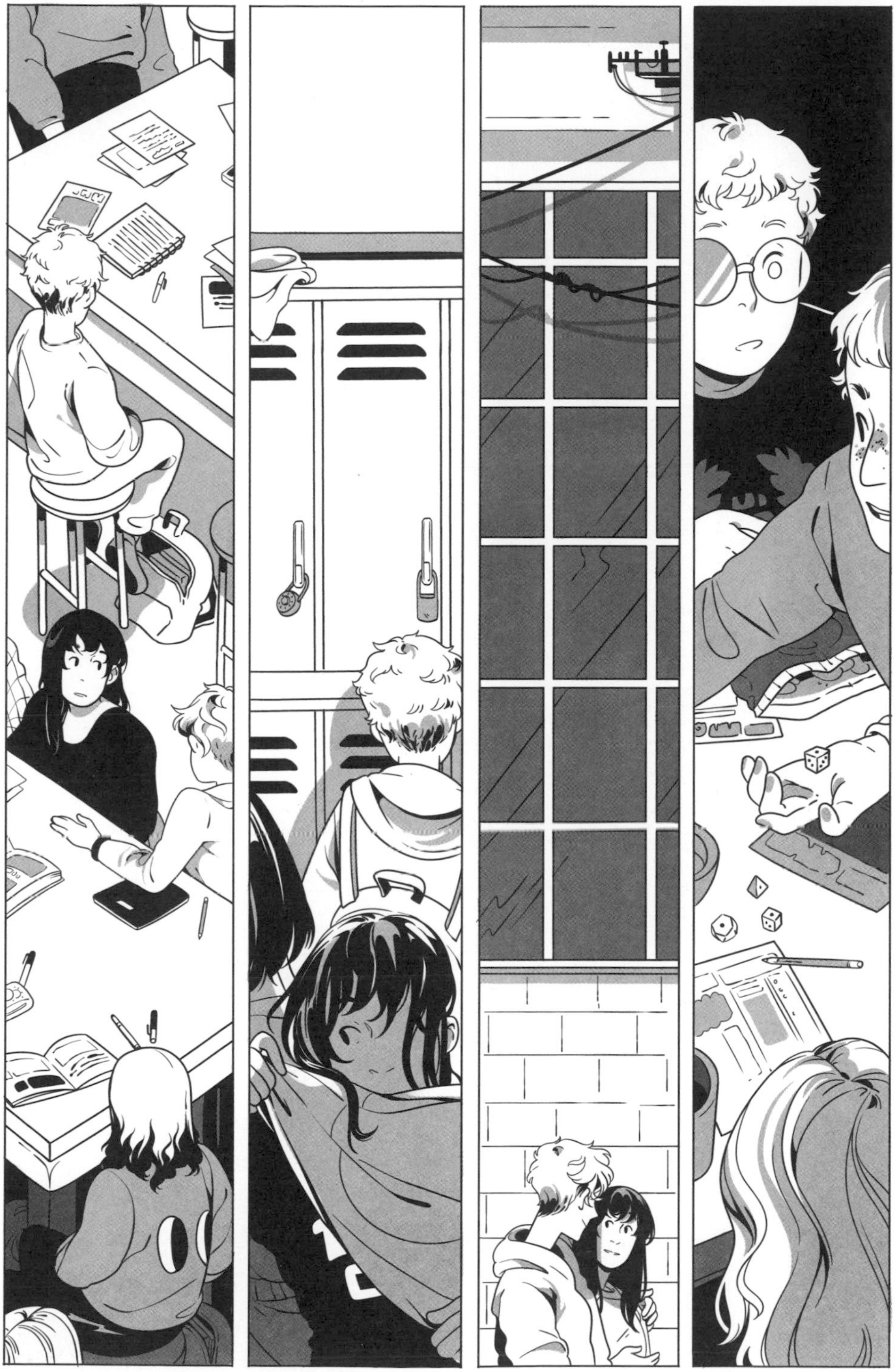

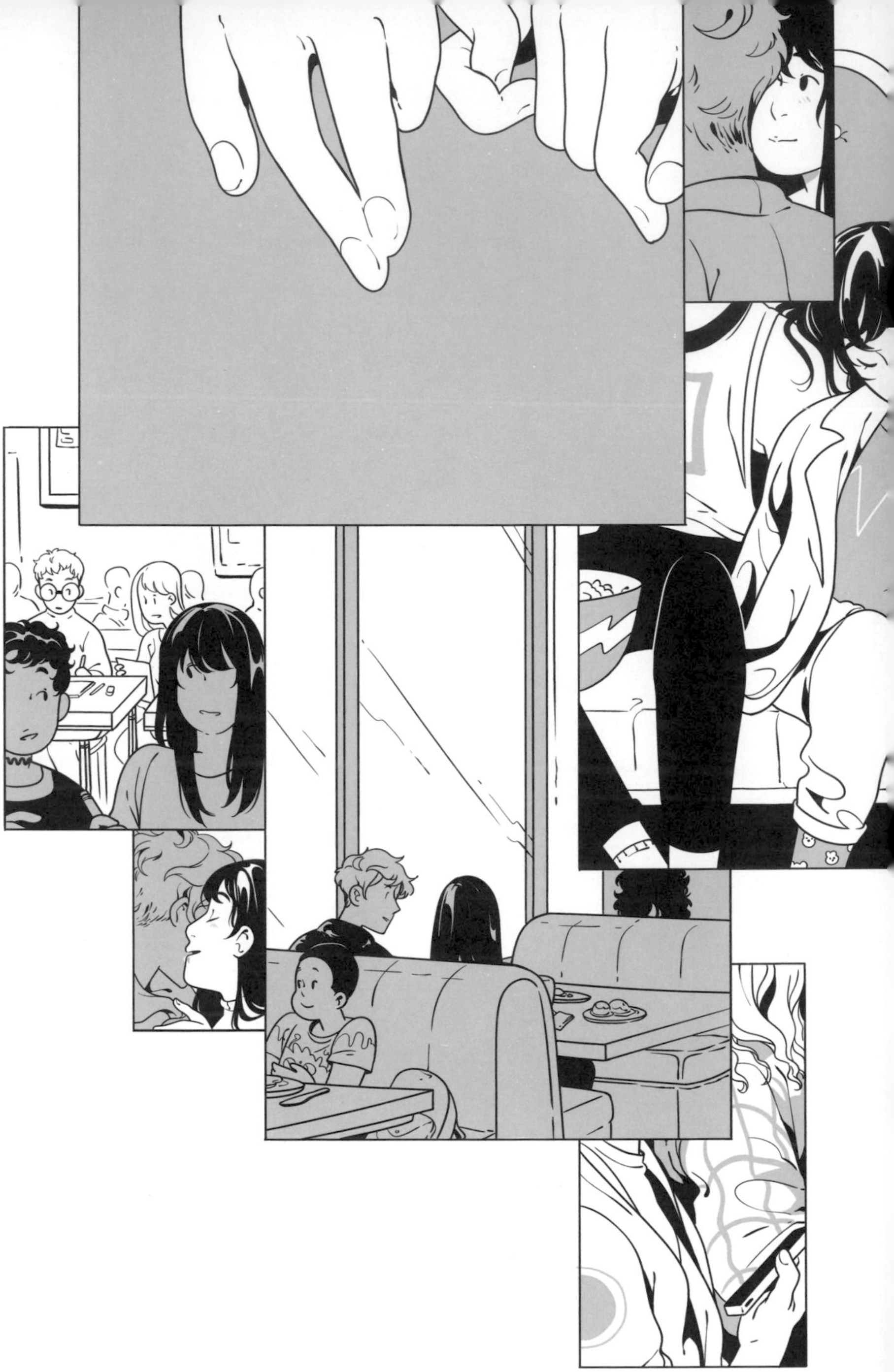

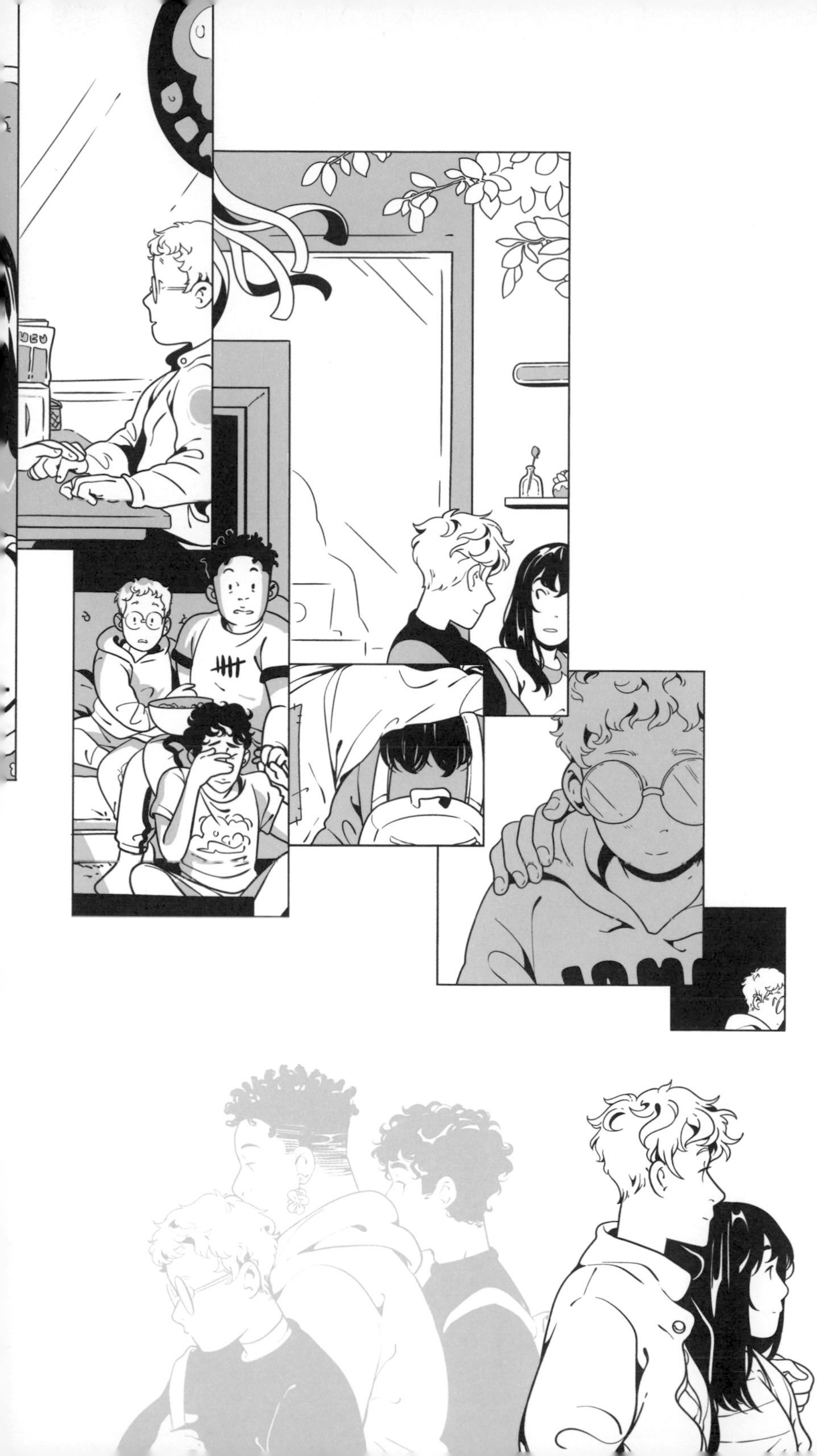

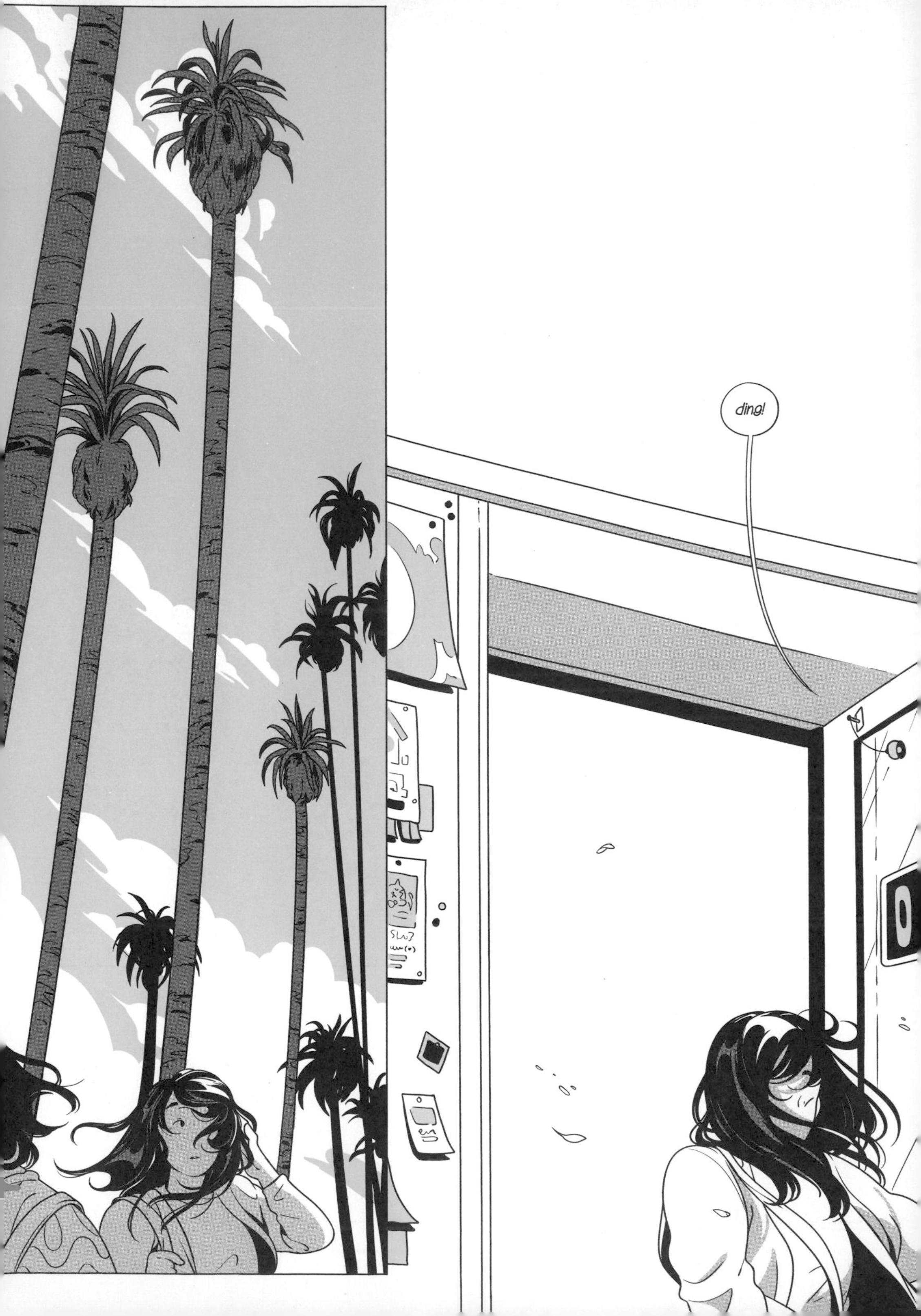
ding!

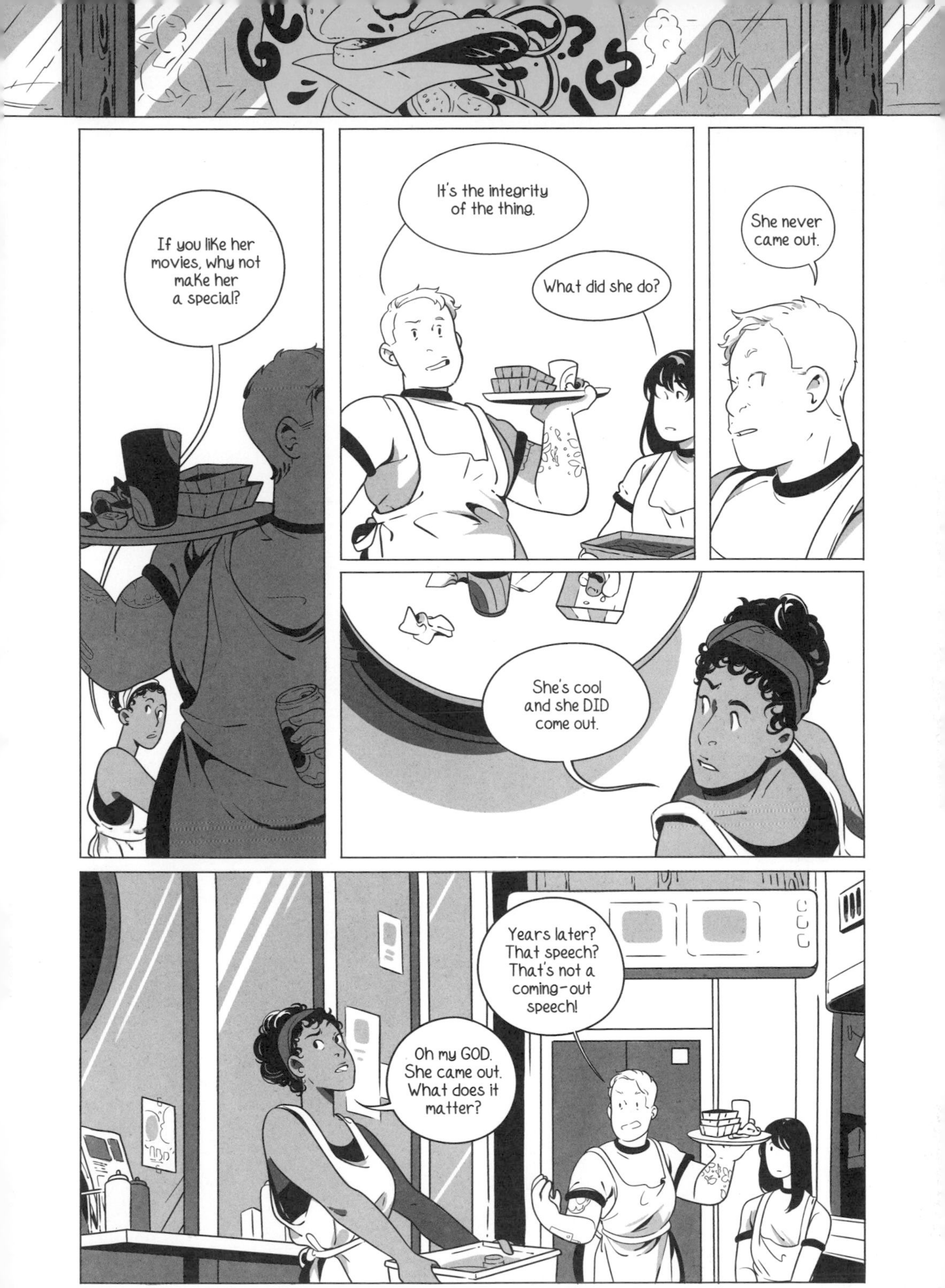
If you like her movies, why not make her a special?
It's the integrity of the thing.
What did she do?
She never came out.
She's cool and she DID come out.
Oh my GOD. She came out. What does it matter?
Years later? That speech? That's not a coming-out speech!

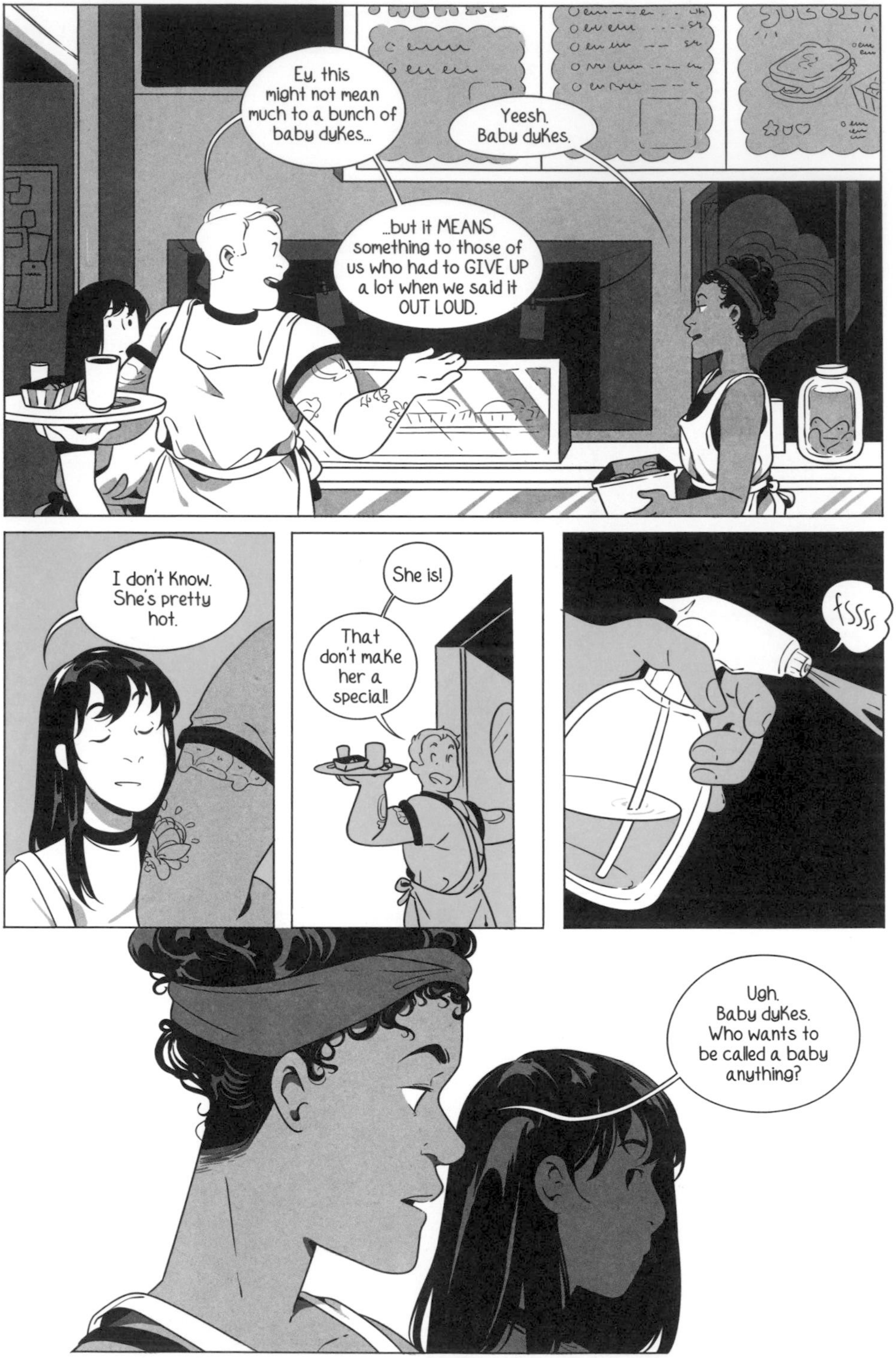
Ey, this might not mean much to a bunch of baby dyKes...
Yeesh. Baby dyKes.
...but it MEANS something to those of us who had to GIVE UP a lot when we said it OUT LOUD.
I don't Know. She's pretty hot.
She is!
That don't maKe her a special!
fssss
Ugh. Baby dyKes. Who wants to be called a baby anything?

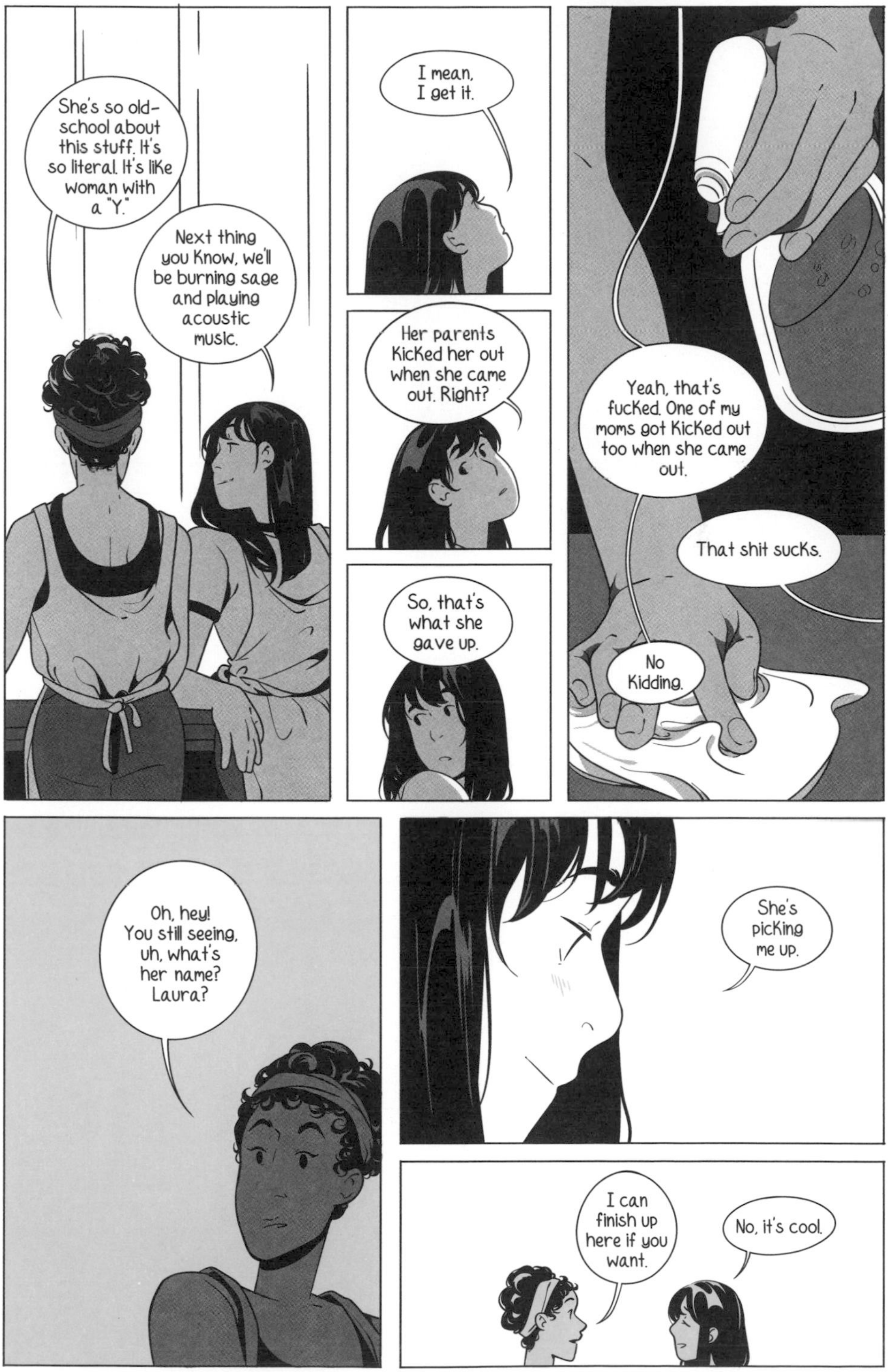
She's so old-school about this stuff. It's so literal. It's like woman with a "Y."
Next thing you Know, we'll be burning sage and playing acoustic music.
I mean, I get it.
Her parents KicKed her out when she came out. Right?
So, that's what she gave up.
Yeah, that's fucKed. One of my moms got KicKed out too when she came out.
No Kidding.
That shit sucKs.
Oh, hey! You still seeing, uh, what's her name? Laura?
She's picKing me up.
I can finish up here if you want.
No, it's cool.

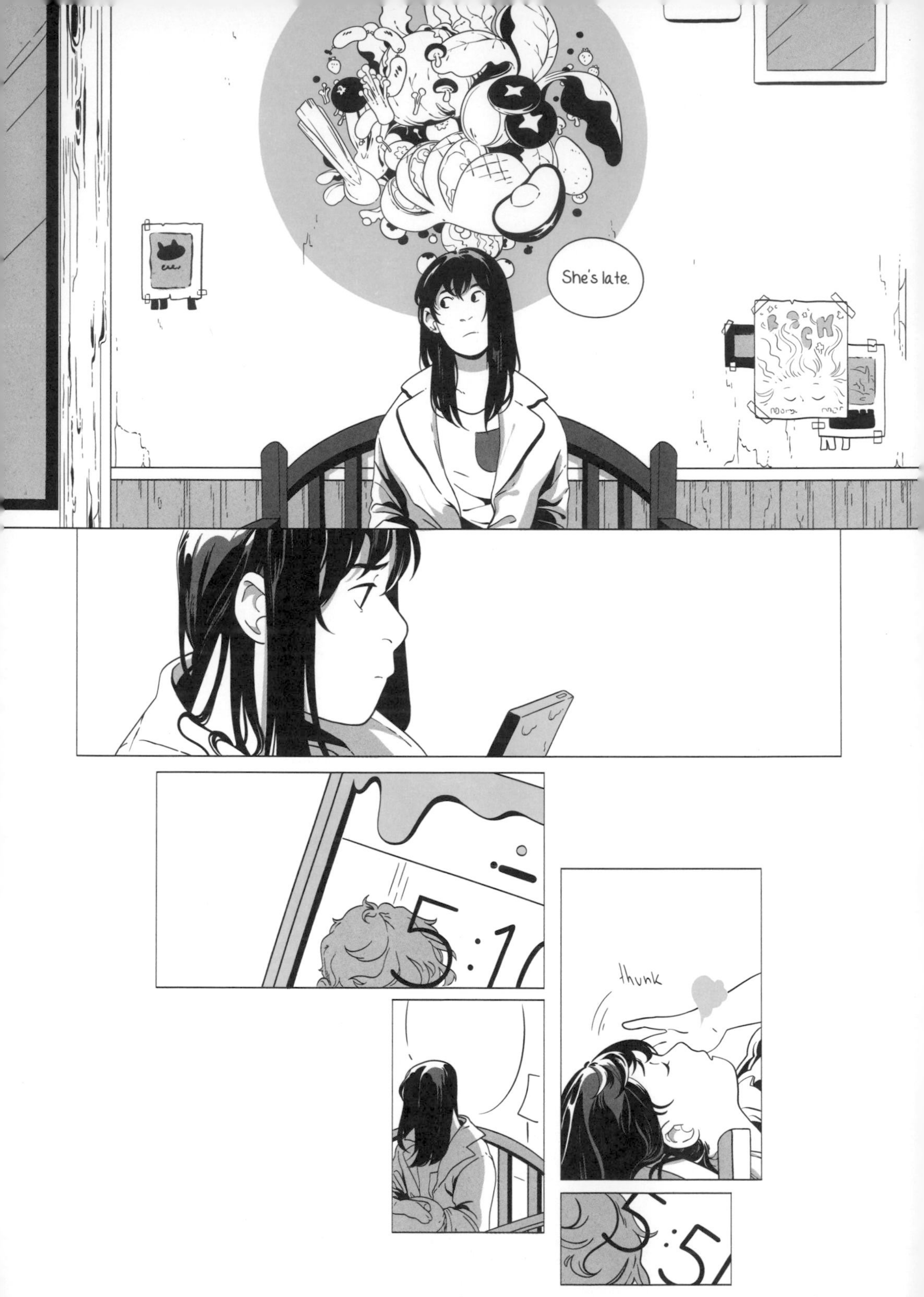
She's late.
thunk

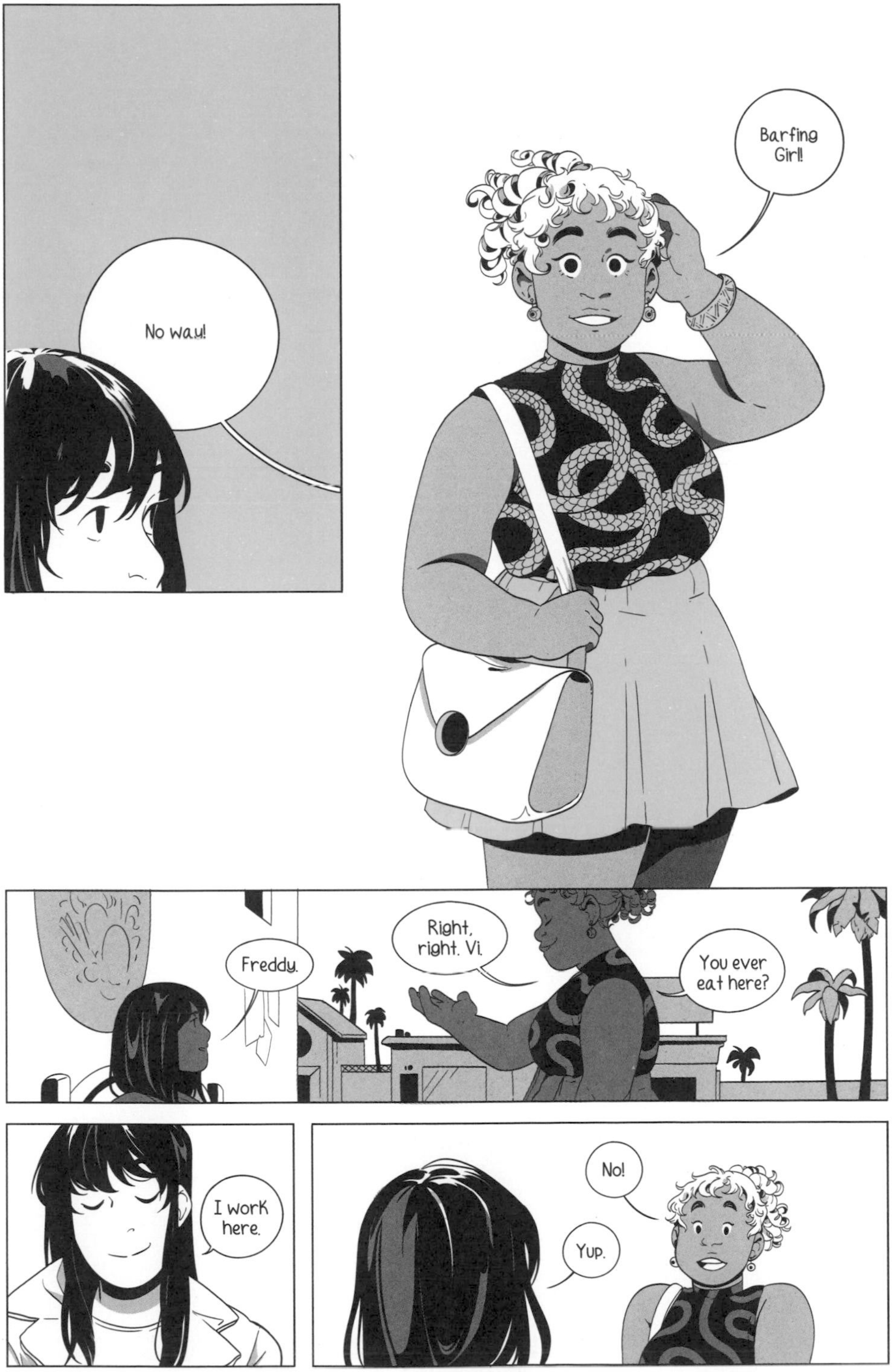
No way!
Barfing Girl!
Freddy.
Right, right. Vi.
You ever eat here?
I work here.
No!
Yup.

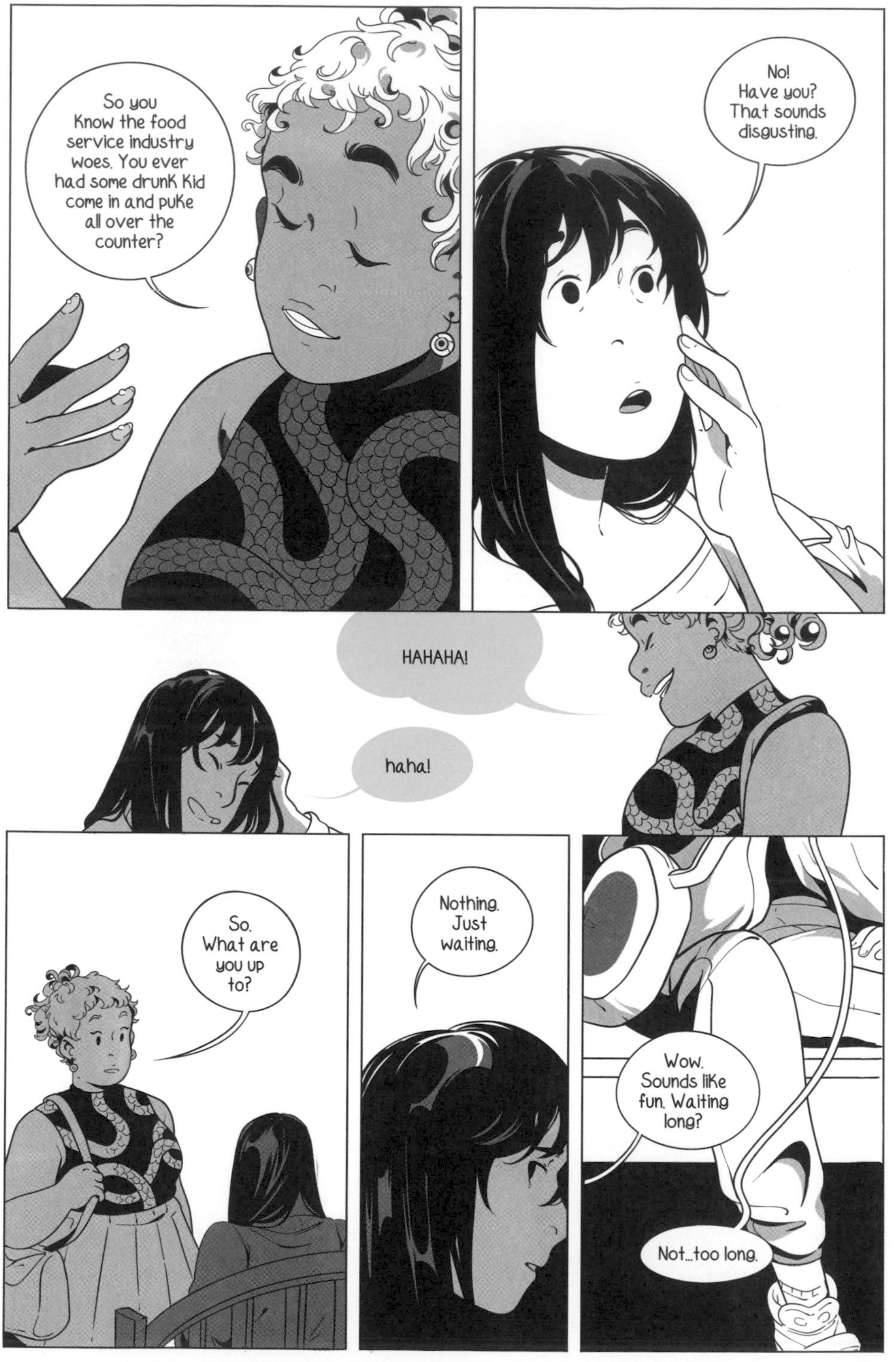
So you Know the food service industry woes. You ever had some drunK Kid come in and puKe all over the counter?
No! Have you? That sounds disgusting.
HAHAHA!
haha!
So. What are you up to?
Nothing. Just waiting.
Wow. Sounds liKe fun. Waiting long?
Not...too long.

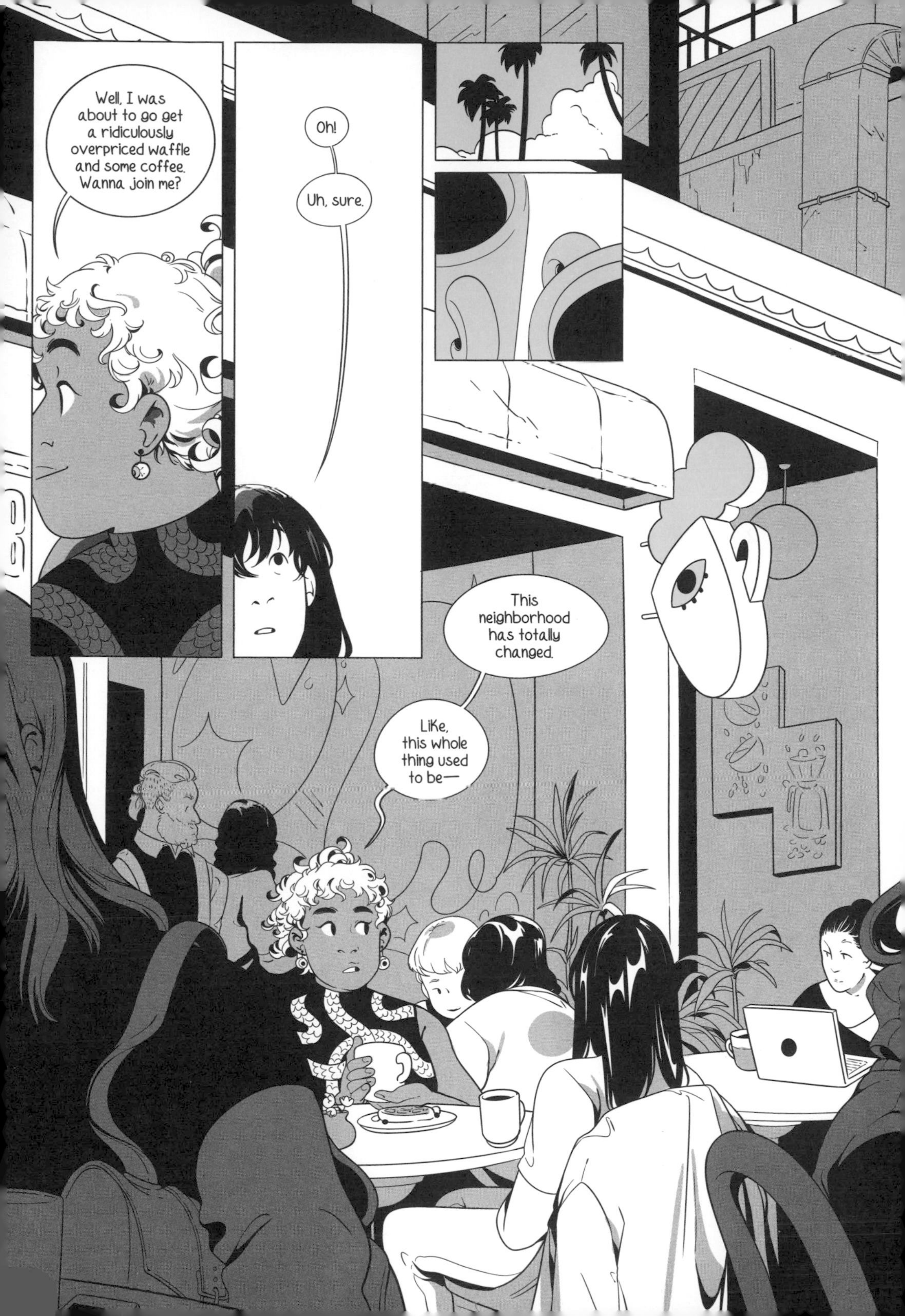
Well, I was about to go get a ridiculously overpriced waffle and some coffee. Wanna join me?
Oh!
Uh, sure.
This neighborhood has totally changed.
Like, this whole thing used to be—

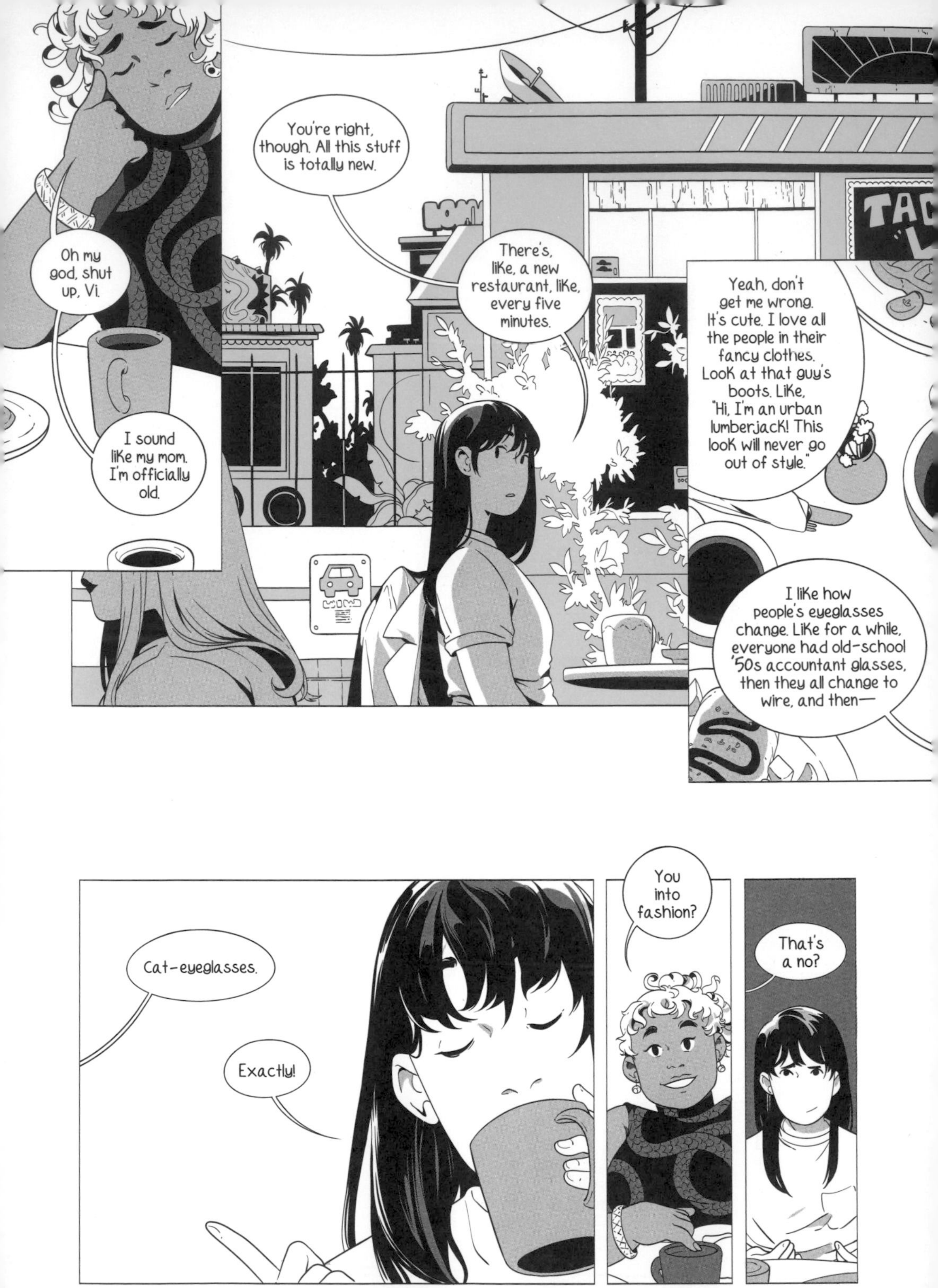
Oh my god, shut up, Vi.
I sound like my mom. I'm officially old.
You're right, though. All this stuff is totally new.
There's, like, a new restaurant, like, every five minutes.
Yeah, don't get me wrong. It's cute. I love all the people in their fancy clothes. Look at that guy's boots. Like, "Hi, I'm an urban lumberjack! This look will never go out of style."
I like how people's eyeglasses change. Like for a while, everyone had old-school '50s accountant glasses, then they all change to wire, and then—
Cat-eyeglasses.
Exactly!
You into fashion?
That's a no?

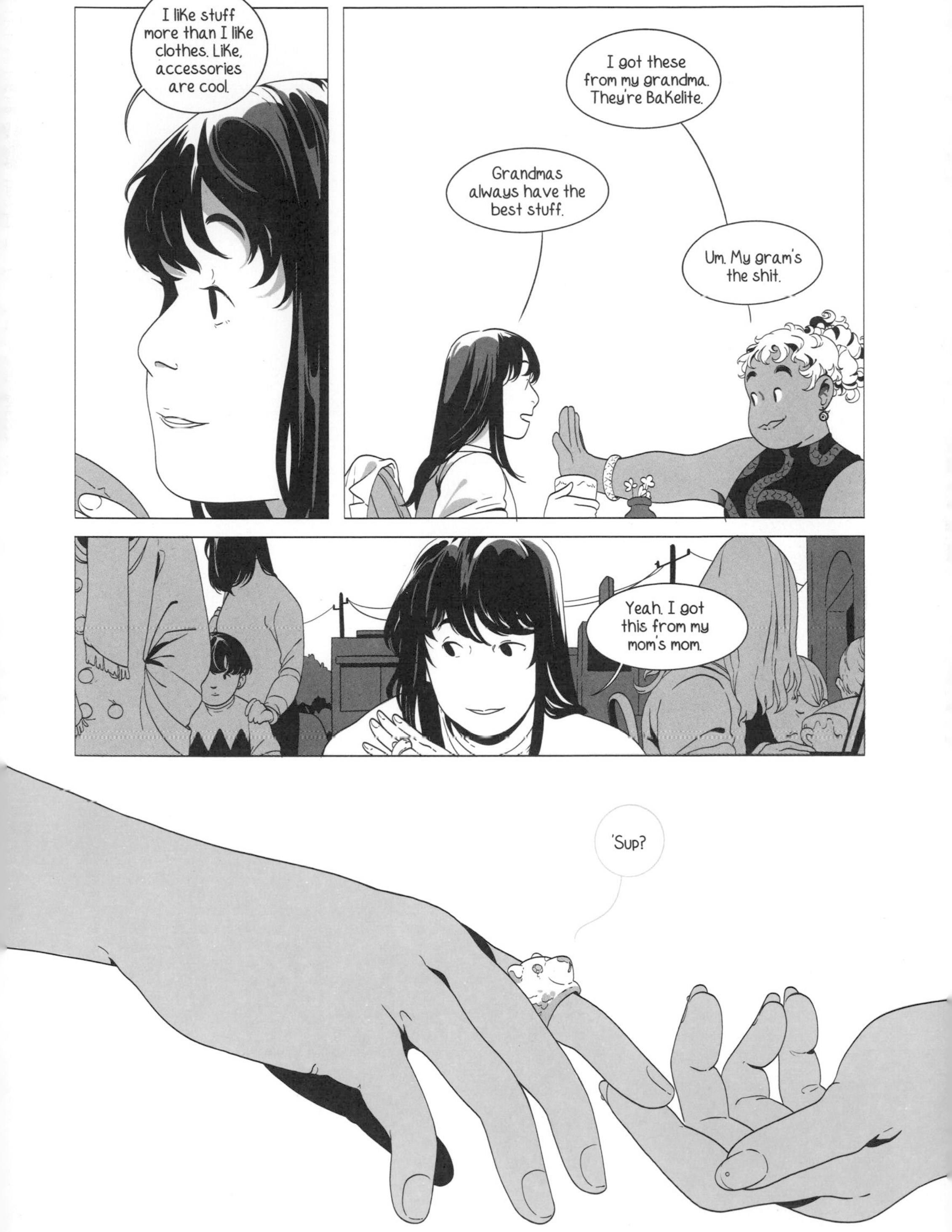
I like stuff more than I like clothes. Like, accessories are cool.
I got these from my grandma. They're Bakelite.
Grandmas always have the best stuff.
Um. My gram's the shit.
Yeah. I got this from my mom's mom.
'Sup?

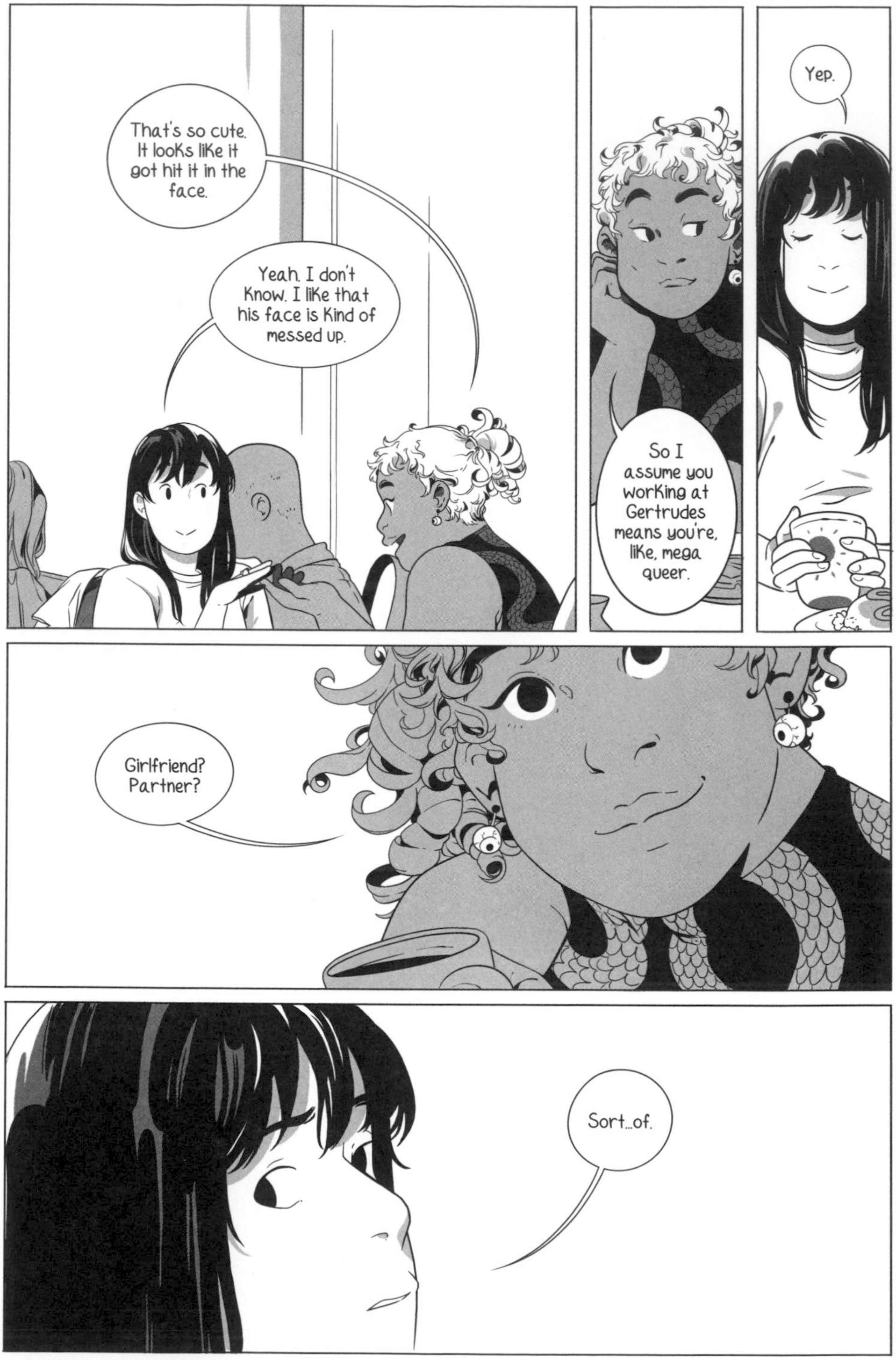
That's so cute. It looks like it got hit it in the face.
Yeah. I don't know. I like that his face is kind of messed up.
So I assume you working at Gertrudes means you're, like, mega queer.
Yep.
Girlfriend? Partner?
Sort...of.

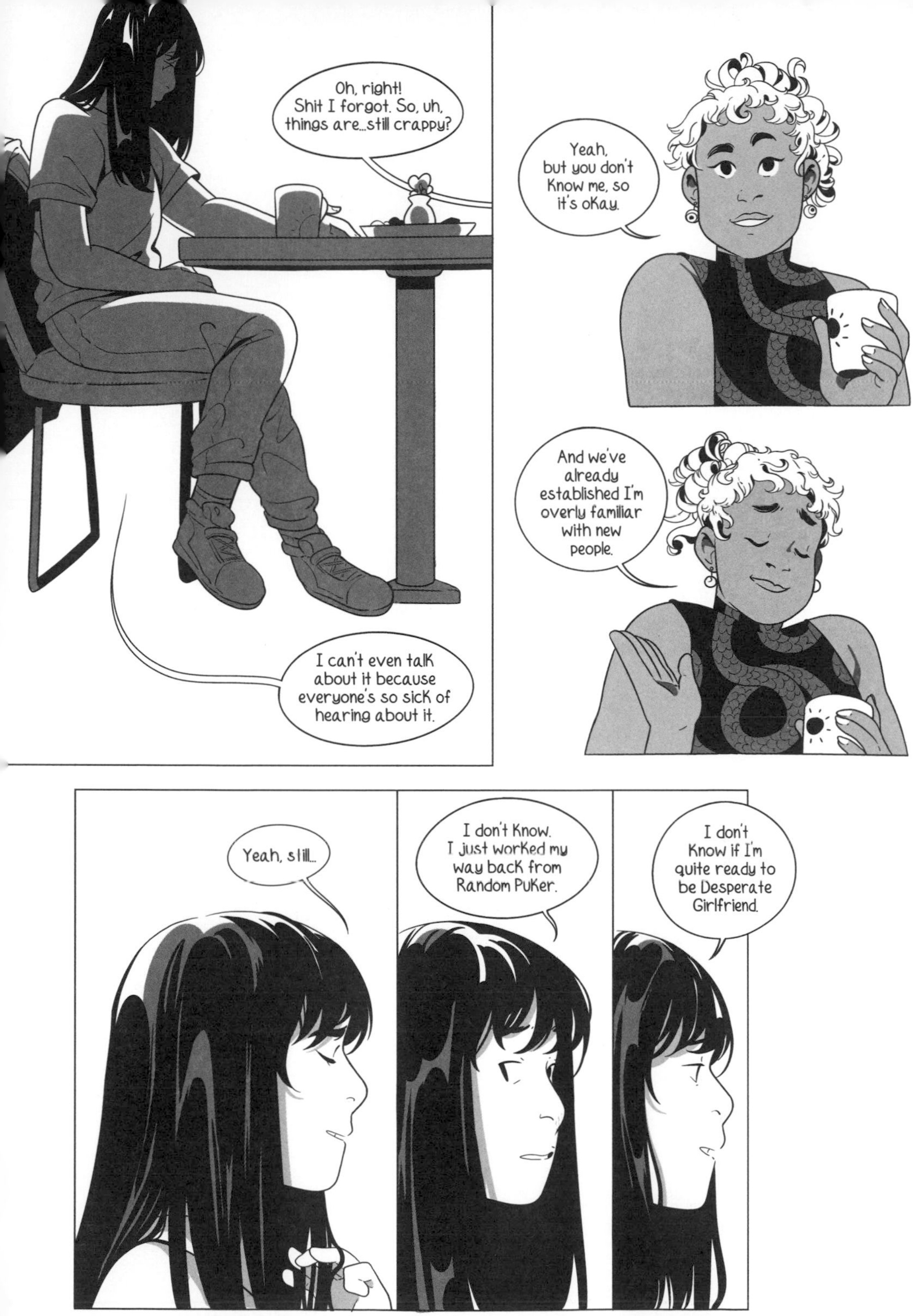
Oh, right! Shit I forgot. So, uh, things are...still crappy?
Yeah, but you don't Know me, so it's oKay.
And we've already established I'm overly familiar with new people.
I can't even talk about it because everyone's so sicK of hearing about it.
Yeah, still...
I don't Know. I just worKed my way bacK from Random PuKer.
I don't Know if I'm quite ready to be Desperate Girlfriend.

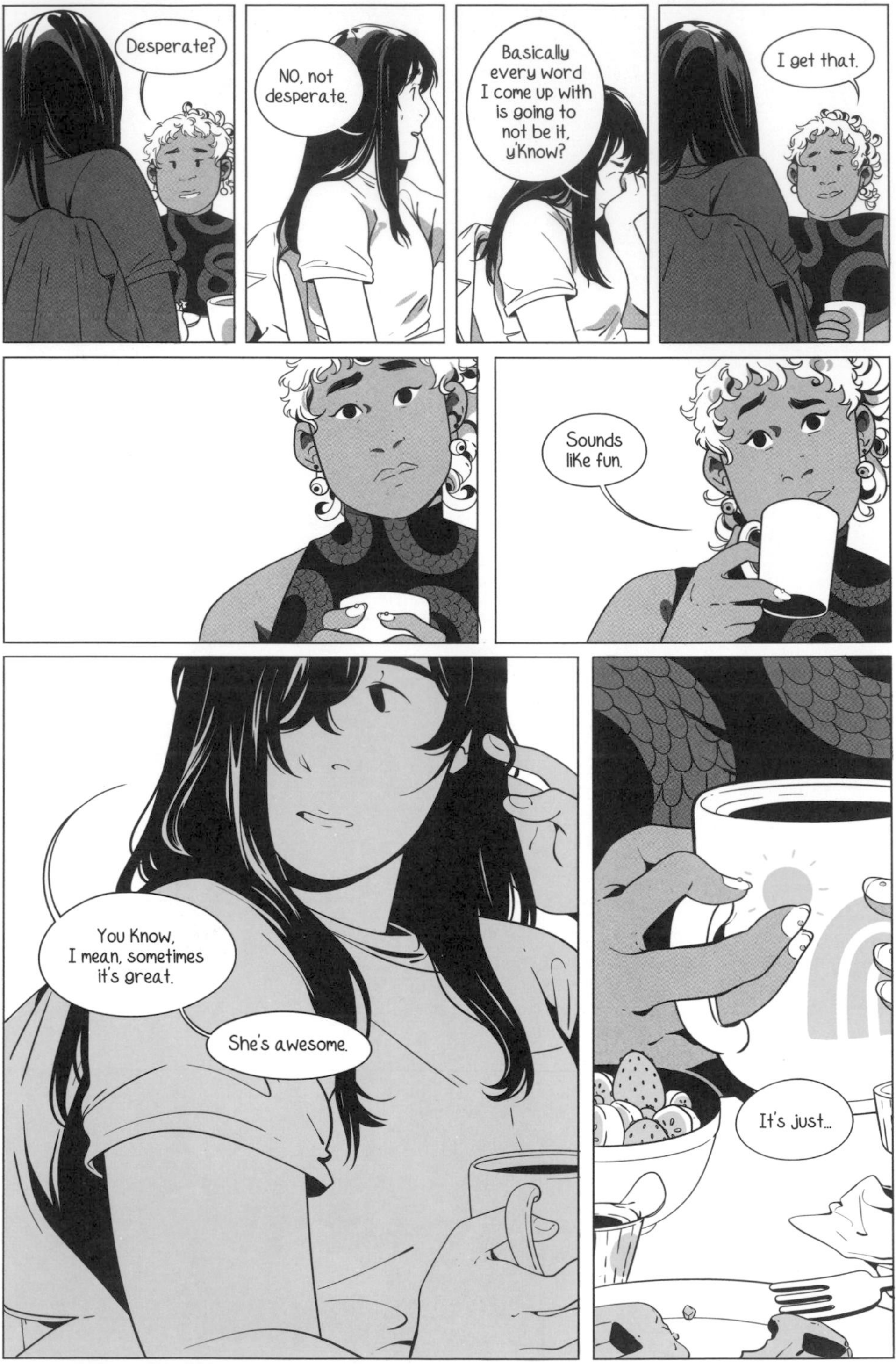
Desperate?
NO, not desperate.
Basically every word I come up with is going to not be it, y'Know?
I get that.
Sounds like fun.
You Know, I mean, sometimes it's great.
She's awesome.
It's just...

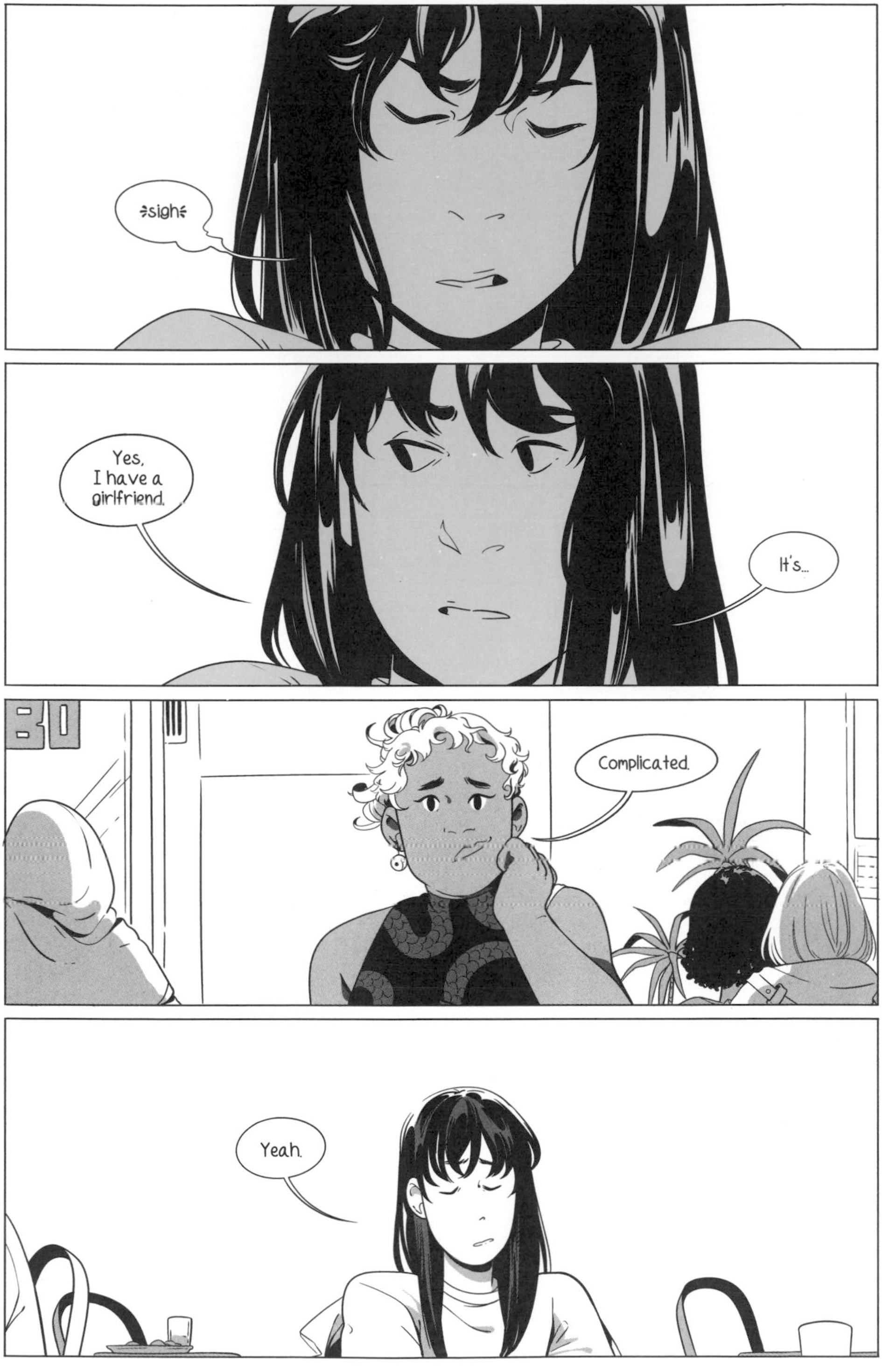

sigh
Yes, I have a girlfriend.
It's...
Complicated.
Yeah.

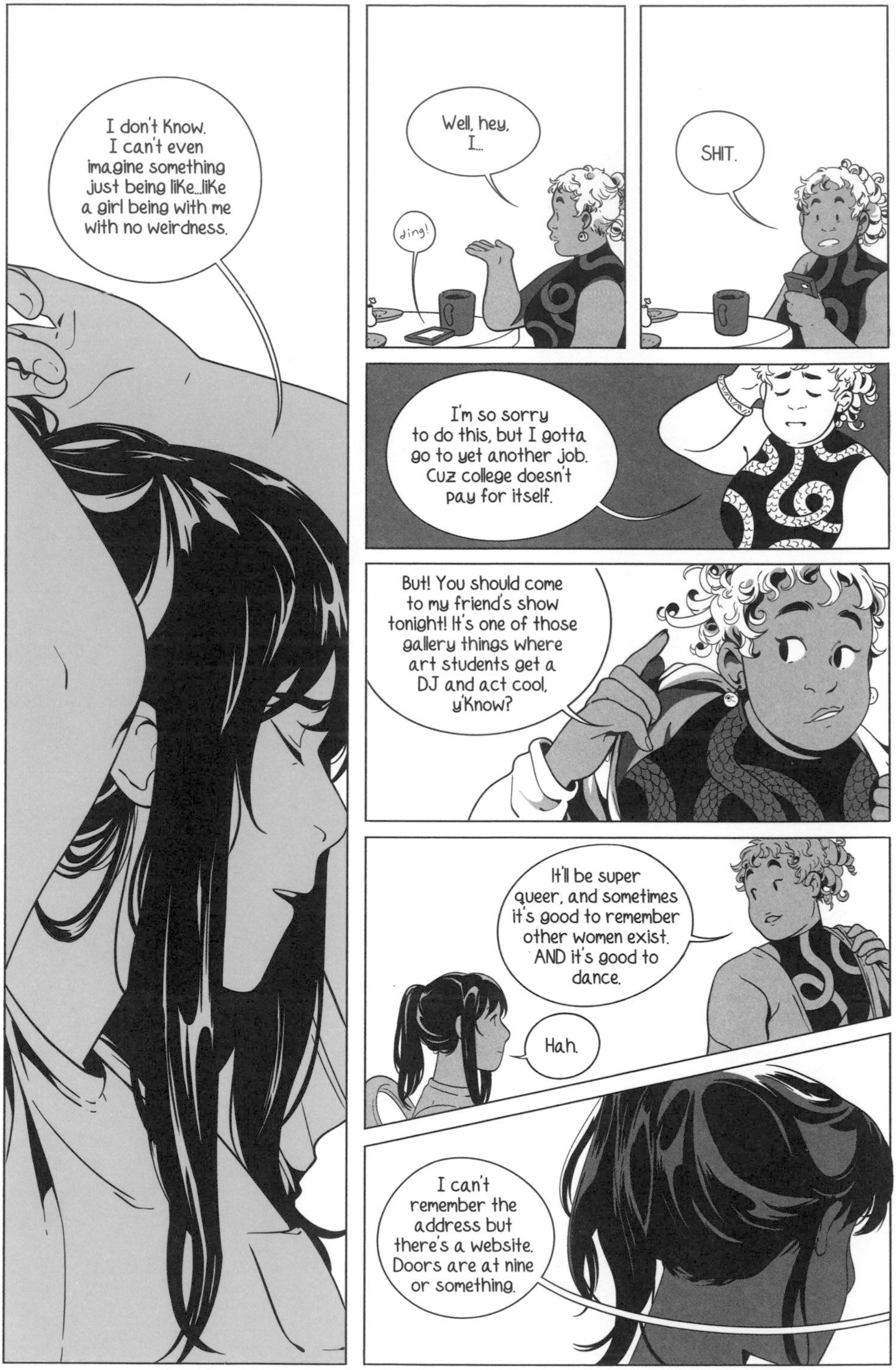
I don't Know. I can't even imagine something just being like...like a girl being with me with no weirdness.
Well, hey, I...
ding!
SHIT.
I'm so sorry to do this, but I gotta go to yet another job. Cuz college doesn't pay for itself.
But! You should come to my friend's show tonight! It's one of those gallery things where art students get a DJ and act cool, y'Know?
It'll be super queer, and sometimes it's good to remember other women exist. AND it's good to dance.
Hah.
I can't remember the address but there's a website. Doors are at nine or something.

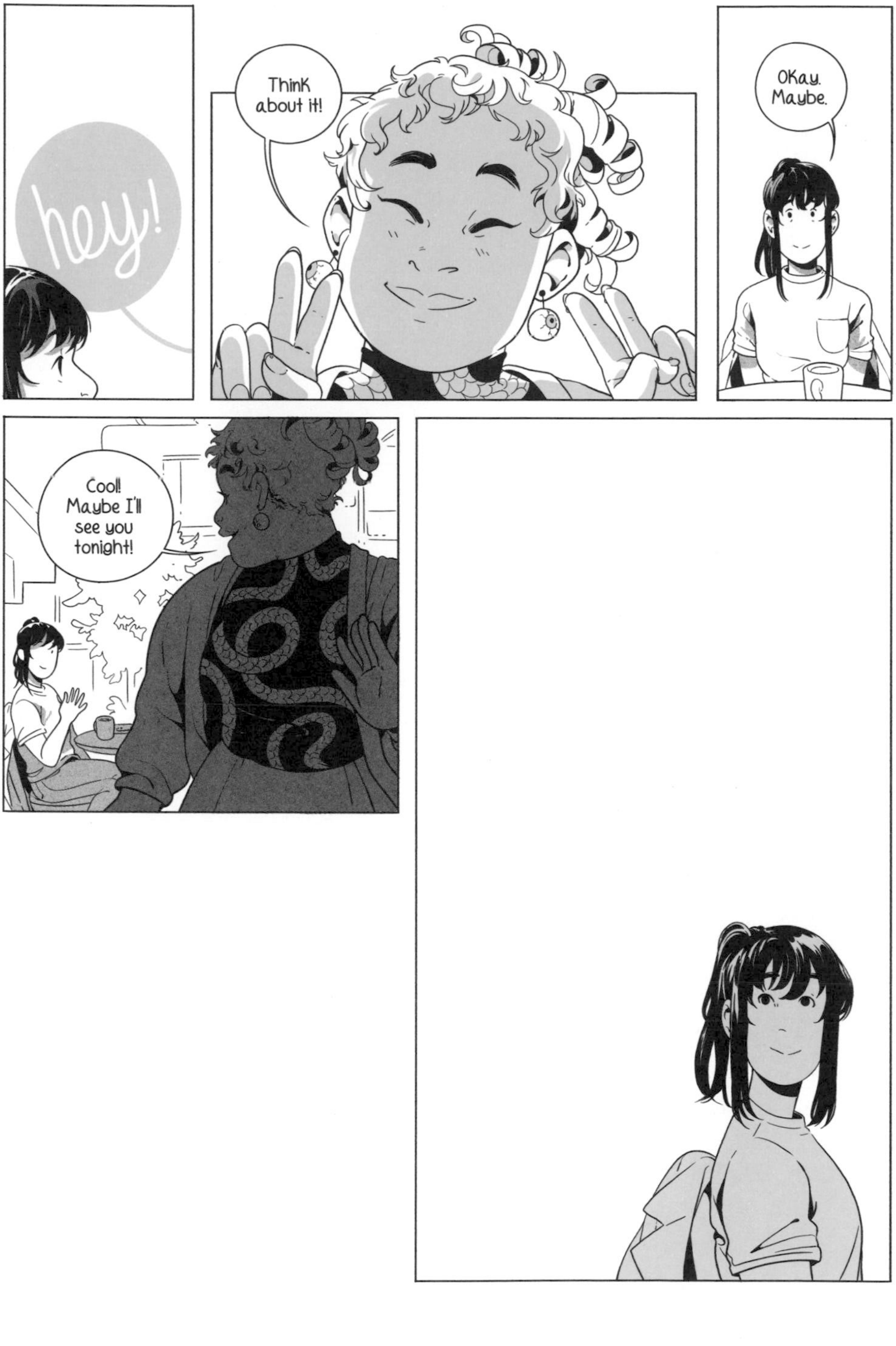
hey!
Think about it!
OKay. Maybe.
Cool! Maybe I'll see you tonight!

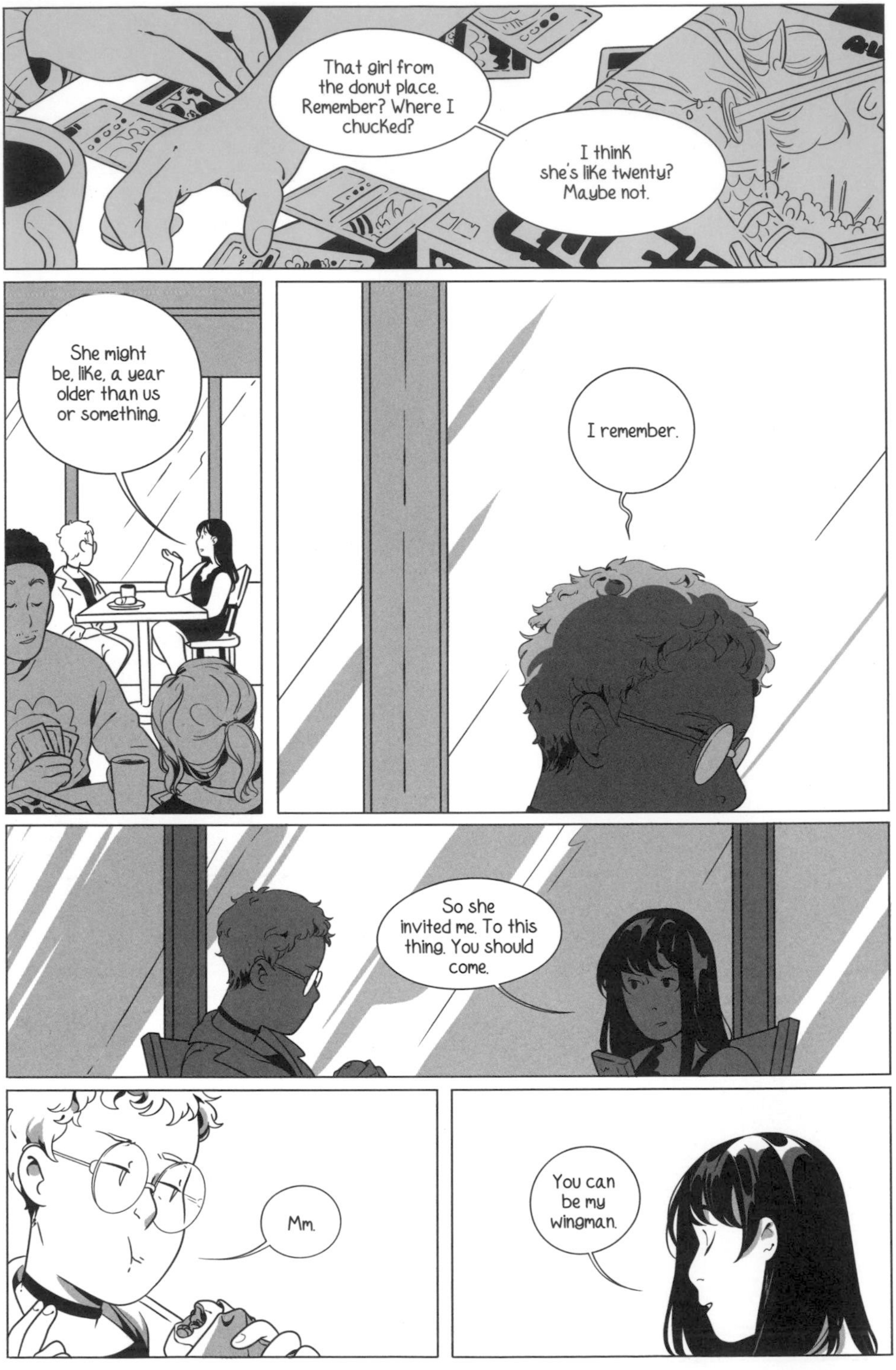
That girl from the donut place. Remember? Where I chucked?
I think she's like twenty? Maybe not.
She might be, like, a year older than us or something.
I remember.
So she invited me. To this thing. You should come.
Mm.
You can be my wingman.

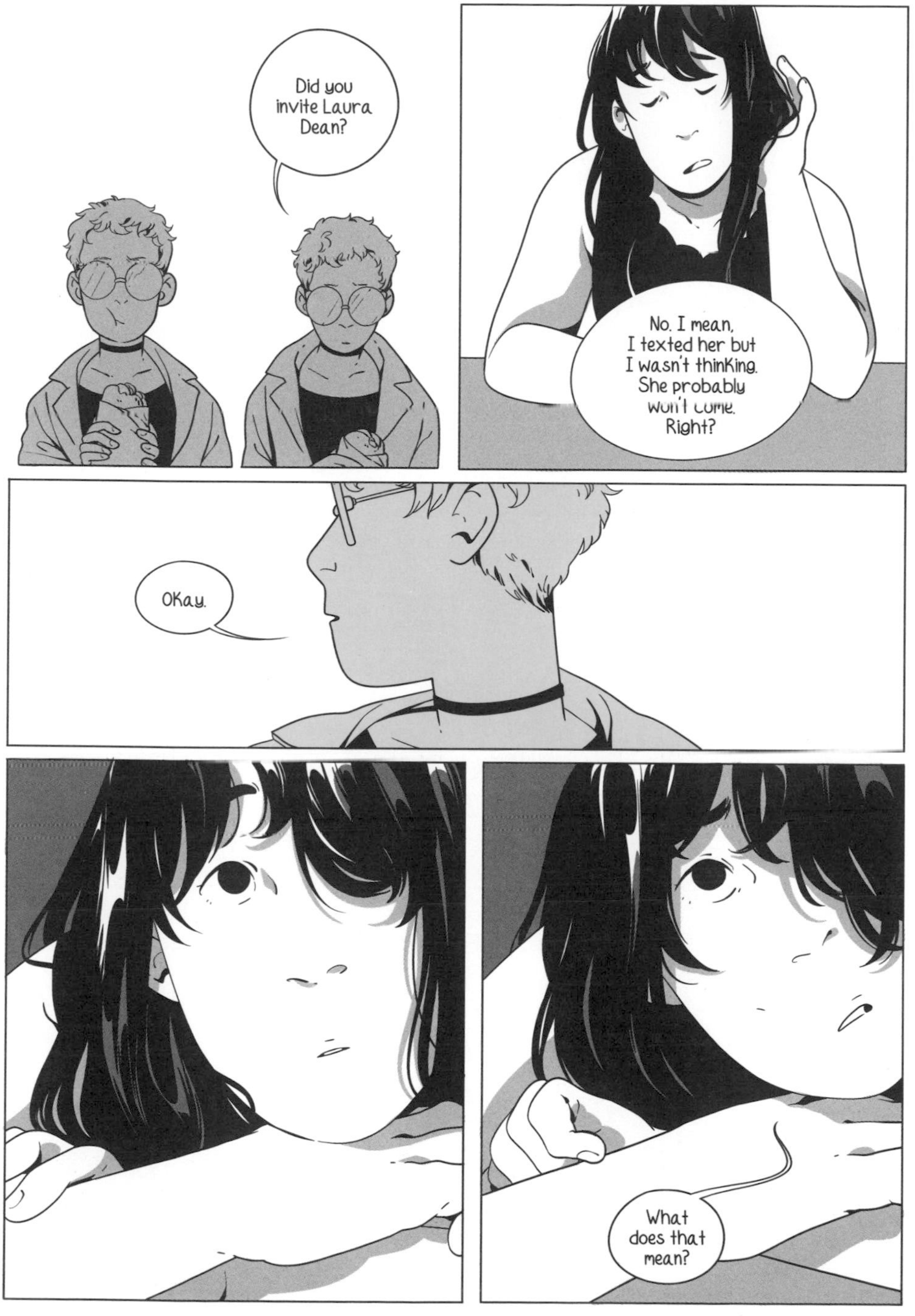

Did you invite Laura Dean?
No. I mean, I texted her but I wasn't thinking. She probably won't come. Right?
Okay.
What does that mean?

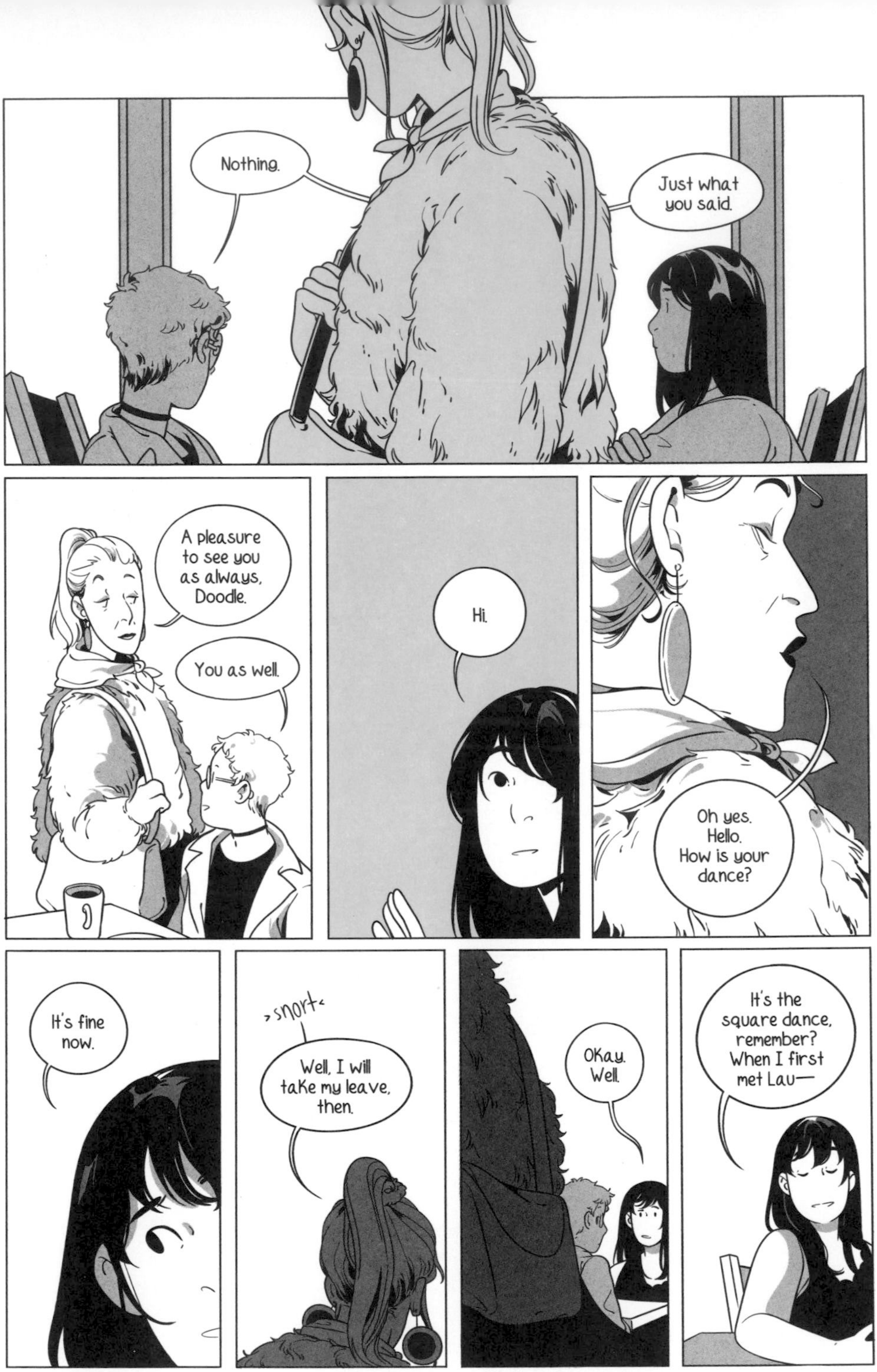

Nothing.
Just what you said.
A pleasure to see you as always, Doodle.
You as well.
Hi.
Oh yes. Hello. How is your dance?
It's fine now.
>snort<
Well, I will take my leave, then.
Okay. Well.
It's the square dance, remember? When I first met Lau—

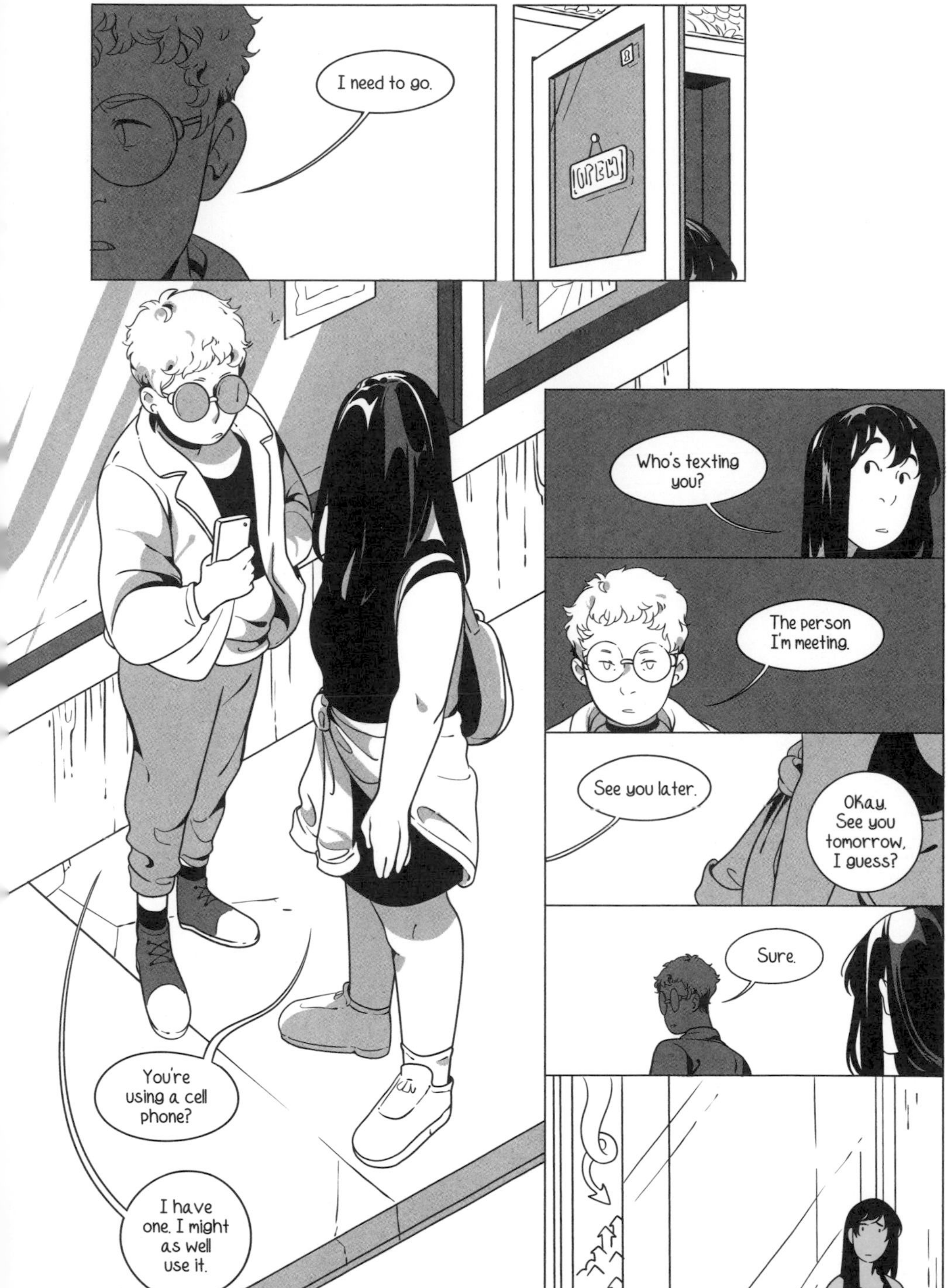

I need to go.
OPEN
Who's texting you?
The person I'm meeting.
You're using a cell phone?
I have one. I might as well use it.
See you later.
OKay. See you tomorrow, I guess?
Sure.

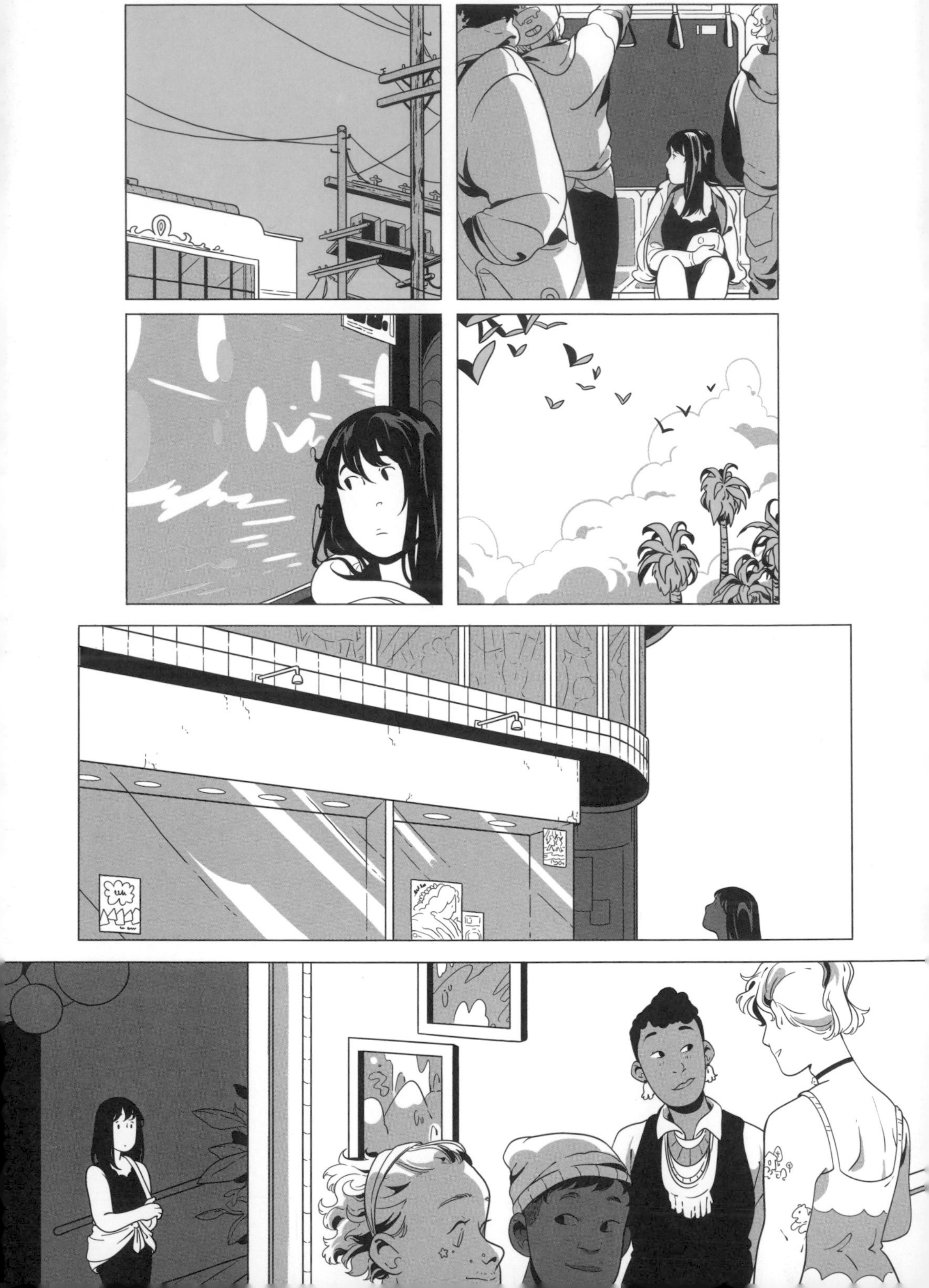

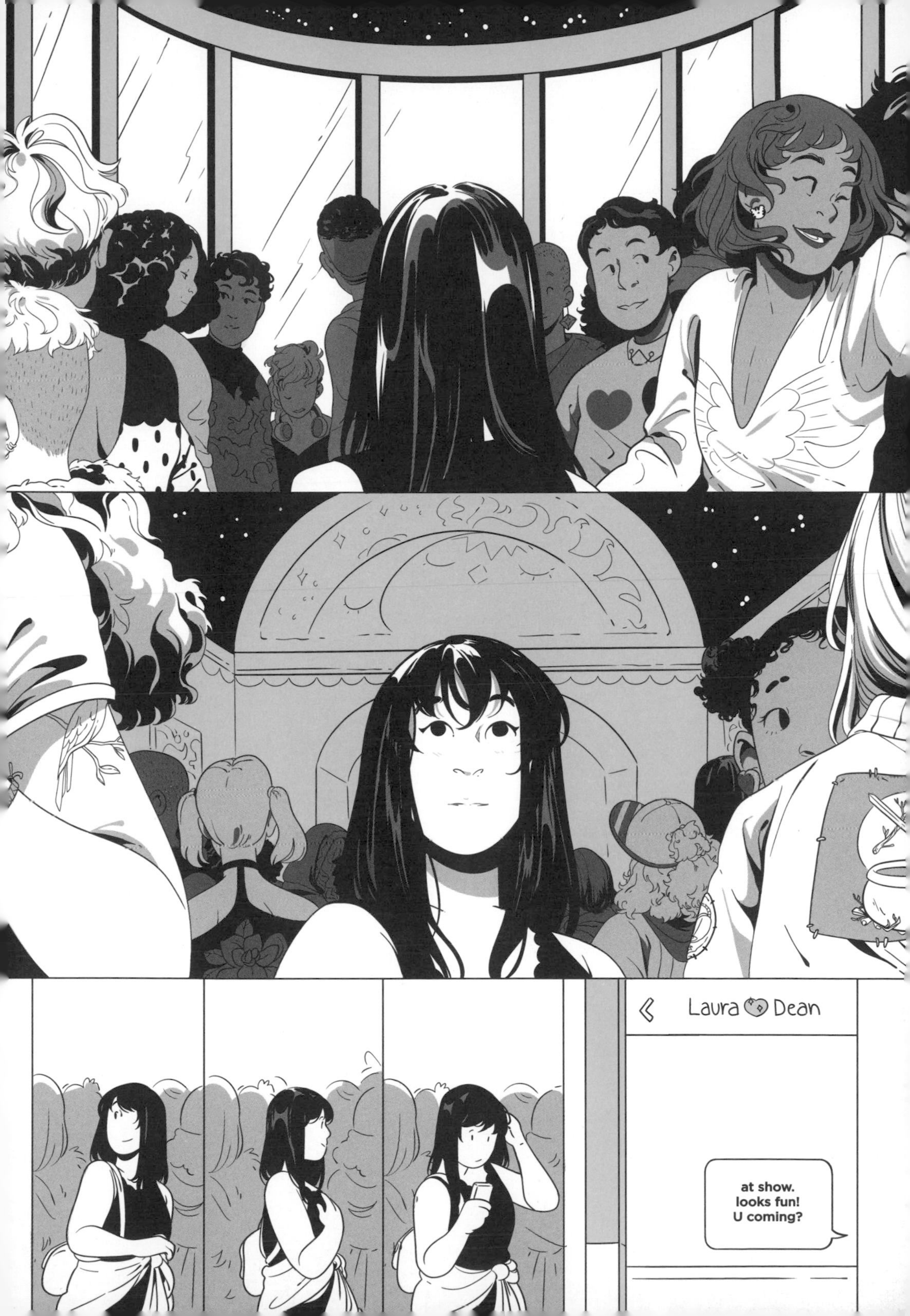
Laura Dean
at show.
looks fun!
U coming?

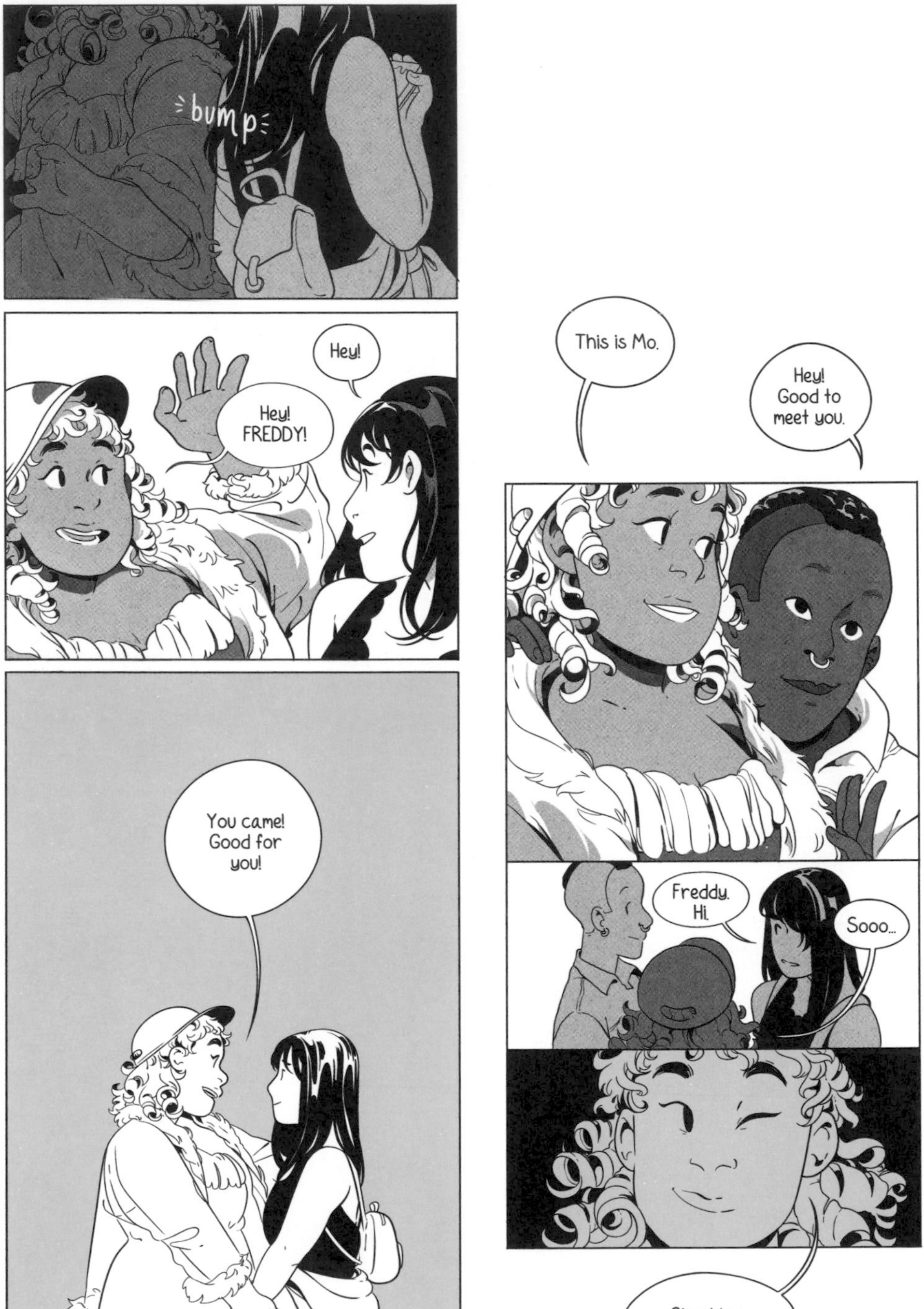
bump
Hey!
Hey! FREDDY!
You came! Good for you!
This is Mo.
Hey! Good to meet you.
Freddy. Hi.
Sooo...
Should we DANCE?

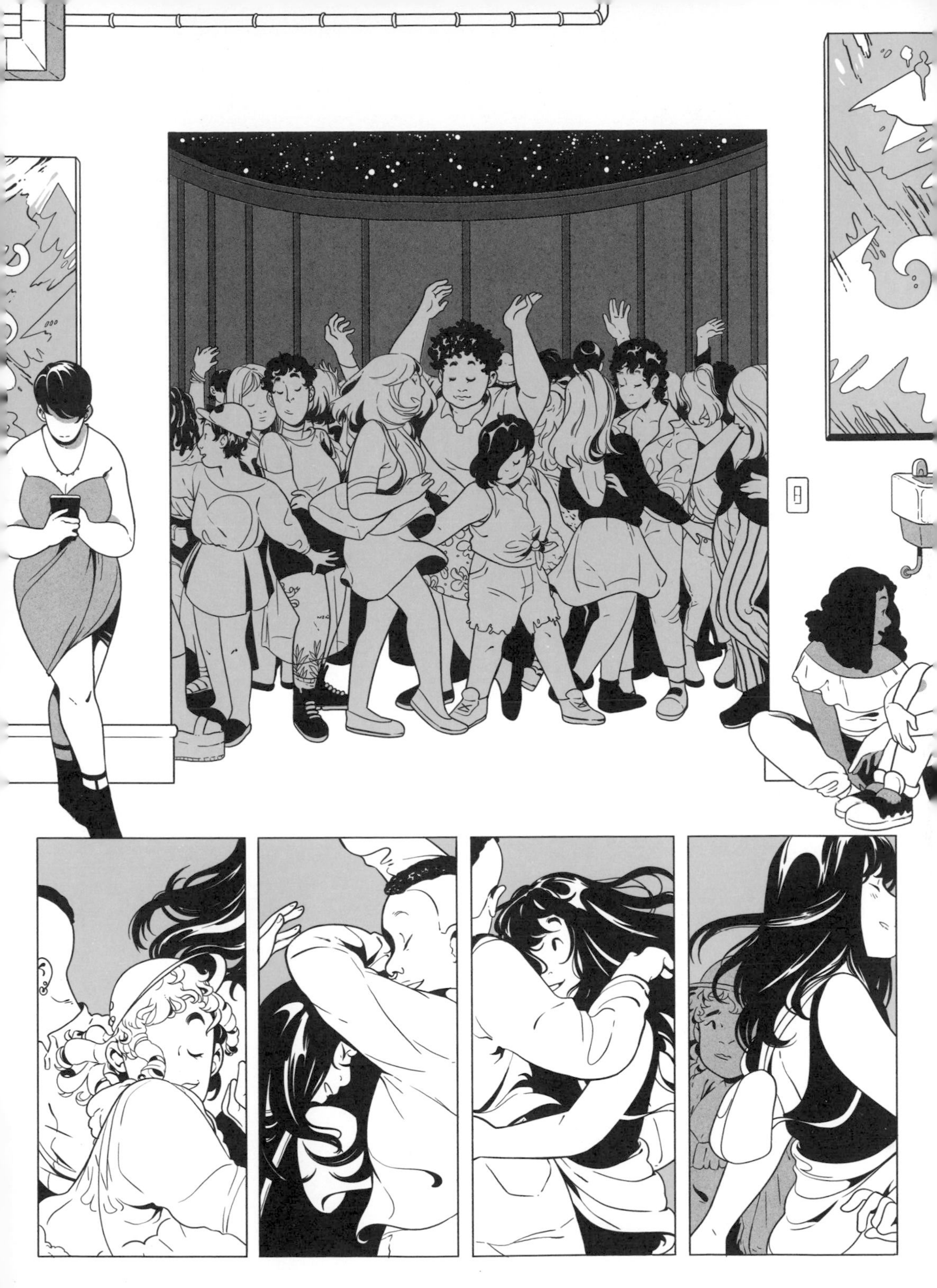

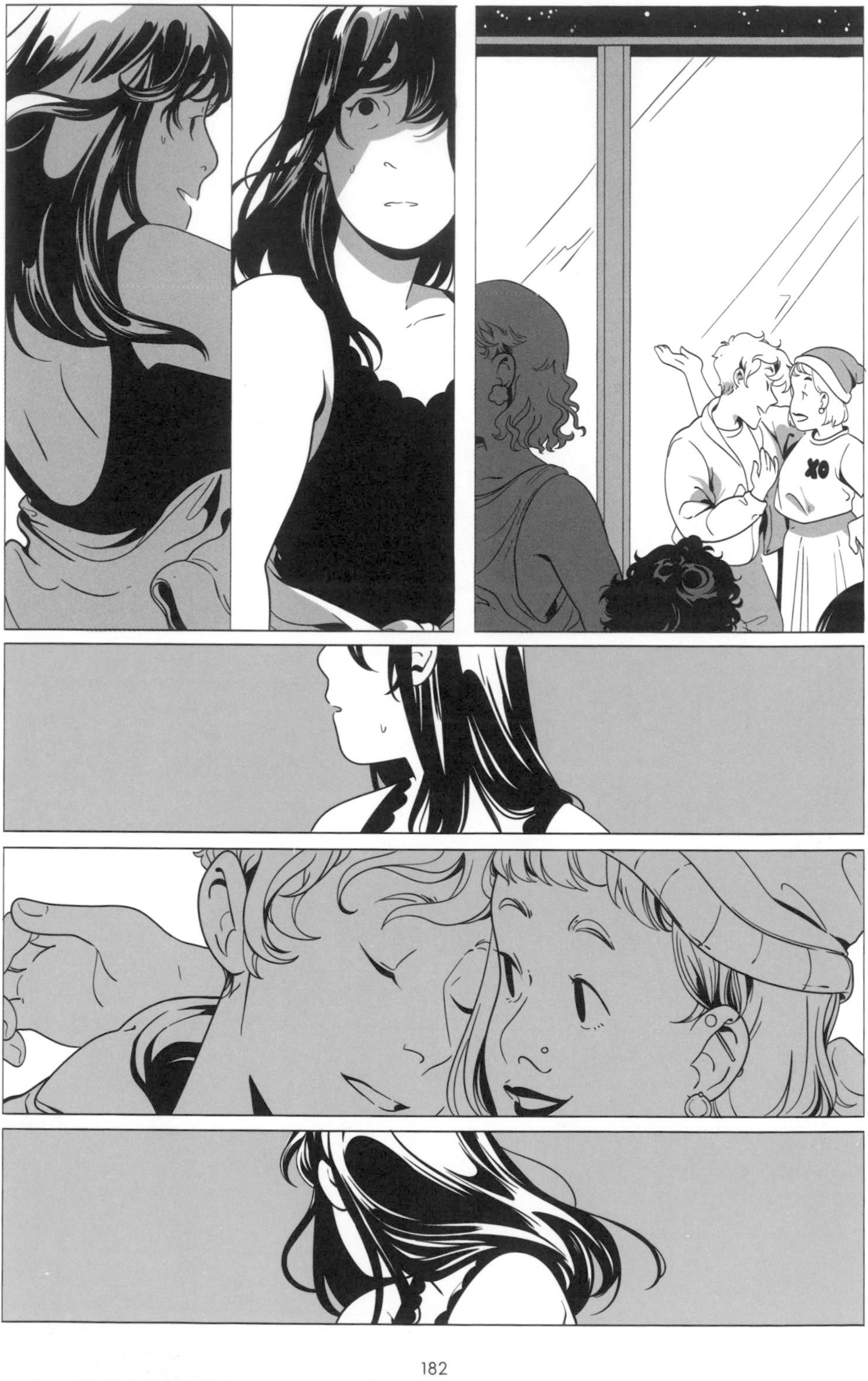
XO

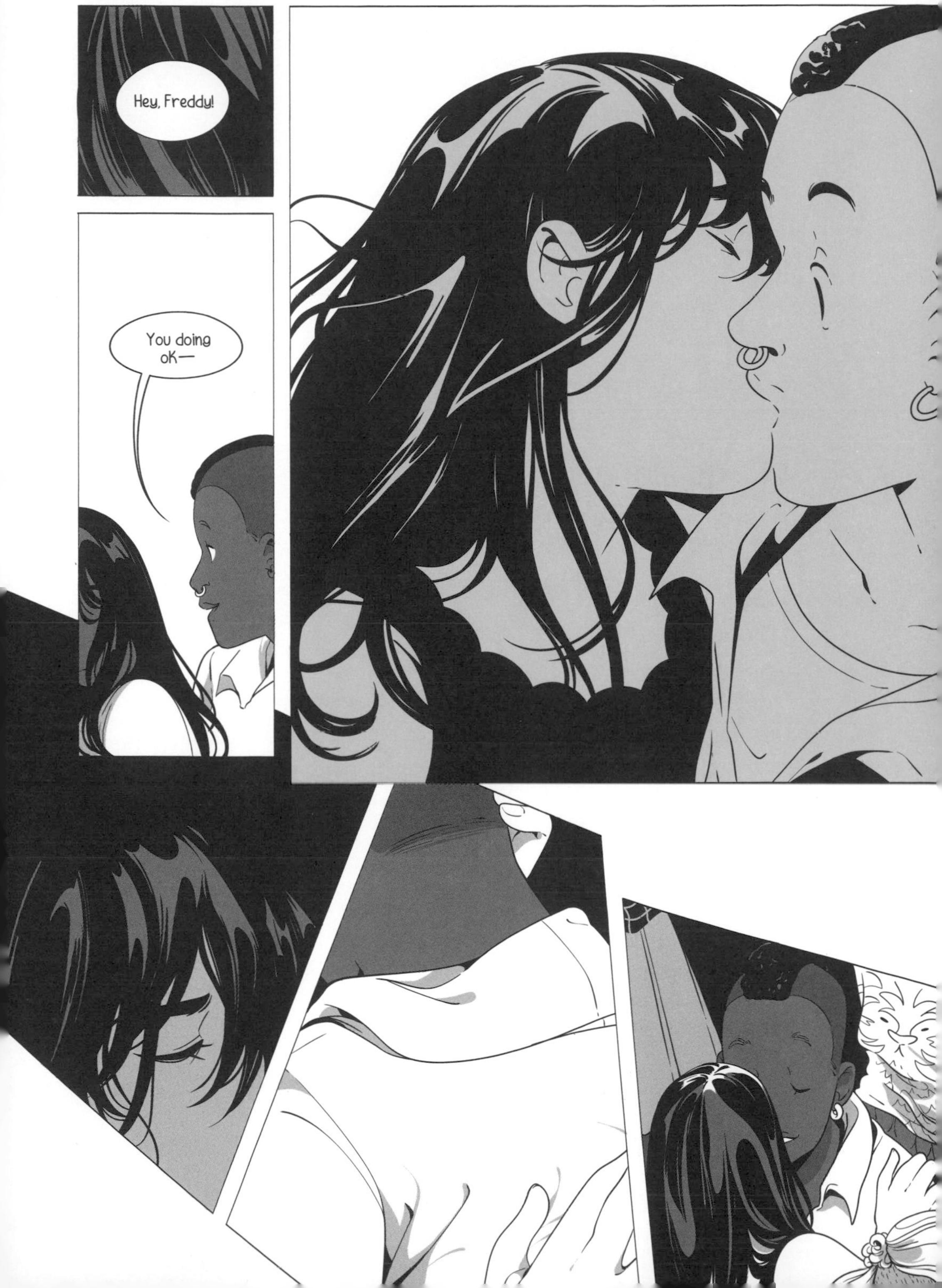
Hey, Freddy!
You doing oK—

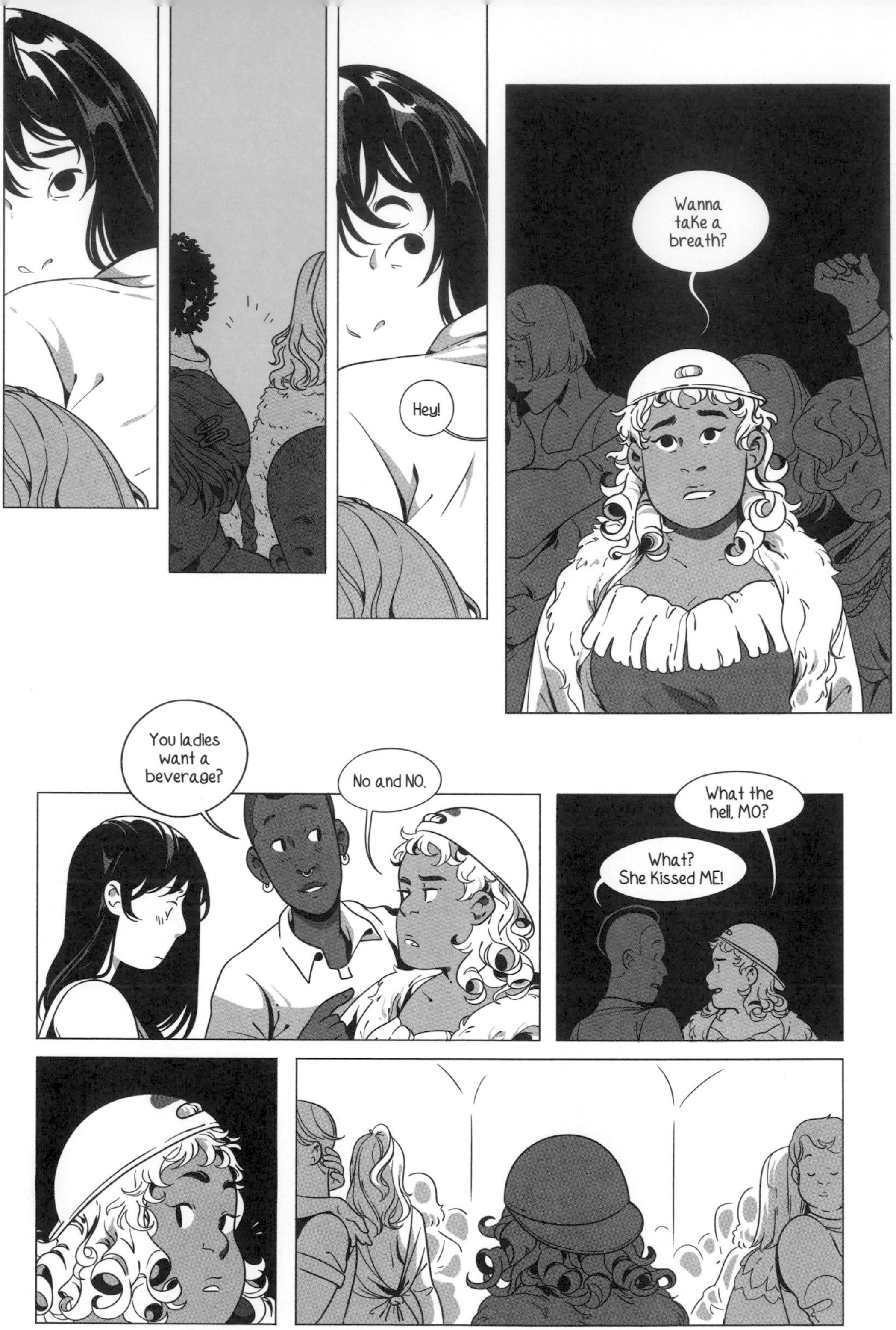
Hey!
Wanna take a breath?
You ladies want a beverage?
No and NO.
What the hell, MO?
What? She Kissed ME!

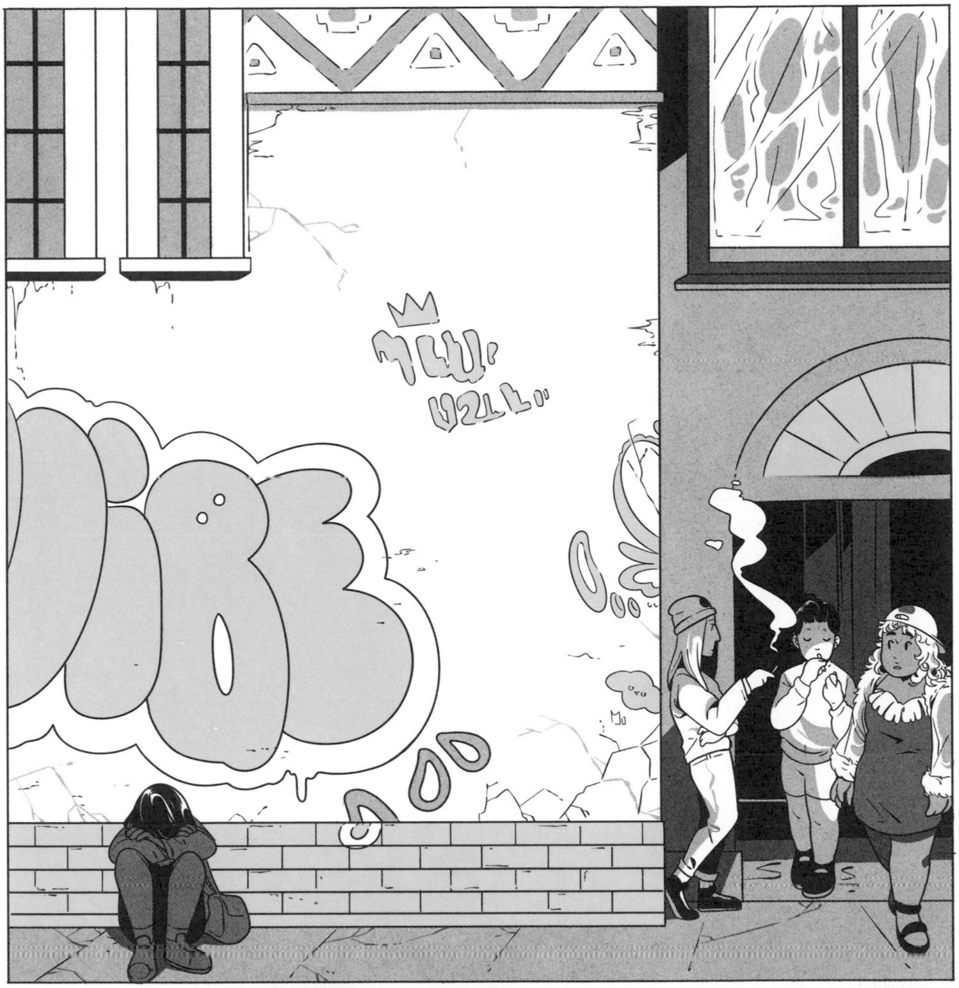

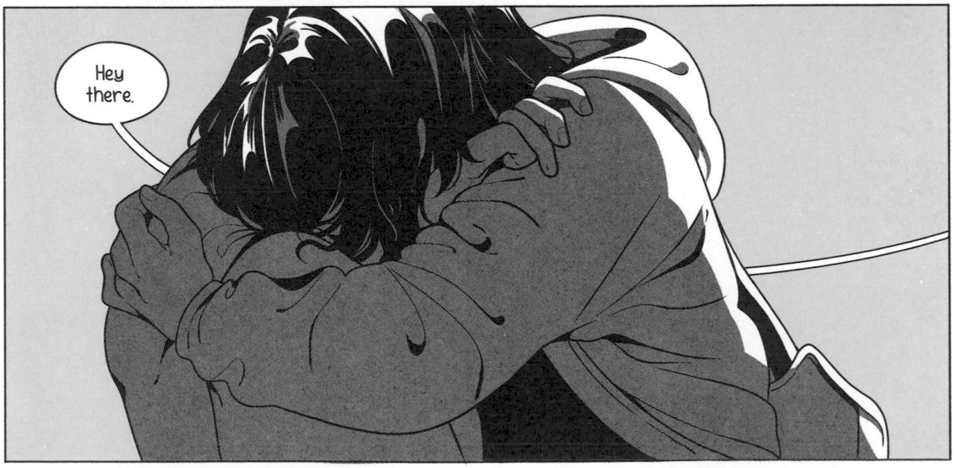
Hey there.

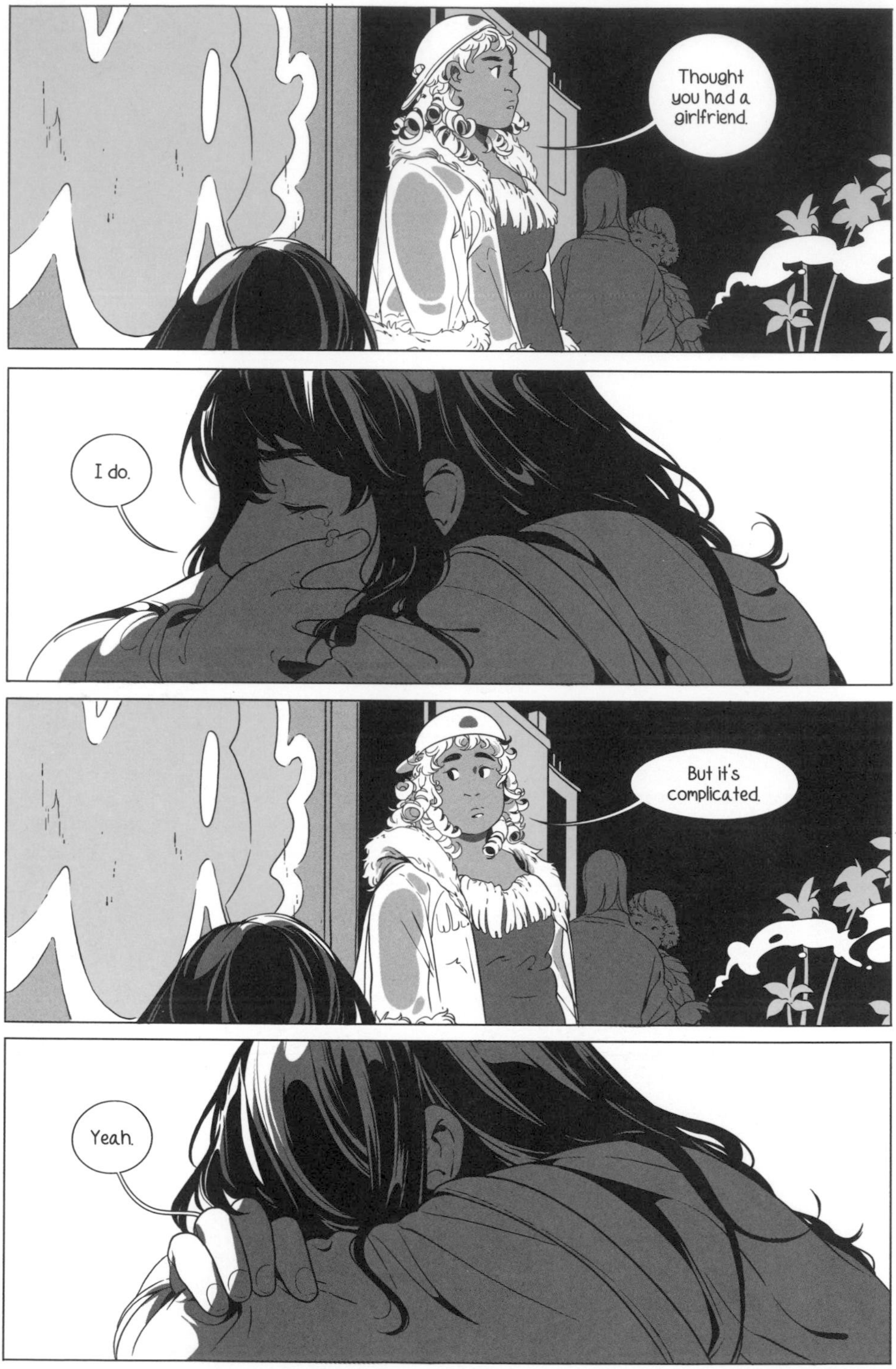
Thought you had a girlfriend.
I do.
But it's complicated.
Yeah.

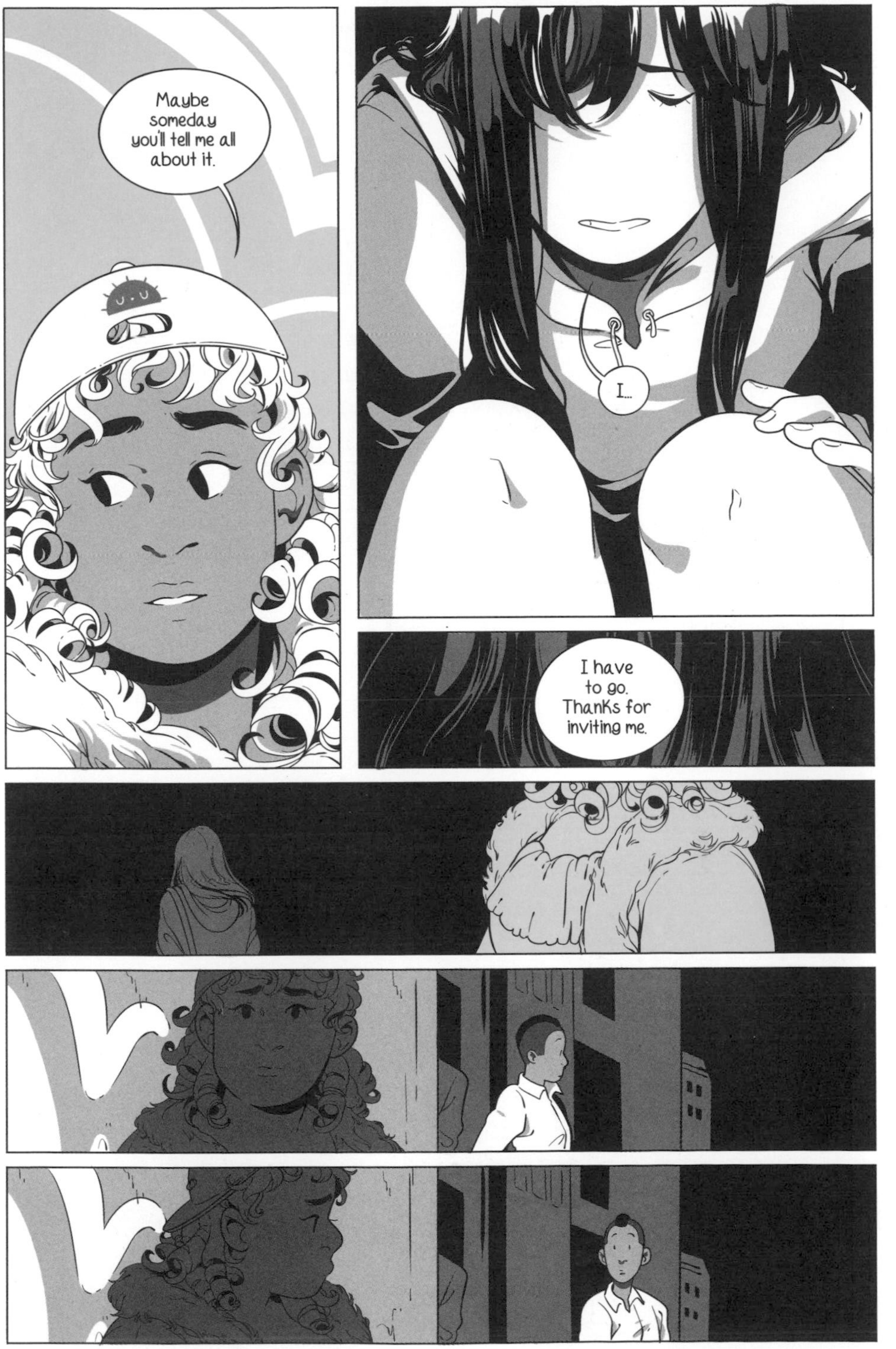
Maybe someday you'll tell me all about it.
I...
I have to go. Thanks for inviting me.

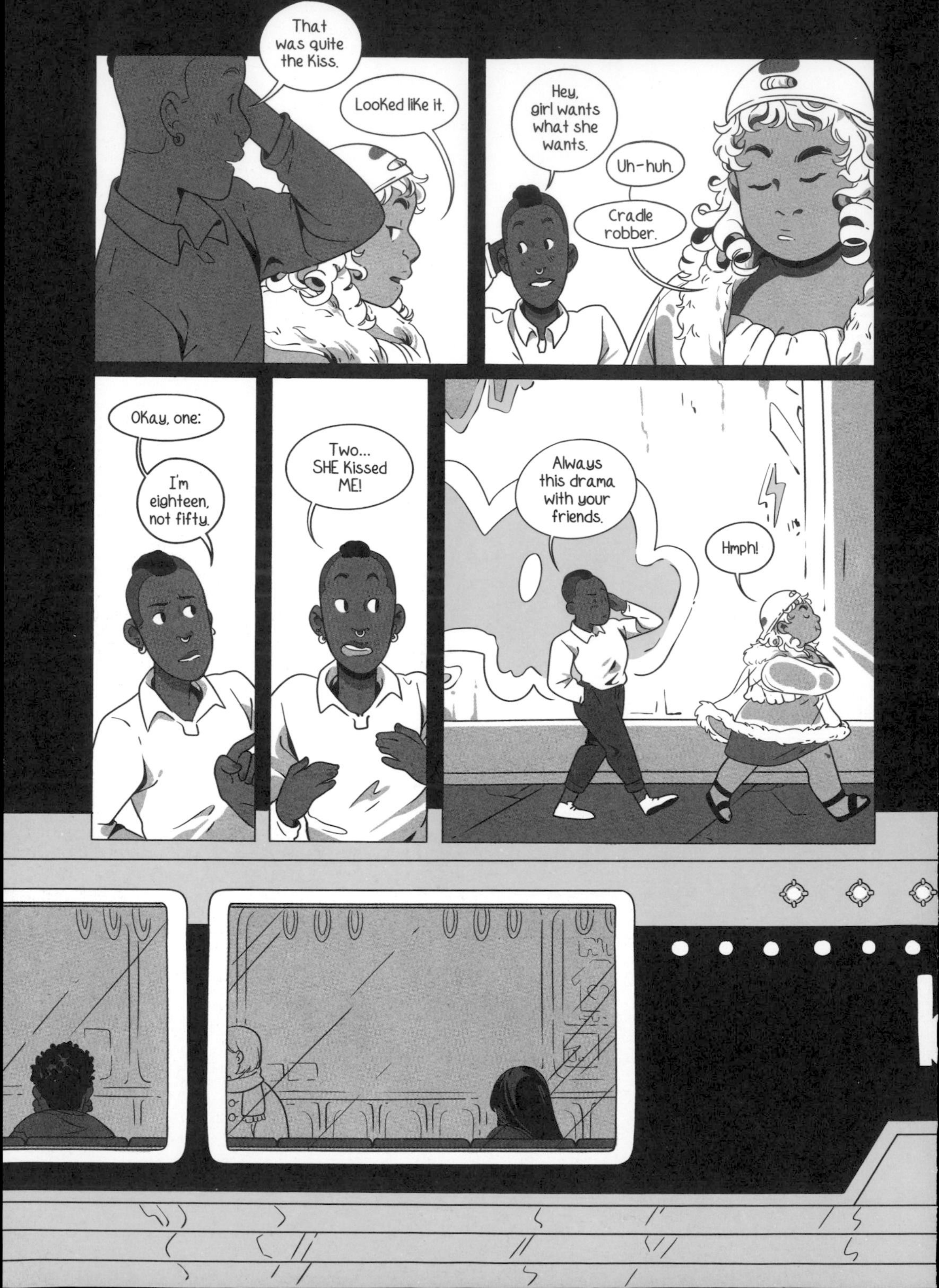
That was quite the kiss.
Looked like it.
Hey, girl wants what she wants.
Uh-huh.
Cradle robber.
Okay, one:
I'm eighteen, not fifty.
Two... SHE kissed ME!
Always this drama with your friends.
Hmph!

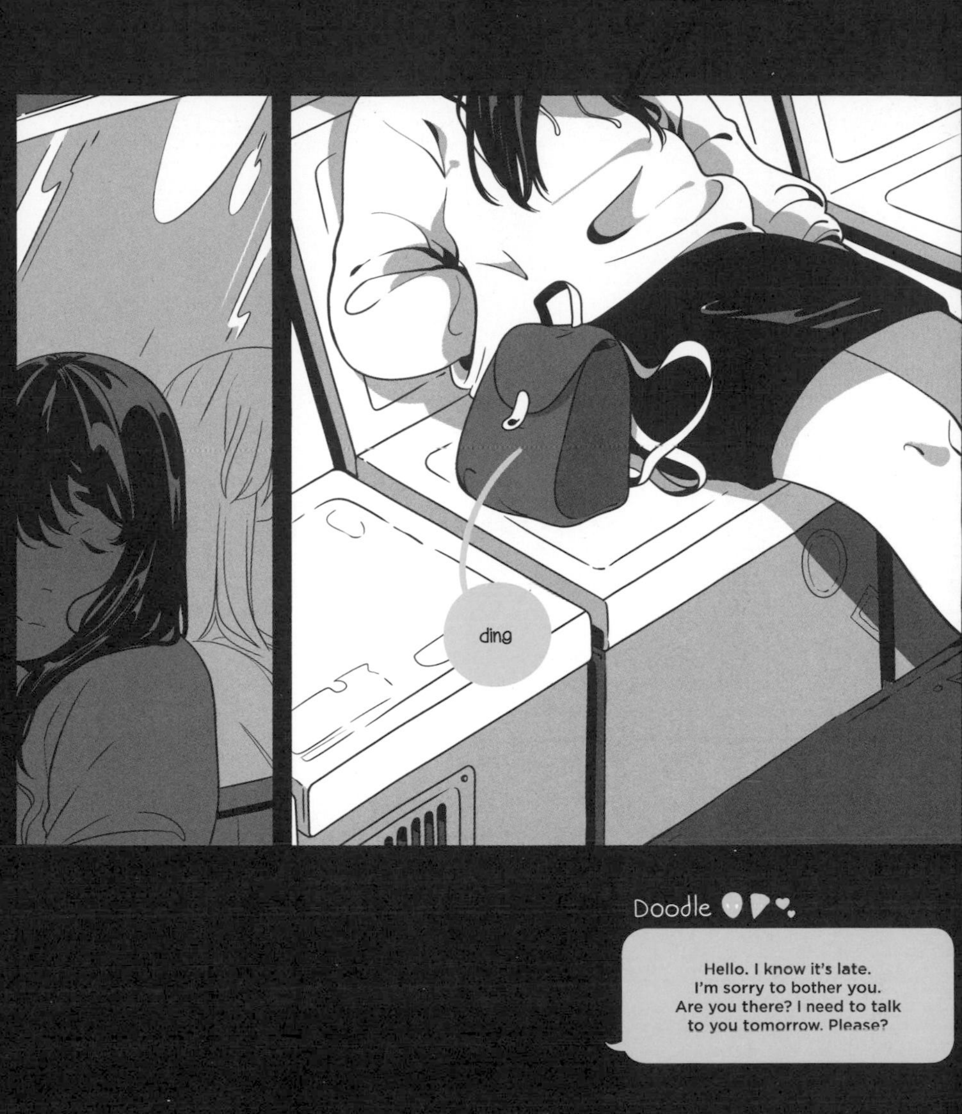
ding
Doodle
Hello. I know it's late.
I'm sorry to bother you.
Are you there? I need to talk
to you tomorrow. Please?

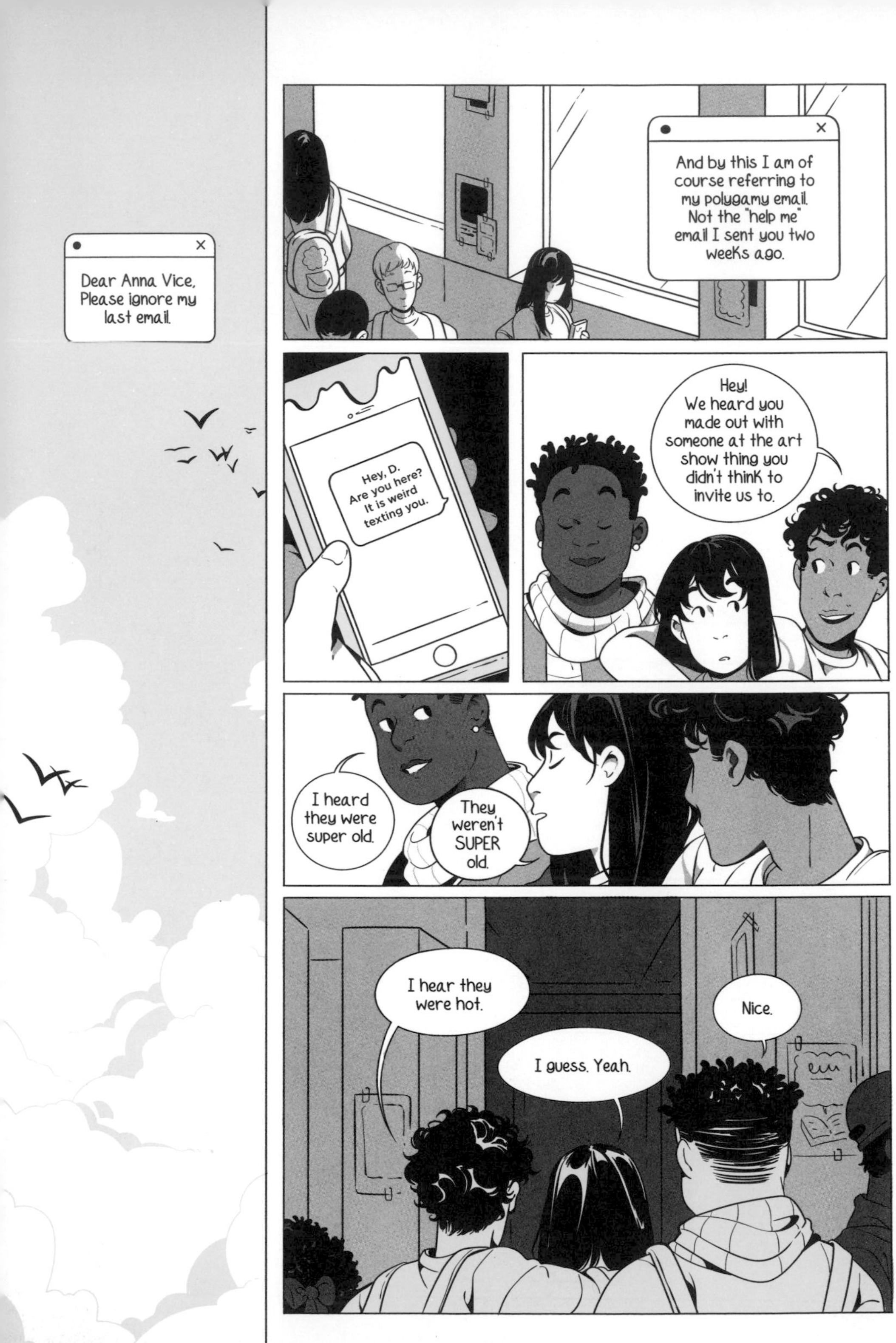
Dear Anna Vice, Please ignore my last email.
And by this I am of course referring to my polygamy email. Not the "help me" email I sent you two weeks ago.
Hey, D. Are you here? It is weird texting you.
Hey! We heard you made out with someone at the art show thing you didn't think to invite us to.
I heard they were super old.
They weren't SUPER old.
I hear they were hot.
Nice.
I guess. Yeah.

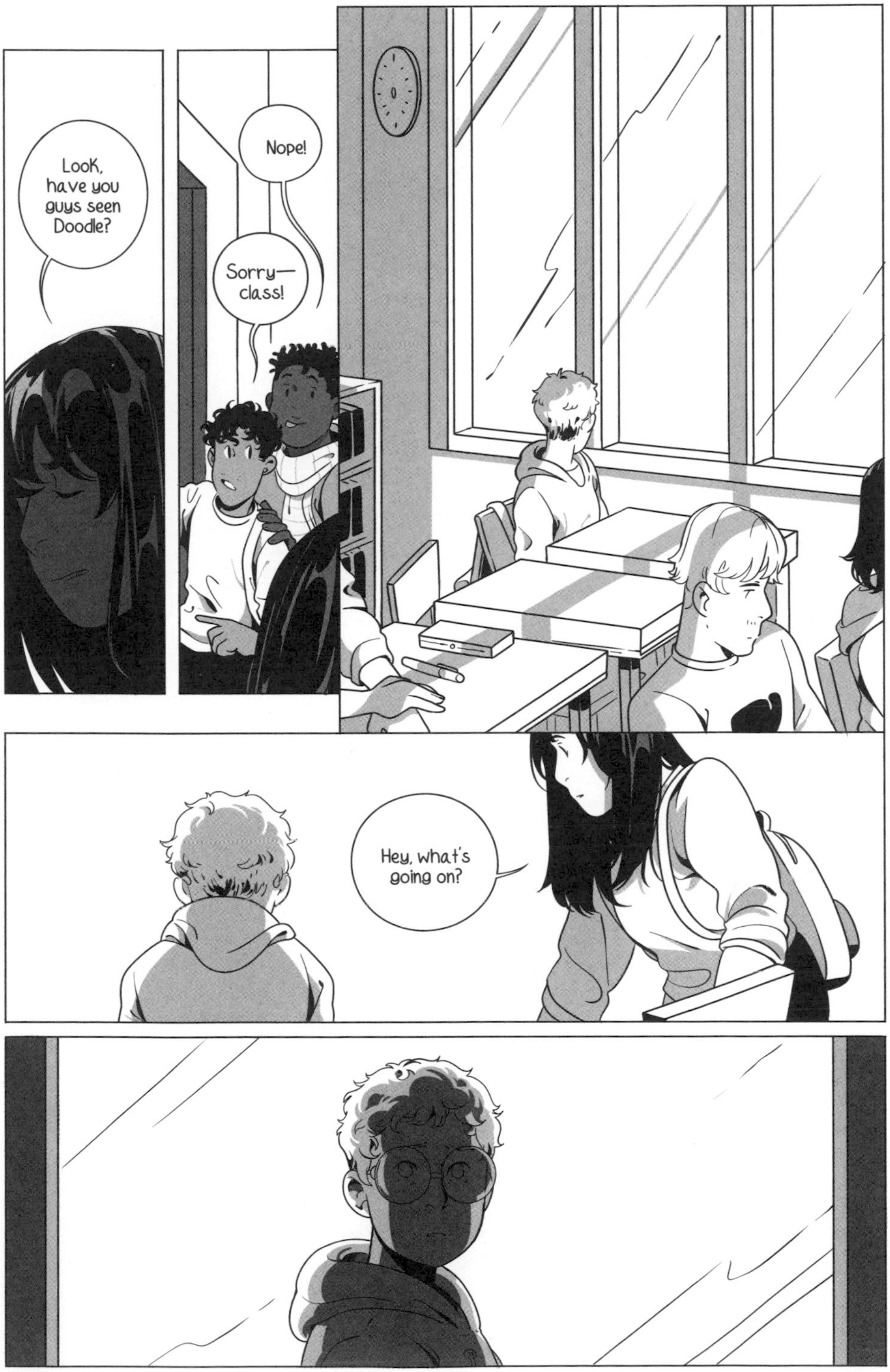
LooK, have you guys seen Doodle?
Nope!
Sorry—class!
Hey, what's going on?

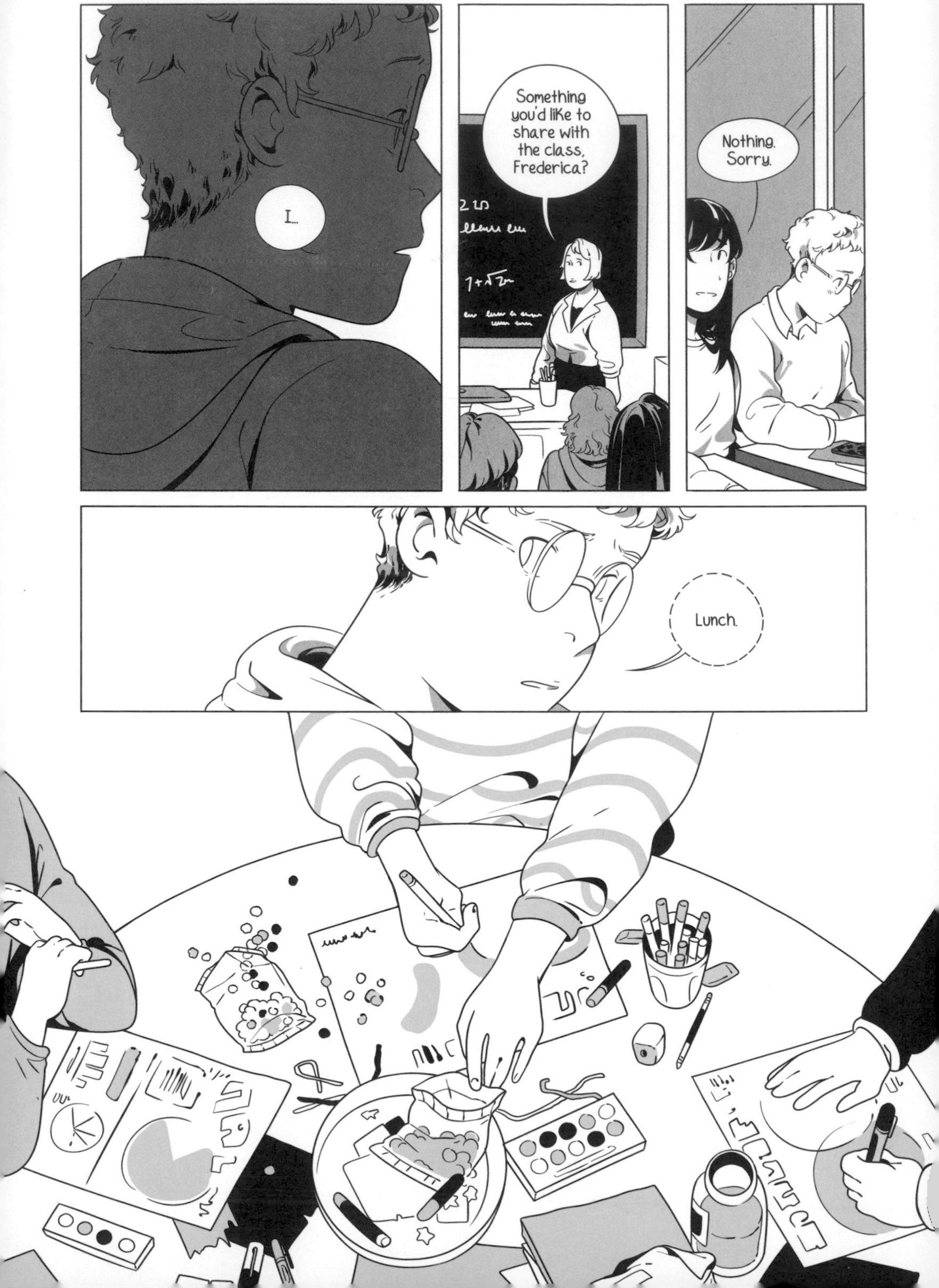
I...
Something you'd like to share with the class, Frederica?
Nothing. Sorry.
Lunch.

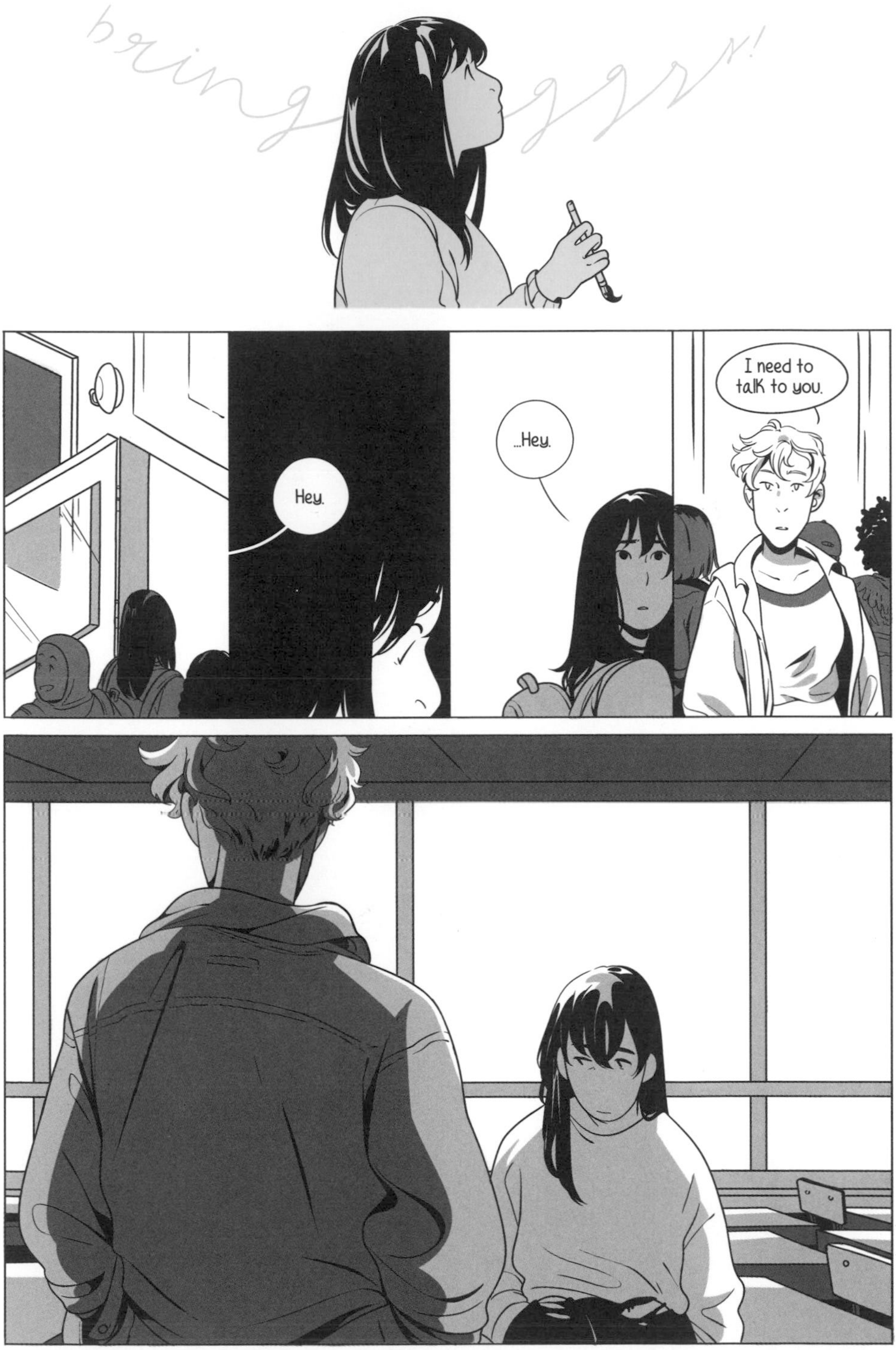
bringggrr!
Hey.
...Hey.
I need to talk to you.

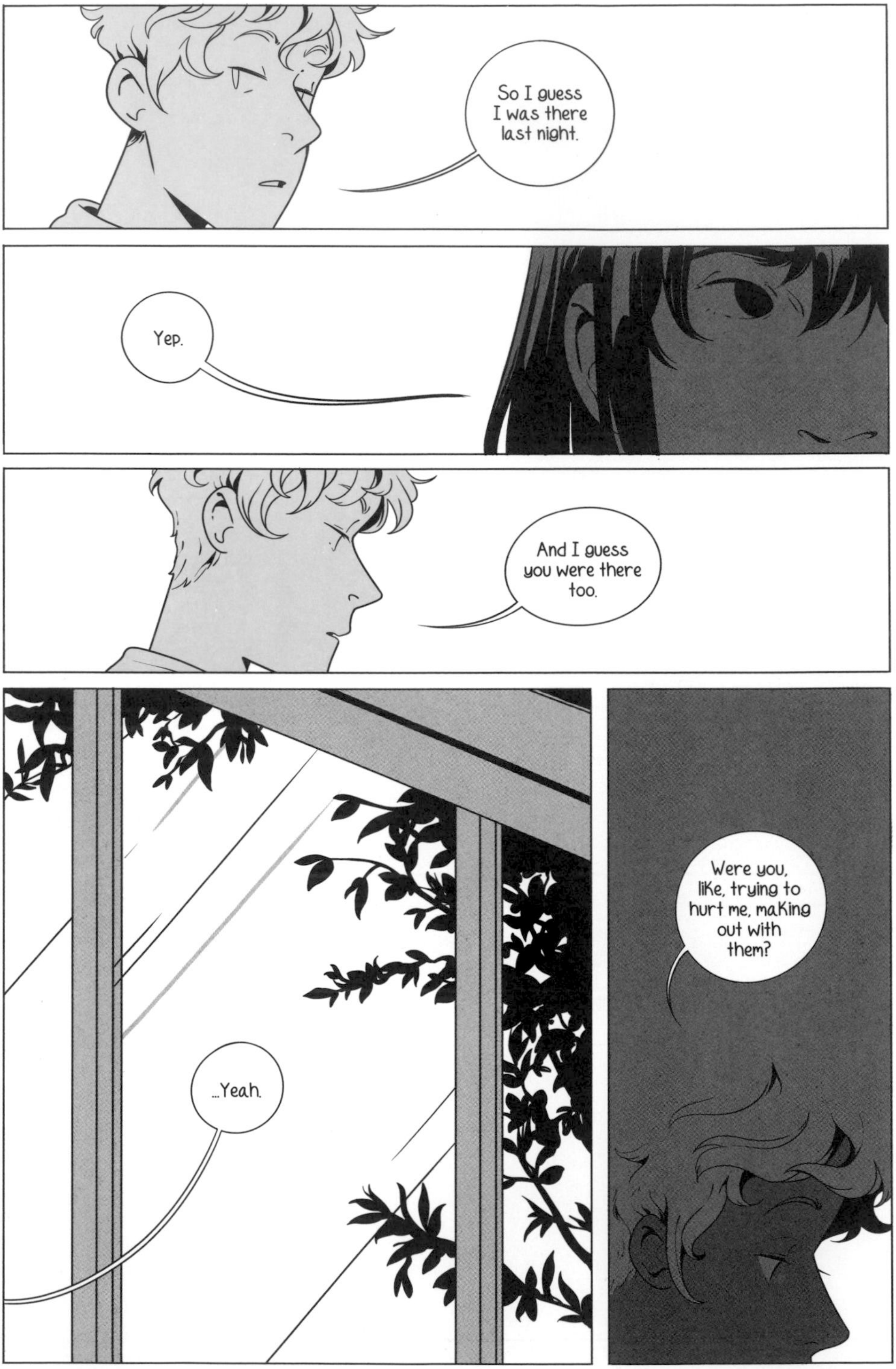
So I guess I was there last night.
Yep.
And I guess you were there too.
Were you, like, trying to hurt me, making out with them?
...Yeah.

No!
Of course
not...

So you
just got
caught up in
the moment.

Yeah.

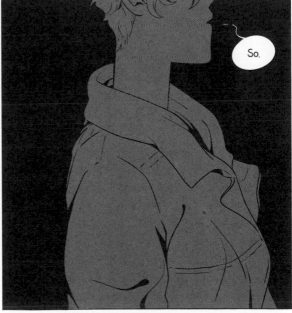

So.

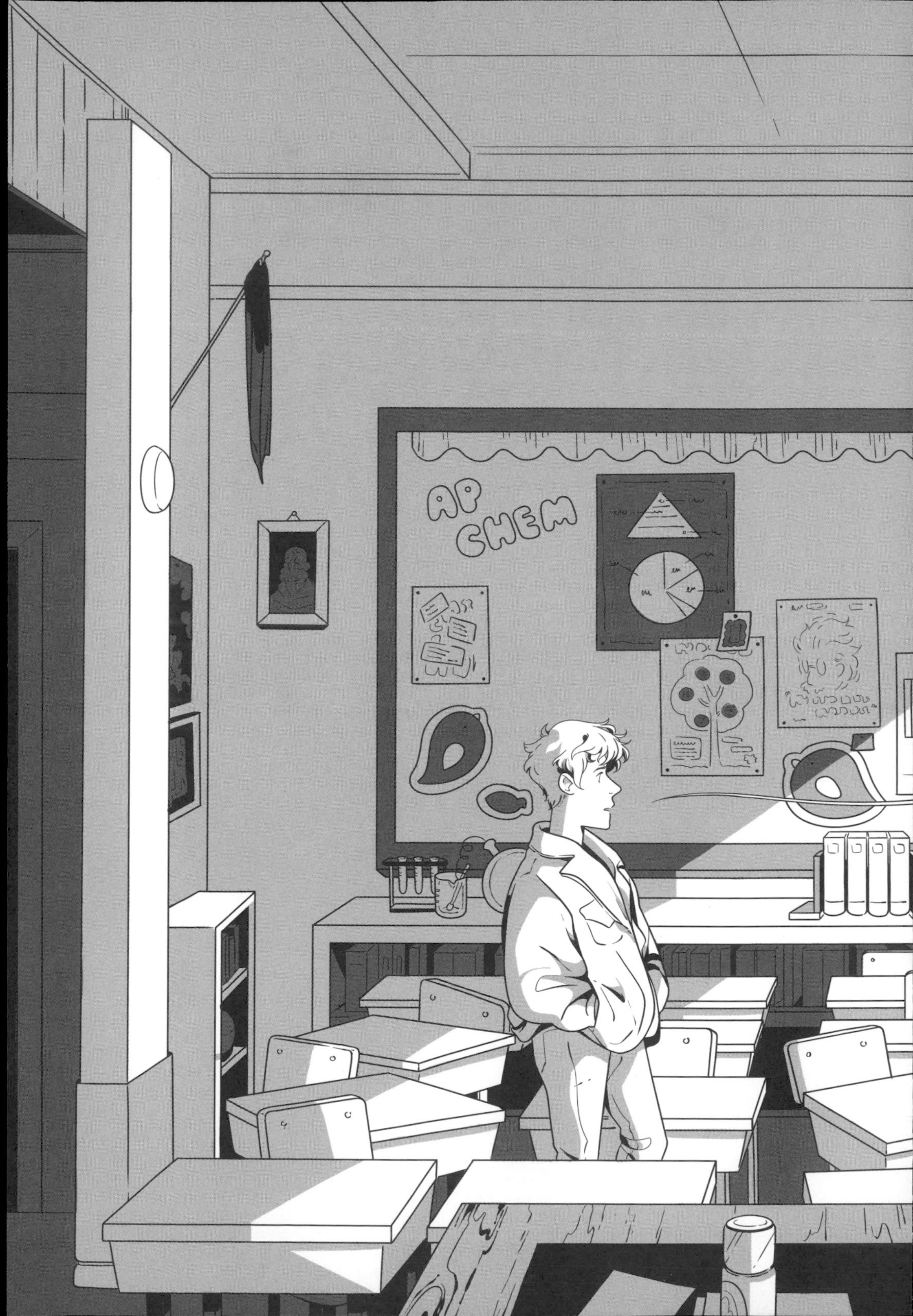
AP
CHEM

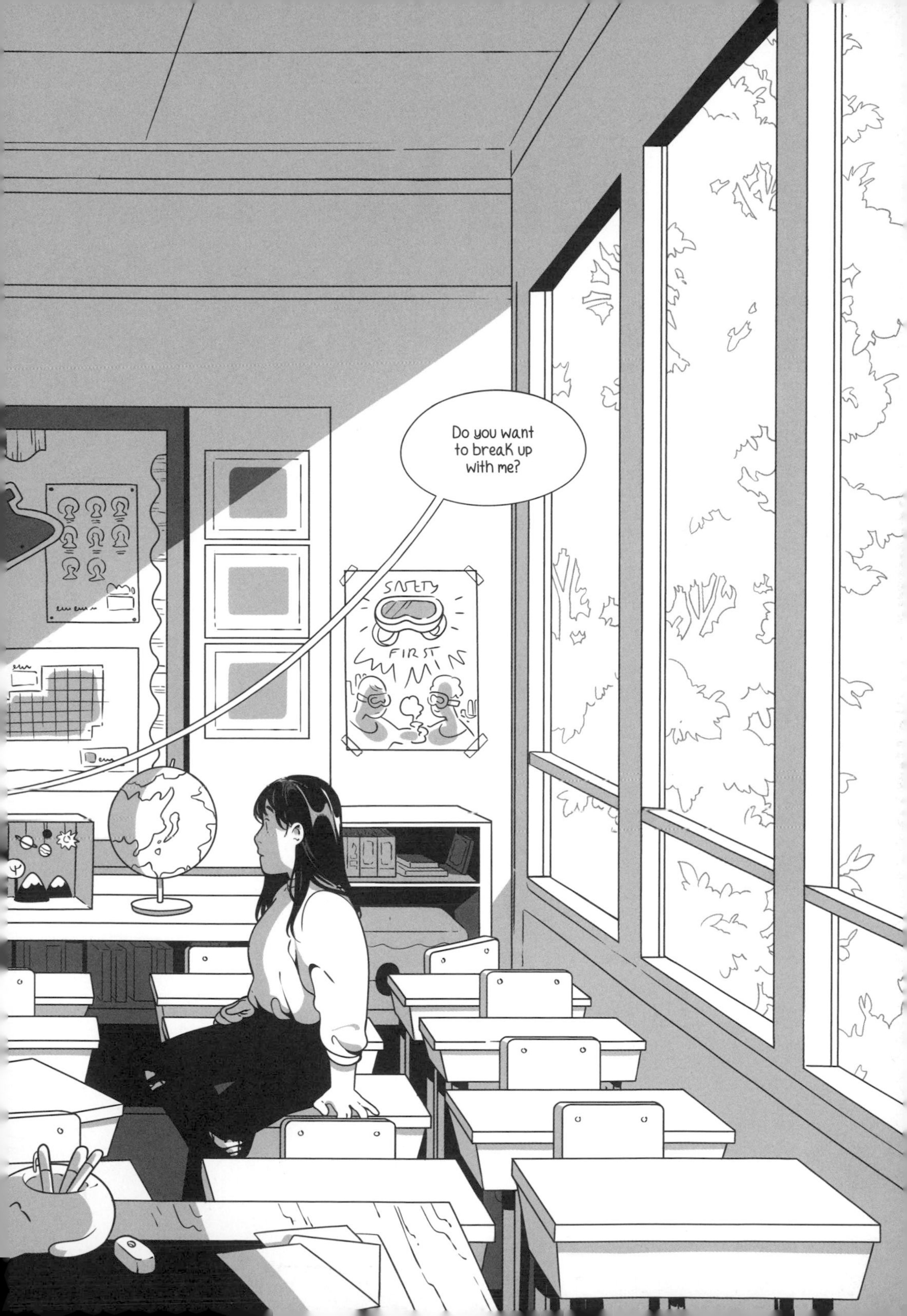
Do you want to break up with me?
SAFETY
FIRST

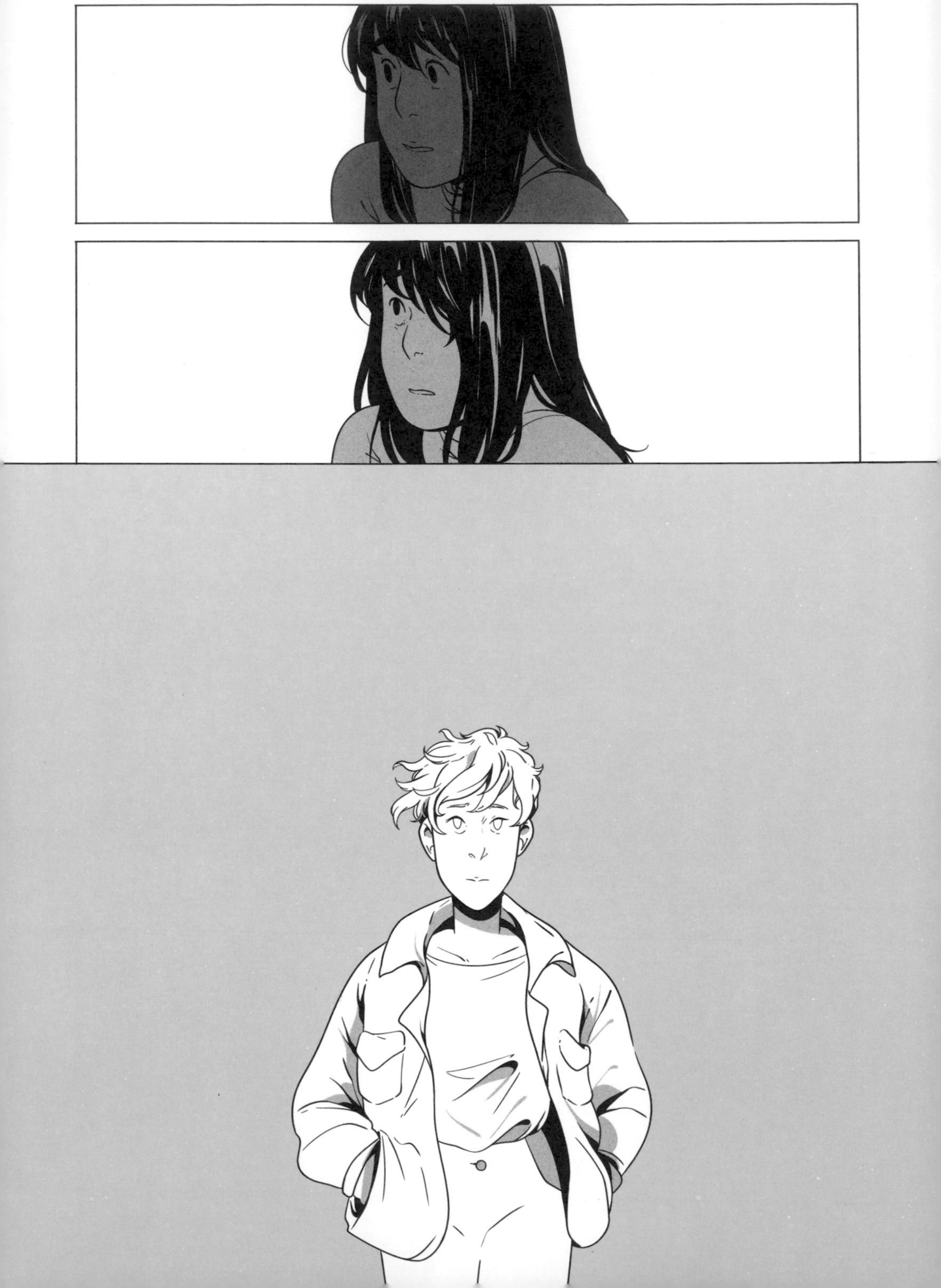

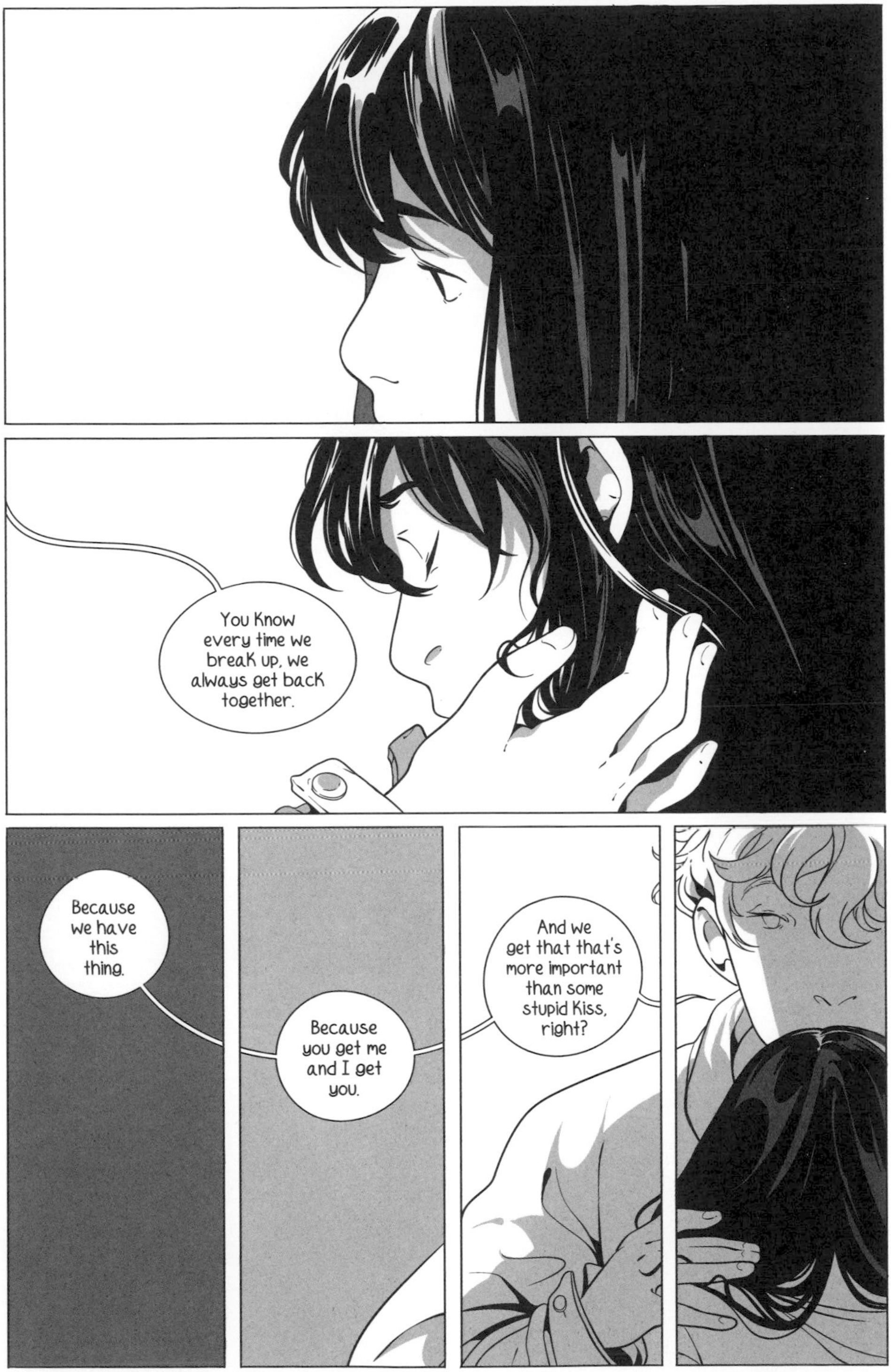
You Know every time we break up, we always get back together.
Because we have this thing.
Because you get me and I get you.
And we get that that's more important than some stupid Kiss, right?

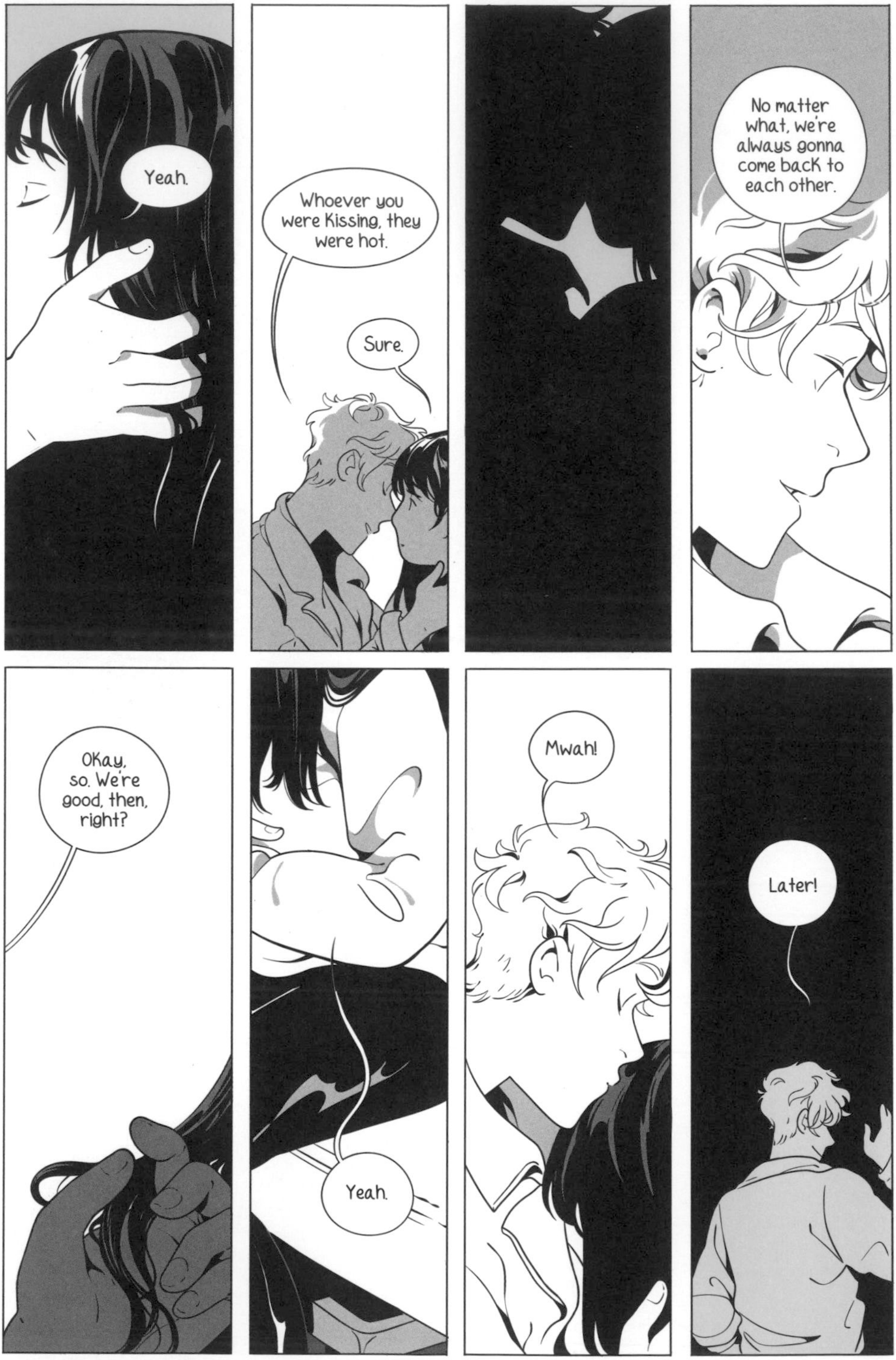
Yeah.
Whoever you were Kissing, they were hot.
Sure.
No matter what, we're always gonna come back to each other.
OKay, so. We're good, then, right?
Yeah.
Mwah!
Later!

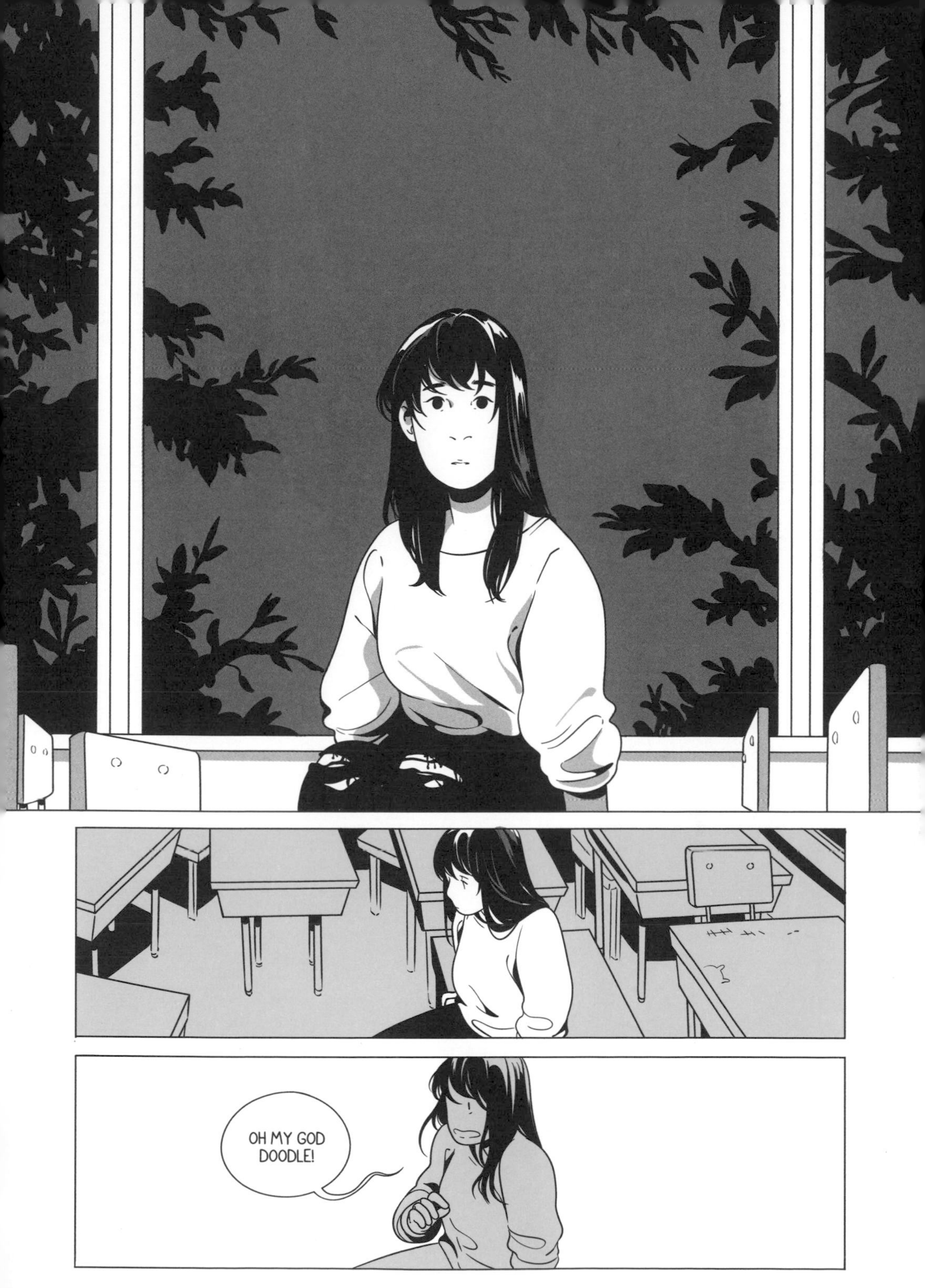
OH MY GOD
DOODLE!

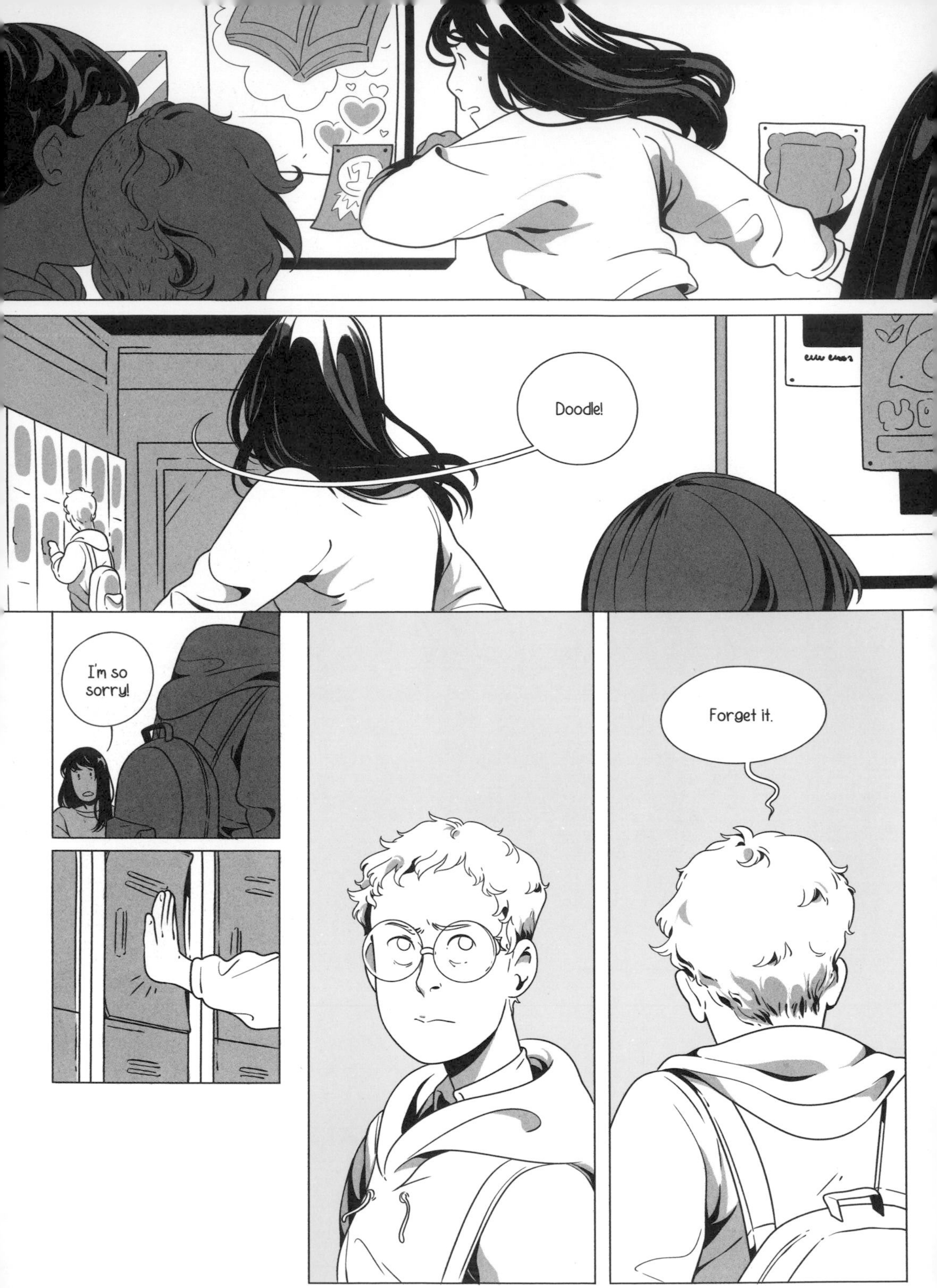
Doodle!
I'm so sorry!
Forget it.

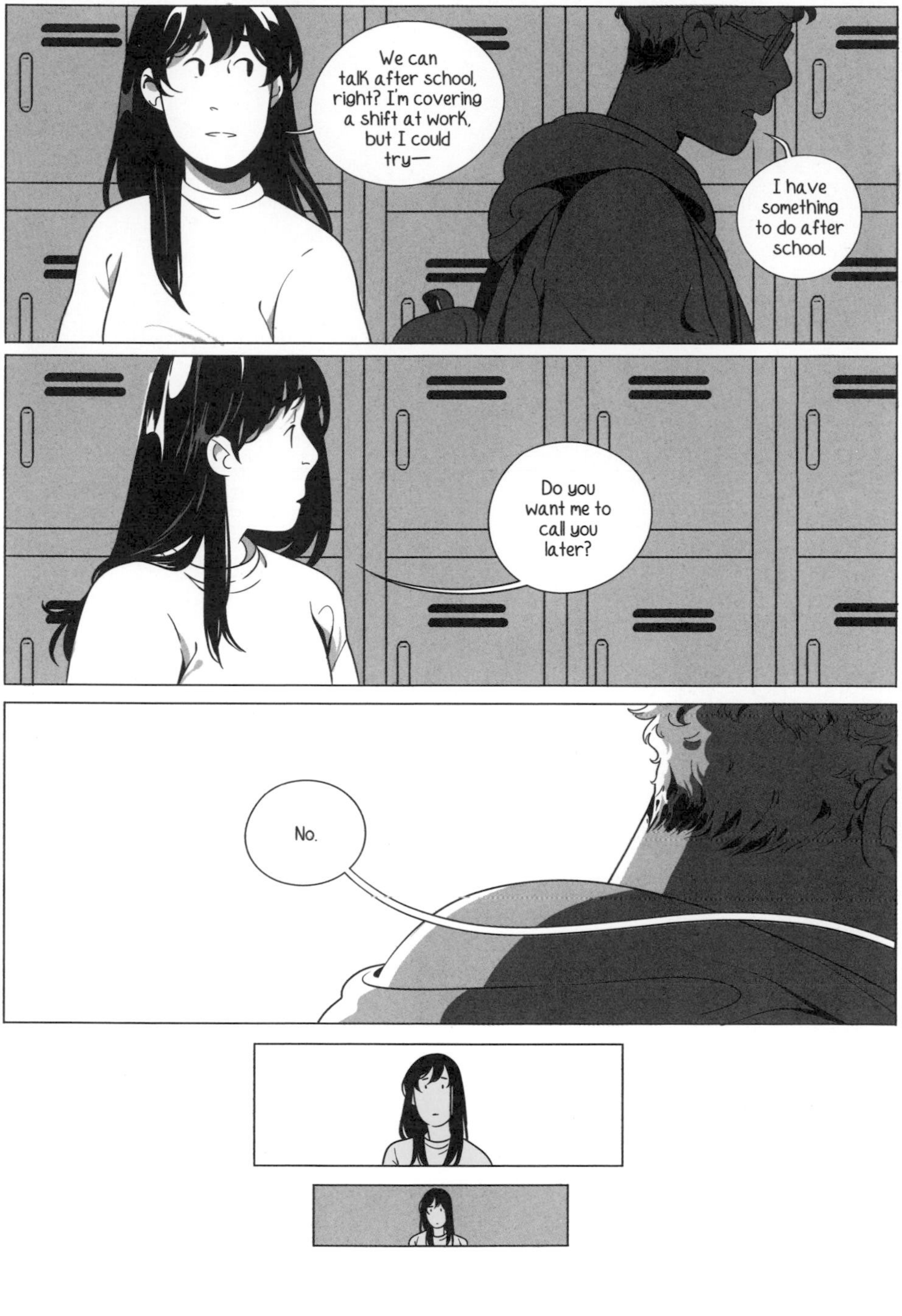
We can talk after school, right? I'm covering a shift at work, but I could try—
I have something to do after school.
Do you want me to call you later?
No.

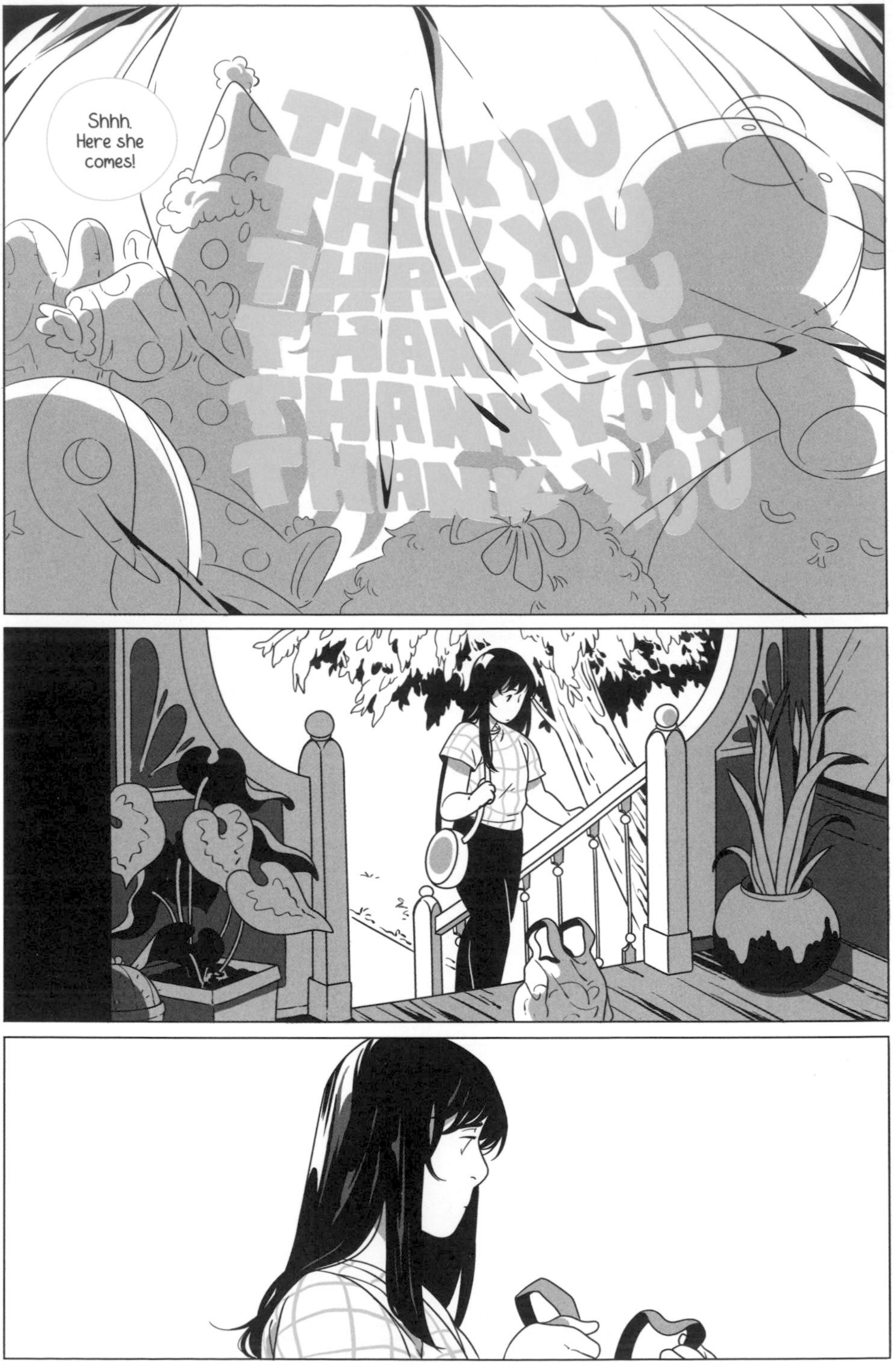
Shhh.
Here she
comes!
THANK YOU
THANK YOU
THANK YOU
THANK YOU
THANK YOU
THANK YOU

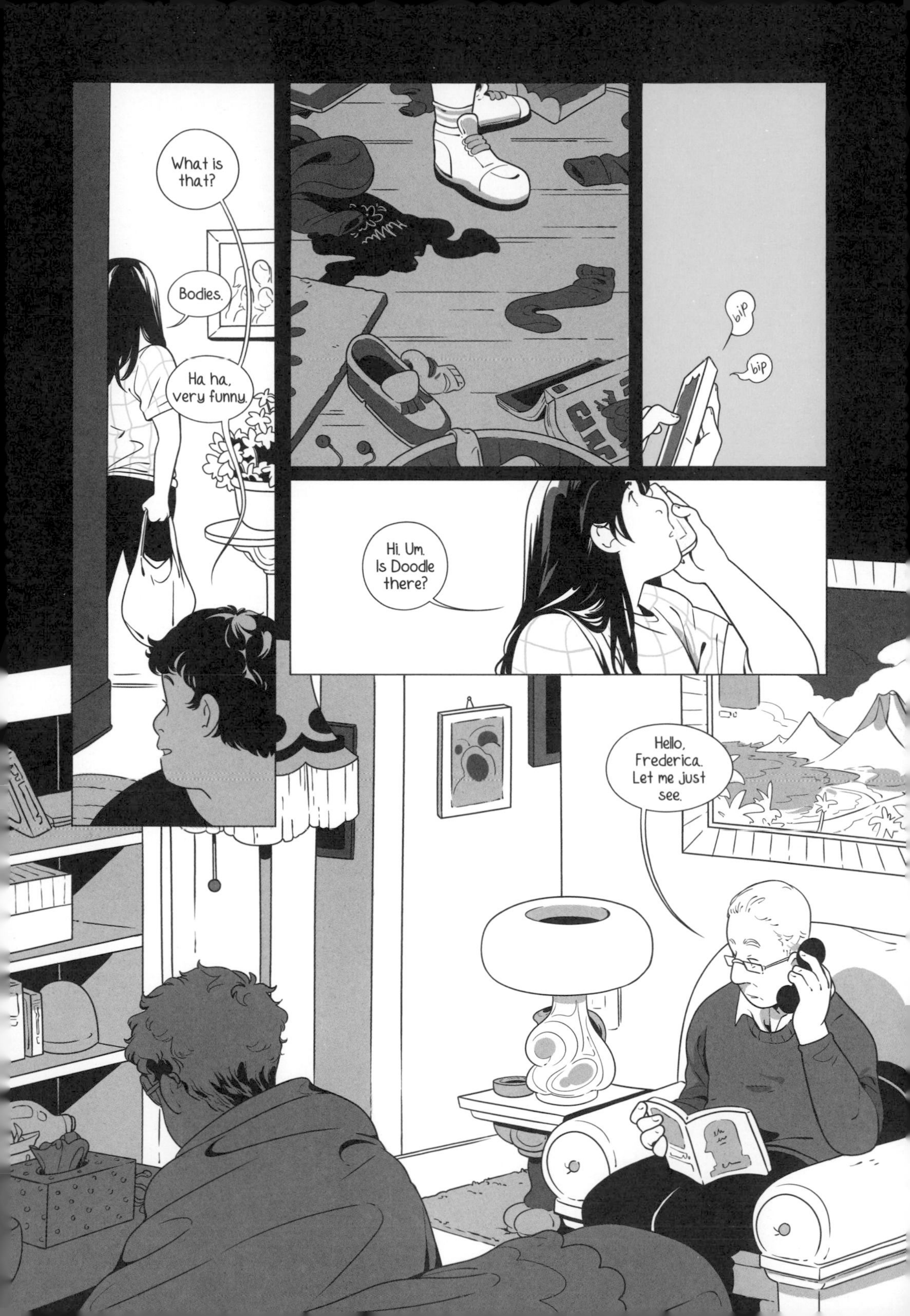
What is that?
Bodies.
Ha ha, very funny.
bip
bip
Hi. Um. Is Doodle there?
Hello, Frederica. Let me just see.

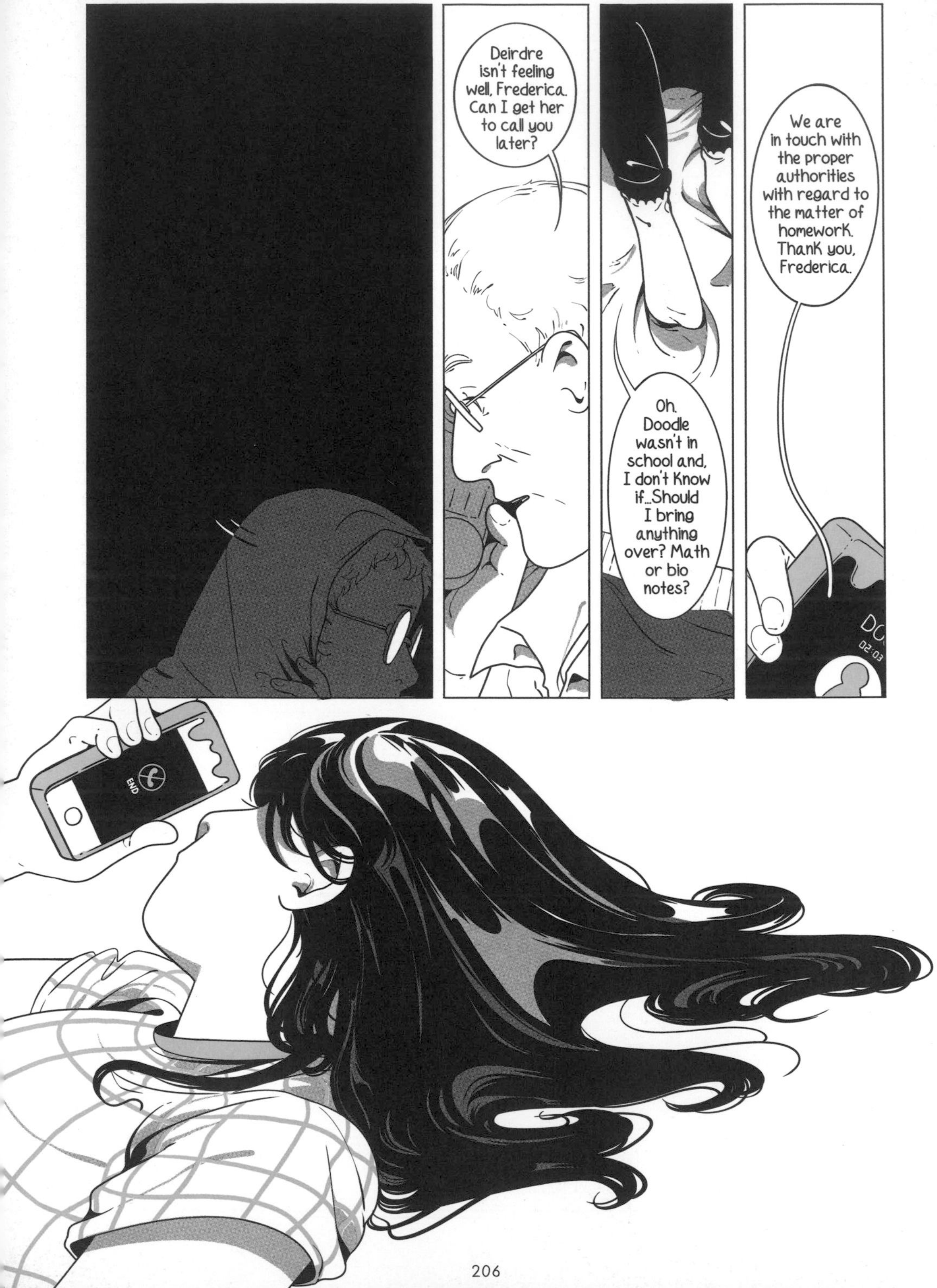

Deirdre isn't feeling well, Frederica. Can I get her to call you later?
Oh. Doodle wasn't in school and, I don't Know if...Should I bring anything over? Math or bio notes?
We are in touch with the proper authorities with regard to the matter of homework. Thank you, Frederica.
END

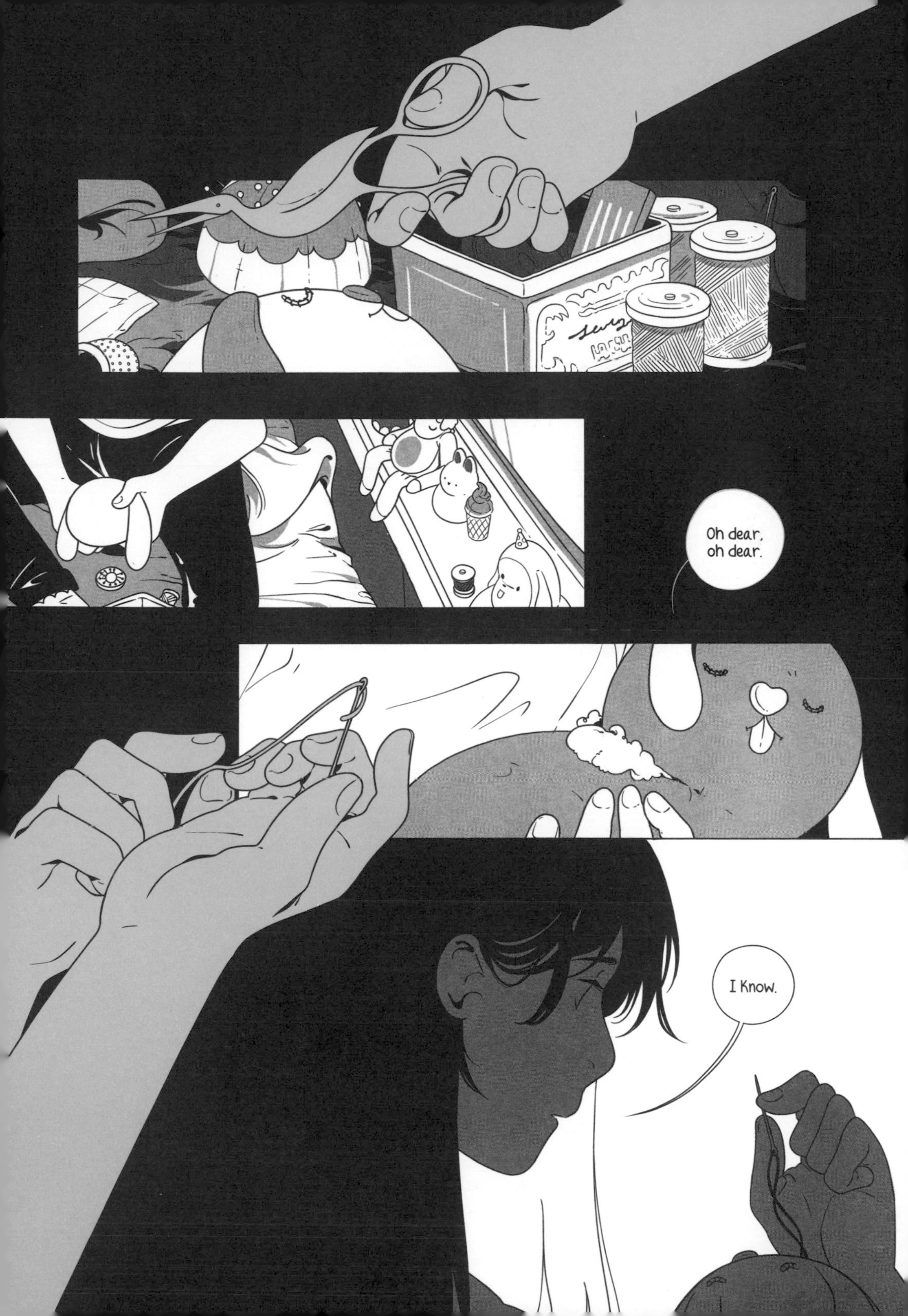
Oh dear, oh dear.
I Know.

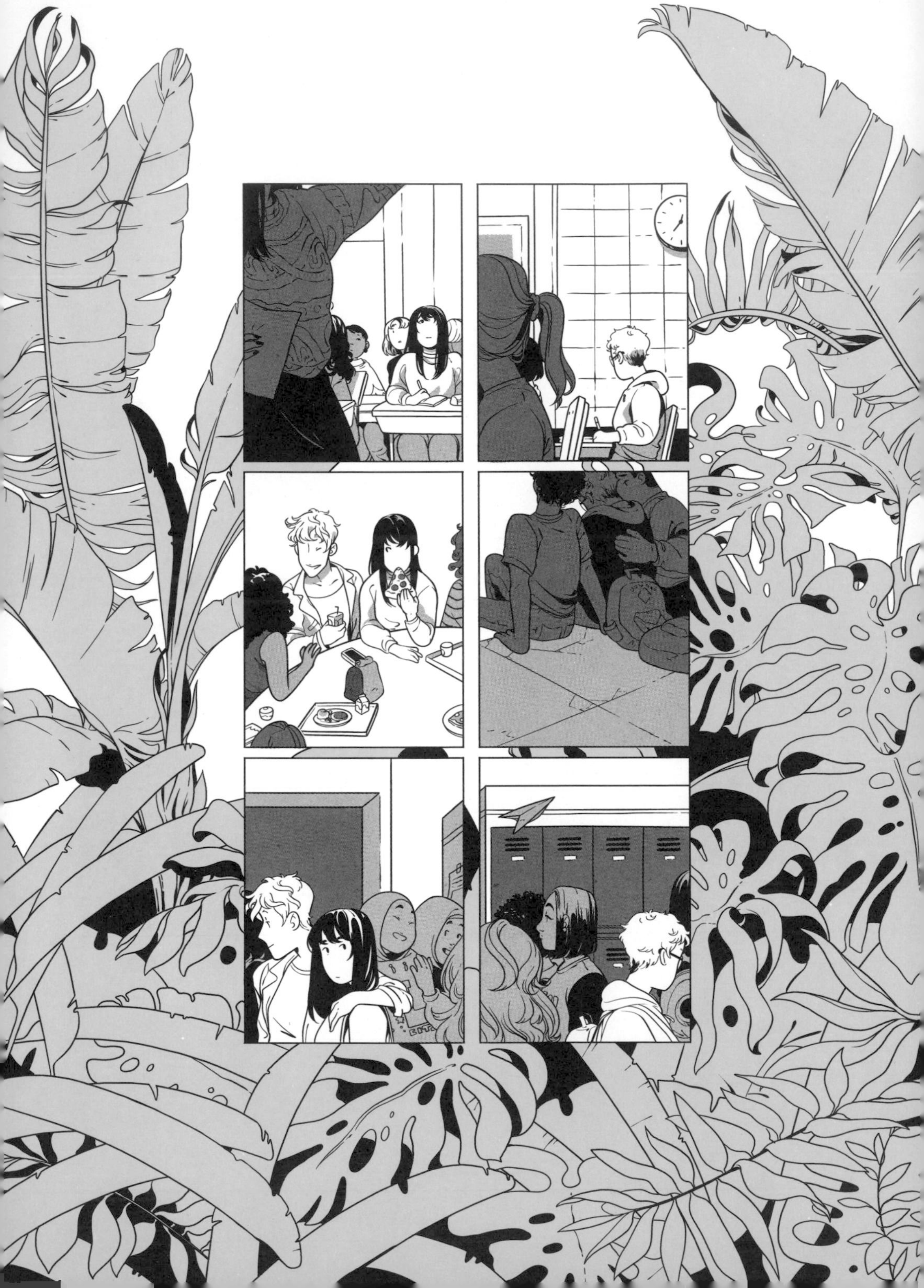

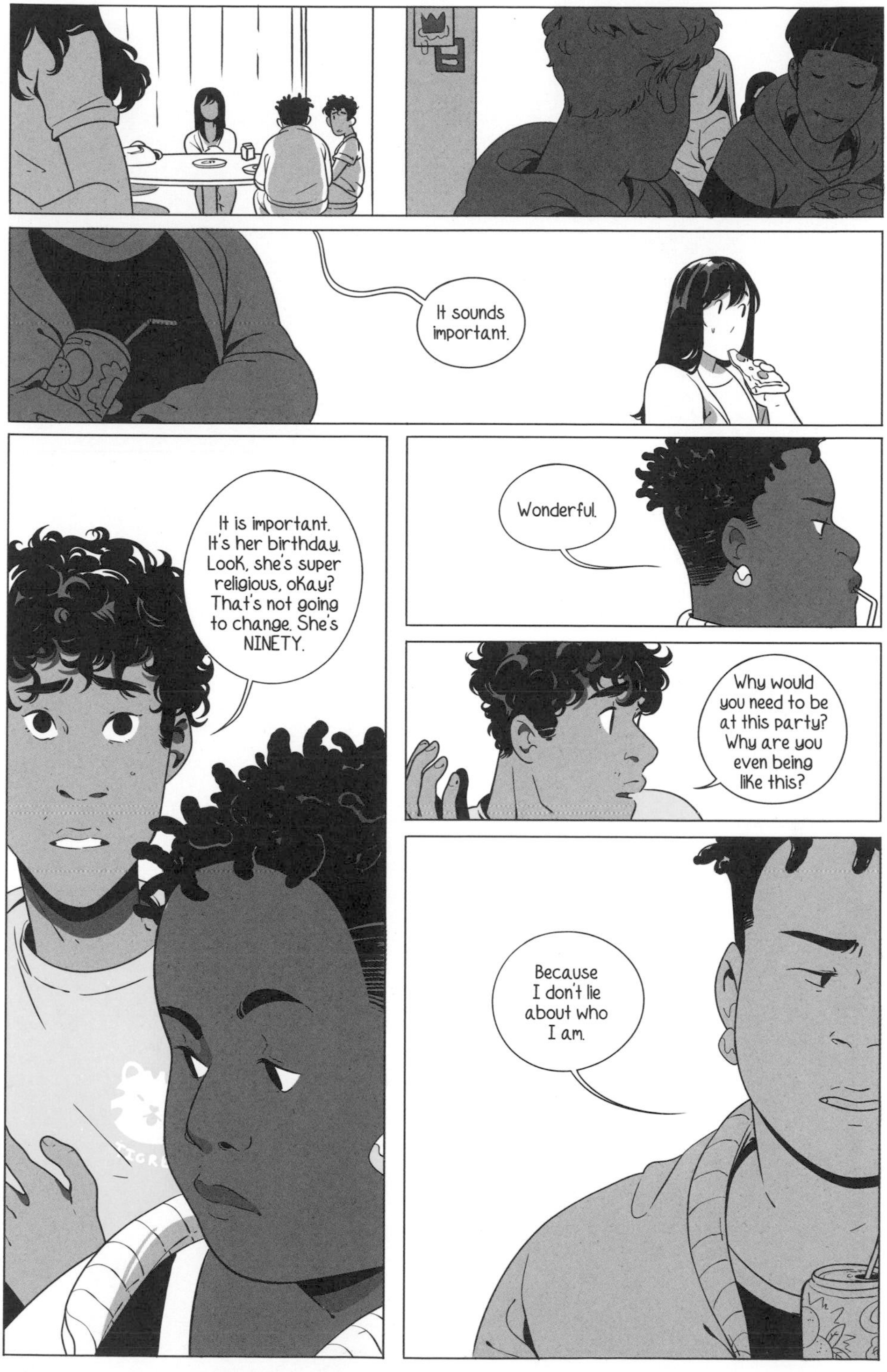
It sounds important.
It is important. It's her birthday. Look, she's super religious, okay? That's not going to change. She's NINETY.
Wonderful.
Why would you need to be at this party? Why are you even being like this?
Because I don't lie about who I am.

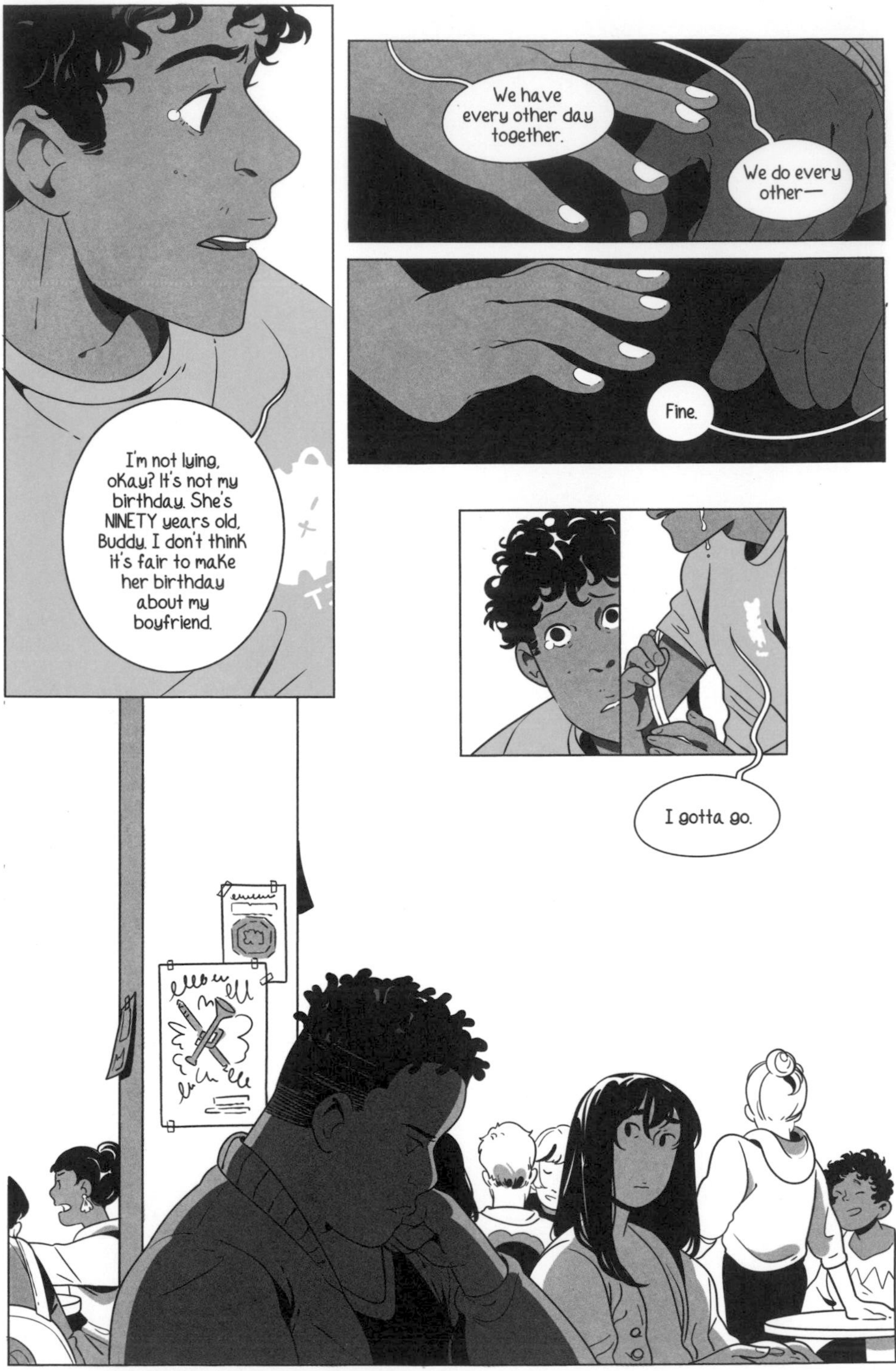
I'm not lying, okay? It's not my birthday. She's NINETY years old, Buddy. I don't think it's fair to make her birthday about my boyfriend.
We have every other day together.
We do every other—
Fine.
I gotta go.

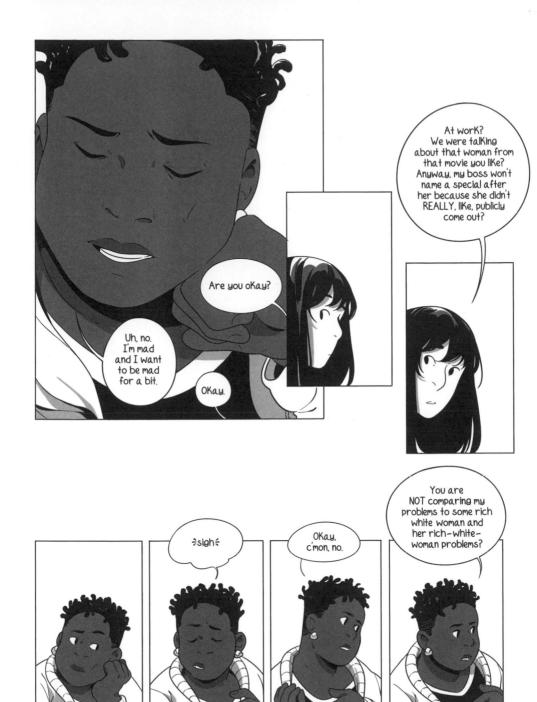

At work?
We were talking about that woman from that movie you like? Anyway, my boss won't name a special after her because she didn't REALLY, like, publicly come out?

Are you okay?

Uh, no. I'm mad and I want to be mad for a bit.

Okay.

You are NOT comparing my problems to some rich white woman and her rich-white-woman problems?

≠sigh≠

Okay, c'mon, no.

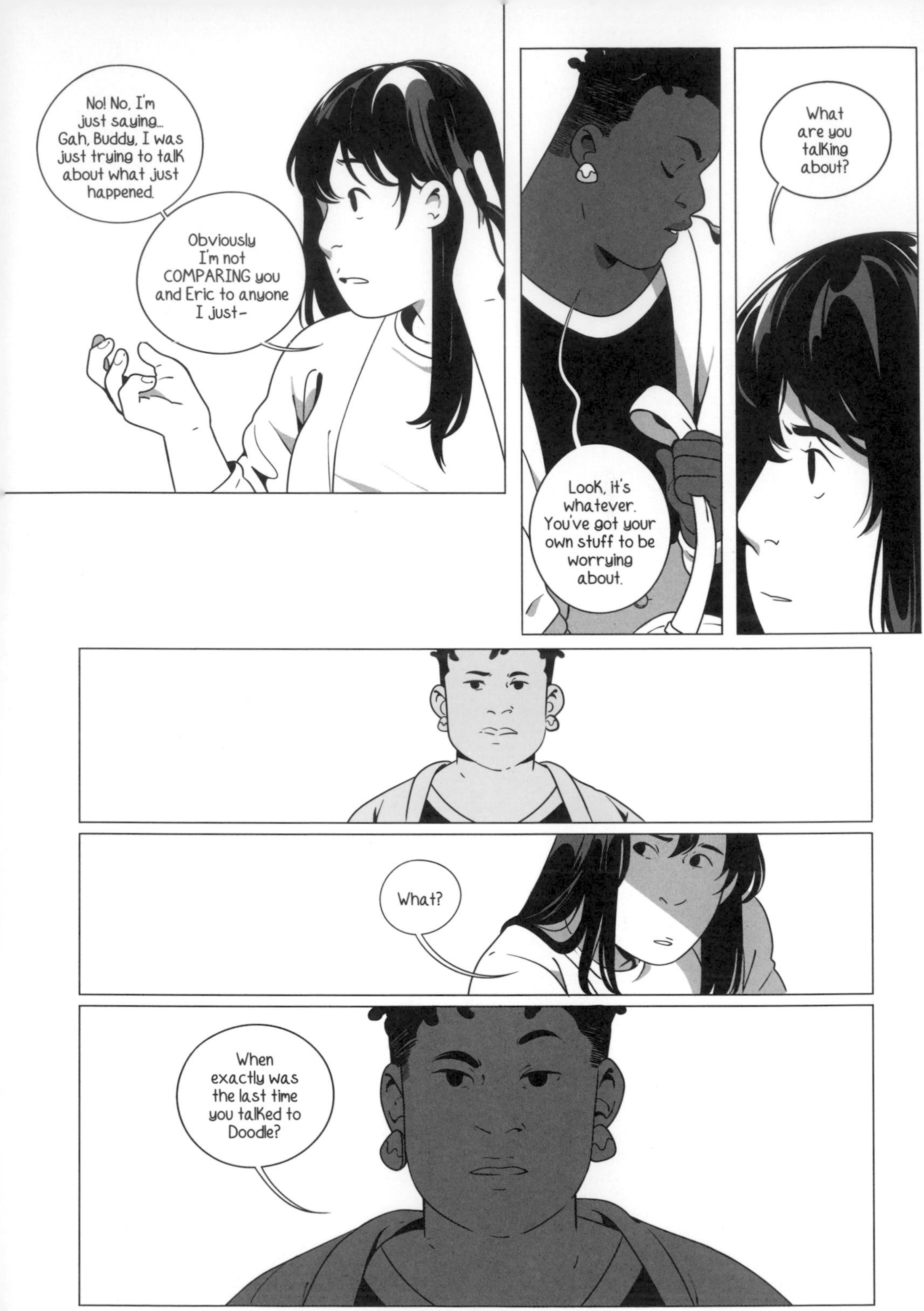
No! No, I'm just saying... Gah, Buddy, I was just trying to talk about what just happened.
Obviously I'm not COMPARING you and Eric to anyone I just-
Look, it's whatever. You've got your own stuff to be worrying about.
What are you talking about?
What?
When exactly was the last time you talked to Doodle?

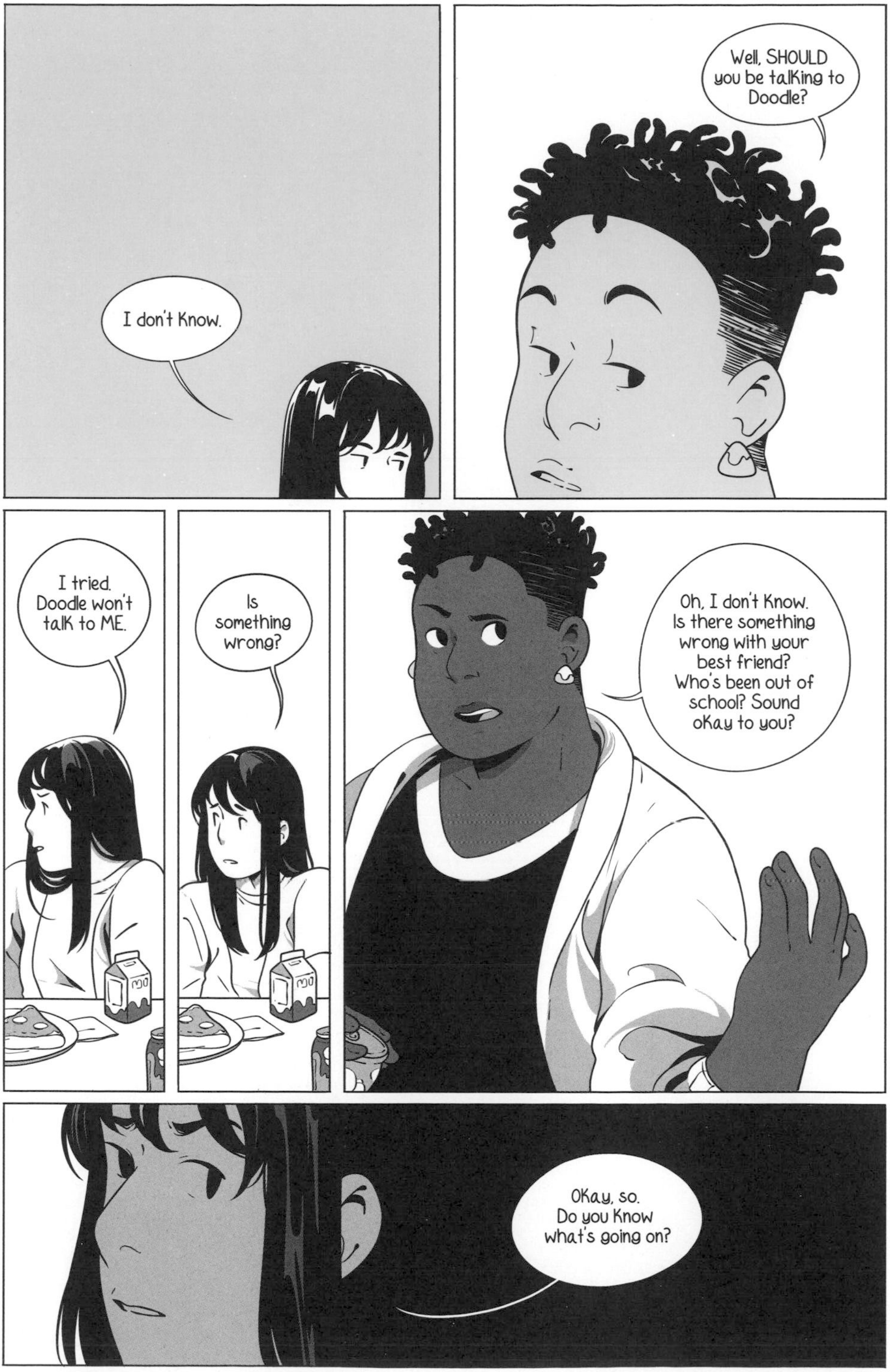
I don't Know.
Well, SHOULD you be talKing to Doodle?
I tried. Doodle won't talK to ME.
Is something wrong?
Oh, I don't Know. Is there something wrong with your best friend? Who's been out of school? Sound oKay to you?
OKay, so. Do you Know what's going on?

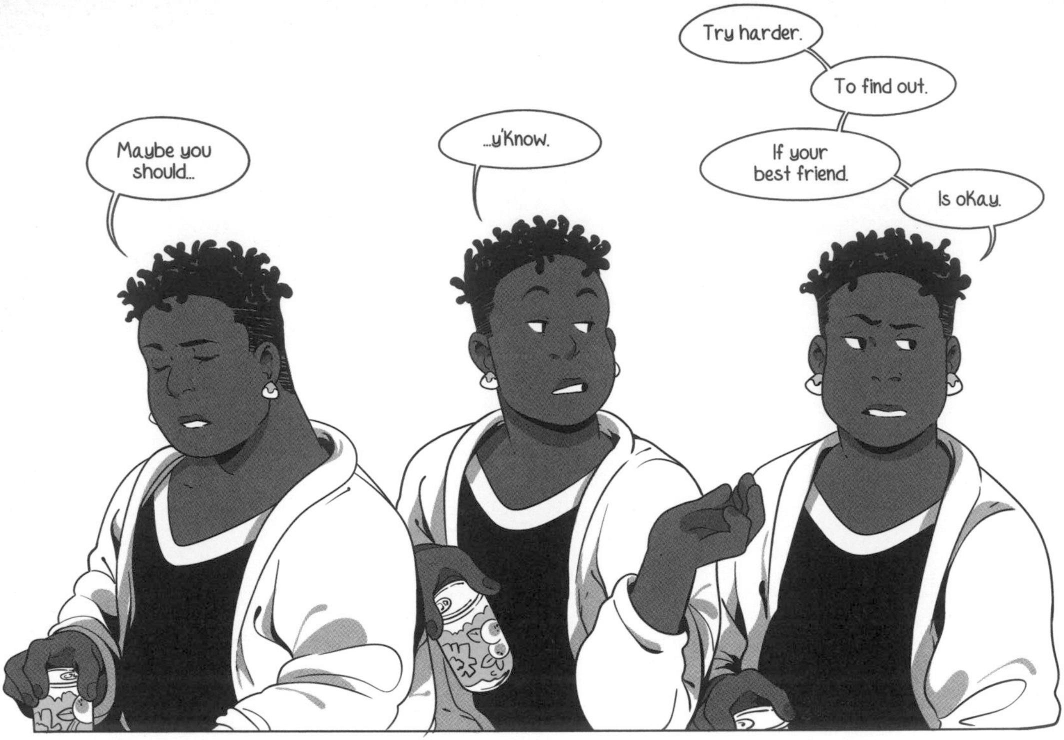
Maybe you should...
...y'know.
Try harder.
To find out.
If your best friend.
Is okay.

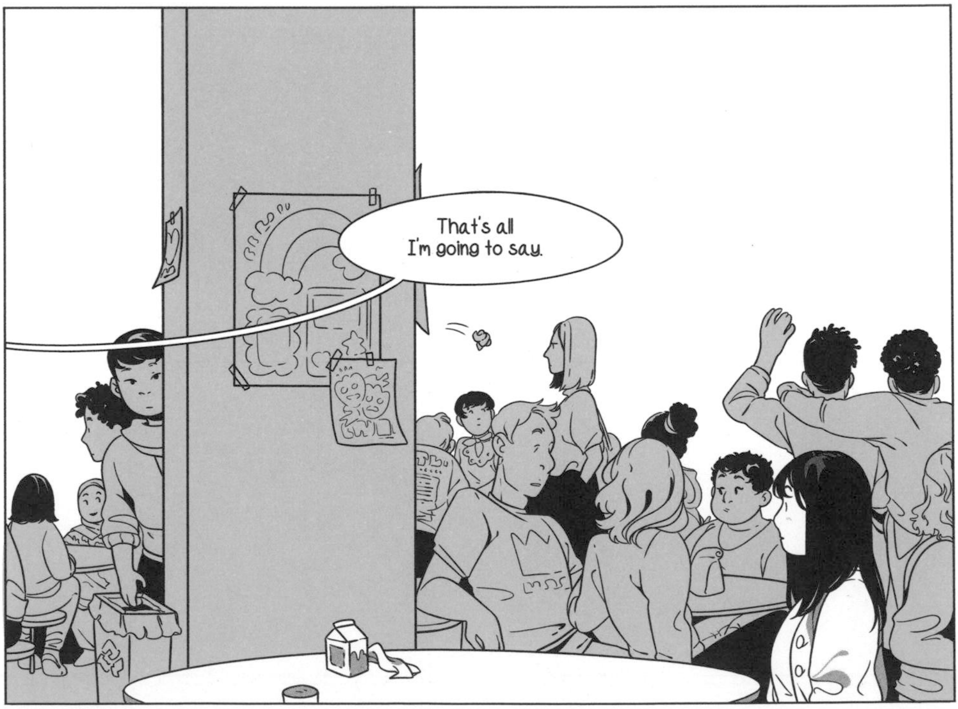
That's all I'm going to say.

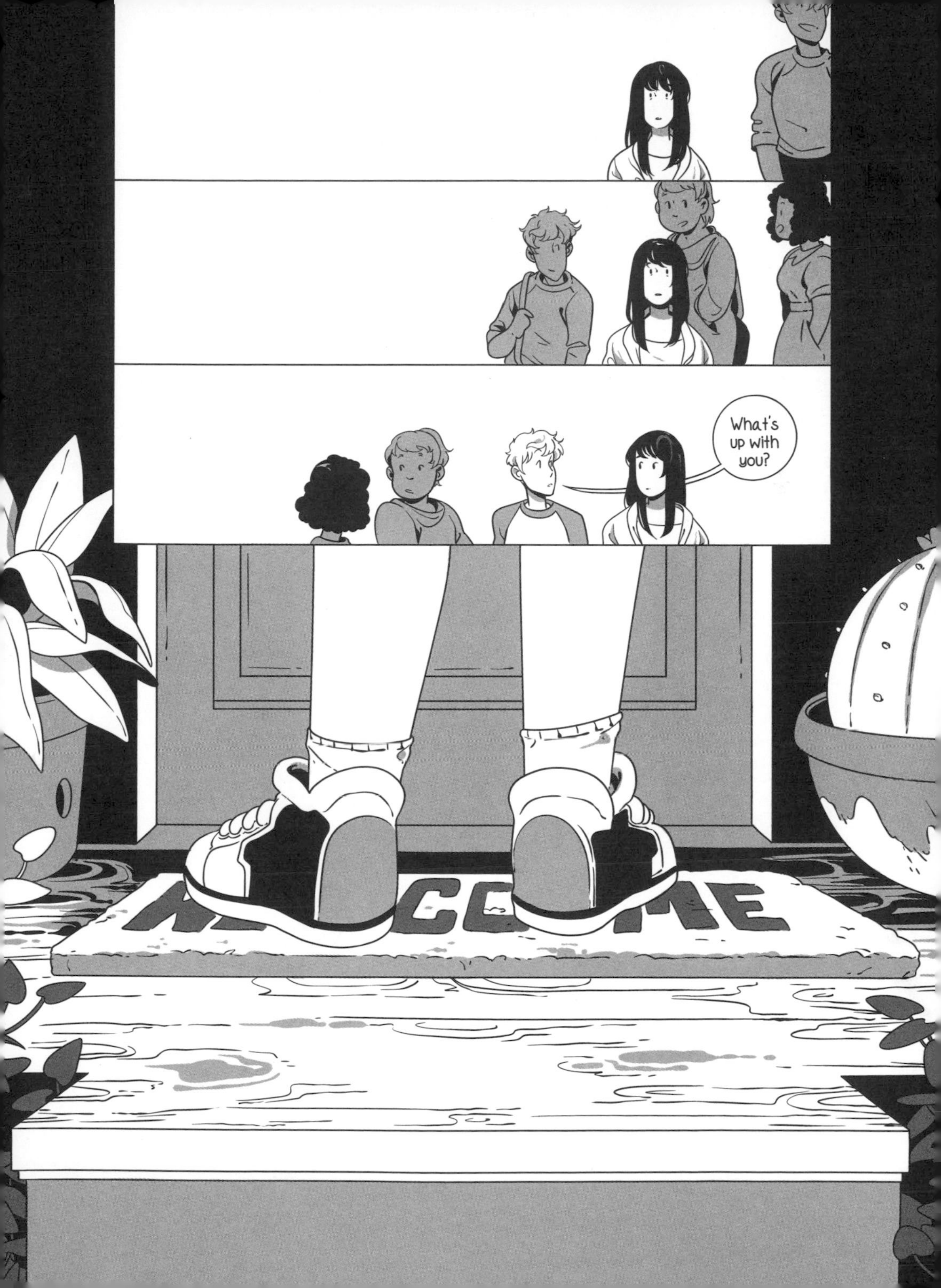
What's up with you?

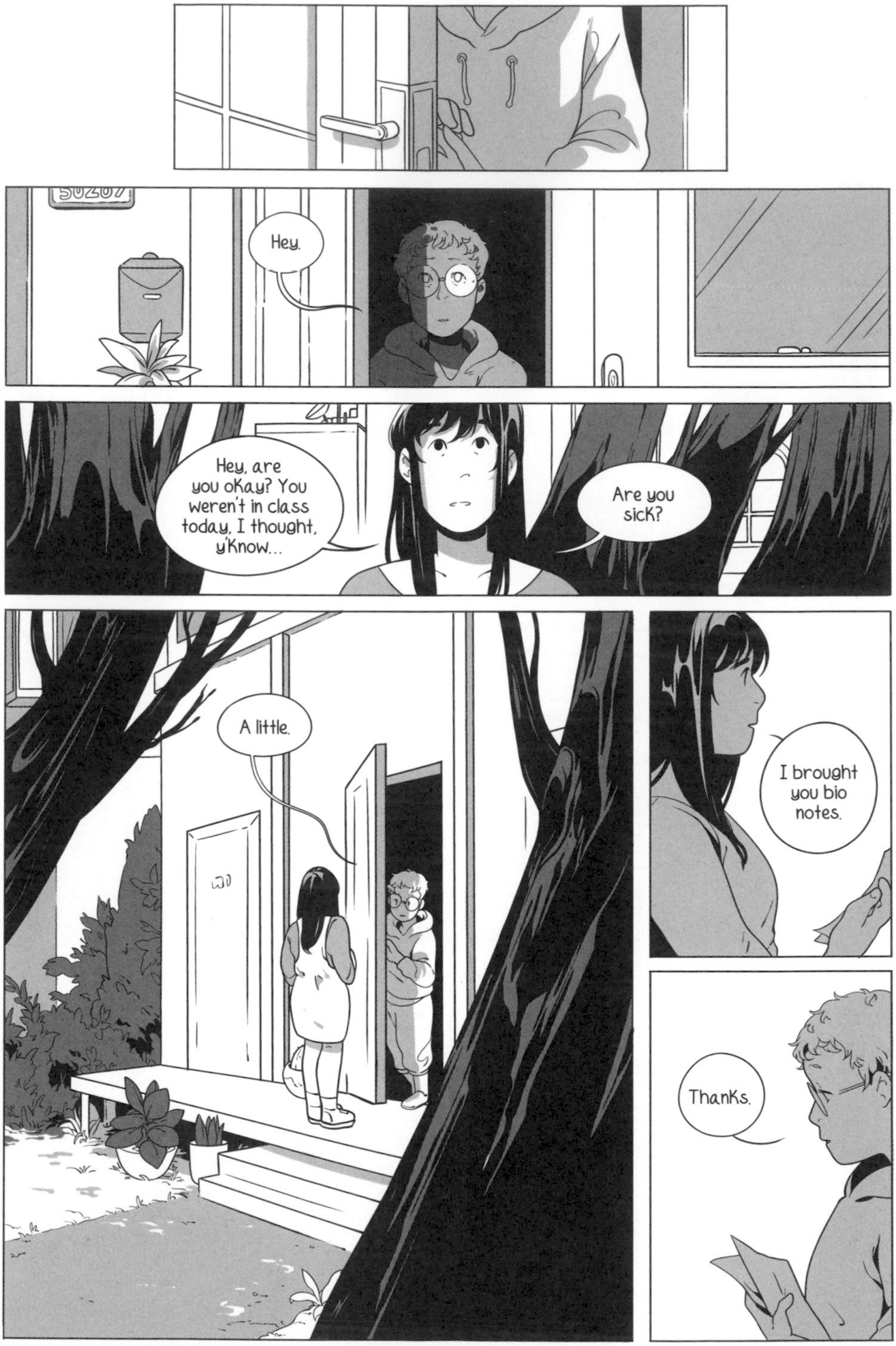
Hey.
Hey, are you okay? You weren't in class today, I thought, y'know...
Are you sick?
A little.
I brought you bio notes.
Thanks.

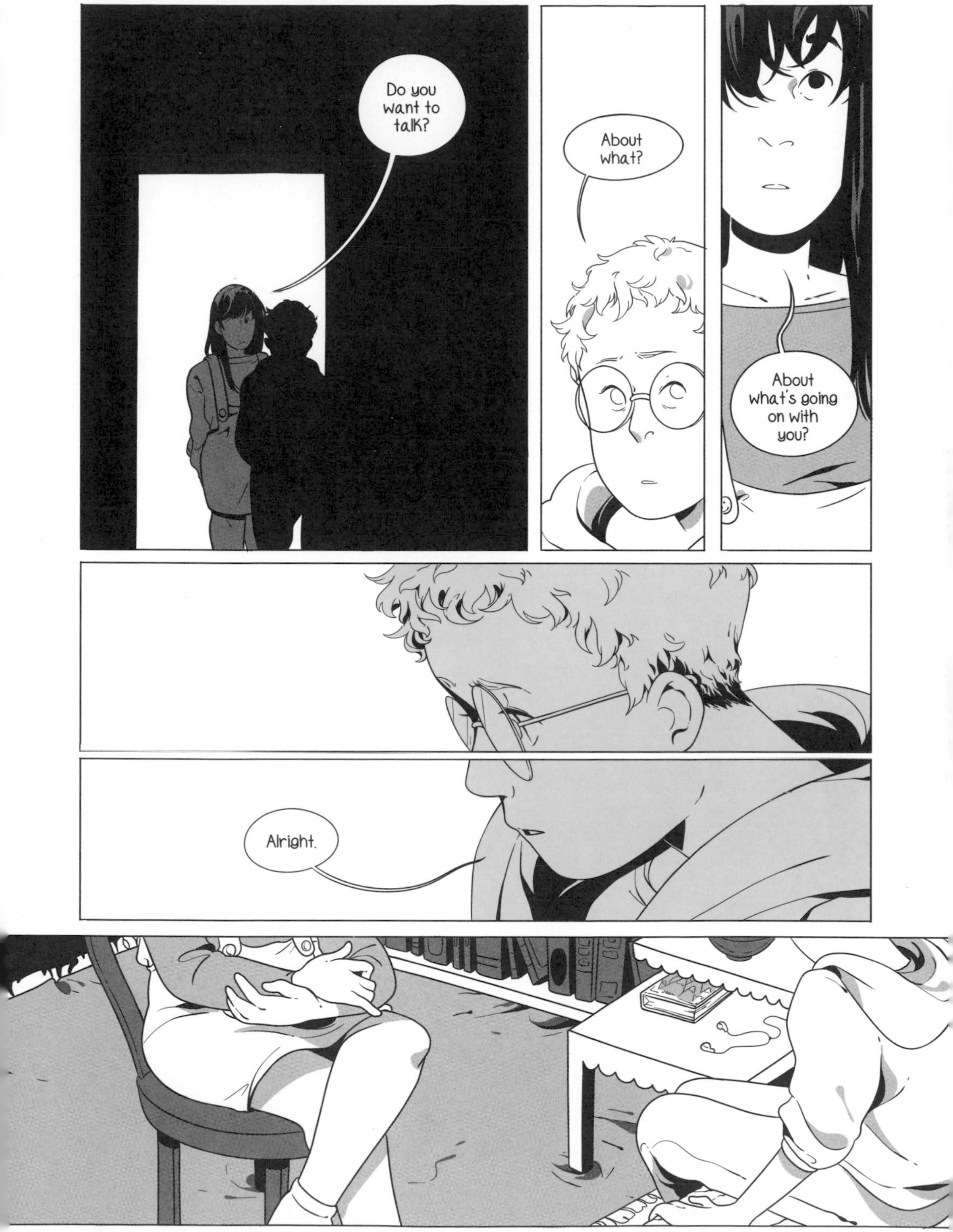
Do you want to talk?
About what?
About what's going on with you?
Alright.

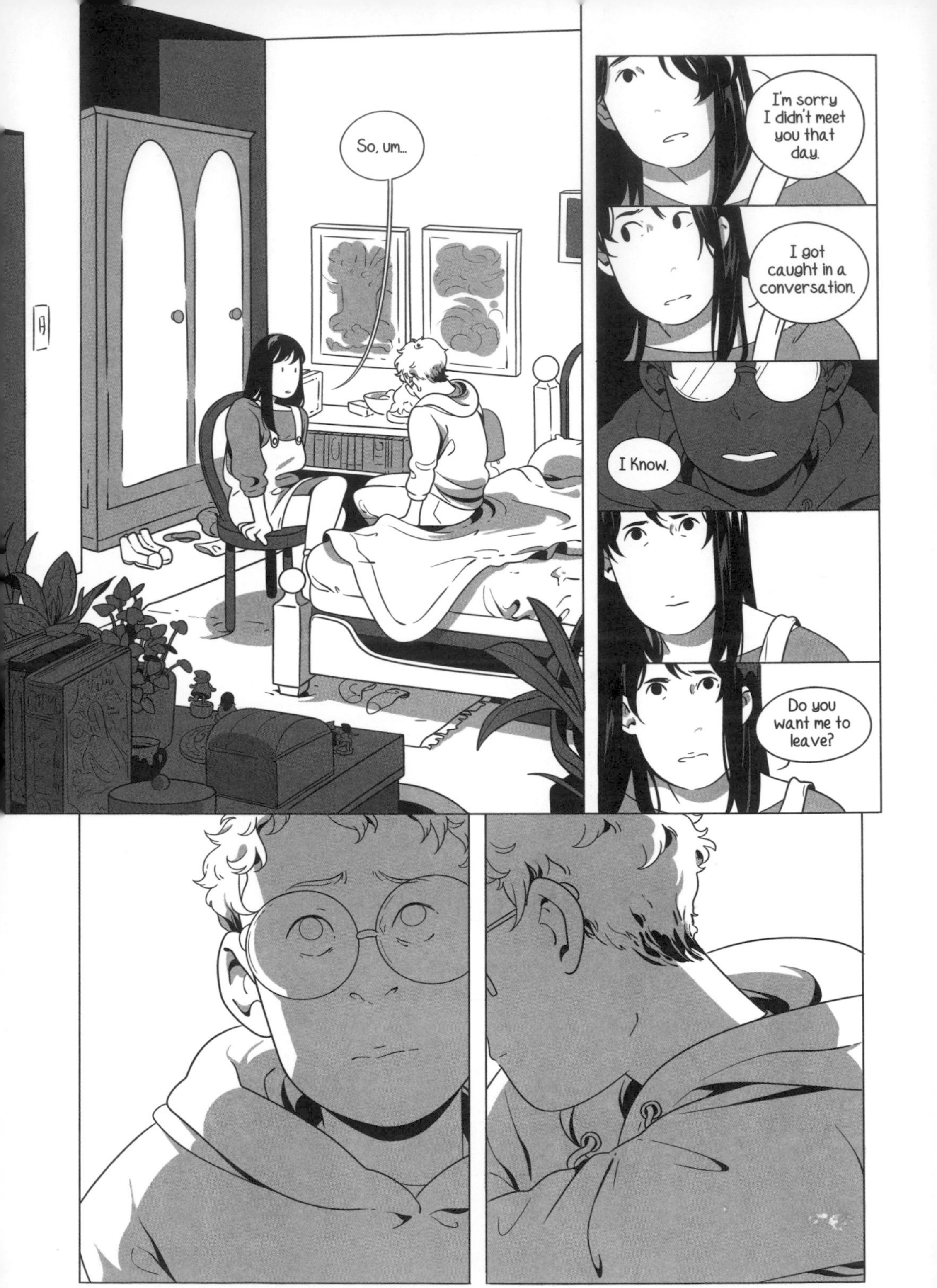
So, um...
I'm sorry I didn't meet you that day.
I got caught in a conversation.
I Know.
Do you want me to leave?

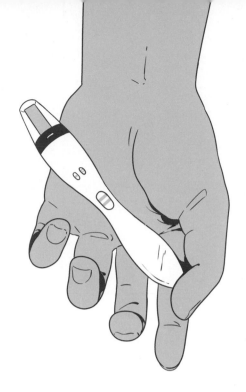

HOLY SHIT!

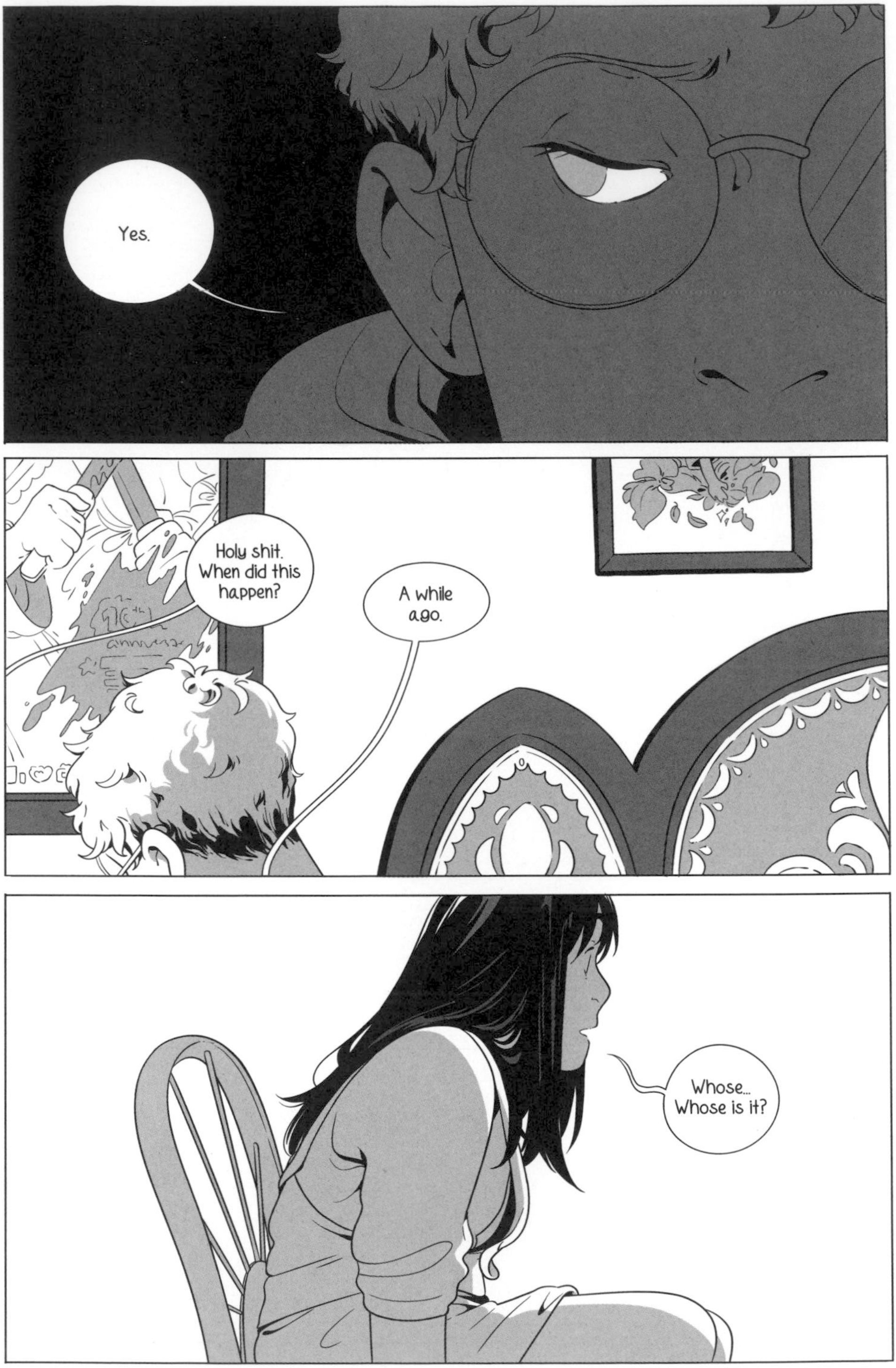

Yes.
Holy shit. When did this happen?
A while ago.
Whose... Whose is it?

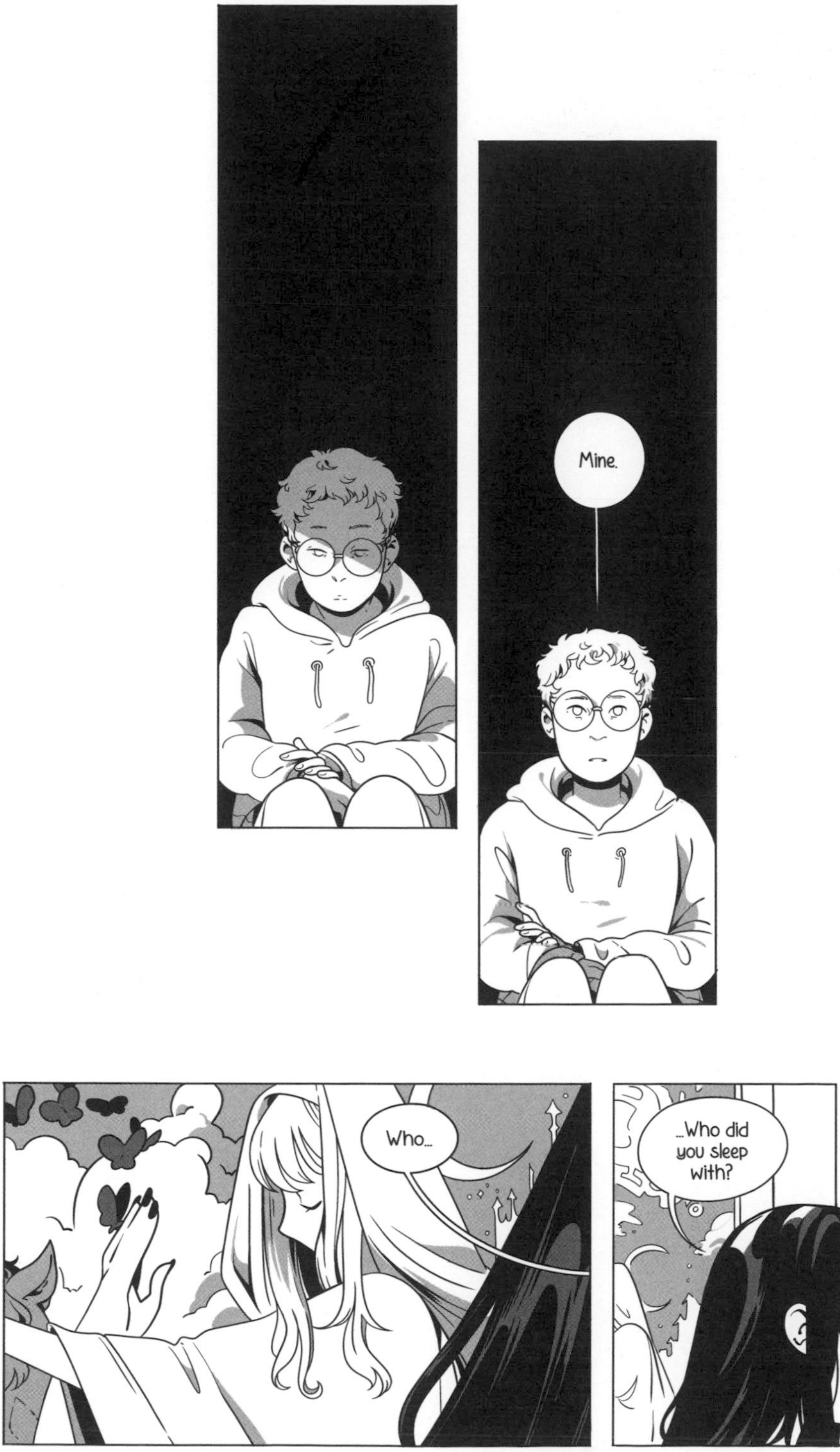
Mine.
Who...
...Who did you sleep with?

You don't know him. He's my DM.

My dungeon master.

His name is Peter.

He's married.

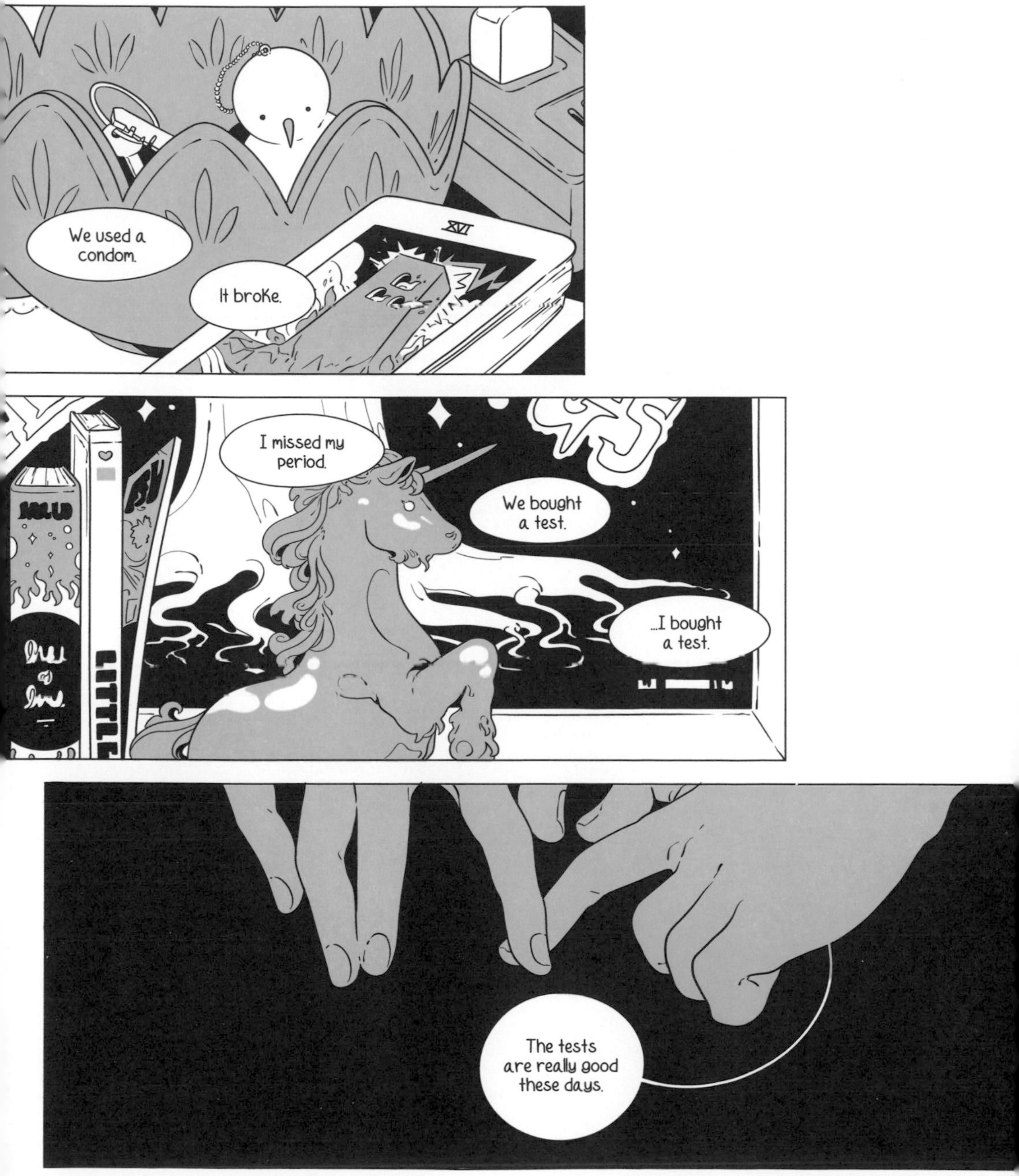
We used a condom.
It broke.
I missed my period.
We bought a test.
...I bought a test.
The tests are really good these days.

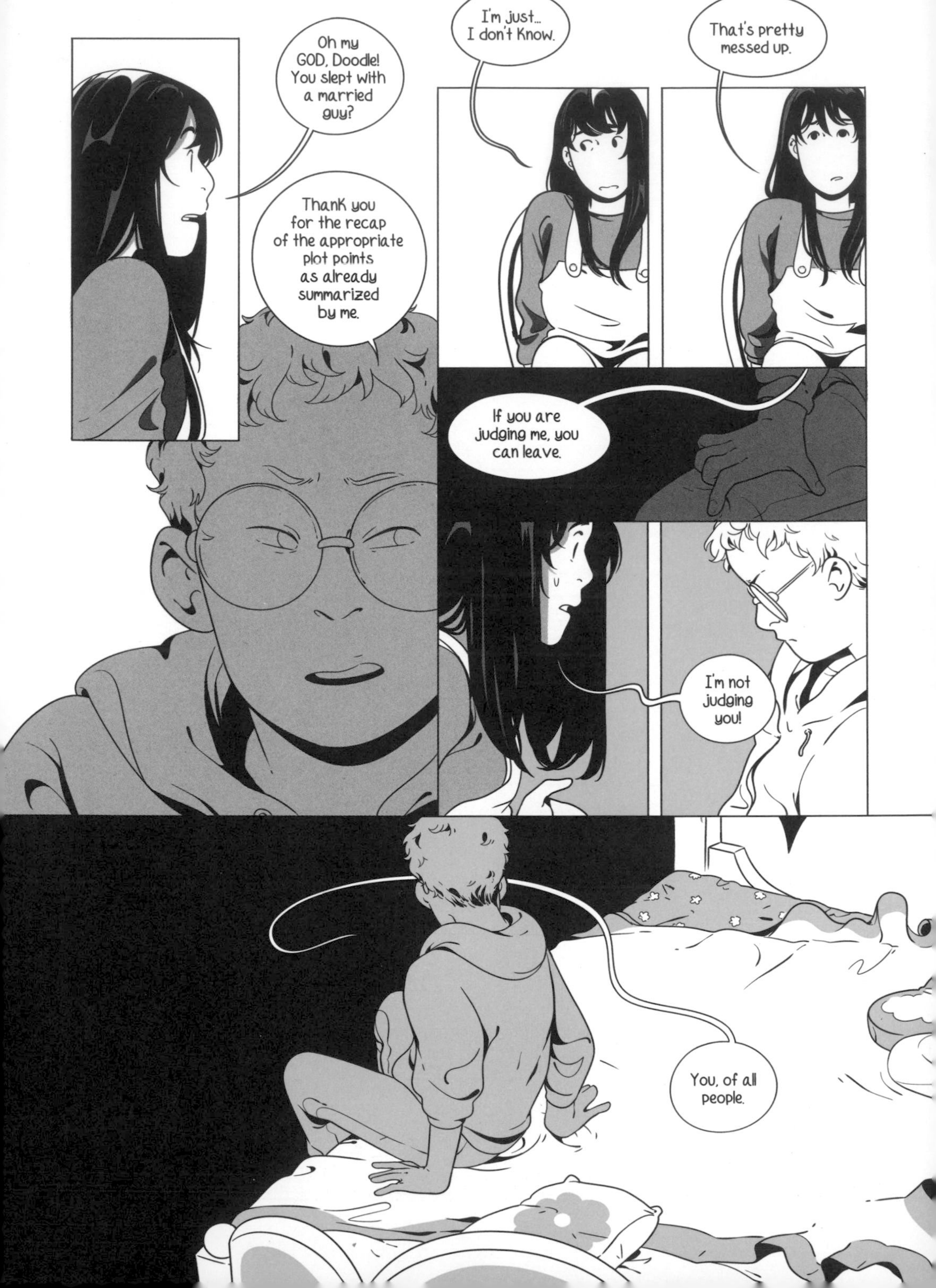
Oh my GOD, Doodle! You slept with a married guy?
Thank you for the recap of the appropriate plot points as already summarized by me.
I'm just... I don't know.
That's pretty messed up.
If you are judging me, you can leave.
I'm not judging you!
You, of all people.

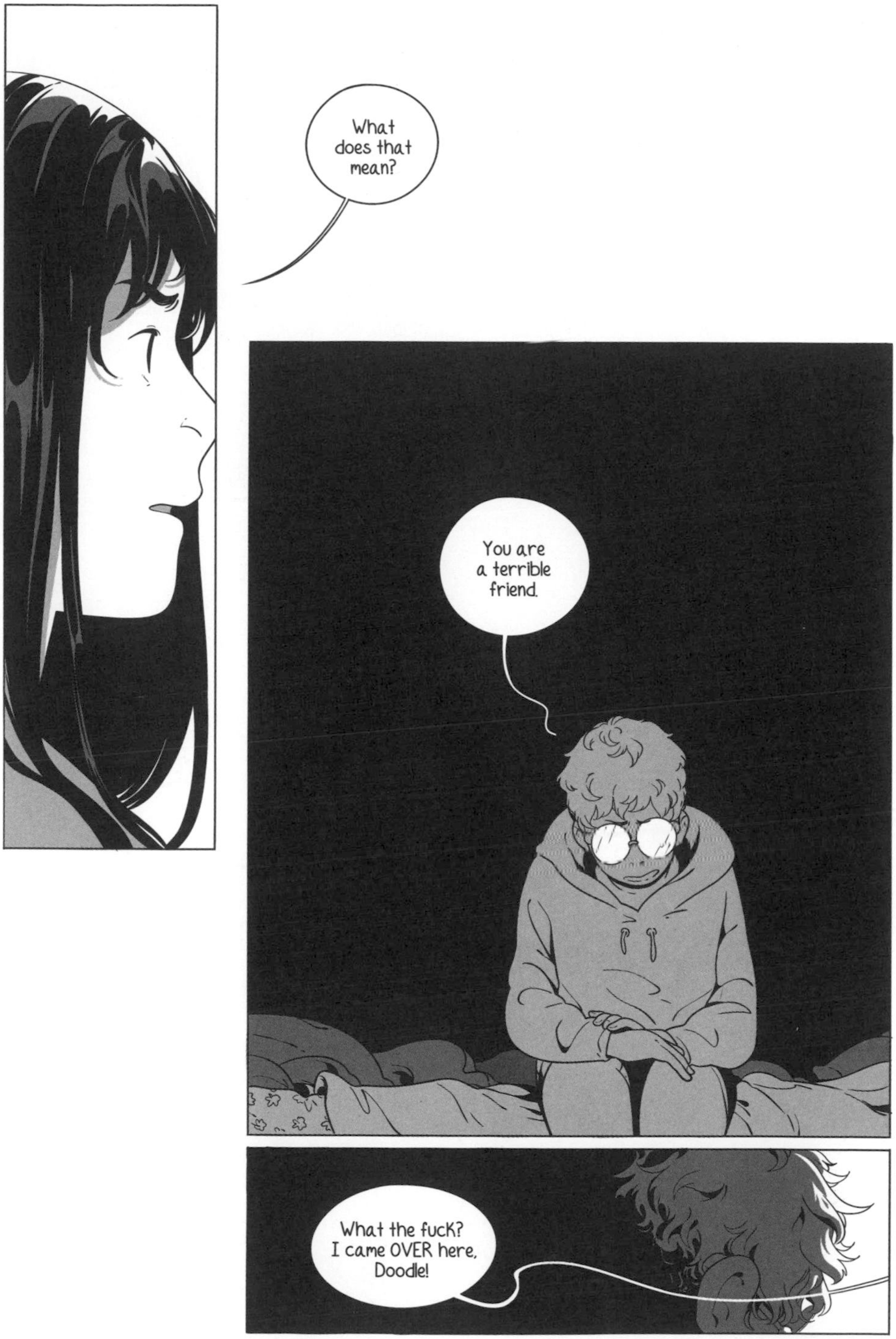
What does that mean?
You are a terrible friend.
What the fuck? I came OVER here, Doodle!

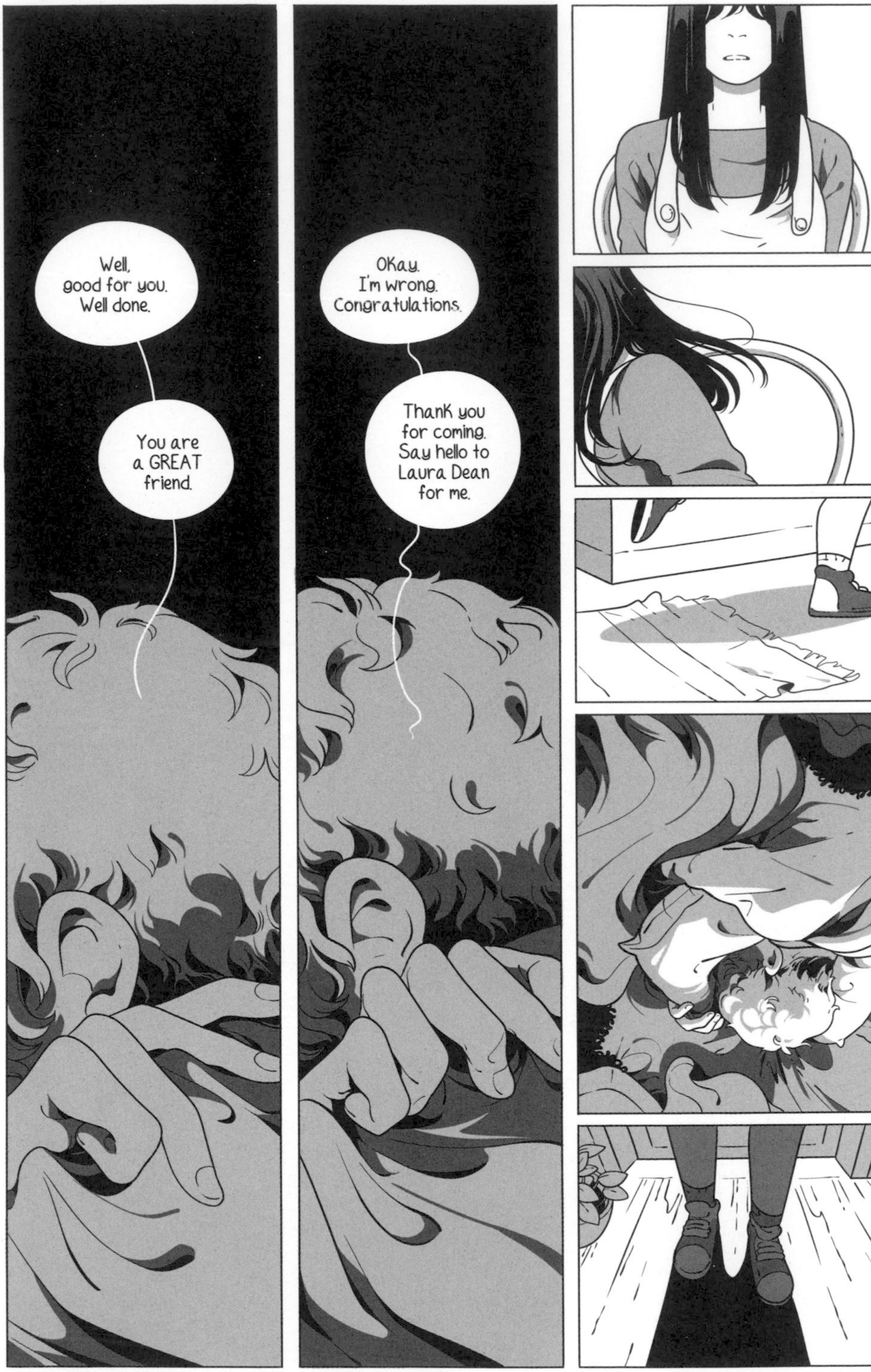

Well, good for you. Well done.
You are a GREAT friend.
Okay. I'm wrong. Congratulations.
Thank you for coming. Say hello to Laura Dean for me.

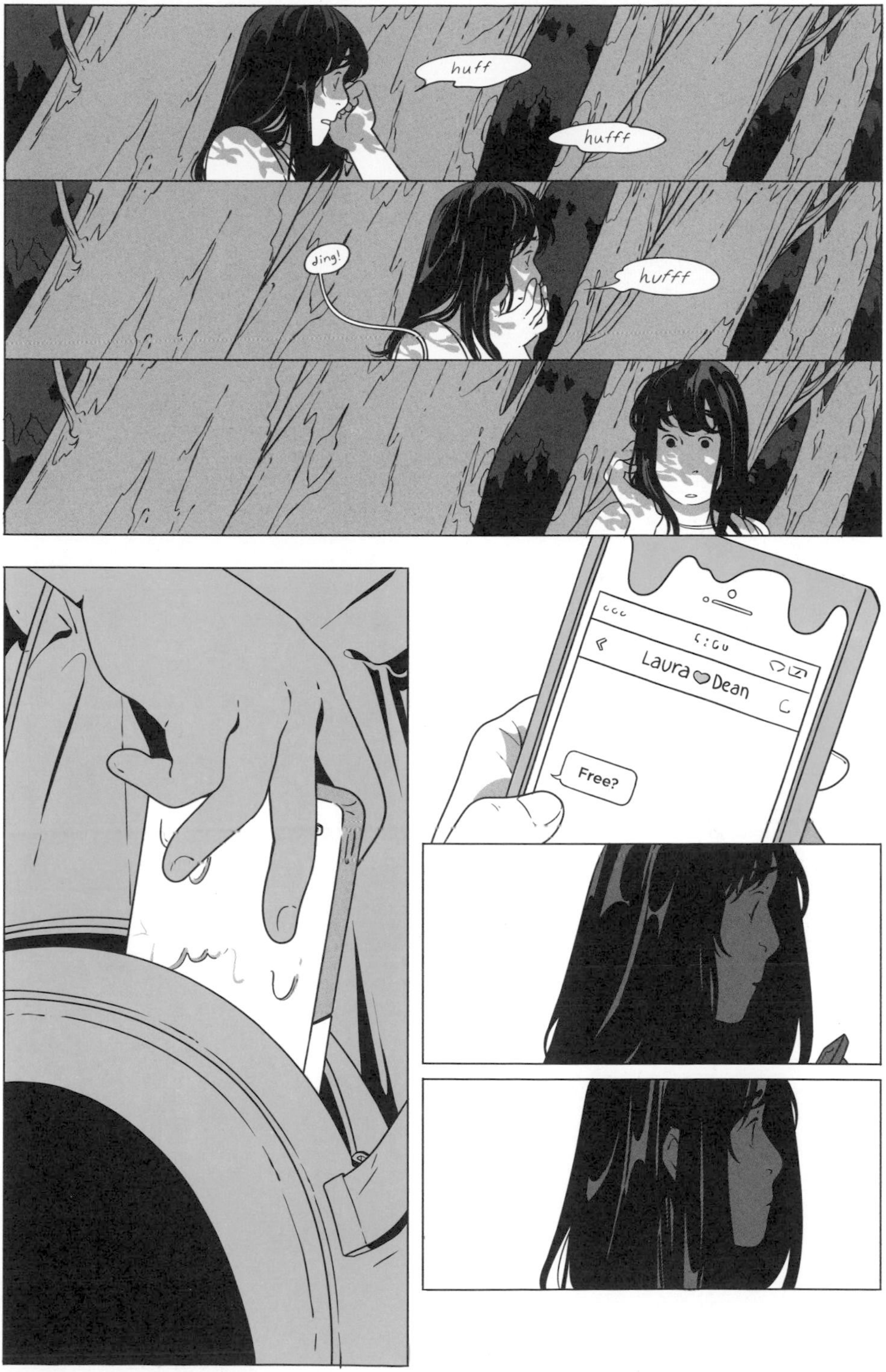
huff
hufff
ding!
hufff
Laura Dean
Free?

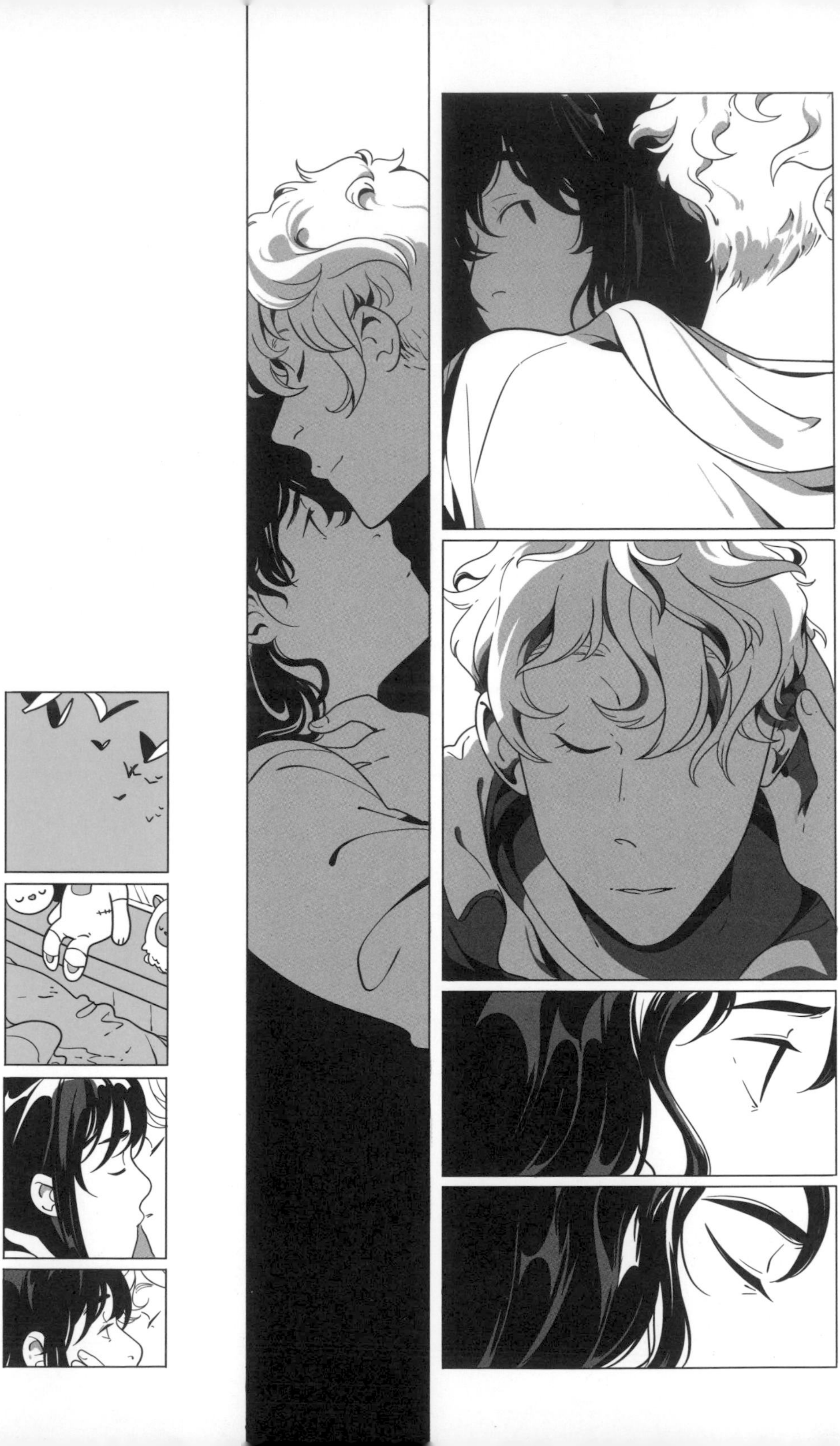

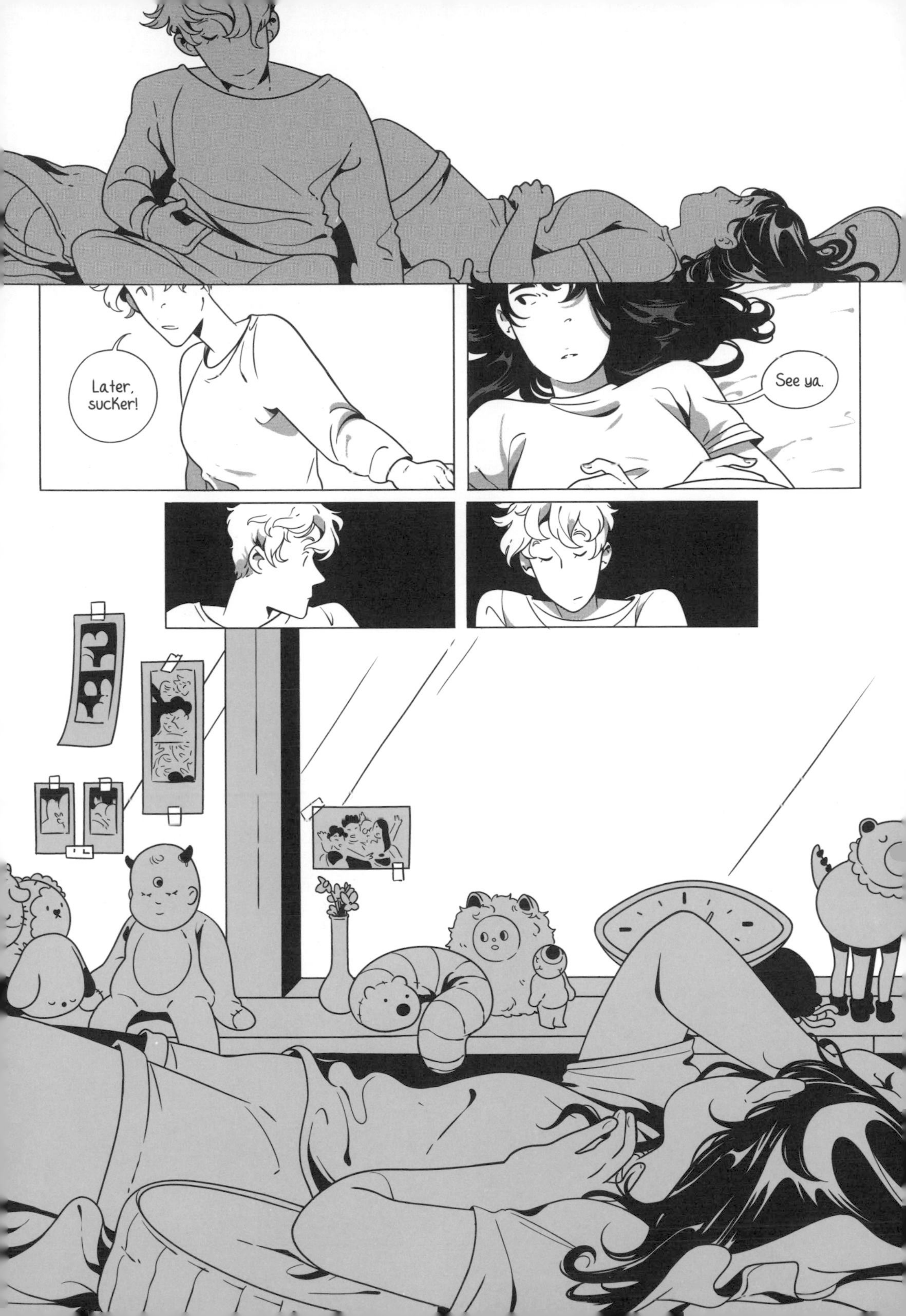
Later, sucker!
See ya.

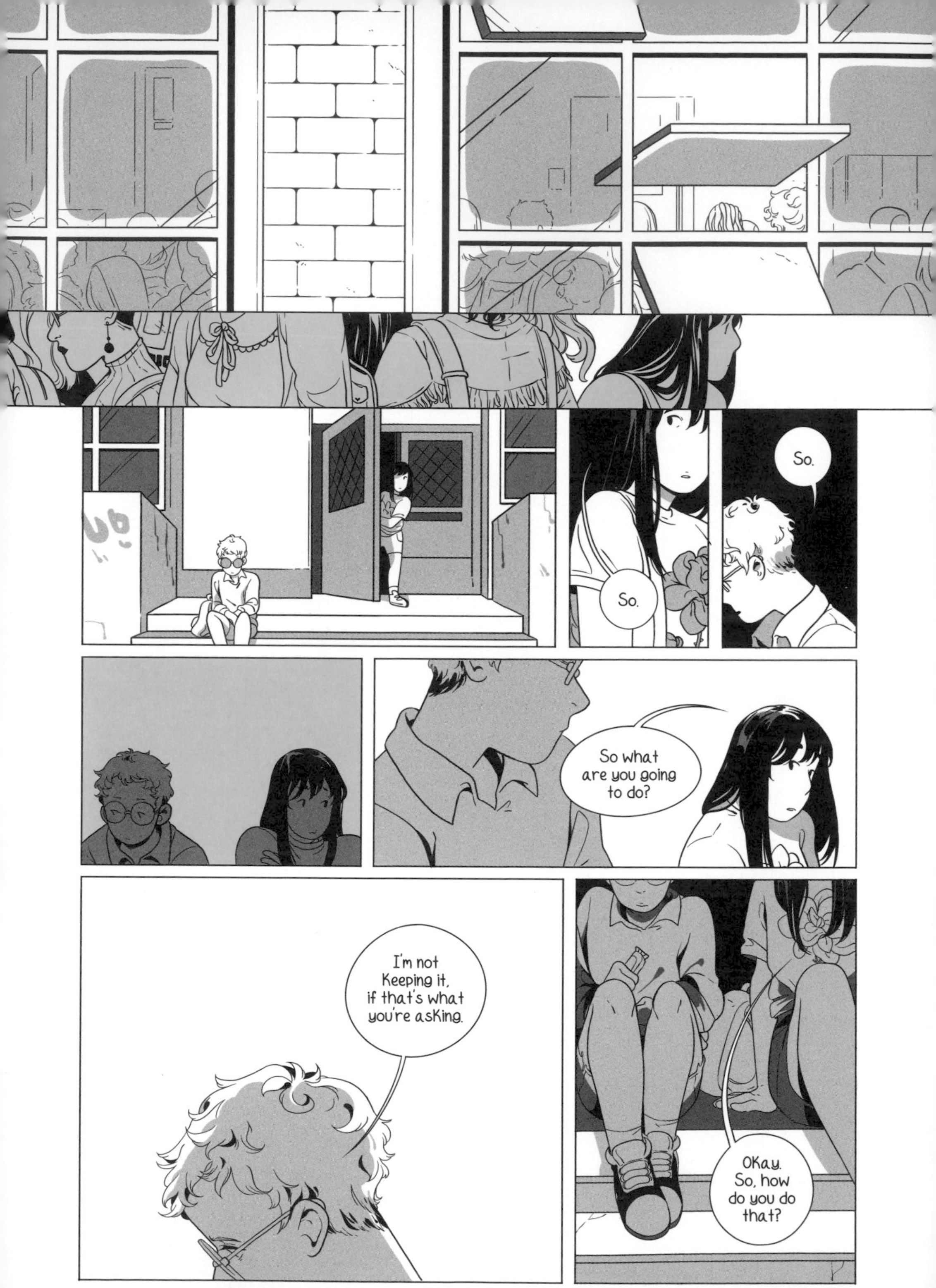
So.
So.
So what are you going to do?
I'm not Keeping it, if that's what you're asking.
OKay. So, how do you do that?

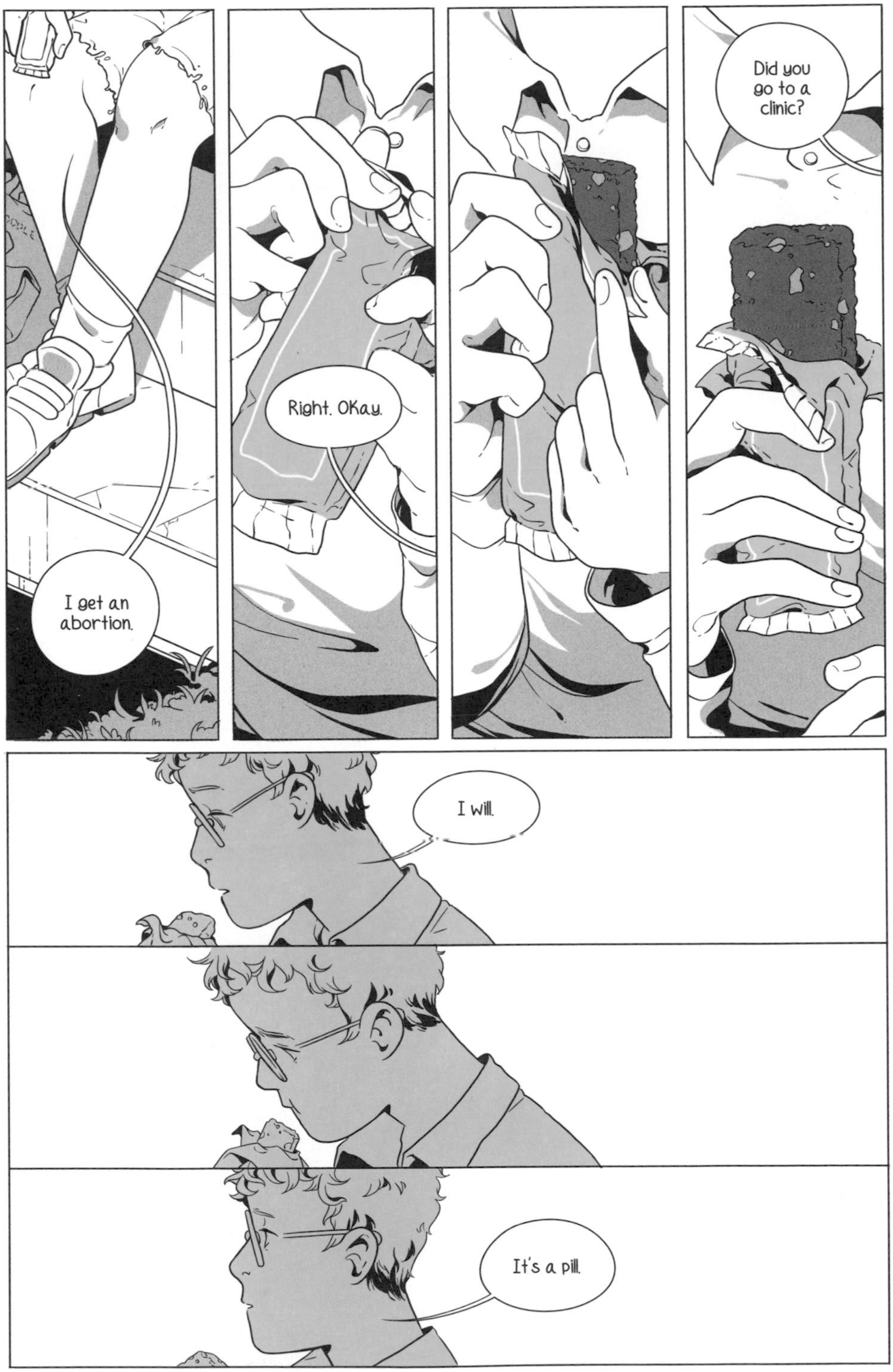
I get an abortion.
Right. OKay.
Did you go to a clinic?
I will.
It's a pill.

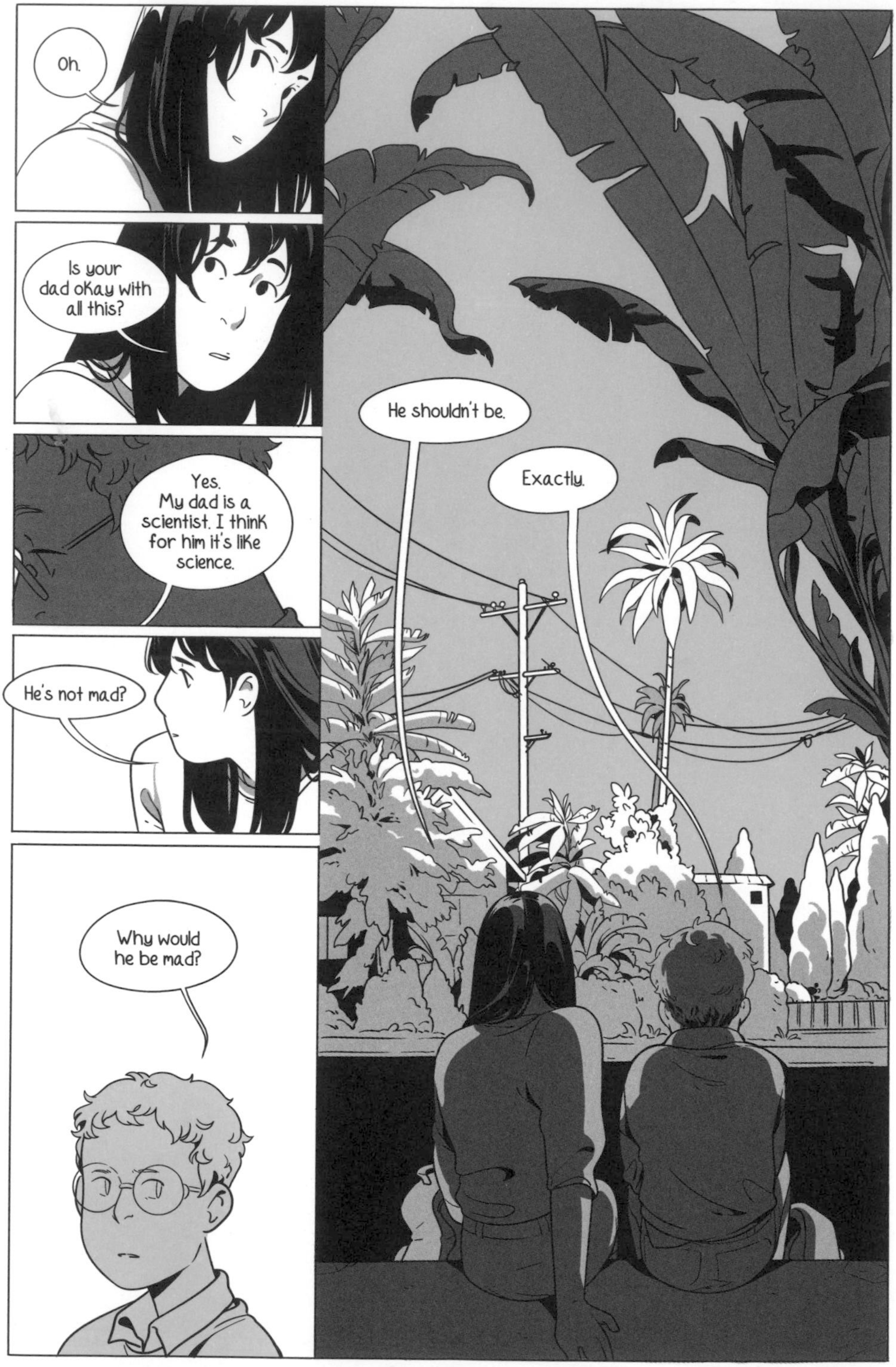
Oh.
Is your dad okay with all this?
Yes. My dad is a scientist. I think for him it's like science.
He's not mad?
Why would he be mad?
He shouldn't be.
Exactly.

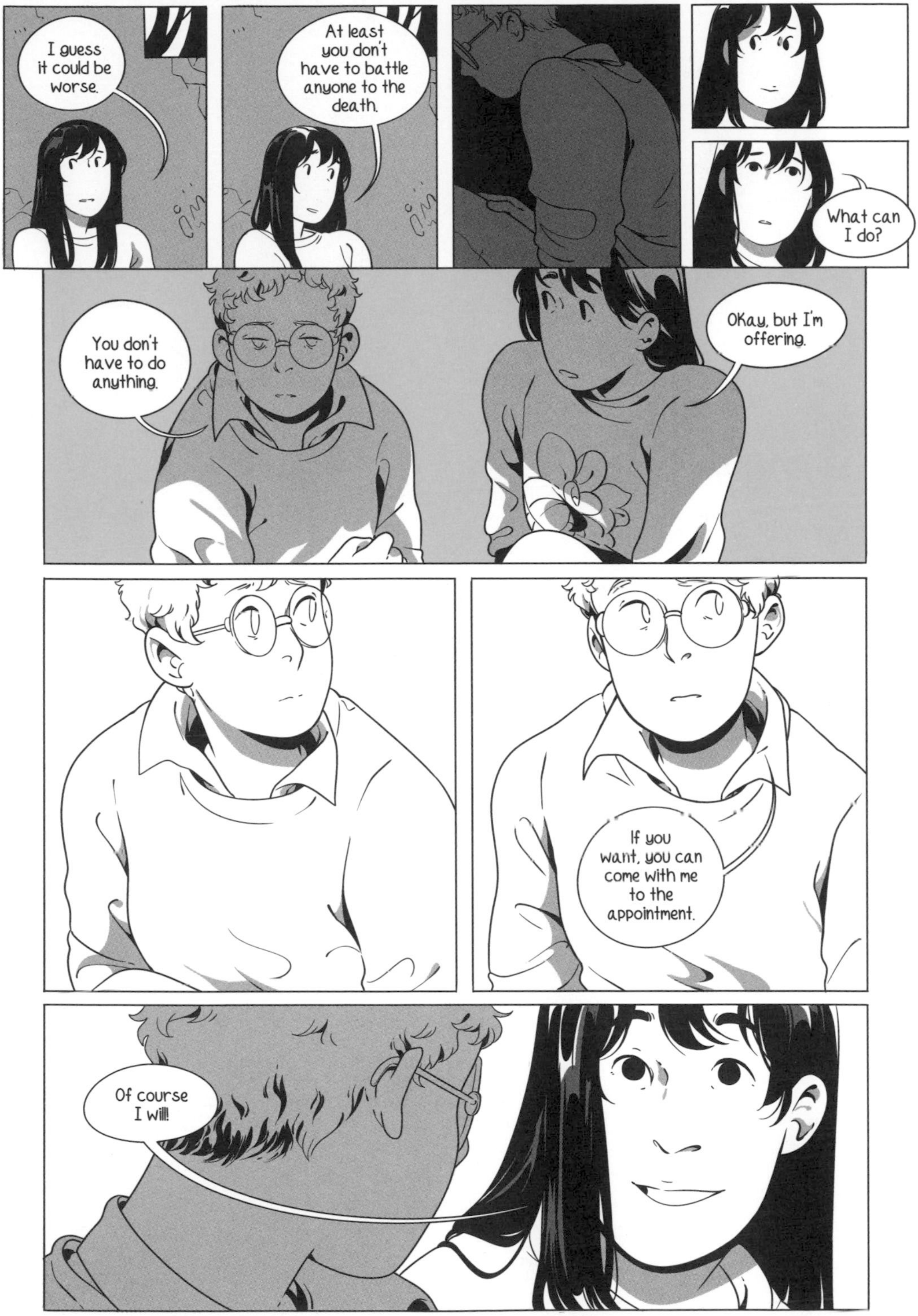

I guess it could be worse.
At least you don't have to battle anyone to the death.
What can I do?
You don't have to do anything.
Okay, but I'm offering.
If you want, you can come with me to the appointment.
Of course I will!

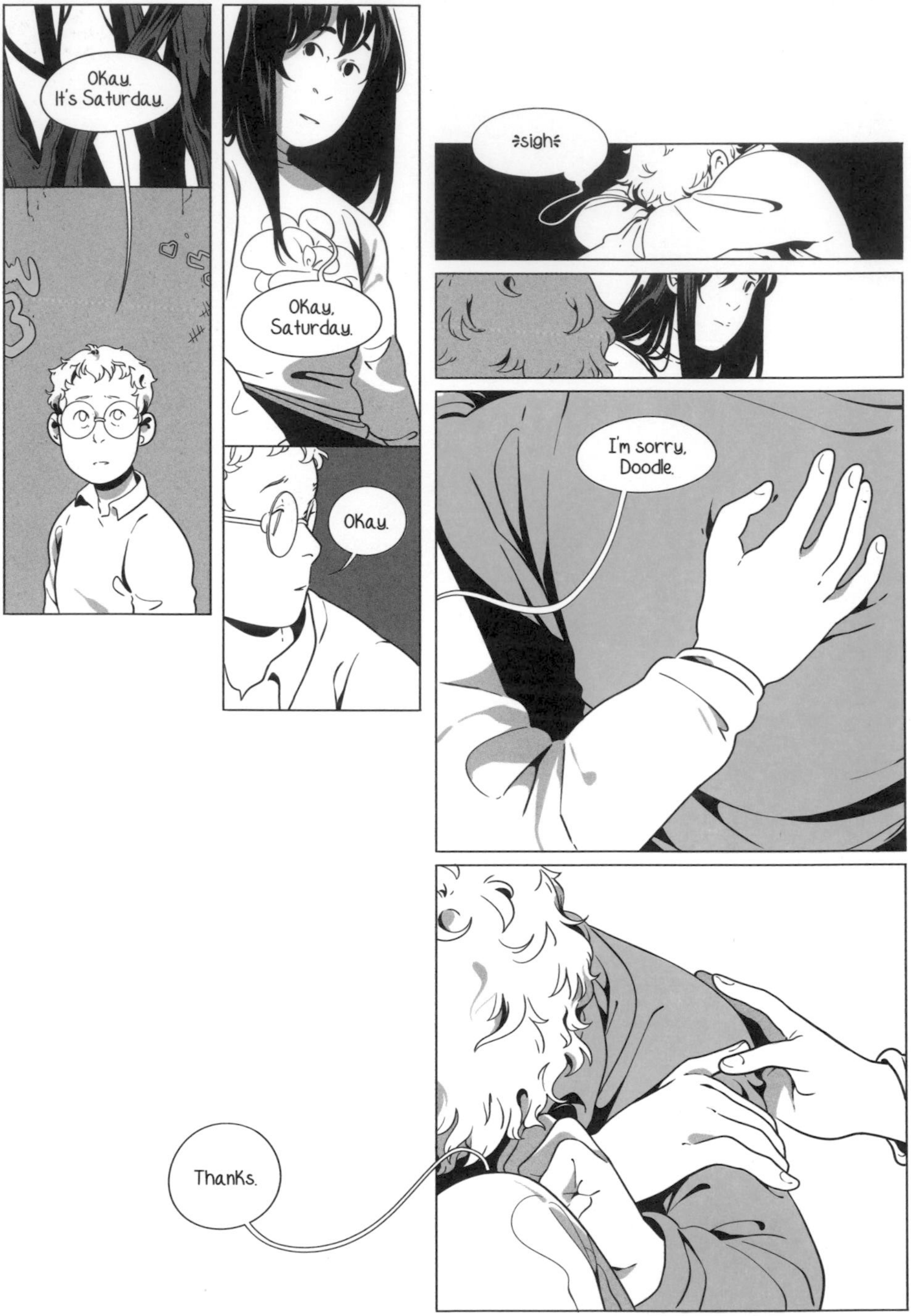
OKay.
It's Saturday.
OKay,
Saturday.
OKay.
sigh
I'm sorry,
Doodle.
ThanKs.

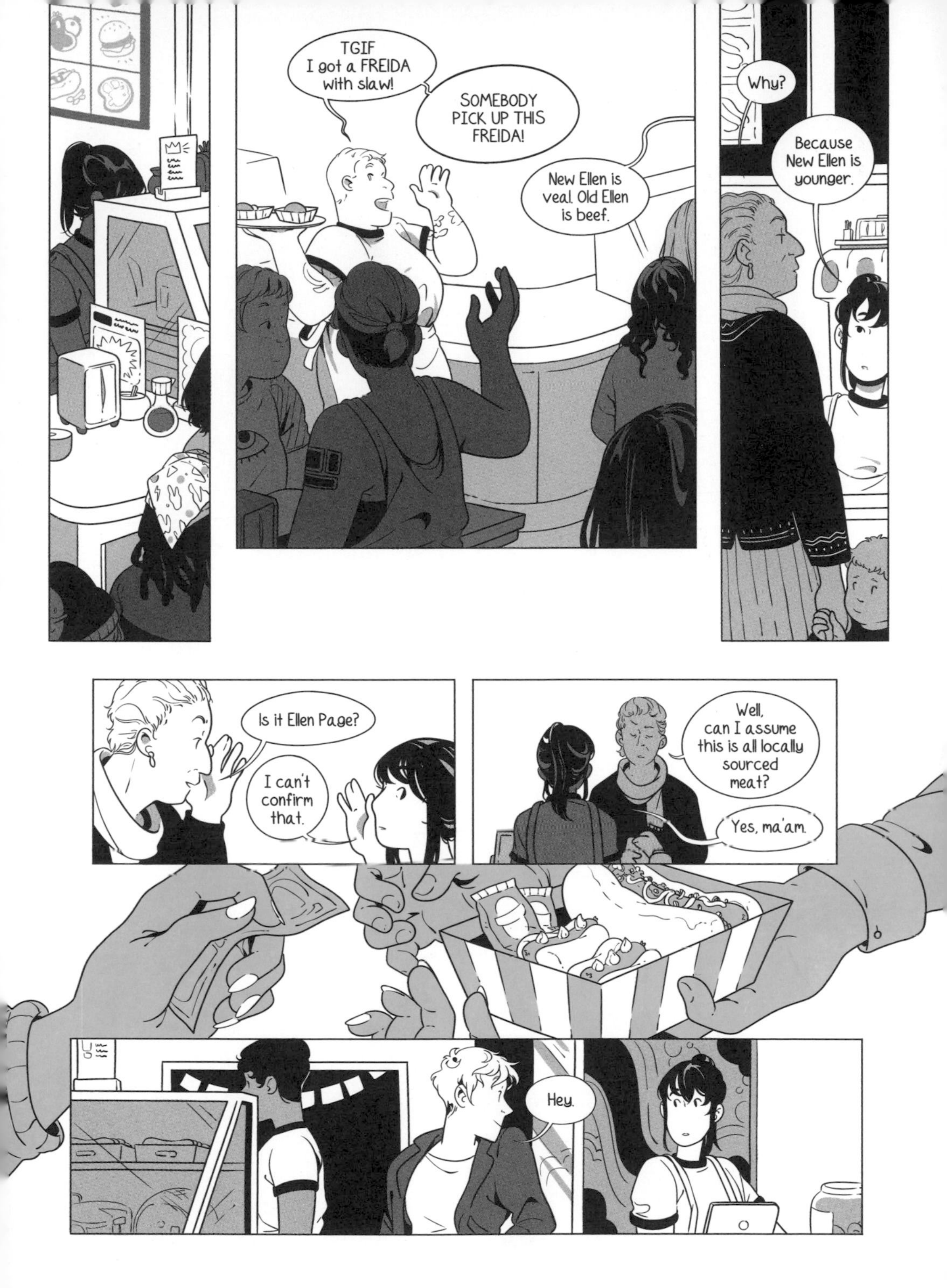
TGIF
I got a FREIDA with slaw!
SOMEBODY PICK UP THIS FREIDA!
New Ellen is veal. Old Ellen is beef.
Why?
Because New Ellen is younger.
Is it Ellen Page?
I can't confirm that.
Well, can I assume this is all locally sourced meat?
Yes, ma'am.
Hey.

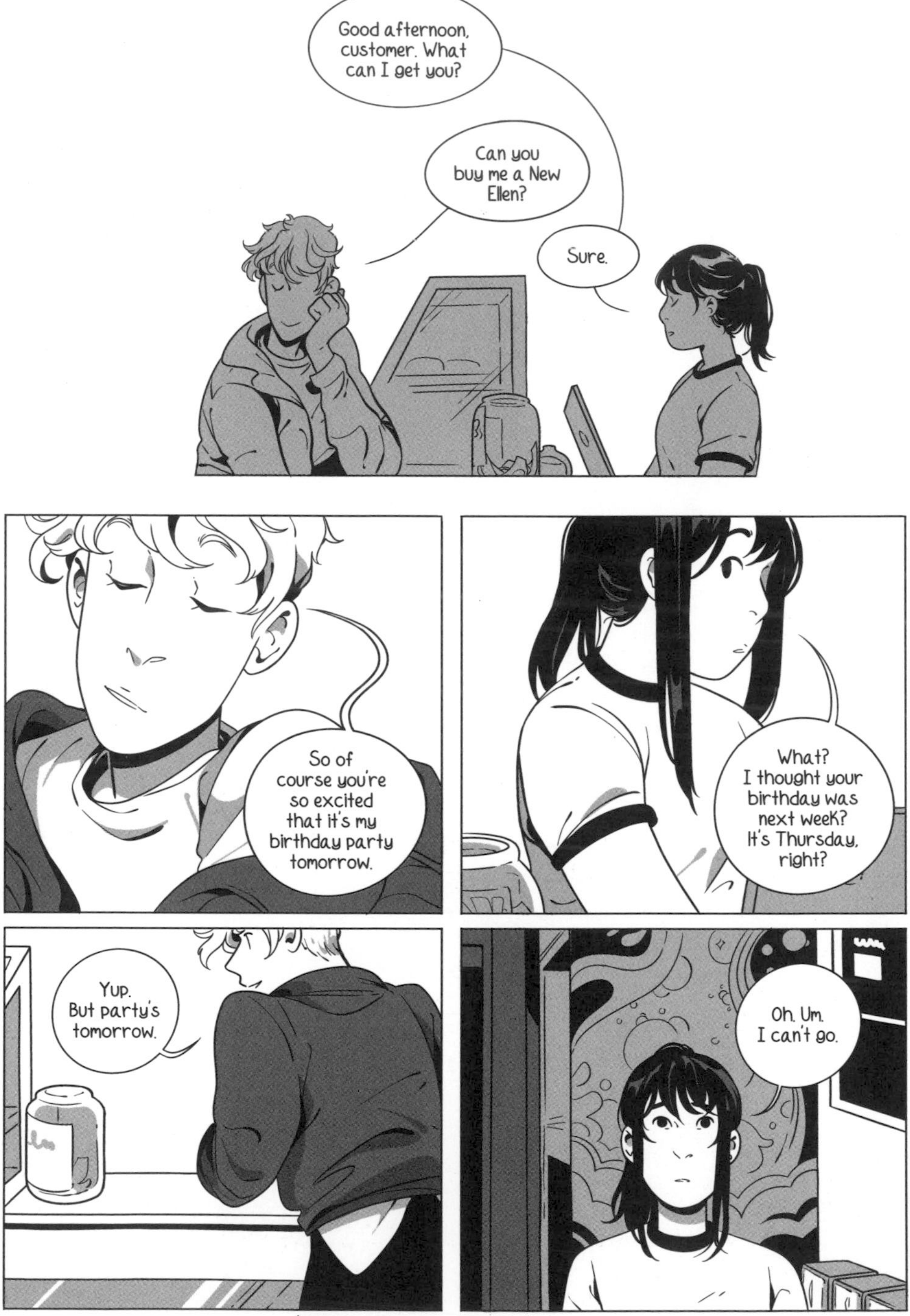
Good afternoon, customer. What can I get you?
Can you buy me a New Ellen?
Sure.
So of course you're so excited that it's my birthday party tomorrow.
What? I thought your birthday was next week? It's Thursday, right?
Yup. But party's tomorrow.
Oh. Um. I can't go.

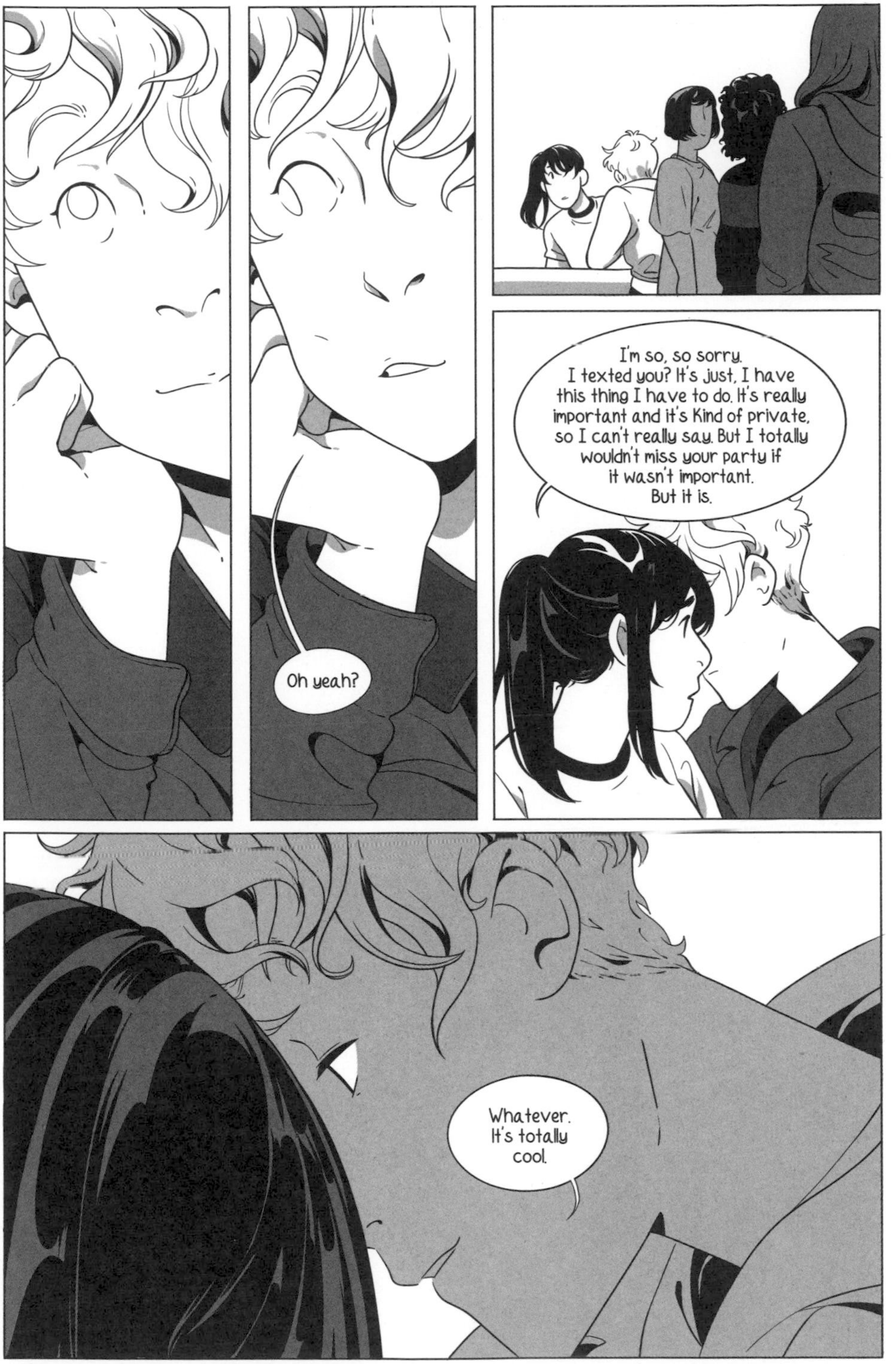
Oh yeah?
I'm so, so sorry. I texted you? It's just, I have this thing I have to do. It's really important and it's Kind of private, so I can't really say. But I totally wouldn't miss your party if it wasn't important. But it is.
Whatever. It's totally cool.

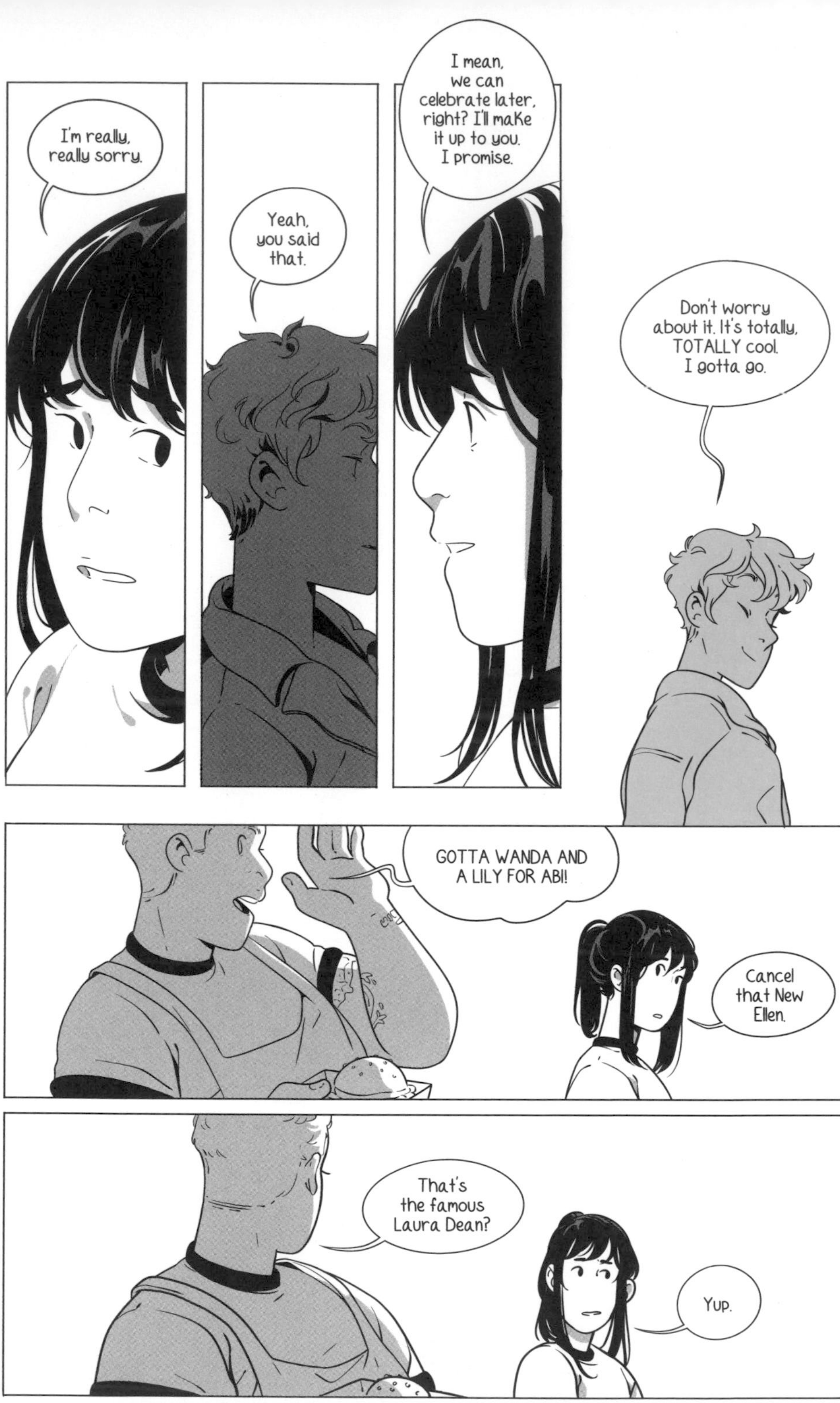
I'm really, really sorry.
Yeah, you said that.
I mean, we can celebrate later, right? I'll make it up to you. I promise.
Don't worry about it. It's totally, TOTALLY cool. I gotta go.
GOTTA WANDA AND A LILY FOR ABI!
Cancel that New Ellen.
That's the famous Laura Dean?
Yup.

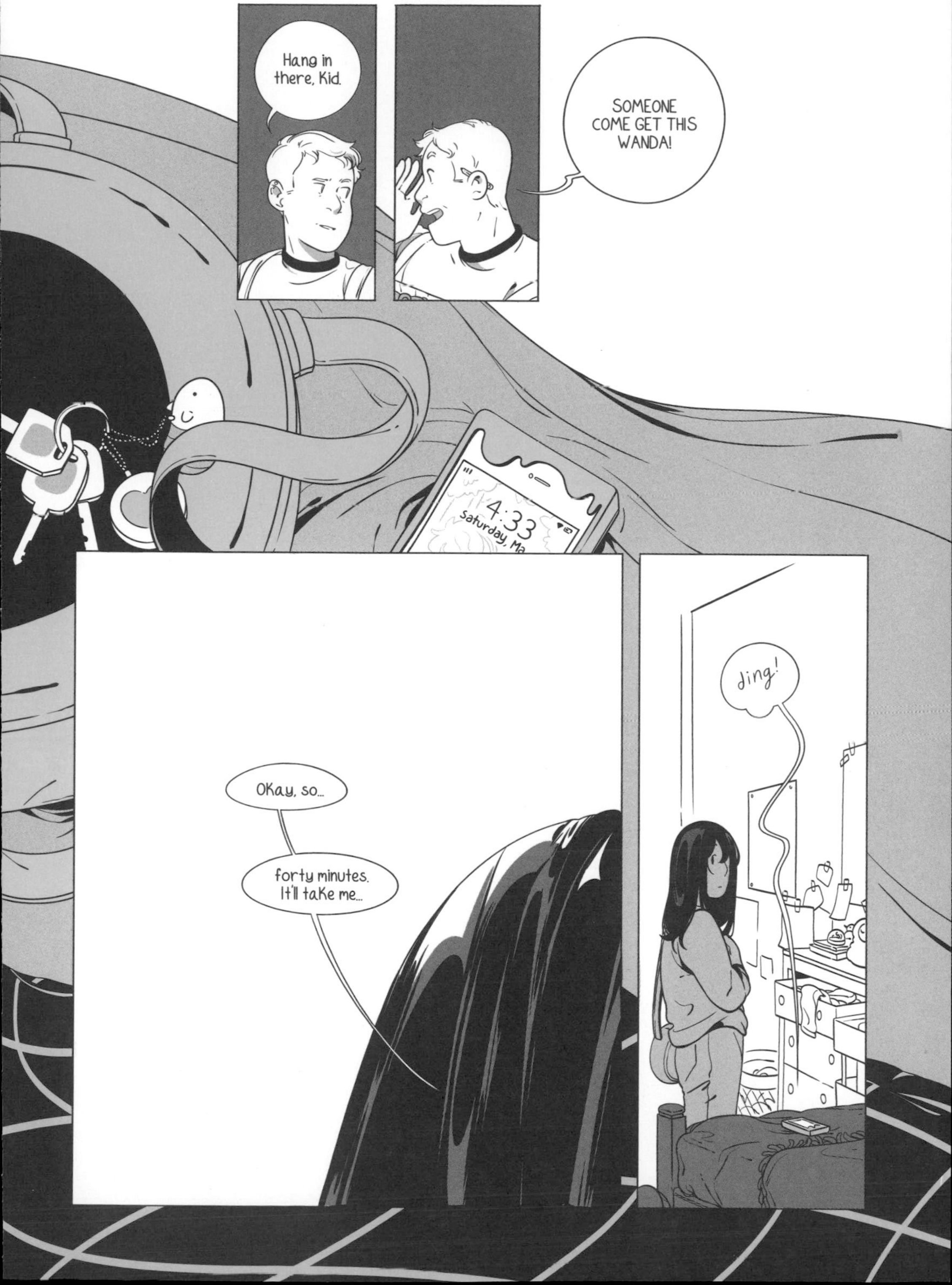
Hang in there, Kid.
SOMEONE COME GET THIS WANDA!
4:33
Saturday, Ma
ding!
OKay, so...
forty minutes. It'll take me...

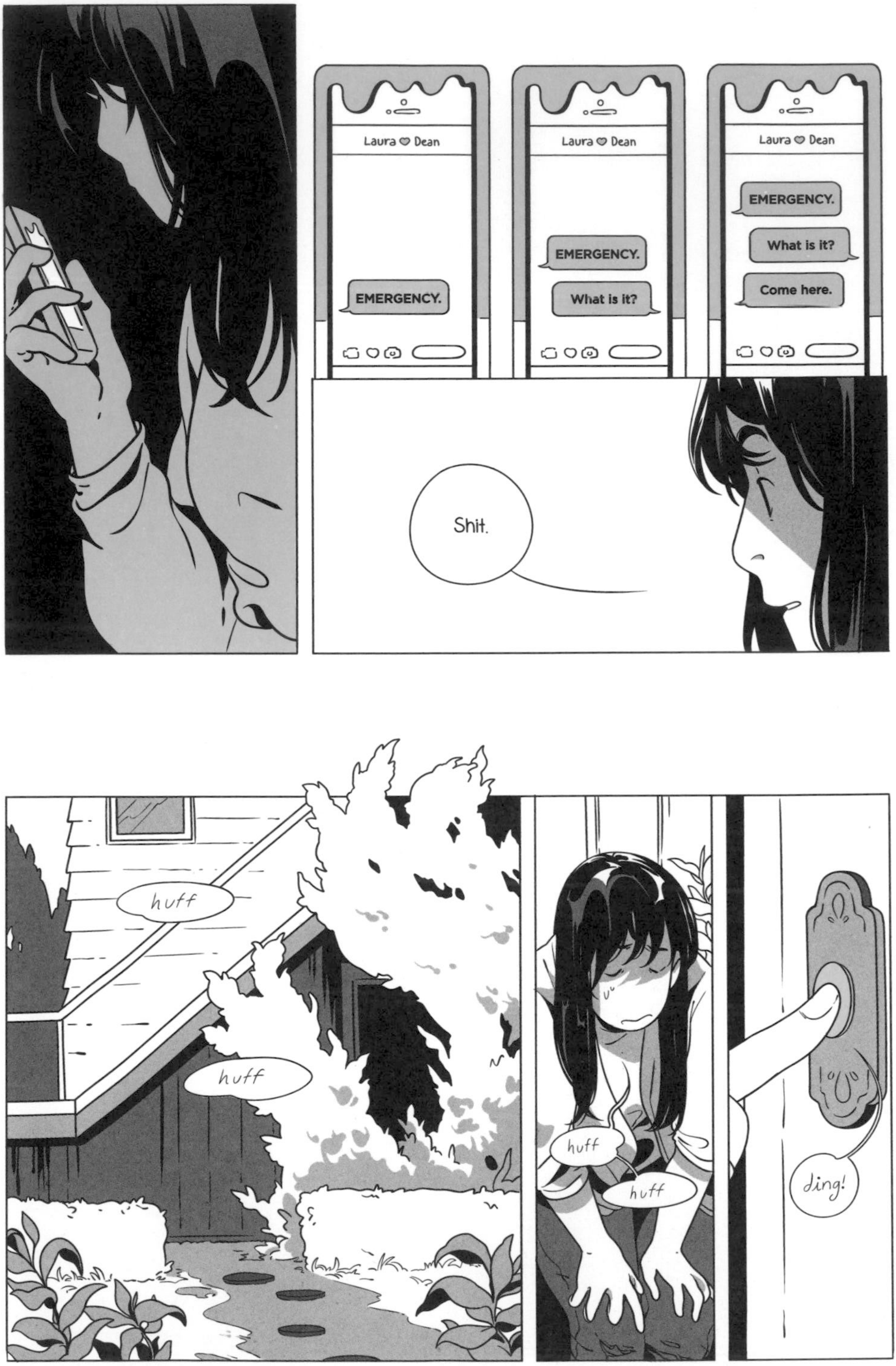

Laura ♥ Dean
EMERGENCY.
Laura ♥ Dean
EMERGENCY.
What is it?
Laura ♥ Dean
EMERGENCY.
What is it?
Come here.
Shit.
huff
huff
huff
huff
ding!

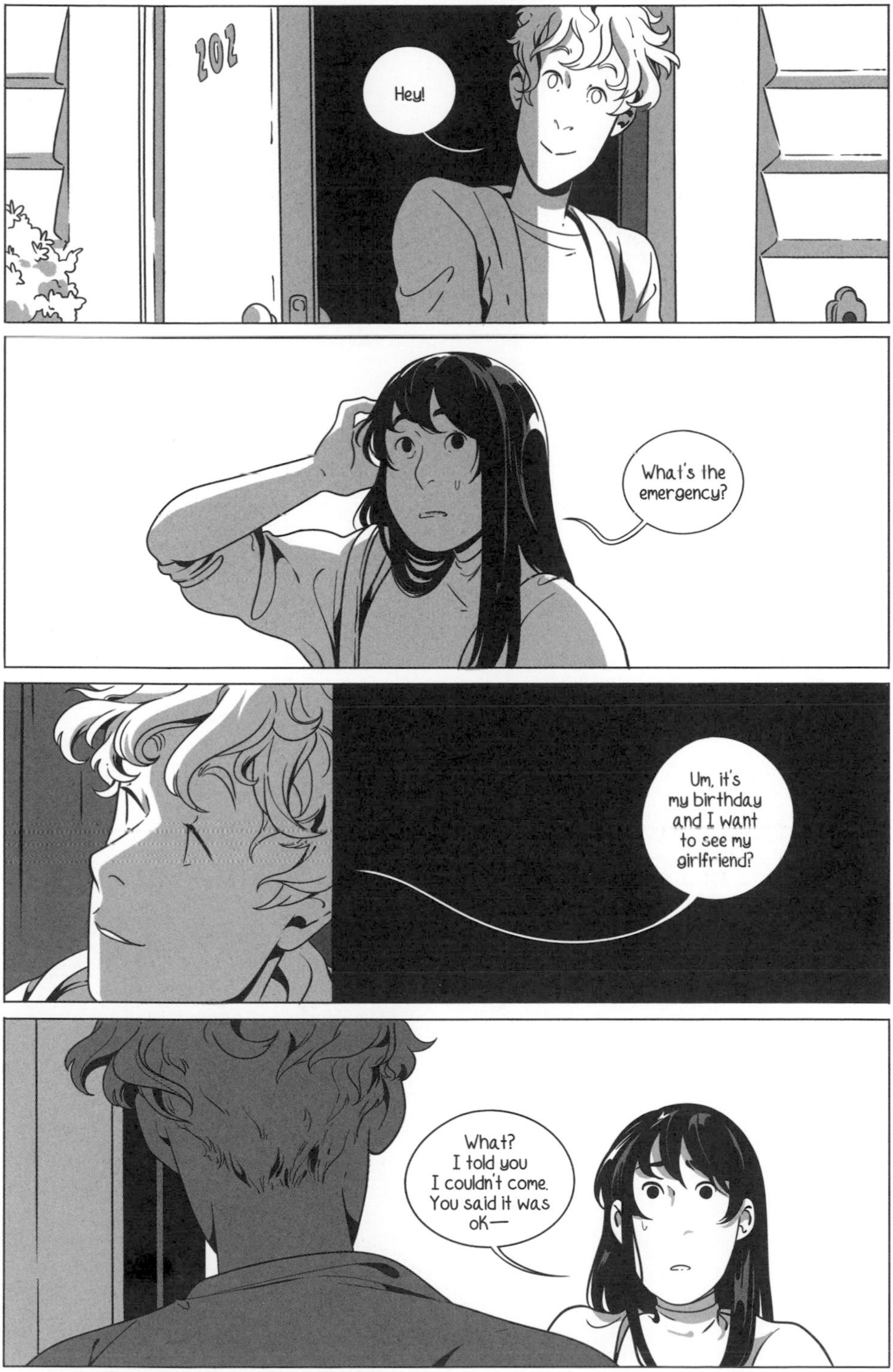

202
Hey!
What's the emergency?
Um, it's my birthday and I want to see my girlfriend?
What? I told you I couldn't come. You said it was oK—

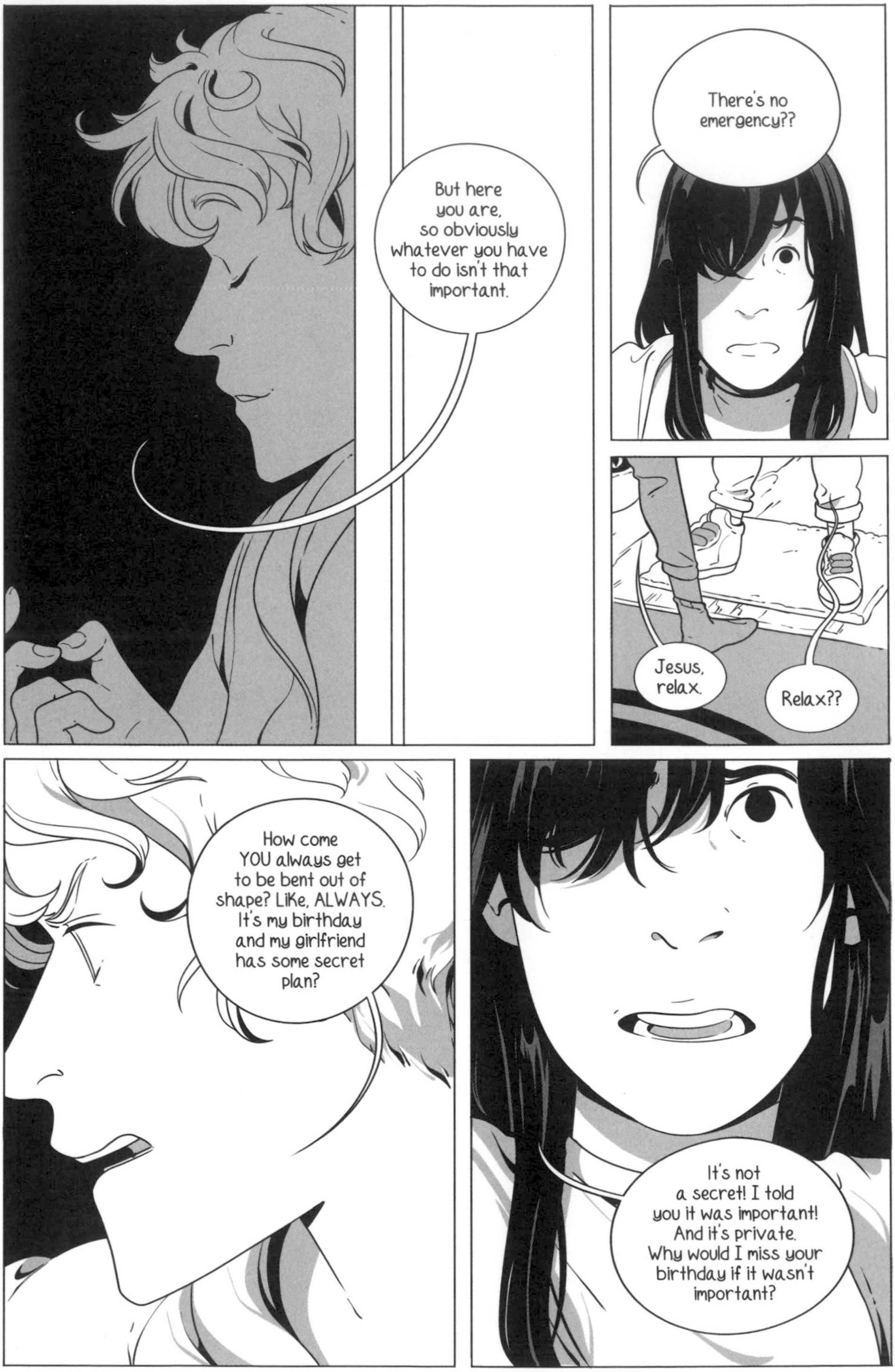
But here you are, so obviously whatever you have to do isn't that important.
There's no emergency??
Jesus, relax.
Relax??
How come YOU always get to be bent out of shape? Like, ALWAYS. It's my birthday and my girlfriend has some secret plan?
It's not a secret! I told you it was important! And it's private. Why would I miss your birthday if it wasn't important?

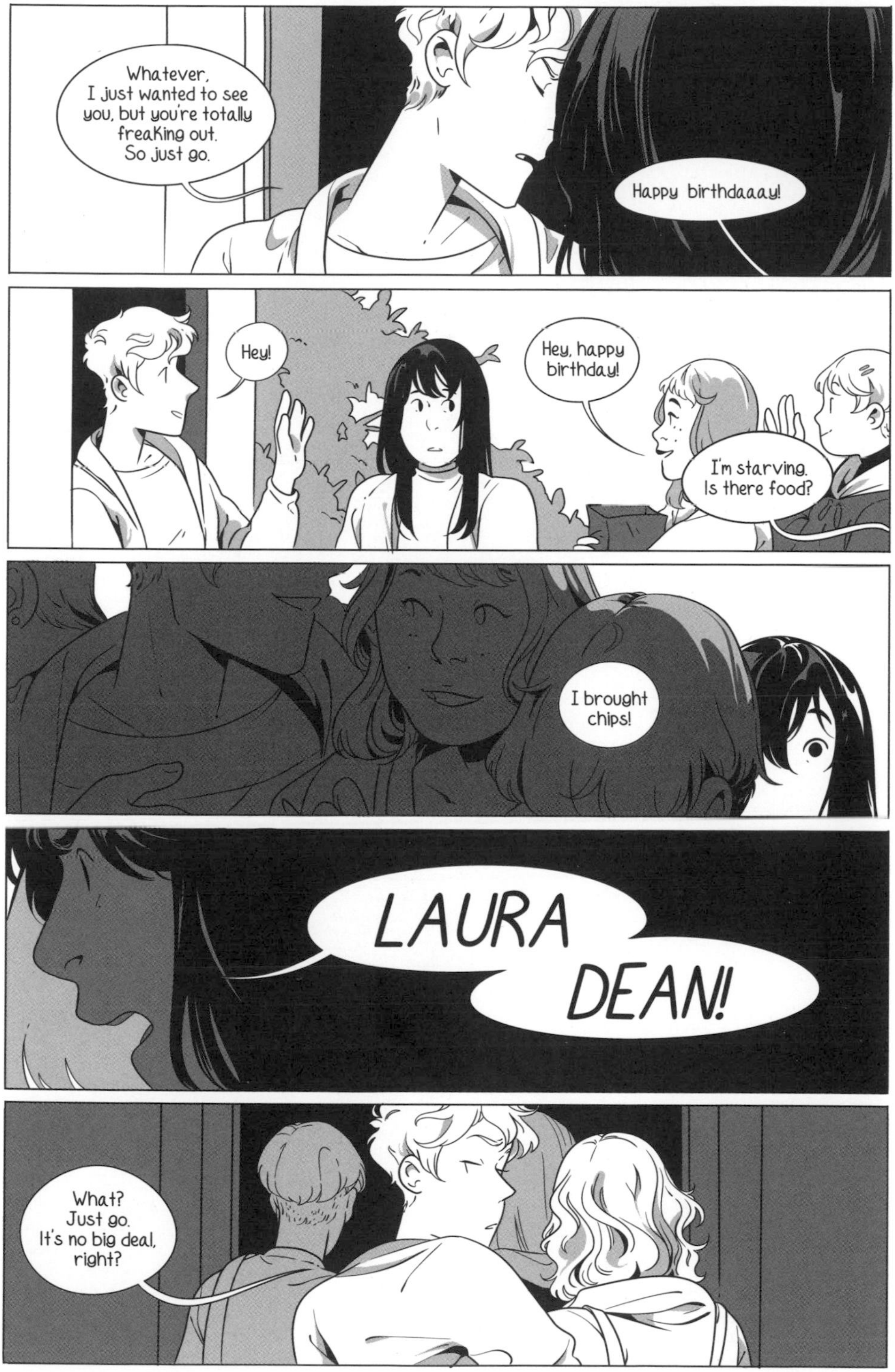
Whatever, I just wanted to see you, but you're totally freaking out. So just go.
Happy birthdaaay!
Hey!
Hey, happy birthday!
I'm starving. Is there food?
I brought chips!
LAURA DEAN!
What? Just go. It's no big deal, right?

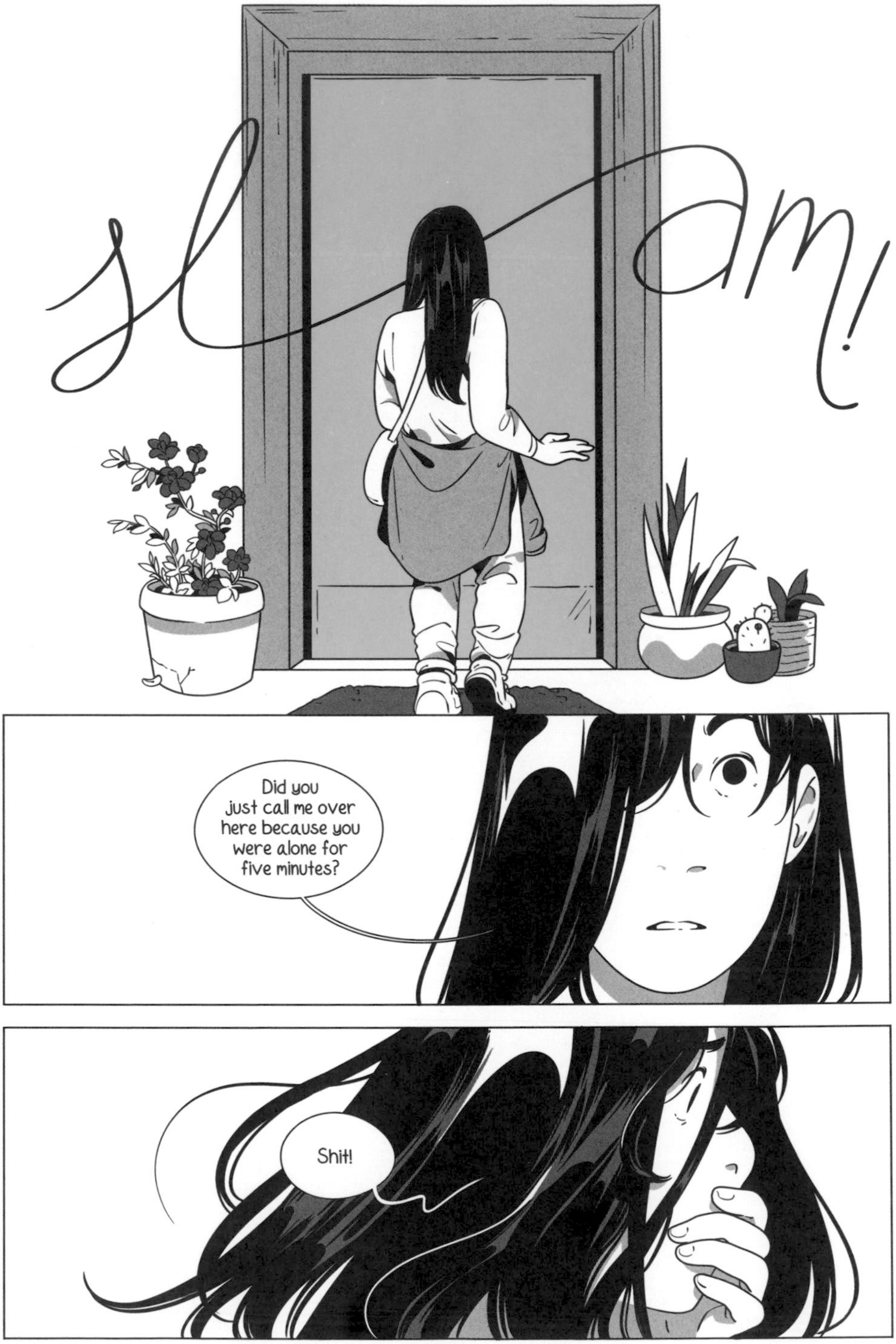
slam!
Did you just call me over here because you were alone for five minutes?
Shit!

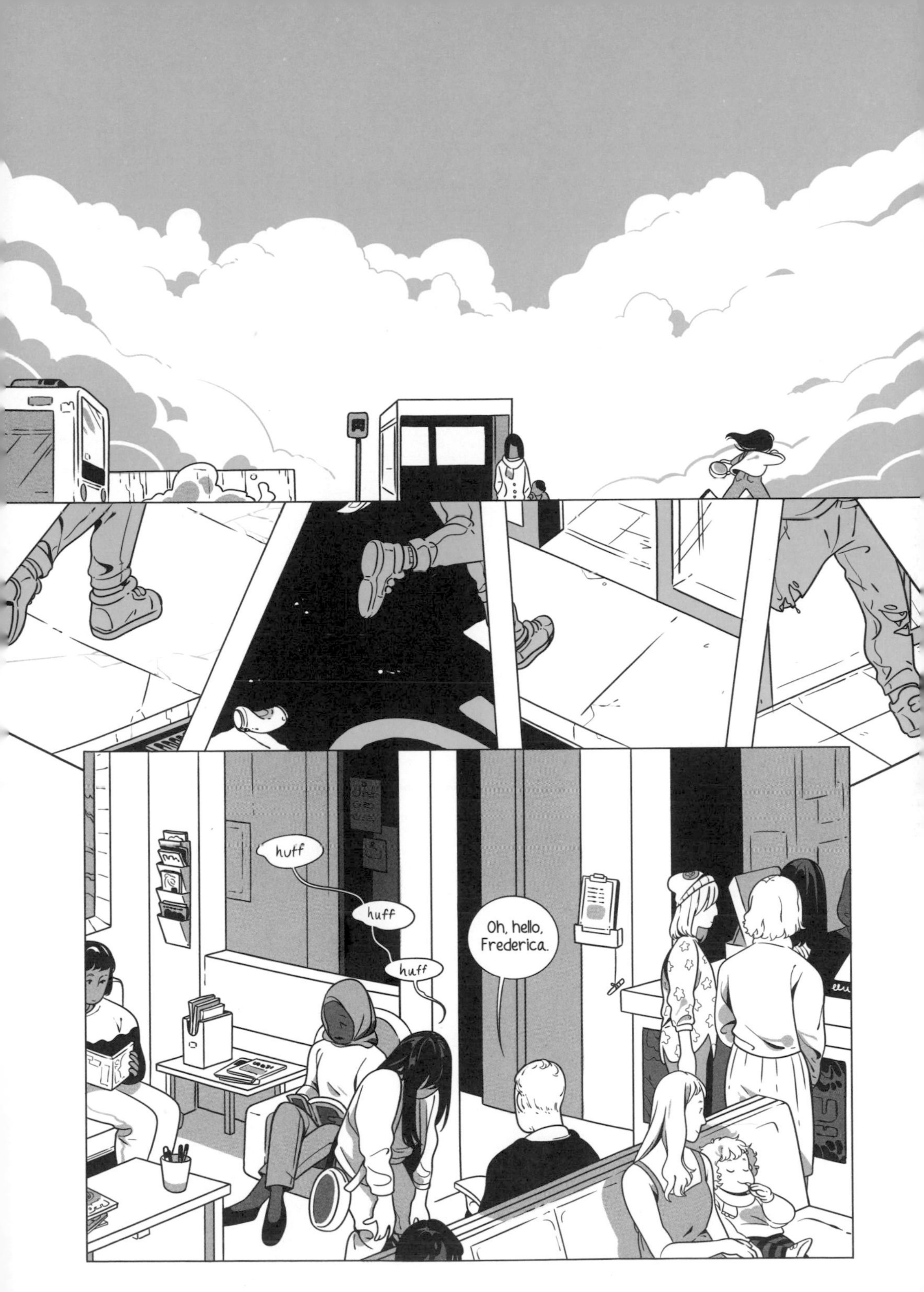
huff
huff
huff
Oh, hello, Frederica.

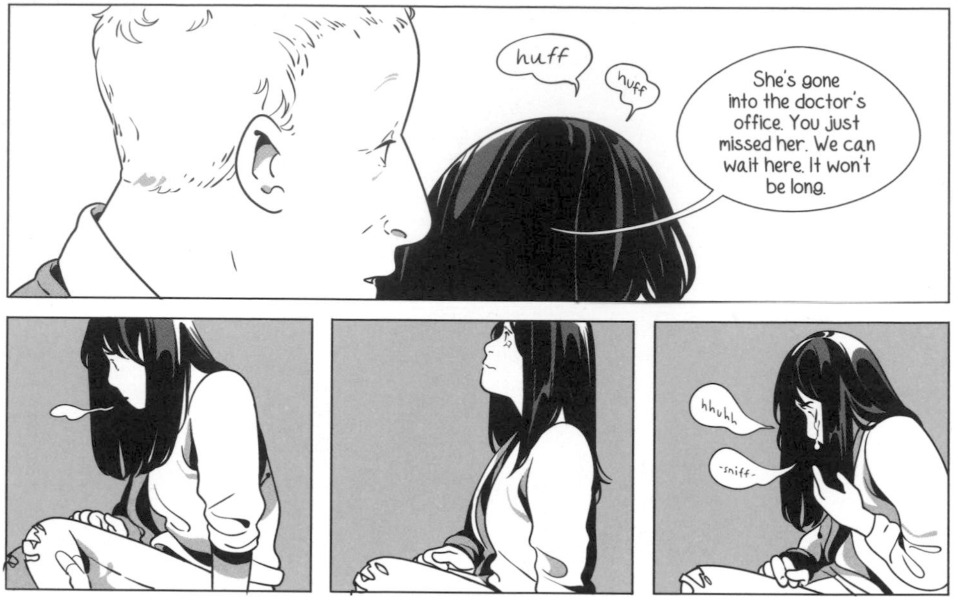
huff
huff
She's gone into the doctor's office. You just missed her. We can wait here. It won't be long.
hhuhh
-sniff-

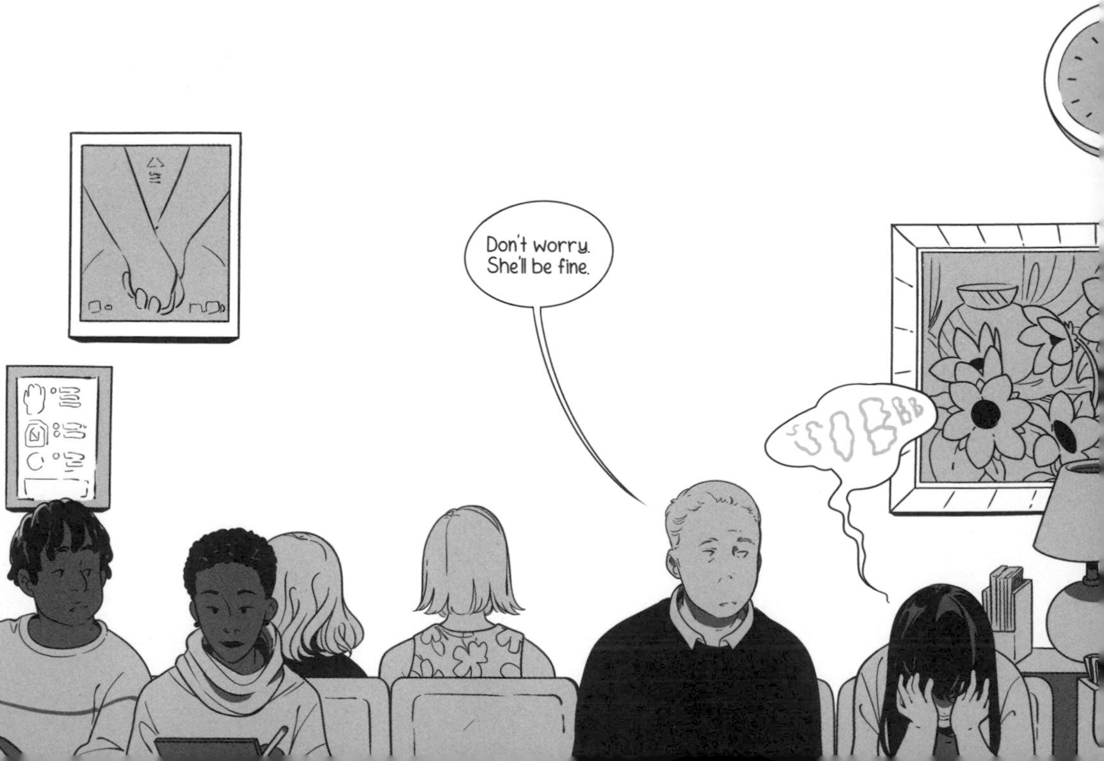
Don't worry. She'll be fine.
SOBBB

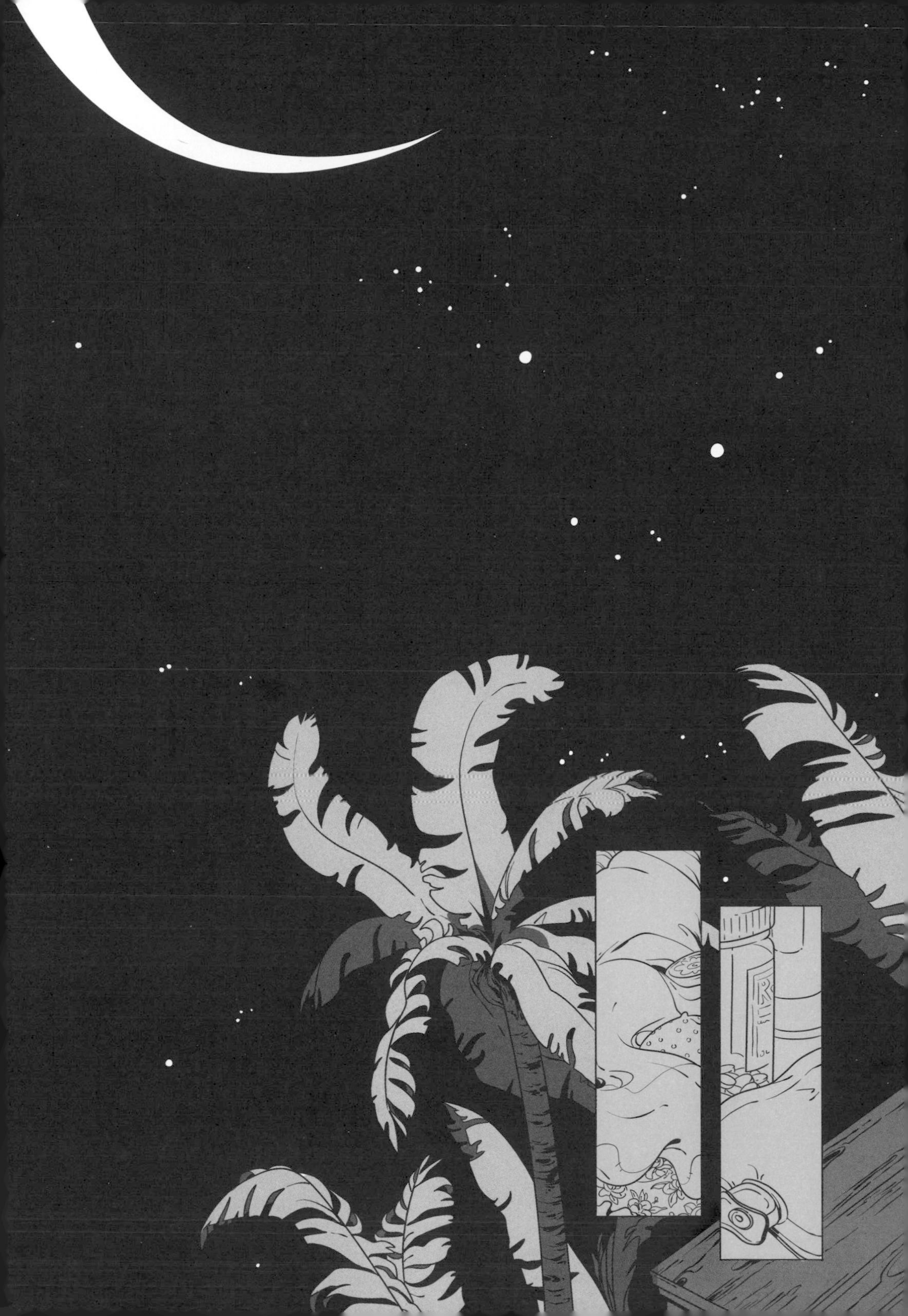

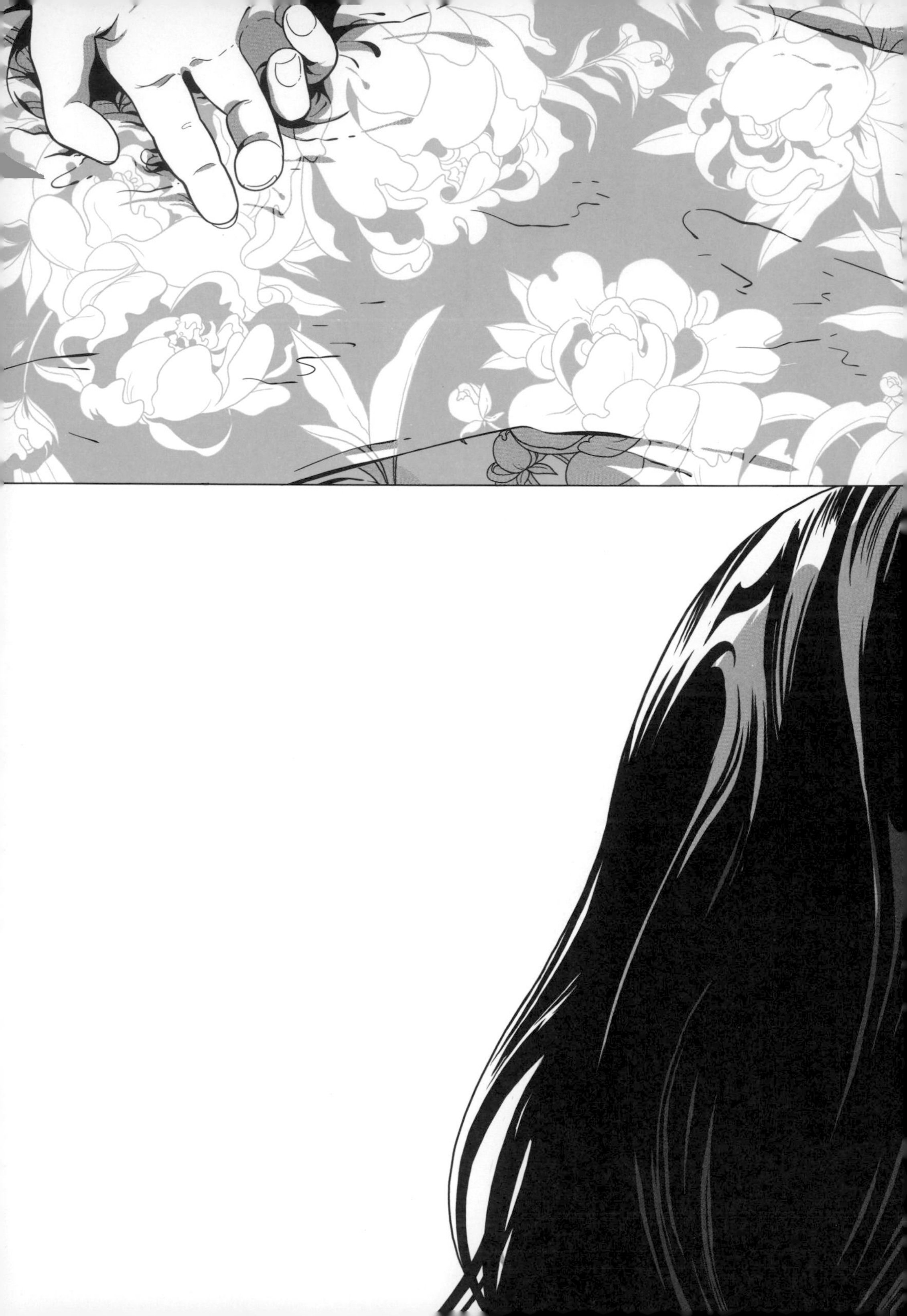

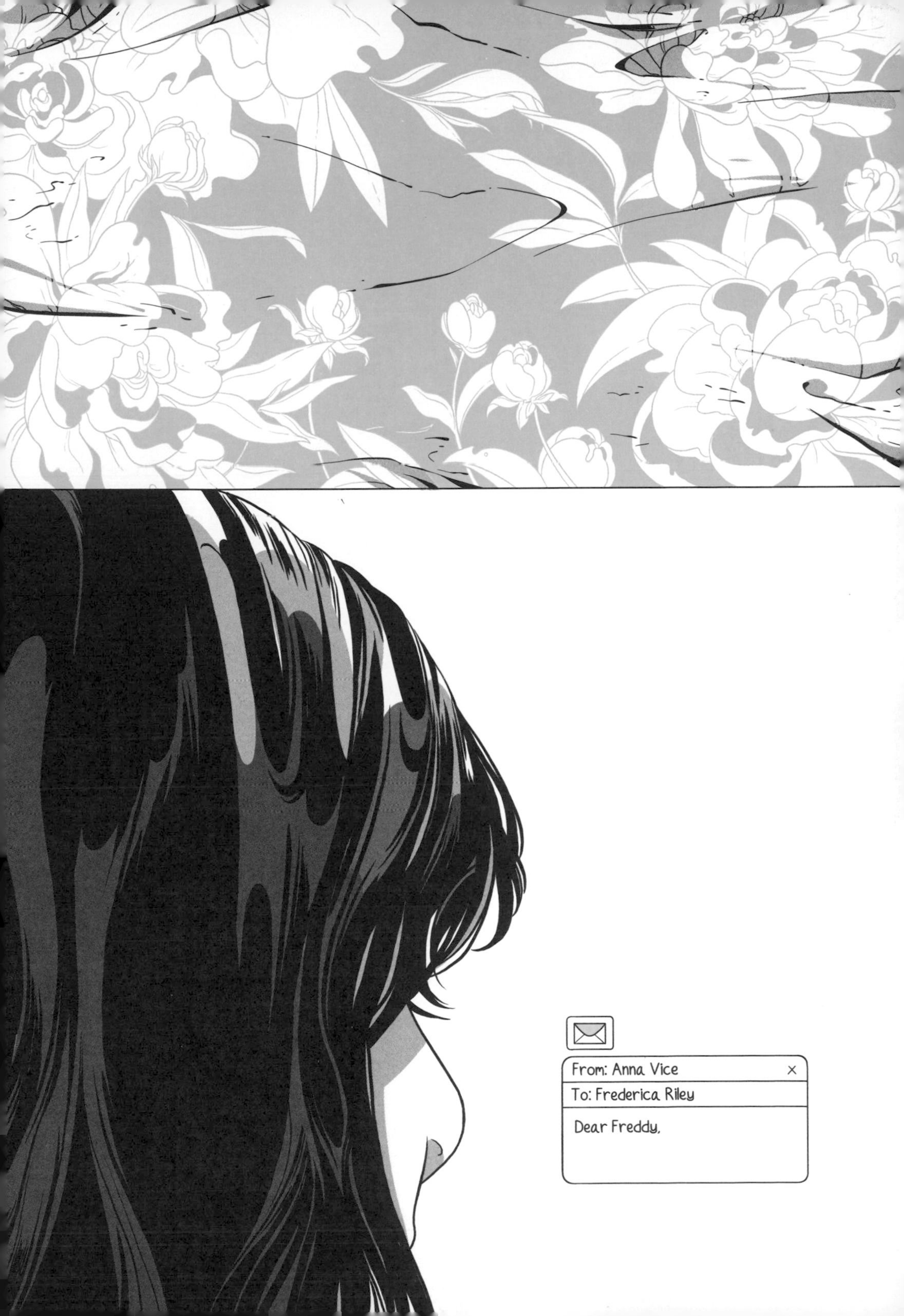
From: Anna Vice
To: Frederica Riley
Dear Freddy,

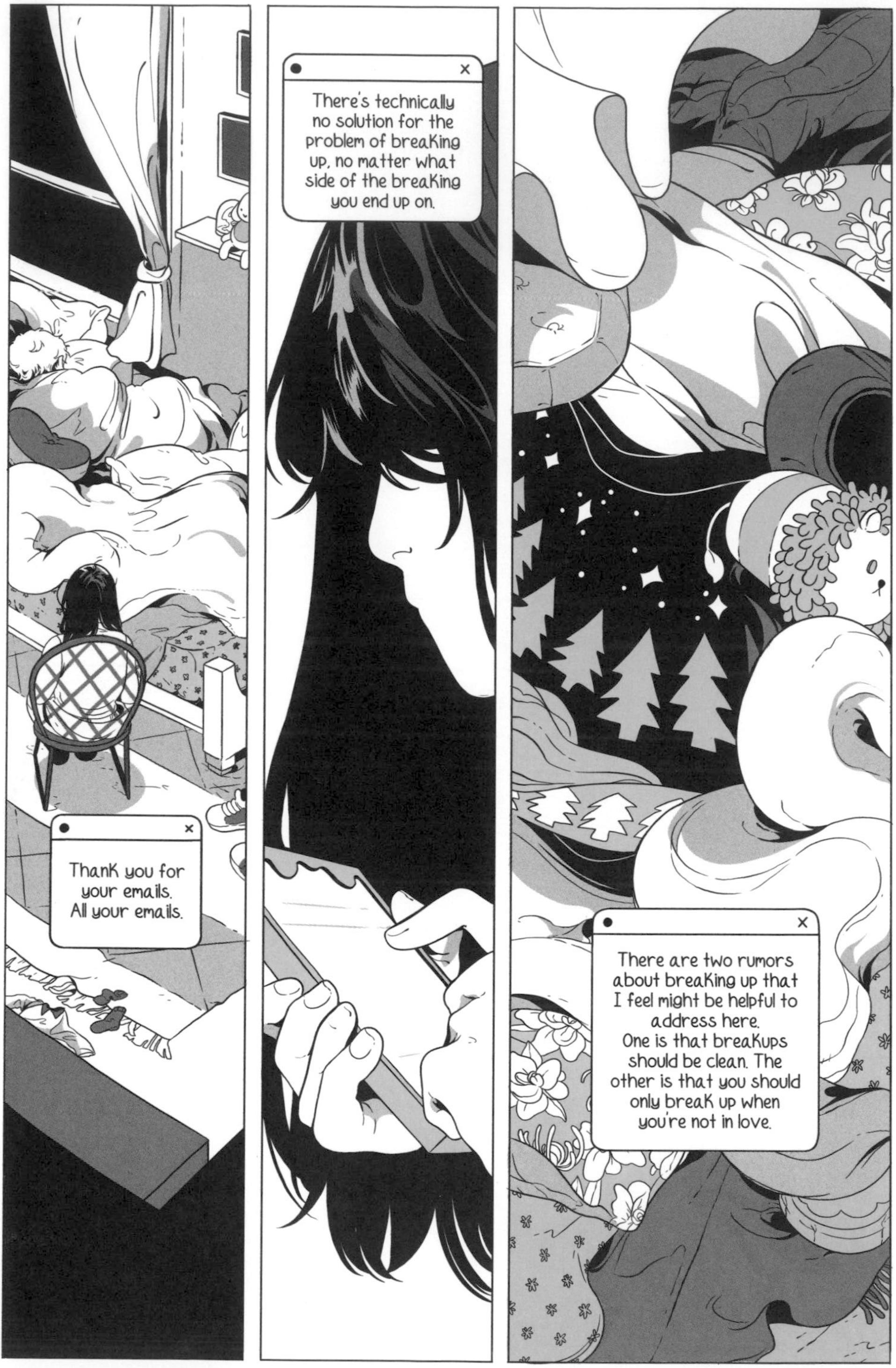
Thank you for your emails. All your emails.
There's technically no solution for the problem of breaking up, no matter what side of the breaking you end up on.
There are two rumors about breaking up that I feel might be helpful to address here. One is that breakups should be clean. The other is that you should only break up when you're not in love.

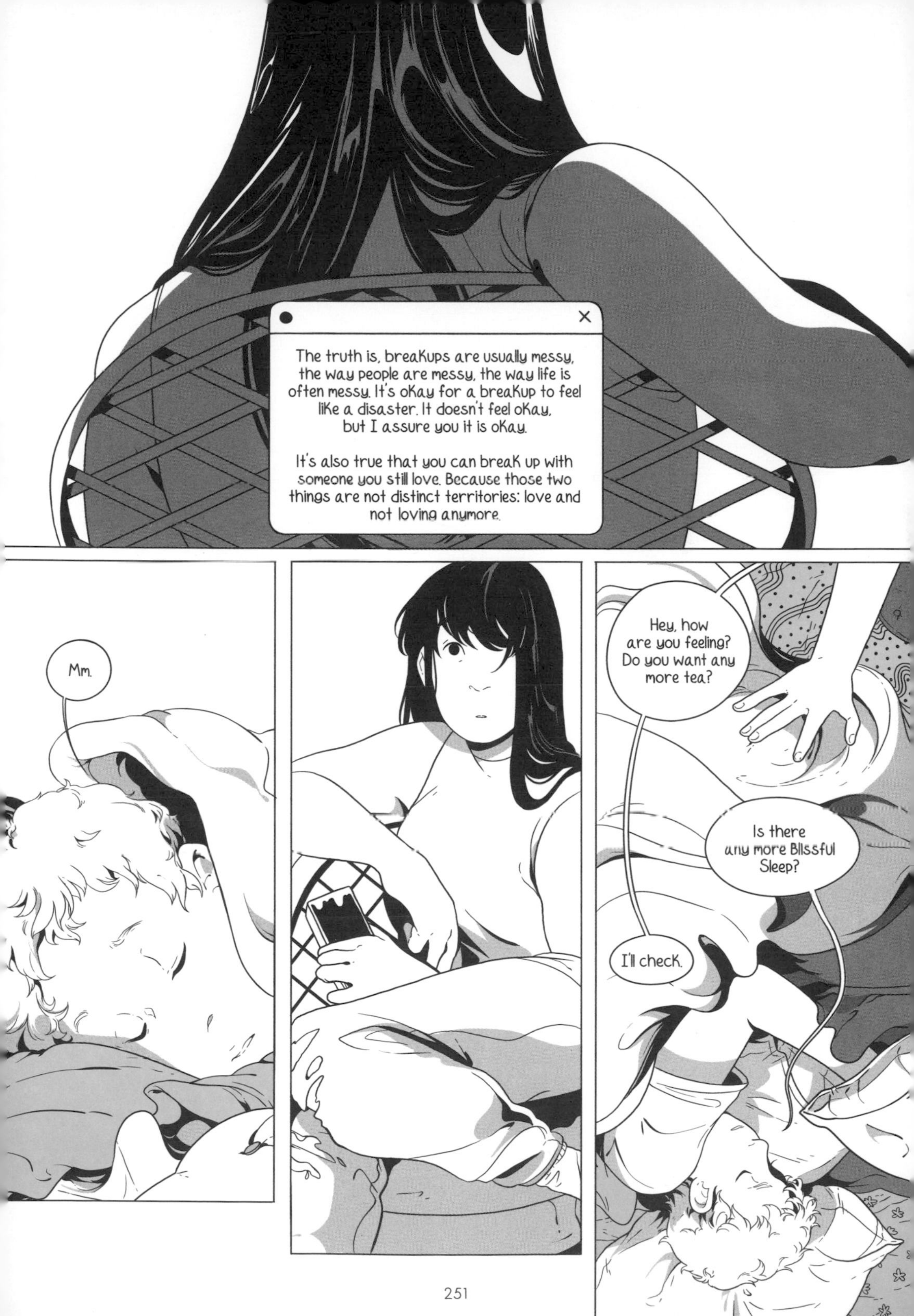
The truth is, breakups are usually messy, the way people are messy, the way life is often messy. It's okay for a breakup to feel like a disaster. It doesn't feel okay, but I assure you it is okay.
It's also true that you can break up with someone you still love. Because those two things are not distinct territories: love and not loving anymore.
Mm.
Hey, how are you feeling? Do you want any more tea?
Is there any more Blissful Sleep?
I'll check.

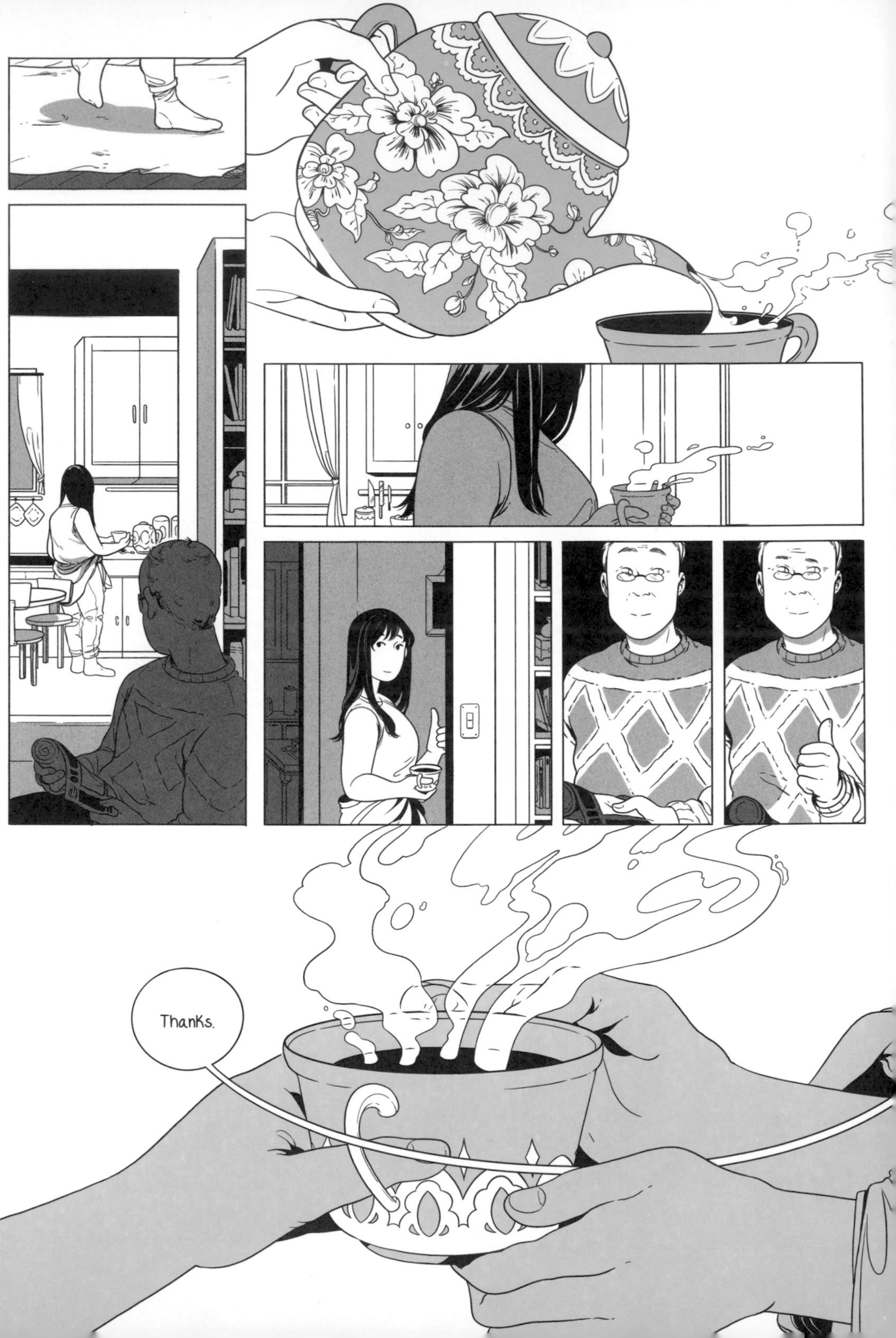
Thanks.

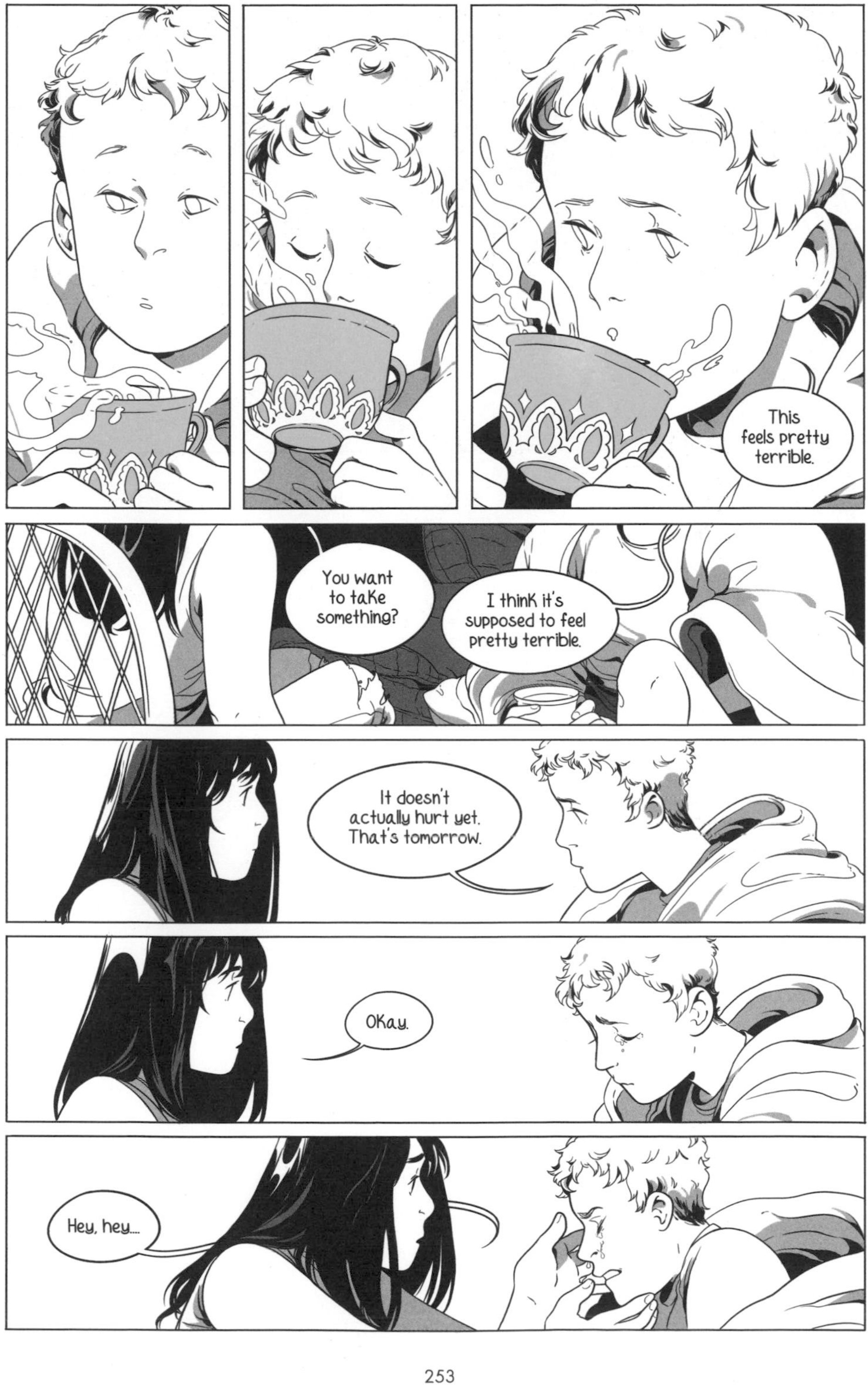
This feels pretty terrible.
You want to take something?
I think it's supposed to feel pretty terrible.
It doesn't actually hurt yet. That's tomorrow.
Okay.
Hey, hey....

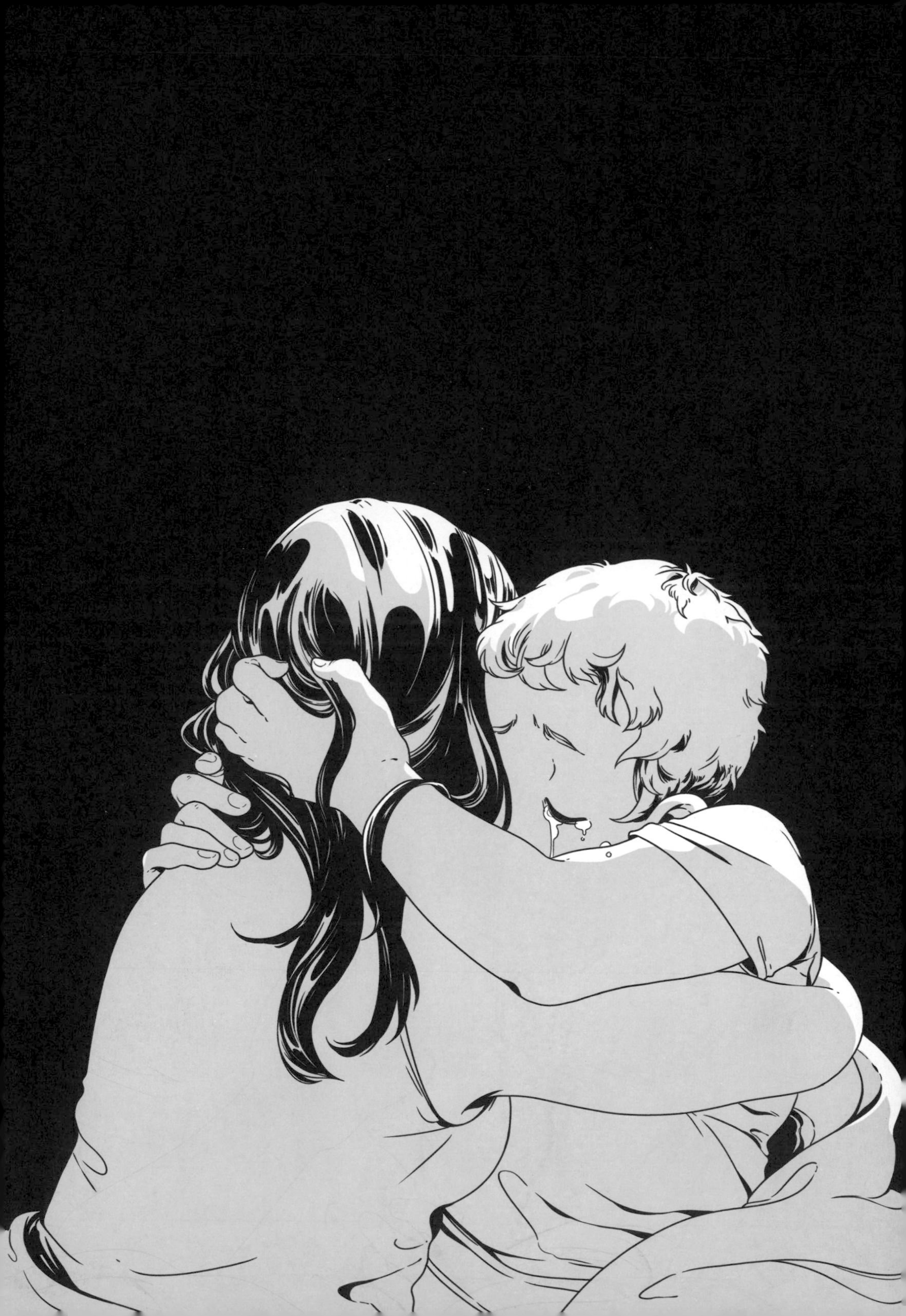

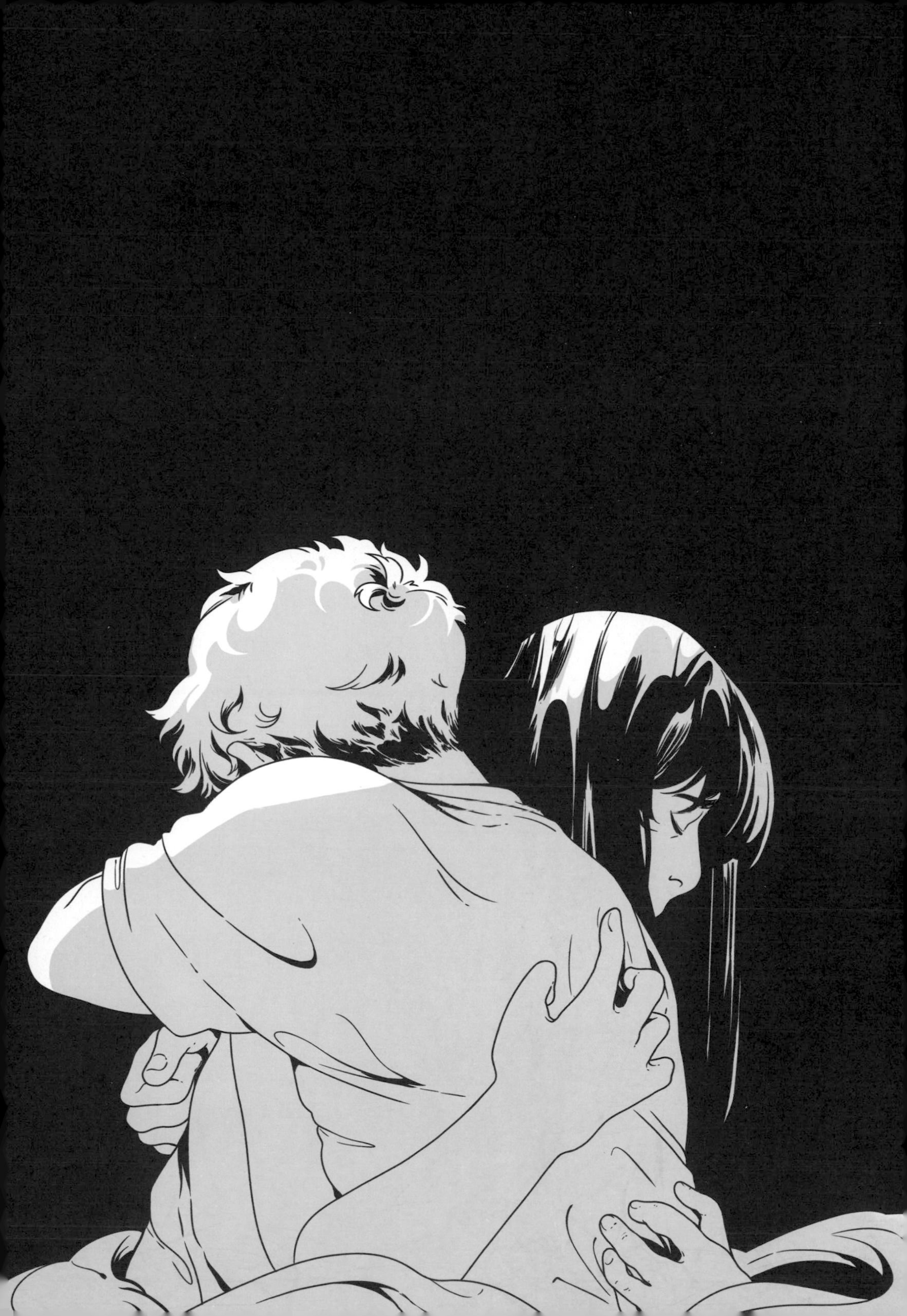

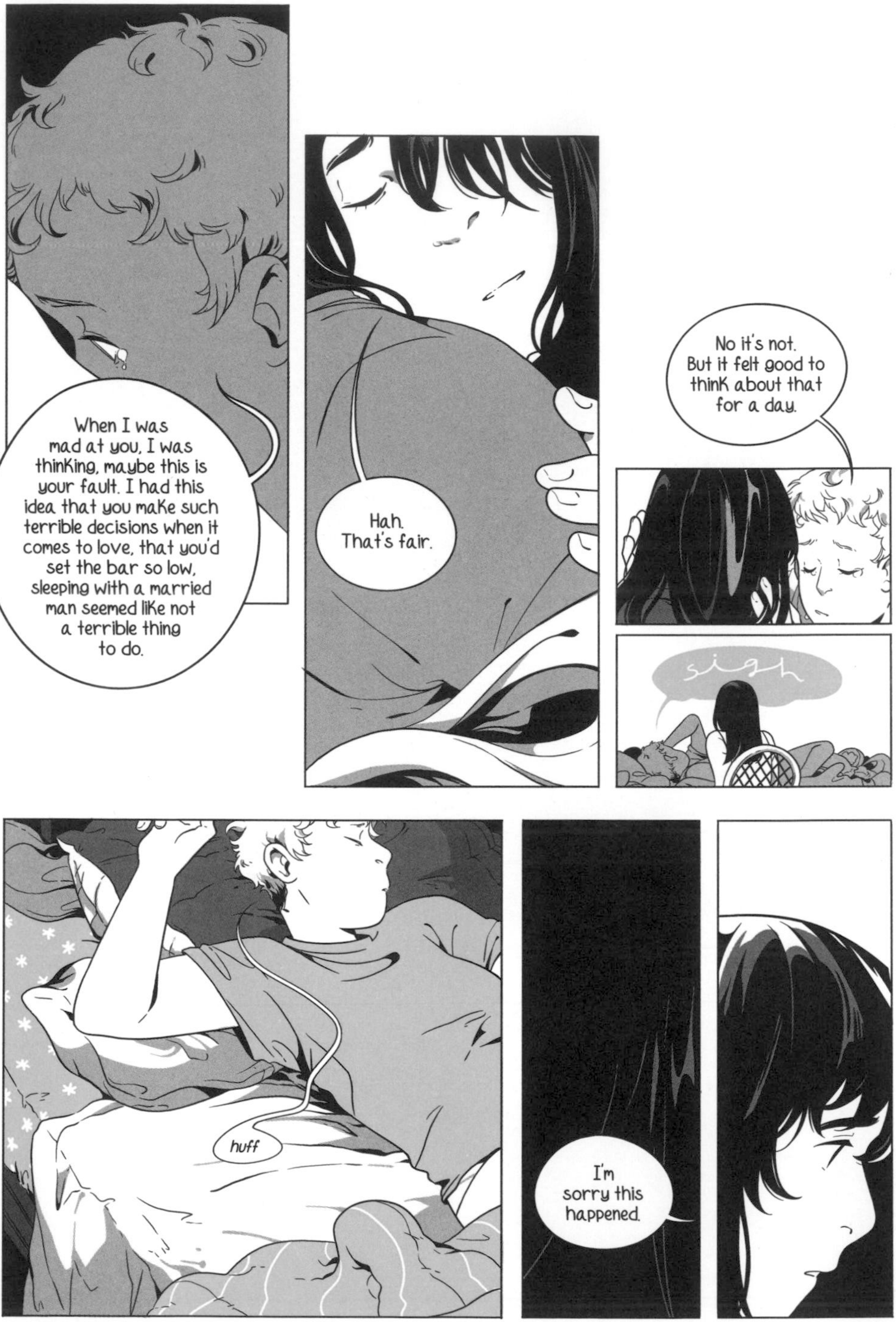
When I was mad at you, I was thinking, maybe this is your fault. I had this idea that you make such terrible decisions when it comes to love, that you'd set the bar so low, sleeping with a married man seemed like not a terrible thing to do.
Hah. That's fair.
No it's not. But it felt good to think about that for a day.
sigh
huff
I'm sorry this happened.

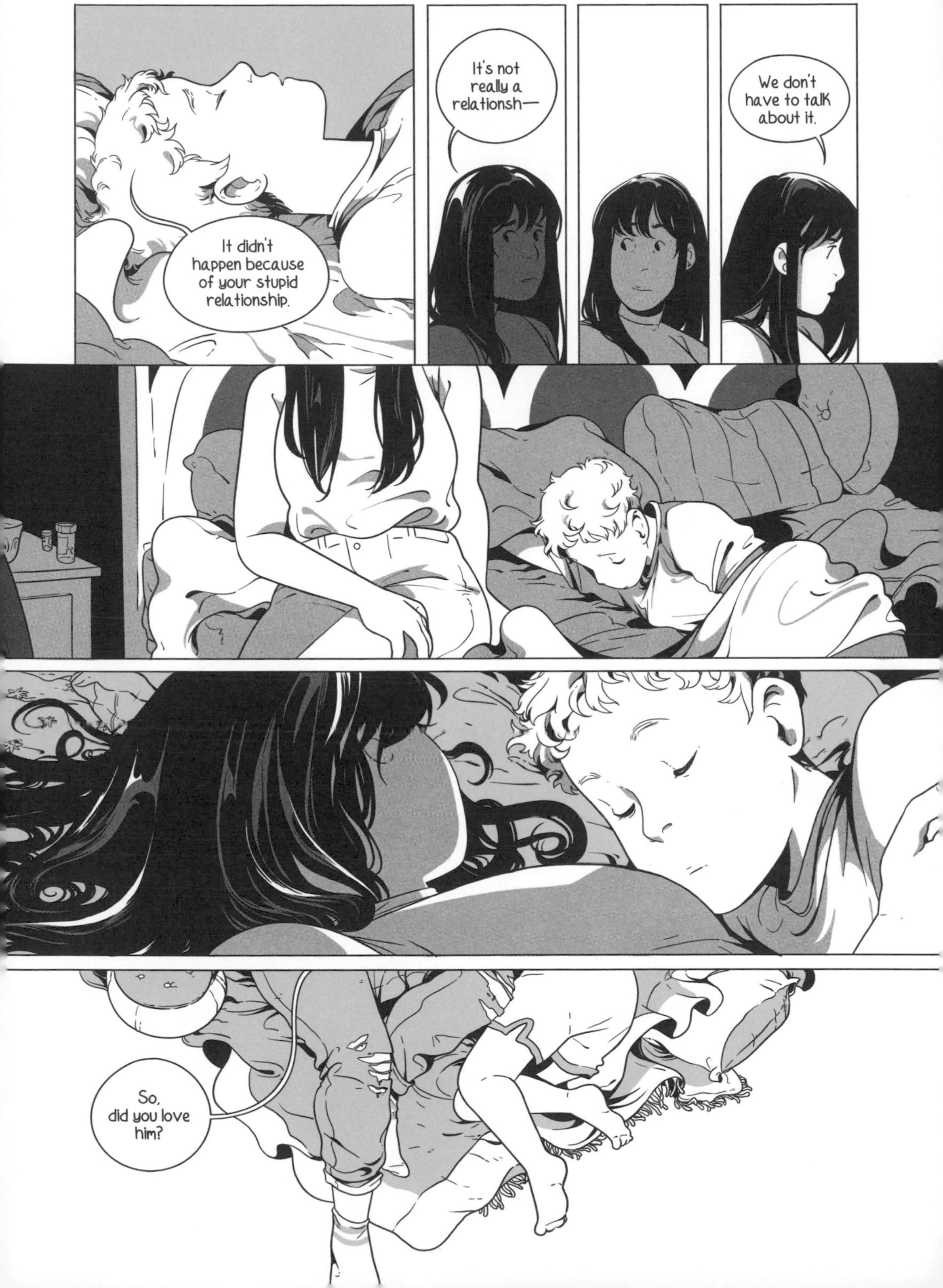
It didn't happen because of your stupid relationship.
It's not really a relationsh—
We don't have to talk about it.
So, did you love him?

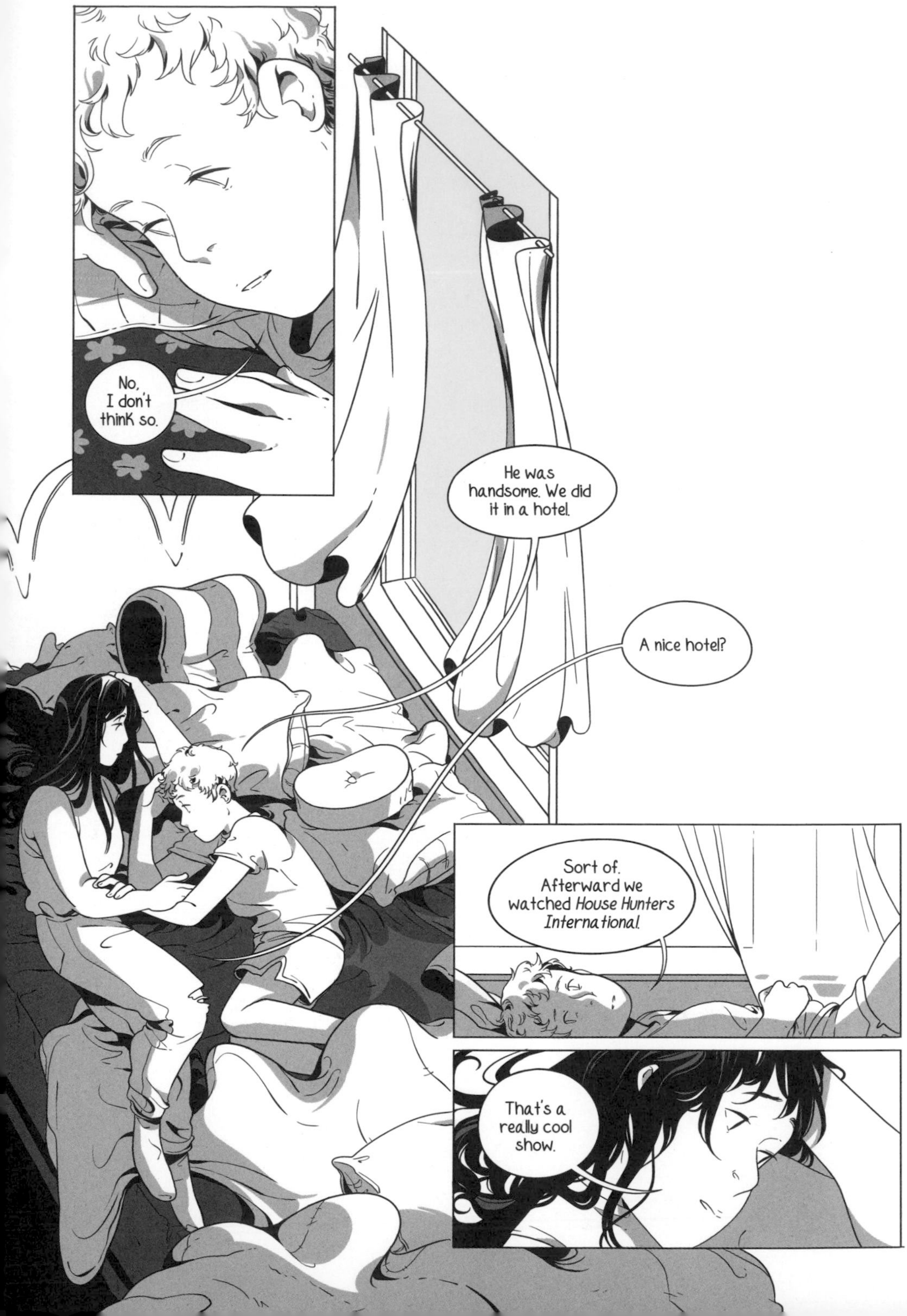
No, I don't think so.
He was handsome. We did it in a hotel.
A nice hotel?
Sort of. Afterward we watched *House Hunters International.*
That's a really cool show.

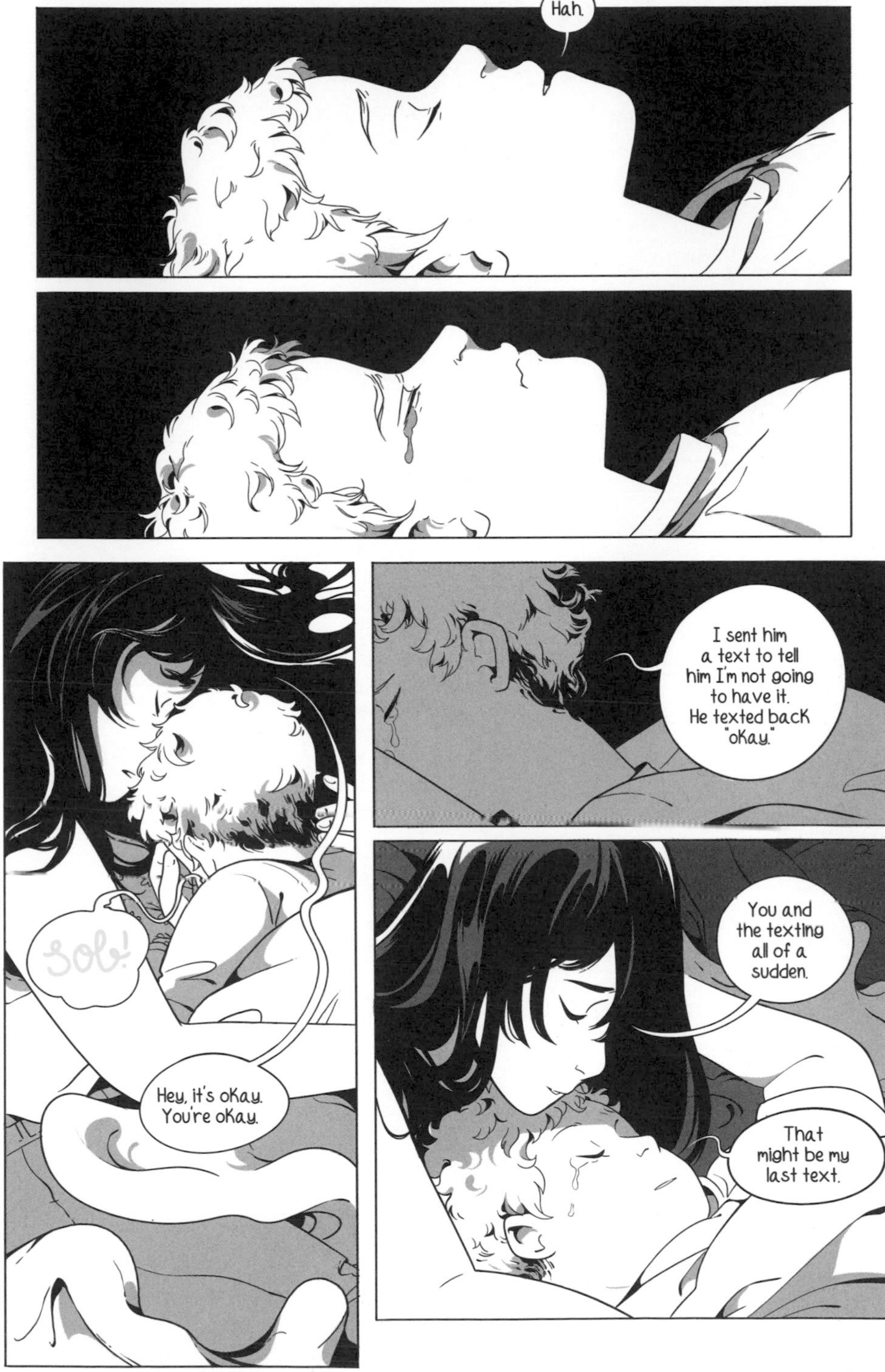
Hah.
Sob!
Hey, it's okay. You're okay.
I sent him a text to tell him I'm not going to have it. He texted back "okay."
You and the texting all of a sudden.
That might be my last text.

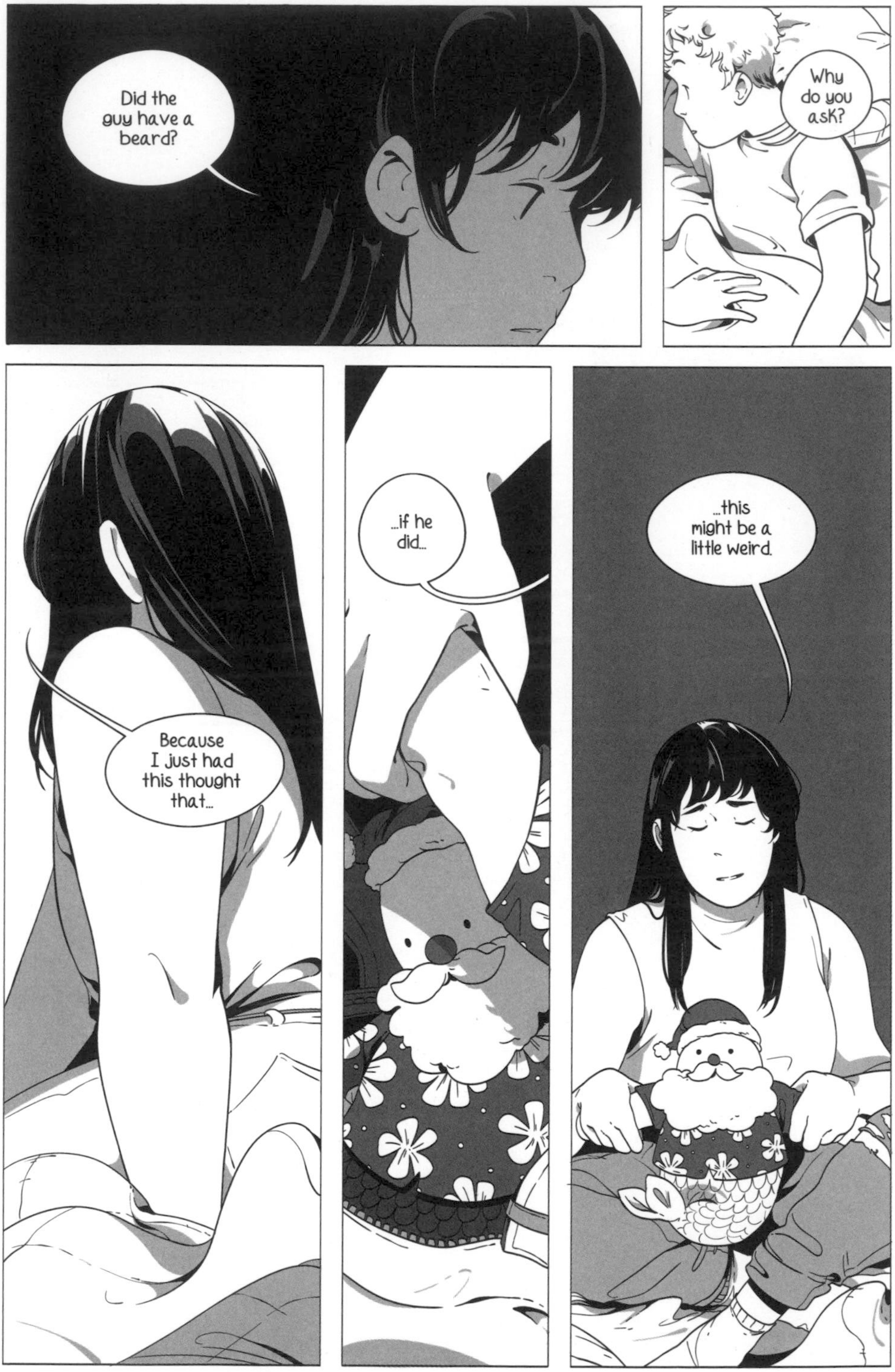
Did the guy have a beard?
Why do you ask?
Because I just had this thought that...
...if he did...
...this might be a little weird.

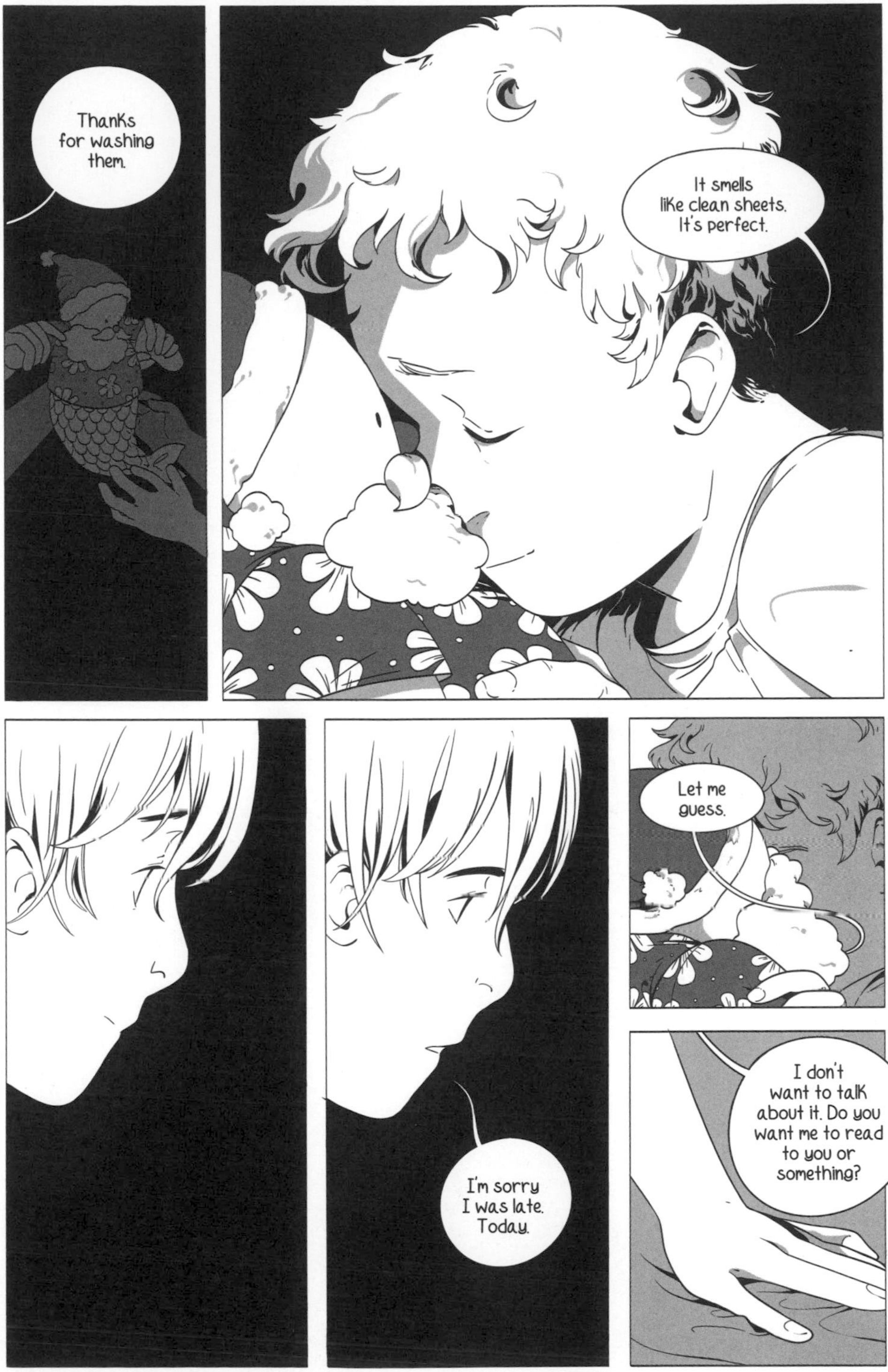

Thanks for washing them.
It smells like clean sheets. It's perfect.
I'm sorry I was late. Today.
Let me guess.
I don't want to talk about it. Do you want me to read to you or something?

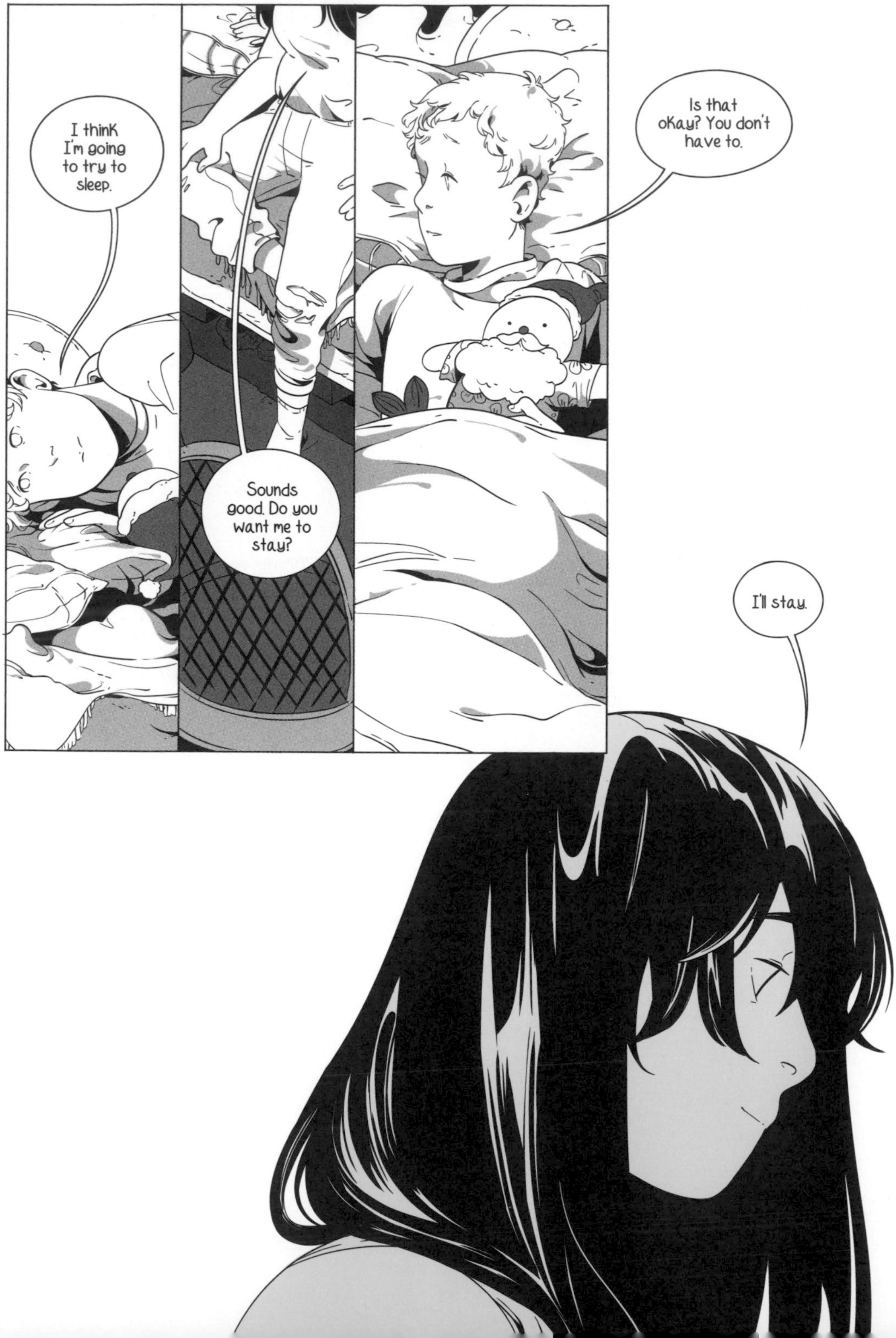
I think I'm going to try to sleep.
Sounds good. Do you want me to stay?
Is that okay? You don't have to.
I'll stay.

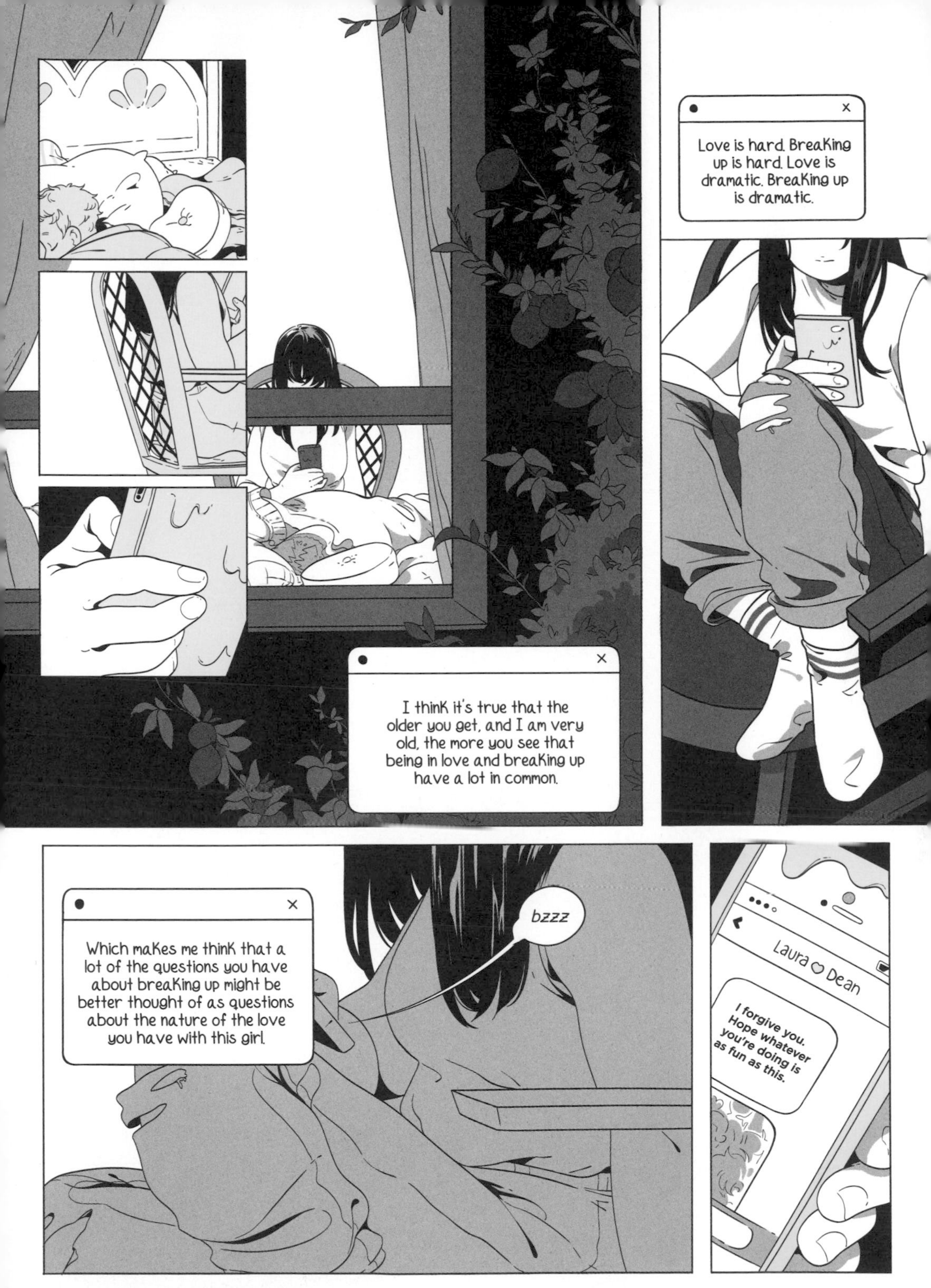
Love is hard. Breaking up is hard. Love is dramatic. Breaking up is dramatic.
I think it's true that the older you get, and I am very old, the more you see that being in love and breaking up have a lot in common.
Which makes me think that a lot of the questions you have about breaking up might be better thought of as questions about the nature of the love you have with this girl.
bzzz
Laura ♡ Dean
I forgive you. Hope whatever you're doing is as fun as this.

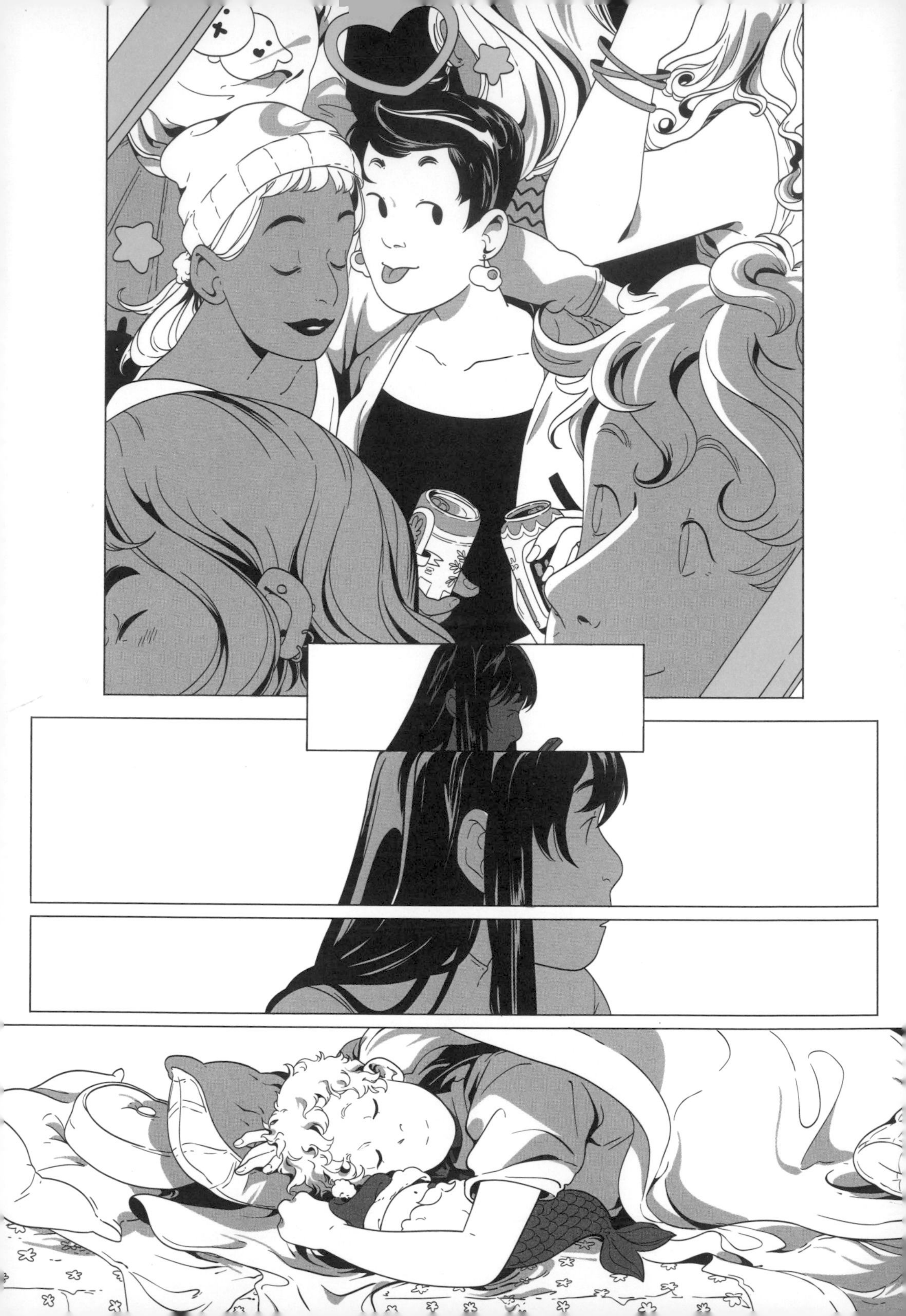

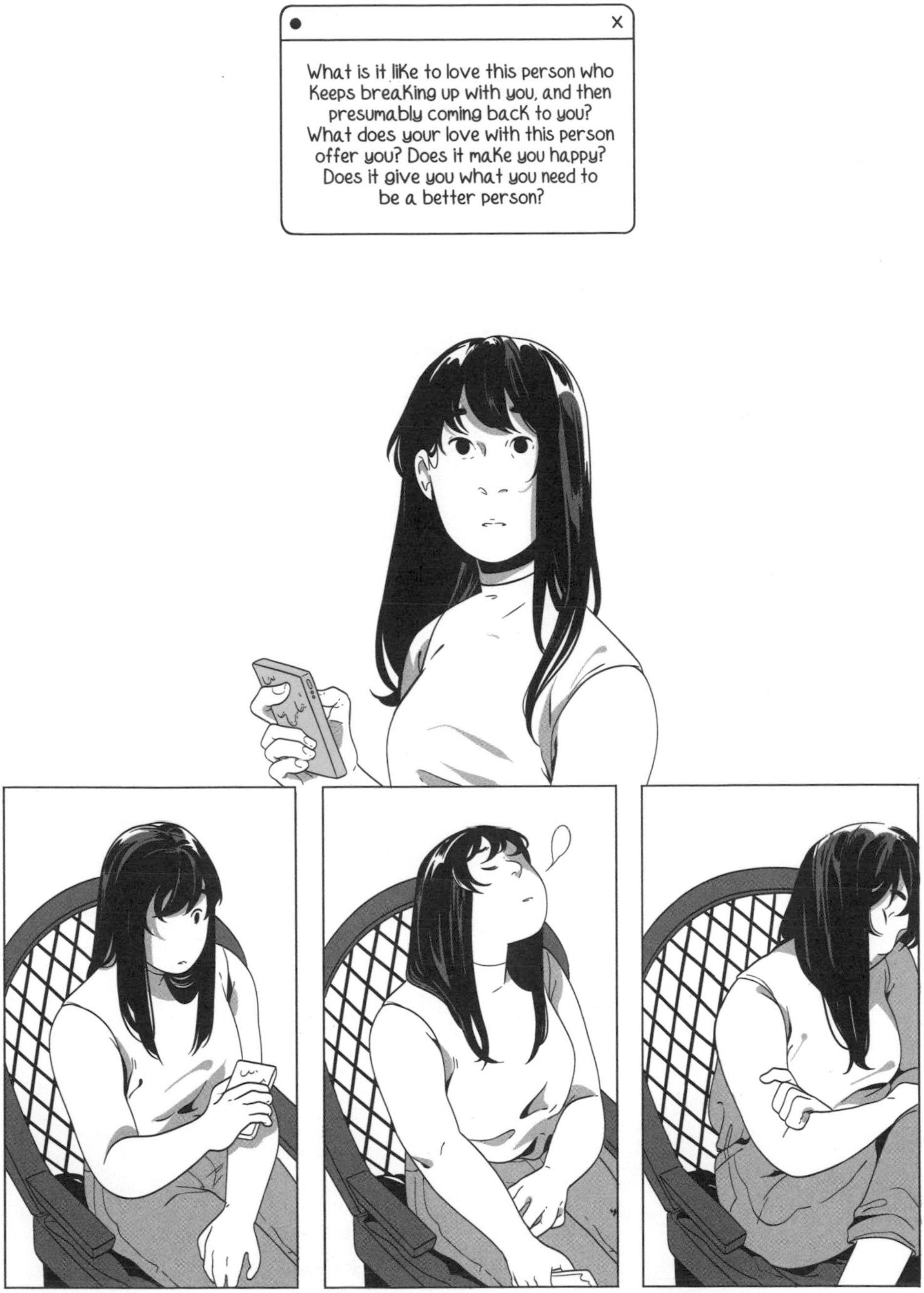
X
What is it like to love this person who Keeps breaKing up with you, and then presumably coming back to you? What does your love with this person offer you? Does it maKe you happy? Does it give you what you need to be a better person?

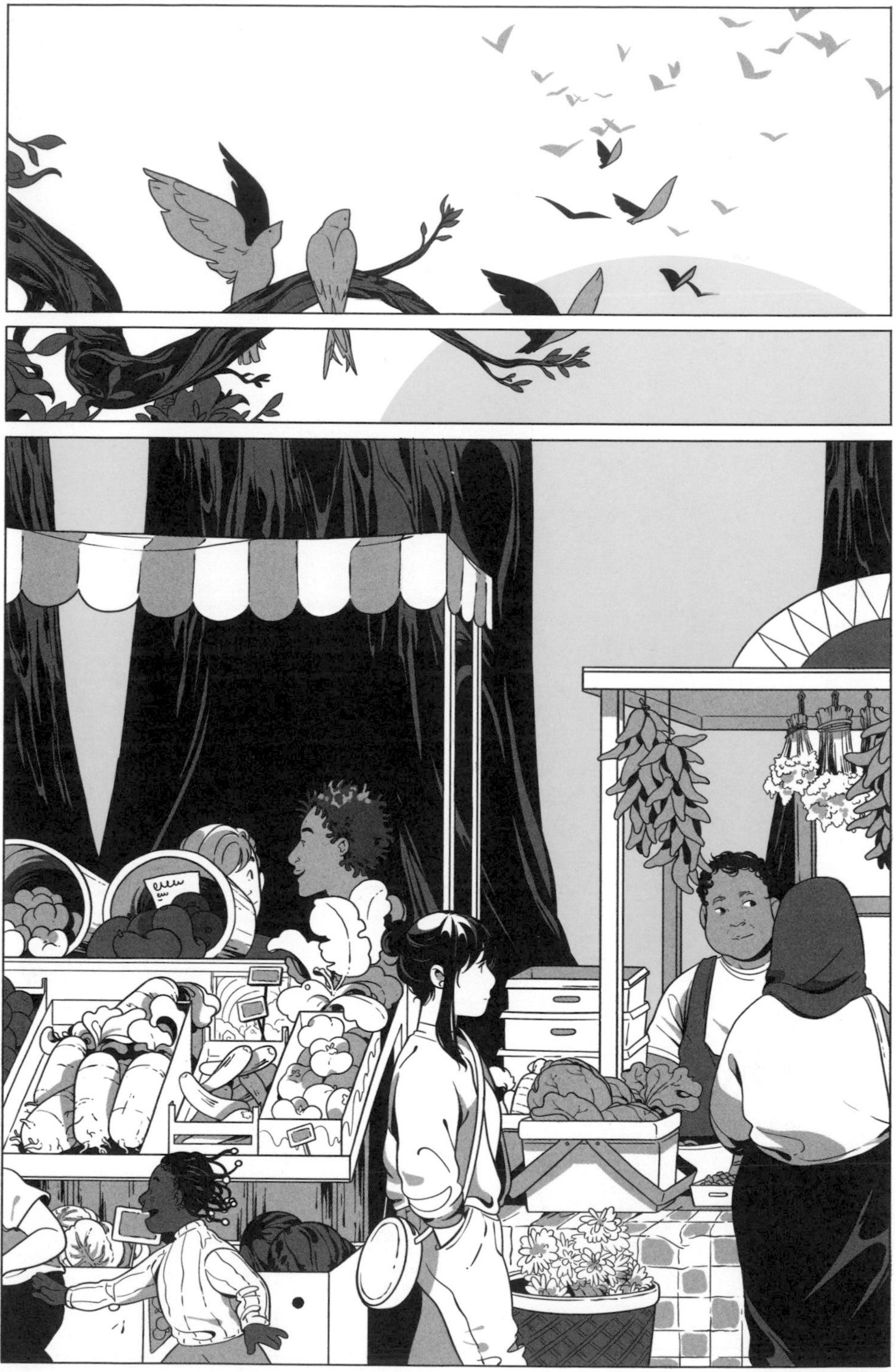

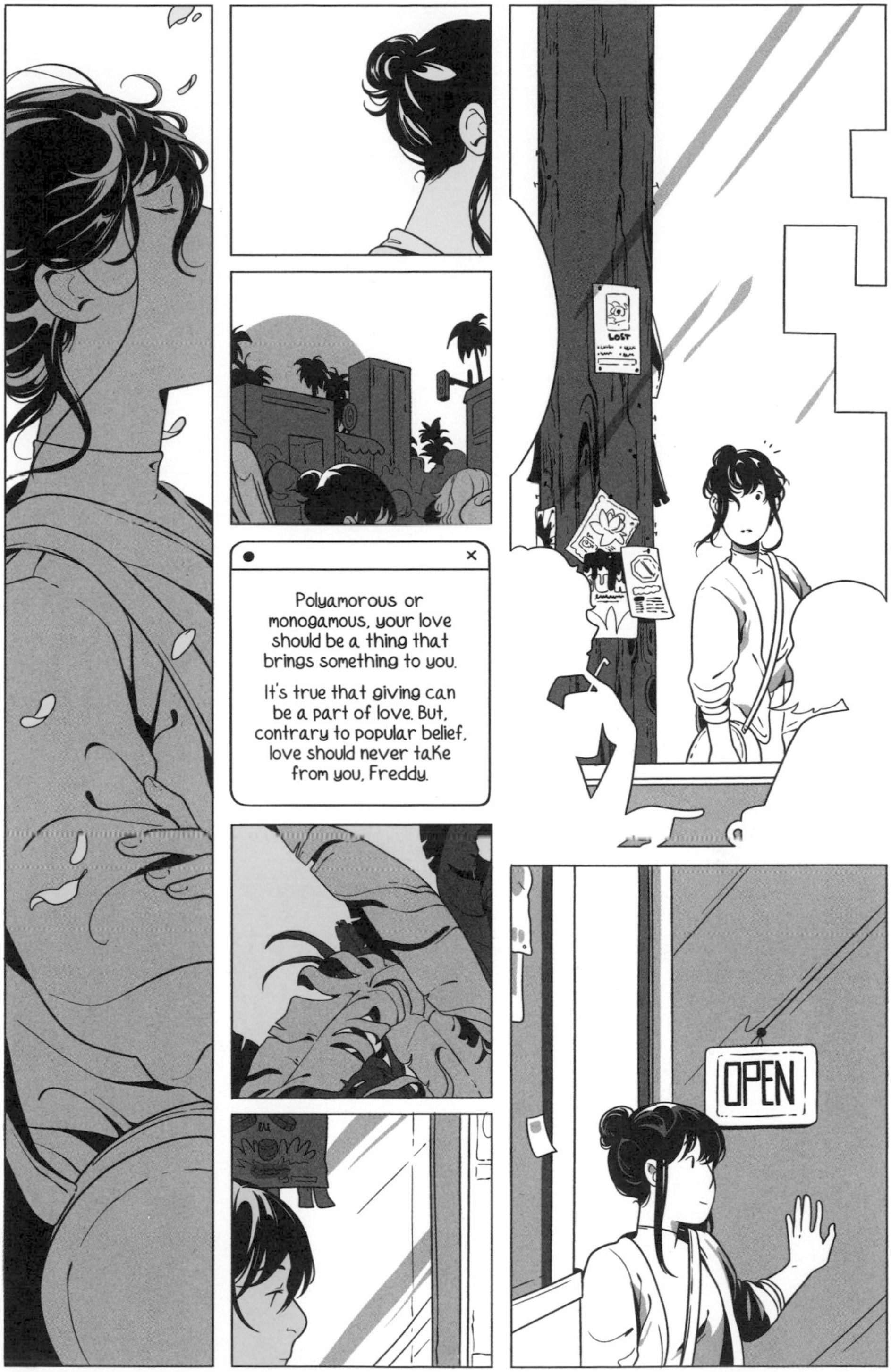

Polyamorous or monogamous, your love should be a thing that brings something to you.
It's true that giving can be a part of love. But, contrary to popular belief, love should never take from you, Freddy.
LOST
OPEN

Hey!

Hey! Wow, you work here too?

Dude, I have a thousand jobs. I'm trying to save for college, remember?

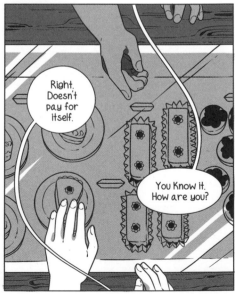

Right. Doesn't pay for itself.

You know it. How are you?

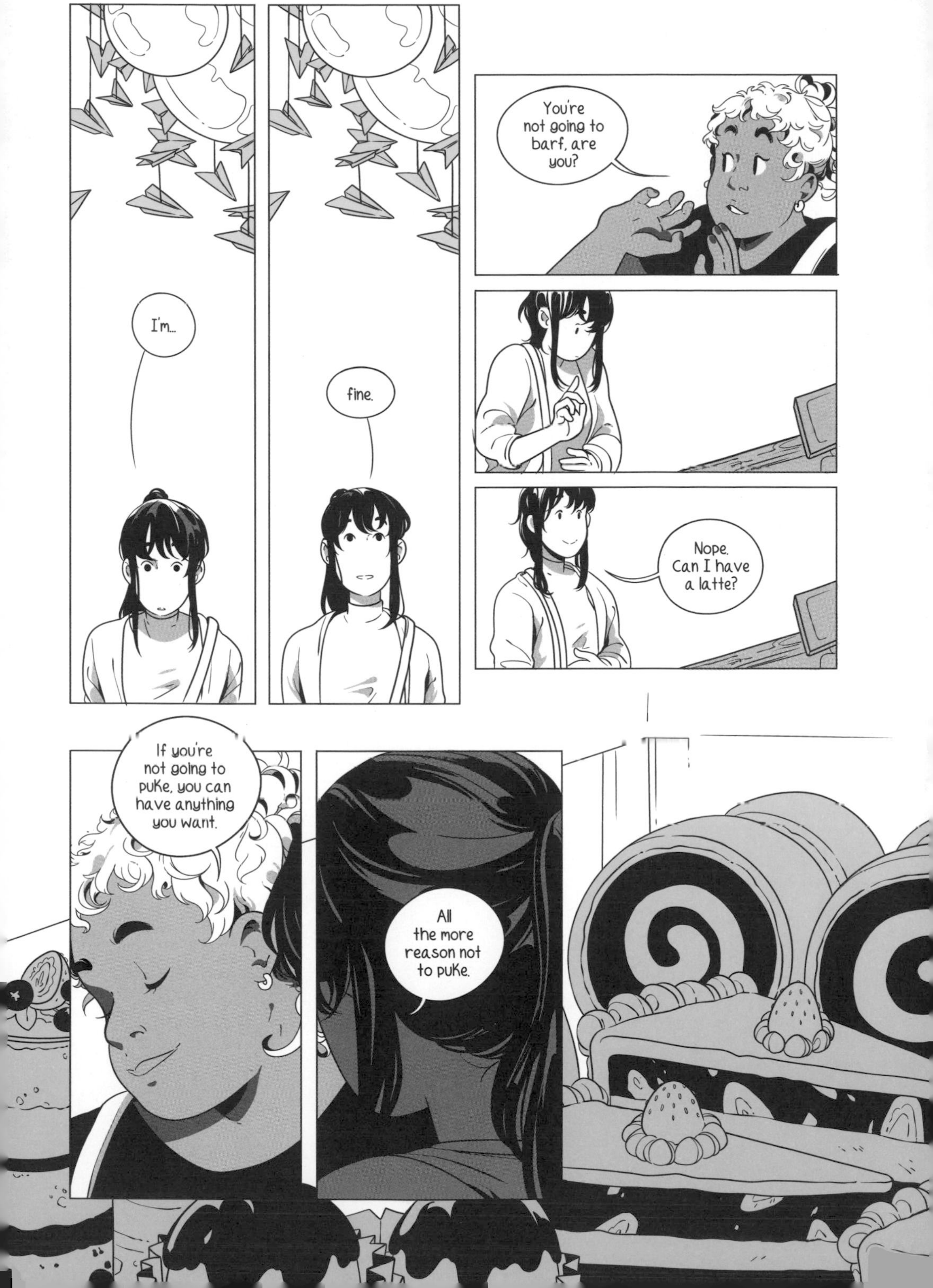
I'm...
fine.
You're not going to barf, are you?
Nope. Can I have a latte?
If you're not going to puke, you can have anything you want.
All the more reason not to puke.

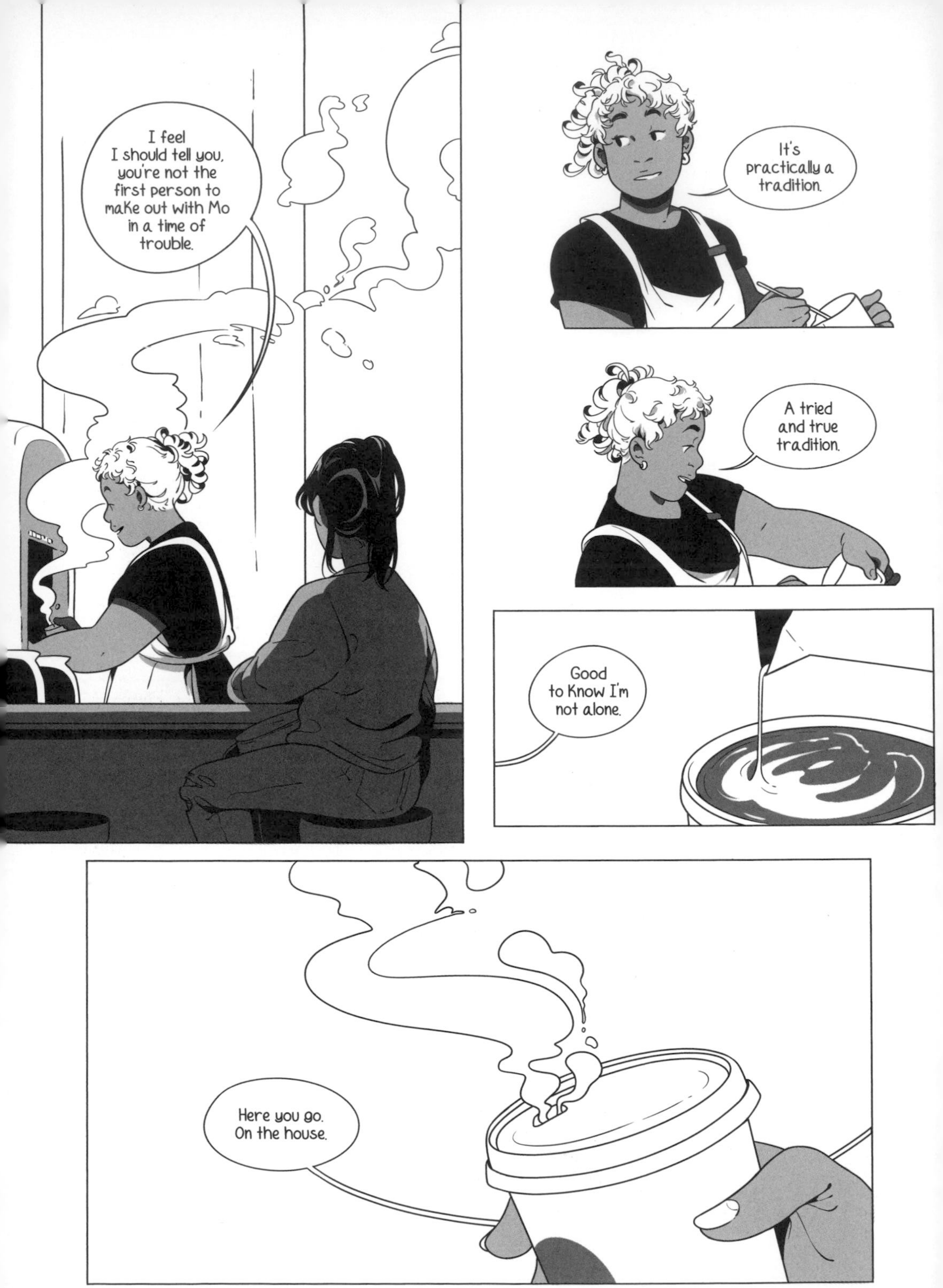
I feel I should tell you, you're not the first person to make out with Mo in a time of trouble.
It's practically a tradition.
A tried and true tradition.
Good to know I'm not alone.
Here you go. On the house.

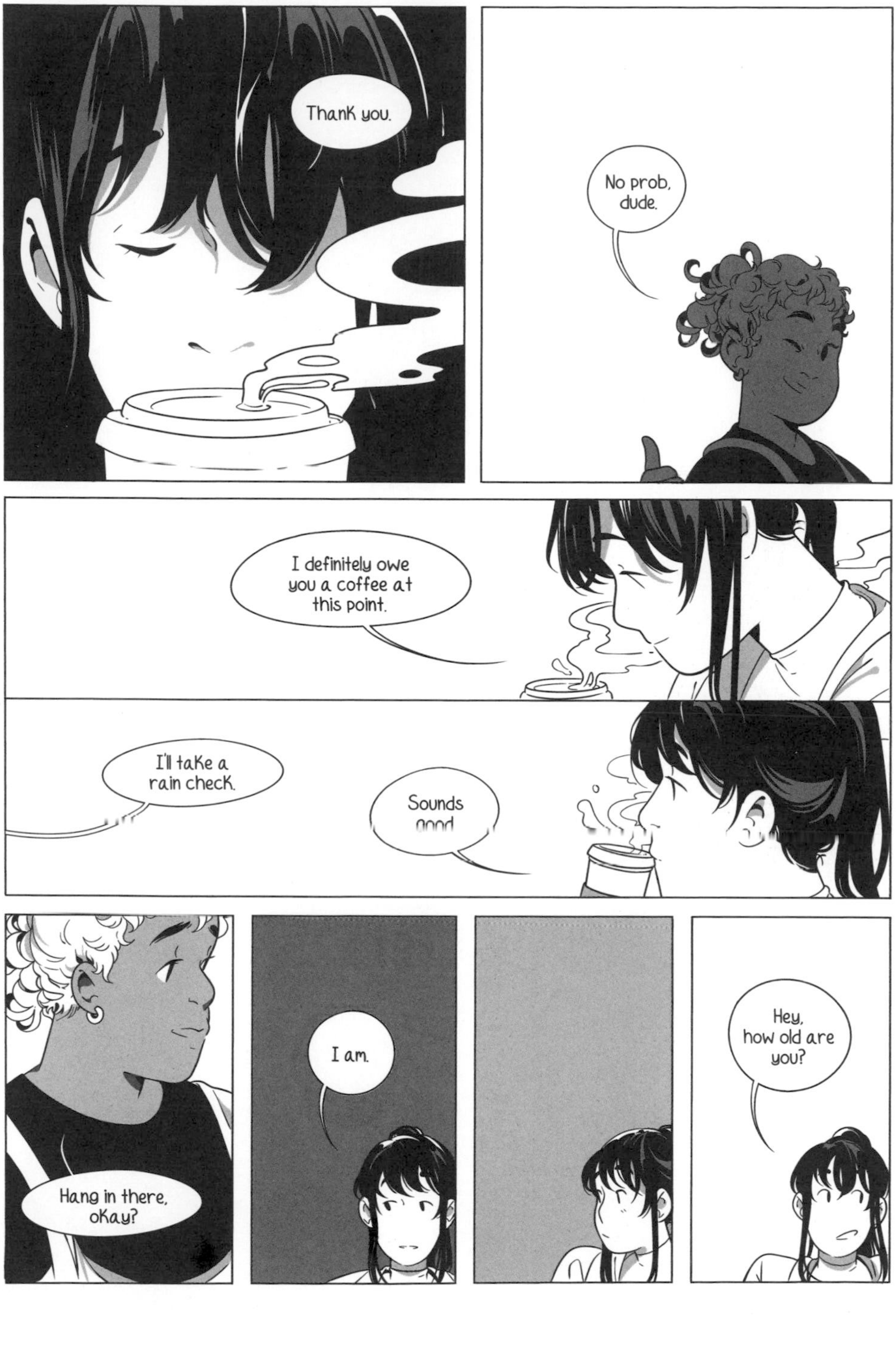
Thank you.
No prob, dude.
I definitely owe you a coffee at this point.
I'll take a rain check.
Sounds
Hang in there, okay?
I am.
Hey, how old are you?

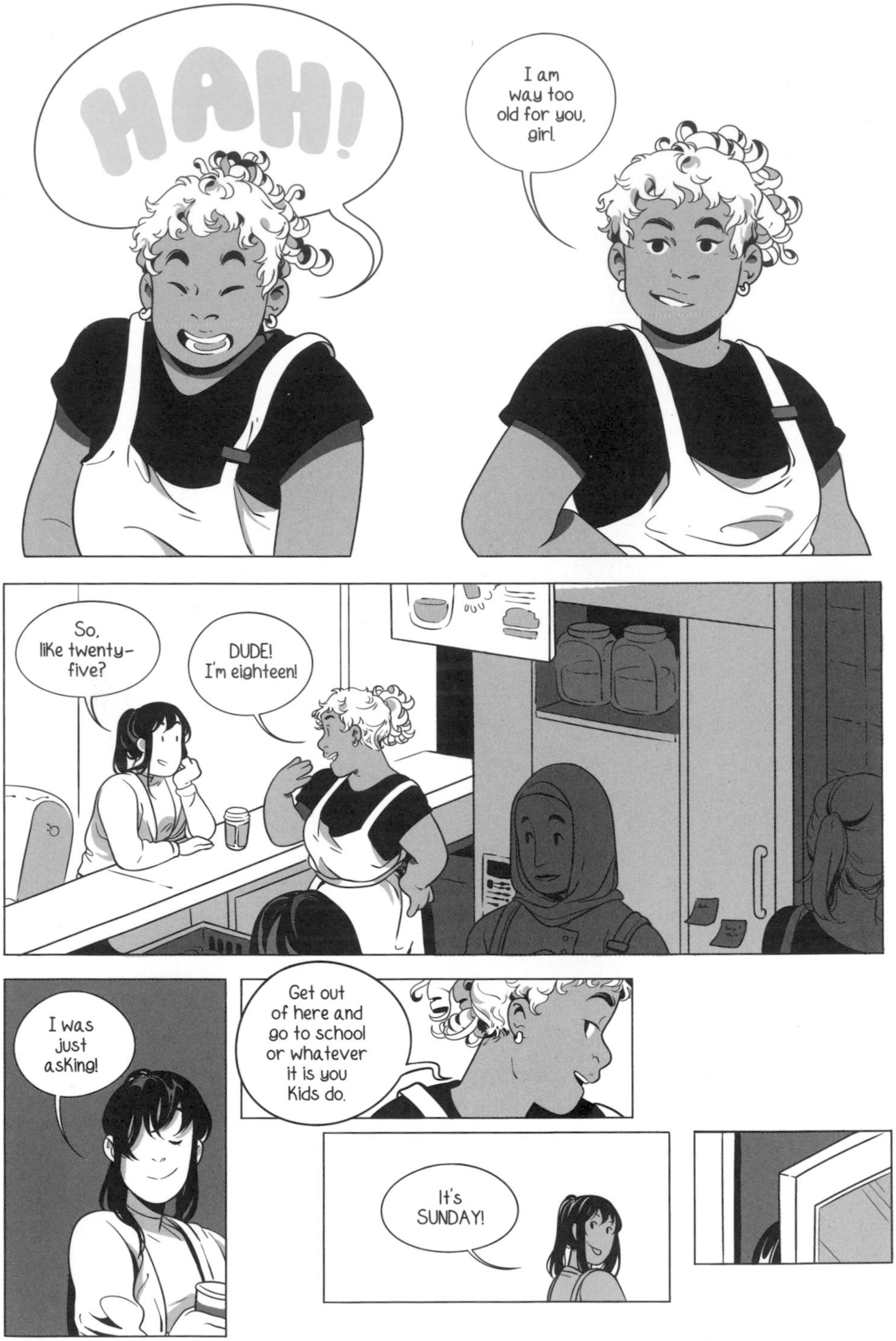
HAH!
I am way too old for you, girl.
So, like twenty-five?
DUDE! I'm eighteen!
I was just asking!
Get out of here and go to school or whatever it is you kids do.
It's SUNDAY!

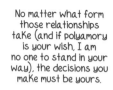

No matter what form those relationships take (and if polyamory is your wish, I am no one to stand in your way), the decisions you make must be yours.

If Laura Dean keeps breaking up with you, what are you doing?

What do you want to do?

273

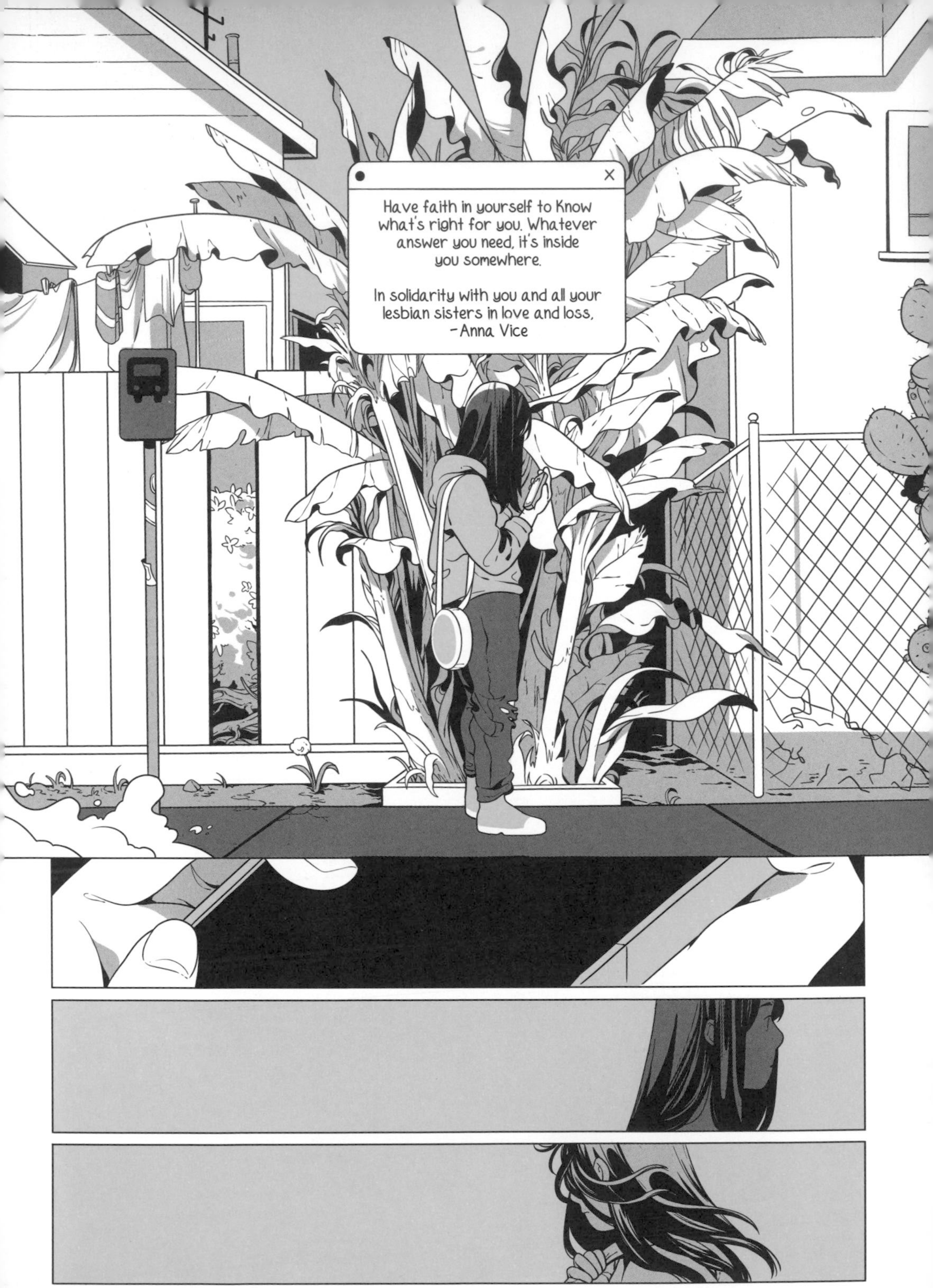
Have faith in yourself to Know what's right for you. Whatever answer you need, it's inside you somewhere.
In solidarity with you and all your lesbian sisters in love and loss,
-Anna Vice

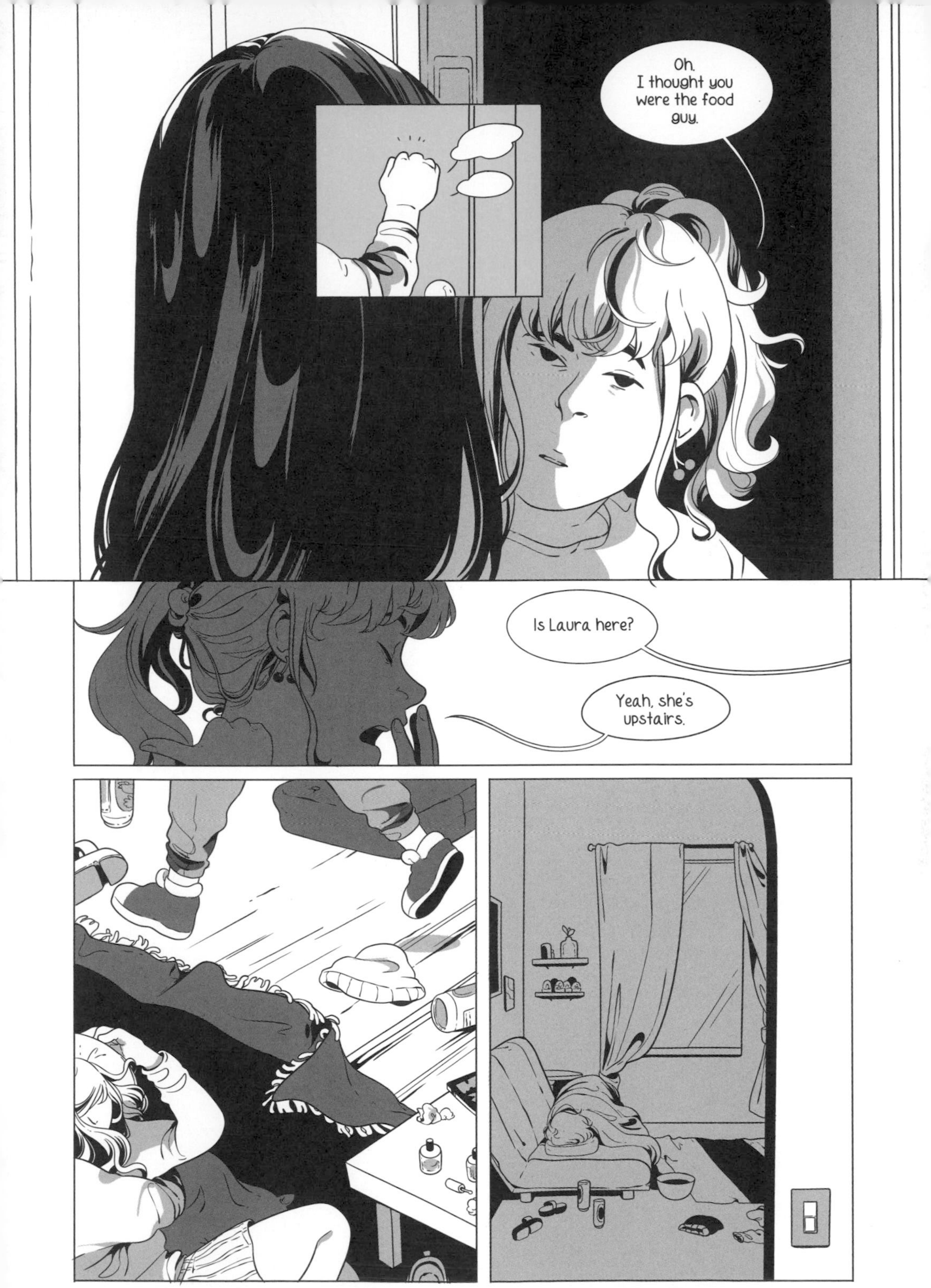
Oh. I thought you were the food guy.
Is Laura here?
Yeah, she's upstairs.

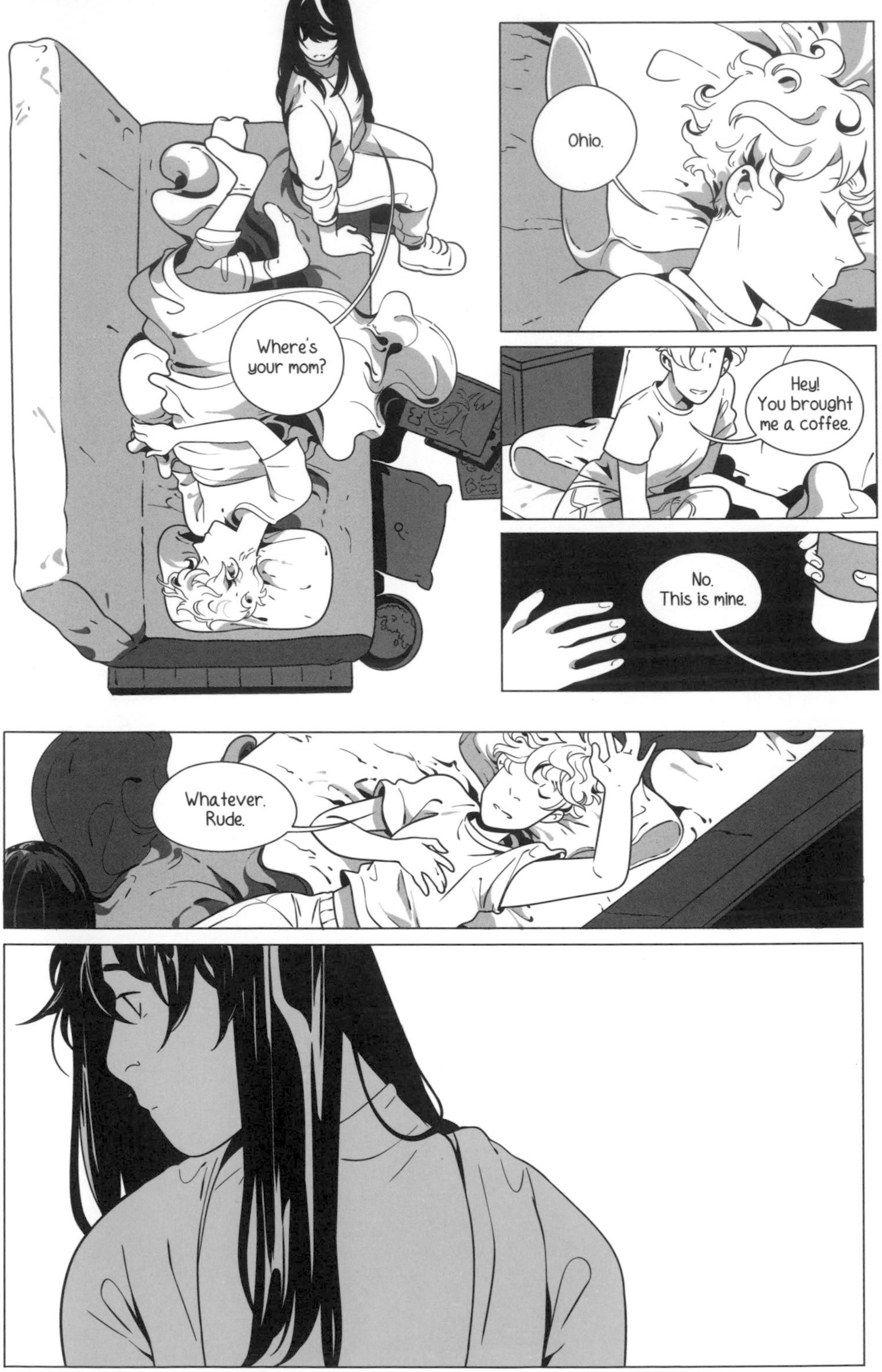
Where's your mom?
Ohio.
Hey! You brought me a coffee.
No. This is mine.
Whatever. Rude.

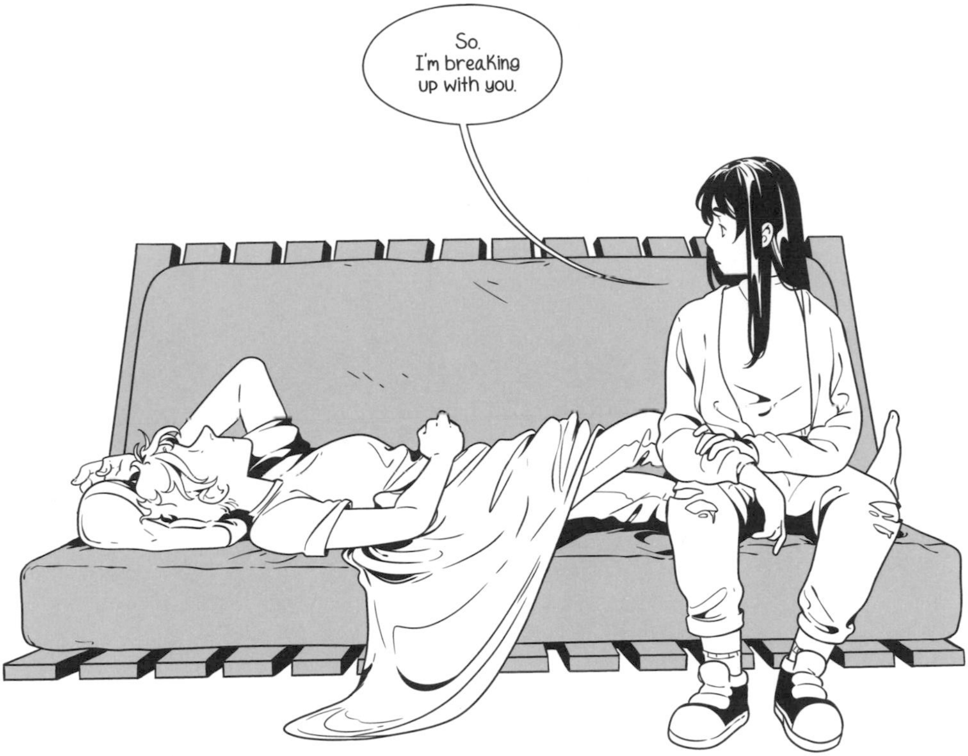
So.
I'm breaking up with you.

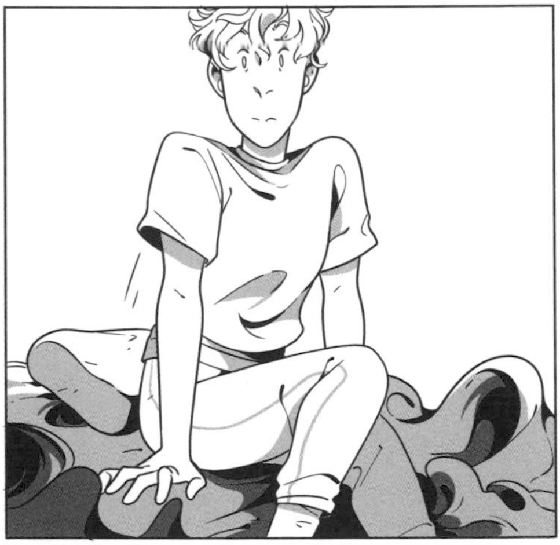

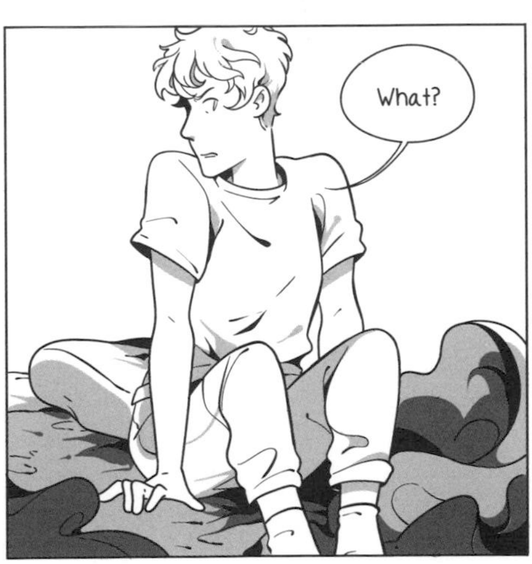
What?

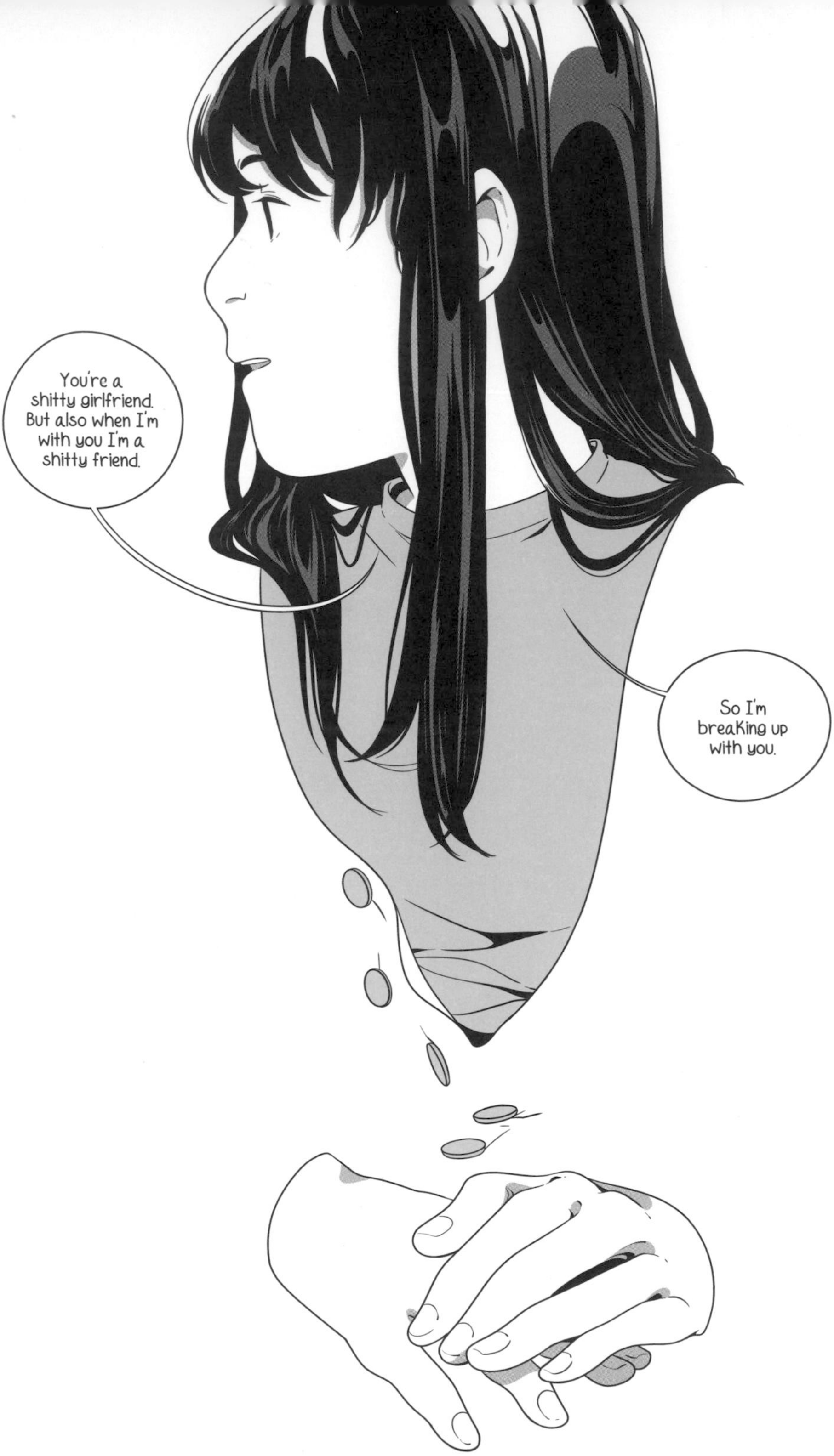
You're a shitty girlfriend. But also when I'm with you I'm a shitty friend.
So I'm breaking up with you.

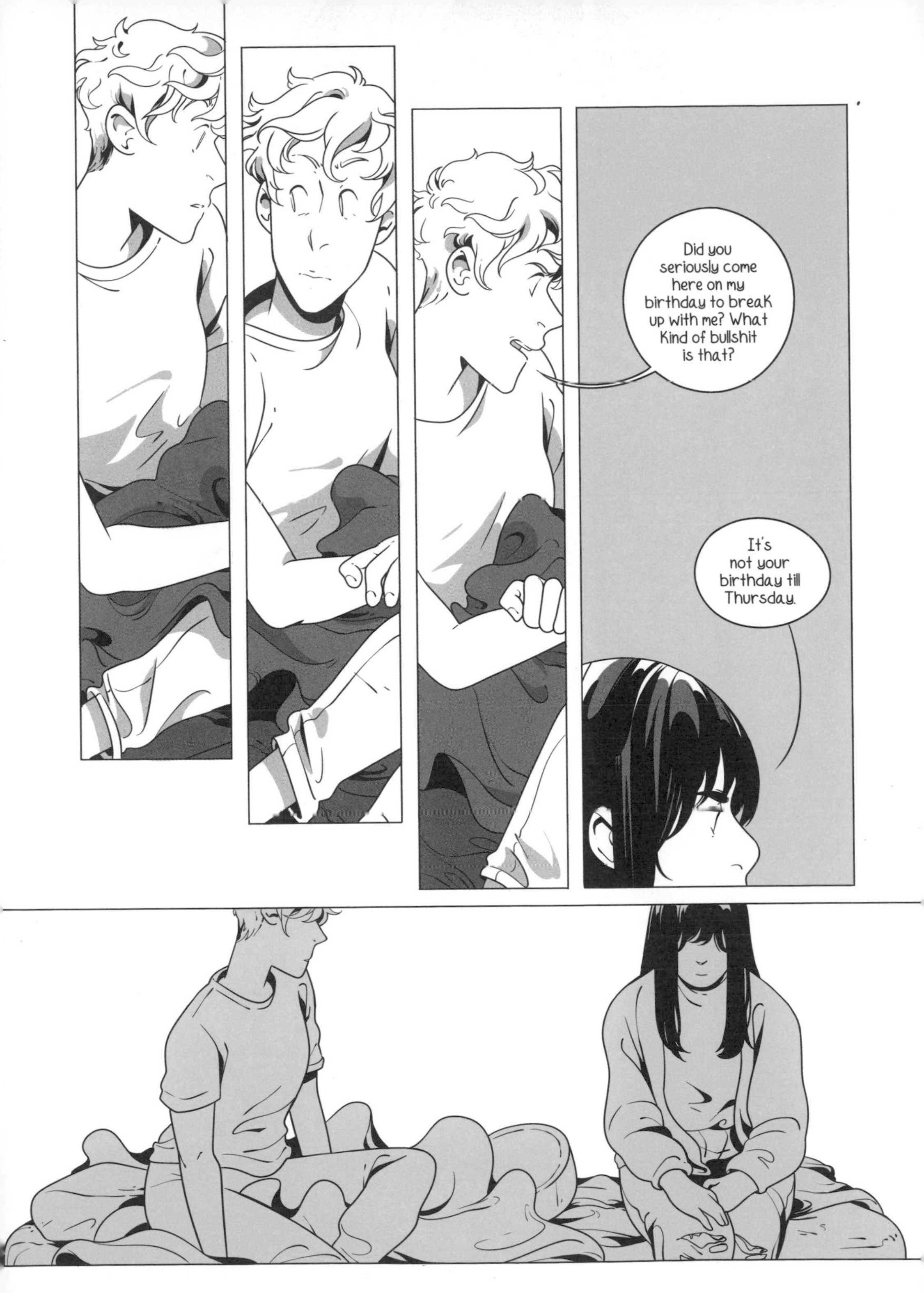
Did you seriously come here on my birthday to break up with me? What kind of bullshit is that?
It's not your birthday till Thursday.

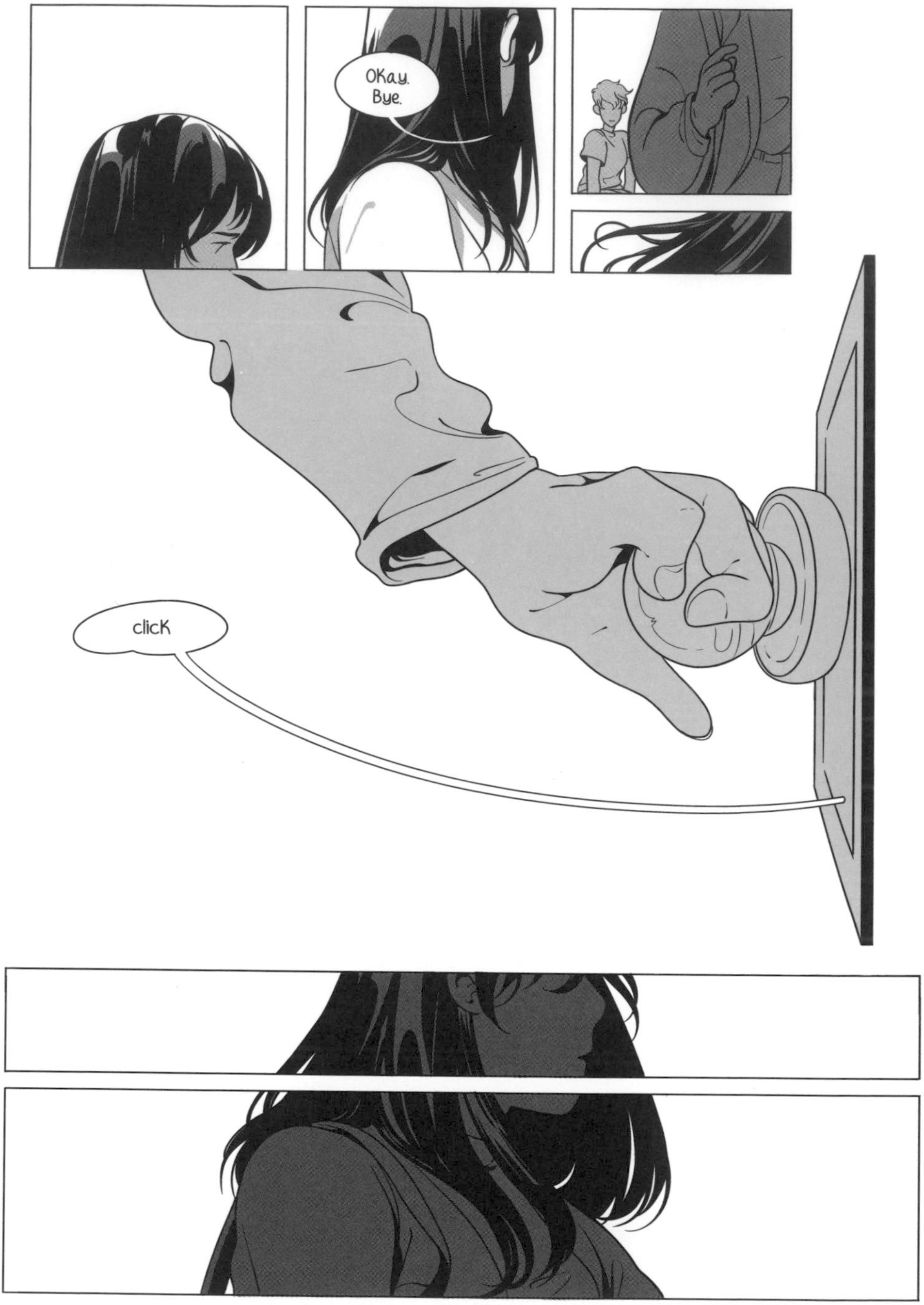
OKay.
Bye.
click

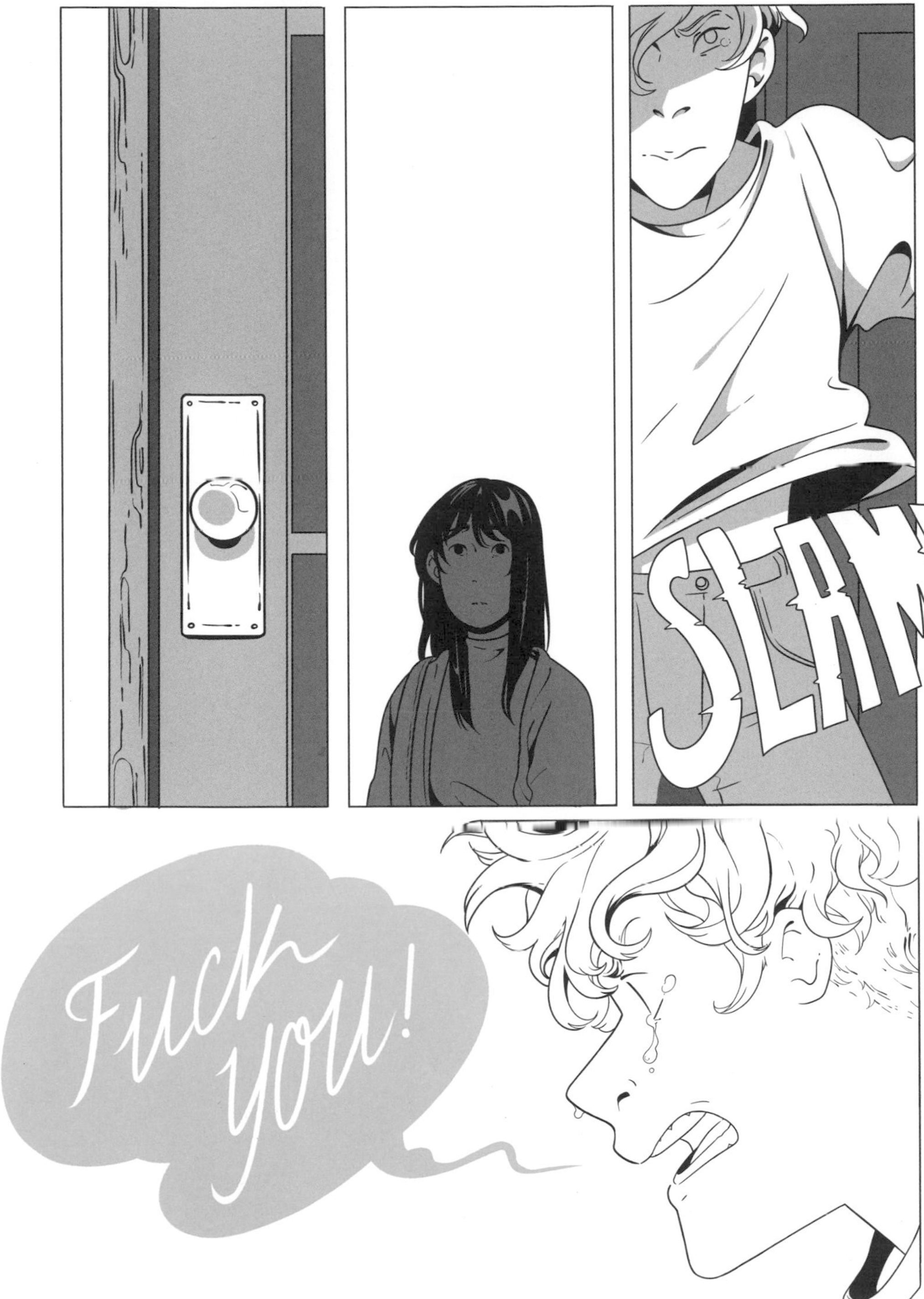
SLAM!
Fuck you!

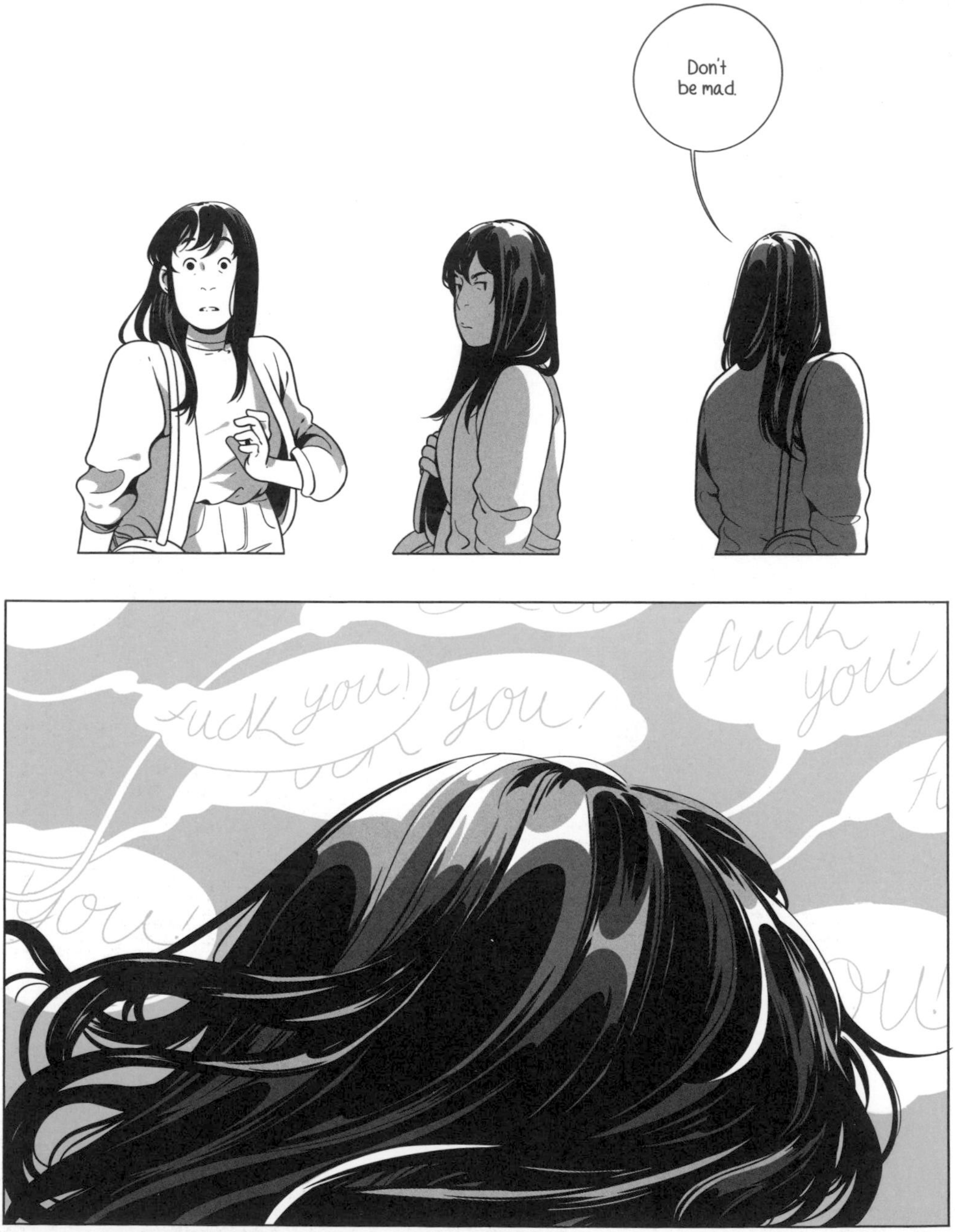
Don't be mad.
fuck you!
you!
fuck you!

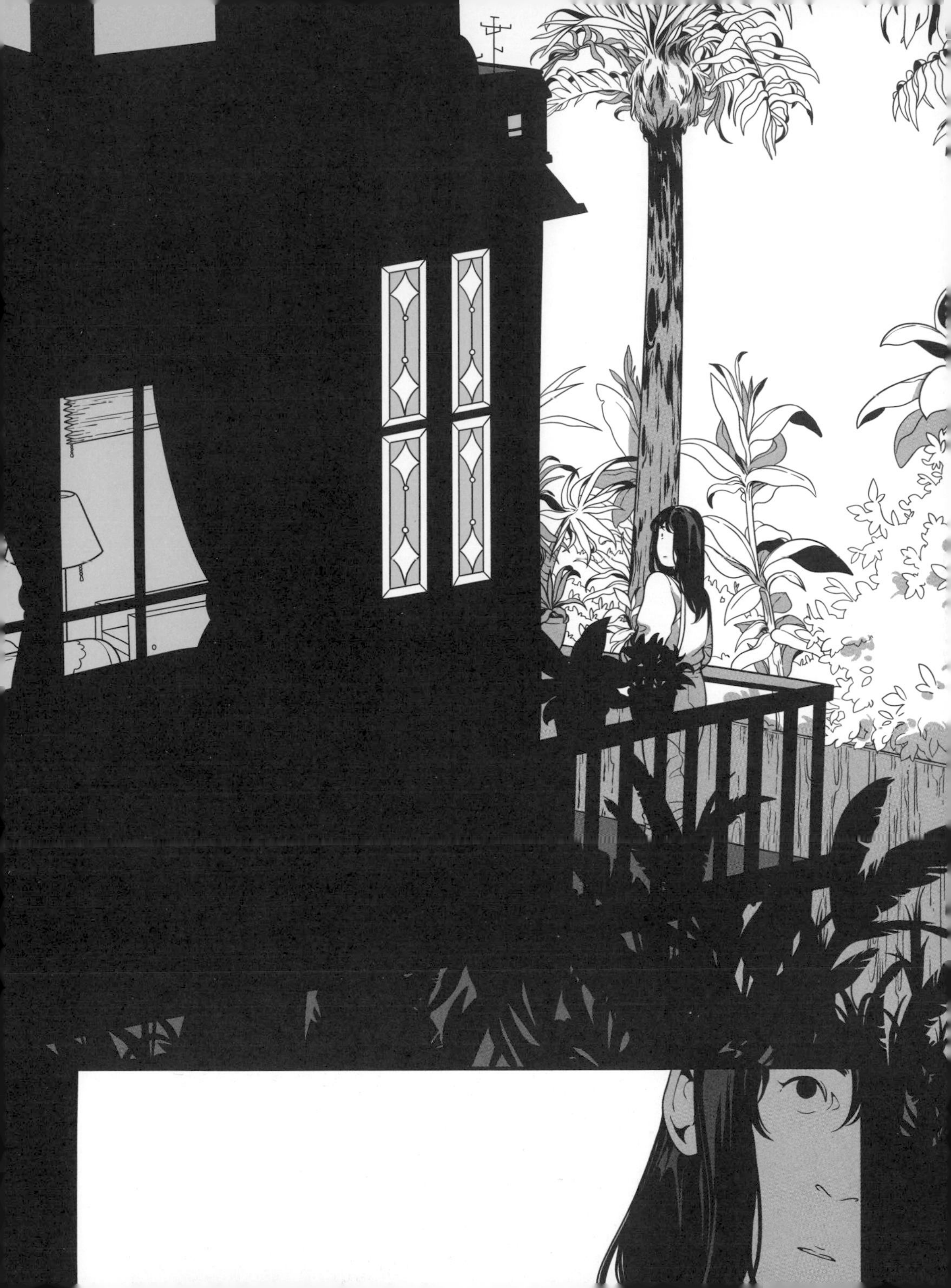

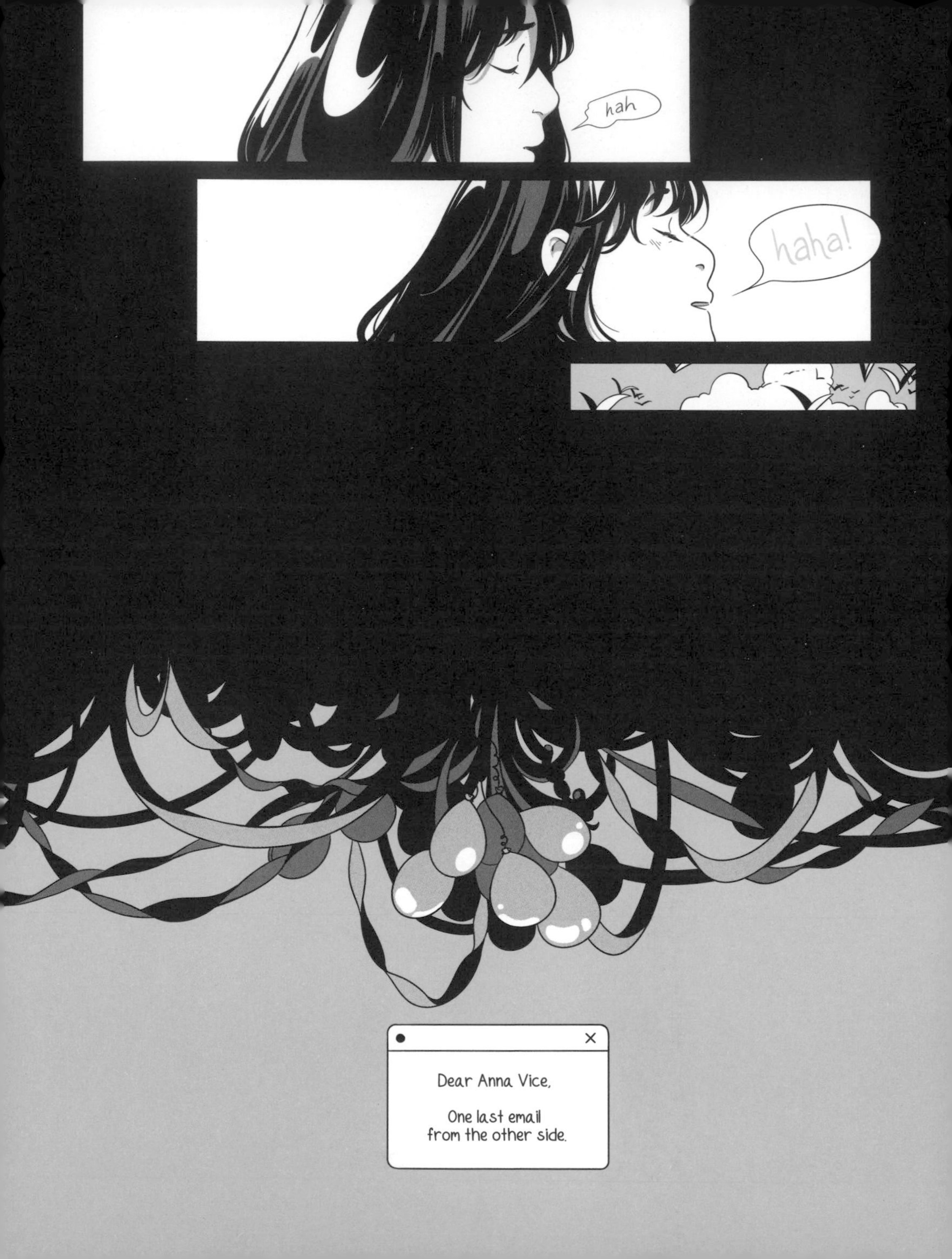
hah
haha!
Dear Anna Vice,
One last email
from the other side.

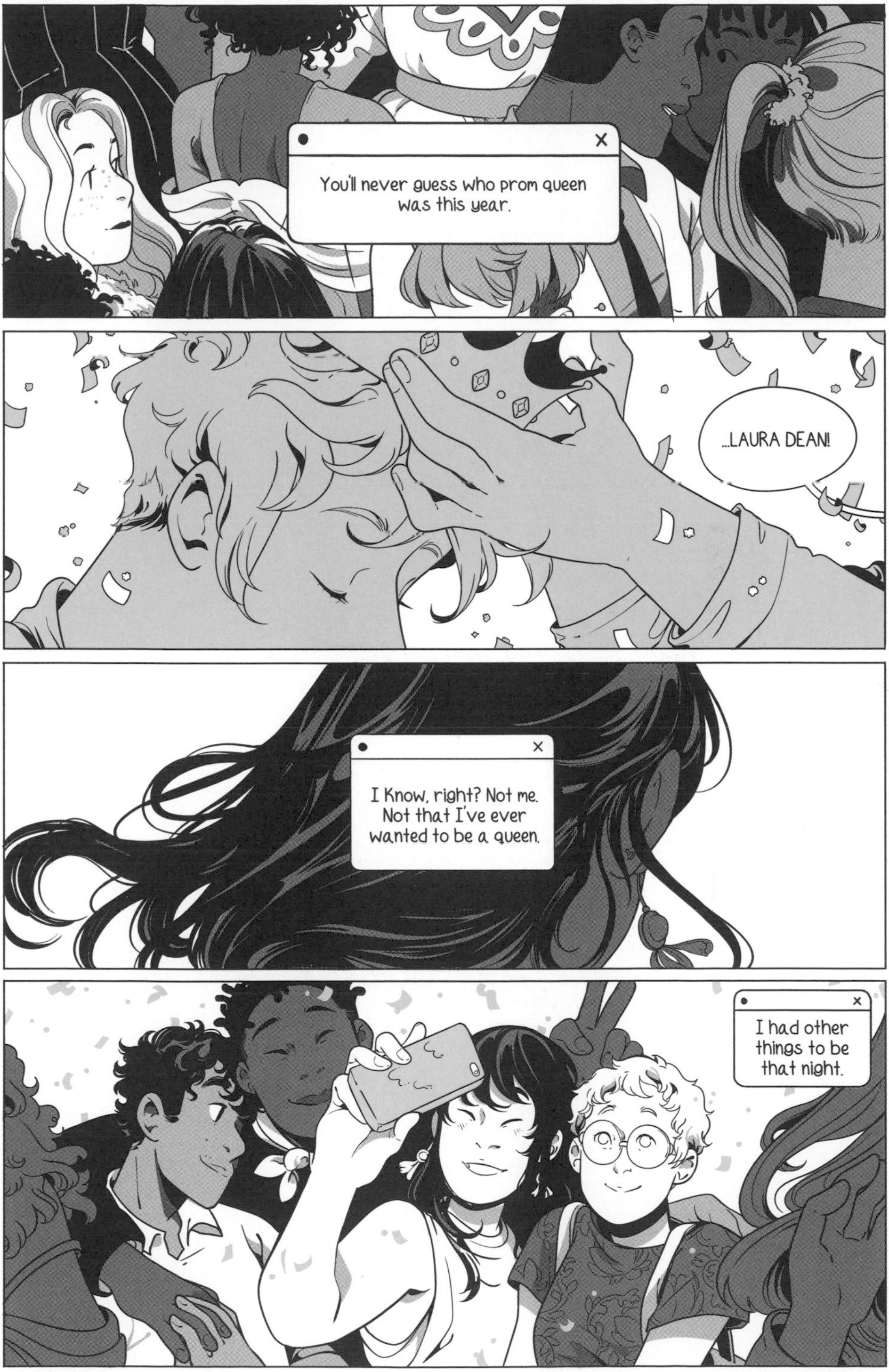
You'll never guess who prom queen was this year.
...LAURA DEAN!
I Know, right? Not me. Not that I've ever wanted to be a queen.
I had other things to be that night.

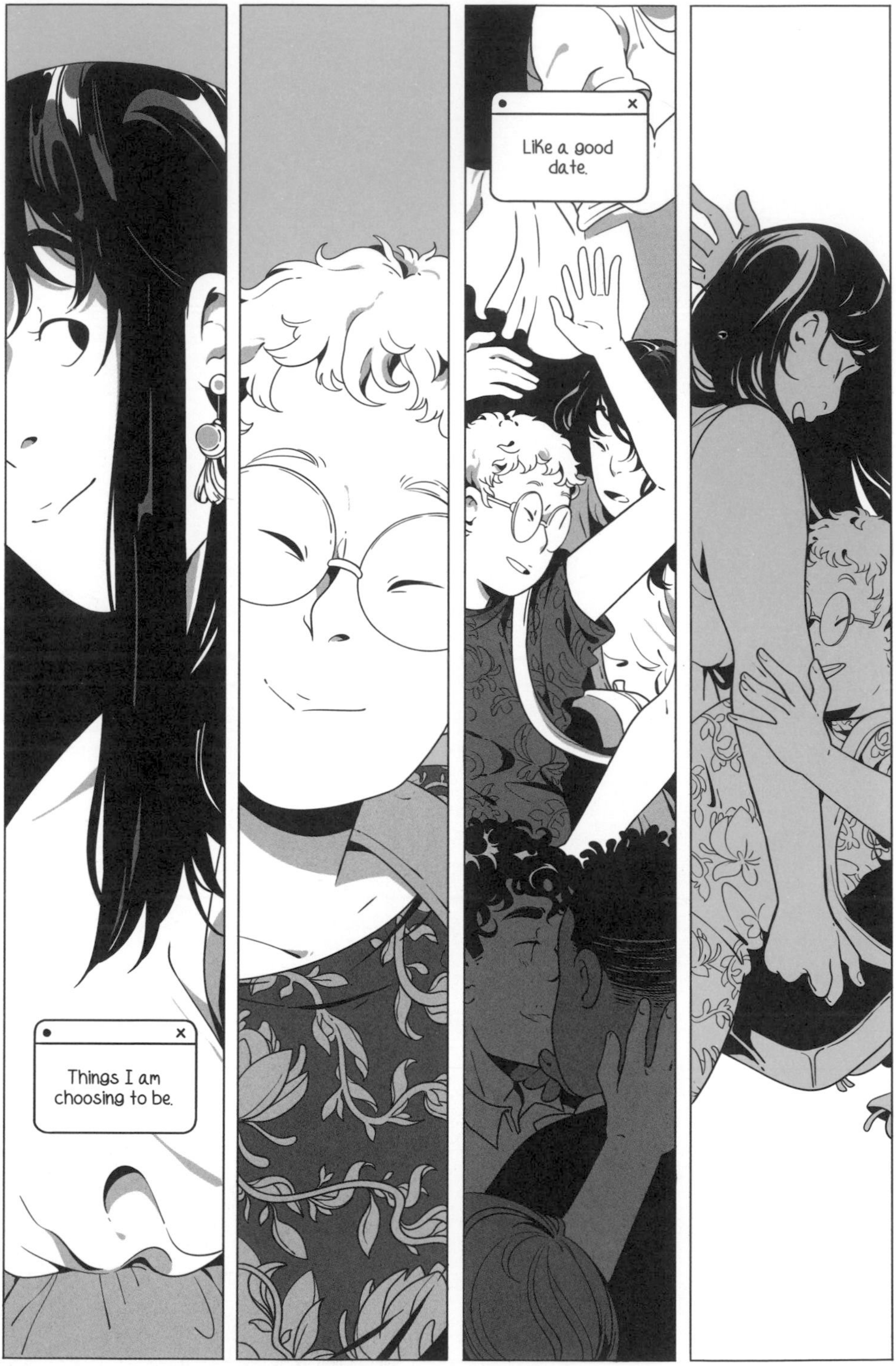
Things I am choosing to be.
Like a good date.

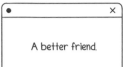

A better friend.

All things that are
something other than
the ex-girlfriend of
Laura Dean.

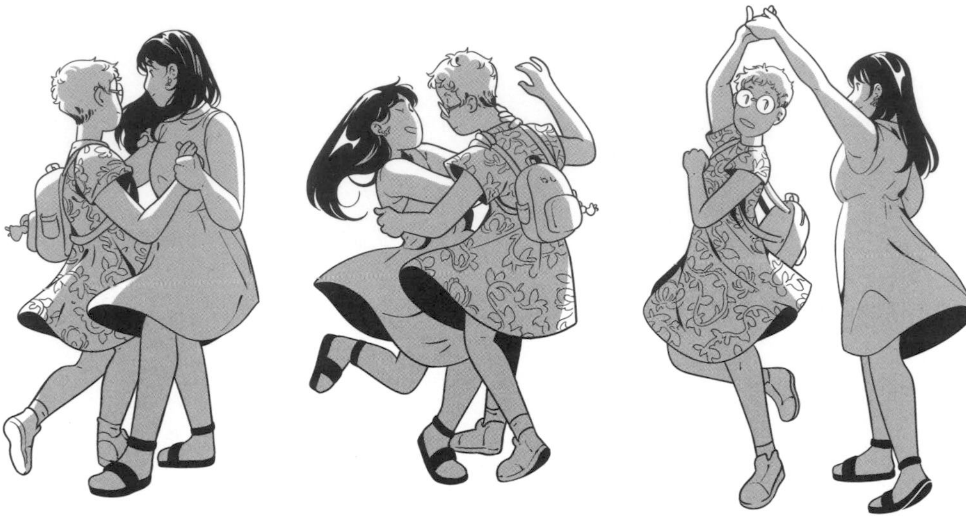

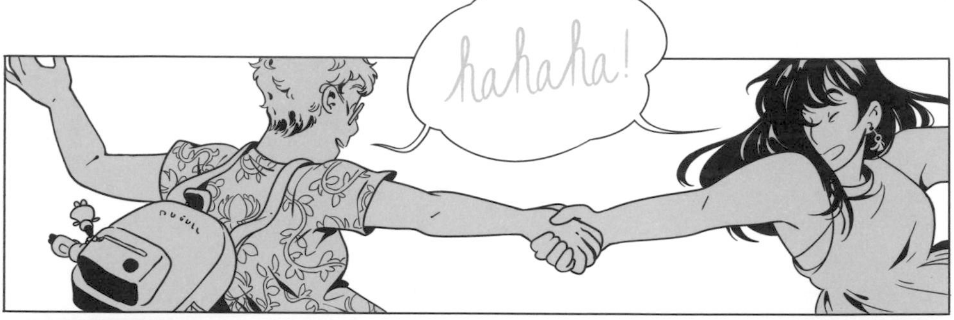
hahaha!

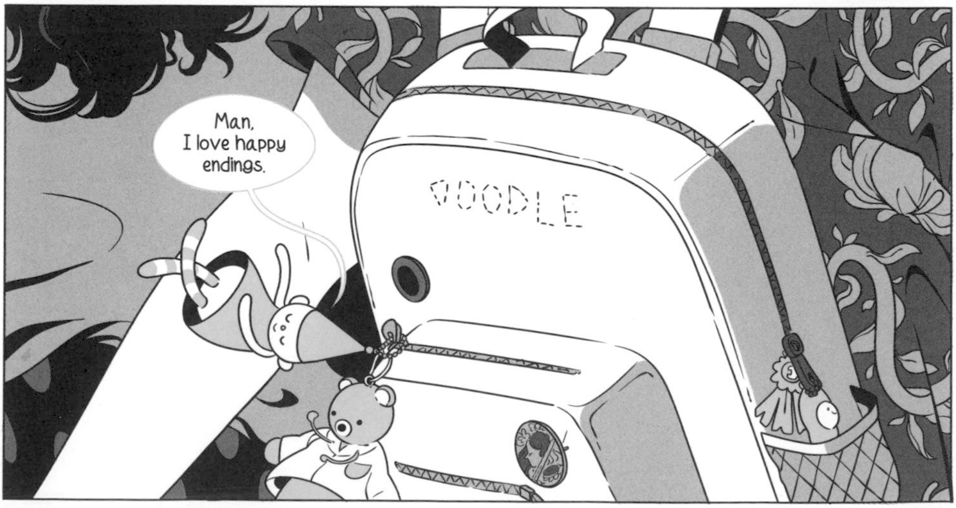
Man, I love happy endings.
VOODLE

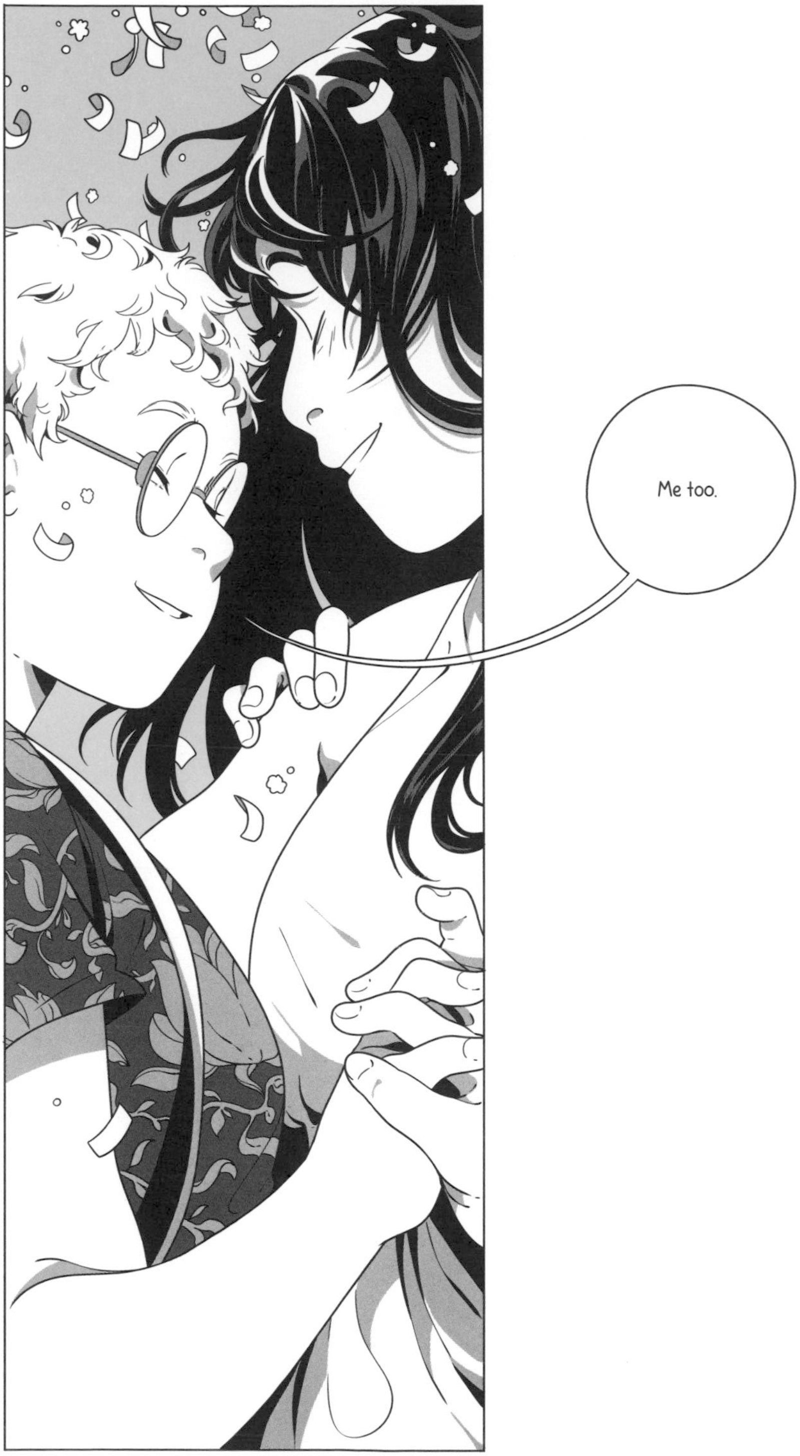
Me too.

ACKNOWLEDGMENTS

Thank you to my agent, Charlotte Sheedy, for her wisdom and guidance. To the many people who read this book, as a manuscript and as an almost fully realized graphic novel, including my editors Calista Brill, Whitney Taylor, Carol Burrell, as well as Kate Schatz, Kim Trusty and Cory Silverberg, thank you for your insight. Thank you to the hard workers at First Second, including Kiara Valdez and Andrew Arnold, who make these books happen in a multitude of unseen but very important ways.

Thank you to all the librarians and educators who I have spoken to over the years at countless conferences for all your support.

Thank you, Rosemary Valero-O'Connell, for working with me and making this book the visual dream that it is. You are so ridiculously talented. You are awesome.

Thank you to my amazing, smart, funny, girlfriend, Heather Gold, my most honest reader, who gives me heart and soul, my real deal love story.

— Mariko Tamaki

Thank you to Charlie Olsen, my incomparable agent, and to Calista Brill, Mark Siegel, Kiara Valdez, Whit Taylor, Andrew Arnold, and everyone else at First Second who worked tirelessly to help bring this book into the world. I will never be able to thank you all enough for the faith you've shown in me, and for the hand you've all played in making my wildest dreams come true. You've changed my life forever.

Thank you to Mariko, whose work lit a fire in my heart when I was a teenager, whose books made me want to throw myself into comics and never look back. You've been a lighthouse to me, and I don't think I'll ever stop having to pinch myself when I remember I got to help you tell this story.

Thank you to Ryan, Maddi, Chase, John, Madeline, Leigh, Lia, Jess, Brando, Spencer, Calvin, Maya, Sage, Corvin, Liz, Andrew, Lizzi, Jack, Chan, Luna, Sawyer, Andy, Mar, Sunmi, Paloma, Kate, Laura, E, Ann, Ashanti, Noella, Sarah, Han, Hannah, Carta, Rii, Carey, Zach, Bryce, Mey, and everyone else who has celebrated with me and encouraged me, who at some point throughout this journey gave me the resolve I needed to take the next step forward.

Thank you to Bob, Zak, Caitlin, and Anders, my mentors, for your guidance, your challenges, and your eternal patience.

Thank you most of all to my mom and my dads, my first and truest cheerleaders, whose unwavering and unflinching love and support keeps my feet on the ground and my eyes unclouded. *Todo lo que soy es gracias a vosotros, y os quiero mil veces más de lo que jamás podre expresar.*

— Rosemary Valero-O'Connell

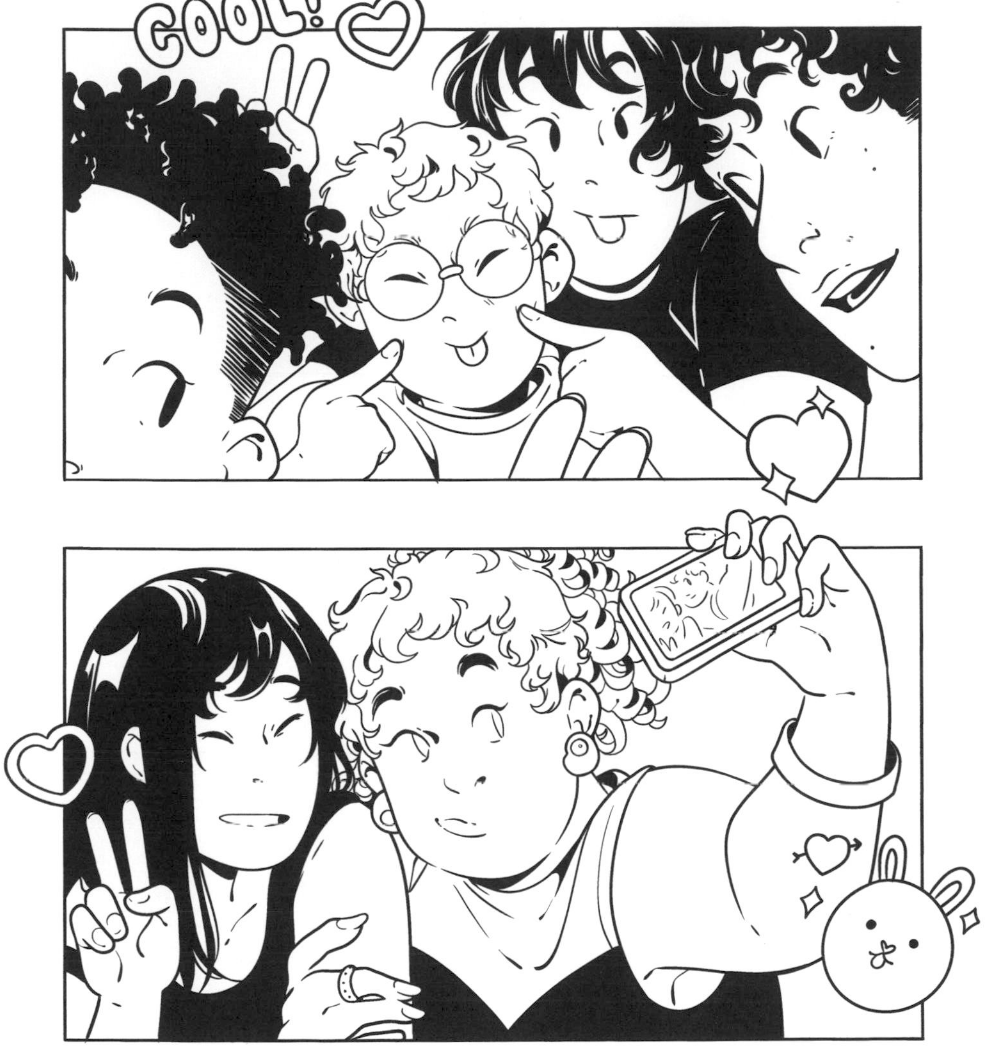
COOL!

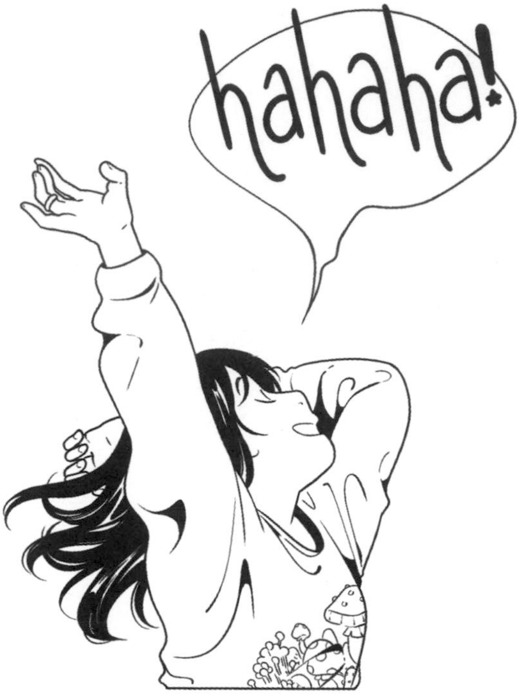
hahaha!

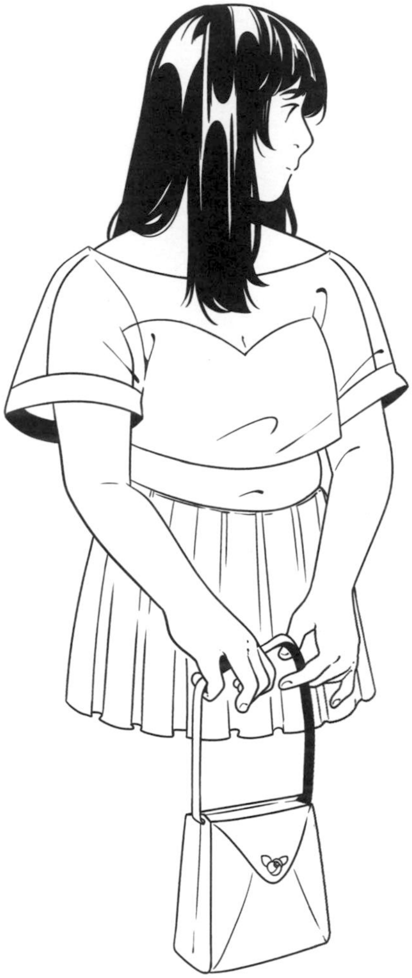

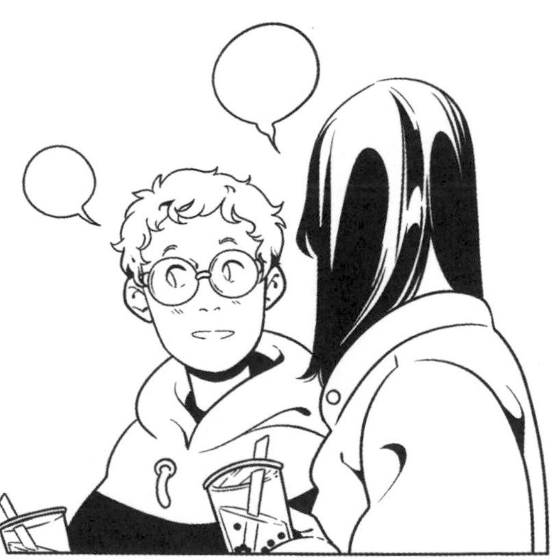

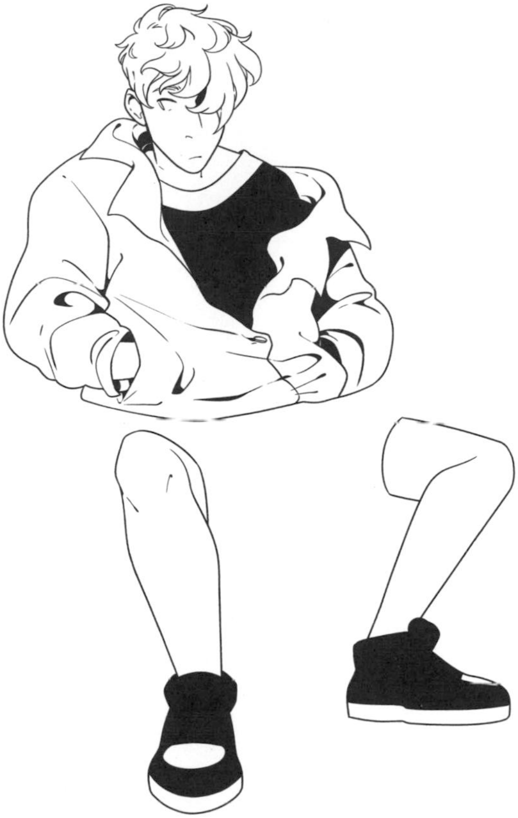

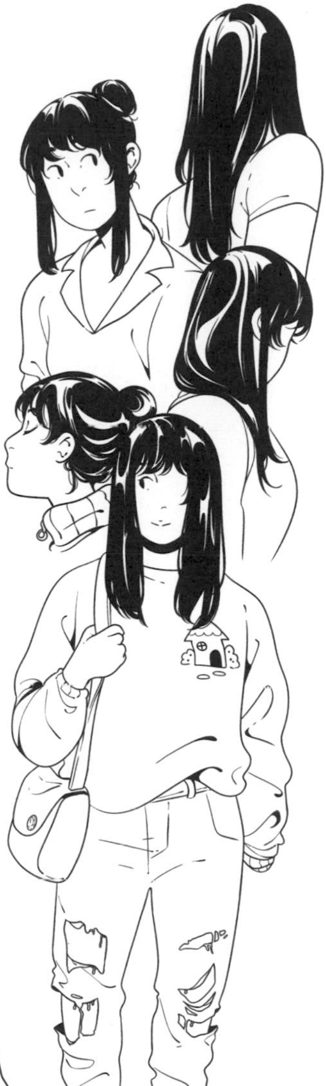

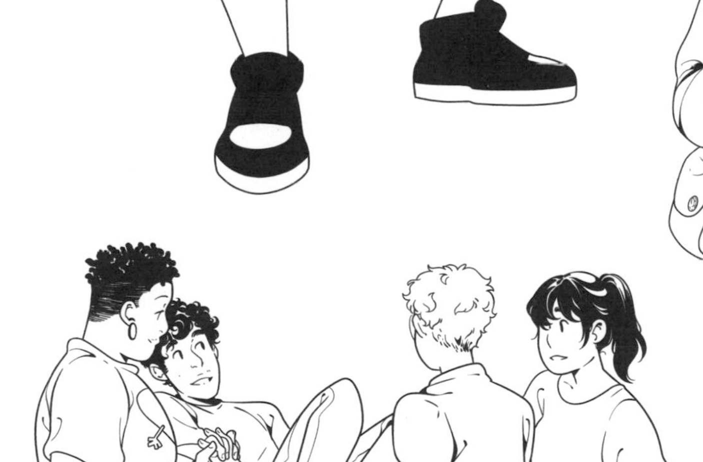

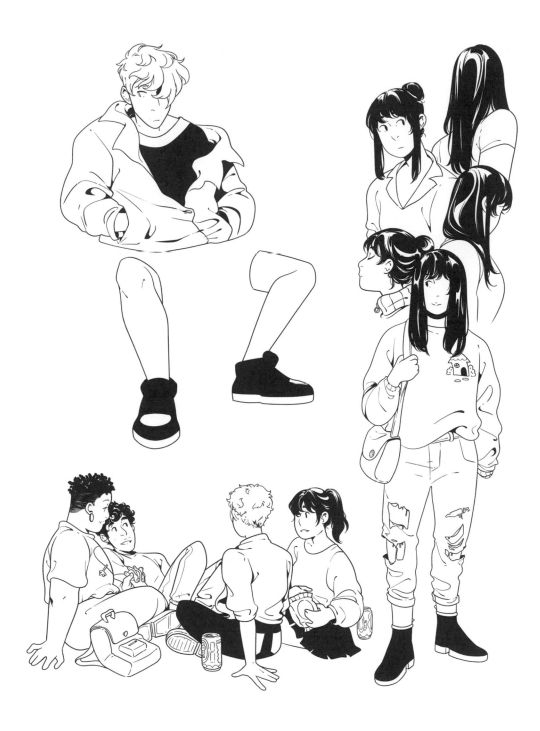

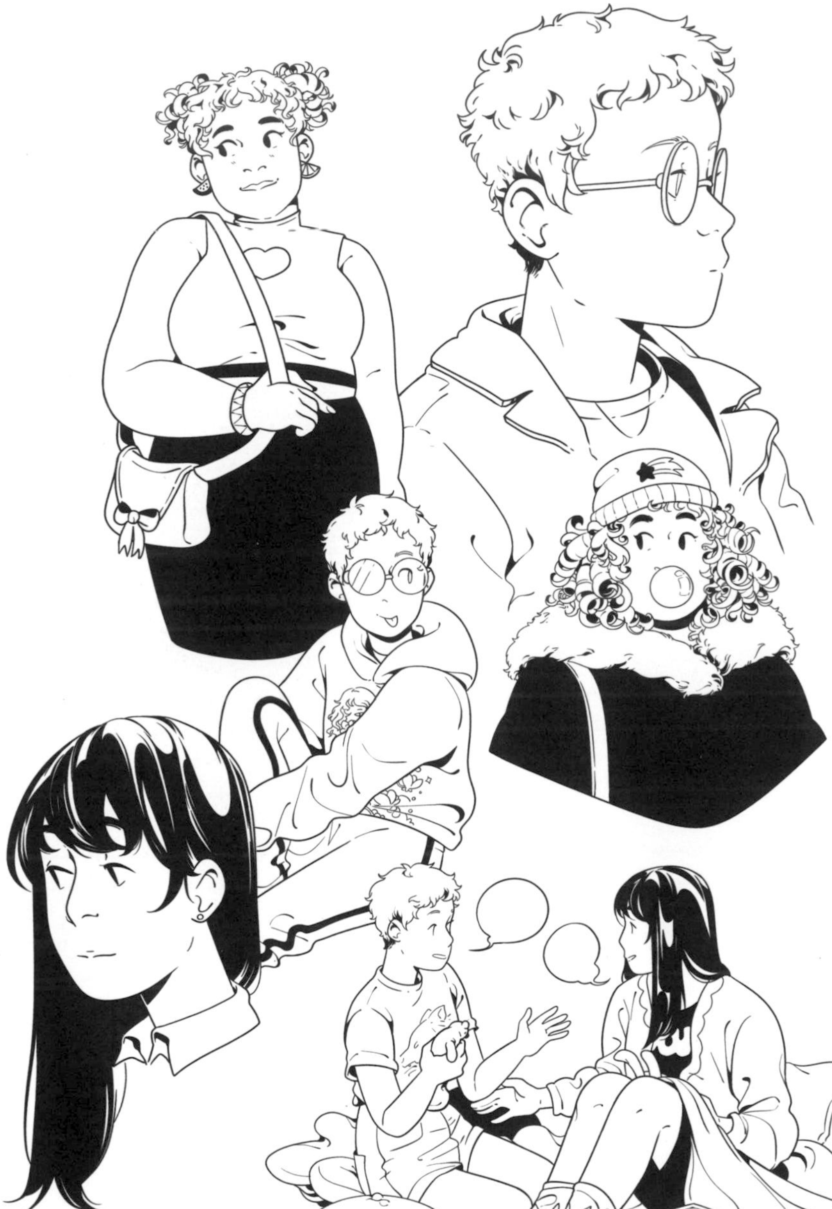

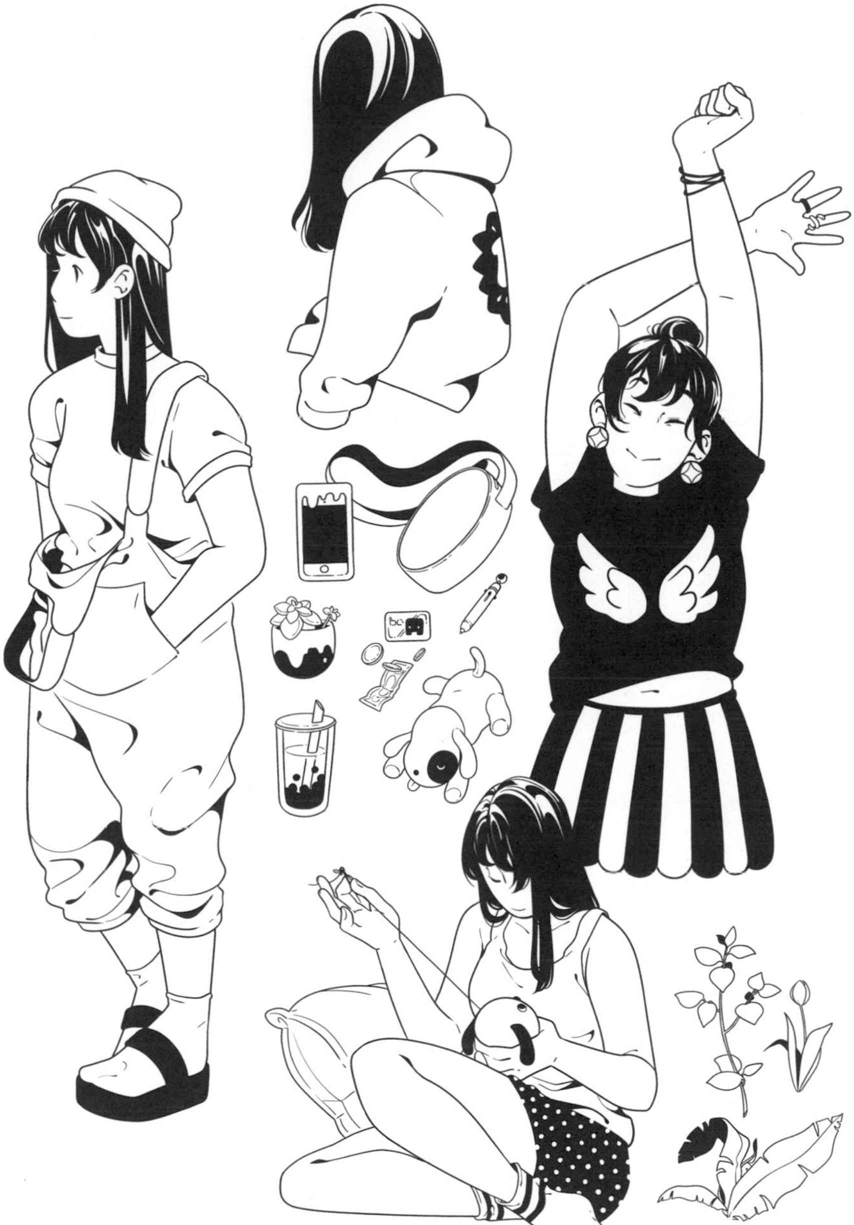

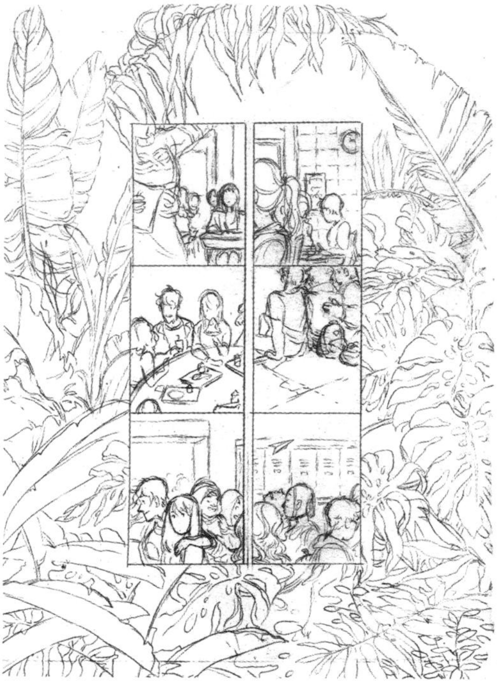

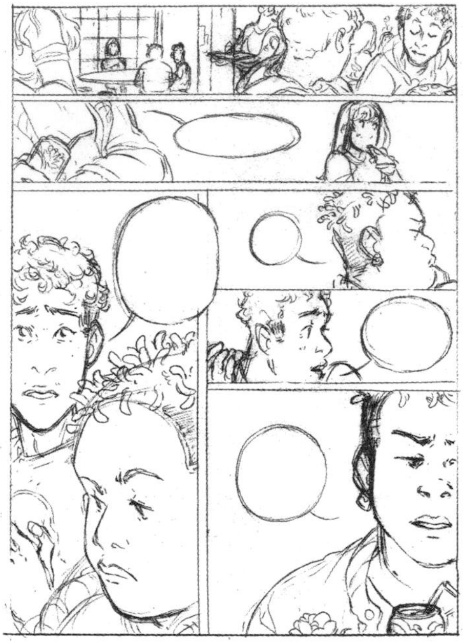

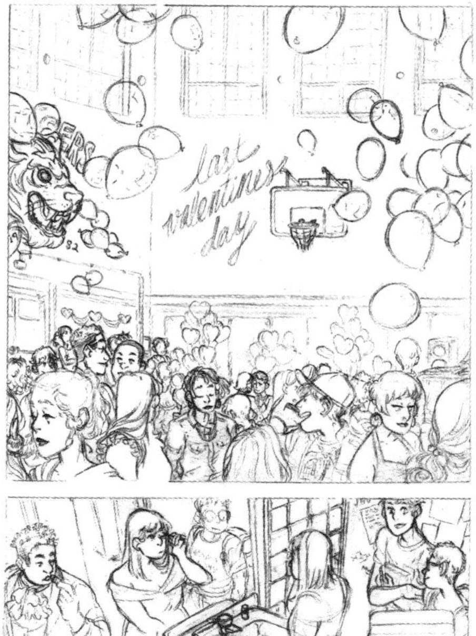
last valentines day

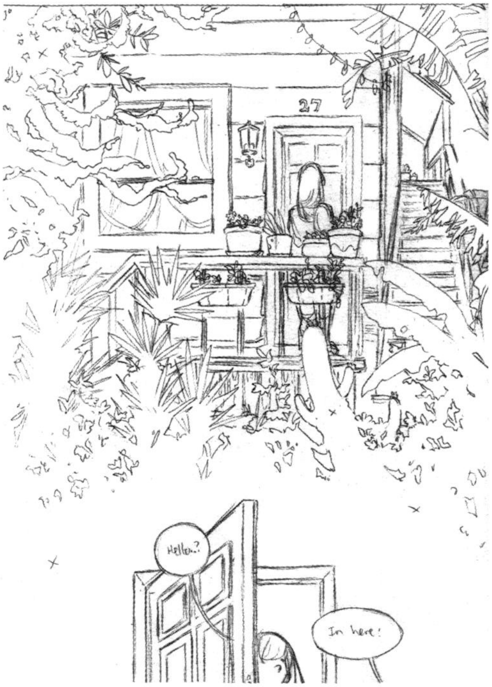
27
Hello..?
In here!

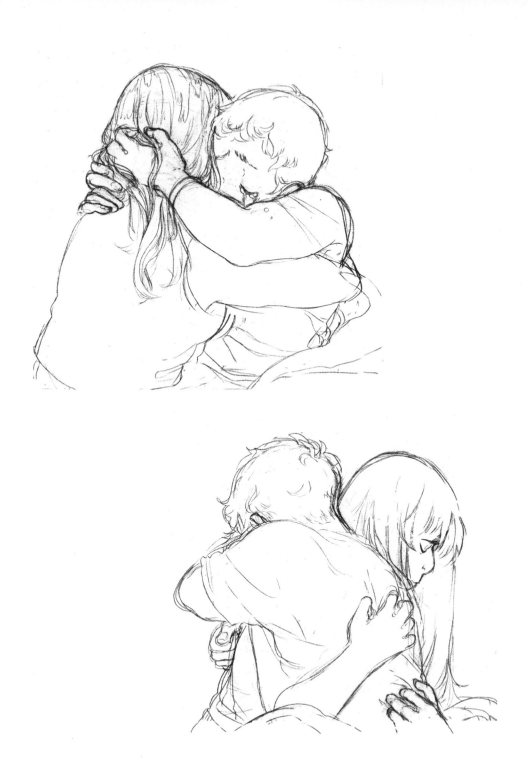

First Second

Text copyright © 2019 by Mariko Tamaki
Illustrations copyright © 2019 by Rosemary Valero-O'Connell

Published by First Second
First Second is an imprint of Roaring Brook Press,
a division of Holtzbrinck Publishing Holdings Limited Partnership
175 Fifth Avenue, New York, NY 10010
All rights reserved

Library of Congress Control Number: 2018944904

Paperback ISBN: 978-1-62672-259-0
Hardcover ISBN: 978-1-250-31284-6

Our books may be purchased in bulk for promotional, educational, or business use. Please
contact your local bookseller or the Macmillan Corporate and Premium Sales Department
at (800) 221-7945 ext. 5442 or by email at MacmillanSpecialMarkets@macmillan.com.

First edition, 2019

Edited by Calista Brill and Whit Taylor
Book design by Chris Dickey and Molly Johanson

Penciled with Bristol and graphite, inked and colored in Photoshop with a Cintiq 21UX and a Surface Pro.
Printed in China by 1010 Printing International Limited, North Point, Hong Kong

Paperback: 10 9 8 7 6 5 4 3 2 1
Hardcover: 10 9 8 7 6 5 4 3 2 1